PENGUIN CLASSICS

AMELIA

ADVISORY EDITOR: BETTY RADICE

Henry Fielding was born in 1707 at Sharpham Park, near Glastonbury. He was educated privately at first and then at Eton. In 1725 he attempted to abduct an heiress and was bound over to keep the peace. He then went to London, where, in 1728, he published a satirical poem, *The Masquerade*, and a comedy, *Love in Several Masques*. From 1728 to 1729 he was a student of literature at Leyden University, returning to London in the autumn of the latter year. Between then and 1737 he wrote some twenty-five dramatic pieces including comedies, adaptations of Molière, farces, ballad operas, burlesques, and a series of topical satires such as *Pasquin* and *The Historical Register for 1736*, which lampooned Sir Robert Walpole and his government; it was partly because of this last play that Walpole introduced the Stage Licensing Act in 1737. Fielding then took up law again, but he had little success as a barrister. In 1734 he married Charlotte Cradock, the model for Sophie Western and also for the heroine of his last novel, *Amelia* (1751).

His novel-writing career began with *Shamela* in 1741, a burlesque written in reaction to what he saw as the smug morality propounded by Richardson's *Pamela*. In the following year he published his own alternative conception of the art and purpose of the novel, *Joseph Andrews*, which achieved immediate popularity. His masterpiece, *Tom Jones*, one of the great comic novels in English literature, was published in 1749. The *Miscellanies* (including *Jonathan Wild*) were published in 1743. After Walpole's fall he wrote pro-government journalism, and he produced two weekly anti-Jacobite papers, *The True Patriot* (1745–6) and *The Jacobite's Journal* (1747–8). Later he ran *The Covent-Garden Journal*, which contained some of his best satire. In 1748 Fielding was commissioned as a Justice of the Peace for Westminster and in the following year became Chairman of the Quarter Sessions of Westminster. He and his brother, John Fielding, were prominent in developing the police force, and between 1749 and 1752 Fielding wrote a good deal on urgent legal and social problems. For many years he suffered from gout and in April 1754 ill health forced him to resign his post. He went to Lisbon and died there on 8 October 1754.

David Blewett, Professor of English at McMaster University, Ontario, is the author of *Defoe's Art of Fiction* and the editor of Defoe's *Roxana* in the Penguin Classics.

PENGUIN CLASSICS

AMELIA

ADVISORY EDITOR: BETTY RADICE

Henry Fielding was born in 1707 at Sharpham Park near Glastonbury. He was educated privately at first and then at Eton. In 1725 he attempted to abduct an heiress and was bound over to keep the peace. He then went to London, where in 1728 he published a satirical poem, *The Masquerade*, and a comedy, *Love in Several Masques*. From 1728 to 1729 he was a student of literature at Leyden University, returning to London in the autumn of that year. Between then and 1737 he wrote some twenty-five dramatic pieces, including comedies, adaptations of Molière, farces, ballad operas, burlesques, and a series of topical satires such as *Pasquin* and *The Historical Register for 1736*, which lampooned Sir Robert Walpole and his government. It was partly because of this last play that Walpole introduced the Stage Licensing Act in 1737. Fielding then took up law again, but he had little success as a barrister. In 1734 he married Charlotte Cradock, the model for Sophia Western and the heroine of his last novel, *Amelia* (1751).

His novel-writing career began with *Shamela* in 1741, a burlesque written in reaction to what he saw as the smug morality propounded by Richardson's *Pamela*. In the following year he published his own alternative conception of the aim and purposes of the novel, *Joseph Andrews*, which achieved immediate popularity. His masterpiece, *Tom Jones*, one of the greatest comic novels in English literature, was published in 1749. The *Miscellanies* (including *Jonathan Wild*) were published in 1743. After Walpole's fall he wrote pro-government journalism, and he produced two weekly anti-Jacobite papers, *The True Patriot* (1745–6) and *The Jacobite's Journal* (1747–8). Later, in 1752, *The Covent-Garden Journal*, which contained some of his best satire. In 1748 Fielding was appointed a Justice of the Peace for Westminster and in 1749 this was extended to the County of Middlesex. He was also Chairman of the Quarter Sessions for Westminster. He and his half-brother, Sir John Fielding, were prominent in developing the police force, and between 1749 and 1753 Fielding wrote a good deal on contemporary legal and social problems. For many years he suffered from gout and in April 1754 ill health forced him to retire. He went to Lisbon and died there on 8 October 1754.

David Blewett, Professor of English at McMaster University, Ontario, is the author of *Defoe's Art of Fiction* and the editor of Defoe's *Roxana* in the Penguin Classics.

Henry Fielding

AMELIA

EDITED BY DAVID BLEWETT

Felices ter & amplius
Quos irrupta tenet copula.

Γυναικὸς οὐδὲν χρῆμ' ἀνὴρ ληίζεται
Ἐσθλῆς ἄμεινον, οὐδὲ ῥίγιον κακῆς

PENGUIN BOOKS

Penguin Books Ltd, Harmondsworth, Middlesex, England
Viking Penguin Inc., 40 West 23rd Street, New York, New York 10010, USA
Penguin Books Australia Ltd, Ringwood, Victoria, Australia
Penguin Books Canada Limited, 2801 John Street, Markham, Ontario, Canada L3R 1B4
Penguin Books (N.Z.) Ltd, 182–190 Wairau Road, Auckland 10, New Zealand

First published 1751
Published in Penguin Books 1987

Made and printed in Great Britain by
Hazell Watson & Viney Ltd, Aylesbury, Bucks

Typeset in Bembo by
Rowland Phototypesetting Ltd
Bury St Edmunds, Suffolk

For Jane, Bill, and Neil, and
especially for Arthur

CONTENTS

INTRODUCTION

FIELDING's last novel, *Amelia* (1751), is the story of a marriage under stress. In his earlier and better-known novels the youthful heroes, Joseph Andrews and Tom Jones, by overcoming the obstacles that chance or malice have thrown in their way, eventually win a paradisal happiness in marriage to the beautiful and virtuous, if somewhat impersonal, heroines, Fanny Goodwin and Sophia Western. Fielding's famous control of narrative voice and of structure gave to both those novels a confidence of tone and an assured outcome; we track the downward course of the hero's misfortunes knowing that by the end the curve of comedy will bring him irresistibly back up again. *Amelia* begins where the earlier novels left off; paradise is not about to be regained but to be lost. Fielding retained few of the features of the immensely successful formula of *Joseph Andrews* (1742) and *Tom Jones* (1749) – the journey motif and the extensiveness of the epic form; a comic vision and mock-heroic irony that sprang from Fielding's own playful sensibility; Jonsonian 'humours' characters that might have walked off the stage; and plots so carefully timed that they seem to tick like clocks. Instead, he darkened the atmosphere to fit the more sombre subject and loosened the structure to accord with the uncertain outcome of the tale.

Like most threatened relationships, the union of William and Amelia Booth is menaced both from without and from within. The internal weakness lies entirely with the husband, whose genuine love for his admirable and charming wife is matched by his impulsive nature, by his naïveté and occasional vanity, and above all by his dangerous and ill-formed ideas about the motives of human behaviour. The character of Amelia is based on Fielding's beloved first wife, Charlotte Cradock, who eloped with Fielding in 1734 and died in his arms ten years later. Amelia is as true and constant as Shakespeare's Desdemona – the parallel with *Othello* is Fielding's and should make us fearful of the outcome – while Booth has affinities with the weaker sides of Othello's personality, particularly his inability to see beyond the outward appearance of other people, the professions of goodwill that they wear as masks to disguise their more sordid intentions. But it is in the analysis of the outward forces that menace the domestic happiness of the Booths, and by extension all ordinary people like them, that Fielding moves beyond his previous depictions of English society. The Booths are the victims of a corrupt social system, the 'institutionalized evil in eighteenth-century society', as one critic has put it,[1] of the law that throws Booth into prison for coming to the aid of an innocent man beaten up by a pair of assailants, of the army that promotes mere boys who can buy commissions over experienced soldiers, of influential noblemen indifferent to merit, of a Church whose priests are motivated more by venality than by piety.

Fielding's dual purpose in *Amelia*, his focus on the domestic life of a young couple and his exposure of public corruption, pulls the novel in contradictory directions, towards a new social realism of the Richardsonian sort (implicit in his choice of a title recalling *Pamela* and *Clarissa*) with its emphasis on the minutiae of daily domestic life; and towards a grim social satire on the 'most glaring evils' of his society, which Fielding saw more closely than ever as a result of his recent appointment (in 1748) to the bench of Bow Street magistrates' court. Social satire came naturally to Fielding, whose first works, a satirical poem called *The Masquerade* (1728) and a comedy, *Love in Several Masques* (1728), betray his fascination with concealment beneath disguise, which was to be a major theme in *Amelia*. Human pretension and hypocrisy are major targets in all his early dramatic works and his later fictional ones, though the high-spirited burlesque in the plays and in *Shamela* (1741), his coarse parody of Samuel Richardson's immensely popular *Pamela*, gives way to a darker satiric indictment of human motives and social conditions, which can be felt as early as his essays in *The Champion* (1739–41) and to some degree in *Joseph*

Andrews, and which establishes the mood of *Amelia*. In 1749 Fielding reached the pinnacle of his literary success with the publication of his masterpiece, *Tom Jones*. But the diseases which were to kill him five years later had already taken hold of his body. Yet until ill health finally forced him to retire in 1754, Fielding worked strenuously to reduce the appallingly high level of street violence and judicial corruption in London. His first-hand knowledge of human misery and official indifference provided the ingredients for his final satiric portrait of domestic London life.

Whether the tension between novelistic and satiric conventions ultimately pulls the novel apart will depend on the reader. Andrew Wright[2] has declared that *Amelia* is 'a deeply flawed conflation of satire and the novel', and certainly readers from the moment *Amelia* was first published have sensed a loss of the narrative unity that the continual authorial presence of Fielding in *Joseph Andrews* and *Tom Jones* gave to those works. But the change of voice is deliberate; Fielding is adjusting the tone to fit his more pessimistic vision of life in mid-eighteenth-century England. His point is that public and private evils are connected, as his dedicatory letter to Ralph Allen suggests, and he bends all his narrative resources, including satire (the characteristic expression of moral indignation in the eighteenth century), to showing the impact of public evil upon private virtue. In the earlier novels those who cannot bear the hurry of the city retire to the quiet of the country, like Mr Wilson in *Joseph Andrews* and the Man of the Hill in *Tom Jones*. In *Amelia* circumstances so restrict the liberty of the Booths that they are not free to make that choice until the penultimate chapter. In this sense *Amelia* may be seen as an expansion and completion of the exemplary tales of Fielding's earlier works.

I

The menacing atmosphere of *Amelia* is conveyed by the powerful themes of enclosure and of deception, exemplified by the dominant images of the prison and the masquerade. Booth is several times imprisoned in a sponging house or in Newgate prison, and as a debtor he lives with his family throughout the book in the verge of the court, the precinct around the royal palace, the only place where he is safe from arrest. Only on Sundays, when arrests for debt could not be made, is he free to move about London, but on other days he is always liable to arrest if tricked into crossing the boundary of the verge of the court – as once happens. In the first quarter of the novel (Books I–III) his situation is especially serious since he is subjected to the indignities of Newgate prison, falsely confined there by sentence of the corrupt and ignorant Justice Thrasher, one of the targets of Fielding's savage indictment of the venal social order. Ironically, Booth's arrest and loss of liberty takes place within the Liberty of Westminster, the legal description of a geographical area not strictly part of City of Westminster (see note 1 to p. 14), but the pun introduces, with a fine Fieldingesque touch, one of the major motifs of the novel. Booth's enclosure within the verge of the court, and his frequent imprisonment thereafter, become a spatial equivalent for the various limitations upon his freedom – social, intellectual, and spiritual. The physical enclosure of Booth and his family reflects their social immobility. A victim of the law, Booth is also a victim of a social system that keeps him in poverty on the salary of a half-pay officer and prevents his escape since he lacks money or political influence. But he is also partly to blame for his own misfortune. Booth is an intellectual drifter who has taken up the popular notion of the predominant passion[3] and uses it to excuse his own lapses in behaviour. The belief that he, like all other individuals, is not responsible for his actions – since these are governed by an inherent disposition that he is powerless to resist – absolves Booth (so he believes) of his moral responsibility and shuts him within an intellectual prison, deprived of free will. His spiritual self-imprisonment, an ultimately more serious matter, is a development of his intellectual beliefs, since his fatalism leads him to doubt the existence of divine providence. His eventual conversion in prison in the final book of the novel when he reads Dr Barrow's sermons, the overdue culmination of his slow growth towards spiritual enlightenment, immediately precedes his release from confinement. The symbolism that ties his physical freedom to his spiritual emancipation is emphasized by Dr Harrison, Booth's friend and protector: 'as the devil hath thought proper to set you free, I will try if I can prevail on the bailiff to do the same' (p. 522).

An even greater impediment to the safety and happiness of Amelia than the oppressive air of confinement is the pervasive pattern of deception in human behaviour. Deprived of her rightful inheritance by her wicked sister and a conniving attorney, Amelia heroically endures the increasing wretchedness of life with her feckless husband (knowing of his adulterous affair with Miss Mathews) while avoiding the snares laid for her virtue by her husband's friend, Colonel James, and later by the sinister and unnamed noble lord. The appropriate place of Colonel James's planned entrapment and seduction of Amelia is a public masquerade at the Opera House in the Haymarket, a fashionable evening entertainment that had acquired a rather shady reputation. Music as well as food and drink were provided, but the main attraction was the opportunity for flirtatious conversation with other masqueraders, often complete strangers, whose identities were more or less successfully hidden by their costumes and masks. Fielding elsewhere attacked the masquerades and similar entertainments on the grounds that they promoted 'idleness, extravagance, and immorality' and, like many of his reform-minded contemporaries, he saw them as 'characteristic of the present age'.[4] In his *Essay on the Knowledge of the Characters of Men* (1743) the masquerade becomes a convenient synecdoche for a world grown corrupt through avarice and deception: 'while the crafty and designing Part of Mankind, consulting only their own separate Advantage, endeavour to maintain one constant Imposition on others, the whole World becomes a vast Masquerade, where the greatest Part appear disguised under false Vizors and Habits'.[5] In *Amelia* the masquerade functions as a microcosm or concentrated expression of a world characterized by artifice, deception, hidden identity, seduction, betrayal, and adultery. When Amelia is apprised of the danger of the masquerade, she avoids it by practising a harmless deception herself. Fielding neatly makes his point; in order to survive in the vast masquerade of life even the virtuous are forced into deception.

The ultimate deception in a novel about marriage is adultery, so that it is significant that Dr Harrison's sermon-letter to Colonel

James on the iniquities of adultery, the core of the moral philosophy of the novel, should be discovered and read aloud by a group of young rakes at the masquerade intended as the scene of Amelia's seduction. For Dr Harrison, as for Fielding, 'Domestic happiness is the end of almost all our pursuits, and the common reward of all our pains' (p. 419). Adultery destroys such happiness, ruining both husband and wife and engulfing the family. The evil spreads like a cancer from private life to society, since the injured man, his life ruined, forgets his own affairs and turns all his thoughts to revenge. Such men 'become bad subjects, bad relations, bad friends and bad men' (p. 419). The scene in which the bucks jeer at the sentiments in Dr Harrison's letter is a Hogarthian icon of sneering, predatory faces, moral ugliness encircling and mocking the letter which forcibly repudiates and condemns such men, willing deceivers enclosed within the circle of their own moral obliquity.

II

Among the more significant departures from his customary way of telling a story is Fielding's method of characterization in *Amelia*. With the rare exception of a name like Justice Thrasher, Fielding for the first time avoids the type names which he had used for comic effect, or to indicate the essential nature of a character such as Mr Allworthy. It is perhaps only a coincidence that many of the names in *Amelia* occur in the list of subscribers to the folio edition (1724) of Bishop Burnet's *History of His Own Times* (which Fielding owned), but it is certainly true that the names of his characters might have been drawn from an eighteenth-century directory.[6] In part the change is due to the darker tone of a novel where comic names are less appropriate, but it also suggests a new and more exploratory approach to character that reflects a world in which deception is rife and where our assessment of human behaviour requires constant adjustment. The neutral names – Mathews, Robinson, James, Ellison – give nothing away and our first impression of characters has to be amended by subsequent revelations. Moreover, the elimination of improbably comic names signals a new realism, since virtually all characters now stand on an equal footing and are capable of development as the novel advances. This fact creates a larger and more realistic social network and a correspondingly greater moral complexity among the characters in it. 'Histories of this kind,' as Fielding says of *Amelia* in the first chapter, 'may properly be called models of HUMAN LIFE.' Fielding's movement towards a heightened realism in his final work of fiction justifies his claim to be teaching a lesson in 'the most useful of all arts . . . the ART OF LIFE'.

One of the more telling instances of the inability to judge the character of other people occurs in Books I–III where Booth in prison brings Miss Mathews up to date with the events of his life since their last meeting. Booth's subjective account introduces several of the characters we will later meet, but scarcely one of them fully corresponds with Booth's description of their personalities. As the novel advances we become increasingly aware of just how poor a judge of character Booth is. His misreading of the character of his friend Colonel James is especially serious, since his persistent naïveté about James's good nature blinds him to the cold egotism and utter ruthlessness of the man. The truth is that Colonel James, like many people, is a complex mixture, capable both of generosity (when he has nothing to lose) and of selfishness (when he has something to gain). Colonel James's plot against Amelia is only possible while Booth thinks of him as a friend, and Amelia's successful counterplot is only possible because she has learned to see him, more accurately than her husband, as an enemy. The discovery that people are not what they seem is one that is constantly made and means that as the characters learn more about one another relationships change. The interconnections among the people who make up the society in which Amelia lives are as unstable as any in reality. Fielding's substitution of an inconsistency of human personality for the stability of character types gives to *Amelia* a greater psychological accuracy than he had achieved in either of his earlier novels.

One of the few characters in whom there is no guile is Dr Harrison, the worthy successor to the benevolent patrons of the young heroes of *Joseph Andrews* and *Tom Jones*. Dr Harrison differs both from Mr Allworthy and from Parson Adams, however, in ways that indicate the shift in narrative strategy in *Amelia*. Unlike Mr Allworthy, whose role in *Tom Jones* is largely confined to the opening movement of the novel, Dr Harrison plays a major part in the action of *Amelia*, appearing at moments of crisis as an agent of providence to affect the lives of the Booths. Nor is he like Parson Adams a figure of fun, the eccentric clerical schoolmaster whose teaching Joseph will in some ways outgrow. His enhanced role springs from Fielding's reluctance, in the interests of a more sombre kind of realism, to allow himself the author's privilege of direct commentary on the actions of his characters. Dr Harrison is the principal spokesman in the novel for Fielding but, unlike an intrusive author, he is not infallible. Dr Harrison makes mistakes, fooled by circumstantial evidence or by consummate hypocrisy, so that like the other characters he too has something to learn about the art of life. One of his chief functions is to show that no one ever fully masters that difficult art.

III

The ending of the story, Booth's sudden conversion and the immediate discovery, as if by consequence, that Amelia is the rightful heiress to her mother's fortune, is difficult for modern readers to accept. The change of mood and direction, although not entirely unexpected, since we are never certain whether *Amelia* is tragedy or comedy, arrives too quickly to be convincing. We prefer the ending to fulfil the expectations that the story has all along aroused. But the tale that can go in either direction, into comedy or into tragedy, has an honourable history. John Butt pointed out that *Amelia* follows epic conventions by introducing an epic discovery (that Amelia is an heiress) and an epic reversal of fortune.[7] Certainly Fielding, who always insisted that the epic poems of Homer and Virgil should be seen as the prototypes of his novels, would have had no objection to such an explanation. And an age that preferred *King Lear* rewritten with a happy ending and that adored Gay's *Beggar's Opera*, which ends tragically until the Beggar arrives and changes the ending to comedy 'to comply with the taste of the town', would have been less troubled than we are by the final book of *Amelia*. Moreover, writers since Fielding have sometimes found that the novels they have written have alternative endings, notably Dickens in *Great Expectations* and John Fowles in *The French Lieutenant's Woman*.

From the opening scene, *Amelia* appears to be cast in the tragic mode, though the introduction of the protective influence of Dr Harrison modifies our first impression, leaving the outcome of the novel problematic. The tragic potential we sense in the menacing and claustrophobic atmosphere is reinforced by the wide range of literary allusions, among which those to the *Aeneid* and to *Othello* are the most significant. In the *Covent-Garden Journal* (No. 8) Fielding called the *Aeneid* the 'noble model' for *Amelia* and on the basis of that claim attempts have been made to find a precise correspondence between the twelve books of the *Aeneid* and the twelve books of *Amelia*.[8] The passion of Miss Mathews for Booth and their brief affair recalls, and parodies, the passion of Dido for Aeneas in the opening books of the *Aeneid*, but it is unlikely that Fielding intended to extend the parallel to the entire novel. Further reference to the *Aeneid* is ironic rather than architectural; Aeneas in his piety and determination throws into relief the irreligion and vacillation of Booth. The shadow that the *Aeneid* casts over *Amelia* darkens the air by contrasting the two men, suggesting that Booth may fail where Aeneas succeeded.

The allusions to *Othello* are more frequent and more sinister.[9] As with the *Aeneid*, no precise correspondence is meant; rather the parallel with *Othello* stirs an undercurrent of suspicion and jealousy. We are never allowed to forget, however often Amelia suffers from Booth's recklessness and inattention and no matter how effectively Dr Harrison intervenes, that the happiness of marriage may be destroyed not just by adultery (which in any case Booth has already committed) but also by the mere suspicion of it. Several other marriages repeat and vary the theme, reinforcing the darker undertones of the story and extending and modifying the *Othello* motif. The ghastly tale of the forcible seduction of Mrs Bennet by the noble lord and its tragic consequence – the discovery by her infuriated husband, momentarily crazed by jealousy and mistakenly believing in her guilt, and the violent events that end with his death – is disclosed to the horrified Amelia just as she is about to walk into a similar trap set by the noble lord. The marriages of Colonel and Mrs James and, an even nastier union, that of the Trents, underline the point and, like the parallel with *Othello*, support the burden of Dr Harrison's letter to Colonel James. When jealousy and suspicion once enter the mind they destroy all inner peace. Hatred and revenge are the frequent result and when extreme, as with Othello, lead to despair, madness, murder, and suicide. The function of these two major literary allusions is to keep the resolution in doubt. The tragic possibility is felt even when the surface of the novel appears comic.

In the nightmare atmosphere of deception and self-delusion that characterizes much of the novel, dreams function as crucially as they do in the *Aeneid* and in *Othello* as omens of future events, either as presages of evil intentions or as tokens of a change of fortune. The most vivid dream is Serjeant Atkinson's delirious vision of Colonel James 'standing by the bed-side of Amelia, with a naked sword in his hand, and threatening to stab her instantly, unless she complied with his desires' (p. 384). Atkinson's delirium is so powerful that he half strangles his sleeping wife, mistaking her for Colonel James, and then, in the commotion that ensues as Booth and Amelia rush in, blurts out to Booth that 'I dreamt I was rescuing your lady from the hands of Colonel James.' When he presses Atkinson for an explanation, Booth's attitude is, like Othello's, that 'dreams denote a foregone conclusion'. The parallel that Fielding calls to mind is Iago's account of Cassio's dream of committing adultery with Desdemona, though the unvoiced allusion to Clarissa's prophetic dream of being stabbed by Lovelace,[10] including its sexual symbolism, is an equally significant antecedent. In *Amelia*, more than in any previous novel, Fielding shows his awareness of the murky depths of sexual and psychological desires and fears.

It is in the uncertain nature of dreams that they can be taken as a sick person's fancy, or as divinely inspired, as delusion or as prophecy, the positions of Horace and of Homer respectively, as Dr Harrison points out (p. 540). When Amelia tries to stop Booth from seeing Colonel James she avers that she has had a dream 'too horrible to be mention'd' about the two men, whom she fears will kill one another, but Booth now dismisses such dreams as 'unreasonable' and wonders how 'a woman of your sense [can] talk of dreams' (p. 510). Amelia's fears, even in the form of a dream, are real and urgent, but Booth is still too headstrong to recognize any viewpoint that runs counter to his own. Earlier, however, Booth had himself suffered the first pangs of jealousy in the form of troubling dreams. Booth was so greatly disturbed by the persistent attention paid to Amelia by both the noble lord and by Colonel James that one night 'he was pursued and haunted by the most frightful and terrifying dreams' (p. 234). On that occasion at least he recognized the origin of his nightmare, vehemently denying that he suffered either from delusions or disease.

Only at the end of the novel do dreams lose their threatening aspect. In order to spare Amelia the shock of the unexpected news of the recovery of her estate, Booth ostensibly recounts a dream in which, after he is released from prison, she arrives with a coach and four to take them with their two children down to her country house. Later Dr Harrison agrees to act, in his words, as 'the oneiropolos', or interpreter of dreams, and gives his view that 'the dream will come to pass'. Though the dream is feigned, it marks the beginning of a new life in which the disturbing visions of the unconscious mind no longer arise to trouble the happiness of the protagonists.

In *Amelia*, after his triumphs with *Joseph Andrews* and with *Tom Jones*, we see Fielding in an innovative mood, striving with considerable (if not complete) success to achieve a new realism in characterization that makes knowledge more tentative and the ultimate lot of the characters uncertain. Although by the end the essential good nature of Booth and the saint-like goodness of Amelia abundantly justify the defeat of the evil forces working against them, Fielding never lets us forget that goodness is not a guarantee of happiness. Through experience Booth has gradually gained a knowledge about human nature and the operation of divine providence in the world that is confirmed by his reading of Dr Barrow's sermons. The conversion of Booth, upon which the happy outcome of the story depends, is delayed until it is largely a formality. It is safe to say that had he read the sermons earlier in the book, he would probably have been unaffected by them.

In its improbabilities *Amelia* shows the strains of a writer's working outside his customary form. But if it is less satisfying than his earlier work, its experimental nature makes it all the more interesting. *Amelia* is the only novel of Fielding's not described on its title-page as a 'history', that is, as a biography; rather it is a social document. The analysis of the moral and social problems that the novel provides, along with its earnest Christian didacticism, which is meant to furnish the answer, gives to *Amelia* an urgency and pathos that are not to be found in English fiction until nineteenth-century novels such as *Bleak House*. To achieve his end Fielding took the unusual step of focusing upon the trials of marriage, rather than those of courtship, and upon a marriage that is assaulted by the forces of institutional corruption as well as by those of personal malignity. And he left the resolution in doubt so that the defeat of Amelia is always a dangerous possibility. Fielding's willingness to take such risks meant that he was attempting not just to repeat his old successes, but rather to enlarge the scope of the novel by pushing it in a new direction.

1. Charles A. Knight, 'The Narrative Structure of Fielding's *Amelia*', *Ariel: A Review of International English Literature*, 11 (1980), 31.
2. *Henry Fielding: Mask and Feast* (Berkeley and Los Angeles, University of California Press, 1966), p. 105.
3. In the eighteenth century the *locus classicus* of the concept of the ruling passion is Pope's *Essay on Man*, II, 131–60. Cf. George Sherburn, 'Fielding's *Amelia*: An Interpretation', *ELH*, III (1936), 1–14.
4. *A Charge Delivered to the Grand Jury at the Sessions of the Peace held for the City and Liberty of Westminster* (1749). This work is included in *The Complete Works of Henry Fielding, Esq.*, ed. W. E. Henley and others (16 vols.; London, Heinemann, 1903); see Vol. 13, p. 214.
5. *Miscellanies*, Vol. I, ed. Henry Knight Miller (The Wesleyan Edition of the Works of Henry Fielding, Oxford, OUP, 1972), p. 155.
6. See Ian Watt, 'The Naming of Characters in Defoe, Richardson, and Fielding', *Review of English Studies*, 25 (1949), 335.
7. *Fielding* (London, Longman, for the British Council, 1954, revised edition, 1959), p. 26.
8. Lyall H. Powers, 'The Influence of the *Aeneid* on Fielding's *Amelia*', *Modern Language Notes*, 71 (1956), 330–36; Maurice Johnson, *Fielding's Art of Fiction* (Philadelphia, University of Pennsylvania Press, 1961).
9. See Eustace Palmer, '*Amelia* – The Decline of Fielding's Art', *Essays in Criticism*, 21 (1971), 135–51; and Robert Folkenflik, 'Purpose and Narration in Fielding's *Amelia*', *Novel*, VII (1974), 168–74.
10. Samuel Richardson, *Clarissa* (1748), ed. Angus Ross (Harmondsworth, Penguin Books, 1985), Letter 84.

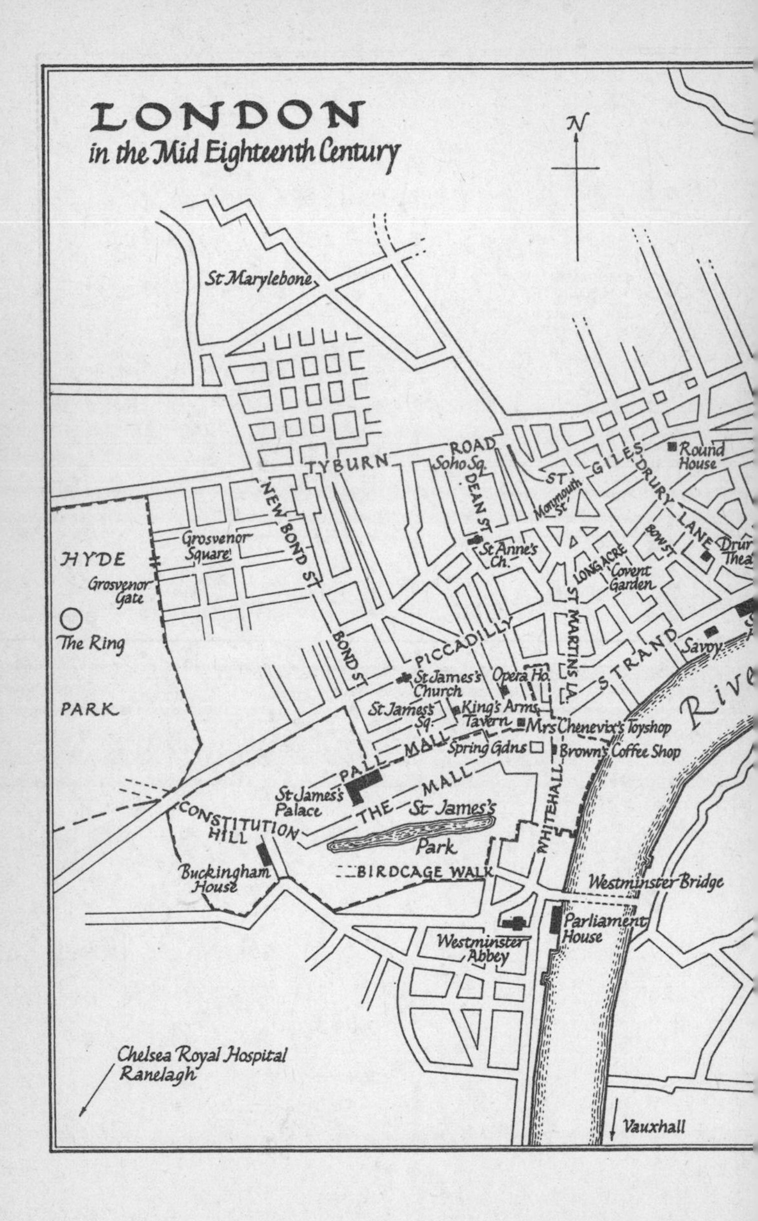
LONDON
in the Mid Eighteenth Century
N
St Marylebone
TYBURN ROAD
Soho Sq.
DEAN ST
ST GILES
Round House
DRURY LANE
Monmouth St
NEW BOND ST
Grosvenor Square
HYDE
Grosvenor Gate
The Ring
PARK
St Anne's Ch.
LONG ACRE
BOW ST
Covent Garden
ST MARTINS LA.
BOND ST
PICCADILLY
St James's Church
Opera Ho.
STRAND
Savoy
St James's Sq.
King's Arms Tavern
Mrs Chenevix's Toyshop
Spring Gdns
Brown's Coffee Shop
PALL MALL
THE MALL
St James's Palace
St James's Park
CONSTITUTION HILL
WHITEHALL
Buckingham House
BIRDCAGE WALK
Westminster Bridge
Parliament House
Westminster Abbey
Chelsea Royal Hospital
Ranelagh
Vauxhall

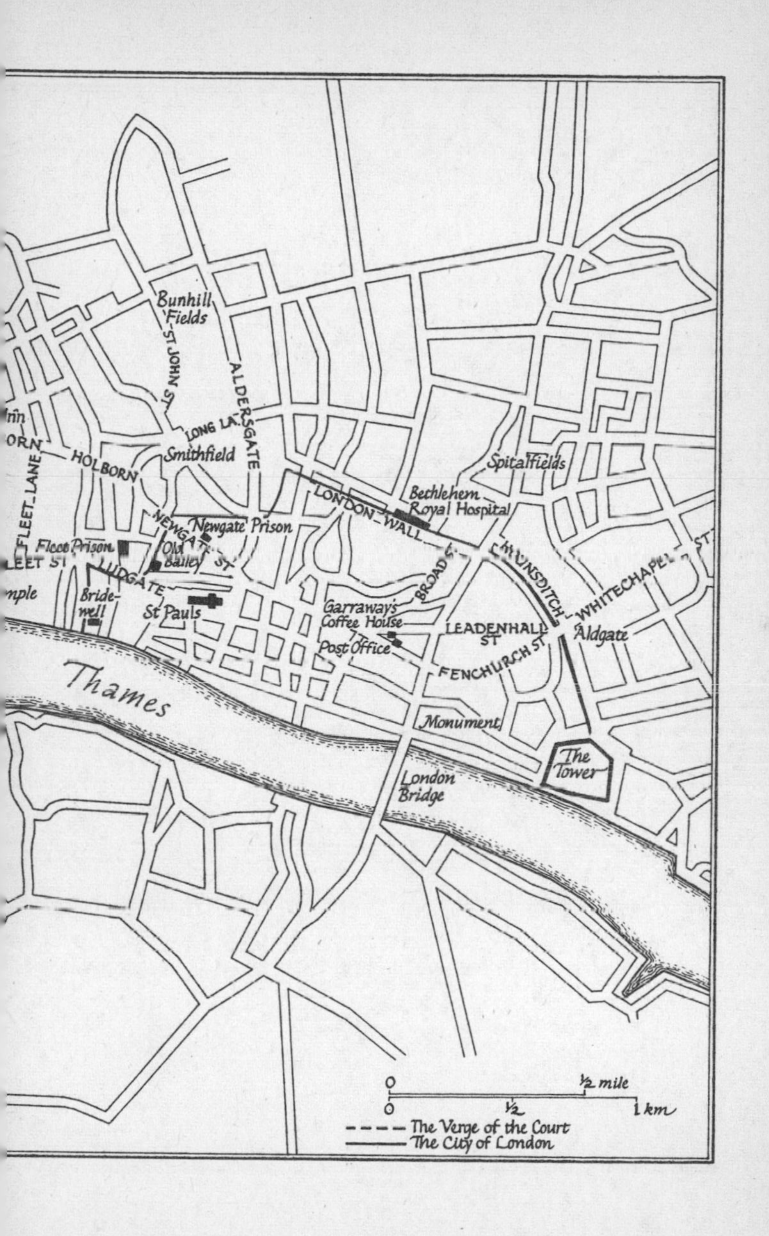

Bunhill Fields
ST JOHN ST
ALDERSGATE
LONG LA.
Smithfield
HOLBORN
FLEET LANE
Fleet Prison
LUDGATE
Bride-well
St Pauls
Old Bailey
Newgate Prison
LONDON WALL
Bethlehem Royal Hospital
Spitalfields
BROAD
WHITECHAPEL
Aldgate
LEADENHALL ST
FENCHURCH ST
Garraway's Coffee House
Post Office
Thames
Monument
The Tower
London Bridge
0 ½ mile
0 ½ 1 km
The Verge of the Court
The City of London

ACKNOWLEDGEMENTS

In the preparation of this edition I have been assisted by 'An Introduction and Annotations for a Critical Edition of *Amelia*', the unpublished doctoral dissertation of A. R. Towers, Jr, and by the authoritative commentary and kind advice of Martin Battestin. Readers who require more detailed information than I have provided should consult Professor Battestin's edition of *Amelia* in the Wesleyan Edition of the Works of Henry Fielding (Oxford, OUP, 1983). I would also like to thank Heather Jones for her assistance in preparing the text; Charlotte Stewart and Bruce Whiteman of Mills Memorial Library, McMaster University, for their helpfulness; and the Arts Research Board of McMaster University for financial support.

ACKNOWLEDGEMENTS

In the preparation of this edition I have been assisted by *An Introduction and Annotations for a Critical Edition of Amelia*, the unpublished doctoral dissertation of A. R. Towers Jr, and by the authoritative commentary and kind advice of Martin C. Battestin. Readers who require more detailed annotation than I have provided should consult Professor Battestin's edition of *Amelia* in the Wesleyan Edition of the Works of Henry Fielding (Oxford, O.U.P., 1983). I would also like to thank Heather Jones for her assistance in preparing the text, Charlotte Stewart and Bruce Whiteman of Mills Memorial Library, McMaster University, for their helpfulness, and the Arts Research Board of McMaster University for financial support.

A NOTE ON THE TEXT

The text of this edition generally follows that of the Wesleyan Edition of the works of Henry Fielding, ed. Martin C. Battestin (Oxford, OUP, 1983), which is based on the first edition (1751) but which incorporates Fielding's substantive revisions for the second edition, published posthumously by Arthur Murphy in *The Works of Henry Fielding, Esq* (1762). I have brought the text into conformity with modern usage by reducing most initial capitals to lower-case letters; by rendering proper names in roman rather than in italic; and by occasionally modifying the spelling. The second chapter of Book V of the first edition ('Containing a brace of doctors, and much physical matter'), omitted in the second edition, is reprinted as an appendix.

A NOTE ON THE TEXT

The text of this edition generally follows that of the Wesleyan Edition of the Works of Henry Fielding, ed. Martin C. Battestin (Oxford, OUP, 1983), which is based on the first edition (1751) but which incorporates Fielding's substantive revisions for the second edition, published posthumously by Arthur Murphy in *The Works of Henry Fielding, Esq.* (1762). I have brought the text into conformity with modern usage by reducing most initial capitals to lower-case letters, by rendering proper names in roman rather than in italic, and by occasionally modifying the spelling. The second chapter of Book V of the first edition ('Containing a brace of doctors, and much physical matter'), omitted in the second edition, is reprinted as an appendix.

A CHRONOLOGY OF HENRY FIELDING

1707 Born, 22 April, at Sharpham Park (his grandfather's house), near Glastonbury in Somerset, son of Edmund Fielding and Sarah Gould. His father, an impecunious lieutenant, later became a lieutenant-general. His mother's father was a Justice of the Queen's Bench.

c. 1710 The family moved to East Stour, Dorset. Fielding educated at home by private tutors.

1714 Death of Queen Anne; accession of George I.

1718 Death of Fielding's mother.

1719 His father remarries. Lady Gould, Fielding's grandmother, wins a Chancery suit for the custody of her daughter's children.

1719–*c.* 1724 Attended Eton.

1721 Birth of Fielding's half-brother John, later Sir John Fielding, a distinguished magistrate.

1725 His attempt to elope with Sarah Andrews at Lyme Regis thwarted by her uncle and guardian, Andrew Tucker.

1727 Death of George I; accession of George II.

1728 Published a verse satire, *The Masquerade*. His *Love in Several Masques* performed at the Theatre Royal, Drury Lane, through the influence of his second cousin, Lady Mary Wortley Montagu.

1728–9 Studied classical literature at the University of Leyden.

1729–37 Career as a playwright. Wrote twenty-five stage pieces (comedies, parodies, adaptations, farces,

	satires, ballad operas) including *Tom Thumb* (1730), *The Covent-Garden Tragedy* (1732), *Pasquin* (1736), and *The Historical Register* (1737).
1734	Married Charlotte Cradock, the model for the heroines of all his novels.
1737	The Licensing Act, brought in by Sir Robert Walpole, the Prime Minister, in part as a response to Fielding's stage satires on his government, ended Fielding's career as a dramatist. He enrolled as a law student in the Middle Temple.
1739–41	Edited (with others) *The Champion*, an opposition newspaper.
1740	Called to the bar and rode the western circuit.
1740	Samuel Richardson's *Pamela* published.
1741	Fielding's *Shamela* published.
1742	*Joseph Andrews*.
1743	*Miscellanies* (including *Jonathan Wild*) published by subscription.
1744	Death of his wife.
1745	The Jacobite uprising.
1747	Married Mary Daniel, his wife's maid.
1748	Fielding commissioned as a Justice of the Peace for Westminster (and later, in 1749, for Middlesex).
1749	*Tom Jones*. Fielding's health begins to deteriorate.
1749–52	Wrote several important legal pamphlets as part of his attack upon widespread crime and corruption in London.
1751	*Amelia*.
1752	*The Covent-Garden Journal*, his most significant periodical.
1754	Resigned because of ill health and left for Lisbon, where he died on 8 October.
1755	*The Journal of a Voyage to Lisbon* published posthumously.

FURTHER READING

BIBLIOGRAPHY

Martin C. Battestin, 'Fielding', in *The English Novel: Select Bibliographical Guides*, ed. A. E. Dyson, Oxford, OUP, 1974.

H. George Hahn, *Henry Fielding: An Annotated Bibliography*, Metuchen, NJ, and London, The Scarecrow Press, 1979.

H. George Hahn and Carl Behm III, 'Henry Fielding', in *The Eighteenth-Century British Novel and Its Background: An annotated bibliography and guide to topics*, Metuchen, NJ, and London, The Scarecrow Press, 1985.

John H. Stoler and Richard D. Fulton, *Henry Fielding: An Annotated Bibliography of Twentieth-Century Criticism 1900–1977*, New York and London, Garland Publishing, 1980.

BIOGRAPHY

W. L. Cross, *The History of Henry Fielding*, 3 vols., New Haven, Yale University Press, 1918.

F. Homes Dudden, *Henry Fielding: His Life, Works, and Times*, 2 vols., Oxford, Clarendon Press, 1951.

Pat Rogers, *Henry Fielding: A Biography*, London, Elek; New York, Scribners, 1979.

GENERAL WORKS ON FIELDING

Robert Alter, *Fielding and the Nature of the Novel*, Cambridge, Mass., Harvard University Press, 1968.

John Butt, *Fielding*, London, Longman, for the British Council, revised edition, 1959.

William B. Coley, 'The Background of Fielding's Laughter', *ELH*, XXVI (1959), 229–52.

Aurélien Digeon, *The Novels of Fielding*, London, Routledge & Kegan Paul, 1925 (translation of *Les Romans de Fielding*, Paris, 1923).

Morris Golden, *Fielding's Moral Psychology*, Amherst, University of Massachusetts Press, 1966.

Glen W. Hatfield, *Fielding and the Language of Irony*, Chicago, University of Chicago Press, 1968.

J. Paul Hunter, *Occasional Form: Henry Fielding and the Chains of Circumstance*, Baltimore, Johns Hopkins University Press, 1975.

Alan D. McKillop, *The Early Masters of English Fiction*, Lawrence, Kan, and London, University Press of Kansas, 1956.

Henry Knight Miller, *Essays on Fielding's Miscellanies: A Commentary on Volume One*, Princeton, Princeton University Press, 1961.

Ronald Paulson, ed., *Fielding: A Collection of Critical Essays*, Englewood Cliffs, NJ, Prentice-Hall, 1962.

George Sherburn, 'Fielding's Social Outlook', *Philological Quarterly*, XXXV (1956), 1–23.

Ian Watt, *The Rise of the Novel: Studies in Defoe, Richardson, and Fielding*, London, Chatto & Windus, 1957; Harmondsworth, Penguin Books, 1963.

James A. Work, 'Henry Fielding, Christian Censor', in *The Age of Johnson: Essays Presented to Chauncey Brewster Tinker*, New Haven, Yale University Press, 1949, pp. 139–48.

Andrew Wright, *Henry Fielding: Mask and Feast*, London, Chatto & Windus, 1965; Berkeley and Los Angeles, University of California Press, 1965.

ON *AMELIA*

Sheridan Baker, 'Fielding's *Amelia* and the Materials of Romance', *Philological Quarterly*, 41 (1962), 437–49.

Martin C. Battestin, 'The Problem of *Amelia*: Hume, Barrow, and the Conversion of Captain Booth', *ELH*, 41 (1974), 613–48.

John S. Coolidge, 'Fielding and "Conservation of Character"', *Modern Philology*, LVII (1960), 245–59. (Reprinted in Paulson.)

Robert Folkenflik, 'Purpose and Narration in Fielding's *Amelia*', *Novel*, VII (1974), 168–74.

Charles A. Knight, 'The Narrative Structure of Fielding's *Amelia*', *Ariel: A Review of International English Literature*, 11 (1980), 31–46.

George Sherburn, 'Fielding's *Amelia*: An Interpretation', *ELH*, III (1936), 1–14. (Reprinted in Paulson.)

D. S. Thomas, 'Fortune and the Passions in Fielding's *Amelia*', *Modern Language Review*, 60 (1965), 176–87.

A. R. Towers, '*Amelia* and the State of Matrimony', *Review of English Studies*, new series, V (1954), 144–57.

Allan Wendt, 'The Naked Virtue of *Amelia*', *ELH*, 27 (1960), 131–48.

AMELIA.

BY

Henry Fielding, Esq;

Felices ter & amplius
Quos irrupta tenet Copula.

Γυναικὸς οὐδὲν χρῆμ' ἀνὴρ ληΐζεται
Ἐσθλῆς ἄμεινον, οὐδὲ ῥίγιον κακῆς.

In FOUR VOLUMES.

VOL. I.

LONDON:
Printed for A. MILLAR, in the *Strand*.
M.DCC.LII.

Facsimile of the title-page of the first edition (1752, for 1751). By permission of Mills Memorial Library, McMaster University.

TO
RALPH ALLEN, ESQ;[1]

SIR,

THE following book is sincerely designed to promote the cause of virtue, and to expose some of the most glaring evils, as well public as private, which at present infest the country; tho' there is scarce, as I remember, a single stroke of satire aimed at any one person throughout the whole.

The best man is the properest patron of such an attempt. This, I believe, will be readily granted; nor will the public voice, I think, be more divided, to whom they shall give that appellation. Should a letter indeed be thus inscribed, DETUR OPTIMO,[2] there are few persons who would think it wanted any other direction.

I will not trouble you with a preface concerning the work; nor endeavour to obviate any criticisms which can be made on it. The good-natured reader, if his heart should be here affected, will be inclined to pardon many faults for the pleasure he will receive from a tender sensation; and for readers of a different stamp, the more faults they can discover, the more, I am convinced, they will be pleased.

Nor will I assume the fulsome stile of common dedicators. I have not their usual design[3] in this epistle; nor will I borrow their language. Long, very long may it be before a most dreadful circumstance shall make it possible for any pen to draw a just and true character of yourself, without incurring a suspicion of flattery in the bosoms of the malignant. This task, therefore, I shall defer till that day (if I should be so unfortunate as ever to see it) when every good man shall pay a tear for the satisfaction of his curiosity; a day which at present, I believe, there is but one good man in the world who can think of with unconcern.

Accept then, sir, this small token of that love, that gratitude, and that respect, with which I shall always esteem it my GREATEST HONOUR to be,

SIR,

Your most obliged,

And most obedient

Humble Servant,

Henry Fielding.

Bow Street,
Dec. 12,
1751

CONTENTS

BOOK I

BOOK II

BOOK III

BOOK IV

BOOK V

BOOK VI

BOOK VII

BOOK VIII

BOOK IX

BOOK X

BOOK XI

BOOK XII

BOOK I

CHAPTER 1

Containing the exordium, &c.

THE various accidents which befel a very worthy couple, after their uniting in the state of matrimony, will be the subject of the following history. The distresses which they waded through, were some of them so exquisite, and the incidents which produced these so extraordinary, that they seemed to require not only the utmost malice, but the utmost invention which superstition hath ever attributed to Fortune: tho' whether any such being interfered in the case, or, indeed, whether there be any such being in the universe, is a matter which I by no means presume to determine in the affirmative. To speak a bold truth, I am, after much mature deliberation, inclined to suspect, that the public voice hath in all ages done much injustice to Fortune, and hath convicted her of many facts in which she had not the least concern. I question much, whether we may not by natural means account for the success of knaves, the calamities of fools, with all the miseries in which men of sense sometimes involve themselves by quitting the directions of prudence, and following the blind guidance of a predominant passion; in short, for all the ordinary phenomena which are imputed to Fortune; whom, perhaps, men accuse with no less absurdity in life, than a bad player complains of ill luck at the game of chess.

But if men are sometimes guilty of laying improper blame on this imaginary being, they are altogether as apt to make her amends, by ascribing to her honours which she as little deserves. To retrieve the ill consequences of a foolish conduct, and by struggling manfully with distress to subdue it, is one of the noblest efforts of wisdom and virtue. Whoever, therefore, calls such a man fortunate, is guilty of no less impropriety in speech, than he would be, who should call the statuary or the poet fortunate, who carved a Venus or who writ an Iliad.

Life may as properly be called an art as any other; and the great incidents in it are no more to be considered as mere accidents, than the several members of a fine statue, or a noble poem. The critics in all these are not content with seeing any thing to be great, without knowing why and how it came to be so. By examining carefully the several gradations which conduce to bring every model to perfection, we learn truly to know that science in which the model is formed: as histories of this kind, therefore, may properly be called models of HUMAN LIFE; so by observing minutely the several incidents which tend to the catastrophe or completion of the whole, and the minute causes whence those incidents are produced, we shall best be instructed in this most useful of all arts, which I call the ART OF LIFE.

CHAPTER 2

The history sets out. Observations on the excellency of the English constitution, and curious examinations before a Justice of Peace.

ON THE first of April, in the year —, the watchmen of a certain parish (I know not particularly which) within the liberty of Westminster,[1] brought several persons whom they had apprehended the preceding night, before Jonathan Thrasher, Esq; one of the Justices of the Peace for that liberty.

But here, reader, before we proceed to the trials of these offenders, we shall, after our usual manner, premise some things which it may be necessary for thee to know.

It hath been observed, I think, by many, as well as the celebrated writer of three letters,[2] that no human institution is capable of consummate perfection. An observation which perhaps that writer at least gathered from discovering some defects in the polity even of this well regulated nation. And, indeed, if there should be any such defect in a constitution which my Lord Coke[3] long ago told us, *the wisdom of all the wise men in the world, if they had all met together at one time, could not have equalled,* which some of our *wisest* men who were met together long before, said was too good to be altered in any particular, and which, nevertheless, hath been mending ever since, by a very great number of the said *wise men*: if, I say, this constitution should be imperfect, we may be allowed, I think, to doubt whether any such faultless model can be found among the institutions of men.

It will probably be objected, that the small imperfections which I am about to produce, do not lie in the laws themselves, but in the ill execution of them; but, with submission, this appears to me to be no less an absurdity, than to say of any machine that it is excellently made, tho' incapable of performing its functions. Good laws should execute themselves in a well regulated state; at least, if the same legislature which provides the laws, doth not provide for the execution of them, they act as Graham[4] would do, if he should ſorm all the parts of a clock in the most exquisite manner, yet put them so together that the clock could not go. In this case, surely we might say that there was a small defect in the constitution of the clock.

To say the truth, Graham would soon see the fault, and would easily remedy it. The fault indeed could be no other than that the parts were improperly disposed.

Perhaps, reader, I have another illustration, which will set my intention in still a clearer light before you. Figure to yourself then a family, the master of which should dispose of the several economical[5] offices in the following manner; *viz.* should put his butler in the coach-box, his steward behind his coach, his coachman in the butlery, and his ſootman in the stewardship, and in the same ridiculous manner should misemploy the talents of every other servant; it is easy to see what a figure such a family must make in the world.

As ridiculous as this may seem, I have often considered some of the lower offices in our civil government to be disposed in this very manner. To begin, I think, as low as I well can, with the watchmen[6] in our metropolis; who being appointed to guard our streets by night from thieves and robbers, an office which at least requires strength of body, are chosen out of those poor old decrepit people, who are from their want of bodily strength rendered incapable of getting a livelihood by work. These men, armed only with a pole, which some of them are scarce able to lift, are to secure the persons and houses of his majesty's subjects from the attacks of gangs of young, bold, stout, desperate and well-armed villains.

Quae non viribus istis
Munera conveniunt.[7]

If the poor old fellows should run away from such enemies, no one I think can wonder, unless it be that they were able to make their escape.

The higher we proceed among our public officers and magistrates, the less defects of this kind will, perhaps, be observable. Mr Thrasher, however, the Justice before whom the prisoners abovementioned were now brought, had some few imperfections in his magistratical capacity. I own, I have been sometimes inclined to think, that this office of a Justice of Peace requires some knowledge of the law: for this simple reason; because in every case which comes before him, he is to judge and act according to law. Again, as these laws are contained in a great variety of books; the statutes which relate to the office of a Justice of Peace, making of themselves at least two large volumes in folio; and that part of his jurisdiction which is founded on the common law being dispersed in above a hundred volumes, I cannot conceive how this knowledge should be acquired without reading; and yet certain it is Mr Thrasher never read one syllable of the matter.

This perhaps was a defect; but this was not all: for where mere ignorance is to decide a point between two litigants, it will always be an even chance whether it decides right or wrong; but sorry am I to say, right was often in a much worse situation than this, and wrong hath often had five hundred to one on his side before that magistrate; who, if he was ignorant of the law of England, was yet well versed in the laws of nature. He perfectly well understood that fundamental principle so strongly laid down in the institutes of the learned Rochefoucault;[8] by which the duty of self-love is so strongly enforced, and every man is taught to consider himself as the centre of gravity, and to attract all things thither. To speak the truth plainly, the Justice was never indifferent in a cause, but when he could get nothing on either side.

Such was the Justice to whose tremendous bar, Mr Gotobed the constable on the day above-mentioned, brought several delinquents, who, as we have said, had been apprehended by the watch for diverse outrages.

The first who came upon his trial was as bloody a spectre as ever the imagination of a murderer or a tragic poet conceived. This poor wretch was charged with a battery by a much stouter man than himself: indeed the accused person bore about him some evidence that he had been in an affray, his cloaths being very bloody; but certain open sluices on his own head sufficiently shewed whence all the scarlet stream had issued; whereas the accuser had not the least mark or appearance of any wound. The Justice asked the defendant, What he meant by breaking the king's peace – To which he answered, – 'Upon my shoul I do love the king very well, and I have not been after breaking any thing of his that I do know; but upon my shoul this man hath brake my head, and my head did brake his stick; that is all, gra.' He then offered to produce several witnesses against this improbable accusation; but the Justice presently interrupted him, saying, 'Sirrah, your tongue betrays your guilt. You are an Irishman, and that is always sufficient evidence with me.'

The second criminal was a poor woman, who was taken up by the watch as a street-walker. It was alledged against her that she was found walking the streets after twelve o'clock, and the watchman declared he believed her to be a common strumpet. She pleaded in her defence (as was really the truth) that she was a servant, and was sent by her mistress, who was a little shopkeeper, and upon the point of delivery, to fetch a midwife; which she offered to prove by several of the neighbours, if she was allowed to send for them. The Justice asked her why she had not done it before. To which she answered, she had no money, and could get no messenger. The Justice then called her several scurrilous names; and declaring she was guilty within the statute of street-walking, ordered her to Bridewell[9] for a month.

A genteel young man and woman were then set forward, and a very grave looking person swore he caught them in a situation which we cannot as particularly describe here as he did before the magistrate; who, having received a wink from his clerk, declared with much warmth that the fact was incredible and impossible. He presently discharged the accused parties, and was going, without any evidence, to commit the accuser of perjury; but this the clerk dissuaded him from, saying, he doubted whether a Justice of Peace had any such power. The Justice at first differed in opinion; and said, 'He had seen a man stand in the pillory about perjury; nay, he had known a man in goal for it too; and how came he there, if he was not committed thither?' 'Why that is true, sir,' answered the clerk. 'And yet I have been told by a very great lawyer, that a man can't be committed for perjury before he is indicted; and the reason is, I believe, because it is not against the peace before the indictment makes it so.' 'Why that may be,' cries the Justice; 'and indeed perjury is but scandalous words, and I know a man can't have no warrant for those, unless you put for rioting* them into the warrant.'

The witness was now about to be discharged, when the lady whom he had accused, declared she would swear the peace against him; for that he had called her a whore several times. 'Oho! you will swear the peace, madam, will you?' cries the Justice, 'Give her the peace, presently; and pray, Mr Constable, secure the prisoner, now we have him, while a warrant is made to take him up.' All which was immediately performed, and the poor witness for want of sureties was sent to prison.

A young fellow, whose name was Booth, was now charged with beating the watchman, in the execution of his office, and breaking his lanthorn. This was deposed by two witnesses; and the shattered remains of a broken lanthorn, which had been long preserved for the sake of its testimony, were produced to corroborate the evidence. The Justice, perceiving the criminal to be but

* *Opus est Interprete.*[10] By the laws of England abusive words are not punishable by the magistrate; some commissioners of the peace therefore, when one scold hath applied to them for a warrant against another, from a too eager desire of doing justice, have construed a little harmless scolding into a riot, which is in law an outragious breach of the peace, committed by several persons, by three at the least, nor can a less number be convicted of it. Under this word rioting, or riotting (for I have seen it spelt both ways) many thousands of old women have been arrested and put to expence, sometimes in prison, for a little intemperate use of their tongues. This practice began to decrease in the year 1749.[11]

shabbily drest, was going to commit him without asking any further questions. At length, however, at the earnest request of the accused, the worthy magistrate submitted to hear his defence. The young man then alledged, as was in reality the case, 'That as he was walking home to his lodging, he saw two men in the street cruelly beating a third, upon which he had stopt and endeavoured to assist the person who was so unequally attacked; that the watch came up during the affray, and took them all four into custody; that they were immediately carried to the round-house,[12] where the two original assailants, who appeared to be men of fortune, found means to make up the matter, and were discharged by the constable; a favour which he himself, having no money in his pocket, was unable to obtain. He utterly denied having assaulted any of the watchmen, and solemnly declared, that he was offered his liberty at the price of half a crown.'

Tho' the bare word of an offender can never be taken against the oath of his accuser; yet the matter of this defence was so pertinent, and delivered with such an air of truth and sincerity, that had the magistrate been endued with much sagacity, or had he been very moderately gifted with another quality very necessary to all who are to administer justice, he would have employed some labour in cross-examining the watchmen; at least he would have given the defendant the time he desired to send for the other persons who were present at the affray; neither of which he did. In short, the magistrate had too great an honour for truth to suspect that she ever appeared in sordid apparel; nor did he ever sully his sublime notions of that virtue, by uniting them with the mean ideas of poverty and distress.

There remained now only one prisoner, and that was the poor man himself in whose defence the last mentioned culprit was engaged. His trial took but a very short time. A cause of battery and broken lanthorn was instituted against him, and proved in the same manner; nor would the Justice hear one word in defence: but tho' his patience was exhausted, his breath was not; for against this last wretch he poured forth a great many vollies of menaces and abuse.

The delinquents were then all dispatched to prison, under a guard of watchmen; and the Justice and the constable adjourned to a neighbouring alehouse, to take their morning repast.

CHAPTER 3

Containing the inside of a prison.

MR BOOTH (for we shall not trouble you with the rest) was no sooner arrived in the prison, than a number of persons gathered round him, all demanding garnish; to which Mr Booth not making a ready answer, as indeed he did not understand the word, some were going to lay hold of him, when a person of apparent dignity came up and insisted that no one should affront the gentleman. This person then, who was no less than the master or keeper of the prison, turning towards Mr Booth, acquainted him, that it was the custom of the place for every prisoner, upon his first arrival there, to give something to the former prisoners to make them drink. This, he said, was what they called garnish; and concluded with advising his new customer to draw his purse upon the present occasion. Mr Booth answered, that he would very readily comply with this laudable custom, was it in his power; but that in reality he had not a shilling in his pocket, and what was worse, he had not a shilling in the world. – 'Oho! if that be the case,' cries the keeper, 'it is another matter, and I have nothing to say.' Upon which he immediately departed, and left poor Booth to the mercy of his companions, who without loss of time applied themselves to uncasing, as they term'd it, and with such dexterity, that his coat was not only stript off, but out of sight in a minute.

Mr Booth was too weak to resist, and too wise to complain of this usage. As soon therefore as he was at liberty, and declared free of the place,[13] he summoned his philosophy, of which he had no inconsiderable share, to his assistance, and resolved to make himself as easy as possible under his present circumstances.

Could his own thoughts indeed have suffered him a moment to forget where he was, the dispositions of the other prisoners might have induced him to believe that he had been in a happier place: for much the greater part of his fellow-sufferers, instead of wailing and repining at their condition, were laughing, singing and diverting themselves with various kinds of sports and gambols.

The first person who accosted him was called Blear-Eyed Moll; a woman of no very comely appearance. Her eye (for she had but one) whence she derived her nick-name was such, as that nick-name bespoke; besides which it had two remarkable qualities; for first, as if nature had been careful to provide for her own defect, it constantly looked towards her blind side; and secondly, the ball consisted almost entirely of white, or rather yellow, with a little grey spot in the corner, so small that it was scarce discernible. Nose she had none;[14] for Venus, envious perhaps at her former charms, had carried off the gristly part; and some earthly damsel, perhaps from the same envy, had levelled the bone with the rest of her face: indeed it was far beneath the bones of her cheeks, which rose proportionally higher than is usual. About half a dozen ebony teeth fortified that large and long canal, which nature had cut from ear to ear, at the bottom of which was a chin, preposterously short, nature having turned up the bottom, instead of suffering it to grow to its due length.

Her body was well adapted to her face; she measured full as much round the middle as from head to foot; for besides the extreme breadth of her back, her vast breasts had long since forsaken their native home, and had settled themselves a little below the girdle.

I wish certain actresses on the stage, when they are to perform characters of no amiable cast, would study to dress themselves with the propriety with which Blear-Eyed Moll was now arrayed. For the sake of our squeamish reader, we shall not descend to particulars. Let it suffice to say, nothing more ragged, or more dirty, was ever emptied out of the round-house at St Giles's.[15]

We have taken the more pains to describe this person for two remarkable reasons; the one is, that this unlovely creature was taken in the fact with a very pretty young fellow; the other, which is more productive of moral lesson, is, that however wretched her fortune may appear to the reader, she was one of the merriest persons in the whole prison.

Blear-Eyed Moll then came up to Mr Booth with a smile, or rather grin on her countenance, and asked him for a dram of gin; and when Booth assured her that he had not a penny of money, she replied, '– D—n your eyes, I thought by your look you had been a clever fellow, and upon the snaffling lay* at least; but d—n your body and eyes, I find you are some sneaking budge† rascal.' She then launched forth a volley of dreadful oaths, interlarded with some language, not proper to be repeated here, and was going to lay hold on poor Booth, when a tall prisoner, who had been very earnestly eyeing Booth for some time, came up, and taking her by the shoulder, flung her off at some distance, cursing her for a b—h, and bidding her let the gentleman alone.

This person was not himself of the most inviting aspect. He was long visaged, and pale, with a red beard of above a fortnight's growth. He was attired in a brownish black coat, which would have shewed more holes than it did, had not the linen which appeared through it, been entirely of the same colour with the cloth.

This gentleman, whose name was Robinson, addressed himself very civilly to Mr Booth, and told him he was sorry to see one of his appearance in that place: 'For as to your being without your coat, sir,' says he, 'I can easily account for that; and indeed dress is the least part which distinguishes a gentleman.' At which words he cast a significant look on his own coat, as if he desired they should be applied to himself. He then proceeded in the following manner:

'I perceive, sir, you are but just arrived in this dismal place, which is, indeed, rendered more detestable by the wretches who inhabit it, than by any other circumstance; but even these a wise man will soon bring himself to bear with indifference: for what is, is; and what must be, must be. The knowledge of this, which, simple as it appears, is in truth the height of all philosophy, renders a wise man superior to every evil which can befal him. I hope, sir, no very dreadful accident is the cause of your coming hither; but whatever it was, you may be assured it could not be otherwise: for all things happen by an inevitable fatality; and a man can no more resist the impulse of fate, than a wheel-barrow can the force of its driver.'

Besides the obligation which Mr Robinson had conferred on Mr Booth, in delivering him from the insults of Blear-Eyed Moll,

* A cant term for robbery on the high-way.
† A cant term for pilfering.

there was something in the manner of Robinson, which, notwithstanding the meanness of his dress, seemed to distinguish him from the crowd of wretches who swarmed in those regions; and above all, the sentiments which he had just declared, very nearly coincided with those of Mr Booth. This gentleman was what they call a freethinker, that is to say, a deist, or, perhaps, an atheist; for tho' he did not absolutely deny the existence of a god, yet he entirely denied his providence: a doctrine which, if it is not downright atheism, hath a direct tendency towards it; and, as Dr Clarke[16] observes, may soon be driven into it. And as to Mr Booth, tho' he was in his heart an extreme well-wisher to religion (for he was an honest man) yet his notions of it were very slight and uncertain. To say truth, he was in the wavering condition so finely described by Claudian:

> *labefacta cadebat*
> *Religio, causaeque viam non sponte sequebar*
> *Alterius; vacuo quae currere semina motu*
> *Affirmat; magnumque novas per inane figuras*
> *Fortuna non arte regi; quae numina sensu*
> *Ambiguo, vel nulla putat, vel nescia nostri.*[17]

This way of thinking, or rather of doubting, he had contracted from the same reasons which Claudian assigns, and which had induced Brutus[18] in his latter days, to doubt the existence of that virtue which he had all his life cultivated. In short, poor Booth imagined, that a larger share of misfortunes had fallen to his lot than he had merited; and this led him, who (tho' a good classical scholar) was not deeply learned in religious matters, into a disadvantageous opinion of providence. A dangerous way of reasoning, in which our conclusions are not only too hasty, from an imperfect view of things; but we are likewise liable to much error from partiality to ourselves; viewing our virtues and vices as through a perspective, in which we turn the glass always to our own advantage, so as to diminish the one, and as greatly to magnify the other.

From the above reasons, it can be no wonder that Mr Booth did not decline the acquaintance of this person, in a place which could not promise to afford him any better. He answered him, therefore, with great courtesy, as indeed he was of a very good and gentle disposition; and after expressing a civil surprize at meeting him there, declared himself to be of the same opinion with regard to the necessity of human actions; adding, however, that he did not believe men were under any blind impulse or direction of fate; but that every man acted merely from the force of that passion which was uppermost in his mind, and could do no otherwise.

A discourse now ensued between the two gentlemen, on the necessity arising from the impulse of fate, and the necessity arising from the impulse of passion, which, as it will make a pretty pamphlet of itself, we shall reserve for some future opportunity. When this was ended, they set forward to survey the goal, and the prisoners, with the several cases of whom Mr Robinson, who had been some time under confinement, undertook to make Mr Booth acquainted.

CHAPTER 4

Disclosing further secrets of the prison-house.

THE first persons whom they past by were three men in fetters, who were enjoying themselves very merrily over a bottle of wine and a pipe of tobacco. These, Mr Robinson informed his friend, were three street-robbers, and were all certain of being hanged the ensuing sessions. So inconsiderable an object, said he, is misery to light minds, when it is at any distance.

A little farther they beheld a man prostrate on the ground, whose heavy groans, and frantic actions, plainly indicated the highest disorder of mind. This person was, it seems, committed for a small felony; and his wife, who then lay-in, upon hearing the news, had thrown herself from a window two pair of stairs high, by which means he had, in all probability, lost both her and his child.

A very pretty girl then advanced towards them, whose beauty Mr Booth could not help admiring the moment he saw her; declaring, at the same time, he thought she had great innocence in her countenance. Robinson said she was committed thither as an idle and disorderly person, and a common street-walker. As she past by Mr Booth, she damn'd his eyes, and discharged a volley of words, every one of which was too indecent to be repeated.

They now beheld a little creature sitting by herself in a corner and crying bitterly. This girl, Mr Robinson said, was committed, because her father-in-law, who was in the Granadier Guards, had sworn that he was afraid of his life, or of some bodily harm, which she would do him, and she could get no sureties for keeping the peace; for which reason Justice Thrasher had committed her to prison.

A great noise now arose, occasioned by the prisoners all flocking to see a fellow whipt for petty larceny, to which he was condemned by the Court of Quarter Sessions; but this soon ended in the disappointment of the spectators; for the fellow, after being stript, having advanced another sixpence, was discharged untouched.

This was immediately followed by another bustle. Blear-Eyed Moll, and several of her companions, having got possession of a man who was committed for certain odious unmanlike practices, not fit to be named, were giving him various kinds of discipline, and would probably have put an end to him, had he not been rescued out of their hands by authority.

When this bustle was a little allayed, Mr Booth took notice of a young woman in rags sitting on the ground, and supporting the head of an old man in her lap, who appeared to be giving up the ghost. These, Mr Robinson informed him, were father and daughter; that the latter was committed for stealing a loaf, in order to support the former, and the former for receiving it knowing it to be stolen.[19]

A well-drest man then walked surlily by them, whom Mr Robinson reported to have been committed on an indictment found against him for a most horrid perjury; 'but', says he, 'we expect him to be bailed to-day.' 'Good Heaven!' cries Booth, 'can such villains find bail, and is no person charitable enough to bail that poor father and daughter?' 'Oh! sir,' answered Robinson, 'the offence of the daughter, being felony, is held not to be bailable in law; whereas perjury is a misdemeanor only; and therefore persons who are even indicted for it, are nevertheless capable of being bailed. Nay of all perjuries that of which this man is indicted, is the worst; for it was with an intention of taking away the life of an innocent person by form of law. As to perjuries in civil matters, they are not so very criminal.' 'They are not,' said Booth, 'and yet even these are a most flagitious offence, and worthy the highest punishment.' 'Surely they ought to be distinguished,' answered Robinson, 'from the others: for what is taking away a little property from a man compared to taking away his life, and his reputation, and ruining his family into the bargain? – I hope there can be no comparison in the crimes, and I think there ought to be none in the punishment. However, at present, the punishment of all perjury is only pillory, and transportation for seven years; and as it is a traversable[20] and bailable offence, methods are often found to escape any punishment at all.'*

Booth exprest great astonishment at this, when his attention was suddenly diverted by the most miserable object that he had yet seen. This was a wretch almost naked, and who bore in his countenance, joined to an appearance of honesty, the marks of poverty, hunger, and disease. He had, moreover, a wooden leg, and two or three scars on his forehead. 'The case of this poor man is indeed unhappy enough,' said Robinson. 'He hath served his country, lost his limb, and received several wounds at the siege of Gibraltar.[22] When he was discharged from the hospital abroad, he came over to get into that of Chelsea,[23] but could not immediately, as none of his officers were then in England; in the mean time, he was one day apprehended and committed hither on suspicion of stealing three herrings from a fishmonger. He was tried several months ago for this offence, and acquitted; indeed his innocence manifestly appeared at the trial; but he was brought back again for his fees,[24] and here he hath lain ever since.'

Booth exprest great horror at this account, and declared if he had only so much money in his pocket, he would pay his fees for him; but added, that he was not possest of a single farthing in the world.

Robinson hesitated a moment, and then said, with a smile, 'I am

* By removing the indictment by *certiorari*[21] into the King's Bench, the trial is so long postponed, and the costs are so highly encreased, that prosecutors are often tired out, and some incapacitated from pursuing. *Verbum sapienti.*

going to make you, sir, a very odd proposal after your last declaration; but what say you to a game at cards? it will serve to pass a tedious hour, and may divert your thoughts from more unpleasant speculations.'

I do not imagine Booth would have agreed to this; for tho' some love of gaming had been formerly amongst his faults; yet he was not so egregiously addicted to that vice, as to be tempted by the shabby plight of Robinson, who had, if I may so express myself, no charms for a gamester. If he had, however, any such inclinations, he had no opportunity to follow them; for before he could make any answer to Robinson's proposal, a strapping wench came up to Booth, and taking hold of his arm, asked him to walk aside with her; saying, 'What a pox, are you such a fresh cull[25] that you do not know this fellow? Why, he is a gambler, and committed for cheating at play. There is not such a pickpocket in the whole quad.'*

A scene of altercation now ensued, between Robinson and the lady, which ended in a bout at fisticuffs, in which the lady was greatly superior to the philosopher.

While the two combatants were engaged, a grave looking man, rather better drest than the majority of the company, came up to Mr Booth, and taking him aside, said, 'I am sorry, sir, to see a gentleman, as you appear to be, in such intimacy with that rascal, who makes no scruple of disowning all revealed religion. As for crimes, they are human errors, and signify but little; nay, perhaps the worse a man is by nature, the more room there is for grace. The spirit is active, and loves best to inhabit those minds where it may meet with the most work. Whatever your crime be, therefore, I would not have you despair; but rather rejoice at it; for perhaps it may be the means of your being called.' He ran on for a considerable time with this cant, without waiting for an answer, and ended in declaring himself a Methodist.[26]

Just as the Methodist had finished his discourse, a beautiful young woman was ushered into the goal. She was genteel and well drest, and did not in the least resemble those females whom Mr Booth had hitherto seen. The constable had no sooner delivered

* A cant word for a prison.

her at the gate, than she asked, with a commanding voice, for the keeper; and, when he arrived, she said to him, 'Well, sir, whither am I to be conducted? I hope I am not to take up my lodging with these creatures.' The keeper answered, with a kind of surly respect, 'Madam, we have rooms for those that can afford to pay for them.' At these words she pulled a handsome purse from her pocket, in which many guineas chinked, saying, with an air of indignation, 'that she was not come thither on account of poverty.' The keeper no sooner viewed the purse, than his features became all softned in an instant, and with all the courtesy of which he was master, he desired the lady to walk with him, assuring her that she should have the best apartment in his house.

Mr Booth was now left alone; for the Methodist had forsaken him, having, as the phrase of the sect is, searched him to the bottom. In fact, he had thoroughly examined every one of Mr Booth's pockets; from which he had conveyed away a pen-knife and an iron snuff-box, these being all the moveables which were to be found.

Booth was standing near the gate of the prison when the young lady above-mentioned was introduced into the yard. He viewed her features very attentively, and was persuaded that he knew her. She was indeed so remarkably handsome, that it was hardly possible for any who had ever seen her to forget her. He enquired of one of the under-keepers, if the name of the prisoner lately arrived was not Mathews; to which he was answered that her name was not Mathews but Vincent, and that she was committed for murder.

The latter part of this information made Mr Booth suspect his memory more than the former: for it was very possible that she might have changed her name; but he hardly thought she could so far have changed her nature as to be guilty of a crime so very incongruous with her former gentle manners; for Miss Mathews had both the birth and education of a gentlewoman. He concluded, therefore, that he was certainly mistaken, and rested satisfied without any further enquiry.

CHAPTER 5

Containing certain adventures which befel Mr Booth in the prison.

THE remainder of the day Mr Booth spent in melancholy contemplation of his present condition. He was destitute of the common necessaries of life, and consequently unable to subsist where he was; nor was there a single person in town to whom he could with any reasonable hope apply for his delivery. Grief for some time banished the thoughts of food from his mind; but, in the morning, nature began to grow uneasy for want of her usual nourishment; for he had not eat a morsel during the last forty hours. A penny loaf, which is, it seems, the ordinary allowance to the prisoners in Bridewell, was now delivered him; and while he was eating this, a man brought him a little packet sealed up, informing him that it came by a messenger who said it required no answer.

Mr Booth now opened his packet, and after unfolding several pieces of blank paper successively, at last discovered a guinea, wrapt with great care in the innermost paper. He was vastly surprised at this sight, as he had few, if any friends, from whom he could expect such a favour, slight as it was; and not one of his friends, as he was apprized, knew of his confinement. As there was no direction to the packet, nor a word of writing contained in it, he began to suspect that it was delivered to the wrong person; and, being one of the most untainted honesty, he found out the man who gave it to him, and again examined him concerning the person who brought it, and the message delivered with it. The man assured Booth that he had made no mistake; saying, 'If your name is Booth, sir, I am positive you are the gentleman to whom the parcel I gave you belongs.'

The most scrupulous honesty would, perhaps, in such a situation, have been well enough satisfied in finding no owner for the guinea; especially when proclamation had been made in the prison, that Mr Booth had received a packet without any direction, to which if any person had any claim, and would discover the contents, he was ready to deliver it to such claimant. No such claimant being found, (I mean none who knew the contents; for many swore that they expected just such a packet, and believed it to be their property) Mr Booth very calmly resolved to apply the money to his own use.

The first thing after redemption of the coat, which Mr Booth, hungry as he was, thought of, was to supply himself with snuff, which he had long, to his great sorrow, been without. On this occasion he presently missed that iron box which the Methodist had so dextrously conveyed out of his pocket, as we mentioned in the last chapter.

He no sooner missed this box, than he immediately suspected that the gambler was the person who had stolen it; nay, so well was he assured of this man's guilt, that it may perhaps be improper to say he barely suspected it. Tho' Mr Booth was, as we have hinted, a man of a very sweet disposition; yet was he rather over-warm. Having, therefore, no doubt concerning the person of the thief, he eagerly sought him out, and very bluntly charged him with the fact.

The gambler, whom I think we should now call the philosopher, received this charge without the least visible emotion either of mind or muscle. After a short pause of a few moments, he answered with great solemnity as follows: 'Young man, I am entirely unconcerned at your groundless suspicion. He that censures a stranger, as I am to you, without any cause, makes a worse compliment to himself than to the stranger. You know yourself, friend; you know not me. It is true indeed you heard me accused of being a cheat and a gamester; but who is my accuser? Look at my apparel, friend, do thieves and gamesters wear such cloaths as these? Play is my folly, not my vice; it is my impulse, and I have been a martyr to it. Would a gamester have asked another to play when he could have lost eighteen pence and won nothing? However, if you are not satisfied you may search my pockets; the outside of all but one will serve your turn, and in that one there is the eighteen pence I told you of.' He then turned up his cloaths; and his pockets entirely resembled the pitchers of the Belides.[27]

Booth was a little staggered at this defence. He said, the real value of the iron box was too inconsiderable to mention; but that he had a capricious value for it, for the sake of the person who gave it him; 'for tho' it is not,' said he, 'worth sixpence, I would willingly give a crown to any one who would bring it me again.'

Robinson answered, 'if that be the case, you have nothing more to do but to signify your intention in the prison; and I am well convinced you will not be long without regaining the possession of your snuff-box.'

This advice was immediately followed, and with success, the Methodist presently producing the box, which, he said, he had found, and should have returned it before, had he known the person to whom it belonged; adding, with uplifted eyes, that the Spirit would not suffer him knowingly to detain the goods of another, however inconsiderable the value was. 'Why so, friend?' said Robinson. 'Have I not heard you often say, the wickeder any man was, the better, provided he was what you call a believer.' 'You mistake me,' cries Cooper (for that was the name of the Methodist) 'no man can be wicked after he is possessed by the Spirit. There is a wide difference between the Days of Sin and the Days of Grace. I have been a sinner myself.' 'I believe thee,' cries Robinson, with a sneer. 'I care not,' answered the other 'what an atheist believes. I suppose you would insinuate that I stole the snuff-box; but I value not your malice; the Lord knows my innocence.' He then walked off with the reward; and Booth turning to Robinson, very earnestly asked pardon for his groundless suspicion; which the other, without any hesitation, accorded him, saying, 'You never accused me, sir; you suspected some gambler, with whose character I have no concern. I should be angry with a friend or acquaintance who should give a hasty credit to any allegation against me; but I have no reason to be offended with you for believing what the woman, and the rascal who is just gone, and who is committed here for a pickpocket, which you did not perhaps know, told you to my disadvantage. And if you thought me to be a gambler, you had just reason to suspect any ill of me; for I myself am confined here by the perjury of one of those villains; who having cheated me of my money at play, and hearing that I intended to apply to a magistrate against him, himself began the attack, and obtained a warrant against me of Justice Thrasher, who, without hearing one speech in my defence, committed me to this place.'

Booth testified great compassion at this account; and he having invited Robinson to dinner, they spent that day together. In the afternoon Booth indulged his friend with a game at cards; at first for halfpence, and afterwards for shillings, when fortune so favoured Robinson, that he did not leave the other a single shilling in his pocket.

A surprising run of luck in a gamester is often mistaken for somewhat else, by persons who are not over zealous believers in the divinity of Fortune. I have known a stranger at Bath, who hath happened fortunately (I might almost say unfortunately) to have four by honours[28] in his hand almost every time he dealt, for a whole evening, shunned universally by the whole company the next day. And certain it is, that Mr Booth, tho' of a temper very little inclined to suspicion, began to waver in his opinion, whether the character given by Mr Robinson of himself, or that which the others gave of him, was the truer.

In the morning hunger paid him a second visit, and found him again in the same situation as before. After some deliberation, therefore, he resolved to ask Robinson to lend him a shilling or two of that money which was lately his own. And this experiment, he thought, would confirm him either in a good or evil opinion of that gentleman.

To this demand Robinson answered with great alacrity, that he should very gladly have complied, had not Fortune played one of her jade tricks with him: 'for, since my winning of you,' said he, 'I have been stript not only of your money, but my own.' He was going to harangue farther; but Booth with great indignation turned from him.

This poor gentleman had very little time to reflect on his own misery, or the rascality, as it appeared to him, of the other, when the same person, who had the day before delivered him the guinea from the unknown hand, again accosted him, and told him a lady in the house (so he expressed himself) desired the favour of his company.

Mr Booth immediately obeyed the message, and was conducted

into a room in the prison, where he was presently convinced that Mrs Vincent was no other than his old acquaintance Miss Mathews.

CHAPTER 6

Containing the extraordinary behaviour of Miss Mathews on her meeting with Booth, and some endeavours to prove by reason and authority, that it is possible for a woman to appear to be what she really is not.

EIGHT or nine years had past since any interview between Mr Booth and Miss Mathews; and their meeting now in so extraordinary a place affected both of them with an equal surprise.

After some immaterial ceremonies, the lady acquainted Mr Booth, that having heard there was a person in the prison who knew her by the name of Mathews, she had great curiosity to enquire who he was, whereupon he had been shewn to her from the window of the house; that she immediately recollected him, and being informed of his distressful situation, for which she expressed great concern, she had sent him that guinea which he had received the day before; and then proceeded to excuse herself for not having desired to see him at that time, when she was under the greatest disorder and hurry of spirits.[29]

Booth made many handsome acknowledgments of her favour; and added, that he very little wondered at the disorder of her spirits, concluding, that he was heartily concerned at seeing her there; 'but I hope, madam,' said he –

Here he hesitated; upon which, bursting into an agony of tears, she cried out, 'O captain, captain, many extraordinary things have past since last I saw you. O gracious Heaven! did I ever expect that this would be the next place of our meeting!'

She then flung herself into her chair, where she gave a loose to her passion, whilst he, in the most affectionate and tender manner, endeavoured to sooth and comfort her; but passion itself did probably more for its own relief than all his friendly consolations.

Having vented this in a large flood of tears, she became pretty well composed; but Booth unhappily mentioning her father, she again relapsed into an agony, and cried out, 'Why? why will you repeat the name of that dear man? I have disgraced him, Mr Booth, I am unworthy the name of his daughter.' – Here passion again stopped her words, and discharged itself in tears.

After this second vent of sorrow or shame; or, if the reader pleases, of rage, she once more recovered from her agonies. To say the truth, these are, I believe, as critical discharges of nature, as any of those which are so called by the physicians; and do more effectually relieve the mind than any remedies with which the whole *materia medica*[30] of philosophy[31] can supply it.

When Mrs Vincent had recovered her faculties, she perceived Booth standing silent, with a mixture of concern and astonishment in his countenance; then addressing herself to him with an air of most bewitching softness, of which she was a perfect mistress, she said, 'I do not wonder at your amazement, Captain Booth; nor indeed at the concern which you so plainly discover for me; for I well know the goodness of your nature; but O Mr Booth! believe me, when you know what hath happened since our last meeting, your concern will be raised, however your astonishment may cease. O, sir, you are a stranger to the cause of my sorrows.'

'I hope, I am, madam,' answered he; 'for I cannot believe what I have heard in the prison – surely murder –' At which words she started from her chair, repeating, 'Murder! oh! 'tis music in my ears. – You have heard then the cause of my commitment, my glory, my delight, my reparation! – Yes, my old friend, this is the hand, this is the arm that drove the penknife to his heart. Unkind fortune, that not one drop of his blood reached my hand. – Indeed, sir, I would never have washed it from it. – But tho' I have not the happiness to see it on my hand, I have the glorious satisfaction of remembring I saw it run in rivers on the floor; I saw it forsake his cheeks. I saw him fall a martyr to my revenge. And is the killing a villain to be called murder? Perhaps the law calls it so. – Let it call it what it will, or punish me as it pleases. – Punish me! – no, no – that is not in the power of man – not of that monster man, Mr Booth. I am undone, am revenged, and have now no more business for life; let them take it from me when they will.'

Our poor gentleman turned pale with horror at this speech, and the ejaculation of *Good Heavens! what do I hear!* burst spontaneously from his lips. Nor can we wonder at this, tho' he was the bravest of men; for her voice, her looks, her gestures, were properly adapted to the sentiments she exprest. Such indeed was her image, that neither could Shakespeare describe, nor Hogarth paint, nor Clive[32] act a Fury in higher perfection.

'What do you hear?' reiterated she. 'You hear the resentment of the most injured of women. You have heard, you say, of the murder; but do you know the cause, Mr Booth? Have you, since your return to England, visited that country where we formerly knew one another? Tell me, do you know my wretched story? tell me that, my friend.'

Booth hesitated for an answer; indeed he had heard some imperfect stories, not much to her advantage. She waited not till he had formed a speech; but cried, 'Whatever you may have heard, you cannot be acquainted with all the strange accidents which have occasioned your seeing me in a place, which, at our last parting, was so unlikely that I should ever have been found in; nor can you know the cause of all that I have uttered, and which, I am convinced, you never expected to have heard from my mouth. If these circumstances raise your curiosity, I will satisfy it.'

He answered, that curiosity was too mean a word to express his ardent desire of knowing her story. Upon which, with very little previous ceremony, she began to relate what is written in the following chapter.

But before we put an end to this, it may be necessary to whisper a word or two to the critics, who have perhaps begun to express no less astonishment than Mr Booth, that a lady, in whom we had remarked a most extraordinary power of displaying softness, should the very next moment after the words were out of our mouth, express sentiments becoming the lips of a Dalila, Jezebel, Medea, Semiramis, Parysatis, Tanaquil, Livilla, Messalina, Agrippina, Brunichilde, Elfrida, Lady Macbeth, Joan of Naples, Christina of Sweden, Katharine Hays, Sarah Malcolm, Con. Philips,* or any other heroine of the tender sex,[33] which

* Tho' last, not least.

history sacred or prophane, antient or modern, false or true, hath recorded.

We desire such critics to remember, that it is the same English climate, in which on the lovely 10th of June,[34] under a serene sky, the amorous Jacobite kissing the odoriferous Zephyr's breath, gathers a nose-gay of white roses to deck the whiter breast of Celia; and in which, on the 11th of June, the very next day, the boisterous Boreas,[35] roused by the hollow thunder, rushes horrible through the air, and driving the wet tempest before him, levels the hope of the husbandman with the earth, dreadful remembrance of the consequences of the Revolution.[36]

Again let it be remembered, that it is the self same Celia, all tender, soft, and delicate, who with a voice, the sweetness of which the sirens might envy, warbles the harmonious song in praise of the young adventurer,[37] and again, the next day, or, perhaps, the next hour, with fiery eyes, wrinkled brows, and foaming lips, roars forth treason and nonsense in a political argument with some fair one, of a different principle.

Or, if the critic be a Whig, and consequently dislikes such kind of similes, as being too favourable to Jacobitism, let him be contented with the following story:

I happened in my youth to sit behind two ladies in a side-box at a play, where, in the balcony on the opposite side was placed the inimitable B—y C—s,[38] in company with a young fellow of no very formal, or indeed sober appearance. One of the ladies, I remember, said to the other – 'Did you ever see any thing look so modest and so innocent as that girl over the way? what pity it is such a creature should be in the way of ruin, as I am afraid she is, by her being alone with that young fellow!' Now this lady was no bad physiognomist; for it was impossible to conceive a greater appearance of modesty, innocence and simplicity, than what nature had displayed in the countenance of that girl; and yet, all appearances notwithstanding, I myself (remember, critic, it was in my youth) had a few mornings before seen that very identical picture of all those engaging qualities in bed with a rake at a bagnio, smoking tobacco, drinking punch, talking obscenity, and swearing and cursing with all the impudence and impiety of the lowest and most abandoned trull of a soldier.

CHAPTER 7

In which Miss Mathews begins her history.

MISS MATHEWS having barred the door on the inside, as securely as it was before barred on the outside, proceeded as follows: 'You may imagine, I am going to begin my history at the time when you left the country; but I cannot help reminding you of something which happened before. You will soon recollect the incident; but I believe you little know the consequence either at that time or since. Alas! I could keep a secret then: now I have no secrets; the world knows all; and it is not worth my while to conceal any thing. Well! – You will not wonder, I believe. – I protest I can hardly tell it you even now. – But I am convinced you have too good an opinion of yourself to be surprised at any conquest you may have made. – Few men want that good opinion – and perhaps very few had ever more reason for it. Indeed, Will, you was a charming fellow in those days; nay you are not much altered for the worse now, at least in the opinion of some women: for your complexion and features are grown much more masculine than they were.' Here Booth made her a low bow, most probably with a compliment; and, after a little hesitation, she again proceeded – 'Do you remember a contest which happened at an assembly, betwixt myself and Miss Johnson, about standing uppermost?[39] You was then my partner; and young Williams danced with the other lady. The particulars are not now worth mentioning, tho' I suppose you have long since forgot them. Let it suffice that you supported my claim, and Williams very sneakingly gave up that of his partner, who was with much difficulty afterwards prevailed on to dance with him. You said, – I am sure I repeat the words exactly, that "you would not for the world affront any lady there; but that you thought you might, without any such danger declare, that there was no assembly in which that lady, meaning your humble servant, was not worthy of the uppermost place; nor will I, said you, suffer the first duke in England, when she is at the uppermost end of the room, and hath called her dance, to lead his partner above her."

'What made this the more pleasing to me was, that I secretly hated Miss Johnson. Will you have the reason? Why then, I will tell you honestly, she was my rival; – that word perhaps astonishes you, as you never, I believe, heard of any one who made his addresses to me; and indeed my heart was till that night entirely indifferent to all mankind. I mean then that she was my rival for praise, for beauty, for dress, for fortune, and consequently for admiration. My triumph on this conquest is not to be expressed, any more than my delight in the person to whom I chiefly owed it. The former, I fancy, was visible to the whole company; and I desired it should be so; but the latter was so well concealed, that no one, I am confident, took any notice of it. And yet you appeared to me that night to be an angel. You looked, you danced, you spoke – every thing charmed me.'

'Good Heavens!' cries Booth, 'is it possible you should do me so much unmerited honour, and I should be dunce enough not to perceive the least symptom!'

'I assure you,' answered she, 'I did all I could to prevent you; and yet I almost hated you for not seeing through what I strove to hide. Why, Mr Booth, was you not more quick-sighted? – I will answer for you – your affections were more happily disposed of to a much better woman than myself, whom you married soon afterwards. I should ask you for her, Mr Booth; I should have asked you for her before; but I am unworthy of asking for her, or of calling her my acquaintance.'

Booth stopt her short, as she was running into another fit of passion, and begged her to omit all former matters, and acquaint him with that part of her history to which he was an entire stranger.

She then renewed her discourse as follows: 'You know, Mr Booth, I soon afterwards left that town, upon the death of my grandmother, and returned home to my father's house; where I had not been long arrived before some troops of dragoons came to quarter in our neighbourhood. Among the officers there was a cornet,[40] whose detested name was Hebbers, a name I could scarce repeat, had I not at the same time the pleasure to reflect that he is now no more. My father, you know, who is a hearty well-wisher to the present government, used always to invite the officers to his house; so did he these. Nor was it long before this cornet, in so particular a manner recommended himself to the poor old gentleman (I cannot think of him without tears) that our house became his principal habitation; and he was rarely at his quarters, unless when his superior officers obliged him to be there. I shall say nothing of his person, nor could that be any recommendation to a man; it was such, however, as no woman could have made an objection to. Nature had certainly wrapt up her odious work in a most beautiful covering. To say the truth, he was the handsomest man, except one only, that I ever saw – I assure you, I have seen a handsomer – but – well – He had besides all the qualifications of a gentleman, was genteel, and extremely polite, spoke French well, and danced to a miracle; but what chiefly recommended him to my father was his skill in music, of which you know that dear man was the most violent lover. I wish he was not too susceptible of flattery on that head; for I have heard Hebbers often greatly commend my father's performance, and have observed, that the good man was wonderfully pleased with such commendations. To say the truth, it is the only way I can account for the extraordinary friendship which my father conceived for this person; such a friendship that he at last became a part of our family.

'This very circumstance, which, as I am convinced, strongly recommended him to my father, had the very contrary effect with me; I had never any delight in music,[41] and it was not without much difficulty I was prevailed on to learn to play on the harpsichord, in which I had made a very slender progress. As this man, therefore, was frequently the occasion of my being importuned to play against my will, I began to entertain some dislike for him on that account; and as to his person, I assure you, I long continued to look on it with great indifference.

'How strange will the art of this man appear to you presently, who had sufficient address to convert that very circumstance which had at first occasioned my dislike, into the first seeds of affection for him.

'You have often, I believe, heard my sister Betty play on the harpsichord; she was indeed reputed the best performer in the whole country.

'I was the farthest in the world from regarding this perfection of hers with envy. In reality, perhaps, I despised all perfection of this kind; at least, as I had neither skill nor ambition to excel this way, I looked upon it as a matter of mere indifference.

'Hebbers first put this emulation in my head. He took great pains to persuade me, that I had much greater abilities of the musical kind than my sister; and that I might, with the greatest ease, if I pleased, excel her; offering me, at the same time, his assistance, if I would resolve to undertake it.

'When he had sufficiently inflamed my ambition, in which perhaps he found too little difficulty, the continual praises of my sister, which before I had disregarded, became more and more nauseous in my ears; and the rather as music being the favourite passion of my father, I became apprehensive (not without frequent hints from Hebbers of that nature) that she might gain too great a preference in his favour.

'To my harpsichord then I applied myself night and day, with such industry and attention, that I soon began to perform in a tolerable manner. I do not absolutely say I excelled my sister; for many were of a different opinion; but indeed there might be some partiality in all that.

'Hebbers, at least, declared himself on my side, and no body could doubt his judgment. He asserted openly, that I played in the better manner of the two; and one day, when I was playing to him alone, he affected to burst into a rapture of admiration, and, squeezing me gently by the hand, said, "There, madam, I now declare you excel your sister as much in music, as," added he, in a whispering sigh, "you do her and all the world in every other charm."

'No woman can bear any superiority in whatever thing she desires to excel in. I now began to hate all the admirers of my sister, to be uneasy at every commendation bestowed on her skill in music, and consequently to love Hebbers for the preference which he gave to mine.

'It was now that I began to survey the handsome person of Hebbers with pleasure. And here, Mr Booth, I will betray to you the grand secret of our sex. – Many women, I believe, do with great innocence, and even with great indifference, converse with men of the finest persons; but this I am confident may be affirmed with truth, that when once a woman comes to ask this question of herself; Is the man whom I like for some other reason, handsome? her fate and his too very strongly depend on her answering in the affirmative.

'Hebbers no sooner perceived that he made an impression on my heart, of which, I am satisfied, I gave him too undeniable tokens, than he affected, on a sudden, to shun me in the most apparent manner. He wore the most melancholy air in my presence, and, by his dejected looks and sighs, firmly persuaded me, that there was some secret sorrow labouring in his bosom; nor will it be difficult for you to imagine to what cause I imputed it.

'Whilst I was wishing for his declaration of a passion, in which, I thought, I could not be mistaken, and, at the same time, trembling, whenever we met, with the apprehension of this very declaration, the widow Cary came from London to make us a visit, intending to stay the whole summer at our house.

'Those who know Mrs Cary, will scarce think I do her an injury, in saying, she is far from being handsome; and yet she is as finished a coquette as if she had the highest beauty to support that character. But, perhaps, you have seen her; and, if you have, I am convinced you will readily subscribe to my opinion.'

Booth answered, he had not; and then she proceeded as in the following chapter.

CHAPTER 8

The history of Miss Mathews continued.

'THIS young lady had not been three days with us, before Hebbers grew so particular with her, that it was generally observed, and my poor father, who, I believe, loved the cornet as if he had been his son, began to jest on the occasion, as one who would not be displeased at throwing a good jointure[42] into the arms of his friend.

'You will easily guess, sir, the disposition of my mind on this occasion; but I was not permitted to suffer long under it; for one day, when Hebbers was alone with me, he took an opportunity of expressing his abhorrence at the thoughts of marrying for interest, contrary to his inclinations. I was warm on the subject, and, I believe, went so far as to say, *that none but fools and villains did so.* He replied, with a sigh, *Yes, madam, but what would you think of a man whose heart is all the while bleeding for another woman, to whom he would willingly sacrifice the world; but, because he must sacrifice her interest as well as his own, never durst even give her a hint of that passion which was preying on his very vitals? Do you believe, Miss Fanny, there is such a wretch on earth?* I answered, with an assumed coldness, *I did not believe there was*; he then took me gently by the hand, and, with a look so tender that I can not describe it, vowed he was himself that wretch. Then starting, as if conscious of an error committed, he cried with a faltering voice, *What am I saying? Pardon me, Miss Fanny; since I beg only your pity, I never will ask for more.* – At these words, hearing my father coming up, I betrayed myself entirely, if, indeed, I had not done it before. I hastily withdrew my hand, crying, *Hush! for Heaven's sake, my father is just coming in*; my blushes, my look, and my accent telling him, I suppose, all which he wished to know.

'A few days now brought matters to an *éclaircissement* between us; the being undeceived in what had given me so much uneasiness, gave me a pleasure too sweet to be resisted. To triumph over the widow, for whom I had, in a very short time, contracted a most inveterate hatred, was a pride not to be described. Hebbers appeared to me to be the cause of all this happiness. I doubted not but that he had the most disinterested passion for me, and thought him every way worthy of its return. I did return it, and accepted him as my lover.

'He declared the greatest apprehensions of my father's suspicion, though I am convinced these were causeless, had his designs been honourable. To blind these, I consented that he should carry on sham addresses to the widow, who was now a constant jest between us; and he pretended, from time to time, to acquaint me faithfully with every thing that past at his interviews with her; nor was this faithless woman wanting in her part of the deceit. She carried herself to me all the while with a shew of affection, and pretended to have the utmost friendship for me. But such are the friendships of women!'

At this remark, Booth, though enough affected at some parts of the story, had great difficulty to refrain from laughter; but, by good luck, he escaped being perceived; and the lady went on without interruption.

'I am come now to a part of my narrative in which it is impossible to be particular, without being tedious; for as to the commerce between lovers, it is, I believe, much the same in all cases; and there is, perhaps, scarce a single phrase that hath not been repeated ten millions of times.

'One thing, however, as I strongly remarked it then, so I will repeat it to you now. In all our conversations, in moments when he fell into the warmest raptures, and exprest the greatest uneasiness at the delay of his joys, he seldom mentioned the word marriage; and never once solicited a day for that purpose. Indeed women cannot be cautioned too much against such lovers; for though I have heard, and perhaps, truly, of some of our sex of a virtue so exalted, that it is proof against every temptation; yet the generality, I am afraid, are too much in the power of a man to whom they have owned an affection. What is called being upon a good footing, is, perhaps, being upon a very dangerous one; and a woman who hath given her consent to marry, can hardly be said to be safe till she is married.

'And now, sir, I hasten to the period of my ruin. We had a wedding in our family; my musical sister was married to a young fellow as musical as herself. Such a match, you may be sure, amongst other festivities, must have a ball. Oh! Mr Booth, shall modesty forbid me to remark to you what past on that occasion? But why do I mention modesty, who have no pretensions to it? Every thing was said, and practised, on that occasion, as if the purpose had been to inflame the mind of every woman present. That effect, I freely own to you, it had with me. Music, dancing, wine, and the most luscious conversation, in which my poor dear father innocently joined, raised ideas in me of which I shall for ever repent; and I wished (why should I deny it?) that it had been my wedding, instead of my sister's.

'The villain Hebbers danced with me that night, and he lost no opportunity of improving the occasion. In short, the dreadful evening came. My father, though it was a very unusual thing with him, grew intoxicated with liquor; most of the men were in the same condition; nay, I myself drank more than I was accustomed to, enough to inflame, though not to disorder. I lost my former bed-fellow, my sister, and, – you may, I think, guess the rest, – the villain found means to steal to my chamber, and I was undone.

'Two months I passed in this detested commerce, buying, even then, my guilty, half-tasted pleasures at too dear a rate, with continual horror and apprehension; but what have I paid since, what do I pay now, Mr Booth? O may my fate be a warning to every woman to keep her innocence, to resist every temptation, since she is certain to repent of the foolish bargain. May it be a warning to her to deal with mankind with care and caution; to shun the least approaches of dishonour, and never to confide too much in the honesty of a man, nor in her own strength, where she has so much at stake; let her remember she walks on a precipice, and the bottomless pit is to receive her, if she slips; nay, if she makes but one false step.

'I ask your pardon, Mr Booth, I might have spared these exhortations, since no woman hears me; but you will not wonder at seeing me affected on this occasion.'

Booth declared he was much more surprised at her being able so well to preserve her temper in recounting her story.

'O sir,' answered she, 'I am at length reconciled to my fate; and I can now die with pleasure, since I die revenged. I am not one of those mean wretches who can sit down and lament their misfortunes. If I ever shed tears, they are the tears of indignation – but I will proceed.

'It was my fate now to solicit marriage; and I failed not to do it in the most earnest manner. He answered me at first with procrastinations, declaring from time to time he would mention it to my father, and still excusing himself for not doing it. At last he thought on an expedient to obtain a longer reprieve. This was by pretending that he should in a very few weeks be preferred to the command of a troop; and then he said, he could with some confidence propose the match.

'In this delay I was persuaded to acquiesce; and was indeed pretty easy; for I had not yet the least mistrust of his honour; but what words can paint my sensations! when one morning he came into my room, with all the marks of dejection in his countenance, and throwing an open letter on the table, said, "There is news, madam, in that letter which I am unable to tell you; nor can it give you more concern than it hath given me."

'This letter was from his captain, to acquaint him, that the rout, as they call it, was arrived, and that they were to march within two days. And this I am since convinced was what he expected, instead of the preferment which had been made the pretence of delaying our marriage.

'The shock which I felt at reading this was inexpressible, occasioned indeed principally by the departure of a villain whom I loved. However, I soon acquired sufficient presence of mind to remember the main point; and I now insisted peremptorily on his making me immediately his wife, whatever might be the consequence.

'He seemed thunderstruck at this proposal, being, I suppose, destitute of any excuse: But I was too impatient to wait for an answer, and cried out with much eagerness, *Sure you cannot hesitate a moment upon this matter. – Hesitate! Madam!* replied he – *What you ask is impossible – Is this a time for me to mention a thing of this kind to your father?* – My eyes were now opened all at once. I fell into a rage little short of madness. *Tell not me*, I cried, *of impossibilities, nor times, nor of my father, – my honour, my reputation, my all are at stake. – I will have no excuse, no delay – make me your wife this instant, or I will proclaim you over the face of the whole earth for the greatest of villains.* – He answered, with a kind of sneer, *what will you proclaim, madam? – whose honour will you injure?* – My tongue faltered when I offered to reply, and I fell into a violent agony, which ended in a fit; nor do I remember anything more that past, till I found myself in the arms of my poor affrighted father.

'O Mr Booth! what was then my situation. I tremble even now from the reflection. – I must stop a moment. I can go no farther.' Booth attempted all in his power to sooth her; and she soon recovered her powers, and proceeded in her story.

CHAPTER 9

In which Miss Mathews concludes her relation.

'BEFORE I had recovered my senses, I had sufficiently betrayed myself to that best of men, who instead of upbraiding me, or exerting any anger, endeavoured to comfort me all he could; with assurances that all should yet be well. This goodness of his affected me with inexpressible sensations; I prostrated myself before him, embraced and kissed his knees, and almost dissolved in tears, and a degree of tenderness hardly to be conceived – But I am running into too minute descriptions.

'Hebbers seeing me in a fit had left me, and sent one of the servants to take care of me. He then ran away like a thief from the house, without taking his leave of my father, or once thanking him for all his civilities. He did not stop at his quarters, but made directly to London, apprehensive, I believe, either of my father or brother's resentment; for I am convinced he is a coward. Indeed his fear of my brother was utterly groundless; for I believe he would rather have thanked any man who had destroyed me; and I am sure I am not in the least behind hand with him in good wishes.

'All his inveteracy to me had, however, no effect on my father, at least at that time; for though the good man took sufficient occasions to reprimand me for my past offence, he could not be brought to abandon me. A treaty of marriage was now set on foot, in which my father himself offered me to Hebbers, with a fortune superior to that which had been given with my sister; nor could all my brother's remonstrances against it, as an act of the highest injustice, avail.

'Hebbers entered into the treaty, tho' not with much warmth. He had even the assurance to make additional demands on my father, which being complied with, every thing was concluded, and the villain once more received into the house. He soon found means to obtain my forgiveness of his former behaviour; indeed he convinced me, so foolishly blind is female love, that he had never been to blame.

'When every thing was ready for our nuptials, and the day of the ceremony was to be appointed, in the midst of my happiness, I received a letter from an unknown hand, acquainting me (guess, Mr Booth, how I was shocked at receiving it) that Mr Hebbers was already married to a woman, in a distant part of the kingdom.

'I will not tire you with all that past at our next interview. I communicated the letter to Hebbers, who, after some little hesitation, owned the fact; and not only owned it, but had the address to improve it to his own advantage, to make it the means of satisfying me concerning all his former delays; which, to say the truth, I was not so much displeased at imputing to any degree of villany, as I should have been to impute it to the want of a sufficient warmth of affection; and tho' the disappointment of all my hopes, at the very instant of their expected fruition, threw me into the most violent disorders; yet when I came a little to myself, he had no great difficulty to persuade me that in every instance, with regard to me, Hebbers had acted from no other motive than from the most ardent and ungovernable love. And there is, I believe, no crime which a woman will not forgive, when she can derive it from that fountain. In short, I forgave him all, and am willing to persuade myself I am not weaker than the rest of my sex. Indeed, Mr Booth, he hath a bewitching tongue, and is master of an address that no woman could resist. I do assure you the charms of his person[43] are his least perfection, at least in my eye.'

Here Booth smiled, but happily without her perceiving it.

'A fresh difficulty (continued she) now arose. This was to excuse the delay of the ceremony to my father, who every day very earnestly urged it. This made me so very uneasy that I at last listened to a proposal, which if any one, in the days of my innocence, or even a few days before, had assured me I could have submitted to have thought of, I should have treated the supposition with the highest contempt and indignation; nay I scarce reflect on it now with more horror than astonishment. In short I agreed to run away with him. To leave my father, my reputation, every thing which was or ought to have been dear to me, and to live with this villain as a mistress, since I could not be his wife.

'Was not this an obligation of the highest and tenderest kind, and had I not reason to expect every return in the man's power on whom I had conferred it?

'I will make short of the remainder of my story: for what is there of a woman worth relating, after what I have told you?

'Above a year I lived with this man in an obscure court in London, during which time I had a child by him, whom Heaven, I thank it, hath been pleased to take to itself.

'During many months he behaved to me with all the apparent tenderness and even fondness imaginable; but alas! how poor was my enjoyment of this compared to what it would have been in another situation? When he was present, life was barely tolerable; but when he was absent, nothing could equal the misery I endured. I past my hours almost entirely alone: for no company, but what I despised, would consort with me. Abroad I scarce ever went, lest I should meet any of my former acquaintance; for their sight would have plunged a thousand daggers in my soul. My only diversion was going very seldom to a play, where I hid myself in the gallery, with a daughter of the woman of the house. A girl indeed of good sense, and many good qualities; but how much beneath me was it to be the companion of a creature so low! O Heavens! When I have seen my equals glittering in a side-box, how have the thoughts of my lost honour torn my soul!'

'Pardon me, dear madam,' cries Booth, 'for interrupting you; but I am under the utmost anxiety to know what became of your poor father, for whom I hve so great a respect, and who, I am convinced, must so bitterly feel your loss.'

'Oh Mr Booth,' answered she, 'he was scarce ever out of my thoughts. His dear image still obtruded itself in my mind, and I believe would have broken my heart, had I not taken a very preposterous way to ease myself. I am indeed almost ashamed to tell you; but necessity put it in my head. – You will think the matter too trifling to have been remembered, and so it surely was; nor should I have remembered it on any other occasion. You must know then, sir, that my brother was always my inveterate enemy, and altogether as fond of my sister. He once prevailed with my father to let him take my sister with him in the chariot, and by that means I was disappointed of going to a ball which I had set my heart on. The disappointment, I assure you, was great at the time;

but I had long since forgotten it. I must have been a very bad woman, if I had not; for it was the only thing in which I can remember that my father ever disobliged me. However, I now revived this in my mind, which I artificially worked up into so high an injury, that I assure you it afforded me no little comfort. When any tender idea intruded into my bosom, I immediately raised this fantom of an injury in my imagination, and it considerably lessened the fury of that sorrow which I should have otherwise felt for the loss of so good a father; who died within a few months of my departure from him.

'And now, sir, to draw to a conclusion. One night as I was in the gallery at Drury Lane play-house, I saw below me, in a side-box – (she was once below me in every place) that widow whom I mentioned to you before – I had scarce cast my eyes on this woman, before I was so shocked with the sight, that it almost deprived me of my senses; for the villain Hebbers came presently in, and seated himself behind her.

'He had been almost a month from me, and I believed him to be at his quarters in Yorkshire. Guess what were my sensations, when I beheld him sitting by that base woman, and talking to her with the utmost familiarity. I could not long endure this sight; and having acquainted my companion that I was taken suddenly ill, I forced her to go home with me at the end of the second act.

'After a restless and sleepless night, when I rose the next morning I had the comfort to receive a visit from the woman of the house, who, after a very short introduction, asked me when I had heard from the captain, and when I expected to see him? I had not strength or spirits to make her any answer; and she proceeded thus: *Indeed I did not think the captain would have used me so. My husband was an officer of the army, as well as himself; and if a body is a little low in the world, I am sure that is no reason for folks to trample on a body. I defy the world to say as I ever was guilty of an ill thing. For Heaven's sake, madam,* says I, *what do you mean! Mean!* cries she, *I am sure if I had not thought you had been Captain Hebbers's lady, his lawful lady too, you should never have set footing in my house. I would have Captain Hebbers know, that tho' I am reduced to let lodgings, I never have entertained any but persons of character.* – In this manner, sir, she ran on, saying many shocking things not worth repeating, till my anger at last got the better of my patience as well as my sorrow, and I pushed her out of the room.

'She had not been long gone before her daughter came to me, and after many expressions of tenderness and pity acquainted me, that her mother had just found out, by means of the captain's servant, that the captain was married to another lady; *which if you did not know before, madam,* said she, *I am sorry to be the messenger of such ill news.*

'Think, Mr Booth, what I must have endured to see myself humbled before such a creature as this, the daughter of a woman who lets lodgings! However, having recollected myself a little, I thought it would be in vain to deny any thing; so knowing this to be one of the best natured and most sensible girls in the world, I resolved to tell her my whole story, and for the future to make her my confidante. I answered her, therefore, with a good deal of assurance, that she need not regret telling me this piece of ill news, for I had known it before I came to her house.

'*Pardon me, madam,* replied the girl, *you cannot possibly have known it so long; for he hath not been married above a week: last night was the first time of his appearing in public with his wife at the play. Indeed I knew very well the cause of your uneasiness there; but would not mention –*

'*His wife at the play!* answered I eagerly, *What wife! whom do you mean?*

'*I mean the widow Cary, madam,* replied she, *to whom the captain was married a few days since. His servant was here last night to pay for your lodging; and he told it my mother.*

'I know not what answer I made, or whether I made any; I presently fell dead on the floor, and it was with great difficulty I was brought back to life by the poor girl: for neither the mother, nor the maid of the house, would lend me any assistance, both seeming to regard me rather as a monster than a woman.

'Scarce had I recovered the use of my senses, when I received a letter from the villain, declaring he had not assurance to see my face, and very kindly advising me to endeavour to reconcile myself to my family; concluding with an offer, in case I did not succeed, to allow me twenty pounds a year to support me in some remote part of the kingdom.

'I need not mention my indignation at these proposals. In the highest agony of rage, I went in a chair to the detested house, where I easily got access to the wretch I had devoted to destruction, whom I no sooner found within my reach, than I plunged a drawn penknife, which I had prepared in my pocket for the purpose, into his accursed heart. For this fact I was immediately seized, and soon after committed hither; and for this fact I am ready to die, and shall with pleasure receive the sentence of the law.

'Thus, sir,' said she, 'I have related to you my unhappy story; and if I have tired your patience, by dwelling too long on those parts which affected me the most, I ask your pardon.'

Booth made a proper speech on this occasion, and having expressed much concern at her present situation, concluded that he hoped her sentence would be milder than she seemed to expect.

Her reply to this was full of so much bitterness and indignation, that we do not think proper to record the speech at length; in which, having vented her passion, she all at once put on a serene countenance, and with an air of great complacency, said, 'Well, Mr Booth, I think I have now a right to satisfy my curiosity, at the expence of your breath. I may say it is not altogether a vain curiosity; for perhaps I have had inclination enough to interest myself in whatever concerns you; – but no matter for that – those days (added she with a sigh) are now over.'

Booth, who was extremely good-natured and well bred, told her that she should not command him twice whatever was in his power; and then, after the usual apology, was going to begin his history, when the keeper arrived and acquainted the lady that dinner was ready, at the same time saying, 'I suppose, madam, as the gentleman is an acquaintance of yours, he must dine with us too.'

Miss Mathews told the keeper that she had only one word to mention in private to the gentleman, and that then they would both attend him. – She then pulled her purse from her pocket, in which were upwards of twenty guineas, being the remainder of the money for which she had sold a gold repeating watch, her father's present, with some other trinkets, and desired Mr Booth to take what he should have occasion for; – saying, 'You know, I believe, dear Will, I never valued money; and now I am sure I shall have very little use for it.' Booth, with much difficulty, accepted of two guineas; and then they both together attended the keeper.

CHAPTER 10

Table talk consisting of a facetious discourse that passed in the prison.

THERE were assembled at the table the governor of these (not improperly called infernal) regions; the lieutenant governor, vulgarly named the first turnkey; Miss Mathews, Mr Booth, Mr Robinson the gambler, several other prisoners of both sexes, and one Murphy an attorney.

The governor took the first opportunity to bring the affair of Miss Mathews upon the carpet, and then turning to Murphy, he said, 'It is very lucky this gentleman happens to be present; I do assure you, madam, your cause cannot be in abler hands. He is, I believe, the best man in England at a defence; I have known him often succeed against the most positive evidence.'

'Fy, sir,' answered Murphy, 'you know I hate all this; but if the lady will trust me with her cause, I will do the best in my power. Come, madam, don't be discouraged, a bit of manslaughter and cold iron,[44] I hope, will be the worst: or perhaps we may come off better, with a slice of chance-medley, or *se defendendo*.'[45]

'I am very ignorant of the law, sir,' cries the lady.

'Yes, madam,' answered Murphy, 'it can't be expected you should understand it. There are very few of us who profess it, that understand the whole; – nor is it necessary we should. There is a great deal of rubbish of little use about indictments and abatements, and bars, and ejectments, and trovers, and such stuff,[46] with which people cram their heads to little purpose. The chapter of evidence is the main business; that is the sheet-anchor: that is the rudder, which brings the vessel safe in *portum*. Evidence is indeed the whole, the *summa totidis*,[47] for *de non apparentibus et non insistentibus eandem est ratio*.'[48]

'If you address yourself to me, sir,' said the lady, 'you are much too learned, I assure you, for my understanding.'

'*Tace*, madam,' answered Murphy, 'is Latin for a candle:[49] I commend your prudence. I shall know the particulars of your case when we are alone.'

'I hope the lady,' said Robinson, 'hath no suspicion of any person here. I hope we are all persons of honour at this table.'

'D—n my eyes!' answered a well-dressed woman, 'I can answer for myself and the other ladies; though I never saw the lady in my life, she need not be shy of us, d—n my eyes! I scorn to rap* against any lady.'

'D—n me, madam!' cried another female, 'I honour what you have done. I once put a knife into a cull myself – so my service to you, madam, and I wish you may come off with *se diffidendo* with all my heart.'

'I beg, good woman,' said Miss Mathews, 'you would talk on some other subject, and give yourself no concern about my affairs.'

'You see, ladies,' cried Murphy, 'the gentlewoman doth not care to talk on this matter before company; so pray do not press her.'

'Nay, I value the lady's acquaintance no more than she values mine,' cries the first woman who spoke – 'I have kept as good company as the lady, I believe, every day in the week. Good woman! I don't use to be so treated – If the lady says such another word to me, d—n me, I'll darken her day-lights.[50] Marry, come up, good woman! – the lady's a whore as well as myself; and though I am sent hither to mill doll,[51] d—n my eyes, I have money enough to buy it off as well as the lady herself.'

Action might perhaps soon have ensued this speech, had not the keeper interposed his authority, and put an end to any further dispute. Soon after which, the company broke up; and none but himself, Mr Murphy, Captain Booth, and Miss Mathews remained together.

Miss Mathews then, at the entreaty of the keeper, began to open her case to Mr Murphy, whom she admitted to be her solicitor,

* A cant word, meaning to swear, or rather to perjure yourself.

though she still declared she was indifferent as to the event of the trial.

Mr Murphy having heard all the particulars with which the reader is already acquainted (as far as related to the murder) shook his head, and said, 'There is but one circumstance, madam, which I wish was out of the case; and that we must put out of it: I mean the carrying the penknife drawn into the room with you; for that seems to imply malice prepensive,[52] as we call it in the law: this circumstance therefore must not appear against you; and if the servant who was in the room observed this, he must be bought off at all hazards. All here, you say, are friends; therefore I tell you openly, you must furnish me with money sufficient for this purpose. Malice is all we have to guard against.'

'I would not presume, sir,' cries Booth, 'to inform you in the law; but I have heard in case of stabbing, a man may be indicted upon the statute; and it is capital, though no malice appears.'

'You say true, sir,' answered Murphy, 'a man may be indicted *contra formam statutis*;[53] and that method, I allow you, requires no malice; I presume you are a lawyer, sir?'

'No, indeed, sir,' answered Booth, 'I know nothing of the law.'

'Then, sir, I will tell you – If a man be indicted *contra formam statutis*, as we say, no malice is necessary; because the form of the statute makes malice; and then what we have to guard against is having struck the first blow – pox on't, it is unlucky this was done in a room – if it had been in the street, we could have had five or six witnesses to have proved the first blow, cheaper, than I am afraid we shall get this one; for when a man knows, from the unhappy circumstances of the case, that you can procure no other witness but himself, he is always dear. It is so in all other ways of business – I am very implicit,[54] you see; but we are all among friends. The safest way is to furnish me with money enough to offer him a good round sum at once; and, I think, (it is for your good I speak) fifty pounds is the least that can be offered him. – I do assure you, I would offer him no less, was it my own case.'

'And do you think, sir,' said she, 'that I would save my life at the expence of hiring another to perjure himself?'

'Ay, surely do I,' cries Murphy; 'for where is the fault, admitting there is some fault in perjury, as you call it; and to be sure, it is such a matter, as every man would rather wish to avoid than not: and yet, as it may be managed, there is not so much as some people are apt to imagine in it; for he need not kiss the book,[55] and then pray where's the perjury? but if the crier[56] is sharper than ordinary, what is it he kisses? is it any thing but a bit of calves-skin? I am sure a man must be a very bad Christian himself, who would not do so much as that to save the life of any Christian whatever, much more of so pretty a lady – Indeed, madam, if we can make out but a tolerable case, so much beauty will go a great ways with the judge and the jury too.'

The latter part of this speech, notwithstanding the mouth it came from, caused Miss Mathews to suppress much of the indignation which began to arise at the former; and she answered with a smile, 'Sir, you are a great casuist in these matters; but we need argue no longer concerning them; for if fifty pounds would save my life, I assure you I could not command that sum. The little money I have in my pocket is all I can call my own; and, I apprehend, in the situation I am in, I shall have very little of that to spare.'

'Come, come, madam,' cries Murphy, 'life is sweet, let me tell you, and never sweeter than when we are near losing it. I have known many a man very brave and undaunted at his first commitment, who, when business began to thicken a little upon him, hath changed his note. – It is no time to be saving in your condition.'

The keeper, who, after the liberality of Miss Mathews, and on seeing a purse of guineas in her hand, had conceived a great opinion of her wealth, no sooner heard that the sum which he had in intention entirely confiscated for his own use, was attempted to be broke in upon, thought it high time to be upon his guard. 'To be sure,' cries he, 'Mr Murphy, life is sweet, as you say, that must be acknowledged; to be sure life is sweet; but sweet as it is, no persons can advance more than they are worth to save it. And indeed, if the lady can command no more money than that little she mentions, she is to be commended for her unwillingness to part with any of it; for, to be sure, as she says, she will want every farthing of that, to live like a gentlewoman till she comes to her trial. And, to be sure, as sweet as life is, people ought to take care to be able to live sweetly while they do live: besides, I can't help saying, the lady shews herself to be what she is, by her abhorrence of perjury, which is certainly a very dreadful crime. And, though the not kissing the book doth, as you say, make a great deal of difference; and, if a man had a great while to live and repent, perhaps he might swallow it well enough; yet when people comes to be near their end, (as who can venture to foretel what will be the lady's case!) they ought to take care not to over-burthen their conscience. I hope the lady's case will not be found murder; for I am sure I always wish well to all my prisoners, who shew themselves to be gentlemen, or gentlewomen; yet one should always fear the worst.'

'Indeed, sir, you speak like an oracle,' answered the lady; 'and one subornation of perjury would sit heavier on my conscience, than twenty such murders as I am guilty of.'

'Nay, to be sure, madam,' answered the keeper, 'no body can pretend to tell what provocation you must have had; and certainly, it can never be imagined, that a lady who behaves herself so handsomely as you have done ever since you have been under my keys, should be guilty of killing a man without being very highly provoked to do it.'

Mr Murphy was, I believe, going to answer, when he was called out of the room; after which, nothing passed between the remaining persons worth relating, till Booth and the lady retired back again into the lady's apartment.

Here they fell immediately to commenting on the foregoing discourse; but as their comments were, I believe, the same with what most readers have made on the same occasion, we shall omit them. At last Miss Mathews reminding her companion of his promise of relating to her what had befallen him since the interruption of their former acquaintance, he began, as is written in the next book of this history.

BOOK II

CHAPTER 1

In which Captain Booth begins to relate his history.

THE tea-table being removed, and Mr Booth and the lady left alone, he proceeded as follows:

'Since you desire, madam, to know the particulars of my courtship to that best and dearest of women, whom I afterwards married; I will endeavour to recollect them as well as I can, at least all those incidents which are most worth relating to you.

'If the vulgar opinion of the fatality in marriage had ever any foundation, it surely appeared in my marriage with my Amelia. I knew her in the first dawn of her beauty; and, I believe, madam, she had as much as ever fell to the share of a woman; but though I always admired her, it was long without any spark of love. Perhaps the general admiration which at that time pursued her, the respect paid her by persons of the highest rank, and the numberless addresses which were made her by men of great fortune, prevented my aspiring at the possession of those charms, which seemed so absolutely out of my reach. However it was, I assure you, the accident which deprived her of the admiration of others, made the first great impression on my heart in her favour. The injury done to her beauty by the overturning of a chaise, by which, as you may well remember, her lovely nose was beat all to pieces, gave me an assurance that the woman who had been so much adored for the charms of her person, deserved a much higher adoration to be paid to her mind: for that she was in the latter respect infinitely more superior to the rest of her sex, than she had ever been in the former.'

'I admire your taste extremely,' cried the lady. 'I remember perfectly well the great heroism with which your Amelia bore that misfortune.'

'Good Heavens! madam,' answered he, 'what a magnanimity of mind did her behaviour demonstrate! If the world have extolled the firmness of soul in a man who can support the loss of fortune; of a general, who can be composed after the loss of a victory; or of a king, who can be contented with the loss of a crown; with what astonishment ought we to behold, with what praises to honour a young lady, who can with patience and resignation submit to the loss of exquisite beauty, in other words, to the loss of fortune, power, glory; every thing which human nature is apt to court and rejoice in! what must be the mind, which can bear to be deprived of all these in a moment, and by an unfortunate trifling accident; which could support all this, together with the most exquisite torments of body, and with dignity, with resignation, without complaining, almost without a tear, undergo the most painful and dreadful operations of surgery in such a situation.' Here he stopt, and a torrent of tears gushed from his eyes; such tears as are apt to flow from a truly noble heart, at the hearing of any thing surprisingly great and glorious. As soon as he was able he again proceeded thus:

'Would you think, Miss Mathews, that the misfortune of my Amelia was capable of any aggravation! I assure you, she hath often told me it was aggravated with a circumstance which outweighed all the other ingredients. This was the cruel insults she received from some of her most intimate acquaintance, several of whom, after many distortions and grimaces, have turned their heads aside, unable to support their secret triumph, and burst into a loud laugh in her hearing.'

'Good heaven!' cry'd Miss Mathews, 'what detestable actions will this contemptible passion of envy prevail on our sex to commit?'

'An occasion of this kind, as she hath since told me, made the first impression on her gentle heart in my favour. I was one day in company with several young ladies, or rather young devils, where poor Amelia's accident was the subject of much mirth and pleasantry. One of these said, *she hoped miss would not hold her head so high for the future*. Another answered, *I don't know, madam, what she may do with her head, but I am convinced she will never more turn up her nose at her betters*. Another cry'd, *what a very proper match might now be made between Amelia and a certain captain*, who had unfortunately received an injury in the same part, though from no shameful cause. Many other sarcasms were thrown out, very unworthy to be repeated. I was hurt with perceiving so much malice in human shape, and cry'd out very bluntly, *Indeed, ladies, you need not express such satisfaction at poor Miss Emily's accident: for she will still be the handsomest woman in England*. This speech of mine was afterwards variously repeated, by some to my honour, and by others represented in a contrary light; indeed it was often reported to be much ruder than it was. However, it at length reached Amelia's ears. She said she was very much obliged to me; since I could have so much compassion for her as to be rude to a lady on her account.

'About a month after the accident, when Amelia began to see company, in a mask, I had the honour to drink tea with her. We were alone together, and I begged her to indulge my curiosity by shewing me her face. She answered in a most obliging manner, "Perhaps, Mr Booth, you will as little know me when my mask is off as when it is on;" and at the same instant unmasked. – The surgeon's skill was the least I considered. A thousand tender ideas rushed all at once on my mind. I was unable to contain myself, and eagerly kissing her hand, I cried – "Upon my soul, madam, you never appeared to me so lovely as at this instant." Nothing more remarkable passed at this visit; but I sincerely believe we were neither of us hereafter indifferent to each other.

'Many months, however, passed after this, before I ever thought seriously of making her my wife. Not that I wanted sufficient love for Amelia. Indeed it arose from the vast affection I bore her. I considered my own as a desperate fortune, hers as entirely dependent on her mother, who was a woman, you know, of violent passions, and very unlikely to consent to a match so highly contrary to the interest of her daughter. The more I loved Amelia, the more firmly I resolved within myself never to propose love to her seriously. Such a dupe was my understanding to my heart; and so foolishly did I imagine I could be master of a flame to which I was every day adding fuel.

'O Miss Mathews! we have heard of men entirely masters of their passions, and of hearts which can carry this fire in them, and conceal it at their pleasure. Perhaps there may be such; but if there are, those hearts may be compared, I believe, to damps, in which it is more difficult to keep fire alive than to prevent its blazing: in mine, it was placed in the midst of combustible matter.

'After several visits, in which looks and sighs had been interchanged on both sides, but without the least mention of passion in private, one day the discourse between us, when alone, happened to turn on love; I say happened, for I protest it was not designed on my side, and I am as firmly convinced not on hers. I was now no longer master of myself; I declared myself the most wretched of all martyrs to this tender passion; that I had long concealed it from its object. At length, after mentioning many particulars, suppressing, however, those which must have necessarily brought it home to Amelia, I concluded with begging her to be the confidante of my amour, and to give me her advice on that occasion.

'Amelia, (O I shall never forget the dear perturbation!) appeared all confusion at this instant. She trembled, turned pale, and discovered how well she understood me, by a thousand more symptoms than I could take notice of, in a state of mind so very little different from her own. At last, with faltering accents, she said, I had made a very ill choice of a counsellor, in a matter in which she was so ignorant. – Adding, at last, *I believe, Mr Booth, you gentlemen want very little advice in these affairs, which you all understand better than we do*.

'I will relate no more of our conversation at present; indeed I am afraid I tire you with too many particulars.'

'O no,' answered she, 'I should be glad to hear every step of an amour which had so tender a beginning. Tell me every thing you said or did, if you can remember it.'

He then proceeded, and so will we in the next chapter.

CHAPTER 2

Mr Booth continues his story. In this chapter there are some passages that may serve as a kind of touchstone, by which a young lady may examine the heart of her lover. I would advise, therefore, that every lover be obliged to read it over in the presence of his mistress, and that she carefully watch his emotions while he is reading.

'I WAS under the utmost concern,' cries Booth, 'when I retired from my visit, and had reflected cooly on what I had said. I now saw plainly that I had made downright love to Amelia; and I feared, such was my vanity, that I had already gone too far, and been too successful. Feared! do I say, could I fear what I hoped? How shall I describe the anxiety of my mind!'

'You need give yourself no great pain,' cried Miss Mathews, 'to describe what I can so easily guess. To be honest with you, Mr Booth, I do not agree with your lady's opinion, that the men have a superior understanding in the matters of love. Men are often blind to the passions of women; but every woman is as quick-sighted as a hawk on these occasions; nor is there one article in the whole science which is not understood by all our sex.'

'However, madam,' said Mr Booth, 'I now undertook to deceive Amelia. I abstained three days from seeing her; to say the truth, I endeavoured to work myself up to a resolution of leaving her for ever; but when I could not so far subdue my passion – But why do I talk nonsense, of subduing passion? I should say when no other passion could surmount my love, I returned to visit her, and now I attempted the strangest project which ever entered into the silly head of a lover. This was to persuade Amelia that I was really in love in another place, and had literally expressed my meaning, when I asked her advice, and desired her to be my confidante.

'I therefore forged a meeting to have been between me and my imaginary mistress, since I had last seen Amelia, and related the particulars as well as I could invent them, which had past at our conversation.

'Poor Amelia presently swallowed this bait, and, as she hath told me since, absolutely believed me to be in earnest. Poor dear love! how should the sincerest of hearts have any idea of deceit? for with all her simplicity I assure you she is the most sensible woman in the world.'

'It is highly generous and good in you,' (said Miss Mathews, with a sly sneer) 'to impute to honesty what others would perhaps call credulity.'

'I protest, madam,' answered he, 'I do her no more than justice. A good heart will at all times betray the best head in the world. – Well, madam, my angel was now, if possible, more confused than before. She looked so silly, you can hardly believe it –'

'Yes, yes, I can,' answered the lady, with a laugh, 'I can believe it. – Well, well, go on.' 'After some hesitation,' cried he, 'my Amelia said faintly to me, "Mr Booth; you use me very ill, you desire me to be your confidante, and conceal from me the name of your mistress."

'"Is it possible then, madam," answered I, "that you cannot guess her, when I tell you she is one of your acquaintance, and lives in this town?"

'"My acquaintance," said she, "La! Mr Booth. – In this town. I – I – I thought I could have guessed for once; but I have an ill talent that way – I will never attempt to guess any thing again." Indeed I do her an injury when I pretend to represent her manner. Her manner, look, voice, every thing was inimitable, such sweetness, softness, innocence, modesty. – Upon my soul, if ever man could boast of his resolution, I think I might now, that I abstained from falling prostrate at her feet and adoring her. However, I triumphed; pride, I believe, triumphed, or perhaps love got the better of love. We once more parted, and I promised, the next time I saw her, to reveal the name of my mistress.

'I now had, I thought, gained a complete victory over myself; and no small compliments did I pay to my own resolution. In short I triumphed as cowards and niggards do when they flatter themselves with having given some supposed instance of courage or generosity; and my triumph lasted as long; that is to say, till my ascendent passion had a proper opportunity of displaying itself in its true and natural colours.

'Having hitherto succeeded so well in my own opinion, and obtained this mighty self-conquest, I now entertained a design of exerting the most romantic generosity, and of curing that unhappy passion which I perceived I had raised in Amelia.

'Among the ladies who had expressed the greatest satisfaction at my Amelia's misfortune, Miss Osborne had distinguished herself in a very eminent degree; she was indeed the next in beauty to my angel, nay she had disputed the preference, and had some among her admirers, who were blind enough to give it in her favour.'

'Well,' cries the lady, 'I will allow you to call them blind; but Miss Osborne was a charming girl.'

'She certainly was handsome,' answered he, 'and a very considerable fortune; so I thought my Amelia would have little difficulty in believing me, when I fixed on her as my mistress. And I concluded, that my thus placing my affections on her known enemy would be the surest method of eradicating every tender idea with which I had been ever honoured by Amelia.

'Well then, to Amelia I went; she received me with more than usual coldness and reserve. In which, to confess the truth, there appeared to me more of anger than indifference, and more of dejection than of either. After some short introduction I revived the discourse of my amour, and presently mentioned Miss Osborne as the lady whose name I had concealed; adding, that the true reason why I did not mention her before, was, that I apprehended there was some little distance between them, which I hoped to have the happiness of accommodating.

'Amelia answered with much gravity. "If you know, sir, that there is any distance between us, I suppose you know the reason of that distance; and then I think I could not have expected to be affronted by her name. I would not have you think, Mr Booth, that I hate Miss Osborne. No! Heaven is my witness, I despise her too much. – Indeed when I reflect how much I loved the woman who hath treated me so cruelly, I own it gives me pain – When I lay, as I then imagined, and as all about me believed, on my death-bed, in all the agonies of pain and misery, to become the object of laughter to my dearest friend. – O Mr Booth, it is a cruel reflection! And could I after this have expected from you: – But why not from you, to whom I am a person entirely indifferent, if such a friend could treat me so barbarously?"

'During the greatest part of this speech the tears streamed from her bright eyes. I could endure it no longer. I caught up the word indifferent, and repeated it, saying, "Do you think then, madam, that Miss Emily is indifferent to me?"

'"Yes surely I do," answered she, "I know I am; indeed why should I not be indifferent to you?"

'"Have my eyes," said I, "then, declared nothing?"

'"O there is no need of your eyes," answered she. "Your tongue hath declared that you have singled out of all woman-kind my greatest, I will say, my basest enemy. – I own I once thought that character would have been no recommendation to you. – But why did I think so? I was born to deceive myself."

'I then fell on my knees before her; and forcing her hand, cried out, "O my Amelia, I can bear no longer. You are the only mistress of my affections; you are the deity I adore." In this stile I ran on for above two or three minutes, what it is impossible to repeat, till a torrent of contending passions, together with the surprize, overpowered her gentle spirits, and she fainted away in my arms.

'To describe my sensation till she returned to herself, is not in my power.' – 'You need not,' cried Miss Mathews. – 'Oh! happy Amelia! why had I not been blest with such a passion?' – 'I am convinced, madam,' continued he, 'you cannot expect all the particulars of the tender scene which ensued. I was not enough in my senses to remember it all. Let it suffice to say, that that behaviour with which Amelia, while ignorant of its motive, had been so much displeased, when she became sensible of that motive, proved the strongest recommendation to her favour; and she was pleased to call it generous.'

'Generous!' repeated the lady, 'and so it was almost beyond the reach of humanity. I question whether you ever had an equal.'

Perhaps the critical reader may have the same doubt with Miss Mathews; and, lest he should, we will here make a gap in our history, to give him an opportunity of accurately considering whether we have in this place maintained or deviated from that strict adherence to universal truth which we profess above all other historians.

CHAPTER 3

The narrative continued. More of the touchstone.

BOOTH made a proper acknowledgment of Miss Mathews's civility, and then renewed his story.

'We were upon the footing of lovers; and Amelia threw off her reserve more and more, till at length I found all that return of my affection which the tenderest lover can require.

'My situation would now have been a paradise, had not my happiness been interrupted with the same reflexions I have already mentioned; had I not, in short, concluded, that I must derive all my joys from the almost certain ruin of that dear creature to whom I should owe them.

'This thought haunted me night and day; till I, at last, grew unable to support it: I therefore resolved, in the strongest manner, to lay it before Amelia.

'One evening then, after the highest professions of the most disinterested love, in which Heaven knows my sincerity, I took an occasion to speak to Amelia, in the following manner:

'"Too true is it, I am afraid, my dearest creature, that the highest human happiness is imperfect. How rich would be my cup, was it not for one poisonous drop, which imbitters the whole! O Amelia, what must be the consequence of my ever having the honour to call you mine! – You know my situation in life, and you know your own: I have nothing more than the poor provision of an ensign's commission to depend on; your sole dependance is on your mother; should any act of disobedience defeat your expectations, how wretched must your lot be with me! O Amelia, how ghastly an object to my mind is the apprehension of your distress! Can I bear to reflect a moment on the certainty of your foregoing all the conveniencies of life; on the possibility of your suffering all its most dreadful inconveniencies! What must be my misery then, to see you in such a situation, and to upbraid myself with being the accursed cause of bringing you to it! Suppose too in such a season I should be summoned from you. Could I submit to see you encounter all the hazards, the fatigues of war, with me! You could not yourself, however willing, support them a single campaign. What then, must I leave you to starve alone, deprived of the tenderness of a husband, deprived too of the tenderness of the best of mothers, through my means? A woman most dear to me, for being the parent, the nurse, and the friend of my Amelia. – But, O my sweet creature, carry your thoughts a little farther. Think of the tenderest consequences, the dearest pledges of our love. Can I bear to think of entailing beggary on the posterity of my Amelia? On our – O Heavens! on our children? – On the other side, is it possible even to mention the word – I will not, must not, cannot, cannot, part with you. – What must we do, Amelia? it is now I sincerely ask your advice."

'"What advice can I give you," said she, "in such an alternative? Would to Heaven we had never met."

'These words were accompanied with a sigh, and a look inexpressibly tender, the tears at the same time overflowing all her lovely cheeks. I was endeavouring to reply, when I was interrupted by what soon put an end to the scene.

'Our amour had already been buzzed all over the town; and it came at last to the ears of Mrs Harris. I had, indeed, observed of late a great alteration in that lady's behaviour towards me, whenever I visited at the house; nor could I, for a long time, before this evening, ever obtain a private interview with Amelia, and now, it seems, I owed it to her mother's intention of over-hearing all that passed between us.

'At the period then abovementioned, Mrs Harris burst from the closet, where she had hid herself, and surprised her daughter, reclining on my bosom, in all that tender sorrow I have just described. I will not attempt to paint the rage of the mother, or the daughter's confusion, or my own. "Here are very fine doings, indeed," cries Mrs Harris, "you have made a noble use, Amelia, of my indulgence, and the trust I reposed in you. – As for you, Mr Booth, I will not accuse you; you have used my child, as I ought to have expected; I may thank myself for what hath happened;" with much more of the same kind, before she would suffer me to speak; but, at last, I obtained a hearing, and offered to excuse my poor Amelia, who was ready to sink into the earth under the oppression of grief, by taking as much blame as I could on myself. Mrs Harris answered, "No, sir, I must say you are innocent in comparison of her; nay, I can say, I have heard you use dissuasive arguments; and I promise you they are of weight. I have, I thank Heaven, one dutiful child, and I shall henceforth think her my only one." She then forc'd the poor, trembling, fainting Amelia out of the room; which when she had done, she began very cooly to reason with me on the folly, as well as iniquity, which I had been guilty of, and repeated to me almost every word I had before urged to her daughter. In fine, she, at last, obtained of me a promise that I would soon go to my regiment, and submit to any misery, rather than that of being the ruin of Amelia.

'I now, for many days, endured the greatest torments which the human mind is, I believe, capable of feeling: and I can honestly say I try'd all the means, and applied every argument which I could raise to cure me of my love. And to make these the more effectual, I spent every night in walking backwards and forwards in sight of Mrs Harris's house, where I never failed to find some object or other, which raised some tender idea of my lovely Amelia, and almost drove me to distraction.'

'And, don't you think, sir,' said Miss Mathews, 'you took a most preposterous method to cure yourself?'

'Alas, madam,' answered he, 'you cannot see it in a more absurd light than I do; but those know little of real love or grief, who do not know how much we deceive ourselves when we pretend to aim at the cure of either. It is with these as it is with some distempers of the body, nothing is, in the least, agreeable to us but what serves to heighten the disease.

'At the end of a fortnight, when I was driven almost to the highest degree of despair, and could contrive no method of conveying a letter to Amelia, how was I surprised when Mrs Harris's servant brought me a card, with an invitation from the mother herself, to drink tea that evening at her house!

'You will easily believe, madam, that I did not fail so agreeable an appointment; on my arrival I was introduced into a large company of men and women, Mrs Harris and my Amelia being part of the company.

'Amelia seemed in my eyes to look more beautiful than ever, and behaved with all the gaiety imaginable. The old lady treated me with much civility; but the young lady took little notice of me, and addressed most of her discourse to another gentleman present. Indeed, she now and then gave me a look of no discouraging kind; and I observed her colour change more than once, when her eyes met mine: circumstances which, perhaps, ought to have afforded me sufficient comfort; but they could not allay the thousand doubts and fears with which I was alarmed: for my anxious thoughts suggested no less to me than that Amelia had made her peace with her mother at the price of abandoning me for ever, and of giving her ear to some other lover. All my prudence now vanish'd at once; and I would that instant have gladly run away with Amelia, and have married her without the least consideration of any consequences.

'With such thoughts I had tormented myself for near two hours, till most of the company had taken their leave. This I was myself incapable of doing; nor do I know when I should have put an end to my visit, had not Dr Harrison taken me away almost by force, telling me in a whisper, that he had something to say to me of great consequence. – You know the doctor, madam –'

'Very well, sir,' answered Miss Mathews, 'and one of the best men in the world he is, and an honour to the sacred order to which he belongs.'

'You will judge,' replied Booth, 'by the sequel, whether I have reason to think him so.' – He then proceeded as in the next chapter.

CHAPTER 4

The story of Mr Booth continued: in this chapter the reader will perceive a glimpse of the character of a very good divine; with some matters of a very tender kind.

'THE doctor conducted me into his study; and then desiring me to sit down, began, as near as I can remember, in these words, or at least to this purpose:

'"You cannot imagine, young gentleman, that your love for Miss Emily is any secret in this place; I have known it some time, and have been, I assure you, very much your enemy in this affair."

'I answered, that I was very much obliged to him.

'"Why so you are," replied he, "and so perhaps you will think yourself when you know all. – I went about a fortnight ago to Mrs Harris, to acquaint her with my apprehensions on her daughter's account: for tho' the matter was much talked of, I thought it might possibly not have reached her ears. I will be very plain with you. I advised her to take all possible care of the young lady, and even to send her to some place, where she might be effectually kept out of your reach, while you remained in the town."

'"And do you think, sir," said I, "that this was acting a kind part by me? Or do you expect that I should thank you on this occasion?"

'"Young man," answered he, "I did not intend you any kindness; nor do I desire any of your thanks. My intention was to preserve a worthy lady from a young fellow of whom I had heard no good character, and whom I imagined to have a design of stealing a human creature for the sake of her fortune."

'"It was very kind of you, indeed," answered I, "to entertain such an opinion of me."

'"Why, sir," replied the doctor, "it is the opinion which, I believe, most of you young gentlemen, of the Order of the Rag[1] deserve. I have known some instances, and have heard of more, where such young fellows have committed robbery under the name of marriage."

'I was going to interrupt him with some anger, when he desired me to have a little patience, and then informed me, that he had visited Mrs Harris, with the abovementioned design, the evening after the discovery I have related; that Mrs Harris, without waiting for his information, had recounted to him all which had happened the evening before; and indeed she must have an excellent memory, for I think she repeated every word I said; and added, that she had confined her daughter to her chamber, where she kept her a close prisoner, and had not seen her since.

'I cannot express, nor would modesty suffer me if I could, all that now past. The doctor took me by the hand, and burst forth into the warmest commendations of the sense and generosity which he was pleased to say discovered themselves in my speech. You know, madam, his strong and singular way of expressing himself on all occasions, especially when he is affected with any thing. *Sir*, said he, *if I knew half a dozen such instances in the army, the painter should put red liveries upon all the saints in my closet.*[2]

'From this instant the doctor told me, he had become my friend and zealous advocate with Mrs Harris, on whom he had at last prevailed, though not without the greatest difficulty, to consent to my marrying Amelia, upon condition that I settled every penny which the mother should lay down;[3] and that she would retain a certain sum in her hands, which she would at any time deposite for my advancement in the army.

'You will, I hope, madam, conceive, that I made no hesitation at these conditions; nor need I mention the joy which I felt on this occasion, or the acknowledgment I paid the doctor, who is indeed, as you say, one of the best of men.

'The next morning I had permission to visit Amelia, who received me in such a manner, that I now concluded my happiness to be complete.

'Every thing was now agreed on all sides, and lawyers employed to prepare the writings, when an unexpected cloud arose suddenly in our serene sky, and all our joys were obscured in a moment.

'When matters were, as I apprehended, drawing near a conclusion, I received an express[4] that a sister, whom I tenderly loved, was seized with a violent fever, and earnestly desired me to come to her. I immediately obeyed the summons, and, as it was then about two in the morning, without staying even to take leave of Amelia, for whom I left a short billet, acquainting her with the reason of my absence.

'The gentleman's house where my sister then was, stood at fifty miles distance, and tho' I used the utmost expedition, the unmerciful distemper had, before my arrival, entirely deprived the poor girl of her senses, as it soon after did of her life.

'Not all the love I bore Amelia, nor the tumultuous delight with which the approaching hour of possessing her filled my heart, could for a while allay my grief at the loss of my beloved Nancy. Upon my soul, I cannot yet mention her name without tears. Never brother and sister had, I believe, a higher friendship for each other. Poor dear girl! whilst I sat by her in her light-headed fits, she repeated scarce any other name but mine: and it plainly appeared that when her dear reason was ravish'd away from her, it had left my image on her fancy, and that the last use she had made of it was to think on me. – "Send for my dear Billy immediately," she cry'd, "I know he will come to me in a moment. Will no body fetch him to me? Pray don't kill me before I see him once more – You durst not use me so if he was here." – Every accent still rings in my ears. – Oh Heavens! to hear this, and at the same time to see the poor delirious creature deriving the greatest horrors from my sight, and mistaking me for a highwayman who had a little before robbed her. – But I ask your pardon, the sensations I felt are to be known only from experience, and to you must appear dull and insipid. – At last she seemed for a moment to know me, and cry'd, "O Heavens! my dearest brother!" upon which she fell into immediate convulsions, and died away in my arms.'

Here Booth stop'd a moment, and wip'd his eyes; and Miss Mathews, perhaps out of complaisance, wip'd hers.

CHAPTER 5

Containing strange revolutions of fortune.

BOOTH proceeded thus:

'This loss, perhaps, madam, you will think had made me miserable enough; but Fortune did not think so; for on the day when my Nancy was to be buried, a courier arrived from Dr Harrison with a letter, in which the doctor acquainted me, that he was just come from Mrs Harris, when he dispatched the express; and earnestly desired me to return the very instant I received his letter, as I valued my Amelia. *Tho' if the daughter,* added he, *should take after her mother (as most of them do) it will be, perhaps, wiser in you to stay away*.

'I presently sent for the messenger into my room, and with much difficulty extorted from him, that a great squire in his coach and six was come to Mrs Harris's, and that the whole town said he was shortly to be married to Amelia.

'I now soon perceived how much superior my love for Amelia was to every other passion; poor Nancy's idea disappeared in a moment: I quitted the dear lifeless corpse, over which I had shed a thousand tears, left the care of her funeral to others, and posted, I may almost say flew, back to Amelia, and alighted at the doctor's house, as he had desired me in his letter.

'The good man presently acquainted me with what had happened in my absence. Mr Winckworth had, it seems, arrived the very day of my departure with a grand equipage,[5] and, without delay, had made formal proposals to Mrs Harris, offering to settle any part of his vast estate, in whatever manner she pleased, on Amelia. These proposals the old lady had, without any deliberation, accepted, and had insisted, in the most violent manner, on her daughter's compliance, which Amelia had as peremptorily refused to give; insisting on her part, on the consent which her mother had before given to our marriage, in which she was heartily seconded by the doctor, who declared to her, as he now did to me, "that we ought as much to be esteemed man and wife, as if the ceremony had already past between us."

'These remonstrances, the doctor told me, had worked no effect on Mrs Harris, who still persisted in her avowed resolution of marrying her daughter to Winckworth, whom the doctor had likewise attacked, telling him that he was paying his addresses to another man's wife; but all to no purpose, the young gentleman was too much in love to hearken to any dissuasives.

'We now entered into a consultation what means to employ. The doctor earnestly protested against any violence to be offered to the person of Winckworth, which I believe, I had rashly threatened; declaring, that if I made any attempt of that kind, he would for ever abandon my cause. I made him a solemn promise of forbearance. At last, he determined to pay another visit to Mrs Harris, and if he found her obdurate, he said he thought himself at liberty to join us together without any further consent of the mother, which every parent, he said, had a right to refuse, but not to retract when given, unless the party himself, by some conduct of his, gave a reason.

'The doctor having made his visit with no better success than before, the matter now debated was, how to get possession of Amelia by stratagem: for she was now a closer prisoner than ever, was her mother's bed-fellow by night, and never out of her sight by day.

'While we were deliberating on this point, a wine merchant of the town came to visit the doctor, to inform him that he had just bottled off a hogshead of excellent old port, of which he offered to spare him a hamper, saying, that he was that day to send in twelve dozen to Mrs Harris.

'The doctor now smiled at a conceit which came into his head; and, taking me aside, asked me if I had love enough for the young lady to venture into the house in a hamper. I joyfully leapt at the proposal, to which the merchant, at the doctor's intercession, consented: for I believe, madam, you know the great authority which that worthy man had over the whole town. The doctor, moreover, promised to procure a licence, and to perform the office for us at his house, if I could find any means of conveying Amelia thither.

'In this hamper then I was carried to the house, and deposited in the entry, where I had not lain long before I was again removed and packed up in a cart, in order to be sent five miles into the country: for I heard the orders given as I lay in the entry; and there I likewise heard that Amelia and her mother were to follow me the next morning.

'I was unloaded from my cart, and set down with the rest of the lumber, in a great hall. Here I remained above three hours, impatiently waiting for the evening, when I determined to quit a posture, which was become very uneasy, and break my prison; but fortune contrived to release me sooner, by the following means. The house where I now was had been left in the care of one maid-servant. This faithful creature came into the hall, with the footman who had driven the cart. A scene of the highest fondness having past between them, the fellow proposed, and the maid consented, to open the hamper and drink a bottle together, which they agreed their mistress would hardly miss in such a quantity. They presently began to execute their purpose. They opened the hamper, and to their great surprise discovered the contents.

'I took an immediate advantage of the consternation which appeared in the countenances of both the servants, and had sufficient presence of mind to improve the knowledge of those secrets to which I was privy. I told them that it entirely depended on their behaviour to me whether their mistress should ever be acquainted, either with what they had done, or with what they had intended to do: for that if they would keep my secret, I would reciprocally keep theirs. I then acquainted them with my purpose of lying concealed in the house, in order to watch an opportunity of obtaining a private interview with Amelia.

'In the situation in which these two delinquents stood, you may be assured it was not difficult for me to seal up their lips. In short they agreed to whatever I proposed. I lay that evening in my dear Amelia's bed-chamber, and was in the morning conveyed into an old lumber garret, where I was to wait till Amelia (whom the maid promised, on her arrival, to inform of my place of concealment) could find some opportunity of seeing me.'

'I ask pardon for interrupting you,' cries Miss Mathews, 'but you bring to my remembrance a foolish story which I heard at that time, tho' at a great distance from you: That an officer had, in confederacy with Miss Harris, broke open her mother's cellar, and stole away a great quantity of her wine. I mention it only to shew you what sort of foundations most stories have.'

Booth told her he had heard some such thing himself, and then continued his story as in the next chapter.

CHAPTER 6

Containing many surprising adventures.

'HERE,' continued he, 'I remained the whole day in hopes of a happiness, the expected approach of which, gave me such a delight, that I would not have exchanged my poor lodgings for the finest palace in the universe.

'A little after it was dark Mrs Harris arrived, together with Amelia and her sister. I cannot express how much my heart now began to flutter; for as my hopes every moment encreased, strange fears which I had not felt before began now to intermingle with them.

'When I had continued full two hours in these circumstances, I heard a woman's step tripping up stairs, which I fondly hoped was my Amelia; but all on a sudden the door flew open, and Mrs Harris herself appeared at it, with a countenance pale as death, her whole body trembling, I suppose, with anger; she fell upon me in the most bitter language. It is not necessary to repeat what she said, nor indeed can I, I was so shocked and confounded on this occasion. – In a word the scene ended with my departing without seeing Amelia.'

'And pray,' cries Miss Mathews, 'how happened this unfortunate discovery?'

Booth answered, 'That the lady at supper ordered a bottle of wine, which neither myself,' said he, 'nor the servants, had presence of mind to provide. Being told there was none in the house, tho' she had been before informed that the things came all safe, she had sent for the maid, who being unable to devise any excuse, had fallen on her knees, and after confessing her design of opening a bottle, which she imputed to the fellow, betrayed poor me to her mistress.

'Well, madam, after a lecture of about a quarter of an hour's duration from Mrs Harris, I suffered her to conduct me to the outward gate of her court-yard, whence I set forward in a disconsolate condition of mind, towards my lodgings. I had five miles to walk in a dark and rainy night; but how can I mention these trifling circumstances as any aggravation of my disappointment.'

'How was it possible,' cried Miss Mathews, 'that you could be got out of the house without seeing Miss Harris?'

'I assure you, madam,' answered Booth, 'I have often wondered at it myself; but my spirits were so much sunk at the sight of her mother, that no man was ever a greater coward than I was at that instant. Indeed I believe my tender concern for the terrors of Amelia were the principal cause of my submission. However it was, I left the house, and walked about a hundred yards, when, at the corner of the garden wall, a female voice, in a whisper, cried out, "Mr Booth." The person was extremely near me, but it was so dark I could scarce see her; nor did I, in the confusion I was in, immediately recognize the voice. I answered in a line of Congreve's, which burst from my lips spontaneously; for I am sure I had no intention to quote plays at that time,

Who calls the wretched thing that was Alphonso?[6]

'Upon which a woman leapt into my arms, crying out, – "O it is indeed my Alphonso, my only Alphonso!" – O Miss Mathews! guess what I felt when I found I had my Amelia in my arms. I embraced her with an extasy not to be described, at the same instant pouring a thousand tendernesses into her ears; at least if I could express so many to her in a minute; for in that time the alarm began at the house, Mrs Harris had missed her daughter, and the court was presently full of lights and noises of all kinds.

'I now lifted Amelia over a gate, and jumping after, we crept along together by the side of a hedge, a different way from what led to the town, as I imagined that would be the road through which they would pursue us. In this opinion I was right: for we heard them pass along that road, and the voice of Mrs Harris herself, who ran with the rest, notwithstanding the darkness and the rain. By these means we luckily made our escape, and clambring over hedge and ditch, my Amelia performing the part of a heroine all the way, we at length arrived at a little green lane, where stood a vast spreading oak, under which we sheltered ourselves from a violent storm.

'When this was over, and the moon began to appear, Amelia declared she knew very well where she was; and a little farther, striking into another lane, to the right, she said, that would lead us to a house where we should be both safe and unsuspected. I followed her directions, and we at length came to a little cottage about three miles distant from Mrs Harris's house.

'As it now rained very violently, we entered this cottage, in which we espied a light, without any ceremony. Here we found an elderly woman sitting by herself at a little fire, who had no sooner viewed us, than she instantly sprung from her seat, and starting back, gave the strongest tokens of amazement; upon which Amelia said, "Be not surprised, nurse, tho' you see me in a strange pickle I own." The old woman, after having several times blessed herself, and expressed the most tender concern for the lady, who stood dripping before her, began to bestir herself in making up the fire; at the same time entreating Amelia that she might be permitted to furnish her with some cloaths, which, she said, tho' not fine, were clean and wholesome, and much dryer than her own. I seconded this motion so vehemently, that Amelia, tho' she declared herself under no apprehension of catching cold, (she hath indeed the best constitution in the world) at last consented, and I retired without doors, under a shed, to give my angel an opportunity of dressing herself in the only room which the cottage afforded below stairs.

'At my return into the room, Amelia insisted on my exchanging my coat for one which belonged to the old woman's son.' – 'I am very glad,' cried Miss Mathews, 'to find she did not forget you. I own I thought it somewhat cruel to turn you out into the rain!' – 'O Miss Mathews,' continued he, taking no notice of her observation, 'I had now an opportunity of contemplating the vast power of exquisite beauty; which nothing almost can add to or diminish. Amelia, in the poor rags of her old nurse, looked scarce less beautiful than I have seen her appear at a ball or an assembly.' –

'Well, well,' cries Miss Mathews, 'to be sure she did; – but pray go on with your story.'

'The old woman,' continued he, 'after having equipped us as well as she could, and placed our wet cloaths before the fire, began to grow inquisitive; and, after some ejaculations, she cried – "O my dear young madam, my mind misgives me hugeously, and pray who is this fine young gentleman? Oh! Miss Emmy, Miss Emmy, I am afraid madam knows nothing of all this matter." "Suppose he should be my husband, nurse," answered Amelia, – "Oh! good! an if he be," replies the nurse, "I hope he is some great gentleman or other, with a vast estate, and a coach and six: for to be sure if an he was the greatest lord in the land you would deserve it all." – But why do I attempt to mimic the honest creature. In short she discovered the greatest affection for my Amelia, with which I was much more delighted than I was offended at the suspicions she shewed of me, or the many bitter curses which she denounced against me, if I ever proved a bad husband to so sweet a young lady.

'I so well improved the hint given me by Amelia, that the old woman had no doubt of our being really married; and comforting herself that if it was not as well as it might have been, yet madam had enough for us both, and that happiness did not always depend on great riches, she began to rail at the old lady for having turned us out of doors, which I scarce told an untruth in asserting. And when Amelia said, "She hoped her nurse would not betray her" – the good woman answered with much warmth, – "Betray you, my dear young madam! no, that I would not if the king would give me all that he is worth. No, not if madam herself would give me the great house, and the whole farm belonging to it."

'The good woman then went out and fetched a chicken from the roost, which she killed, and began to pick, without asking any questions. Then summoning her son, who was in bed, to her assistance, she began to prepare this chicken for our supper. This she afterwards set before us in so neat, I may almost say elegant a manner, that whoever would have disdained it, either doth not know the sensation of hunger, or doth not deserve to have it gratified. Our food was attended with some ale, which our kind hostess said she intended not to have tap'd till Christmas; "but," added she, "I little thought ever to have the honour of seeing my dear honoured lady in this poor place."

'For my own part, no human being was then an object of envy to me, and even Amelia seemed to be in pretty good spirits; she softly whispered to me, *that she perceived there might be happiness in a cottage*.'

'A cottage!' cries Miss Mathews sighing, 'A cottage with the man one loves is a palace.'

'When supper was ended,' continued Booth, 'the good woman began to think of our further wants, and very earnestly recommended her bed to us, saying it was a very neat, tho' homely one, and that she could furnish us with a pair of clean sheets. She added some persuasives which painted my angel all over with vermillion. As for myself I behaved so aukwardly and foolishly, and so readily agreed to Amelia's resolution of sitting up all night, that if it did not give the nurse any suspicion of our marriage, it ought to have inspired her with the utmost contempt for me.

'We both endeavoured to prevail with nurse to retire to her own bed, but found it utterly impossible to succeed; she thanked Heaven she understood breeding better than that. And so well bred was the good woman, that we could scarce get her out of the room the whole night. Luckily for us we both understood French, by means of which we consulted together, even in her presence, upon the measures we were to take in our present exigency. At length, it was resolved that I should send a letter by this young lad whom I have just before mentioned, to our worthy friend the doctor, desiring his company at our hut, since we thought it utterly unsafe to venture to the town, which we knew would be in an uproar on our account before the morning.'

Here Booth made a full stop, smiled, and then said, he was going to mention so ridiculous a distress, that he could scarce think of it without laughing. – What this was the reader shall know in the next chapter.

CHAPTER 7

The story of Booth continued. More surprising adventures.

'FROM what trifles, dear Miss Mathews,' cried Booth, 'may some of our greatest distresses arise! Do you not perceive I am going to tell you we had neither pen, ink, nor paper in our present exigency.

'A verbal message was now our only resource; however, we contrived to deliver it in such terms, that neither nurse nor her son could possibly conceive any suspicion from it of the present situation of our affairs. Indeed, Amelia whisper'd me, I might safely place any degree of confidence in the lad; for he had been her foster brother, and she had a great opinion of his integrity. He was in truth a boy of very good natural parts;[7] and Dr Harrison, who had received him into his family, at Amelia's recommendation, had bred him up to write and read very well, and had taken some pains to infuse into him the principles of honesty and religion. He was not, indeed, even now discharged from the doctor's service; but had been at home with his mother for some time on account of the small-pox, from which he was lately recovered.

'I have said so much,' continued Booth, 'of the boy's character, that you may not be surprised at some stories which I shall tell you of him hereafter.

'I am going now, madam, to relate to you one of those strange accidents, which are produced by such a train of circumstances, that mere chance hath been thought incapable of bringing them together; and which have therefore given birth, in superstitious minds, to Fortune, and to several other imaginary beings.

'We were now impatiently expecting the arrival of the doctor; our messenger had been gone much more than a sufficient time, which to us, you may be assured, appeared not at all shorter than it was, when nurse, who had gone out of doors on some errand, came running hastily to us, crying out, "O my dear young madam, her ladyship's coach is just at the door." Amelia turned pale as death at these words; indeed I feared she would have fainted, if I could be said to fear, who had scarce any of my senses left, and was in a condition little better than my angel's.

'While we were both in this dreadful situation, Amelia fallen back in her chair with the countenance in which ghosts are painted, myself at her feet, with a complexion of no very different colour, and nurse screaming out, and throwing water in Amelia's face, Mrs Harris entered the room. At the sight of this scene, she threw herself likewise into a chair, and called immediately for a glass of water, which Miss Betty her daughter supplied her with: for, as to nurse, nothing was capable of making any impression on her, whilst she apprehended her young mistress to be in danger.

'The doctor had now entered the room, and coming immediately up to Amelia, after some expressions of surprize, he took her by the hand, called her his little sugar-plumb, and assured her there were none but friends present. He then led her tottering across the room to Mrs Harris. Amelia then fell upon her knees before her mother, but the doctor caught her up saying, "Use that posture, child, only to the Almighty;" but I need not mention this singularity of his to you who know him so well, and must have heard him often dispute against addressing ourselves to man in the humblest posture which we use towards the Supreme Being.

'I will tire you with no more particulars; we were soon satisfied that the doctor had reconciled us and our affairs to Mrs Harris, and we now proceeded directly to church, the doctor having before provided a licence for us.'

'But where is the strange accident?' cried Miss Mathews. 'Sure you raised more curiosity than you have satisfied.'

'Indeed, madam,' answered he, 'your reproof is just; I had like to have forgotten it; but you cannot wonder at me when you reflect on that interesting part of my story, which I am now relating. – But before I mention this accident, I must tell you what happened after Amelia's escape from her mother's house. Mrs Harris at first ran out into the lane among her servants, and pursued us (so she imagined) along the road leading to the town; but that being very dirty, and a violent storm of rain coming, she took shelter in an alehouse, about half a mile from her own house, whither she sent for her coach: she then drove together with her daughter to town; where soon after her arrival, she sent for the doctor, her usual privy counsellor in all her affairs. They sat up all night together, the doctor endeavouring by arguments and persuasions to bring Mrs Harris to reason; but all to no purpose, tho', as he hath informed me, Miss Betty seconded him with the warmest entreaties.'

Here Miss Mathews laughed; of which Booth begged to know the reason; she, at last, after many apologies, said, 'It was the first good thing she ever heard of Miss Betty; nay,' said she, 'and asking your pardon for my opinion of your sister, since you will have it, I always conceived her to be the deepest of hypocrites.'

Booth fetched a sigh, and said, he was afraid she had not always acted so kindly; – and then after a little hesitation proceeded.

'You will be pleased, madam, to remember, the lad was sent with a verbal message to the doctor; which message was no more than to acquaint him where we were, and to desire the favour of his company, or that he would send a coach to bring us to whatever place he would please to meet us at. This message was to be delivered to the doctor himself, and the messenger was ordered, if he found him not at home, to go to him wherever he was. He fulfilled his orders, and told it to the doctor in the presence of Mrs Harris.'

'Oh! the idiot,' cried Miss Mathews. 'Not at all,' answered Booth: 'He is a very sensible fellow, as you will, perhaps, say hereafter. He had not the least reason to suspect that any secrecy was necessary: for we took the utmost care he should not suspect it. – Well, madam, this accident, which appeared so unfortunate, turned in the highest degree to our advantage. Mrs Harris no sooner heard the message delivered, than she fell into the most violent passion imaginable, and accused the doctor of being in the plot, and of having confederated with me in the design of carrying off her daughter.

'The doctor, who had hitherto used only soothing methods, now talked in a different strain. He confessed the accusation, and justified his conduct. He said, he was no meddler in the family-affairs of others, nor should he have concerned himself with hers, but at her own request; but that since Mrs Harris herself had made him an agent in this matter, he would take care to acquit himself with honour, and above all things to preserve a young lady for whom he had the highest esteem; "for she is," cries he, and by Heavens he said true, "the most worthy, generous, and noble of all human beings. You have yourself, madam," said he, "consented to the match. I have, at your request, made the match;" and then he added some particulars relating to his opinion of me, which my modesty forbids me to repeat.' – 'Nay, but,' cries Miss Mathews, 'I insist on your conquest of that modesty for once. – We women do not love to hear one another's praises, and I will be made amends by hearing the praises of a man, and of a man, whom perhaps,' added she with a leer, 'I shall not think much the better of upon that account.' – 'In obedience to your commands then, madam,' continued he, 'the doctor was so kind to say, he had enquired into my character, and had found that I had been a dutiful son, and an affectionate brother. Relations, said he, in which, whoever discharges his duty well, gives us a well-grounded hope, that he will behave as properly in all the rest. – He concluded with saying, that Amelia's happiness, her heart, nay, her very reputation, were all concerned in this matter, to which, as he had been made instrumental, he was resolved to carry her thro' it; and then taking the licence from his pocket, declared to Mrs Harris that he would go that instant and marry her daughter wherever he found her. This speech, the doctor's voice, his look, and his behaviour, all which are sufficiently calculated to inspire awe, and even terror, when he pleases, frightened poor Mrs Harris, and wrought a more sensible effect than it was in his power to produce by all his arguments and entreaties; and I have already related what followed.

'Thus the strange accident of our wanting pen, ink, and paper, and our not trusting the boy with our secret, occasioned the discovery to Mrs Harris: that discovery put the doctor upon his metal, and produced that blessed event which I have recounted to you, and which, as my mother[8] hath since confessed, nothing but the spirit which he had exerted after the discovery, could have brought about.

'Well, madam, you now see me married to Amelia; in which situation you will, perhaps, think my happiness incapable of addition. Perhaps it was so; and yet I can with truth say, that the love which I then bore Amelia was not comparable to what I bear her now.' 'Happy Amelia!' cried Miss Mathews. 'If all men were like you, all women would be blessed; nay the whole world would be so in a great measure: for upon my soul, I believe that from the damned inconstancy of your sex to ours proceeds half the miseries of mankind.'

That we may give the reader leisure to consider well the foregoing sentiment, we will here put an end to this chapter.

CHAPTER 8

In which our readers will probably be divided in their opinion of Mr Booth's conduct.

BOOTH proceeded as follows:

'The first months of our marriage produced nothing remarkable enough to mention. I am sure I need not tell Miss Mathews that I found in my Amelia every perfection of human nature. Mrs Harris at first gave us some little uneasiness. She had rather yielded to the doctor than given a willing consent to the match; however, by degrees, she became more and more satisfied, and at last seemed perfectly reconciled. This we ascribed a good deal to the kind offices of Miss Betty, who had always appeared to be my friend. She had been greatly assisting to Amelia in making her escape, which I had no opportunity of mentioning to you before, and in all things behaved so well, outwardly at least, to myself as well as her sister, that we regarded her as our sincerest friend.

'About half a year after our marriage, two additional companies were added to our regiment, in one of which I was preferred to the command of a lieutenant. Upon this occasion Miss Betty gave the first intimation of a disposition which we have since too severely experienced.'

'Your servant, sir,' says Miss Mathews, 'then I find I was not mistaken in my opinion of the lady. – No, no, shew me any goodness in a censorious prude and –'

As Miss Mathews hesitated for a simile or an execration, Booth proceeded. 'You will please to remember, madam, there was formerly an agreement between myself and Mrs Harris, that I should settle all my Amelia's fortune on her, except a certain sum, which was to be laid out in my advancement in the army; but as our marriage was carried on in the manner you have heard, no such agreement was ever executed. And since I was become Amelia's husband, not a word of this matter was ever mentioned by the old lady; and as for myself, I declare I had not yet awakened from that delicious dream of bliss in which the possession of Amelia had lulled me.'

Here Miss Mathews sighed, and cast the tenderest of looks on Booth, who thus continued his story:

'Soon after my promotion, Mrs Harris one morning took an occasion to speak to me on this affair. She said, that as I had been promoted gratis to a lieutenancy, she would assist me with money to carry me yet a step higher; and if more was required than was formerly mentioned, it should not be wanting, since she was so perfectly satisfied with my behaviour to her daughter. Adding, that she hoped I had still the same inclination to settle on my wife the remainder of her fortune.

'I answered with very warm acknowledgments of my mother's goodness, and declared, if I had the world I was ready to lay it at my Amelia's feet. – And so, Heaven knows, I would ten thousand worlds.

'Mrs Harris seemed pleased with the warmth of my sentiments, and said, she would immediately send to her lawyer and give him the necessary orders; and thus ended our conversation on this subject.

'From this time there was a very visible alteration in Miss Betty's behaviour. She grew reserved to her sister as well as to me. She was fretful and captious on the slightest occasion; nay she affected much to talk on the ill consequences of an imprudent marriage, especially before her mother; and if ever any little tenderness or endearments escaped me in public towards Amelia, she never failed to make some malicious remark on the short duration of violent passions; and when I have expressed a fond sentiment for my wife, her sister would kindly wish she might hear as much seven years hence.

'All these matters have been since suggested to us by reflection: for while they actually past, both Amelia and myself had our thoughts too happily engaged to take notice of what discovered itself in the mind of any other person.

'Unfortunately for us, Mrs Harris's lawyer happened at this time to be at London, where business detained him upwards of a month; and as Mrs Harris would on no occasion employ any other, our affair was under an entire suspension till his return.

'Amelia, who was now big with child, had often expressed the deepest concern at her apprehensions of my being sometime commanded abroad, a circumstance which she declared, if it should ever happen to her, even tho' she should not then be in the same situation as at present, would infallibly break her heart. These remonstrances were made with such tenderness, and so much affected me, that to avoid any probability of such an event, I endeavoured to get an exchange into the Horse-guards, a body of troops which very rarely goes abroad unless where the king himself commands in person. I soon found an officer for my purpose, the terms were agreed on, and Mrs Harris had ordered the money which I was to pay to be ready, notwithstanding the opposition made by Miss Betty, who openly dissuaded her mother from it; alledging that the exchange was highly to my disadvantage; that I could never hope to rise in the army after it; not forgetting, at the same time, some insinuations very prejudicial to my reputation as a soldier.

'When every thing was agreed on, and the two commissions were actually made out, but not signed by the king, one day, at my return from hunting, Amelia flew to me, and eagerly embracing me, cried out, "O Billy, I have news for you, which delights my soul. Nothing sure was ever so fortunate as the exchange you have made. The regiment you was formerly in is ordered for Gibraltar."

'I received this news with far less transport than it was delivered. I answered coldly, since the case was so, I heartily hoped the commissions might be both signed. *What do you say?* replied Amelia eagerly, – *Sure you told me every thing was entirely settled. That look of yours frightens me to death.* – But I am running into too minute particulars. In short, I received a letter by that very post, from the officer with whom I had exchanged, insisting that tho' his majesty had not signed the commissions, that still the bargain was valid, partly urging it as a right, and partly desiring it as a favour, that he might go to Gibraltar in my room.

'This letter convinced me in every point. I was now informed that the commissions were not signed, and consequently that the exchange was not compleated. Of consequence the other could have no right to insist on going; and as for granting him such a favour, I too clearly saw I must do it at the expence of my honour. I was now reduced to a dilemma, the most dreadful which I think any man can experience; in which I am not ashamed to own, I found love was not so over-matched by honour as he ought to have been. The thoughts of leaving Amelia, in her present condition, to misery, perhaps to death or madness, were insupportable; nor could any other consideration but that, which now tormented me on the other side, have combated them a moment.'

'No woman upon earth,' cries Miss Mathews, 'can despise want of spirit in a man more than myself; and yet I cannot help thinking you was rather too nice on this occasion.'

'You will allow, madam,' answered Booth, 'that whoever offends against the laws of honour in the least instance, is treated as the highest delinquent. Here is no excuse, no pardon; and he doth nothing who leaves any thing undone. But if the conflict was so terrible with myself alone, what was my situation in the presence of Amelia? How could I support her sighs, her tears, her agonies, her despair! Could I bear to think myself the cruel cause of her sufferings, for so I was! Could I endure the thought of having it in my power to give her instant relief, for so it was, and refuse it her!

'Miss Betty was now again become my friend. She had scarce been civil to me for a fortnight last past, yet now she commended me to the skies, and as severely blamed her sister, whom she arraigned of the most contemptible weakness, in preferring my safety to my honour: she said many ill-natured things on the occasion, which I shall not now repeat.

'In the midst of this hurricane the good doctor came to dine with Mrs Harris, and at my desire delivered his opinion on the matter.'

Here Mr Booth was interrupted in his narrative, by the arrival of a person whom we shall introduce in the next chapter.

CHAPTER 9

Containing a scene of a different kind from any of the preceding.

THE gentleman who now arrived was the keeper; or if you please, (for so he pleased to call himself) the governor of the prison.

He used so little ceremony at his approach, that the bolt, which was very slight on the inside, gave way, and the door immediately flew open. He had no sooner entered the room than he acquainted Miss Mathews that he had brought her very good news, for which he demanded a bottle of wine, as his due.

This demand being complied with, he acquainted Miss Mathews that the wounded gentleman was not dead, nor was his wound thought to be mortal: that loss of blood, and, perhaps, his fright had occasioned his fainting away; 'but I believe, madam,' said he, 'if you take the proper measures, you may be bailed to-morrow. I expect the lawyer here this evening, and if you put the business into his hands, I warrant it will be done. Money to be sure must be parted with, that's to be sure. People to be sure will expect to touch[9] a little in such cases. For my own part, I never desire to keep a prisoner longer than the law allows, not I: I always inform them they can be bailed as soon as I know it. I never make any bargain, not I; I always love to leave those things to the gentlemen and ladies themselves. I never suspect gentlemen and ladies of wanting generosity.'

Miss Mathews made a very slight answer to all these friendly professions. She said she had done nothing she repented of, and was indifferent as to the event. 'All I can say,' cries she, 'is, that if the wretch is alive, there is no greater villain in life than himself;' and instead of mentioning any thing of the bail, she begged the keeper to leave her again alone with Mr Booth. The keeper replied, 'Nay, madam, perhaps it may be better to stay a little longer here, if you have not bail ready, than to buy them too dear. Besides, a day or two hence, when the gentleman is past all danger of recovery, to be sure some folks that would expect an extraordinary fee now, can't expect to touch any thing. And to be sure you shall want nothing here. The best of all things are to be had here for money, both eatable and drinkable; tho' I say it, I shan't turn my back to any of the taverns for either eatables or wind.[10] The captain there need not have been so shy of owning himself when he first came in; we have had captains and other great gentlemen here before now; and no shame to them, tho' I say it. Many a great gentleman is sometimes found in places that don't become them half so well, let me tell them that, Captain Booth, let me tell them that.'

'I see, sir,' answered Booth, a little discomposed, 'that you are acquainted with my title as well as my name.'

'Ay, sir,' cries the keeper, 'and I honour you the more for it. I love the gentlemen of the army. I was in the army myself formerly; in the Lord of Oxford's Horse.[11] It is true I rode private; but I had money enough to have bought in quarter-master, when I took it into my head to marry, and my wife she did not like that I should continue a soldier, she was all for a private life; and so I came to this business.'

'Upon my word, sir,' answered Booth, 'you consulted your wife's inclinations very notably; but pray, will you satisfy my curiosity in telling me how you became acquainted that I was in the army? For my dress, I think, could not betray me.'

'Betray!' replied the keeper. 'There is no betraying here, I hope – I am not a person to betray people. – But you are so shy and peery,[12] you would almost make one suspect there was more in the matter. And if there be, I promise you, you need not be afraid of telling it me. You will excuse me giving you a hint; but the sooner the better, that's all. Others may be before-hand with you, and first come first serv'd on these occasions, that's all. Informers are odious, there's no doubt of that, and no one would care to be an informer if he could help it, because of the ill usage they always receive from the mob;[13] yet it is dangerous to trust too much; and when safety and a good part of the reward[14] too are on one side, and the gallows on the other – I know which a wise man would chuse.'

'What the devil do you mean by all this?' cries Booth.

'No offence, I hope,' answered the keeper; 'I speak for your good, and if you have been upon the snaffling lay[15] – you understand me, I'm sure.'

'Not I,' answered Booth, 'upon my honour.'

'Nay, nay,' replied the keeper, with a contemptuous sneer, 'if you are so peery as that comes to, you must take the consequence. – But for my part, I know I would not trust Robinson with two-pence untold.'

'What do you mean?' cries Booth. 'Who is Robinson?'

'And you don't know Robinson!' answered the keeper with great emotion. To which Booth replying in the negative, the keeper, after some tokens of amazement, cried out; 'Well, captain, I must say you are the best at it, of all the gentlemen I ever saw. However, I will tell you this: The lawyer and Mr Robinson have been laying their heads together about you above half an hour this afternoon. I overheard them mention Captain Booth, several times; and for my part, I would not answer that Mr Murphy is not now gone about the business; but if you will impeach[16] any to me of the road,[17] or any thing else, I will step away to his worship Thrasher this instant, and I am sure I have interest enough with him to get you admitted an evidence.'[18]

'And so,' cries Booth, 'you really take me for a highwayman.'

'No offence, captain, I hope,' said the keeper: 'As times go, there are many worse men in the world than those. Gentlemen may be driven to distress, and when they are, I know no more genteeler way than the road. It hath been many a brave man's case, to my knowledge, and men of as much honour too as any in the world.'

'Well, sir,' said Booth, 'I assure you I am not that gentleman of honour you imagine me.'

Miss Mathews, who had long understood the keeper no better than Mr Booth, no sooner heard his meaning explained, than she was fired with greater indignation than the gentleman had expressed. 'How dare you, sir,' said she to the keeper, 'insult a man of fashion, and who hath had the honour to bear his majesty's commission in the army, as you yourself own you know. If his misfortunes have sent him hither, sure we have no laws that will protect such a fellow as you in insulting him.' 'Fellow!' mutter'd the keeper – 'I would not advise you, madam, to use such language to me.' – 'Do you dare threaten me,' reply'd Miss Mathews in a rage; 'Venture in the least instance to exceed your authority, with regard to me, and I will prosecute you with the utmost vengeance.'

A scene of very high altercation now ensued, till Booth interposed, and quieted the keeper, who was, perhaps, enough inclined to an accommodation; for, in truth, he waged unequal war. He was besides unwilling to incense Miss Mathews, whom he expected to be bailed out the next day, and who had more money left than he intended she should carry out of the prison with her; and as for any violent or unjustifiable methods, the lady had discovered much too great a spirit to be in danger of them. The governor therefore, in a very gentle tone, declared, that if he had given any offence to the gentleman, he heartily asked his pardon: That if he had known him to be really a captain, he should not have entertained any such suspicions; but that captain was a very common title in that place, and belonged to several gentlemen that had never been in the army, or at most had rid private like himself. 'To be sure, captain,' said he, 'as you yourself own, your dress is not very military;' (for he had on a plain fustian suit) 'and besides, as the lawyer says, *Noscitur a sosir*[19] is a very good rule. And I don't believe there is a greater rascal upon earth than that same Robinson that I was talking of. Nay, I assure you, I wish there may be no mischief hatching against you. But if there is, I will do all I can with the lawyer to prevent it. To be sure Mr Murphy is one of the cleverest men in the world at the law: That even his enemies must own; and as I recommend him to all the business I can, (and it is not a little to be sure that arises in this place) why, one good turn deserves another. And I may expect that he will not be concerned in any plot to ruin any friend of mine; at least, when I desire him not. I am sure he could not be an honest man if he would.'

Booth was then satisfied that Mr Robinson, whom he did not yet know by name, was the gamester who had won his money at play. And now, Miss Mathews, who had very impatiently borne this long interruption, prevailed on the keeper to withdraw. As soon as he was gone, Mr Booth began to felicitate her upon the news of the wounded gentleman being in a fair likelihood of recovery. To which, after a short silence, she answered, 'There is something, perhaps, which you will not easily guess, that makes your congratulations more agreeable to me than the first account I heard of the villain's having escaped the fate he deserves: for, I do assure you, at first, it did not make me amends for the interruption of my curiosity. Now, I hope, we shall be disturbed no more, till you have finish'd your whole story. – You left off, I think, somewhere in the struggle about leaving Amelia, the happy Amelia.' – 'And can you call her happy at such a period?' cries Booth. 'Happy, ay happy, in any situation,' answer'd Miss Mathews, 'with such a husband. I, at least, may well think so, who have experienced the very reverse of her fortune; but I was not born to be happy. I may say with the poet:

The blackest ink of fate was sure my lot,
And when fate writ my name, it made a blot.'[20]

'Nay, nay, dear Miss Mathews,' answered Booth, 'you must, and shall banish such gloomy thoughts. Fate hath, I hope, many happy days in store for you.' – 'Do you believe it, Mr Booth,' replied she, 'indeed you know the contrary – you must know – for you can't have forgot. No Amelia in the world can have quite obliterated – forgetfulness is not in our own power. If it was, indeed, I have reason to think – but I know not what I am saying. – Pray, do proceed in that story.'

Booth so immediately complied with this request, that it is possible he was pleased with it. To say the truth, if all which unwittingly dropt from Miss Mathews was put together, some conclusions might, it seems, be drawn from the whole, which could not convey a very agreeable idea to a constant husband. Booth therefore proceeded to relate what is written in the third book of this history.

BOOK III

CHAPTER 1

In which Mr Booth resumes his story.

'If I am not mistaken, madam,' continued Booth, 'I was just going to acquaint you with the doctor's opinion, when we were interrupted by the keeper.

'The doctor having heard counsel on both sides, that is to say, Mrs Harris for my staying, and Miss Betty for my going, at last delivered his own sentiments. As for Amelia, she sat silent, drown'd in her tears; nor was I myself in a much better situation.

'"As the commissions are not signed," said the doctor, "I think you may be said to remain in your former regiment; and therefore I think you ought to go on this expedition, your duty to your king and country, whose bread you have eaten, requires it; and this is a duty of too high a nature to admit the least deficiency. Regard to your character likewise requires you to go: for the world, which might justly blame your staying at home if the case was even fairly stated, will not deal so honestly by you: You must expect to have every circumstance against you heightened, and most of what makes for your defence omitted; and thus you will be stigmatiz'd as a coward, without any palliation. As the malicious disposition of mankind is too well known, and the cruel pleasure which they take in destroying the reputations of others; the use we are to make of this knowledge is to afford no handle to reproach: for bad as the world is, it seldom falls on any man who hath not given some slight cause for censure, tho' this, perhaps, is often aggravated ten thousand fold; and when we blame the malice of the aggravation, we ought not to forget our own imprudence in giving the occasion. Remember, my boy, your honour is at stake; and you know how nice the honour of a soldier is in these cases. This is a treasure, which he must be your enemy indeed who would attempt to rob you of. Therefore you ought to consider every one as your enemy, who by desiring you to stay would rob you of your honour."

'"Do you hear that, sister?" cries Miss Betty. – "Yes, I do hear it," answered Amelia, with more spirit than I ever saw her exert before, "and would preserve his honour at the expence of my life. I will preserve it, if it should be at that expence; and since it is Dr Harrison's opinion that he ought to go, I give my consent. Go, my dear husband," cry'd she, falling upon her knees, "may every angel of Heaven guard and preserve you." – I cannot repeat her words without being affected,' said he, wiping his eyes, 'the excellence of that woman, no words can paint; Miss Mathews, she hath every perfection in human nature.

'I will not tire you with the repetition of any more that past on that occasion; nor with the quarrel that ensued between Mrs Harris and the doctor; for the old lady could not submit to my leaving her daughter in her present condition. She fell severely on the army, and cursed the day in which her daughter was married to a soldier, not sparing the doctor for having had some share in the match. I will omit likewise the tender scene which past between Amelia and myself previous to my departure.'

'Indeed I beg you would not,' cries Miss Mathews, 'nothing delights me more than scenes of tenderness. I should be glad to know, if possible, every syllable which was uttered on both sides.'

'I will indulge you then,' cries Booth, 'as far as is in my power. Indeed, I believe, I am able to recollect much the greatest part; for the impression is never to be effaced from my memory.'

He then proceeded as Miss Mathews desired; but lest all our readers should not be of her opinion, we will, according to our usual custom, endeavour to accommodate ourselves to every taste, and shall therefore place this scene in a chapter by itself, which we desire all our readers who do not love, or who perhaps do not know the pleasure of tenderness, to pass over; since they may do this without any prejudice to the thread of the narrative.

CHAPTER 2

Containing a scene of the tender kind.

'THE doctor, madam,' continued Booth, 'spent his evening at Mrs Harris's house, where I sat with him whilst he smok'd his pillow pipe, as his phrase is. Amelia was retired above half an hour, to her chamber, before I went to her. At my entrance, I found her on her knees, a posture in which I never disturbed her. In a few minutes she arose, came to me, and embracing me, said, she had been praying for resolution to support the cruellest moment she had ever undergone, or could possibly undergo. I reminded her how much more bitter a farewel would be on a death-bed, when we never could meet in this world, at least, again. I then endeavour'd to lessen all those objects which alarmed her most, and particularly the danger I was to encounter; upon which head I seemed a little to comfort her; – but the probable length of my absence, and the certain length of my voyage were circumstances which no oratory of mine could even palliate. "Oh! Heavens," said she, bursting into tears, "can I bear to think that hundreds, thousands, for ought I know, of miles or leagues, that lands and seas are between us. What is the prospect from that mount in our garden, where I have sat so many happy hours with my Billy? what is the distance between that and the farthest hill which we see from thence, compared to the distance which will be between us? You cannot wonder at this idea; you must remember, my Billy, at this place, this very thought came formerly into my foreboding mind. I then begged you to leave the army. Why would you not comply? Did I not tell you then that the smallest cottage we could survey from the mount, would be with you a paradise to me; it would be so still, why can't my Billy think so? Am I so much his superior in love? Where is the dishonour, Billy? or if there be any, will it reach our ears in our little hutt? Are glory and fame, and not his Amelia, the happiness of my husband? Go then, purchase them at my expence. You will pay a few sighs, perhaps a few tears at parting, and then new scenes will drive away the thoughts of poor Amelia from your bosom; but what assistance shall I have in my affliction? Not that any change of scene could drive you one moment from my remembrance; yet here every object I behold will place your lov'd idea in the liveliest manner before my eyes. This is the bed in which you have reposed; that is the chair on which you sat. Upon these boards you have stood. These books you have read to me. Can I walk among our beds of flowers, without viewing your favourites, nay those which you have planted with your own hands? Can I see one beauty from our beloved mount, which you have not pointed out to me?" – Thus she went on, the woman, madam, you see still prevailing.' – 'Since you mention it,' says Miss Mathews, with a smile, 'I own the same observation occurred to me. It is too natural to us to consider ourselves only, Mr Booth.' – 'You shall hear,' he cry'd, – 'At last, the thoughts of her present condition suggested themselves. – "But if," said she, "my situation, even in health, will be so intolerable, how shall I, in the danger and agonies of child-birth, support your absence!" – Here she stop'd, and looking on me with all the tenderness imaginable, cried out, "And am I then such a wretch to wish for your presence at such a season; ought I not to rejoice that you are out of the hearing of my cries, or the knowledge of my pains? If I die, will you not have escaped the horrors of a parting ten thousand times more dreadful than this? Go, go, my Billy; the very circumstance which made me most dread your departure, hath perfectly reconciled me to it. I perceive clearly now that I was only wishing to support my own weakness with your strength, and to relieve my own pains at the price of yours. Believe me, my love, I am ashamed of myself." – I caught her in my arms with raptures not to be exprest in words, called her my heroine; sure none ever better deserved that name; after which we remained for sometime speechless, and lock'd in each other's embraces.' – 'I am convinced,' said Miss Mathews, with a sigh, 'there are moments in life worth purchasing with worlds.' –

'At length the fatal morning came. I endeavoured to hide every pang of my heart, and to wear the utmost gaiety in my countenance. Amelia acted the same part. In these assumed characters we met the family at breakfast; at their breakfast, I mean: for we were both full already. The doctor had spent above an hour that morning in discourse with Mrs Harris, and had in some measure reconciled her to my departure. He now made use of every art to relieve the poor distressed Amelia; not by inveighing against the folly of grief, or by seriously advising her not to grieve; both which were sufficiently performed by Miss Betty. The doctor, on the contrary, had recourse to every means which might cast a veil over the idea of grief, and raise comfortable images in my angel's mind. He endeavoured to lessen the supposed length of my absence, by discoursing on matters which were more distant in time. He said, he intended next year to rebuild a part of his parsonage-house. "– And you, captain," says he, "shall lay the corner-stone, I promise you;" with many other instances of the like nature, which produced, I believe, some good effect on us both.

'Amelia spoke but little; indeed more tears than words dropt from her; however, she seemed resolved to bear her affliction with resignation. But when the dreadful news arrived that the horses were ready, and I, having taken my leave of all the rest, at last approached her; she was unable to support the conflict with nature any longer; and clinging round my neck, she cried, – "Farewel, farewel for ever: for I shall never, never, see you more." At which words the blood entirely forsook her lovely cheeks, and she became a lifeless corps in my arms.

'Amelia continued so long motionless, that the doctor, as well as Mrs Harris, began to be under the most terrible apprehensions: so they informed me afterwards; for at that time I was incapable of making any observation. I had indeed very little more use of my senses than the dear creature whom I supported. At length, however, we were all delivered from our fears; and life again visited the loveliest mansion that human nature ever afforded it.

'I had been, and yet was, so terrified with what had happened, and Amelia continued yet so weak and ill, that I determined, whatever might be the consequence, not to leave her that day: which resolution she was no sooner acquainted with, than she fell on her knees, crying, "Good Heaven, I thank thee for this reprieve at least. Oh! that every hour of my future life could be crammed into this dear day."

'Our good friend the doctor remained with us. He said, he had intended to visit a family in some affliction; "but I don't know," says he, "why I should ride a dozen miles after affliction, when we have enough here." Of all mankind the doctor is the best of comforters. As his excessive good-nature makes him take vast delight in the office; so his great penetration into the human mind, joined to his great experience, renders him the most wonderful proficient in it; and he so well knows when to sooth, when to reason, and when to ridicule, that he never applies any of those arts improperly, which is almost universally the case with the physicians of the mind, and which it requires very great judgment and dexterity to avoid.

'The doctor principally applied himself to ridiculing the dangers of the siege, in which he succeeded so well, that he sometimes forced a smile even into the face of Amelia. But what most comforted her, were the arguments he used to convince her of the probability of my speedy, if not immediate return. He said, the general opinion was, that the place would be taken before our arrival there. In which case, we should have nothing more to do, than to make the best of our way home again.

'Amelia was so lulled by these arts, that she passed the day much better than I expected. Though the doctor could not make pride strong enough to conquer love; yet, he exalted the former to make some stand against the latter; insomuch that my poor Amelia, I believe more than once, flattered herself, to speak the language of the world, that her reason had gained an entire victory over her passion; till love brought up a re-inforcement, if I may use that term, of tender ideas, and bore down all before him.

'In the evening, the doctor and I passed another half hour together, when he proposed to me to endeavour to leave Amelia asleep in the morning, and promised me to be at hand when she awaked, and to support her with all the assistance in his power. He added, that nothing was more foolish, than for friends to take leave of each other. "It is true indeed," says he, "in the common acquaintance and friendship of the world, this is a very harmless ceremony; but between two persons, who really love each other, the Church of Rome never invented a penance half so severe as this, which we absurdly impose on ourselves."

'I greatly approved the doctor's proposal; thanked him, and

promised, if possible, to put it in execution. He then shook me by the hand, and heartily wished me well, saying, in his blunt way; "Well, boy, I hope to see thee crowned with laurels at thy return; one comfort I have, at least, that stone walls and a sea will prevent thee from running away."

'When I had left the doctor, I repaired to my Amelia, whom I found in her chamber, employed in a very different manner from what she had been the preceding night; she was busy in packing up some trinkets in a casket, which she desired me to carry with me. This casket was her own work, and she had just fastened it as I came to her.

'Her eyes very plainly discovered what had passed while she was engaged in her work; however, her countenance was now serene, and she spoke, at least, with some chearfulness. But after some time, "You must take care of this casket, Billy," said she. – "You must indeed, Billy – for –" here passion almost choaked her, till a flood of tears gave her relief, and then she proceeded – "For I shall be the happiest woman that ever was born when I see it again." – I told her, with the blessing of God that day would soon come. "Soon!" answered she, – "No, Billy, not soon; a week is an age; – but yet the happy day may come. It shall, it must, it will! – Yes, Billy, we shall meet never to part again: – even in this world I hope." – Pardon my weakness, Miss Mathews, but upon my soul I cannot help it,' cried he, wiping his eyes – 'Well, I wonder at your patience, and I will try it no longer. Amelia, tired out with so long a struggle between variety of passions, and having not closed her eyes during three successive nights, towards the morning fell into a profound sleep. In which sleep I left her – and having drest myself with all the expedition imaginable, singing, whistling, hurrying, attempting by every method to banish thought, I mounted my horse, which I had overnight ordered to be ready, and galloped away from that house where all my treasure was deposited.

'Thus, madam, I have, in obedience to your commands, run through a scene, which if it hath been tiresome to you, you must yet acquit me of having obtruded upon you. This I am convinced of, that no one is capable of tasting such a scene, who hath not a heart full of tenderness, and perhaps not even then, unless he hath been in the same situation.'

CHAPTER 3

In which Mr Booth sets forward on his journey.

'WELL, madam, we have now taken our leave of Amelia. I rode a full mile before I once suffered myself to look back; but now being come to the top of a little hill, the last spot I knew which could give me a prospect of Mrs Harris's house, my resolution failed; I stopt and cast my eyes backward. Shall I tell you what I felt at that instant? I do assure you I am not able. So many tender ideas crowded at once into my mind, that, if I may use the expression, they almost dissolved my heart. And now, madam, the most unfortunate accident came first into my head. This was, that I had in the hurry and confusion left the dear casket behind me. The thought of going back at first suggested itself; but the consequences of that were too apparent. I therefore resolved to send my man, and in the mean time to ride on softly on my road. He immediately executed my orders, and after some time, feeding my eyes with that delicious and yet heart-felt prospect, I at last turned my horse to descend the hill, and proceeded about a hundred yards, when, considering with myself, that I should lose no time by a second indulgence, I again turned back, and once more feasted my sight with the same painful pleasure, till my man returned, bringing me the casket, and an account that Amelia still continued in the sweet sleep I left her. – I now suddenly turned my horse for the last time, and with the utmost resolution pursued my journey.

'I perceived my man at his return – But before I mention any thing of him, it may be proper, madam, to acquaint you who he was. He was the foster-brother of my Amelia. This young fellow had taken it into his head to go into the army; and he was desirous to serve under my command. The doctor consented to discharge him; his mother at last yielded to his importunities; and I was very easily prevailed on to list one of the handsomest young fellows in England.

'You will easily believe I had some little partiality to one whose milk Amelia had sucked; but as he had never seen the regiment, I had no opportunity to shew him any great mark of favour. Indeed he waited on me as my servant; and I treated him with all the tenderness which can be used to one in that station.

'When I was about to change into the Horse-guards, the poor fellow began to droop, fearing that he should no longer be in the same corps with me, tho' certainly that would not have been the case. However, he had never mentioned one word of his dissatisfaction. – He is indeed a fellow of a noble spirit; but when he heard that I was to remain where I was, and that we were to go to Gibraltar together, he fell into transports of joy little short of madness. In short, the poor fellow had imbibed a very strong affection for me; tho' this was what I knew nothing of till long after.

'When he returned to me then, as I was saying, with the casket, I observed his eyes all over blubbered with tears. I rebuked him a little too rashly on this occasion. *Heyday!* says I, *what is the meaning of this? I hope I have not a milksop with me. If I thought you would shew such a face to the enemy, I would leave you behind. – Your honour need not fear that*, answered he, *I shall find no body there that I shall love well enough to make me cry*. I was highly pleased with this answer, in which I thought I could discover both sense and spirit. I then asked him what had occasioned those tears since he had left me; (for he had no sign of any at that time) and whether he had seen his mother at Mrs Harris's. He answered in the negative, and begged that I would ask him no more questions; adding, that he was not very apt to cry, and he hoped he should never give me such another opportunity of blaming him. I mention this only as an instance of his affection towards me: for I never could account for those tears, any otherwise than by placing them to the account of that distress in which he left me at that time. We travelled full forty miles that day without baiting, when arriving at the inn where I intended to rest that night, I retired immediately to my chamber, with my dear Amelia's casket, the opening of which was the nicest repast, and to which every other hunger gave way.

'It is impossible to mention to you all the little matters with which Amelia had furnished this casket. It contained medicines of all kinds, which her mother, who was the Lady Bountiful[1] of that country, had supplied her with. The most valuable of all to me was a lock of her dear hair, which I have from that time to this worn in my bosom. What would I have then given for a little picture of my dear angel, which she had lost from her chamber about a month before? and which we had the highest reason in the world to imagine her sister had taken away: for the suspicion lay only between her and Amelia's maid, who was of all creatures the honestest, and whom her mistress had often trusted with things of much greater value: for the picture, which was set in gold, and had two or three little diamonds round it, was worth about twelve guineas only; whereas Amelia left jewels in her care of much greater value.'

'Sure,' cries Miss Mathews, 'she could not be such a paultry pilferer.'

'Not on account of the gold or the jewels,' cries Booth. 'We imputed it to mere spite, with which I assure you she abounds; and she knew that next to Amelia herself, there was nothing which I valued so much as this little picture: for such a resemblance did it bear of the original, that Hogarth himself did never, I believe, draw a stronger likeness. Spite therefore was the only motive to this cruel depredation; and indeed her behaviour on the occasion sufficiently convinced us both of the justice of our suspicion, tho' we neither of us durst accuse her; and she herself had the assurance to insist very strongly (tho' she could not prevail) with Amelia to turn away her innocent maid, saying, she would not live in the house with a thief.'

Miss Mathews now discharged some curses on Miss Betty, not much worth repeating, and then Mr Booth proceeded in his relation.

CHAPTER 4

A sea-piece.

'THE next day we joined the regiment, which was soon after to embark. Nothing but mirth and jollity were in the countenance of every officer and soldier; and as I now met several friends whom I had not seen for above a year before, I passed several happy hours, in which poor Amelia's image seldom obtruded itself to interrupt my pleasure. To confess the truth, dear Miss Mathews, the tenderest of passions is capable of subsiding; nor is absence from our dearest friends so unsupportable as it may at first appear. Distance of time and place do really cure what they seem to aggravate; and taking leave of our friends resembles taking leave of the world, concerning which it hath been often said, that it is not death but dying which is terrible.' – Here Miss Mathews burst into a fit of laughter, and cried, 'I sincerely ask your pardon; but I cannot help laughing at the gravity of your philosophy.' Booth answered, that the doctrine of the passions had been always his favourite study; that he was convinced every man acted entirely from that passion which was uppermost; 'Can I then think,' said he, 'without entertaining the utmost contempt for myself, that any pleasure upon earth could drive the thoughts of Amelia one instant from my mind?

'At length we embarked aboard a transport, and sailed for Gibraltar, but the wind, which was at first fair, soon chopped about; so that we were obliged, for several days, to beat to windward, as the sea phrase is. During this time the taste which I had of a sea-faring life did not appear extremely agreeable. We rolled up and down in a little narrow cabbin, in which were three officers, all of us extremely sea-sick; our sickness being much aggravated by the motion of the ship, by the view of each other, and by the stench of the men. But this was but a little taste indeed of the misery which was to follow: for we were got about six leagues to the westward of Scilly,[2] when a violent storm arose at north-east, which soon raised the waves to the height of mountains. The horror of this is not to be adequately described to those who have never seen the like. The storm began in the evening, and as the clouds brought on the night apace, it was soon entirely dark; nor had we during many hours any other light than what was caused by the jarring elements, which frequently sent forth flashes, or rather streams of fire; and whilst these presented the most dreadful objects to our eyes, the roaring of the winds, the dashing of the waves against the ship and each other, formed a sound altogether as horrible for our ears; while our ship, sometimes lifted up as it were to the skies, and sometimes swept away at once as into the lowest abyss, seemed to be the sport of the winds and seas. The captain himself almost gave all for lost, and exprest his apprehension of being inevitably cast on the rocks of Scilly, and beat to pieces. And now, while some on board were addressing themselves to the Supreme Being, and others applying for comfort to strong liquors, my whole thoughts were entirely engaged by my Amelia. A thousand tender ideas crowded into my mind. I can truly say, that I had not a single consideration about myself, in which she was not concerned. Dying to me was leaving her, and the fear of never seeing her more was a dagger stuck in my heart. Again, all the terrors with which this storm, if it reached her ears, must fill her gentle mind on my account, and the agonies which she must undergo, when she heard of my fate, gave me such intolerable pangs, that I now repented my resolution, and wished, I own I wished, that I had taken her advice, and preferred love and a cottage to all the dazzling charms of honour.

'While I was tormenting myself with those meditations, and had concluded myself as certainly lost, the master came into the cabbin, and with a chearful voice, assured us that we had escaped the danger, and that we had certainly past to the westward of the rock. This was comfortable news to all present; and my captain, who had been some time on his knees, leapt suddenly up and testified his joy with a great oath.

'A person unused to the sea would have been astonished at the satisfaction which now discovered itself in the master or in any on board: for the storm still raged with great violence, and the day-light which now appeared, presented us with sights of horror sufficient to terrify minds which were not absolute slaves to the passion of fear; but so great is the force of habit, that what inspires a landman with the highest apprehension of danger, gives not the least concern to a sailor, to whom rocks and quick-sands are almost the only objects of terror.

'The master, however, was a little mistaken in the present instance; for he had not left the cabbin above an hour, before my man came running to me, and acquainted me that the ship was half full of water; that the sailors were going to hoist out the boat and save themselves, and begged me to come that moment along with him, as I tendered my preservation. With this account, which was conveyed to me in a whisper, I acquainted both the captain and ensign, and we all together immediately mounted the deck, where we found the master making use of all his oratory to persuade the sailors that the ship was in no danger; and at the same time employing all his authority to set the pumps a-going, which he assured them would keep the water under, and save his dear *Lovely Peggy*, (for that was the name of the ship) which he swore he loved as dearly as his own soul.

'Indeed this sufficiently appeared; for the leak was so great, and the water flowed in so plentifully, that his *Lovely Peggy* was half filled, before he could be brought to think of quitting her; but now the boat was brought along-side the ship; and the master himself, notwithstanding all his love for her, quitted his ship; and leapt into the boat. Every man present attempted to follow his example, when I heard the voice of my servant roaring forth my name in a kind of agony. I made directly to the ship side, but was too late: for the boat being already over laden put directly off. And now, madam, I am going to relate to you an instance of heroic affection in a poor fellow towards his master, to which love itself, even among persons of superior education, can produce but few similar instances. My poor man being unable to get me with him into the boat, leapt suddenly into the sea and swam back to the ship; and when I gently rebuked him for his rashness, he answered, he chose rather to die with me, than to live to carry the account of my death to my Amelia; at the same time bursting into a flood of tears, he cried, "Good Heavens! what will that poor lady feel when she hears of this!" This tender concern for my dear love endeared the poor fellow more to me than the gallant instance which he had just before given of his affection towards myself.

'And now, madam, my eyes were shocked with a sight, the horror of which can scarce be imagined: for the boat had scarce got four hundred yards from the ship, when it was swallowed up by the merciless waves, which now ran so high, that out of the number of persons which were in the boat none recovered the ship; tho' many of them we saw miserably perish before our eyes, some of them very near us, without any possibility of giving them the least assistance.

'But whatever we felt for them, we felt, I believe, more for ourselves, expecting every minute when we should share the same fate. Among the rest one of our officers appeared quite stupified with fear. I never indeed saw a more miserable example of the great power of that passion: I must not, however, omit doing him justice, by saying that I afterwards saw the same man behave well in an engagement, in which he was wounded. Tho' there likewise he was said to have betrayed the same passion of fear in his countenance.

'The other of our officers was no less stupified (if I may so express myself) with fool-hardiness, and seemed almost insensible of his danger. To say the truth, I have, from this and some other instances which I have seen, been almost inclined to think, that the courage as well as cowardice of fools proceeds from not knowing what is or what is not the proper object of fear: indeed, we may account for the extreme hardiness of some men, in the same manner as for the terrors of children at a bugbear. The child knows not but that the bugbear is the proper object of fear, the block-head knows not that a cannon ball is so.

'As to the remaining part of the ship's crew, and the soldiery, most of them were dead drunk; and the rest were endeavouring, as fast as they could, to prepare for death in the same manner.

'In this dreadful situation we were taught that no human condition should inspire men with absolute despair: for as the storm had ceased for some time, the swelling of the sea began considerably to abate; and we now perceived the man of war which convoyed us, at no great distance a-stern. Those aboard her easily perceived our distress, and made towards us. When they came pretty near, they hoisted out two boats to our assistance. These no sooner approached the ship, than they were instantaneously filled, and I myself got a place in one of them, chiefly by the aid of my honest servant, of whose fidelity to me on all occasions I cannot speak or think too highly. Indeed I got into the boat so much the more easily as a great number on board the ship were rendered by drink incapable of taking any care for themselves. There was time, however, for the boat to pass and repass; so that when we came to call over names, three only, of all that remained in the ship, after the loss of her own boat, were missing.

'The captain, ensign, and myself were received with many

congratulations by our officers on board the man of war. – The sea officers too, all except the captain, paid us their compliments, tho' these were of the rougher kind, and not without several jokes on our escape. As for the captain himself, we scarce saw him during many hours; and when he appeared he presented a view of majesty beyond any that I had ever seen. The dignity which he preserved, did indeed give me rather the idea of a Mogul, or a Turkish emperor, than of any of the monarchs of Christendom. To say the truth, I could resemble his walk on the deck to nothing but to the image of Captain Gulliver strutting among the Lilliputians; he seemed to think himself a being of an order superior to all around him, and more especially to us of the land service. Nay such was the behaviour of all the sea officers and sailors to us and our soldiers, that instead of appearing to be subjects of the same prince, engaged in one quarrel, and joined to support one cause; we land-men rather seemed to be captives on board an enemy's vessel. This is a grievous misfortune, and often proves so fatal to the service, that it is great pity some means could not be found of curing it.'

Here Mr Booth stopt a while, to take breath. We will therefore give the same refreshment to the reader.

CHAPTER 5

The arrival of Booth at Gibraltar, with what there befel him.

'THE adventures,' continued Booth, 'which happened to me from this day till my arrival at Gibraltar, are not worth recounting to you. After a voyage, the remainder of which was tolerably prosperous, we arrived in that garrison, the natural strength of which is so well known to the whole world.

'About a week after my arrival, it was my fortune to be ordered on a sally-party, in which my left leg was broke with a musket ball; and I should most certainly have either perish'd miserably, or must have owed my preservation to some of the enemy, had not my faithful servant carried me off on his shoulders, and afterwards, with the assistance of one of his comrades, brought me back into the garrison.

'The agony of my wound was so great, that it threw me into a fever, from whence my surgeon apprehended much danger. I now began again to feel for my Amelia, and for myself on her account: and the disorder of my mind occasioned by such melancholy contemplations, very highly aggravated the distemper of my body; insomuch that it would probably have proved fatal, had it not been for the friendship of one Captain James, an officer of our regiment, and an old acquaintance, who is undoubtedly one of the pleasantest companions, and one of the best-natured men in the world. This worthy man, who had a head and a heart perfectly adequate to every office of friendship, stay'd with me almost day and night during my illness; and by strengthening my hopes, raising my spirits, and cheering my thoughts, preserved me from destruction.

'The behaviour of this man alone is a sufficient proof of the truth of my doctrine, that all men act entirely from their passions; for Bob James can never be supposed to act from any motive of virtue or religion; since he constantly laughs at both; and yet his conduct towards me alone demonstrates a degree of goodness, which, perhaps, few of the votaries of either virtue or religion can equal.'

'You need not take much pains,' answered Miss Mathews, with a smile, 'to convince me of your doctrine. I have been always an advocate for the same. I look upon the two words you mention, to serve only as cloaks under which hypocrisy may be the better enabled to cheat the world. I have been of that opinion ever since I read that charming fellow Mandevil.'[3]

'Pardon me, madam,' answered Booth, 'I hope you do not agree with Mandevil neither, who hath represented human nature in a picture of the highest deformity. He hath left out of his system the best passion which the mind can possess, and attempts to derive the effects or energies of that passion, from the base impulses of pride or fear. Whereas, it is as certain that love exists in the mind of man, as that its opposite hatred doth, and the same reasons will equally prove the existence of the one as the existence of the other.'

'I don't know, indeed,' replied the lady, 'I never thought much about the matter. This I know, that when I read Mandevil, I thought all he said was true; and I have been often told, that he proves religion and virtue to be only mere names. However, if he denies there is any such thing as love, that is most certainly wrong. – I am afraid I can give him the lye myself.'

'I will join with you, madam, in that,' answered Booth, 'at any time.'

'Will you join with me?' answered she, looking eagerly at him – 'O Mr Booth, I know not what I was going to say – What – Where did you leave off? – I would not interrupt you – but I am impatient to know something.'

'What, madam?' cries Booth, 'if I can give you any satisfaction –'

'No, no,' said she, 'I must hear all, I would not for the world break the thread of your story – Besides, I am afraid to ask – Pray, pray, sir, go on.'

'Well, madam,' cries Booth, 'I think I was mentioning the extraordinary acts of friendship done me by Captain James; nor can I help taking notice of the almost unparallel'd fidelity of poor Atkinson (for that was my man's name) who was not only constant in the assiduity of his attendance, but during the time of my danger demonstrated a concern for me which I can hardly account for, as my prevailing on his captain to make him a serjeant was the first favour he ever received at my hands, and this did not happen till I was almost perfectly recovered of my broken leg. Poor fellow! I shall never forget the extravagant joy his halbert gave him; I remember it the more because it was one of the happiest days of my own life; for it was upon this day that I received a letter from my dear Amelia, after a long silence, acquainting me that she was out of all danger from her lying-in.

'I was now once more able to perform my duty; when (so unkind was the fortune of war) the second time I mounted the guard, I received a violent contusion from the bursting of a bomb. I was felled to the ground, where I lay breathless by the blow, till honest Atkinson came to my assistance, and conveyed me to my room, where a surgeon immediately attended me.

'The injury I had now received, was much more dangerous in my surgeon's opinion than the former; it caused me to spit blood, and was attended with a fever, and other bad symptoms; so that very fatal consequences were apprehended.

'In this situation the image of my Amelia haunted me day and night; and the apprehensions of never seeing her more were so intolerable, that I had thoughts of resigning my commission, and returning home, weak as I was, that I might have, at least, the satisfaction of dying in the arms of my love. Captain James, however, persisted in dissuading me from any such resolution. He told me my honour was too much concerned, attempted to raise my hopes of recovery to the utmost of his power; but chiefly he prevailed on me by suggesting, that if the worst which I apprehended, should happen, it was much better for Amelia, that she should be absent than present in so melancholy an hour. "I know," cry'd he, "the extreme joy which must arise in you from meeting again with Amelia, and the comfort of expiring in her arms; but consider what she herself must endure upon the dreadful occasion, and you would not wish to purchase any happiness at the price of so much pain to her." This argument, at length, prevailed on me; and it was after many long debates resolved, that she should not even know my present condition till my doom either for life or death was absolutely fixed.'

'Oh! Heavens! how great! how generous!' cried Miss Mathews. 'Booth, thou art a noble fellow; and I scarce think there is a woman upon earth worthy so exalted a passion.'

Booth made a modest answer to the compliment which Miss Mathews had paid him. This drew more civilities from the lady; and these again more acknowledgments. All which we shall pass by, and proceed with our history.

CHAPTER 6

Containing matters which will please some readers.

'TWO months, and more, had I continued in a state of uncertainty, sometimes with more flattering, and sometimes with more alarming symptoms; when one afternoon poor Atkinson came running into my room, all pale and out of breath, and begged me not to be surprised at his news. I asked him eagerly what was the matter, and if it was any thing concerning Amelia? – I had scarce utter'd the dear name, when she herself rushed into the room, and ran hastily to me, crying, "Yes, it is, it is your Amelia herself."

'There is nothing so difficult to describe, and generally so dull when described, as scenes of excessive tenderness.'

'Can you think so?' says Miss Mathews, 'surely there is nothing so charming! – O! Mr Booth, our sex is d—n'd by the want of tenderness in yours – O were they all like you – certainly no man was ever your equal.'

'Indeed, madam,' cries Booth, 'you honour me too much – But – well – when the first transports of our meeting were over, Amelia began gently to chide me for having concealed my illness from her; for in three letters which I had writ her since the accident had happened, there was not the least mention of it, or any hint given by which she could possibly conclude I was otherwise than in perfect health. And when I had excused myself, by assigning the true reason, she cry'd, – "O Mr Booth! and do you know so little of your Amelia, as to think I could or would survive you! – Would it not be better for one dreadful sight to break my heart all at once, than to break it by degrees? – O Billy! can any thing pay me for the loss of this embrace –" But I ask your pardon – how ridiculous doth my fondness appear in your eyes?'

'How often,' answered she, 'shall I assert the contrary? – What would you have me say, Mr Booth? Shall I tell you I envy Mrs Booth of all the women in the world? Would you believe me if I did? I hope you – What am I saying? – Pray make no farther apology, but go on.'

'After a scene,' continued he, 'too tender to be conceived by many, Amelia informed me that she had received a letter from an unknown hand, acquainting her with my misfortune, and advising her, if she ever desired to see me more to come directly to Gibraltar. She said, she should not have delayed a moment after receiving this letter, had not the same ship brought her one from me written with rather more than usual gaiety, and in which there was not the least mention of my indisposition. This, she said, greatly puzzled her and her mother, and the worthy divine endeavoured to persuade her to give credit to my letter, and to impute the other to a species of wit with which the world greatly abounds. This consists entirely in doing various kinds of mischief to our fellow-creatures; by belying one, deceiving another, exposing a third, and drawing in a fourth to expose himself; in short, by making some the objects of laughter, others of contempt; and indeed not seldom, by subjecting them to very great inconveniences, perhaps to ruin, for the sake of a jest.

'Mrs Harris and the doctor derived the letter from this species of wit. Miss Betty, however, was of a different opinion, and advised poor Amelia to apply to an officer whom the Governor had sent over in the same ship, by whom the report of my illness was so strongly confirmed, that Amelia immediately resolved on her voyage.

'I had a great curiosity to know the author of this letter; but not the least trace of it could be discovered. The only person with whom I lived in any great intimacy was Captain James; and he, madam, from what I have already told you, you will think to be the last person I could suspect; besides, he declared upon his honour, that he knew nothing of the matter; and no man's honour is, I believe, more sacred. There was indeed an ensign of another regiment who knew my wife, and who had sometimes visited me in my illness; but he was a very unlikely man to interest himself much in any affairs which did not concern him; and he too declared he knew nothing of it.'

'And did you never discover this secret?' cried Miss Mathews.

'Never to this day,' answered Booth.

'I fancy,' said she, 'I could give a shrewd guess – What so likely as that Mrs Booth, when you left her, should have given her foster-brother orders to send her word of whatever befel you? – Yet stay – that could not be neither: for then she would not have doubted whether she should leave dear England on the receipt of the letter. – No, it must have been by some other means; – yet that I owned appeared extremely natural to me: for if I had been left by such a husband, I think I should have pursued the same method.'

'No, madam,' cried Booth, 'it must have been conveyed by some other channel; for my Amelia, I am certain, was entirely ignorant of the manner; and as for poor Atkinson, I am convinced he would not have ventured to take such a step without acquainting me. Besides, the poor fellow had, I believe, such a regard for my wife, out of gratitude for the favours she hath done his mother, that I make no doubt he was highly rejoiced at her absence from my melancholy scene. Well, whoever writ it is a matter very immaterial; yet as it seemed so odd and unaccountable an incident I could not help mentioning it.

'From the time of Amelia's arrival nothing remarkable happened till my perfect recovery, unless I should observe her remarkable behaviour, so full of care and tenderness that it was perhaps without a parallel.'

'O no, Mr Booth,' cries the lady. – 'It is fully equalled, I am sure, by your gratitude. There is nothing, I believe, so rare as gratitude in your sex, especially in husbands. So kind a remembrance is indeed more than a return to such an obligation: for where is the mighty obligation which a woman confers, who being possessed of an inestimable jewel is so kind to herself as to be careful and tender of it? I do not say this to lessen your opinion of Mrs Booth. I have no doubt but that she loves you as well as she is capable. But I would not have you think so meanly of our sex, as to imagine there are not a thousand women susceptible of true tenderness towards a meritorious man. – Believe me, Mr Booth, if I had received such an account of an accident having happened to such a husband, a mother and a parson would not have held me a moment. I should have leapt into the first fishing-boat I could have found, and bid defiance to the winds and waves. – O there is no true tenderness but in a woman of spirit. I would not be understood all this while to reflect on Mrs Booth. I am only defending the cause of my sex; for upon my soul such compliments to a wife are a satire on all the rest of womankind.'

'Sure you jest, Miss Mathews,' answered Booth, with a smile. 'However, if you please, I will proceed in my story.'

CHAPTER 7

The captain continuing his story, recounts some particulars which we doubt not to many good people will appear unnatural.

'I WAS scarce sooner recovered from my indisposition than Amelia herself fell ill. This, I am afraid, was occasioned by the fatigues which I could not prevent her from undergoing on my account; for as my disease went off with violent sweats, during which the surgeon strictly ordered that I should lie by myself, my Amelia could not be prevailed upon to spend many hours in her own bed. During my restless fits she would sometimes read to me several hours together; indeed it was not without difficulty that she ever quitted my bed-side. These fatigues, added to the uneasiness of her mind, overpowered her weak spirits, and threw her into one of the worst disorders that can possibly attend a woman. A disorder very common among the ladies, and our physicians have not agreed upon its name. Some call it the fever on the spirits, some a nervous fever, some the vapours, and some the hysterics.'[4]

'O say no more,' cries Miss Mathews, 'I pity you, I pity you from my soul. A man had better be plagued with all the curses of Egypt[5] than with a vapourish wife.'

'Pity me, madam!' answered Booth. 'Pity rather that dear creature, who, from her love and care of my unworthy self, contracted a distemper, the horrors of which are scarce to be imagined. It is indeed a sort of complication of all diseases together, with almost madness added to them. In this situation, the siege being at an end, the Governor[6] gave me leave to attend my wife to Montpelier,[7] the air of which was judged to be most likely to restore her to health. Upon this occasion she wrote to her mother to desire a remittance, and set forth the melancholy condition of her health, and her necessity for money, in such terms as would have touched any bosom not void of humanity, tho' a stranger to the unhappy sufferer. Her sister answered it, and I believe I have a copy of the answer in my pocket. I keep it by me as a curiosity, and you would think it more so, could I shew you my Amelia's letter.' He then searched his pocket-book, and finding the letter, among many others, he read it in the following words:

'Dear Sister,

My mamma being much disordered, hath commanded me to tell you, she is both shocked and surprised at your extraordinary request, or, as she chuses to call it, order for money. You know, my dear, she says, that your marriage with this red-coat man was entirely against her consent, and the opinion of all your family, (I am sure I may here include myself in that number) and yet after this fatal act of disobedience, she was prevailed on to receive you as her child; not, however, nor are you so to understand it, as the favourite which you was before. She forgave you; but this was as a Christian and a parent; still preserving in her own mind a just sense of your disobedience, and a just resentment on that account. And yet, notwithstanding this resentment, she desires you to remember, that when you a second time ventured to oppose her authority, and nothing would serve you but taking a ramble (an indecent one I can't help saying) after your fellow, she thought fit to shew the excess of a mother's tenderness, and furnished you with no less than fifty pounds for your foolish voyage. How can she then be otherwise than surprised at your present demand? which, should she be so weak to comply with, she must expect to be every month repeated, in order to supply the extravagance of a young rakish officer. – You say she will compassionate your sufferings; yes, surely she doth greatly compassionate them, and so do I too, tho' you was neither so kind, nor so civil as to suppose I should. But I forgive all your slights to me, as well now as formerly. Nay, I not only forgive, but I pray daily for you. – But, dear sister, what could you expect less than what hath happened? You should have believed your friends, who were wiser and older than you. I do not here mean myself, tho' I own I am eleven months and some odd weeks your superior; tho' had I been younger, I might perhaps have been able to advise you: for wisdom and what some may call beauty do not always go together. You will not be offended at this: for I know in your heart you have always held your head above some people, whom perhaps other people have thought better of; but why do I mention what I scorn so much? – No, my dear sister, heaven forbid it should ever be said of me, that I value myself upon my face – not but if I could believe men perhaps – but I hate and despise men – you know I do, my dear, and I wish you had despised them as much; but *jacta est alia*,[8] as the doctor says. – You are to make the best of your fortune. What fortune I mean my mamma may please to give you: for you know all is in her power. Let me advise you then to bring your mind to your circumstances, and remember (for I can't help writing it, as it is for your own good) the vapours are a distemper which very ill become a knapsack.[9] Remember, my dear, what you have done; remember what my mamma hath done; remember we have something of yours to keep, and do not consider yourself as an only child – No, nor as a favourite child, but be pleased to remember,

Dear sister,
Your most affectionate sister,
And most obedient humble servant.

E. HARRIS.'

'O brave Miss Betty,' cried Miss Mathews, 'I always held her in high esteem; but I protest she exceeds even what I could have expected from her.'

'This letter, madam,' cries Booth, 'you will believe was an excellent cordial for my poor wife's spirits. So dreadful indeed was the effect it had upon her, that as she had read it in my absence, I found her at my return home in the most violent fits; and so long was it before she recovered her senses, that I despaired of that blest event ever happening, and my own senses very narrowly escaped from being sacrificed to my despair. However, she came at last to herself, and I began to consider of every means of carrying her immediately to Montpelier, which was now become much more necessary than before.

'Tho' I was greatly shocked at the barbarity of the letter; yet I apprehended no very ill consequence from it: for as it was believed all over the army that I had married a great fortune, I had received offers of money, if I wanted it, from more than one. Indeed, I might have easily carried my wife to Montpelier at any time; but she was extremely averse to the voyage, being desirous of our returning to England, as I had leave to do; and she grew daily so much better, that had it not been for the receipt of that cursed — which I have just read to you, I am persuaded she might have been able to return to England in the next ship.

'Among others there was a colonel in the garrison, who had not only offered, but importuned me to receive money of him: I now therefore repaired to him; and as a reason of altering my resolution, I produced the letter, and at the same time acquainted him with the true state of my affairs. The colonel read the letter, shook his head, and after some silence, said, he was sorry I had refused to accept his offer before; but that he had now so ordered matters, and disposed of his money, that he had not a shilling left to spare from his own occasions.

'Answers of the same kind I had from several others; but not one penny could I borrow of any: for I have been since firmly persuaded that the honest colonel was not content with denying me himself; but took effectual means, by spreading the secret I had so foolishly trusted him with, to prevent me from succeeding elsewhere: for such is the nature of men, that whoever denies himself to do you a favour, is unwilling that it should be done to you by any other.

'This was the first time I had ever felt that distress which arises from the want of money; a distress very dreadful indeed in a married state: for what can be more miserable than to see any thing necessary to the preservation of a beloved creature, and not be able to supply it?

'Perhaps you may wonder, madam, that I have not mentioned Captain James on this occasion; but he was at that time laid up at Algiers, (whither he had been sent by the Governor) in a fever. However, he returned time enough to supply me, which he did with the utmost readiness, on the very first mention of my distress; and the good colonel, notwithstanding his having disposed of his money, discounted the captain's draught.[10] You see, madam, an instance in the generous behaviour of my friend James, how false are all universal satires against human kind. He is indeed one of the worthiest men the world ever produced.

'But, perhaps, you will be more pleased still with the extravagant generosity of my serjeant. The day before the return of Mr James, the poor fellow came to me, with tears in his eyes, and begged I would not be offended at what he was going to mention. He then pulled a purse from his pocket, which contained, he said, the sum of twelve pounds, and which he begged me to accept, crying he was sorry it was not in his power to lend me whatever I wanted. I was so struck with this instance of generosity and friendship in such a person, that I gave him an opportunity of pressing me a second time before I made him an answer. Indeed I was greatly surprised how he came to be worth that little sum, and no less at his being acquainted with my own wants. In both which points he presently satisfied me. As to the first, it seems he had plundered a Spanish officer of fifteen pistoles; and as to the second, he confessed he had it from my wife's maid, who had overheard some discourse between her mistress and me. Indeed people, I believe, always deceive themselves who imagine they can conceal distrest circumstances from their servants: for these are always extremely quick-sighted on such occasions.'

'Good Heaven!' cries Miss Mathews, 'how astonishing is such behaviour in so low a fellow!'

'I thought so myself,' answered Booth; 'and yet I know not, on a more strict examination into the matter, why we should be more surprised to see greatness of mind discover itself in one degree, or rank of life, than in another. Love, benevolence, or what you will please to call it, may be the reigning passion in a beggar as well as in a prince; and wherever it is, its energies will be the same.

'To confess the truth, I am afraid, we often compliment what we call upper life, with too much injustice, at the expence of the lower. As it is no rare thing to see instances which degrade human nature, in persons of the highest birth and education; so I apprehend, that examples of whatever is really great and good, have been sometimes found amongst those who have wanted all such advantages. In reality, palaces, I make no doubt, do sometimes contain nothing but dreariness and darkness, and the sun of righteousness[11] hath shone forth with all its glory in a cottage.'

CHAPTER 8

The story of Booth continued.

MR BOOTH thus went on:

'We now took leave of the garrison, and having landed at Marseilles, arrived at Montpelier, without any thing happening to us worth remembrance, except the extreme sea-sickness of poor Amelia, but I was afterwards well repaid for the terrors which it occasioned me, by the good consequences which attended it: for I believe it contributed even more than the air of Montpelier, to the perfect re-establishment of her health.'

'I ask your pardon for interrupting you,' cries Miss Mathews, 'but you never satisfied me whether you took the serjeant's money. – You have made me half in love with that charming fellow.'

'How can you imagine, madam,' answered Booth, 'I should have taken from a poor fellow what was of so little consequence to me, and at the same time of so much to him? – Perhaps now you will derive this from the passion of pride.'

'Indeed,' says she, 'I neither derive it from the passion of pride, nor from the passion of folly; but methinks you should have accepted the offer, and I am convinced you hurt him very much when you refused it. But pray proceed in your story.' Then Booth went on as follows:

'As Amelia recovered her health and spirits daily, we began to pass our time very pleasantly at Montpelier: for the greatest enemy to the French will acknowledge, that they are the best people in the world to live amongst for a little while. In some countries it is almost as easy to get a good estate as a good acquaintance. In England, particularly, acquaintance is of almost as slow growth as an oak; so that the age of man scarce suffices to bring it to any perfection, and families seldom contract any great intimacy till the third, or at least the second generation. So shy indeed are we English of letting a stranger into our houses, that one would imagine we regarded all such as thieves. Now the French are the very reverse. Being a stranger among them entitles you to the better place, and to the greater degree of civility; and if you wear but the appearance of a gentleman, they never suspect you are not one. Their friendship indeed seldom extends so far as their purse; nor is such friendship usual in other countries. To say the truth, politeness carries friendship far enough in the ordinary occasions of life, and those who want this accomplishment rarely make amends for it by their sincerity: for bluntness, or rather rudeness, as it commonly deserves to be called, is not always so much a mark of honesty as it is taken to be.

'The day after our arrival we became acquainted with Mons. Bagillard. He was a Frenchman of great wit and vivacity, with a greater share of learning than gentlemen are usually possessed of. As he lodged in the same house with us, we were immediately acquainted, and I liked his conversation so well, that I never thought I had too much of his company. Indeed I spent so much of my time with him, that Amelia (I know not whether I ought to mention it) grew uneasy at our familiarity, and complained of my being too little with her, from my violent fondness for my new acquaintance; for our conversation turning chiefly upon books, and principally Latin ones (for we read several of the classics together) she could have but little entertainment by being with us. When my wife had once taken it into her head that she was deprived of my company by Mr Bagillard, it was impossible to change her opinion; and tho' I now spent more of my time with her than I had ever done before, she still grew more and more dissatisfied, till, at last, she very earnestly desired me to quit my lodgings, and insisted upon it with more vehemence than I had ever known her express before. To say the truth, if that excellent woman could ever be thought unreasonable, I thought she was so on this occasion.

'But in what light soever her desires appeared to me, as they manifestly arose from an affection of which I had daily the most endearing proofs, I resolved to comply with her, and accordingly removed to a distant part of the town: for it is my opinion that we can have but little love for the person whom we will never indulge in an unreasonable demand. Indeed, I was under a difficulty with regard to Mons. Bagillard; for as I could not possibly communicate to him the true reason for quitting my lodgings; so I found it as difficult to deceive him by a counterfeit one; besides, I was apprehensive I should have little less of his company than before. I could, indeed, have avoided this dilemma by leaving Montpelier; for Amelia had perfectly recovered her health; but I had faithfully promised Captain James to wait his return from Italy, whither he was gone some time before from Gibraltar, nor was it proper for Amelia to take any long journey, she being now near six months gone with child.

'This difficulty, however, proved to be less than I had imagined it; for my French friend, whether he suspected any thing from my wife's behaviour, tho' she never, as I observed, shew'd him the least incivility, became suddenly as cold on his side. After our leaving the lodgings he never made above two or three formal visits; indeed his time was soon after entirely taken up by an intrigue with a certain countess, which blazed all over Montpelier.

'We had not been long in our new apartments before an English officer arrived at Montpelier, and came to lodge in the same house with us. This gentleman, whose name was Bath, was of the rank of a major, and had so much singularity in his character, that, perhaps, you never heard of any like him. He was far from having any of those bookish qualifications, which had before caused my Amelia's disquiet. It is true, his discourse generally turned on matters of no feminine kind, war and martial exploits being the ordinary topics of his conversation: however, as he had a sister with whom Amelia was greatly pleased, an intimacy presently grew between us, and we four lived in one family.

'The major was a great dealer in the marvellous, and was constantly the little hero of his own tale. This made him very entertaining to Amelia, who of all persons in the world hath the truest taste and enjoyment of the ridiculous,[12] for whilst no one sooner discovers it in the character of another, no one so well conceals her knowledge of it from the ridiculous person. I cannot help mentioning a sentiment of hers on this head, as I think it doth her great honour. "If I had the same neglect," said she, "for ridiculous people with the generality of the world, I should rather think them the objects of tears than laughter; but in reality, I have known several who in some parts of their characters have been extremely ridiculous, in others have been altogether as amiable. For instance," said she, "here is the major who tells us of many things which he hath never seen, and of others which he hath never done, and both in the most extravagant excess; and yet how amiable is his behaviour to his poor sister, whom he hath not only brought over hither for her health, at his own expence, but is come to bear her company." I believe, madam, I repeat her very words; for I am very apt to remember what she says.

'You will easily believe, from a circumstance I have just mentioned in the major's favour, especially when I have told you that his sister was one of the best of girls, that it was entirely necessary to hide from her all kind of laughter at any part of her brother's behaviour. To say the truth, this was easy enough to do; for the poor girl was so blinded with love and gratitude, and so highly honoured and reverenced her brother, that she had not the least suspicion that there was a person in the world capable of laughing at him.

'Indeed, I am certain she never made the least discovery of our ridicule; for I am well convinced she would have resented it: for besides the love she bore her brother, she had a little family pride, which would sometimes appear. To say the truth, if she had any fault, it was that of vanity; but she was a very good girl upon the whole; and none of us are entirely free from faults.'

'You are a good-natured fellow, Will,' answered Miss Mathews, 'but vanity is a fault of the first magnitude in a woman, and often the occasion of many others.'

To this Booth made no answer; but continued his story.

'In this company we passed two or three months very agreeably till the major and I both betook ourselves to our several nurseries; my wife being brought to bed of a girl, and Miss Bath confined to her chamber by a surfeit,[13] which had like to have occasioned her death.'

Here Miss Mathews burst into a loud laugh, of which when Booth asked the reason, she said she could not forbear at the thoughts of two such nurses: 'And did you really,' says she, 'make your wife's caudle[14] yourself?'

'Indeed, madam,' said he, 'I did, and do you think that so extraordinary?'

'Indeed I do,' answered she, 'I thought the best husbands had looked on their wives lying in as a time of festival and jollity. What, did you not even get drunk in the time of your wife's delivery? Tell me honestly how you employ'd yourself at this time.'

'Why then honestly,' replied he, 'and in defiance of your laughter, I lay behind her bolster, and supported her in my arms, and upon my soul, I believe I felt more pain in my mind than she underwent in her body. And now answer me as honestly: Do you really think it a proper time of mirth, when the creature one loves to distraction is undergoing the most racking torments, as well as in the most imminent danger? And – but I need not express any more tender circumstances.'

'I am to answer honestly,' cry'd she. – 'Yes, and sincerely,' cries Booth – 'Why then honestly and sincerely,' says she, 'may I never see Heaven, if I don't think you an angel of a man.'

'Nay, madam,' answered Booth – 'but, indeed, you do me too much honour, there are many such husbands – Nay, have we not an example of the like tenderness in the major? Tho' as to him, I believe, I shall make you laugh. While my wife lay in, Miss Bath being extremely ill, I went one day to the door of her apartment, to enquire after her health, as well as for the major, whom I had not seen during a whole week. I knocked softly at the door, and being bid to open it, I found the major in his sister's antichamber warming her posset.[15] His dress was certainly whimsical enough, having on a woman's bed-gown, and a very dirty flannel night-cap, which being added to a very odd person (for he is a very aukward thin man near seven feet high) might have formed, in the opinion of most men, a very proper object of laughter. The major started from his seat at my entring into the room, and with much emotion, and a great oath, cry'd out, "Is it you, sir?" I then enquired after his and his sister's health. He answer'd, that his sister was better, and he was very well, "Tho' I did not expect, sir," cry'd he, with not a little confusion, "to be seen by you in this situation." I told him, I thought it impossible he could appear in a situation more becoming his character. "You do not?" answered he. "By G— I am very much obliged to you for that opinion; but I believe, sir, however my weakness may prevail on me to descend from it, no man can be more conscious of his own dignity than myself.'' His sister then called to him from the inner room; upon which he rang the bell for her servant, and then after a stride or two across the room, he said with an elated aspect, "I would not have you think, Mr Booth, because you have caught me in this dishabille, by coming upon me a little too abruptly, I can't help saying, a little too abruptly, that I am my sister's nurse. I know better what is due to the dignity of a man, and I have shewn it in a line of battle. – I think I have made a figure there, Mr Booth, and becoming my character; by G— I ought not to be despised too much, if my nature is not totally without its weaknesses.'' He utter'd this, and some more of the same kind, with great majesty, or as he call'd it, dignity. Indeed, he used some hard words that I did not understand; for all his words are not to be found in a dictionary. Upon the whole, I could not easily refrain from laughter; however, I conquered myself, and soon after retired from him, astonished that it was possible for a man to possess true goodness, and be, at the same time, ashamed of it.

'But if I was surprised at what had past at this visit, how much more was I surprised the next morning, when he came very early to my chamber, and told me he had not been able to sleep one wink at what had past between us! "There were some words of yours,'' says he, "which must be further explained before we part. You told me, sir, when you found me in that situation, which I cannot bear to recollect, that you thought I could not appear in one more becoming my character; these were the words, I shall never forget them. Do you imagine that there is any of the dignity of a man wanting in my character? Do you think that I have, during my sister's illness, behaved with a weakness that savours too much of effeminacy? I know how much it is beneath a man to whine and whimper about a trifling girl as well as you, or any man; and if my sister had died, I should have behaved like a man on the occasion. I would not have you think I confined myself from company merely upon her account. I was very much disorder'd myself. And when you surprised me in that situation, I repeat again in that situation, her nurse had not left the room three minutes, and I was blowing the fire for fear it should have gone out.'' – In this manner he ran on almost a quarter of an hour, before he would suffer me to speak. At last, looking stedfastly in his face, I asked him if I must conclude that he was in earnest. – "In earnest," says he, repeating my words; "Do you then take my character for a jest!" "Lookee, sir," said I, very gravely, "I think we know one another very well; and I have no reason to suspect you should impute it to fear, when I tell you, I was so far from intending to affront you, that I meant you one of the highest compliments. Tenderness for women is so far from lessening, that it proves a true manly character. The manly Brutus shewed the utmost tenderness to his Porcia;[16] and the great King of Sweden,[17] the bravest, and even fiercest of men, shut himself up three whole days in the midst of a campaign, and would see no company on the death of a favourite sister." At these words, I saw his features soften; and he cry'd out, "D—n me, I admire the King of Sweden of all the men in the world; and he is a rascal that is ashamed of doing any thing which the King of Sweden did. – And yet if any King of Sweden in France was to tell me that his sister had more merit than mine; by G— I'd knock his brains about his ears. Poor little Betsy! she is the honestest, worthiest girl that ever was born. Heaven be praised, she is recovered; for, if I had lost her, I never should have enjoyed another happy moment." – In this manner he ran on some time, till the tears began to overflow – which when he perceived, he stopt; perhaps he was unable to go on; for he seemed almost choaked; – after a short silence, however, having wip'd his eyes with his handkerchief, he fetched a deep sigh, and cry'd, "I am ashamed you should see this, Mr Booth; but d—n me, nature will get the better of dignity." I now comforted him with the example of Xerxes,[18] as I had before done with that of the King of Sweden; and soon after we sat down to breakfast together with much cordial friendship: for I assure you, with all his oddity there is not a better-natured man in the world than the major.'

'Good-natured, indeed!' cries Miss Mathews, with great scorn. – 'A fool! How can you mention such a fellow with commendation?'

Booth spoke as much as he could in defence of his friend; indeed he had represented him in as favourable a light as possible, and had particularly left out those hard words, with which, as he hath observed a little before, the major interlarded his discourse. Booth then proceeded as in the next chapter.

CHAPTER 9

Containing very extraordinary matters.

'MISS BATH', continued Booth, 'now recovered so fast, that she was abroad as soon as my wife. Our little party quarrée[19] began to grow agreeable again; and we mix'd with the company of the place more than we had done before. Mons. Bagillard now again renewed his intimacy; for the countess his mistress was gone to Paris. At which my wife at first shewed no dissatisfaction; and I imagined that as she had a friend and companion of her own sex (for Miss Bath and she had contracted the highest fondness for each other) she would the less miss my company. However, I was disappointed in this expectation; for she soon began to express her former uneasiness, and her impatience for the arrival of Captain James, that we might entirely quit Montpelier.

'I could not avoid conceiving some little displeasure at this humour of my wife, which I was forced to think a little unreasonable.' – 'A little, do you call it,' says Miss Mathews, 'Good Heavens! what a husband are you!' – 'How little worthy,' answered he, 'as you will say hereafter of such a wife as my Amelia. One day as we were sitting together, I heard a violent scream, upon which my wife starting up, cry'd out, "Sure that's Miss Bath's voice," and immediately ran towards the chamber whence it proceeded. I followed her; and when we arrived, we there beheld the most shocking sight imaginable; Miss Bath lying dead on the floor, and the major all bloody kneeling by her, and roaring out for assistance. Amelia, tho' she was herself in little better condition than her friend, ran hastily to her, bared her neck, and attempted to loosen her stays, while I ran up and down, scarce knowing what I did, calling for water and cordials, and dispatching several servants one after another for doctors and surgeons.

'Water, cordials, and all necessary implements being brought, Miss Bath was, at length, recovered, and placed in her chair, when the major seated himself by her. And now the young lady being restored to life, the major, who, till then, had engaged as little of his own, as of any other person's attention, became the object of all our considerations, especially his poor sister's, who had no sooner recovered sufficient strength, than she began to lament her brother, crying out, that he was killed; and bitterly bewailing her fate, in having revived from her swoon to behold so dreadful a spectacle. While Amelia applied herself to sooth the agonies of her friend, I began to enquire into the condition of the major. In which I was assisted by a surgeon, who now arrived. The major declared with great chearfulness, that he did not apprehend his wound to be in the least dangerous, and therefore begged his sister to be comforted, saying, he was convinced the surgeon would soon give her the same assurance; but that good man was not so liberal of assurances as the major had expected; for as soon as he had probed the wound, he afforded no more than hopes, declaring that it was a very ugly wound; but added, by way of consolation, that he had cured many much worse.

'When the major was drest, his sister seemed to possess his whole thoughts, and all his care was to relieve her grief. He solemnly protested, that it was no more than a flesh wound, and not very deep, nor could, as he apprehended, be in the least dangerous; and as for the cold expressions of the surgeon, he very well accounted for them from a motive too obvious to be mentioned. From these declarations of her brother, and the interposition of her friends; and above all, I believe, from that vast vent which she had given to her fright, Miss Bath seemed a little pacify'd; Amelia therefore at last prevailed; and as terror abated, curiosity became the superior passion. I therefore now began to enquire what had occasioned that accident, whence all the uproar arose.

"The major took me by the hand, and looking very kindly at me, said, "My dear Mr Booth, I must begin by asking your pardon; for I have done you an injury, for which nothing but the height of friendship in me can be an excuse; and therefore nothing but the height of friendship in you can forgive." This preamble, madam, you will easily believe, greatly alarmed all the company, but especially me. – I answered, "dear major, I forgive you, let it be what it will; but what is it possible you can have done to injure me?" "That," replied he, "which I am convinced a man of your honour and dignity of nature, by G— must conclude to be one of the highest injuries. I have taken out of your own hands the doing yourself justice. I am afraid I have killed the man who hath injured your honour. I mean that villain Bagillard – but I cannot proceed; for you, madam," said he to my wife, "are concerned; and I know what is due to the dignity of your sex." – Amelia, I observed, turn'd pale at these words, but eagerly begg'd him to proceed. – "Nay, madam," answered he, "if I am commanded by a lady, it is a part of my dignity to obey." He then proceeded to tell us, that Bagillard had rallied him upon a supposition that he was pursuing my wife, with a view of gallantry; telling him that he could never succeed; giving hints that if it had been possible, he should have succeeded himself; and ending with calling my poor Amelia an accomplished prude; upon which the major gave Bagillard a box in the ear, and both immediately drew their swords.

'The major had scarce ended his speech, when a servant came into the room, and told me there was a friar below who desired to speak with me in great haste. I shook the major by the hand, and told him I not only forgave him, but was extremely obliged to his friendship; and then going to the friar, I found that he was Bagillard's confessor, from whom he came to me, with an earnest desire of seeing me, that he might ask my pardon, and receive my forgiveness before he dy'd, for the injury he had intended me. My wife at first opposed my going from some sudden fears on my account; but when she was convinced they were groundless, she consented.

'I found Bagillard in his bed; for the major's sword had passed up to the very hilt through his body. After having very earnestly asked my pardon, he made me many compliments on the possession of a woman, who, joined to the most exquisite beauty, was mistress of the most impregnable virtue; as a proof of which, he acknowledged the vehemence as well as ill success of his attempts; and to make Amelia's virtue appear the brighter, his vanity was so predominant, he could not forbear running over the names of several women of fashion who had yielded to his passion, which, he said, had never raged so violently for any other as for my poor Amelia; and that this violence, which he had found wholly unconquerable, he hoped would procure his pardon at my hands. It is unnecessary to mention what I said on the occasion. I assured him of my entire forgiveness; and so we parted. To say the truth, I afterwards thought myself almost obliged to him for a meeting with Amelia, the most luxuriously delicate[20] that can be imagined.

'I now ran to my wife, whom I embraced with raptures of love and tenderness. When the first torrent of these was a little abated, "Confess to me, my dear," said she, "could your goodness prevent you from thinking me a little unreasonable in expressing so much uneasiness at the loss of your company, while I ought to have rejoiced in the thoughts of your being so well entertained? I know you must; and then consider what I must have felt, while I knew I was daily lessening myself in your esteem, and forced into a conduct, which I was sensible must appear to you, who was ignorant of my motive, to be mean, vulgar, and selfish. And yet what other course had I to take, with a man whom no denial, no scorn could abash. – But if this was a cruel task, how much more wretched still was the constraint I was obliged to wear in his presence before you, to shew outward civility to the man whom my soul detested, for fear of any fatal consequence from your suspicion; and this too, while I was afraid he would construe it to be an encouragement. – Do you not pity your poor Amelia when you reflect on her situation?" – "Pity!" cry'd I, "my love, is pity an adequate expression for esteem, for adoration? – But how, my love, could he carry this on so secretly – by letters?" "O no, he offered me many; but I never would receive but one, and that I return'd him. Good G— I would not have such a letter in my possession for the universe, I thought my eyes contaminated with reading it."' – 'O brave,' cry'd Miss Mathews, 'heroic, I protest.

Had I a wish that did not bear
The stamp and image of my dear,
I'd pierce my heart through every vein,
And die to let it out again.'[21]

'And can you really,' cry'd he, 'laugh at so much tenderness?' 'I laugh at tenderness! O Mr Booth,' answered she, 'Thou knowest but little of Calista.'[22] 'I thought formerly,' cry'd he, 'I knew a great deal, and thought you of all women in the world to have the greatest – of all women!' – 'Take care, Mr Booth,' said she. – 'By

Heaven, if you thought so, you thought truly – But what is the object of my tenderness – such an object as –' 'Well, madam,' says he, 'I hope you will find one.' – 'I thank you for that hope, however,' says she, 'cold as it is; but pray go on with your story;' which command he immediately obeyed.

CHAPTER 10

Containing a letter of a very curious kind.

'THE major's wound,' continued Booth, 'was really as slight as he believed it; so that in a very few days he was perfectly well; nor was Bagillard, tho' run through the body, long apprehending to be in any danger of his life. The major then took me aside, and wishing me heartily joy of Bagillard's recovery, told me I should now, by the gift (as it were) of Heaven, have an opportunity of doing myself justice. I answered, I could not think of any such thing: for that when I imagined he was on his death-bed, I had heartily and sincerely forgiven him. "Very right," replied the major, "and consistent with your honour,[23] when he was on his death-bed; but that forgiveness was only conditional, and is revoked by his recovery." I told him I could not possibly revoke it; for that my anger was really gone. – "What hath anger," cry'd he, "to do with the matter? The dignity of my nature hath been always my reason for drawing my sword; and when that is concerned, I can as readily fight with the man I love, as with the man I hate." – I will not tire you with the repetition of the whole argument, in which the major did not prevail; and I really believe, I sunk a little in his esteem upon that account, till Captain James, who arrived soon after, again perfectly reinstated me in his favour.

'When the captain was come, there remained no cause of our longer stay at Montpelier; for as to my wife, she was in a better state of health than I had ever known her, and Miss Bath had not only recovered her health, but her bloom, and from a pale skeleton, was become a plump, handsome, young woman. James was again my cashier; for far from receiving any remittance, it was now a long time since I had received any letter from England, tho' both myself and my dear Amelia had written several both to my mother and sister; and now at our departure from Montpelier, I bethought myself of writing to my good friend the doctor, acquainting him with our journey to Paris, whither I desired he would direct his answer.

'At Paris we all arrived, without encountring any adventure on the road worth relating; nor did any thing of consequence happen here during the first fortnight: for as you know neither Captain James nor Miss Bath, it is scarce worth telling you, that an affection, which afterwards ended in a marriage, began now to appear between them, in which it may appear odd to you that I made the first discovery of the lady's flame, and my wife of the captain's.

'The seventeenth day after our arrival at Paris, I received a letter from the doctor, which I have in my pocket-book; and if you please I will read it you: for I would not willingly do any injury to his words.'

The lady, you may easily believe, desired to hear the letter, and Booth read it as follows:

> 'My dear Children,
>
> For I will now call you so, as you have neither of you now any other parent in this world. Of this melancholy news I should have sent you earlier notice, if I had thought you ignorant of it, or indeed if I had known whither to have writ. If your sister hath received any letters from you, she hath kept them a secret, and perhaps out of affection to you hath reposited them in the same place where she keeps her goodness, and, what I am afraid is much dearer to her, her money. The reports concerning you have been various; so is always the case in matters where men are ignorant: for when no man knows what the truth is, every man thinks himself at liberty to report what he pleases. Those who wish you well, son Booth, say simply that you are dead; others that you ran away from the siege, and was cashiered. As for my daughter, all agree that she is a saint above; and there are not wanting those who hint that her husband sent her thither. From this beginning you will expect, I suppose, better news than I am going to tell you; but pray, my dear children, why

may not I, who have always laughed at my own afflictions, laugh at yours, without the censure of much malevolence? I wish you could learn this temper from me; for, take my word for it, nothing truer ever came from the mouth of a heathen than that sentence,

– *Leve fit quod bene fertur onus.*★

'And tho' I must confess, I never thought Aristotle[25] (whom I do not take for so great a blockhead as some who have never read him) doth not very well resolve the doubt which he hath raised in his Ethics, *viz.* how a man, in the midst of King Priam's misfortunes, can be called happy?[26] yet I have long thought that there is no calamity so great that a Christian philosopher may not reasonably laugh at it. If the heathen Cicero, doubting of immortality (for so wise a man must have doubted of that which had such slender arguments to support it) could assert it as the office of wisdom, *Humanas res despicere atque infra se positas arbitrari.*†

'Which passage, with much more to the same purpose, you will find in the third book of his *Tusculan Questions.*

'With how much great confidence may a good Christian despise and even deride all temporary and short transitory evils![28] If the poor wretch, who is trudging on to his miserable cottage, can laugh at the storms and tempests, the rain and whirlwinds which surround him, while his richest hope is only that of rest, how much more chearfully must a man pass through such transient evils whose spirits are buoyed up with the certain expectation of finding a noble palace, and the most sumptuous entertainment ready to receive him? I do not much like the simile; but I cannot think of a better. And yet, inadequate as the simile is, we may, I think, from the actions of mankind, conclude that they will consider it as much too strong; for in the case I have put of the entertainment, is there any man so tender or poor-spirited as not to despise and often to deride the fiercest of those inclemencies which I have mentioned? but in our journey to the glorious mansions of everlasting

★ The burden becomes light by being well borne.[24]

† To look down on all human affairs as matters below his consideration.[27]

bliss, how severely is every little rub, every trifling accident lamented; and if Fortune showers down any of her heavier storms upon us, how wretched do we presently appear to ourselves and to others! The reason of this can be no other than that we are not in earnest in our faith; at the best we think with too little attention on this our great concern. While the most paultry matters of this world, even those pitiful trifles, those childish gewgaws, riches and honours, are transacted with the utmost earnestness, and most serious application, the grand and weighty affair of immortality is postponed and disregarded, nor ever brought into the least competition with our affairs here. If one of my cloth should begin a discourse of Heaven in the scenes of business or pleasure; in the court of requests,[29] at Garaway's or at White's,[30] would he gain a hearing, unless perhaps of some sorry jester who would desire to ridicule him? would he not presently acquire the name of the mad parson, and be thought by all men worthy of Bedlam?[31] or would he not be treated as the Romans treated their Aretalogi,* and considered in the light of a buffoon? But why should I mention those places of hurry and worldly pursuit? – What attention do we engage even in the pulpit? Here, if a sermon be prolonged a little beyond the usual hour, doth it not set half the audience asleep? as I question not I have by this time both my children. – Well then, like a good-natured surgeon, who prepares his patient for a painful operation, by endeavouring as much as he can to deaden his sensation, I will now communicate to you, in your slumbring condition, the news with which I threatened you. Your good mother, you are to know, is dead at last, and hath left her whole fortune to her elder daughter. – This is all the ill news I have to tell you. Confess now, if you are awake, did you not expect it was much worse? Did not you apprehend that your charming child was dead? Far from it, he is in perfect health, and the admiration of every body; what is more, he will be taken care of, with the tenderness of a parent, till your return. What pleasure must this give you! If indeed any thing can add to the happiness of a married couple, who are extremely

* A set of beggarly philosphers, who diverted great men at their table with burlesque discourses on virtue.[32]

and deservedly fond of each other, and as you write me, in perfect health. A superstitious heathen would have dreaded the malice of Nemesis in your situation; but as I am a Christian I shall venture to add another circumstance to your felicity, by assuring you that you have besides your wife a faithful and zealous friend. – Do not therefore, my dear children, fall into that fault which the excellent Thucydides observes,[33] is too common in human nature, *to bear heavily the being deprived of the smaller good, without conceiving at the same time any gratitude for the much greater blessings which we are suffered to enjoy*. I have only farther to tell you, my son, that when you call at Mr Morand's, Rue Dauphine, you will find yourself worth a hundred pounds. Good Heaven! how much richer are you than millions of people who are in want of nothing! Farewel, and know me for

'Your sincere and affectionate friend.

'There, madam,' cries Booth, 'how do you like the letter?'

'Oh! extremely,' answered she, 'the doctor is a charming man, I always loved dearly to hear him preach. I remember to have heard of Mrs Harris's death above a year before I left the country; but never knew the particulars of her will before. I am extremely sorry for it, upon my honour.'

'Oh fy! madam,' cries Booth, 'have you so soon forgot the chief purport of the doctor's letter?'

'Ay, ay,' cried she, 'these are very pretty things to read, I acknowledge; but the loss of fortune is a serious matter; and I am sure a man of Mr Booth's understanding must think so.' 'One consideration, I must own, madam,' answered he, 'a good deal baffled all the doctor's arguments. This was the concern for my little growing family, who must one day feel the loss; nor was I so easy upon Amelia's account as upon my own, tho' she herself put on the utmost chearfulness; and stretched her invention to the utmost to comfort me. – But sure, madam, there is something in the doctor's letter to admire beyond the philosophy of it; what think you of that easy, generous, friendly manner in which he sent me the hundred pounds?'

'Very noble and great indeed,' replied she, 'but pray go on with your story; for I long to hear the whole.'

CHAPTER 11

In which Mr Booth relates his return to England.

'NOTHING remarkable, as I remember, happened during our stay at Paris, which we left soon after and came to London. Here we rested only two days, and then, taking leave of our fellow-travellers, we set out for Wiltshire, my wife being so impatient to see the child, which she had left behind her, that the child she carried with her was almost killed with the fatigue of the journey.

'We arrived at our inn late in the evening. Amelia, tho' she had no great reason to be pleased with any part of her sister's behaviour, resolved to behave to her, as if nothing wrong had ever happened. She therefore sent a kind note to her the moment of our arrival, giving her her option whether she would come to us at the inn, or whether we should that evening wait on her. The servant, after waiting an hour, brought us an answer, excusing her from coming to us so late, as she was disordered with a cold, and desiring my wife by no means to think of venturing out after the fatigue of her journey, saying, she would on that account defer the great pleasure of seeing her till the morning, without taking any more notice of your humble servant, than if no such person had been in the world, tho' I had very civilly sent my compliments to her. I should not mention this trifle, if it was not to shew you the nature of the woman, and that it will be a kind of key to her future conduct.

'When the servant returned, the good doctor, who had been with us almost all the time of his absence, hurried us away to his house, where we presently found a supper and a bed prepared for us. My wife was eagerly desirous to see her child that night; but the doctor would not suffer it; and as he was at nurse at a distant part of the town, and the doctor assured her he had seen him in perfect health that evening, she suffered herself at last to be dissuaded.

'We spent that evening in the most agreeable manner: for the doctor's wit and humour, joined to the highest chearfulness and good-nature, made him the most agreeable companion in the world; and he was now in the highest spirits, which he was pleased to place to our account. We sat together to a very late hour: for so excellent is my wife's constitution, that she declared she was scarce sensible of any fatigue from her late journies.

'Amelia slept not a wink all night, and in the morning early the doctor accompanied us to the little infant. The transports we felt on this occasion were really enchanting, nor can any but a fond parent conceive, I am certain, the least idea of them. Our imaginations suggested a hundred agreeable circumstances, none of which had perhaps any foundation. We made words and meaning out of every sound, and in every feature found out some resemblance to my Amelia, as she did to me.

'But I ask your pardon for dwelling on such incidents; and will proceed to scenes which to most persons will be more entertaining.

'We went hence to pay a visit to Miss Harris,[34] whose reception of us was, I think, truly ridiculous; and as you know the lady, I will endeavour to describe it particularly. At our first arrival we were ushered into a parlour, where we were suffered to wait almost an hour. At length the lady of the house appeared in deep mourning, with a face, if possible, more dismal than her dress, in which, however, there was every appearance of art. Her features were indeed skrewed up to the very height of grief. With this face, and in the most solemn gait, she approached Amelia, and coldly saluted[35] her. After which she made me a very distant formal courtesy, and we all sat down. A short silence now ensued, which Miss Harris at length broke, with a deep sigh, and said, "Sister, here is a great alteration in this place since you saw it last; Heaven hath been pleased to take my poor mother to itself." – (Here she wiped her eyes, and then continued) "I hope I know my duty, and have learned a proper resignation to the divine will; but something is to be allowed to grief for the best of mothers; for so she was to us both: and if at last she made any distinction, she must have had her reasons for so doing. I am sure I can truly say I never wished, much less desired it." The tears now stood in poor Amelia's eyes; indeed she had paid too many already for the memory of so unnatural a parent. She answered with the sweetness of an angel, that she was far from blaming her sister's emotions on so tender an occasion;

that she heartily joined with her in her grief: for that nothing which her mother had done in the latter part of her life, could efface the remembrance of that tenderness which she had formerly shewn her. Her sister caught hold of the word efface, and rung the changes upon it. – "Efface!" cried she, "O Miss Emily[36] (for you must not expect me to repeat names that will be for ever odious) I wish indeed every thing could be effaced. – Effaced! O that that was possible; we might then have still enjoyed my poor mother: for I am convinced she never recovered her grief on a certain occasion." – Thus she ran on, and after many bitter strokes upon her sister, at last directly charged her mother's death on my marriage with Amelia. I could be silent then no longer. I reminded her of the perfect reconciliation between us before my departure, and the great fondness which she expressed for me; nor could I help saying in very plain terms, that if she had ever changed her opinion of me, as I was not conscious of having deserved such a change by my own behaviour, I was well convinced to whose good offices I owed it. Guilt hath very quick ears to an accusation. Miss Harris immediately answered to the charge. She said such suspicions were no more than she expected; that they were of a piece with every other part of my conduct, and gave her one consolation, that they served to account for her sister Emily's unkindness, as well to herself as to her poor deceased mother, and in some measure lessened the guilt of it with regard to her, since it was not easy to know how far a woman is in the power of her husband. My dear Amelia reddened at this reflexion on me; and begged her sister to name any single instance of unkindness or disrespect, in which she had ever offended. To this the other answered, (I am sure I repeat her words, tho' I cannot mimic either the voice or air with which they were spoken) – "Pray, Miss Emily, which is to be the judge, yourself or that gentleman? I remember the time when I could have trusted to your judgment in any affair; but you are now no longer mistress of yourself, and are not answerable for your actions. Indeed it is my constant prayer that your actions may not be imputed to you. – It was the constant prayer of that blessed woman, my dear mother, who is now a saint above; a saint whose name I can never mention without a tear, tho' I find you can hear it without one. – I cannot help observing some concern on so melancholy an occasion; it seems due to decency; but perhaps (for I always wish to excuse you) you are forbid to cry." The idea of being bid or forbid to cry struck so strongly on my fancy, that indignation only could have prevented me from laughing. But my narrative, I am afraid, begins to grow tedious. – In short, after hearing, for near an hour, every malicious insinuation which a fertile genius could invent, we took our leave, and separated as persons who would never willingly meet again.

'The next morning, after this interview, Amelia received a long letter from Miss Harris, in which, after many bitter invectives against me, she excused her mother, alledging that she had been driven to do as she did, in order to prevent Amelia's ruin, if her fortune had fallen into my hands. She likewise very remotely hinted that she would be only a trustee for her sister's children, and told her, that on one condition only she would consent to live with her as a sister. This was, if she could by any means be separated from that man, as she was pleased to call me, who had caused so much mischief in the family.

'I was so enraged at this usage, that had not Amelia intervened, I believe I should have applied to a magistrate for a search-warrant for that picture, which there was so much reason to suspect she had stolen; and which, I am convinced, upon a search, we should have found in her possession.'

'Nay, it is possible enough,' cries Miss Mathews; 'for I believe there is no wickedness of which the lady is not capable.'

'This agreeable letter was succeeded by another of the like comfortable kind, which informed me that the company in which I was, being an additional one raised in the beginning of the war, was reduced; so that I was now a lieutenant on half-pay.

'Whilst we were meditating on our present situation, the good doctor came to us. When we related to him the manner in which my sister had treated us, he cried out, "Poor soul! I pity her heartily;" for this is the severest resentment he ever expresses; indeed I have often heard him say, that a wicked soul is the greatest object of compassion in the world.' – A sentiment which we shall leave the reader a little time to digest.

CHAPTER 12

In which Mr Booth concludes his story.

'THE next day the doctor set out for his parsonage, which was about thirty miles distant, whither Amelia and myself accompanied him, and where we stayed with him all the time of his residence there, being almost three months.

'The situation of the parish under my good friend's care is very pleasant. It is placed among meadows washed by a clear trout stream, and flanked on both sides with downs. His house indeed would not much attract the admiration of the virtuoso. He built it himself, and it is remarkable only for its plainness; with which the furniture so well agrees, that there is no one thing in it that may not be absolutely necessary, except books, and the prints of Mr Hogarth, whom he calls a moral satirist.

'Nothing, however, can be imagined more agreeable than the life that the doctor leads in this homely house, which he calls his earthly paradise. All his parishioners, whom he treats as his children, regard him as their common father. Once in a week he constantly visits every house in the parish, examines, commends, and rebukes, as he finds occasion. This is practised likewise by his curate in his absence; and so good an effect is produced by this their care, that no quarrels ever proceed either to blows or law-suits; no beggar is to be found in the whole parish; nor did I ever hear a very profane oath all the time I lived in it.

'But to return, from so agreeable a digression, to my own affairs, that are much less worth your attention. In the midst of all the pleasures I tasted in this sweet place, and in the most delightful company, the woman and man whom I loved above all things, melancholy reflexions concerning my unhappy circumstances would often steal into my thoughts. My fortune was now reduced to less than forty pounds a year; I had already two children, and my dear Amelia was again with child.

'One day the doctor found me sitting by myself, and employed in melancholy contemplations on this subject. He told me he had observed me growing of late very serious; that he knew the occasion, and neither wondered at, nor blamed me. He then asked me if I had any prospect of going again into the army; if not, what scheme of life I proposed to myself.

'I told him, that as I had no powerful friends, I could have but little expectations in a military way; that I was as incapable of thinking of any other scheme, as all business required some knowledge or experience, and likewise money to set up with; of all which I was destitute.

'"You must know then, child," said the doctor, "that I have been thinking on this subject as well as you: for I can think, I promise you, with a pleasant countenance." These were his words. "As to the army, perhaps means might be found of getting you another commission; but my daughter seems to have a violent objection to it; and to be plain, I fancy you yourself will find no glory make you amends for your absence from her. And for my part," said he, "I never think those men wise who for any worldly interest forego the greatest happiness of their lives. If I mistake not," said he, "a country life, where you could be always together, would make you both much happier people."

'I answered, that of all things I preferred it most; and I believed Amelia was of the same opinion.

'The doctor, after a little hesitation, proposed to me to turn farmer, and offered to let me his parsonage, which was then become vacant. He said, it was a farm which required but little stock, and that little should not be wanting.

'I embraced this offer very eagerly, and with great thankfulness, and immediately repaired to Amelia to communicate it to her, and to know her sentiments.

'Amelia received the news with the highest transports of joy; she said that her greatest fear had always been of my entring again into the army. She was so kind as to say, that all stations of life were equal to her, unless as one afforded her more of my company than another. "And as to our children," said she, "let us breed them up to an humble fortune; and they will be contented with it: for none," added my angel, "deserve happiness, or indeed, are capable of it, who make any particular station a necessary ingredient."

'Thus, madam, you see me degraded from my former rank

in life; no longer Captain Booth, but Farmer Booth at your service.

'During my first year's continuance in this new scene of life, nothing, I think, remarkable happened; the history of one day would, indeed, be the history of the whole year.'

'Well, pray then,' said Miss Mathews, 'do let us hear the history of that day; I have a strange curiosity to know how you could kill your time; and do, if possible, find out the very best day you can.'

'If you command me, madam,' answered Booth, 'you must yourself be accountable for the dulness of the narrative. Nay, I believe, you have imposed a very difficult task on me; for the greatest happiness is incapable of description.

'I rose then, madam –'

'O the moment you waked, undoubtedly,' said Miss Mathews. –

'Usually,' said he, 'between five and six.'

'I will have no usually,' cry'd Miss Mathews, 'you are confined to a day, and it is to be the best and happiest in the year.'

'Nay, madam,' cries Booth, 'then I must tell you the day in which Amelia was brought to bed, after a painful and dangerous labour; for that I think was the happiest day of my life.'

'I protest,' said she, 'you are become Farmer Booth, indeed. What a happiness have you painted to my imagination! You put me in mind of a news-paper, where my lady such-a-one is delivered of a son, to the great joy of some illustrious family.'

'Why then, I do assure you, Miss Mathews,' cries Booth, 'I scarce know a circumstance that distinguished one day from another. The whole was one continued series of love, health, and tranquillity. Our lives resembled a calm sea.' –

'The dullest of all ideas,' cries the lady.

'I know,' said he, 'it must appear dull in description; for who can describe the pleasures which the morning air gives to one in perfect health; the flow of spirits which springs up from exercise; the delights which parents feel from the prattle, and innocent follies of their children; the joy with which the tender smile of a wife inspires a husband; or lastly, the chearful, solid comfort which a fond couple enjoy in each other's conversation. – All these pleasures, and every other of which our situation was capable, we tasted in the highest degree. Our happiness was, perhaps, too great; for fortune seemed to grow envious of it, and interposed one of the most cruel accidents that could have befallen us, by robbing us of our dear friend the doctor.'

'I am sorry for it,' said Miss Mathews. 'He was indeed a valuable man, and I never heard of his death before.'

'Long may it be before any one hears of it,' cries Booth. 'He is, indeed, dead to us; but will, I hope, enjoy many happy years of life. You know, madam, the obligations he had to his patron the earl;[37] indeed, it was impossible to be once in his company without hearing of them; I am sure you will neither wonder that he was chosen to attend the young lord in his travels as his tutor, nor that the good man, however disagreeable it might be (as in fact it was) to his inclination, should comply with the earnest request of his friend and patron.

'By this means I was bereft not only of the best companion in the world, but of the best counsellor; a loss of which I have since felt the bitter consequence: for no greater advantage, I am convinced, can arrive to a young man who hath any degree of understanding, than an intimate converse with one of riper years, who is not only able to advise, but who knows the manner of advising. By this means alone youth can enjoy the benefit of the experience of age, and that at a time of life when such experience will be of more service to a man, than when he hath lived long enough to acquire it of himself.

'From want of my sage counsellor I now fell into many errors. The first of these was in enlarging my business, by adding a farm of £100 a year to the parsonage; in renting which I had also as bad a bargain as the doctor had before given me a good one. The consequence of which was, that whereas at the end of the first year, I was worth upwards of fourscore pounds, at the end of the second, I was near half that sum worse (as the phrase is) than nothing.

'A second folly I was guilty of, in uniting families with the curate of the parish, who had just married, as my wife and I thought, a very good sort of a woman. We had not, however, lived one month together before I plainly perceived this good sort of woman had taken a great prejudice against my Amelia; for which, if I had not known something of the human passions, and that high place which envy holds among them, I should not have been able to account: for so far was my angel from having given her any cause of dislike, that she had treated her not only with civility but kindness.

'Besides superiority in beauty, which, I believe, all the world would have allowed to Amelia, there was another cause of this envy, which I am almost ashamed to mention, as it may well be called my greatest folly. You are to know then, madam, that from a boy I had been always fond of driving a coach, in which I valued myself on having some skill. This, perhaps, was an innocent, but I allow it to have been a childish vanity. As I had an opportunity, therefore, of buying an old coach and harness very cheap, (indeed they cost me but twelve pound) and as I considered that the same horses which drew my waggons, would likewise draw my coach, I resolved on indulging myself in the purchase.

'The consequence of setting up this poor old coach is inconceivable. Before this, as my wife and myself had very little distinguished ourselves from the other farmers and their wives, either in our dress, or our way of living, they treated us as their equals; but now they began to consider us as elevating ourselves into a state of superiority, and immediately began to envy, hate, and declare war against us. The neighbouring little squires too were uneasy to see a poor renter become their equal in a matter in which they placed so much dignity; and not doubting but it arose in me from the same ostentation, they began to hate me likewise, and to turn my equipage into ridicule; asserting that my horses, which were as well matched as any in the kingdom, were of different colours and sizes, with much more of that kind of wit, the only basis of which is lying.

'But what will appear most surprising to you, madam, was, that the curate's wife, who being lame, had more use of the coach than my Amelia, (indeed, she seldom went to church in any other manner) was one of my bitterest enemies on the occasion. If she had ever any dispute with Amelia, which all the sweetness of my poor girl could not sometimes avoid, she was sure to introduce with a malicious sneer, *Tho' my husband doth not keep a coach, madam.* Nay, she took this opportunity to upbraid my wife with the loss of her fortune, alledging, *that some folks might have had as good pretensions to a coach as other folks, and a better too, as they brought a better fortune to their husbands. But that all people had not the art of making brick without straw*.

'You will wonder, perhaps, madam, how I can remember such stuff, which, indeed, was a long time only matter of amusement to both Amelia and myself; but we, at last, experienced the mischievous nature of envy, and that it tends rather to produce tragical than comical events. My neighbours now began to conspire against me. They nick-named me in derision, THE SQUIRE FARMER. Whatever I bought, I was sure to buy dearer; and when I sold, I was obliged to sell cheaper than any other. In fact, they were all united; and while they every day committed trespasses on my lands with impunity, if any of my cattle escaped into their fields, I was either forced to enter into a law-suit, or to make amends four-fold for the damage sustained.

'The consequences of all this could be no other than that ruin which ensued. Without tiring you with particulars, before the end of four years, I became involved in debt near £300 more than the value of all my effects. My landlord seized my stock for rent; and to avoid immediate confinement in prison, I was forced to leave the country, with all that I hold dear in the world, my wife, and my poor little family.

'In this condition, I arrived in town five or six days ago. I had just taken a lodging in the verge of the court,[38] and had writ my dear Amelia word, where she might find me, when she had settled her affairs in the best manner she could. That very evening, as I was returning home from a coffee-house, a fray happening in the street, I endeavour'd to assist the injured party, when I was seized by the watch, and after being confined all night in the round-house, was conveyed in the morning before a Justice of Peace, who committed me hither; where I should probably have starved, had I not, from your hands, found a most unaccountable preservation. – And here, give me leave to assure you, my dear Miss Mathews, that whatever advantage I may have reaped from your misfortune, I sincerely lament it; nor would I have purchased any relief to myself at the price of seeing you in this dreadful place.'

He spake these last words with great tenderness: for he was a man of consummate good-nature, and had formerly had much affection for this young lady; indeed, more than the generality of people are capable of entertaining for any person whatsoever.

BOOK IV

CHAPTER 1

Containing very mysterious matter.

MISS MATHEWS did not in the least fall short of Mr Booth in expressions of tenderness. Her eyes, the most eloquent orators on such occasions, exerted their utmost force; and at the conclusion of his speech, *she cast a look as languishingly sweet*, as ever Cleopatra gave to Anthony.[1] In real fact, this Mr Booth had been her first love, and had made those impressions on her young heart, which the learned in this branch of philosophy affirm, and perhaps truly, are never to be eradicated.

When Booth had finished his story, a silence ensued of some minutes; an interval which the painter would describe much better than the writer. Some readers may however be able to make pretty pertinent conjectures, by what I have said above, especially when they are told that Miss Mathews broke the silence by a sigh, and cried, 'why is Mr Booth unwilling to allow me the happiness of thinking my misfortunes have been of some little advantage to him? Sure the happy Amelia would not be so selfish to envy me that pleasure. No; not if she was as much the fondest as she is the happiest of women.' 'Good Heavens! madam,' said he, 'do you call my poor Amelia the happiest of women?' 'Indeed I do,' answered she briskly. – 'O Mr Booth, there is a speck of white in her fortune, which when it falls to the lot of a sensible woman, makes her full amends for all the crosses which can attend her – Perhaps she may not be sensible of it; but if it had been my blest fate – O Mr Booth, could I have thought when we were first acquainted, that the most agreeable man in the world had been capable of making the kind, the tender, the affectionate husband – the happy Amelia in those days was unknown; Heaven had not then given her a prospect of the happiness it intended her – but yet it did intend it her: for sure there is a fatality in the affairs of love; and the more I reflect on my own life, the more I am convinced of it. O Heavens! how a thousand little circumstances crowd into my mind. When you first marched into our town, you had then the colours in your hand; as you passed under the window where I stood, my glove by accident dropt into the street; you stoopt, took up my glove, and putting it upon the spike belonging to your colours, lifted it up to the window. Upon this, a young lady, who stood by, said, "So, miss, the young officer hath accepted your challenge." I blush'd then, and I blush now, when I confess to you, I thought you the prettiest young fellow I had ever seen; and, upon my soul, I believe you was then the prettiest fellow in the world.' – Booth here made a low bow, and cried – 'O dear madam, how ignorant was I of my own happiness!' 'Would you really have thought so?' answered she, 'however, there is some politeness, if there be no sincerity in what you say.' Here the governor of the enchanted castle interrupted them, and entering the room without any ceremony, acquainted the lady and gentleman, that it was locking-up time;[2] and addressing Booth, by the name of captain, asked him if he would not please to have a bed; adding, that he might have one in the next room to the lady, but that it would come dear; for that he never let a bed in that room under a guinea, nor could he afford it cheaper to his father.

No answer was made to this proposal; but Miss Mathews, who had already learnt some of the ways of the house, said, she believed Mr Booth would like to drink a glass of something; upon which, the governor immediately trumpeted forth the praises of his rack-punch,[3] and without waiting for any farther commands, presently produced a large bowl of that liquor.

The governor having recommended the goodness of his punch by a hearty draught, began to revive the other matter, saying that he was just going to bed, and must first lock up. – 'But suppose,' said Miss Mathews, with a smile, 'the captain and I should have a mind to sit up all night.' – 'With all my heart,' said the governor; 'but I expect a consideration for those matters. For my part, I don't enquire into what doth not concern me; but single and double are two things. If I lock up double, I expect half a guinea; and I'm sure the captain cannot think that's out of the way – It is but the price of a bagnio.'[4]

Miss Mathews's face became of the colour of scarlet at those words – However, she mustered up her spirits, and turning to Booth, said, 'what say you, captain? for my own part, I had never less inclination to sleep; which hath the greater charms for you, the punch or the pillow?' 'I hope, madam,' answered Booth, 'you have a better opinion of me, than to doubt my preferring Miss Mathews's conversation to either.' 'I assure you,' replied she, 'it is no compliment to you, to say I prefer yours to sleep at this time.'

The governor then, having received his fee, departed; and turning the key, left the gentleman and the lady to themselves.

In imitation of him, we will lock up likewise a scene which we do not think proper to expose to the eyes of the public. If any over curious readers should be disappointed on this occasion, we will recommend such readers to the apologies with which certain gay[5] ladies have lately been pleased to oblige the world, where they will possibly find every thing recorded, that past at this interval.

But tho' we decline painting the scene, it is not our intention to conceal from the world the frailty of Mr Booth, or of his fair partner, who certainly past that evening, in a manner inconsistent with the strict rules of virtue and chastity.

To say the truth, we are much more concerned for the behaviour of the gentleman, than of the lady, not only for his sake, but for the sake of the best woman in the world, whom we should be sorry to consider as yoked to a man of no worth nor honour.

We desire therefore the good-natured and candid reader will be pleased to weigh attentively the several unlucky circumstances which concurred so critically, that fortune seemed to have used her utmost endeavours to ensnare poor Booth's constancy. Let the reader set before his eyes a fine young woman, in a manner a first love, conferring obligations, and using every art to soften, to allure, to win, and to enflame; let him consider the time and place; let him remember that Mr Booth was a young fellow, in the highest vigour of life; and lastly, let him add one single circumstance, that the parties were alone together; and then if he will not acquit the defendant, he must be convicted; for I have nothing more to say in his defence.

CHAPTER 2

The latter part of which we expect will please our reader better than the former.

A WHOLE week did our lady and gentleman live in this criminal conversation,[6] in which the happiness of the former was much more perfect than that of the latter; for tho' the charms of Miss Mathews, and her excessive endearments, sometimes lulled every thought in the sweet lethargy of pleasure; yet in the intervals of his fits, his virtue alarmed and roused him, and brought the image of poor injured Amelia to haunt and torment him. In fact, if we regard this world only, it is the interest of every man to be either perfectly good, or completely bad. He had better destroy his conscience, than gently wound it. The many bitter reflections which every bad action costs a mind in which there are any remains of goodness, are not to be compensated by the highest pleasures which such an action can produce.

So it happened to Mr Booth. Repentance never failed to follow his transgressions; and yet so perverse is our judgment, and so slippery is the descent of vice, when once we are entered into it; the same crime which he now repented of, became a reason for doing that which was to cause his future repentance; and he continued to sin on, because he had begun. His repentance however returned still heavier and heavier, till at last it flung him into a melancholy, which Miss Mathews plainly perceived, and at which she could not avoid expressing some resentment in obscure hints, and ironical compliments on Amelia's superiority to her whole sex, who could not cloy a gay young fellow by many years possession. She would then repeat the compliments which others had made to her own beauty – and could not forbear once crying out: 'Upon my soul! my dear Billy, I believe the chief disadvantage on my side, is in my superior fondness; for love, in the minds of men, hath one quality at least of a fever, which is to prefer coldness in the object. Confess, dear Will, is there not something vastly refreshing in the cool air of a prude.' – Booth fetched a deep sigh, and begged her never more to mention Amelia's name. – 'O Will,' cries she, 'did that request proceed from the motive I could wish, I should be the happiest of womankind.' – 'You would not sure, madam,' said Booth, 'desire a sacrifice, which I must be a villain to make to any?' 'Desire!' answered she, 'are there any bounds to the desires of love! Have not I been sacrificed? Hath not my first love been torn from my bleeding heart? – I claim a prior right – As for sacrifices, I can make them too; and would sacrifice the whole world at the least call of my love.'

Here she delivered a letter to Booth, which she had received within an hour, the contents of which were these:

Dearest Madam,

Those only who truly know what love is, can have any conception of the horrors I felt at hearing of your confinement at my arrival in town, which was this morning. I immediately sent my lawyer to enquire into the particulars, who brought me the agreeable news that the man, whose heart's blood ought not to be valued at the rate of a single hair of yours, is entirely out of all danger, and that you might be admitted to bail. I presently ordered him to go with two of my tradesmen, who are to be bound in any sum for your appearance, if he should be mean enough to prosecute you. Tho' you may expect my attorney with you soon, I would not delay sending this, as I hope the news will be agreeable to you. My chariot will attend at the same time to carry you where-ever you please. You may easily guess what a violence I have done to myself in not waiting on you in person; but I who know your delicacy, feared it might offend, and that you might think me ungenerous enough to hope from your distresses that happiness, which I am resolved to owe to your free gift alone, when your good-nature shall induce you to bestow on me what no man living can merit. I beg you will pardon all the contents of this hasty letter, and do me the honour of believing me,

Dearest madam,
Your most passionate admirer,
and most obedient humble servant,

DAMON

Booth thought he had somewhere before seen the same hand; but in his present hurry of spirits could not recollect whose it was; nor did the lady give him any time for reflection: for he had scarce read the letter when she produced a little bit of paper, and cried out, 'here, sir, here are the contents which he fears will offend me.' She then put a bank-bill of £100 into Mr Booth's hands, and asked him with a smile, if he did not think she had reason to be offended with so much insolence.

Before Booth could return any answer the governor arrived and introduced Mr Rogers the attorney, who acquainted the lady that he had brought her discharge from her confinement, and that a chariot waited at the door to attend her where-ever she pleased.

She received the discharge from Mr Rogers, and said she was very much obliged to the gentleman who employed him, but that she would not make use of the chariot, as she had no notion of leaving that wretched place in a triumphant manner; in which resolution when the attorney found her obstinate, he withdrew, as did the governor with many bows, and as many ladyships.

They were no sooner gone, than Booth asked the lady why she would refuse the chariot of a gentleman who had behaved with such excessive respect. She looked earnestly upon him, and cry'd, 'How unkind is that question! Do you imagine I would go and leave you in such a situation? Thou knowest but little of Calista.[7] Why, do you think I would accept this hundred pound from a man I dislike, unless it was to be serviceable to the man I love? I insist on your taking it as your own, and using whatever you want of it.'

Booth protested in the solemnest manner, that he would not touch a shilling of it, saying, he had already received too many obligations at her hands, and more than ever he should be able, he feared, to repay. 'How unkind,' answered she, 'is every word you say? Why will you mention obligations? Love never confers any. It doth every thing for its own sake. I am not therefore obliged to the man whose passion makes him generous: for I feel how inconsiderable the whole world would appear to me, if I could throw it after my heart.'

Much more of this kind past, she still pressing the bank-note upon him, and he as absolutely refusing, till Booth left the lady to dress herself, and went to walk in the area of the prison.

Miss Mathews now applied to the governor to know by what means she might procure the captain his liberty. The governor answered, 'as he cannot get bail, it will be a difficult matter; and money to be sure there must be: for people no doubt expect to touch[8] on these occasions. When prisoners have not wherewithal as the law requires to entitle themselves to justice, why they must be beholden to other people, to give them their liberty; and people will not to be sure suffer others to be beholden to them for nothing, whereof there is good reason: for how should we all live if it was not for these things!' – 'Well, well,' said she, 'and how much will it cost.' – 'How much!' answered he, – 'How much! – why, let me see.' – Here he hesitated some time, and then answered, 'that for five guineas he would undertake to procure the captain his discharge.' That being the sum which he computed to remain in the lady's pocket; for as to the gentleman's, he had long been acquainted with the emptiness of it.

Miss Mathews, to whom money was as dirt, (indeed she may be thought not to have known the value of it) delivered him the bank-bill, and bid him get it changed: 'for if the whole,' says she, 'will procure him his liberty, he shall have it this evening.'

'The whole, madam,' answered the governor, as soon as he had recovered his breath: for it almost forsook him at the sight of the black word hundred. 'No, no. – There might be people indeed – but I am not one of those. A hundred! no, nor nothing like it. – As for myself, as I said, I will be content with five guineas, and I am sure that's little enough. What other people will expect, I can't exactly say. – To be sure his worship's clerk will expect to touch pretty handsomely, as for his worship himself he never touches any thing, that is, not to speak of; but then the constable will expect something, and the watchmen must have something, and the lawyers on both sides they must have their fees for finishing.' – 'Well,' said she, 'I leave all to you. If it costs me £20 I will have him discharged this afternoon. – But you must give his discharge into my hands, without letting the captain know any thing of the matter.'

The governor promised to obey her commands in every particular; nay, he was so very industrious, that tho' dinner was just then coming upon the table, at her earnest request, he set out immediately on the purpose, and went, as he said, in pursuit of the lawyer.

All the other company assembled at table as usual, where poor Booth was the only person out of spirits. This was imputed by all present to a wrong cause; nay, Miss Mathews herself either could not, or would not, suspect that there was any thing deeper than the despair of being speedily discharged, that lay heavy on his mind.

However, the mirth of the rest, and a pretty liberal quantity of punch, which he swallowed after dinner (for Miss Mathews had ordered a very large bowl at her own expence, to entertain the good company at her farewell) so far exhilarated his spirits, that when the young lady and he retired to their tea, he had all the marks of gayety in his countenance, and his eyes sparkled with good humour.

The gentleman and lady had spent about two hours in tea and conversation, when the governor returned, and privately delivered to the lady the discharge for her friend, and the sum of eighty-two pounds five shillings; the rest having been, he said, disbursed in the business, of which he was ready at any time to render an exact account.

Miss Mathews being again alone with Mr Booth, she put the discharge into his hands, desiring him to ask her no questions; and adding, 'I think, sir, we have neither of us now any thing more to do at this place.' She then summoned the governor, and ordered a bill of that day's expence, for long scores were not usual there; and at the same time ordered a hackney coach, without having yet determined whither she would go, but fully determined she was wherever she went, to take Mr Booth with her.

The governor was now approaching with a long roll of paper, when a faint voice was heard to cry out hastily, 'where is he?' – and presently a female spectre, all pale and breathless, rushed into the room, and fell into Mr Booth's arms, where she immediately fainted away.

Booth made a shift to support his lovely burthen; tho' he was himself in a condition very little different from hers. Miss Mathews likewise, who presently recollected the face of Amelia, was struck motionless with the surprize; nay, the governor himself, tho' not easily moved at sights of horrour, stood aghast, and neither offered to speak nor stir.

Happily for Amelia, the governess of the mansions had out of curiosity followed her into the room, and was the only useful person present on this occasion; she immediately called for water, and ran to the lady's assistance, fell to loosening her stays, and performed all the offices proper at such a season; which had so good an effect, that Amelia soon recovered the disorder which the violent agitation of her spirits[9] had caused, and found herself alive and awake in her husband's arms.

Some tender caresses, and a soft whisper or two past privately between Booth and his lady; nor was it without great difficulty, that poor Amelia put some restraint on her fondness, in a place so improper for a tender interview. She now cast her eyes round the room, and fixing them on Miss Mathews, who stood like a statue; she soon recollected her, and addressing her by her name, said, 'sure, madam, I cannot be mistaken in those features; tho' meeting you here might almost make me suspect my memory.'

Miss Mathews's face was now all covered with scarlet. The reader may easily believe she was on no account pleased with Amelia's presence; indeed, she expected from her some of those insults, of which virtuous women are generally so liberal to a frail sister; but she was mistaken, Amelia was not one,

Who thought the nation ne'er would thrive,
Till all the whores were burnt alive.[10]

Her virtue could support itself with its own intrinsic worth, without borrowing any assistance from the vices of other women; and she considered their natural infirmities as the objects of pity, not of contempt or abhorrence.

When Amelia therefore perceived the visible confusion in Miss Mathews, she presently called to remembrance some stories which she had imperfectly heard; for as she was not naturally attentive to scandal, and had kept very little company since her return to England, she was far from being a mistress of the lady's whole history. However she had heard enough to impute her confusion to the right cause; she advanced to her, and told her she was extremely sorry to meet her in such a place, but hoped that no very great misfortune was the occasion of it.

Miss Mathews began, by degrees, to recover her spirits. She answered with a reserved air, 'I am much obliged to you, madam, for your concern; we are all liable to misfortunes in this world. Indeed I know not why I should be much ashamed of being in any place where I am in such good company.'

Here Booth interposed. He had before acquainted Amelia in a whisper, that his confinement was at an end. 'The unfortunate accident, my dear,' said he, 'which brought this young lady to this melancholy place, is entirely determined; and she is now as absolutely at her liberty as myself.'

Amelia imputing the extreme coldness and reserve of the lady to the cause already mentioned, advanced still more and more in proportion as she drew back; till the governor, who had withdrawn some time, returned, and acquainted Miss Mathews that her coach was at the door; upon which the company soon separated. Amelia and Booth went together in Amelia's coach, and poor Miss Mathews was obliged to retire alone, after having satisfied the demands of the governor, which in one day only had amounted to a pretty considerable sum; for he with great dexterity proportioned his bills to the abilities of his guests.

It may seem perhaps wonderful to some readers, that Miss Mathews should have maintained that cold reserve towards Amelia, so as barely to keep within the rules of civility, instead of embracing an opportunity which seemed to offer, of gaining some degree of intimacy with a wife, whose husband she was so fond of; but besides that her spirits were entirely disconcerted by so sudden and unexpected a disappointment; and besides the extreme horrors which she conceived at the presence of her rival, there is, I believe, something so outrageously suspicious in the nature of all vice, especially when joined with any great degree of pride, that the eyes of those whom we imagine privy to our failings, are intolerable to us, and we are apt to aggravate their opinions to our disadvantage far beyond the reality.

CHAPTER 3

Containing wise observations of the author, and other matters.

THERE is nothing more difficult than to lay down any fixed and certain rules for happiness; or indeed to judge with any precision of the happiness of others, from the knowledge of external circumstances. There is sometimes a little speck of black in the brightest and gayest colours of fortune, which contaminates and deadens the whole. On the contrary, when all without looks dark and dismal, there is often a secret ray of light within the mind, which turns every thing to real joy and gladness.

I have in the course of my life seen many occasions to make this observation; and Mr Booth was at present a very pregnant instance of its truth. He was just delivered from a prison, and in the possession of his beloved wife and children; and (which might be imagined greatly to augment his joy) Fortune had done all this for him within an hour, without giving him the least warning or reasonable expectation of this strange reverse in his circumstances; and yet it is certain, that there were very few men in the world, more seriously miserable than he was at this instant. A deep melancholy[11] seized his mind, and cold damp sweats over-spread his person, so that he was scarce animated; and poor Amelia, instead of a fond warm husband, bestowed her caresses on a dull lifeless lump of clay. He endeavoured however at first, as much as possible, to conceal what he felt, and attempted what is the hardest of all tasks, to act the part of a happy man; but he found no supply of spirits to carry on this deceit, and would have probably sunk under his attempt, had not poor Amelia's simplicity helped him to another fallacy, in which he had much better success.

This worthy woman very plainly perceived the disorder in her husband's mind; and having no doubt of the cause of it, especially when she saw the tears stand in his eyes at the sight of his children, threw her arms round his neck, and embracing him with rapturous fondness, cried out, 'my dear Billy, let nothing make you uneasy.

Heaven will, I doubt not, provide for us and these poor babes. Great fortunes are not necessary to happiness. For my own part, I can level my mind with any state; and for those poor little things, whatever condition of life we breed them to, that will be sufficient to maintain them in. How many thousands abound in affluence, whose fortunes are much lower than ours! for it is not from nature, but from education and habit, that our wants are chiefly derived. Make yourself easy therefore, my dear love; for you have a wife who will think herself happy with you, and endeavour to make you so in any situation. Fear nothing, Billy, industry will always provide us a wholesome meal; and I will take care, that neatness and cheerfulness shall make it a pleasant one.'

Booth presently took the cue, which she had given him. He fixed his eyes on her for a minute, with great earnestness and inexpressible tenderness; and then cried, 'O my Amelia, how much are you my superior in every perfection! How wise, how great, how noble are your sentiments! Why can I not imitate what I so much admire? Why can I not look with your constancy, on those dear little pledges of our loves? All my philosophy is baffled with the thought, that my Amelia's children are to struggle with a cruel hard unfeeling world, and to buffet those waves of fortune, which have overwhelmed their father. – Here I own I want your firmness, and am not without an excuse for wanting it; for am I not the cruel cause of all your wretchedness? Have I not stept between you and fortune, and been the cursed obstacle to all your greatness and happiness?'

'Say not so, my love,' answered she. 'Great I might have been, but never happy with any other man. Indeed, dear Billy, I laugh at the fears you formerly raised in me; what seemed so terrible at a distance, now it approaches nearer, appears to have been a mere bugbear – and let this comfort you, that I look on myself at this day as the happiest of women; nor have I done any thing which I do not rejoice in, and would, if I had the gift of prescience, do again.'

Booth was so overcome with this behaviour, that he had no words to answer. To say the truth, it was difficult to find any worthy of the occasion. He threw himself prostrate at her feet, whence poor Amelia was forced to use all her strength as well as entreaties to raise, and place him in his chair.

Such is ever the fortitude of perfect innocence, and such the depression of guilt in minds not utterly abandoned. Booth was naturally of a sanguine temper; nor would any such apprehensions as he mentioned have been sufficient to have restrained his joy, at meeting with his Amelia. In fact, a reflection on the injury he had done her was the sole cause of his grief. This it was that enervated his heart, and threw him into agonies, which all that profusion of heroic tenderness that the most excellent of women intended for his comfort, served only to heighten and aggravate; as the more she rose in his admiration, the more she quickened his sense of his own unworthiness.

After a disagreeable evening, the first of that kind that he had ever past with his Amelia, in which he had the utmost difficulty to force a little cheerfulness, and in which her spirits were at length over-powered by discerning the oppresion on his, they retired to rest, or rather to misery, which need not be described.

The next morning at breakfast, Booth began to recover a little from his melancholy, and to taste the company of his children. He now first thought of enquiring of Amelia, by what means she had discovered the place of his confinement. Amelia, after gently rebuking him for not having himself acquainted her with it, informed him, that it was known all over the country, and that she had traced the original of it to her sister; who had spread the news with a malicious joy, and added a circumstance, which would have frightened her to death, had not her knowledge of him made her give little credit to it, which was, that he was committed for murder. But tho' she had discredited this part, she said, the not hearing from him during several successive posts made her too apprehensive of the rest. That she got a conveyance therefore for herself and children to Salisbury; from whence the stage-coach had brought them to town, and having deposited the children at his lodging, of which he had sent her an account on his first arrival in town, she took a hack,[12] and came directly to the prison where she heard he was, and where she found him.

Booth excused himself, and with truth as to his not having writ: for in fact, he had writ twice from the prison, tho' he had mentioned nothing of his confinement; but as he sent away his letters after nine at night, the fellow, to whom they were entrusted, had burnt them both for the sake of putting the two pence in his own pocket, or rather in the pocket of the keeper of the next gin-shop.

As to the account which Amelia gave him, it served rather to raise than to satisfy his curiosity. He began to suspect, that some person had seen both him and Miss Mathews together in the prison, and had confounded her case with his; and this the circumstance of murder made the more probable. But who this person should be, he could not guess. After giving himself therefore some pains in forming conjectures to no purpose, he was forced to rest contented with his ignorance of the real truth.

Two or three days now past without producing any thing remarkable; unless it were, that Booth more and more recovered his spirits, and had now almost regained his former degree of cheerfulness, when the following letter arrived again to torment him:

Dear Billy,

To convince you I am the most reasonable of women, I have given you up three whole days to the unmolested possession of my fortunate rival; I can refrain no longer from letting you know that I lodge in Dean Street, not far from the church,[13] at the sign of the Pelican and Trumpet; where I expect this evening to see you – Believe me, I am with more affection than any other woman in the world can be,

My dear Billy,

Your affectionate, fond, doating

F. MATHEWS.

Booth tore the letter with rage, and threw it into the fire; resolving never to visit the lady more, unless it was to pay her the money she had lent him, which he was determined to do the very first opportunity: for it was not at present in his power.

This letter threw him back into his fit of dejection, in which he had not continued long, when a packet from the country brought him the following from his friend Dr Harrison:

SIR, Lyons, January 21. N.S.[14]

Tho' I am now on my return home, I have taken up my pen to communicate to you some news I have heard from England, which gives me much uneasiness, and concerning which I can indeed deliver my sentiments with much more ease this way than any other. In my answer to your last I very freely gave you my opinion, in which it was my misfortune to disapprove of every step you had taken; but those were all pardonable errors. Can you be so partial to yourself, upon cool and sober reflexion, to think what I am going to mention is so? I promise you, it appears to me a folly of so monstrous a kind, that had I heard it from any but a person of the highest honour, I should have rejected it as utterly incredible. I hope you already guess what I am about to name; since Heaven forbid your conduct should afford you any choice of such gross instances of weakness. In a word then you have set up an equipage. What shall I invent in your excuse, either to others, or to myself? In truth, I can find no excuse for you, and what is more, I am certain you can find none for yourself. I must deal therefore very plainly and sincerely with you. Vanity is always contemptible; but when joined with dishonesty, it becomes odious and detestable. At whose expence are you to support this equipage? Is it not entirely at the expence of others; and will it not finally end in that of your poor wife and children? You know you are two years in arrears to me. If I could impute this to any extraordinary or common accident, I think I should never have mentioned it; but I will not suffer my money to support the ridiculous, and I must say, criminal vanity of any one. I expect therefore to find at my return, that you have either discharged my whole debt, or your equipage. Let me beg you seriously to consider your circumstances and condition in life, and to remember that your situation will not justify any the least unnecessary expence. *Simply to be poor*, says my favourite Greek historian,[15] *was not held scandalous by the wise Athenians, but highly so, to owe that poverty to our own indiscretion.* Present my affections to Mrs Booth, and be assured, that I shall not without great reason, and great pain too, ever cease to be,

Your most faithful friend,

R. HARRISON.

Had this letter come at any other time, it would have given Booth the most sensible affliction; but so totally had the affair of

Miss Mathews possessed his mind, that like a man in a most raging fit of the gout, he was scarce capable of any additional torture; nay, he even made a use of this latter epistle, as it served to account to Amelia for that concern which he really felt on another account. The poor deceived lady therefore applied herself to give him comfort where he least wanted it. She said he might easily perceive that the matter had been misrepresented to the doctor, who would not, she was sure, retain the least anger against him when he knew the real truth.

After a short conversation on this subject, in which Booth appeared to be greatly consoled by the arguments of his wife, they parted. He went to take a walk in the Park, and she remained at home to prepare him his dinner.

He was no sooner departed than his little boy, not quite six years old, said to Amelia, 'La! mamma, what is the matter with poor papa, what makes him look so as if he was going to cry? He is not half so merry as he used to be in the country.' Amelia answered, 'Oh! my dear! your papa is only a little thoughtful, he will be merry again soon.' – Then looking fondly on her children, she burst into an agony of tears, and cried, 'Oh Heavens! what have these poor little infants done? why will the barbarous world endeavour to starve them, by depriving us of our only friend? – O my dear, your father is ruined, and we are undone.' – The children presently accompanied their mother's tears, and the daughter cried – 'Why, will any body hurt poor papa? Hath he done any harm to any body?' – 'No, my dear child,' said the mother, 'he is the best man in the world, and therefore they hate him.' Upon which the boy, who was extremely sensible at his years, answered, 'Nay, mamma, how can that be? Have not you often told me, that if I was good, every body would love me?' 'All good people will,' answered she. 'Why don't they love papa then?' replied the child, 'for I am sure he is very good.' 'So they do, my dear,' said the mother, 'but there are more bad people in the world, and they will hate you for your goodness.' 'Why then bad people,' cries the child, 'are loved by more than the good.' – 'No matter for that, my dear,' said she, 'the love of one good person is more worth having, than that of a thousand wicked ones; nay, if there was no such person in the world, still you must be a good boy: for there is one in

Heaven who will love you; and his love is better for you than that of all mankind.'

This little dialogue we are apprehensive will be read with contempt by many; indeed we should not have thought it worth recording, was it not for the excellent example which Amelia here gives to all mothers. This admirable woman never let a day pass, without instructing her children in some lesson of religion and morality. By which means, she had in their tender minds so strongly annexed the ideas of fear and shame to every idea of evil of which they were susceptible, that it must require great pains and length of habit to separate them. Tho' she was the tenderest of mothers, she never suffered any symptom of malevolence to shew itself in their most trifling actions without discouragement, without rebuke; and if it broke forth with any rancour, without punishment. In which she had such success, that not the least marks of pride, envy, malice, or spite discovered itself in any of their little words or deeds.

CHAPTER 4

In which Amelia appears in no unamiable light.

AMELIA, with the assistance of a little girl, who was their only servant, had drest her dinner; and she had likewise drest herself as neat as any lady who had a regular set of servants could have done; when Booth returned, and brought with him his friend James, whom he had met with in the Park; and who, as Booth absolutely refused to dine away from his wife, to whom he had promised to return, had invited himself to dine with him. Amelia had none of that paultry pride, which possesses so many of her sex, and which disconcerts their tempers, and gives them the air and looks of furies, if their husbands bring in an unexpected guest, without giving them timely warning to provide a sacrifice to their own vanity. Amelia received her husband's friend with the utmost complaisance and good humour: she made indeed some apology for the homeliness of her dinner; but it was politely turned as a compliment to Mr James's friendship, which could carry him where he was sure of being so ill entertained; and gave not the least hint how magnificently she would have provided, *had she expected the favour of so much good company*. A phrase which is generally meant to contain not only an apology for the lady of the house, but a tacit satire on her guests for their intrusion, and is at least a strong insinuation that they are not welcome.

Amelia failed not to enquire very earnestly after her old friend Mrs James, formerly Miss Bath, and was very sorry to find that she was not in town. The truth was, as James had married out of a violent liking of, or appetite to her person, possession had surfeited him, and he was now grown so heartily tired of his wife, that she had very little of his company; she was forced therefore to content herself with being the mistress of a large house and equipage in the country, ten months in the year by herself. The other two he indulged her with the diversions of the town; but then, tho' they lodged under the same roof, she had little more of her husband's society, than if they had been one hundred miles a-part. With all this, as she was a woman of calm passions, she made herself contented; for she had never had any violent affection for James; the match was of the prudent kind, and to her advantage: for his fortune, by the death of an uncle, was become very considerable; and she had gained every thing by the bargain but a husband, which her constitution suffered her to be very well satisfied without.

When Amelia after dinner retired to her children, James began to talk to his friend concerning his affairs. He advised Booth very earnestly to think of getting again into the army, in which he himself had met with such success, that he had obtained the command of a regiment, to which his brother-in-law was lieutenant-colonel. These preferments they both owed to the favour of fortune only: for tho' there was no objection to either of their military characters; yet neither of them had any extraordinary desert; and if merit in the service was a sufficient recommendation, Booth, who had been twice wounded in the siege, seemed to have the fairest pretensions; but he remained a poor half-pay lieutenant, and the others were, as we have said, one of them a lieutenant-colonel, and the other had a regiment. Such rises we often see in life, without being able to give any satisfactory account of the means, and therefore ascribe them to the good fortune of the person.

Both Colonel James and his brother-in-law were Members of Parliament: for as the uncle of the former had left him, together with his estate, an almost certain interest in a borough, so he chose to confer this favour on Colonel Bath; a circumstance which would have been highly immaterial to mention here; but as it serves to set forth the goodness of James, who endeavoured to make up in kindness to the family, what he wanted in fondness for his wife.

Colonel James then endeavoured all in his power to persuade Booth to think again of a military life, and very kindly offered him his interest towards obtaining him a company in the regiment under his command. Booth must have been a madman in his present circumstances to have hesitated one moment at accepting such an offer, and he well knew Amelia, notwithstanding her aversion to the army, was much too wise to make the least scruple of giving her consent. Nor was he, as it appeared afterwards, mistaken in his opinion of his wife's understanding: for she made not the least objection when it was communicated to her, but contented herself with an express stipulation, that wherever he was commanded to go (for the regiment was now abroad) she would accompany him.

Booth therefore accepted his friend's proposal with a profusion of acknowledgments; and, it was agreed, that Booth should draw up a memorial of his pretensions,[16] which Colonel James undertook to present to some man of power, and to back it with all the force he had.

Nor did the friendship of the colonel stop here. 'You will excuse me, dear Booth,' said he, 'if after what you have told me' (for he had been very explicit in revealing his affairs to him) 'I suspect you must want money at this time. If that be the case, as I am certain it must be, I have fifty pieces[17] at your service.' This generosity brought the tears into Booth's eyes; and he at length confest, that he had not five guineas in the house; upon which James gave him a bank-bill for £20 and said he would give him thirty more the next time he saw him.

Thus did this generous colonel (for generous he really was to the highest degree) restore peace and comfort to this little family; and by this act of beneficence make two of the worthiest people, two of the happiest that evening.

Here, reader, give me leave to stop a minute, to lament that so few are to be found of this benign disposition; that while wantonness, vanity, avarice and ambition are every day rioting and triumphing in the follies and weakness, the ruin and desolation of mankind, scarce one man in a thousand is capable of tasting the happiness of others. Nay, give me leave to wonder that pride, which is constantly struggling, and often imposing on itself to gain some little pre-eminence, should so seldom hint to us the only certain as well as laudable way of setting ourselves above another man, and that is by becoming his benefactor.

CHAPTER 5

Containing an eulogium upon innocence, and other grave matters.

BOOTH past that evening, and all the succeeding day with his Amelia, without the interruption of almost a single thought concerning Miss Mathews, after having determined to go on the Sunday, the only day he could venture[18] without the verge in the present state of his affairs, and pay her what she had advanced for him in the prison. But she had not so long patience; for the third day, while he was sitting with Amelia, a letter was brought to him. As he knew the hand, he immediately put it in his pocket unopened, not without such an alteration in his countenance, that had Amelia, who was then playing with one of the children, cast her eyes towards him, she must have remarked it. This accident however, luckily gave him time to recover himself: for Amelia was so deeply engaged with the little one, that she did not even remark the delivery of the letter. The maid soon after returned into the room, saying the chairman[19] desired to know if there was any answer to the letter. – 'What letter,' cries Booth. – 'The letter I gave you just now,' answered the girl. – 'Sure,' cries Booth, 'the child is mad, you gave me no letter.' – 'Yes, indeed I did, sir,' said the poor girl. 'Why then, as sure as fate,' cries Booth, 'I threw it into the fire in my reverie, why, child, why did you not tell me it was a letter? Bid the chairman come up – stay, I will go down myself; for he will otherwise dirt the stairs with his feet.'

Amelia was gently chiding the girl for her carelessness, when Booth returned, saying, it was very true that she had delivered him a letter from Colonel James, and that perhaps it might be of consequence. 'However,' says he, 'I will step to the coffee-house, and send him an account of this strange accident, which I know he will pardon in my present situation.'

Booth was overjoyed at this escape which poor Amelia's total want of all jealousy and suspicion, made it very easy for him to accomplish: but his pleasure was considerably abated, when upon opening the letter, he found it to contain, mixed with several very strong expressions of love, some pretty warm ones of the upbraiding kind; but what most alarmed him was a hint, that it was in her power (Miss Mathews's power), to make Amelia as miserable as herself. Besides the general knowledge of

– furens quid femina possit,[20]

he had more particular reasons to apprehend the rage of a lady, who had given so strong an instance how far she could carry her revenge. She had already sent a chairman to his lodgings, with a positive command not to return without an answer to her letter. This might of itself have possibly occasioned a discovery; and he thought he had great reason to fear, that if she did not carry matters so far as purposely and avowedly to reveal the secret to Amelia, her indiscretion would at least effect the discovery of that which he would at any price have concealed. Under these terrours he might, I believe, be considered as the most wretched of human beings.

O Innocence, how glorious and happy a portion art thou to the breast that possesses thee! Thou fearest neither the eyes nor the tongues of men. Truth, the most powerful of all things, is thy strongest friend; and the brighter the light is in which thou art displayed, the more it discovers thy transcendent beauties. Guilt, on the contrary, like a base thief, suspects every eye that beholds him to be privy to his transgressons, and every tongue that mentions his name to be proclaiming them. Fraud and Falsehood are his weak and treacherous allies; and he lurks trembling in the dark, dreading every ray of light, lest it should discover him, and give him up to shame and punishment.

While Booth was walking in the Park with all these horrors in his mind, he again met his friend Colonel James, who soon took notice of that deep concern which the other was incapable of hiding. After some little conversation, Booth said, 'my dear colonel, I am sure I must be the most insensible of men, if I did not look on you as the best and the truest friend; I will therefore without scruple repose a confidence in you of the highest kind. I have often made you privy to my necessities, I will now acquaint you with my shame, provided you have leisure enough to give me a hearing: for I must open to you a long history, since I will not reveal my fault, without informing you, at the same time, of those circumstances, which, I hope, will in some measure excuse it.'

The colonel very readily agreed to give his friend a patient hearing. So they walked directly to a coffee-house at the corner of Spring Garden,[21] where being in a room by themselves, Booth opened his whole heart, and acquainted the colonel with his amour with Miss Mathews from the very beginning, to his receiving that letter which had caused all his present uneasiness, and which he now delivered into his friend's hand.

The colonel read the letter very attentively twice over: (he was silent indeed long enough to have read it oftener) and then turning to Booth said, 'Well, sir; and is it so grievous a calamity to be the object of a young lady's affection; especially of one whom you allow to be so extremely handsome?' 'Nay, but my dear friend,' cries Booth, 'do not jest with me; you who know my Amelia.' 'Well, my dear friend,' answered James, 'and you know Amelia, and this lady too – But what would you have me do for you?' 'I would have you give me your advice,' says Booth, 'by what method I shall get rid of this dreadful woman without a discovery.' 'And do you really,' cries the other, 'desire to get rid of her?' 'Can you doubt it,' said Booth, 'after what I have communicated to you, and after what you yourself have seen in my family? for I hope, notwithstanding this fatal slip, I do not appear to you in the light of a profligate.' 'Well,' answered James, 'and whatever light I may appear to you in, if you are really tired of the lady, and if she be really what you have represented her, I'll endeavour to take her off your hands; but I insist upon it, that you do not deceive me in any particular.' Booth protested in the most solemn manner that every word which he had spoken was strictly true; and being asked whether he would give his honour never more to visit the lady, he assured James that he never would. He then, at his friend's request, delivered him Miss Mathews's letter, in which was a second direction to her lodgings, and declared to him, that if he could bring him safely out of this terrible affair, he should think himself to have a still higher obligation to his friendship, than any which he had already received from it.

Booth pressed the colonel to go home with him to dinner, but he excused himself, being, as he said, already engaged. However, he undertook in the afternoon to do all in his power, that Booth should receive no more alarms from the quarter of Miss Mathews, whom the colonel undertook to pay all the demands she had on his friend. They then separated. The colonel went to dinner at the King's Arms,[22] and Booth returned in high spirits to meet his Amelia.

The next day early in the morning, the colonel came to the coffee-house, and sent for his friend, who lodged but at a little distance. The colonel told him he had a little exaggerated the lady's beauty; however, he said, he excused that; 'for you might think perhaps,' cries he, 'that your inconstancy to the finest woman in the world, might want some excuse. Be that as it will,' said he, 'you may make yourself easy, as it will be, I am convinced, your own fault, if you have ever any further molestation from Miss Mathews.'

Booth poured forth very warmly a great profusion of gratitude on this occasion; and nothing more any-wise material past at this interview, which was very short, the colonel being in a great hurry, as he had, he said, some business of very great importance to transact that morning.

The colonel had now seen Booth twice, without remembring to give him the thirty pound. This the latter imputed entirely to forgetfulness; for he had always found the promises of the former to be equal in value with the notes or bonds of other people. He was more surprized at what happened the next day, when meeting his friend in the Park, he received only a cold salute from him; and tho' he past him five or six times, and the colonel was walking with a single officer of no great rank, and with whom he seemed in no earnest conversation; yet could not Booth, who was alone, obtain any further notice from him.

This gave the poor man some alarm; tho' he could scarce persuade himself there was any design in all this coldness or forgetfulness. Once he imagined that he had lessened himself in the colonel's opinion, by having discovered his inconstancy to Amelia; but the known character of the other, presently cured him of this suspicion, for he was a perfect libertine with regard to women; that being indeed the principal blemish in his character, which otherwise might have deserved much commendation for good-nature, generosity, and friendship. But he carried this one to a most unpardonable height; and made no scruple of openly declaring, that if he ever liked a woman well enough to be uneasy on her account, he would cure himself, if he could, by enjoying her, whatever might be the consequence.

Booth could not therefore be persuaded that the colonel would so highly resent in another a fault, of which he was himself most notoriously guilty. After much consideration, he could derive this behaviour from nothing better than a capriciousness in his friend's temper, from a kind of inconstancy of mind, which makes men grow weary of their friends, with no more reason than they often are of their mistresses. To say the truth, there are jilts in friendship as well as in love; and by the behaviour of some men in both, one would almost imagine that they industriously sought to gain the affections of others, with a view only of making the parties miserable.

This was the consequence of the colonel's behaviour to Booth. Former calamities had afflicted him; but this almost distracted him; and the more so, as he was not able well to account for such conduct, nor to conceive the reason of it.

Amelia at his return, presently perceived the disturbance in his mind, tho' he endeavoured with his utmost power to hide it; and he was at length prevailed upon by her entreaties to discover to her the cause of it; which she no sooner heard, than she applied as judicious a remedy to his disordered spirits, as either of those great mental physicians, Tully[23] or Aristotle, could have thought of. She used many arguments to persuade him that he was in an error; and had mistaken forgetfulness and carelessness for a design'd neglect.

But as this physic was only eventually good, and as its efficacy depended on her being in the right, a point in which she was not apt to be too positive; she thought fit to add some consolation of a more certain and positive kind. 'Admit,' said she, 'my dear, that Mr James should prove the unaccountable person you have suspected, and should, without being able to alledge any cause, withdraw his friendship from you, (for surely the accident of burning his letter is too trifling and ridiculous to mention) why should this grieve you? The obligations he hath confer'd on you, I allow, ought to make his misfortunes almost your own; but they should not, I think, make you see his faults so very sensibly, especially when by one of the greatest faults in the world committed against yourself, he hath considerably lessened all obligations: For sure, if the same person who hath contributed to my happiness at one time, doth every thing in his power maliciously and wantonly to make me miserable at another, I am very little obliged to such a person. And let it be a comfort to my dear Billy, that however other friends may prove false and fickle to him, he hath one friend, whom no inconstancy of her own, nor any change of his fortune, nor time, nor age, nor sickness, nor any accident can ever alter; but who will esteem, will love, and doat on him for ever.' So saying, she flung her snowy arms about his neck, and gave him a caress so tender, that it seemed almost to balance all the malice of his fate.

And, indeed, the behaviour of Amelia would have made him completely happy, in defiance of all adverse circumstances, had it not been for those bitter ingredients which he himself had thrown into his cup; and which prevented him from truly relishing his Amelia's sweetness, by cruelly reminding him how unworthy he was of this excellent creature.

Booth did not long remain in the dark as to the conduct of James, which at first appeared to him to be so great a mystery; for this very afternoon he received a letter from Miss Mathews, which unravelled the whole affair. By this letter, which was full of bitterness and upbraiding, he discovered that James was his rival with that lady, and was indeed the identical person who had sent the £100 note to Miss Mathews, when in the prison. He had reason to believe likewise, as well by the letter as by other circumstances, that James had hitherto been an unsuccessful lover: for the lady, tho' she had forfeited all title to virtue, had not yet so far forfeited all pretensions to delicacy, as to be, like the dirt in the street, indifferently common to all. She distributed her favours only to those she liked, in which number that gentleman had not the happiness of being included.

When Booth had made this discovery, he was not so little versed in human nature, as any longer to hesitate at the true motive to the colonel's conduct; for he well knew how odious a sight a happy rival is to an unfortunate lover. I believe he was in reality glad to assign the cold treatment he had received from his friend, to a cause which, however unjustifiable, is at the same time highly natural; and to acquit him of a levity, fickleness, and caprice, which he must have been unwillingly obliged to have seen in a much worse light.

He now resolved to take the first opportunity of accosting the colonel, and of coming to a perfect explanation upon the whole matter. He debated likewise with himself, whether he should not throw himself at Amelia's feet, and confess a crime to her, which he found so little hopes of concealing, and which he foresaw would occasion him so many difficulties and terrors to endeavour to conceal. Happy had it been for him, had he wisely pursued this step; since in great probability he would have received immediate forgiveness from that best of women; but he had not sufficient resolution; or to speak, perhaps, more truly, he had too much pride to confess his guilt, and preferred the danger of the highest inconveniences to the certainty of being put to the blush.

CHAPTER 6

In which may appear that violence is sometimes done to the name of love.

WHEN that happy day came, in which unhallowed hands are forbidden to contaminate the shoulders of the unfortunate, Booth went early to the colonel's house, and being admitted to his presence, began with great freedom, though with great gentleness, to complain of his not having dealt with him with more openness. 'Why, my dear colonel,' said he, 'would you not acquaint me with that secret which this letter hath disclosed?' James read the letter, at which his countenance changed more than once, and then after a short silence, said, 'Mr Booth, I have been to blame, I own it; and you upbraid me with justice. The true reason was, that I was ashamed of my own folly. D—n me, Booth, if I have not been a most consummate fool, a very dupe to this woman; and she hath a particular pleasure in making me so. I know what the impertinence of virtue is, and I can submit to it; but to be treated thus by a whore. – You must forgive me, dear Booth; but your success was a kind of triumph over me which I could not bear. I own I have not the least reason to conceive any anger against you; and yet, curse me, if I should not have been less displeased at your lying with my own wife; nay I could almost have parted with half my fortune to you more willingly, than have suffered you to receive that trifle of my money, which you received at her hands. However, I ask your pardon, and I promise you, I will never more think of you with the least ill-will, on the account of this woman; but as for her, d—n me, if I do not enjoy her by some means or other, whatever it costs me; for I am already above £200 out of pocket, without having scarce had a smile in return.'

Booth exprest much astonishment at this declaration; he said, he could not conceive how it was possible to have such an affection for a woman, who did not shew the least inclination to return it. – James gave her a hearty curse; and said, 'Pox of her inclination; I want only the possession of her person; and that you will allow is a very fine one. But, besides my passion for her, she hath now piqued my pride; for how can a man of my fortune brook being refused by a whore?' 'Since you are so set on the business,' cries Booth; 'you will excuse my saying so; I fancy you had better change your method of applying to her: for, as she is perhaps the vainest woman upon earth, your bounty may probably do you little service, nay, may rather actually disoblige her. Vanity is plainly her predominant passion, and, if you will administer to that, it will infallibly throw her into your arms. To this I attribute my own unfortunate success. While she relieved my wants and distresses, she was daily feeding her own vanity; whereas as every gift of yours asserted your superiority, it rather offended than pleased her. Indeed women generally love to be of the obliging side; and if we examine their favourites, we shall find them to be much oftner such as they have conferred obligations on, than such as they have received them from.'

There was something in this speech which pleased the colonel; and he said with a smile, 'I don't know how it is, Will; but you know women better than I.' 'Perhaps colonel,' answered Booth, 'I have studied their minds more.' 'I don't however much envy you your knowledge,' reply'd the other: 'for I never think their minds worth considering. However, I hope I shall profit a little by your experience with Miss Mathews. Damnation seize the proud insolent harlot! The devil take me if I don't love her more than I ever loved a woman!'

The rest of their conversation turned on Booth's affairs. The colonel again reassumed the part of a friend, gave him the remainder of the money, and promised to take the first opportunity of laying his memorial before a great man.

Booth was greatly overjoyed at this success. Nothing now lay on his mind, but to conceal his frailty from Amelia, to whom he was afraid Miss Mathews in the rage of her resentment would communicate it. This apprehension made him stay almost constantly at home; and he trembled at every knock at the door. His fear moreover betrayed him into a meanness, which he would have heartily despised on any other occasion. This was to order the maid to deliver him any letter directed to Amelia, at the same time strictly charging her not to acquaint her mistress with her having received any such orders.

A servant of any acuteness would have formed strange conjectures from such an injunction; but this poor girl was of perfect simplicity; so great indeed was her simplicity, that had not Amelia been void of all suspicion of her husband, the maid would have soon after betrayed her master.

One afternoon while they were drinking tea, little Betty, so was the maid called, came into the room; and calling her master forth, delivered him a card which was directed to Amelia. Booth having read the card, on his return into the room, chid the girl for calling him, saying, 'if you can read, child, you must see it was directed to your mistress.' – To this the girl answered pertly enough. 'I am sure, sir, you ordered me to bring every letter first to you.' This hint with many women would have been sufficient to have blown up the whole affair; but Amelia who heard what the girl said, through the medium of love and confidence, saw the matter in a much better light than it deserved; and looking tenderly on her husband, said, 'Indeed, my love, I must blame you for a conduct, which perhaps I ought rather to praise, as it proceeds only from the extreme tenderness of your affection. But why will you endeavour to keep any secrets from me? Believe me, for my own sake you ought not: for as you cannot hide the consequences, you make me always suspect ten times worse than the reality. While I have you and my children well before my eyes, I am capable of facing any news which can arrive: for what ill news can come (unless indeed it concerns my little babe in the country) which doth not relate to the badness of our circumstances? and those, I thank Heaven, we have now a fair prospect of retrieving. Besides, dear Billy, though my understanding be much inferiour to yours, I have sometimes had the happiness of luckily hitting on some argument which hath afforded you comfort. This you know, my dear, was the case with regard to Colonel James, whom I persuaded you to think you had mistaken, and you see the event proved me in the right.' So happily, both for herself and Mr Booth, did the excellence of this good woman's disposition deceive her, and force her to see every thing in the most advantageous light to her husband.

The card being now inspected was found to contain the compliments of Mrs James to Mrs Booth, with an account of her being arrived in town, and having brought with her a very great cold. Amelia was overjoyed at the news of her arrival; and having drest herself in the utmost hurry, left her children to the care of her husband, and ran away to pay her respects to her friend, whom she loved with a most sincere affection. But how was she disappointed, when eager with the utmost impatience, and exulting with the thoughts of presently seeing her beloved friend, she was answered at the door that the lady was not at home? nor could she, upon telling her name, obtain any admission. This, considering the account she had received of the lady's cold, greatly surprized her; and she returned home very much vexed at her disappointment.

Amelia, who had no suspicion that Mrs James was really at home, and, as the phrase is, was denied, would have made a second visit the next morning, had she not been prevented by a cold, which she herself now got, and which was attended with a slight fever. This confined her several days to her house, during which Booth officiated as her nurse, and never stirred from her.

In all this time she heard not a word from Mrs James, which gave her some uneasiness, but more astonishment. The tenth day when she was perfectly recovered, about nine in the evening, when she and her husband were just going to supper, she heard a most violent thundering at the door, and presently after a rustling of silk upon her stair-case, at the same time a female voice cried out pretty loud – 'Bless me! what am I to climb up another pair of stairs?' Upon which, Amelia, who well knew the voice, presently ran to the door, and ushered in Mrs James most splendidly drest; who put on as formal a countenance, and made as formal a courtesie to her old friend, as if she had been her very distant acquaintance.

Poor Amelia, who was going to rush into her friend's arms, was struck motionless by this behaviour; but recollecting her spirits, as she had an excellent presence of mind, she presently understood what the lady meant, and resolved to treat her in her own way. Down therefore the company sat, and silence prevailed for some time, during which Mrs James surveyed the room with more attention than she would have bestowed on one much finer. At length the conversation began, in which the weather and the diversions of the town, were well canvassed. Amelia, who was a woman of great humour, performed her part to admiration; so that a by-stander would have doubted, in every other article than dress, which of the two was the most accomplished fine lady.

After a visit of twenty minutes, during which not a word of any former occurrences was mentioned, nor indeed any subject of discourse started, except only those two above-mentioned, Mrs James rose from her chair, and retired in the same formal manner in which she had approached. We will pursue her, for the sake of the contrast, during the rest of the evening. She went from Amelia directly to a rout,[24] where she spent two hours in a croud of company, talked again and again over the diversions and news of the town, played two rubbers at whist, and then retired to her own apartment, where having past another hour in undressing herself, she went to her own bed.

Booth and his wife, the moment their companion was gone, sat down to supper on a piece of cold meat, the remains of their dinner. After which, over a pint of wine, they entertained themselves for a while with the ridiculous behaviour of their visitant. But Amelia declaring she rather saw her as the object of pity than anger, turned the discourse to pleasanter topics. The little actions of their children, the former scenes, and future prospects of their life, furnished them with many pleasant ideas, and the contemplation of Amelia's recovery threw Booth into raptures. At length they retired, happy in each other.

It is possible some readers may be no less surprized at the behaviour of Mrs James, than was Amelia herself, since they may have perhaps received so favourable an impression of that lady from the account given of her by Mr Booth, that her present demeanour may seem unnatural and inconsistent with her former character. But they will be pleased to consider the great alteration in her circumstances, from a state of dependency on a brother, who was himself no better than a soldier of fortune, to that of being wife to a man of a very large estate, and considerable rank in life. And what was her present behaviour more than that of a fine lady, who considered form and show as essential ingredients of human happiness, and imagined all friendship to consist in ceremony, courtesies, messages and visits? In which opinion she hath the honour to think with much the larger part of one sex, and no small number of the other.

CHAPTER 7

Containing a very extraordinary and pleasant incident.

THE next evening Booth and Amelia went to walk in the Park with their children. They were now on the verge of the Parade,[25] and Booth was describing to his wife the several buildings round it; when on a sudden Amelia missing her little boy cried out, 'where's little Billy;' upon which Booth casting his eyes over the grass saw a foot-soldier shaking the boy at a little distance. At this sight, without making any answer to his wife, he leapt over the rails; and running directly up to the fellow, who had a firelock with a bayonet fixed in his hand, he seized him by the collar, and tript up his heels, and at the same time wrested his arms from him. A serjeant upon duty seeing the affray at some distance ran presently up, and being told what had happened, gave the sentinel a hearty curse, and told him he deserved to be hanged. A bystander gave this information; for Booth was returned with his little boy to meet Amelia, who staggered towards him as fast as she could, all pale and breathless, and scarce able to support her tottering limbs. The serjeant now came up to Booth, to make an apology for the behaviour of the soldier, when of a sudden he turned almost as pale as Amelia herself. He stood silent whilst Booth was employed in comforting and recovering his wife; and then addressing himself to him, said, 'bless me! lieutenant, could I imagine it had been your honour; and was it my little master that the rascal used so – I am glad I did not know it, for I should certainly have run my halbert into him.'

Booth presently recognized his old faithful servant Atkinson, and gave him a hearty greeting; saying he was very glad to see him in his present situation. 'Whatever I am,' answered the serjeant, 'I shall always think I owe it to your honour.' Then taking the little boy by the hand – he cried, 'what a vast fine young gentleman master is grown!' and cursing the soldier's inhumanity swore heartily he would make him pay for it.

As Amelia was much disordered with her fright, she did not recollect her foster-brother, till he was introduced to her by Booth; but she no sooner knew him, than she bestowed a most obliging smile on him; and calling him by the name of honest Joe said she was heartily glad to see him in England. – 'See, my dear,' cries Booth, 'what preferment your old friend is come to. You would scarce know him, I believe, in his present state of finery.' 'I am very well pleased to see it,' answered Amelia, 'and I wish him joy of being made an officer, with all my heart.' In fact, from what Mr Booth said, joined to the serjeant's laced coat, she believed that he had obtained a commission. So weak and absurd is human vanity, that this mistake of Amelia's possibly put poor Atkinson out of countenance; for he looked at this instant more silly than he had ever done in his life; and making her a most respectful bow muttered something about obligations, in a scarce articulate or intelligible manner.

The serjeant had indeed among many other qualities, that modesty which a Latin author[26] honours by the name of ingenuous. Nature had given him this, notwithstanding the meanness of his birth; and six years conversation in the army, had not taken it away. To say the truth, he was a noble fellow; and Amelia by supposing he had a commission in the Guards[27] had been guilty of no affront to that honourable body.

Booth had a real affection for Atkinson, tho' in fact he knew not half his merit. He acquainted him with his lodgings, where he earnestly desired to see him.

Amelia, who was far from being recovered from the terrors into which the seeing her husband engaged with the soldier had thrown her, desired to go home; nor was she well able to walk without some assistance. While she supported herself therefore on her husband's arm, she told Atkinson, she should be obliged to him, if he would take care of the children. He readily accepted the office; but upon offering his hand to Miss, she refused, and burst into tears. Upon which the tender mother resigned Booth to her children, and put herself under the serjeant's protection; who conducted her safe home, tho' she often declared she feared she should drop down by the way. The fear of which so affected the serjeant, (for besides the honour which he himself had for the lady, he knew how tenderly his friend loved her) that he was unable to speak; and had not his nerves been so strongly braced that nothing could shake them, he had enough in his mind to have set him a trembling equally with the lady.

When they arrived at the lodgings, the mistress of the house opened the door, who, seeing Amelia's condition, threw open the parlour, and begged her to walk in; upon which she immediately flung herself into a chair; and all present thought she would have fainted away. – However she escaped that misery, and having drank a glass of water with a little white wine mixed in it, she began in a little time to regain her complexion, and at length assured Booth that she was perfectly recovered; but declared she had never undergone so much, and earnestly begged him never to be so rash for the future. She then called her little boy, and gently chid him; saying, 'you must never do so more, Billy; you see what mischief you might have brought upon your father; and what you have made me suffer.' 'La! mamma,' said the child, 'what harm did I do? I did not know that people might not walk in the green fields in London. I am sure if I did a fault, the man punished me enough for it; for he pinched me almost through my slender arm.' He then bared his little arm, which was greatly discoloured by the injury it had received. – Booth uttered a most dreadful execration at this sight; and the serjeant, who was now present, did the like.

Atkinson now returned to his guard, and went directly to the officer to acquaint him with the soldier's inhumanity; but he who was about fifteen years of age,[28] gave the serjeant a great curse, and said the soldier had done very well; for that idle boys ought to be corrected. This however did not satisfy poor Atkinson, who the next day, as soon as the guard was relieved, beat the fellow most unmercifully, and told him he would remember him as long as he stayed in the regiment.

Thus ended this trifling adventure, which some readers will perhaps be pleased with seeing related at full length. None, I think, can fail drawing one observation from it; namely, how capable the most insignificant accident is of disturbing human happiness, and of producing the most unexpected and dreadful events.

A reflection which may serve to many moral and religious uses.

This accident produced the first acquaintance between the mistress of the house, and her lodgers; for hitherto they had scarce exchanged a word together. But the great concern which the good woman had shewn on Amelia's account at this time, was not likely to pass unobserved, or unthanked either by the husband or wife. Amelia therefore, as soon as she was able to go up stairs, invited Mrs Ellison (for that was her name) to her apartment, and desired the favour of her to stay to supper. She readily complied; and they past a very agreeable evening together, in which the two women seemed to have conceived a most extraordinary liking to each other.

Tho' beauty in general doth not greatly recommend one woman to another, as it is too apt to create envy; yet in cases where this passion doth not interfere, a fine woman is often a pleasing object even to some of her own sex; especially when her beauty is attended with a certain air of affability, as was that of Amelia in the highest degree. She was, indeed, a most charming woman; and I know not whether the little scar on her nose did not rather add to, than diminish her beauty.

Mrs Ellison therefore was as much charmed with the loveliness of her fair lodger, as with all her other engaging qualities. She was indeed so taken with Amelia's beauty, that she could not refrain from crying out in a kind of transport of admiration, 'upon my word, Captain Booth, you are the happiest man in the world. Your lady is so extremely handsome, that one cannot look at her without pleasure.'

This good woman herself had none of these attractive charms to the eye. Her person was short, and immoderately fat; her features were none of the most regular; and her complexion (if indeed she ever had a good one) had considerably suffered by time.

Her good humour and complaisance, however, were highly pleasing to Amelia. Nay, why should we conceal the secret satisfaction which that lady felt from the compliments paid to her person? since such of my readers as like her best will not be sorry to find that she was a woman.

CHAPTER 8

Containing various matters.

A FORTNIGHT had now past, since Booth had seen or heard from the colonel; which did not a little surprize him, as they had parted so good friends, and as he had so cordially undertaken his cause concerning the memorial, on which all his hopes depended.

The uneasiness which this gave him, farther encreased on finding that his friend refused to see him: for he had paid the colonel a visit at nine in the morning, and was told he was not stirring; and at his return back an hour afterwards, the servant said his master was gone out; of which Booth was certain of the falsehood; for he had, during that whole hour, walked backwards and forwards within sight of the colonel's door, and must have seen him, if he had gone out within that time.

The good colonel however did not long suffer his friend to continue in the deplorable state of anxiety; for the very next morning Booth received his memorial inclosed in a letter, acquainting him that Mr James had mentioned his affair to the person he proposed; but that the great man[29] had so many engagements on his hands, that it was impossible for him to make any further promises at this time.

The cold and distant stile of this letter, and indeed the whole behaviour of James, so different from what it had been formerly, had something so mysterious in it, that it greatly puzzled and perplexed poor Booth; and it was so long before he was able to solve it, that the reader's curiosity will perhaps be obliged to us for not leaving him so long in the dark as to this matter. The true reason then of the colonel's conduct was this: his unbounded generosity, together with the unbounded extravagance, and consequently the great necessity[30] of Miss Mathews, had at length overcome the cruelty of that lady, with whom he likewise had luckily no rival. Above all, the desire of being revenged on Booth, with whom she was to the highest degree enraged, had perhaps contributed not a little to his success: for she had no sooner condescended to a familiarity with her new lover, and discovered that Captain James, of whom she had heard so much from Booth, was no other than the identical colonel, than she employed every art of which she was mistress, to make an utter breach of friendship between these two. For this purpose she did not scruple to insinuate, that the colonel was not at all obliged to the character given of him by his friend; and to the account of this latter she placed most of the cruelty which she had shewn to the former.

Had the colonel made a proper use of his reason, and fairly examined the probability of the fact, he could scarce have been imposed upon to believe a matter so inconsistent with all he knew of Booth, and in which that gentleman must have sinned against all the laws of honour without any visible temptation. But in solemn fact, the colonel was so intoxicated with his love, that it was in the power of his mistress to have persuaded him of any thing; besides, he had an interest in giving her credit: for he was not a little pleased with finding a reason for hating the man, whom he could not help hating without any reason, at least, without any which he durst fairly assign even to himself. Henceforth therefore he abandoned all friendship for Booth, and was more inclined to put him out of the world, than to endeavour any longer at supporting him in it.

Booth communicated this letter to his wife, who endeavoured, as usual, to the utmost of her power to console him under one of the greatest afflictions which, I think, can befal a man, namely, the unkindness of a friend; but he had luckily at the same time the greatest blessing in his possession, the kindness of a faithful and beloved wife. A blessing however, which tho' it compensates most of the evils of life, rather serves to aggravate the misfortune of distress'd circumstances, from the consideration of the share which she is to bear in them.

This afternoon Amelia received a second visit from Mrs Ellison, who acquainted her that she had a present of a ticket for the oratorio,[31] which would carry two persons into the gallery; and therefore begged the favour of her company thither.

Amelia with many thanks acknowledged the civility of Mrs Ellison; but declined accepting her offer; upon which Booth very strenuously insisted on her going, and said to her, 'my dear, if you knew the satisfaction I have in any of your pleasures, I am convinced you would not refuse the favour Mrs Ellison is so kind to offer you; for as you are a lover of music, you, who have never been at an oratorio, cannot conceive how you will be delighted.' 'I well know your goodness, my dear,' answered Amelia, 'but I cannot think of leaving my children without some person more proper to take care of them than this poor girl.' Mrs Ellison removed this objection, by offering her own servant, a very discreet matron, to attend them; but notwithstanding this, and all she could say with the assistance of Booth, and of the children themselves, Amelia still persisted in her refusal; and the mistress of the house, who knew how far good breeding allows persons to be pressing on these occasions, took her leave.

She was no sooner departed, than Amelia looking tenderly on her husband said, 'how can you, my dear creature, think that music hath any charms for me at this time – or indeed do you believe that I am capable of any sensation worthy the name of pleasure, when neither you nor my children are present, or bear any part of it?'

An officer of the regiment to which Booth had formerly belonged, hearing from Atkinson where he lodged, now came to pay him a visit. He told him that several of their old acquaintance were to meet the next Wednesday at a tavern, and very strongly pressed him to be one of the company. Booth was in truth what is called a hearty fellow, and loved now and then to take a chearful glass with his friends; but he excused himself at this time. His friend declared he would take no denial, and he growing very importunate, Amelia at length seconded him. Upon this Booth answered, 'well, my dear, since you desire me, I will comply, but on one condition, that you go at the same time to the oratorio.' Amelia thought this request reasonable enough, and gave her consent; of which Mrs Ellison presently received the news, and with great satisfaction.

It may perhaps be asked why Booth could go to the tavern, and not to the oratorio with his wife. In truth then, the tavern was within hallowed ground, that is to say, in the verge of the court: for of five officers that were to meet there, three besides Booth were confined to that air, which hath been always found extremely wholesome to a broken military constitution. And here if the good reader will pardon the pun,[32] he will scarce be offended at the observation; since how is it possible that without running in debt, any persons should maintain the dress and appearance of a gentleman, whose income is not half so good as that of a porter? It is true, that this allowance, small as it is, is a great expence to the public; but if several more unnecessary charges were spared, the public might perhaps bear a little encrease of this without much feeling it. They would not, I am sure, have equal reason to complain at contributing to the maintenance of a set of brave fellows, who, at the hazard of their health, their limbs and their lives, have maintained the safety and honour of their country; as when they find themselves taxed to the support of a set of drones, who have not the least merit or claim to their favour; and who, without contributing in any manner to the good of the hive, live luxuriously on the labours of the industrious bee.[33]

CHAPTER 9

In which Amelia, with her friend, goes to the oratorio.

NOTHING happened between the Monday and the Wednesday worthy a place in this history. Upon the evening of the latter the two ladies went to the oratorio, and were there time enough to get a first row in the galery. Indeed there was only one person in the house when they came: for Amelia's inclinations, when she gave a loose to them, were pretty eager for this diversion, she being a great lover of music, and particularly of Mr Handel's compositions. Mrs Ellison was, I suppose, a great lover likewise of music, for she was the more impatient of the two; which was rather the more extraordinary, as these entertainments were not such novelties to her as they were to poor Amelia.

Tho' our ladies arrived full two hours before they saw the back of Mr Handel; yet this time of expectation did not hang extremely heavy on their hands; for besides their own chat, they had the company of the gentleman, whom they found at their first arrival in the galery; and who, though plainly, or rather roughly dressed, very luckily for the women happened to be not only well-bred, but a person of very lively conversation. The gentleman on his part seemed highly charmed with Amelia, and in fact was so: for, though he restrained himself entirely within the rules of good-breeding, yet was he in the highest degree officious to catch at every opportunity of shewing his respect, and doing her little services. He procured her a book and wax-candle, and held the candle for her himself during the whole entertainment.

At the end of the oratorio, he declared he would not leave the ladies till he had seen them safe into their chairs or coach; and at the same time very earnestly entreated that he might have the honour of waiting on them. Upon which Mrs Ellison, who was a very good-humoured woman, answered, 'Ay sure, sir, if you please; you have been very obliging to us; and a dish of tea shall be at your service at any time;' and then told him where she lived.

The ladies were no sooner seated in their hackney-coach, than Mrs Ellison burst into a loud laughter, and cried, 'I'll be hanged, madam, if you have not made a conquest to night; and what is very pleasant, I believe the poor gentleman takes you for a single lady.' 'Nay,' answered Amelia very gravely, 'I protest I began to think at last he was rather too particular, though he did not venture at a word that I could be offended at; but if you fancy any such thing, I am sorry you invited him to drink tea.' 'Why so?' replied Mrs Ellison, 'Are you angry with a man for liking you? If you are, you will be angry with almost every man that sees you. If I was a man myself, I declare I should be in the number of your admirers. Poor gentleman, I pity him heartily; he little knows that you have not a heart to dispose of. For my own part, I should not be surprized at seeing a serious proposal of marriage: for I am convinced he is a man of fortune, not only by the politeness of his address, but by the fineness of his linen, and that valuable diamond-ring on his finger. But you will see more of him when he comes to tea.' 'Indeed I shall not,' answered Amelia, 'tho' I believe you only rally me; I hope you have a better opinion of me, than to think I would go willingly into the company of a man, who had an improper liking for me.' Mrs Ellison, who was one of the gayest women in the world, repeated the words, improper liking, with a laugh; and cried, 'My dear Mrs Booth, believe me, you are too handsome and too good-humour'd for a prude. How can you affect being offended at what I am convinced is the greatest pleasure of woman-kind, and chiefly I believe of us virtuous women? for I assure you, notwithstanding my gaiety, I am as virtuous as any prude in Europe.' 'Far be it from me, madam,' said Amelia, 'to suspect the contrary of abundance of women, who indulge themselves in much greater freedoms than I should take, or have any pleasure in taking: for I solemnly protest, if I know my own heart, the liking of all men, but of one, is a matter quite indifferent to me, or rather would be highly disagreeable.'

This discourse brought them home, where Amelia finding her children asleep, and her husband not returned, invited her companion to partake of her homely fare, and down they sat to supper together. The clock struck twelve; and no news being arrived of Booth, Mrs Ellison began to express some astonishment at his stay, whence she launched into a general reflexion on husbands, and soon past to some particular invectives on her own. 'Ah, my dear madam,' says she, 'I know the present state of your mind by what I have myself often felt formerly. I am no stranger to the melancholy tone of a midnight clock. It was my misfortune to drag on a heavy chain above fifteen years with a sottish yoke-fellow. But how can I wonder at my fate; since I see even your superiour charms can't confine a husband from the bewitching pleasures of a bottle.' 'Indeed, madam,' says Amelia, 'I have no reason to complain, Mr Booth is one of the soberest of men; but now and then to spend a late hour with his friend, is, I think, highly excusable.' 'O, no doubt,' cries Mrs Ellison, 'if he can excuse himself; but if I was a man –' Here Booth came in and interrupted the discourse. Amelia's eyes flashed with joy the moment he appeared; and he discovered no less pleasure in seeing her. His spirits were indeed a little elevated with wine, so as to heighten his good-humour, without in the least disordering his understanding, and made him such delightful company, that though it was past one in the morning, neither his wife, nor Mrs Ellison, thought of their beds during a whole hour.

Early the next morning the serjeant came to Mr Booth's lodgings, and with a melancholy countenance acquainted him, that he had been the night before at an ale-house, where he heard one Mr Murphy an attorney declare, that he would get a warrant backed against one Captain Booth at the next Board of Green-Cloth.[34] 'I hope, sir,' said he, 'your honour will pardon me; but by what he said, I was afraid he meant your honour; and therefore I thought it my duty to tell you; for I knew the same thing happen to a gentleman here t'other day.'

Booth gave Mr Atkinson many thanks for his information. 'I doubt not,' said he, 'but I am the person meant; for it would be foolish in me to deny that I am liable to apprehensions of that sort.' 'I hope, sir,' said the serjeant, 'your honour will soon have reason to fear no man living; but in the mean time, if any accident should happen, my bail is at your service as far as it will go; and I am a housekeeper, and can swear myself worth £100.' Which hearty and friendly declaration received all those acknowledgments from Booth, which it really deserved.

The poor gentleman was greatly alarmed at this news; but he was altogether as much surprized at Murphy's being the attorney employed against him, as all his debts, except only to Colonel James, arose in the country, where he did not know that Mr Murphy had any acquaintance. However, he made no doubt that he was the person intended, and resolved to remain a close prisoner in his own lodgings, till he saw the event of a proposal which had been made him the evening before at the tavern, where an honest gentleman, who had a post under the government, and who was one of the company, had promised to serve him with the Secretary at War, telling him, that he made no doubt of procuring him whole pay in a regiment abroad, which in his present circumstances was very highly worth his acceptance; when indeed that, and a goal, seemed to be the only alternatives that offered themselves to his choice.

Mr Booth and his lady spent that afternoon with Mrs Ellison. An incident which we should scarce have mentioned, had it not been that Amelia gave, on this occasion, an instance of that prudence which should never be off its guard in married women of delicacy: for before she would consent to drink tea with Mrs Ellison, she made conditions, that the gentleman who had met them at the oratorio should not be let in. Indeed this circumspection proved unnecessary in the present instance; for no such visitor ever came; a circumstance which gave great content to Amelia: for that lady had been a little uneasy at the raillery of Mrs

Ellison, and had upon reflexion magnified every little compliment made her, and every little civility shewn her by the unknown gentleman, far beyond the truth. These imaginations, now all subsided again; and she imputed all that Mrs Ellison had said, either to raillery or mistake.

A young lady made a fourth with them at whist, and likewise stayed the whole evening. Her name was Bennet. She was about the age of five and twenty; but sickness had given her an older look, and had a good deal diminished her beauty; of which, young as she was, she plainly appeared to have only the remains in her present possession. She was in one particular the very reverse of Mrs Ellison, being altogether as remarkably grave as the other was gay. This gravity was not however attended with any sourness of temper: on the contrary, she had much sweetness in her countenance, and was perfectly well-bred. In short, Amelia imputed her grave deportment to her ill health, and began to entertain a compassion for her, which in good minds, that is to say, in minds capable of compassion, is certain to introduce some little degree of love or friendship.

Amelia was in short so pleased with the conversation of this lady, that, though a woman of no impertinent curiosity, she could not help taking the first opportunity of enquiring who she was. Mrs Ellison said, that she was an unhappy lady, who had married a young clergyman for love, who, dying of a consumption, had left her a widow in very indifferent circumstances.[35] This account made Amelia still pity her more, and consequently added to the liking which she had already conceived for her. Amelia therefore desired Mrs Ellison to bring her acquainted with Mistress Bennet, and said she would go any day with her to make that lady a visit. 'There need be no ceremony,' cried Mrs Ellison, 'she is a woman of no form: and as I saw plainly she was extremely pleased with Mrs Booth, I am convinced I can bring her to drink tea with you any afternoon you please.'

The two next days Booth continued at home, highly to the satisfaction of his Amelia, who really knew no happiness out of his company, nor scarce any misery in it. She had indeed at all times so much of his company when in his power, that she had no occasion to assign any particular reason for his staying with her, and consequently it could give her no cause of suspicion. The Saturday one of her children was a little disordered with a feverish complaint, which confined her to her room, and prevented her drinking tea in the afternoon with her husband in Mrs Ellison's apartment, where a noble lord, a cousin of Mrs Ellison's, happened to be present: for though that lady was reduced in her circumstances, and obliged to let out part of her house in lodgings, she was born of a good family, and had some considerable relations.

His lordship was not himself in any office of state; but his fortune gave him great authority with those who were. Mrs Ellison therefore very bluntly took an opportunity of recommending Booth to his consideration. She took the first hint from my lord's calling the gentleman captain – to which she answered – 'Ay, I wish your lordship would make him so. It would be but an act of justice, and I know it is in your power to do much greater things.' She then mentioned Booth's services, and the wounds he had received at the siege, of which she had heard a faithful account from Amelia. – Booth blushed, and was as silent as a young virgin at the hearing her own praises. His lordship answered, 'Cousin Ellison, you know you may command my interest; nay, I shall have a pleasure in serving one of Mr Booth's character: for my part, I think merit in all capacities ought to be encouraged; but I know the Ministry are greatly pestered with solicitations at this time. However, Mr Booth may be assured I will take the first opportunity; and in the mean time I shall be glad of seeing him any morning he pleases.' For all these declarations, Booth was not wanting in acknowledgments to the generous peer, any more than he was in secret gratitude to the lady, who had shewn so friendly and uncommon a zeal in his favour.

The reader, when he knows the character of this nobleman, may perhaps conclude that his seeing Booth alone was a lucky circumstance; for he was so passionate an admirer of women, that he could scarce have escaped the attraction of Amelia's beauty. And few men, as I have observed, have such disinterested generosity as to serve a husband the better, because they are in love with his wife, unless she will condescend to pay a price beyond the reach of a virtuous woman.

BOOK V

CHAPTER 1

In which the reader will meet with an old acquaintance.

BOOTH's affairs were put on a better aspect than they had ever worn before, and he was willing to make use of the opportunity of one day in seven to taste the fresh air.

At nine in the morning he went to pay a visit to his old friend Colonel James, resolving, if possible, to have a full explanation of that behaviour which appeared to him so mysterious; but the colonel was as inaccessible as the best defended fortress; and it was as impossible for Booth to pass beyond his entry, as the Spaniards found it to take Gibraltar. He received the usual answers; first, that the colonel was not stirring, and an hour after that he was gone out. All that he got by asking further questions was only to receive still ruder and ruder answers; by which, if he had been very sagacious, he might have been satisfied how little worth his while it was to desire to go in: for the porter at a great man's door is a kind of thermometer, by which you may discover the warmth or coldness of his master's friendship. Nay, in the highest stations of all, as the great man himself hath his different kinds of salutation, from an hearty embrace with a kiss, and my dear Lord, or dear Sir Charles, down to, well Mr — what would you have me do? So the porter to some bows with respect, to others with a smile, to some he bows more, to others less low, to others not at all. Some he just lets in, and others he just shuts out. And in all this they so well correspond, that one would be inclined to think that the great man and his porter had compared their lists together, and like two actors concerned to act different parts in the same scene, had rehearsed their parts privately together, before they ventured to perform in public.

Tho' Booth did not perhaps see the whole matter in this just light, for that in reality it is; yet he was discerning enough to conclude, from the behaviour of the servant, especially when he considered that of the master likewise, that he had entirely lost the friendship of James; and this conviction gave him a concern, that not only the flattering prospect of his lordship's favour was not able to compensate; but which even obliterated, and made him for a while forget the situation in which he had left his Amelia; and he wandered about almost two hours, scarce knowing where he went, till at last he dropt into a coffee-house near St James's, where he sat himself down.

He had scarce drank his dish of coffee, before he heard a young officer of the Guards cry to another, 'Od d—m me Jack, here he comes – here's old honour and dignity, faith.' Upon which he saw a chair open, and out issued a most erect and stately figure indeed, with a vast perriwig on his head, and a vast hat under his arm. This august personage having entered the room walked directly up to the upper end, where having paid his respects to all present of any note, to each according to seniority, he at last cast his eyes on Booth, and very civilly, tho' somewhat coldly, asked him how he did.

Booth, who had long recognized the features of his old acquaintance Major Bath, returned the compliment with a very low bow; but did not venture to make the first advance to familiarity, as he was truly possessed of that quality which the Greeks considered in the highest light of honour, and which we term modesty;[1] tho' indeed neither ours nor the Latin language hath any word adequate to the idea of the original.

The colonel, after having discharged himself of two or three articles of news, and made his comments upon them, when the next chair to him became vacant, called upon Booth to fill it. He then asked him several questions relating to his affairs; and when he heard he was out of the army, advised him earnestly to use all means to get in again, saying, that he was a pretty lad, and they must not lose him.

Booth told him in a whisper, that he had a great deal to say to him on that subject, if they were in a more private place; upon this the colonel proposed a walk in the Park, which the other readily accepted.

During their walk, Booth opened his heart, and among other matters acquainted Colonel Bath that he feared he had lost the friendship of Colonel James; 'though I am not,' said he, 'conscious of having done the least thing to deserve it.'

Bath answered, 'You are certainly mistaken, Mr Booth. I have indeed scarce seen my brother since my coming to town: for I have been here but two days; however I am convinced he is a man of too nice honour to do any thing inconsistent with the true dignity of a gentleman.' Booth answered, 'he was far from accusing him of any thing dishonourable.' – 'D—n me,' said Bath, 'if there is a man alive can, or dare accuse him: if you have the least reason to take any thing ill, why don't you go to him? you are a gentleman, and his rank doth not protect him from giving you satisfaction.' 'The affair is not of any such kind,' says Booth, 'I have great obligations to the colonel, and have more reason to lament than complain; and if I could but see him, I am convinced I should have no cause for either; but I cannot get within his house; it was but an hour ago, a servant of his turned me rudely from the door.' 'Did a servant of my brother use you rudely?' said the colonel, with the utmost gravity. 'I do not know, sir, in what light you see such things; but to me the affront of a servant is the affront of the master; and if he doth not immediately punish it, by all the dignity of man, I would see that master's nose between my fingers.' Booth offered to explain, but to no purpose; the colonel was got into his stilts; and it was impossible to take him down, nay, it was as much as Booth could possibly do to part with him without an actual quarrel; nor would he perhaps have been able to have accomplished it, had not the colonel by accident turned at last to take Booth's side of the question; and before they separated, he swore many oaths that James should give him proper satisfaction.

Such was the end of this present interview, so little to the content of Booth, that he was heartily concerned he had ever mentioned a syllable of the matter to his honourable friend.

CHAPTER 2

In which Booth pays a visit to the noble lord.

WHEN that day of the week returned in which Mr Booth chose to walk abroad, he went to wait on the noble peer according to his kind invitation.

Booth now found a very different reception with this great man's porter, from what he had met with at his friend the colonel's. He no sooner told his name, than the porter with a bow told him his lordship was at home; the door immediately flew wide open; and he was conducted to an antichamber, where a servant told him he would acquaint his lordship with his arrival. Nor did he wait many minutes before the same servant returned, and ushered him to his lordship's apartment.

He found my lord alone, and was received by him in the most courteous manner imaginable. After the first ceremonials were over, his lordship began in the following words: 'Mr Booth, I do assure you you are very much obliged to my cousin Ellison. She hath given you such a character that I shall have a pleasure in doing any thing in my power to serve you. – But it will be very difficult, I am afraid, to get you a rank at home. In the West Indies perhaps, or in some regiment abroad it may be more easy; and when I consider your reputation as a soldier, I make no doubt of your readiness to go to any place where the service of your country shall call you.' Booth answered, 'that he was highly obliged to his lordship, and assured him, he would with great chearfulness attend his duty in any part of the world. The only thing grievous in the exchange of countries,' said he, 'in my opinion is to leave those I love behind me, and I am sure, I shall never have a second trial equal to my first. It was very hard, my lord, to leave a young wife big with her first child, and so affected with my absence, that I had the utmost reason to despair of ever seeing her more. After such a demonstration of my resolution to sacrifice every other consideration to my duty, I hope your lordship will honour me with some confidence, that I shall make no objection to serve in any country.' 'My dear

Mr Booth,' answered the lord, 'you speak like a soldier, and I greatly honour your sentiments. Indeed I own the justice of your inference from the example you have given: for, to quit a wife as you say, in the very infancy of marriage, is, I acknowledge, some trial of resolution.' Booth answered with a low bow, and then after some immaterial conversation, his lordship promised to speak immediately to the Minister, and appointed Mr Booth to come to him again on the Wednesday morning, that he might be acquainted with his patron's success. The poor man now blushed and looked silly, till after some time, he summoned up all his courage to his assistance, and relying on the other's friendship, he opened the whole affair of his circumstances, and confessed that he did not dare stir from his lodgings above one day in seven. His lordship expressed great concern at this account, and very kindly promised to take some opportunity of calling on him at his cousin Ellison's, when he hoped, he said, to bring him comfortable tidings.

Booth soon afterwards took his leave with the most profuse acknowledgments for so much goodness, and hastened home to acquaint his Amelia with what had so greatly overjoyed him. She highly congratulated him on his having found so generous and powerful a friend, towards whom both their bosoms burnt with the warmest sentiments of gratitude. She was not however contented, till she had made Booth renew his promise in the most solemn manner of taking her with him. After which they sat down with their little children to a scrag[2] of mutton and broth, with the highest satisfaction, and very heartily drank his lordship's health in a pot of porter.

In the afternoon this happy couple, if the reader will allow me to call poor people happy, drank tea with Mrs Ellison, where his lordship's praises being again repeated by both the husband and wife were very loudly echoed by Mrs Ellison. While they were here, the young lady, whom we have mentioned at the end of the last book to have made a fourth at whist, and with whom Amelia seemed so much pleased, came in: she was just returned to town from a short visit in the country, and her present visit was unexpected. It was however very agreeable to Amelia, who liked her still better upon a second interview, and was resolved to solicit her further acquaintance.

Mrs Bennet still maintained some little reserve, but was much more familiar and communicative than before. She appeared moreover to be as little ceremonious as Mrs Ellison had reported her, and very readily accepted Amelia's apology for not paying her the first visit, and agreed to drink tea with her the very next afternoon.

Whilst the above-mentioned company were sitting in Mrs Ellison's parlour, Serjeant Atkinson passed by the window, and knocked at the door. Mrs Ellison no sooner saw him, than she said, 'pray, Mr Booth, who is that genteel young serjeant? He was here every day last week, to enquire after you.' This was indeed a fact; the serjeant was apprehensive of the design of Murphy; but as the poor fellow had received all his answers from the maid or Mrs Ellison, Booth had never heard a word of the matter. He was however greatly pleased with what he was now told, and burst forth into great praises of the serjeant, which were seconded by Amelia, who added that he was her foster-brother, and she believed one of the honestest fellows in the world.

'And I'll swear,' cries Mrs Ellison, 'he is one of the prettiest – Do, Mr Booth, desire him to walk in. A serjeant of the Guards is a gentleman, and I had rather give such a man as you describe a dish of tea, than any Beau Fribble[3] of them all.'

Booth wanted no great solicitation to shew any kind of regard to Atkinson; and accordingly the serjeant was ushered in, tho' not without some reluctance on his side. There is perhaps nothing more uneasy than those sensations which the French call the *mauvaise honte*,[4] nor any more difficult to conquer; and poor Atkinson would, I am persuaded, have mounted a breach with less concern, than he shewed in walking cross a room before three ladies, two of whom were his avowed well wishers.

Tho' I do not entirely agree with the late learned Mr Essex[5] the celebrated dancing-master's opinion, that dancing is the rudiment of polite education, as he would, I apprehend, exclude every other art and science; yet is it certain, that persons whose feet have never been under the hands of the professors of that art, are apt to discover this want in their education in every motion, nay, even when they stand or sit still. They seem indeed to be over-burthened with limbs, which they know not how to use, as if when nature hath finished her work, the dancing-master still is necessary to put it in motion.

Atkinson was at present an example of this observation, which doth so much honour to a profession for which I have a very high regard. He was handsome and exquisitely well made; and yet, as he had never learnt to dance, he made so awkward an appearance in Mrs Ellison's parlour, that the good lady herself, who had invited him in, could at first scarce refrain from laughter at his behaviour.

He had not however been long in the room, before admiration of his person got the better of such risible ideas. So great is the advantage of beauty in men as well as women, and so sure is this quality in either sex of procuring some regard from the beholder.

The exceeding courteous behaviour of Mrs Ellison, joined to that of Amelia and Booth, at length dissipated the uneasiness of Atkinson; and he gained sufficient confidence to tell the company some entertaining stories of accidents, that had happened in the army within his knowledge; which tho' they greatly pleased all present, are not however of consequence enough to have a place in this history.

Mrs Ellison was so very importunate with her company to stay supper, that they all consented. As for the serjeant, he seemed to be none of the least welcome guests. She was indeed so pleased with what she had heard of him, and what she saw of him, that when a little warmed with wine, for she was no flincher at the bottle, she began to indulge some freedoms in her discourse towards him, that a little offended Amelia's delicacy, nay, they did not seem to be highly relished by the other lady. Tho' I am far from insinuating that these exceeded the bounds of decorum, or were indeed greater liberties than ladies of the middle age, and especially widows, do frequently allow to themselves.

CHAPTER 3

Relating principally to the affairs of Serjeant Atkinson.

THE next day, when all the same company, Atkinson only excepted, assembled in Amelia's apartment, Mrs Ellison presently began to discourse of him, and that in terms not only of approbation, but even of affection. She called him her clever serjeant, and her dear serjeant, repeated often that he was the prettiest fellow in the army, and said it was a thousand pities he had not a commission; for that if he had, she was sure he would become a general.

'I am of your opinion, madam,' answered Booth; 'and he hath got £100 of his own already, if he could find a wife now to help him to two or three hundred more, I think he might easily get a commission in a marching regiment; for I am convinced there is no colonel in the army would refuse him.'

'Refuse him indeed!' said Mrs Ellison, 'no. He would be a very pretty colonel that did. And upon my honour, I believe there are very few ladies who would refuse him, if he had but a proper opportunity of soliciting them. The colonel and the lady both would be better off, than with one of those pretty masters that I see walking about, and dragging their long swords after them, when they should rather drag their leading-strings.'[6]

'Well said,' cries Booth, 'and spoken like a woman of spirit. – Indeed, I believe, they would be both better served.'

'True captain,' answered Mrs Ellison, 'I would rather leave the two first syllables out of the word gentleman, than the last.'

'Nay I assure you,' replied Booth, 'there is not a quieter creature in the world. Tho' the fellow hath the bravery of a lion, he hath the meekness of a lamb. I can tell you stories enow of that kind, and so can my dear Amelia when he was a boy.'

'O if the match sticks there,' cries Amelia, 'I positively will not spoil his fortune by my silence. I can answer for him from his infancy, that he was one of the best natured lads in the world. I will tell you a story or two of him, the truth of which I can testify from my own knowledge. When he was but six years old, he was at play with me at my mother's house, and a great pointing-dog bit him through the leg. The poor lad in the midst of the anguish of his wound, declared he was overjoyed it had not happened to miss, (for the same dog had just before snapt at me, and my petticoats had been my defence.) Another instance of his goodness which greatly recommended him to my father, and which I have loved him for ever since, was this: my father was a great lover of birds, and strictly forbad the spoiling of their nests. Poor Joe was one day caught upon a tree, and being concluded guilty, was severely lashed for it; but it was afterwards discovered that another boy, a friend of Joe's, had robbed the nest of its young ones, and poor Joe had climbed the tree in order to restore them, notwithstanding which he submitted to the punishment rather than he would impeach his companion. But if these stories appear childish and trifling, the duty of kindness he hath shewn to his mother, must recommend him to every one. Ever since he hath been fifteen years old, he hath more than half supported her; and when my brother died, I remember particularly Joe at his desire, for he was much his favourite, had one of his suits given him, but instead of his becoming finer on that occasion, another young fellow came to church in my brother's cloaths, and my old nurse appeared the same Sunday in a new gown, which her son had purchased for her with the sale of his legacy.'

'Well, I protest, he is a very worthy creature,' said Mrs Bennet.

'He is a charming fellow,' cries Mrs Ellison, – 'but then the name of serjeant, Captain Booth, there, as the play says, my pride brings me off again.

> *And whatsoever the sages charge on pride,*
> *The angels fall, and twenty other good faults beside;*
> *On earth I'm sure – I'm sure – something – calling*
> *Pride saves man and our sex too from falling.*'[7]

Here a footman's rap at the door shook the room. Upon which Mrs Ellison running to the window, cry'd out, 'let me die if it is not my lord, what shall I do? I must be at home to him, but suppose he should enquire for you, captain, what shall I say? or will you go down with me?'

The company were in some confusion at this instant, and before they had agreed on any thing, Booth's little girl came running into the room, and said, 'there was a prodigious great gentleman coming up stairs.' She was immediately followed by his lordship, who, as he knew Booth must be at home, made very little or no enquiry at the door.

Amelia was taken somewhat at a surprize, but she was too polite to shew much confusion: for though she knew nothing of the town, she had had a genteel education, and kept the best company the country afforded. The ceremonies therefore past as usual, and they all sat down.

His lordship soon addressed himself to Booth, saying, 'As I have what I think good news for you, sir, I could not delay giving myself the pleasure of communicating it to you. I have mentioned your affair where I promised you, and I have no doubt of my success. One may easily perceive, you know, from the manner of people's behaving upon such occasions; and indeed, when I related your case I found there was much inclination to serve you. Great men, Mr Booth, must do things in their own time; but I think you may depend on having something done very soon.'

Booth made many acknowledgments for his lordship's goodness, and now a second time paid all the thanks which would have been due, even had the favour been obtained. This art of promising is the economy[8] of a great man's pride, a sort of good husbandry in conferring favours, by which they receive ten-fold in acknowledgments for every obligation, I mean among those who really intend the service: for there are others who cheat poor men of their thanks, without ever designing to deserve them at all.

This matter being sufficiently discussed, the conversation took a gayer turn; and my lord began to entertain the ladies with some of that elegant discourse, which tho' most delightful to hear, it is impossible should ever be read.

His lordship was so highly pleased with Amelia, that he could not help being somewhat particular to her; but this particularity distinguished itself only in a higher degree of respect, and was so very polite and so very distant, that she herself was pleased, and at his departure, which was not till he had far exceeded the length of a common visit, declared he was the finest gentleman she had ever seen, with which sentiment her husband and Mrs Ellison both entirely concurred.

Mrs Bennet on the contrary exprest some little dislike to my lord's complaisance, which she called excessive. 'For my own part,' said she, 'I have not the least relish for those very fine gentlemen; what the world generally calls politeness, I term insincerity; and I am more charmed with the stories which Mrs Booth told us of the honest serjeant, than with all that the finest gentlemen in the world ever said in their lives.'

'O to be sure,' cries Mrs Ellison, '*All for Love, or the World well Lost*,[9] is a motto very proper for some folks to wear in their coat of arms; but the generality of the world will, I believe, agree with that lady's opinion of my cousin, rather than with Mrs Bennet.'

Mrs Bennet seeing Mrs Ellison took offence at what she said, thought proper to make some apology, which was very readily accepted, and so ended the visit.

We cannot however put an end to the chapter without observing, that such is the ambitious temper of beauty, that it may always apply to itself that celebrated passage in Lucan,

> *Nec quenquam jam ferre potest Caesarve priorem*
> *Pompeiusve parem.*[10] –

Indeed, I believe, it may be laid down as a general rule, that no woman who hath any great pretensions to admiration, is ever well pleased in a company, where she perceives herself to fill only the second place. This observation however I humbly submit to the judgment of the ladies, and hope it will be considered as retracted by me, if they shall dissent from my opinon.

CHAPTER 4

Containing matters that require no preface.

WHEN Booth and his wife were left alone together, they both extremely exulted in their good fortune, in having found so good a friend as his lordship; nor were they wanting in very warm expressions of their gratitude towards Mrs Ellison. After which they began to lay down schemes of living when Booth should have his commission of captain, and after the exactest computation, concluded that with economy, they should be able to save, at least, fifty pounds a year out of their income, in order to pay their debts.

These matters being well settled, Amelia asked Booth what he thought of Mrs Bennet. 'I think, my dear,' answered Booth, 'that she hath been formerly a very pretty woman.' 'I am mistaken,' replied she, 'if she be not a very good creature. I don't know I ever took such a liking to any one on so short an acquaintance. I fancy she hath been a very spritely woman: for if you observe, she discovers by starts a great vivacity in her countenance.' 'I made the same observation,' cries Booth: 'sure some strange misfortune hath befallen her.' 'A misfortune indeed!' answered Amelia, 'sure child, you forget what Mrs Ellison told us, that she had lost a beloved husband. A misfortune which I have often wondered at any woman's surviving,' – at which words, she cast a tender look at Booth, and presently afterwards throwing herself upon his neck, cried – 'O Heavens! what a happy creature am I; when I consider the dangers you have gone through, how I exult in my bliss!' The good natured reader will suppose that Booth was not deficient in returning such tenderness, after which the conversation became too fond to be here related.

The next morning Mrs Ellison addressed herself to Booth as follows: 'I shall make no apology, sir, for what I am going to say, as it proceeds from my friendship to yourself and your dear lady. I am convinced then, sir, there is something more than accident in your going abroad only one day in the week. Now, sir, if, as I am afraid, matters are not altogether as well as I wish them, I beg, since I do not believe you are provided with a lawyer, that you will suffer me to recommend one to you. The person I shall mention is, I assure you, of much ability in his profession, and I have known him do great services to gentlemen under a cloud. Do not be ashamed of your circumstances, my dear friend. They are a much greater scandal to those, who have left so much merit unprovided for.'

Booth gave Mrs Ellison abundance of thanks of her kindness, and explicitely confest to her that her conjectures were right, and without hesitation accepted the offer of her friend's assistance.

Mrs Ellison then acquainted him with her apprehensions on his account. She said she had both yesterday and this morning seen two or three very ugly suspicious fellows pass several times by her window. 'Upon all accounts,' said she, 'my dear sir, I advise you to keep yourself close confined till the lawyer hath been with you. I am sure he will get you your liberty, at least of walking about within the verge – There's something to be done with the Board of Green Cloth, I don't know what; but this I know, that several gentlemen have lived here a long time very comfortably, and have defied all the vengance of their creditors. However, in the mean time you must be a close prisoner with your lady; and I believe there is no man in England but would exchange his liberty for the same goal.'

She then departed, in order to send for the attorney, and presently afterwards the serjeant arrived with news of the like kind. He said he had scraped an acquaintance with Murphy. 'I hope your honour will pardon me,' cries Atkinson, 'but I pretended to have a small demand upon your honour myself, and offered to employ him in the business. Upon which he told me, that if I would go with him to the Marshal's Court,[11] and make affidavit of my debt, he should be able very shortly to get it me; "for I shall have the captain in hold," cries he, "within a day or two." I wish,' said the serjeant, 'I could do your honour any service. Shall I walk about all day before the door? or shall I be porter and watch it in the inside, till your honour can find some means of securing yourself? I hope you will not be offended at me, but I beg you would take care of falling into Murphy's hands; for he hath the character of the greatest villain upon earth. I am afraid you will think me too bold, sir; but I have a little money, if it can be of any service, do, pray your honour, command it. It can never do me so much good any other way. Consider, sir, I owe all I have to yourself, and my dear mistress.'

Booth stood a moment, as if he had been thunder-struck, and then, the tears bursting from his eyes, he said: 'Upon my soul, Atkinson, you overcome me. I scarce ever heard of so much goodness, nor do I know how to express my sentiments of it. But be assured, as for your money, I will not accept it, and let it satisfy you, that in my present circumstances it would do me no essential service; but this be assured of likewise, that whilst I live, I shall never forget the kindness of the offer – However, as I apprehend I may be in some danger of fellows getting into the house, for a day or two, as I have no guard but a poor little girl, I will not refuse the goodness you offer to shew in my protection. And I make no doubt but Mrs Ellison will let you sit in her parlour for that purpose.'

Atkinson with the utmost readiness undertook the office of porter; and Mrs Ellison as readily allotted him a place in her back-parlour, where he continued three days together, from eight in the morning till twelve at night; during which time he had sometimes the company of Mrs Ellison, and sometimes of Booth, Amelia, and Mrs Bennet too; for this last had taken as great a fancy to Amelia, as Amelia had to her, and therefore as Mr Booth's affairs were now no secret in the neighbourhood, made her frequent visits during the confinement of her husband, and consequently her own.

Nothing, as I remember, happened in this interval of time, more worthy notice than the following card, which Amelia received from her old acquaintance Mrs James. 'Mrs James sends her compliments to Mrs Booth, and desires to know how she does; for as she hath not had the favour of seeing her at her own house, or of meeting her in any public place, in so long time, fears it may be owing to ill health.'

Amelia had long given over all thoughts of her friend, and doubted not but that she was as entirely given over by her; she was very much surprized at this message, and under some doubt whether it was not meant as an insult, especially from the mention of public places, which she thought so inconsistent with her present circumstances, of which she supposed Mrs James was well apprized. However, at the entreaty of her husband, who languished for nothing more than to be again reconciled to his friend James, Amelia undertook to pay the lady a visit, and to examine into the mystery of this conduct, which appeared to her so unaccountable.

Mrs James received her with a degree of civility that amazed Amelia, no less than her coldness had done before. She resolved to come to an *éclaircissement*, and having sat out some company that came in, when they were alone together, Amelia, after some silence, and many offers to speak, at last said, 'my dear Jenny, (if you will now suffer me to call you by so familiar a name,) have you entirely forgot a certain young lady who had the pleasure of being your intimate acquaintance at Montpelier?' – 'Whom do you mean, dear madam?' cries Mrs James, with great concern. 'I mean myself,' answered Amelia. – 'You surprize me, madam,' replied Mrs James. 'How can you ask me that question?' 'Nay, my dear, I do not intend to offend you,' cries Amelia; 'but I am really desirous to solve to myself the reason of that coldness which you shewed me, when you did me the favour of a visit. Can you think, my dear, I was not disappointed when I expected to meet an intimate friend, to receive a cold formal visitant? I desire you to examine your own heart, and answer me honestly, if you do not think I had some little reason to be dissatisfied with your behaviour?' 'Indeed, Mrs Booth,' answered the other lady, 'you surprize me very much; if there was any thing displeasing to you in my behaviour, I am extremely concerned at it. I did not know I had been defective in any of the rules of civility, but if I was, madam, I ask your pardon.' 'Is civility then, my dear,' replied Amelia, 'a synonymous term with friendship? Could I have expected when I parted the last time with Miss Jenny Bath, to have met her the next time in the shape of a fine lady, complaining of the hardship of climbing up two pair of stairs to visit me, and then approaching me with the distant air of a new or a slight acquaintance? Do you think, my dear Mrs James, if the tables had been turned, if my fortune had been as high in the world as yours, and you in my distress and abject condition, that I would not have climbed as high as the Monument[12] to visit you?' 'Sure, madam,' cries Mrs James, 'I mistake you, or you have greatly mistaken me. Can you complain of my not visiting you, who have owed me a visit almost these three weeks? Nay, did I not even then send you a card, which sure was doing more than all the friendship and good breeding in the world required; but indeed as I had met you in no public place, I really thought you was ill?' 'How can you mention public places to me,' said Amelia, 'when you can hardly be a stranger to my present situation? Did you not know, madam, that I was ruined?' 'No indeed, madam, did I not,' replied Mrs James, 'I am sure I should have been highly concerned if I had.'

'Why sure, my dear,' cries Amelia, 'you could not imagine that we were in affluent circumstances, when you found us in such a place, and in such a condition.' 'Nay, my dear,' answered Mrs James, 'since you are pleased to mention it first yourself, I own I was a little surprized to see you in no better lodgings; but I concluded you had your own reasons for liking them; and for my own part, I have laid it down as a positive rule, never to enquire into the private affairs of any one, especially of my friends. I am not of the humour of some ladies, who confine the circle of their acquaintance to one part of the town, and would not be known to visit in the City[13] for the world. For my part, I never dropt an acquaintance with any one, while it was reputable to keep it up; and I can solemnly declare, I have not a friend in the world for whom I have a greater esteem than I have for Mrs Booth.'

At this instant the arrival of a new visitant put an end to the discourse, and Amelia soon after took her leave without the least anger, but with some little unavoidable contempt for a lady, in whose opinion, as we have hinted before, outward form and ceremony constituted the whole essence of friendship; who valued all her acquaintance alike, as each individual served equally to fill up a place in her visiting roll, and who in reality had not the least concern for the good qualities or well-being of any of them.

CHAPTER 5

Containing much heroic matter.

AT the end of three days Mrs Ellison's friend had so far purchased Mr Booth's liberty, that he could walk again abroad within the verge, without any danger of having a warrant backed against him by the Board before he had notice. As for the ill-looked persons that had given the alarm, it was now discovered that another unhappy gentleman, and not Booth was the object of their pursuit.

Mr Booth now being delivered from his fears, went, as he had formerly done, to take his morning-walk in the Park. Here he met Colonel Bath in company with some other officers, and very civilly paid his respects to him. But instead of returning the salute, the colonel looked him full in the face with a very stern countenance; and if he could be said to take any notice of him, it was in such a manner as to inform him he would take no notice of him.

Booth was not more hurt than surprized at this behaviour, and resolved to know the reason of it. He therefore watched an opportunity till the colonel was alone, and then walked boldly up to him, and desired to know if he had given him any offence, – the colonel answered hastily, 'Sir, I am above being offended with you, nor do I think it consistent with my dignity to make you any answer.' Booth replied, 'I don't know, sir, that I have done any thing to deserve this treatment.' – 'Look'ee, sir,' cries the colonel, 'if I had not formerly had some respect for you, I should not think you worth my resentment. However, as you are a gentleman born and an officer, and as I have had an esteem for you, I will give you some marks of it by putting it in your power to do yourself justice. I will tell you therefore, sir, that you have acted like a scoundrel.' – 'If we were not in the Park,' answered Booth warmly, 'I would thank you very properly for the compliment.' – 'O sir!' cries the colonel, 'we can be soon in a convenient place.' Upon which Booth answered he would attend him wherever he pleased. – The Colonel then bid him come along, and strutted forward directly up Constitution Hill to Hyde Park, Booth following him at first, and afterwards walking before him, till they came to that place which may be properly called the field of blood, being that part a little to the left of the Ring,[14] which heroes have chosen for the scene of their exit out of this world.

Booth reached the Ring some time before the colonel; for he mended not his pace any more than a Spaniard.[15] To say truth, I believe it was not in his power; for he had so long accustomed himself to one and the same strut, that as a horse used always to trotting can scarce be forced into a gallop, so could no passion force the colonel to alter his pace.

At length, however, both parties arrived at the lists, where the colonel very deliberately took off his wig and coat, and laid them on the grass, and then drawing his sword, advanced to Booth, who had likewise his drawn weapon in his hand, but had made no other preparation for the combat.

The combatants now engaged with great fury, and after two or three passes, Booth run the colonel through the body and threw him on the ground, at the same time possessing himself of the colonel's sword.

As soon as the colonel was become master of his speech, he called out to Booth in a very kind voice, and said, 'you have done my business, and satisfied me that you are a man of honour, and that my brother James must have been mistaken: for I am convinced, that no man who will draw his sword in so gallant a manner, is capable of being a rascal, d—n me, give me a buss, my dear boy, I ask your pardon for that infamous appellation I dishonoured your dignity with; but, d—n me, if it was not purely out of love, and to give you an opportunity of doing yourself justice, which I own you have done like a man of honour. What may be the consequence I know not, but, I hope, at least I shall live to reconcile you with my brother.'

Booth shewed great concern and even horror in his countenance. 'Why, my dear colonel,' said he, 'would you force me to this? For Heaven's sake, tell me, what I have ever done to offend you.'

'Me!' cried the colonel. 'Indeed, my dear child, you never did any thing to offend me. Nay, I have acted the part of a friend to you in the whole affair. I maintained your cause with my brother as long as decency would permit, I could not flatly contradict him, tho' indeed I scarce believed him. But what could I do; if I had not fought with you, I must have been obliged to have fought with him? However, I hope, what is done will be sufficient, and that matters may be *discomodated* without your being put to the necessity of fighting any more on this occasion.'

'Never regard me,' cried Booth eagerly, 'for Heaven's sake think of your own preservation. Let me put you into a chair, and get you a surgeon.'

'Thou art a noble lad,' cries the colonel, who was now got on his legs, 'and I am glad the business is so well over. For tho' your sword went quite through, it slanted so, that I apprehend there is little danger of life. However, I think there is enough done to put an honourable end to the affair, especially as you was so hasty to disarm me. I bleed a little, but I can walk to the house by the water;[16] and if you will send me a chair thither I shall be obliged to you.'

As the colonel refused any assistance, (indeed he was very able to walk without it, tho' with somewhat less dignity than usual) Booth set forward to Grosvenor Gate,[17] in order to procure the chair, and soon after returned with one to his friend; whom having conveyed into it, he attended himself on foot into Bond Street, where then lived a very eminent surgeon.[18]

The surgeon having probed the wound turned towards Booth who was apparently the guilty person, and said with a smile, 'Upon my word, sir, you have performed the business with great dexterity.'

'Sir,' cries the colonel to the surgeon, 'I would not have you imagine I am afraid to die. I think I know more what belongs to the dignity of a man; and, I believe, I have shewn it at the head of a line of battle. Do not impute my concern to that fear, when I ask you whether there is or is not any danger?'

'Really, colonel,' answered the surgeon, who well knew the complexion[19] of the gentleman then under his hands, 'it would appear like presumption to say, that a man who hath been just run through the body, is in no manner of danger. But this, I think, I may assure you, that I yet perceive no very bad symptoms, and unless something worse should appear, or a fever be the consequence, I hope you may live to be again, with all your dignity, at the head of a line of battle.'

'I am glad to hear that is your opinion,' quoth the colonel, 'for I am not desirous of dying, tho' I am not afraid of it. But if any thing worse than you apprehend should happen, I desire you will be a witness of my declaration, that this young gentleman is entirely innocent. I forced him to do what he did. My dear Booth, I am pleased matters are as they are. You are the first man that ever gained an advantage over me; but it was very lucky for you that you disarmed me, and I doubt not, but you have the *equannanimity* to think so. If the business therefore hath ended without doing any thing to the purpose, it was fortune's pleasure, and neither of our faults.'

Booth heartily embraced the colonel, and assured him of the great satisfaction he had received from the surgeon's opinion; and soon after the two combatants took their leave of each other. The colonel after he was drest, went in a chair to his lodgings, and

Booth walked on foot to his; where he luckily arrived without meeting any of Mr Murphy's gang; a danger which never once occurred to his imagination till he was out of it.

The affair he had been about had indeed so entirely occupied his mind, that it had obliterated every other idea; among the rest, it caused him so absolutely to forget the time of the day, that tho' he had exceeded the time of dining above two hours, he had not the least suspicion of being at home later than usual.

CHAPTER 6

In which the reader will find matter worthy his consideration.

AMELIA having waited above an hour for her husband concluded, as he was the most punctual man alive, that he had met with some engagement abroad, and sat down to her meal with her children; which, as it was always uncomfortable in the absence of her husband, was very short; so that before his return all the apparatus of dining was entirely removed.

Booth sat some time with his wife, expecting every minute when the little maid would make her appearance; at last curiosity, I believe, rather than appetite, made him ask, how long it was to dinner? 'To dinner! my dear,' answered Amelia; 'sure you have dined, I hope?' Booth replied in the negative; upon which his wife started from her chair, and bestirred herself as nimbly to provide him a repast, as the most industrious hostess in the kingdom doth, when some unexpected guest of extraordinary quality arrives at her house.

The reader hath not, I think, from any passages hitherto recorded in this history had much reason to accuse Amelia of a blameable curiosity; he will not, I hope, conclude that she gave an instance of any such fault, when, upon Booth's having so long overstaid his time, and so greatly mistaken the hour of the day, and upon some other circumstances of his behaviour: (for he was too honest to be good at concealing any of his thoughts) she said to him, after he had done eating, 'My dear, I am sure something more than ordinary hath happened to-day, and I beg you will tell me what it is.'

Booth answered, that nothing of any consequence had happened; that he had been detained by a friend, whom he met accidentally, longer than he expected. In short, he made many shuffling and evasive answers, not boldly lying out, which perhaps would have succeeded, but poorly and vainly endeavouring to reconcile falsehood with truth. An attempt which seldom fails to betray the most practised deceiver.

How impossible was it therefore for poor Booth to succeed in an art for which nature had so entirely disqualified him. His countenance indeed confessed faster than his tongue denied; and the whole of his behaviour gave Amelia an alarm, and made her suspect something very bad had happened; and as her thoughts turned presently on the badness of their circumstances, she feared some mischief from his creditors had befallen him: for she was too ignorant of such matters to know, that if he had fallen into the hands of the Philistines,[20] (which is the name given by the faithful to bailiffs) he would hardly have been able so soon to recover his liberty. Booth at last perceived her to be so uneasy, that as he saw no hopes of contriving any fiction to satisfy her, he thought himself obliged to tell her the truth, or at least part of the truth, and confessed that he had had a little skirmish with Colonel Bath, in which he said the colonel had received a slight wound, not at all dangerous; and this, says he, is all the whole matter. 'If it be so,' cries Amelia, 'I thank Heaven no worse hath happened; but why, my dear, will you ever converse with that madman, who can embrace a friend one moment, and fight with him the next?' 'Nay, my dear,' answered Booth, 'you yourself must confess, though he be a little too much on the *qui vive*,[21] he is a man of great honour and good-nature.' 'Tell me not,' replied she, 'of such good-nature and honour as would sacrifice a friend and a whole family to a ridiculous whim. O Heaven,' cried she, falling upon her knees, 'from what misery have I escaped, from what have these poor babes escaped thro' your gracious providence this day!' – Then turning to her husband – she cry'd – 'But are you sure the monster's wound is no more dangerous than you say? a monster surely I may call him, who can quarrel with a man that could not, that I am convinced would not offend him.'

Upon this question Booth repeated the assurances which the surgeon had given them, perhaps with a little enlargement, which pretty well satisfied Amelia; and instead of blaming her husband for what he had done, she tenderly embraced him, and again returned thanks to Heaven for his safety.

In the evening Booth insisted on paying a short visit to the colonel, highly against the inclination of Amelia, who by many arguments and entreaties endeavoured to dissuade her husband from continuing an acquaintance; in which she said she should always foresee much danger for the future. However, she was at last prevailed upon to acquiesce; and Booth went to the colonel, whose lodgings happened to be in the verge as well as his own.

He found the colonel in his night-gown and his great chair, engaged with another officer at a game at chess. He rose immediately, and having heartily embraced Booth, presented him to his friend, saying he had the honour to introduce to him as brave and as *fortitudinous* a man as any in the king's dominions. – He then took Booth with him into the next room, and desired him not to mention a word of what had happened in the morning, saying, 'I am very well satisfied that no more hath happened; however, as it ended in nothing, I could wish it might remain a secret.' Booth told him he was heartily glad to find him so well, and promised never to mention it more to any one.

The game at chess being but just begun, and neither of the parties having gained any considerable advantage, they neither of them insisted on continuing it; and now the colonel's antagonist took his leave, and left the colonel and Booth together.

As soon as they were alone, the latter earnestly entreated the former to acquaint him with the real cause of his anger; 'for may I perish,' cries Booth, 'if I can even guess what I have ever done to offend either you, or your brother Colonel James.'

'Look'ee, child,' cries the colonel, 'I tell you I am for my own part satisfied: for I am convinced that a man who will fight can never be a rascal; and therefore why should you enquire any more of me at present? When I see my brother James, I hope to reconcile all matters, and perhaps no more swords need be drawn on this occasion.' But Booth still persisting in his desire, the colonel after some hesitation, with a tremendous oath, cry'd out, 'I do not think myself at liberty to refuse you after the indignity I offered you; so since you demand it of me, I will inform you. My brother told me you had used him dishonourably, and had *divellicated* his character behind his back. He gave me his word too that he was well assured of what he said. What could I have done, though I own to you I did not believe him, and your behaviour since hath convinced me I was in the right, I must either have given him the lye, and fought with him, or else I was obliged to behave as I did, and fight with you. And now, my lad, I leave it to you to do as you please; but if you are laid under any necessity to do yourself further justice, it is your own fault.'

'Alas! colonel,' answered Booth, 'besides the obligations I have to the colonel, I have really so much love for him, that I think of nothing less than resentment.[22] All I wish is to have this affair brought to an *éclaircissement*, and to satisfy him that he is in an error: for though his assertions are cruelly injurious, and I have never deserved them; yet I am convinced he would not say what he did not himself think. Some rascal envious of his friendship for me hath belied me to him; and the only resentment[23] I desire is to convince him of his mistake.'

At these words – the colonel *grinned horribly a ghastly smile*,[24] or rather sneer, and answered, 'Young gentleman, you may do as you please; but by the eternal dignity of man, if any man breathing had taken a liberty with my character, – here, here – Mr Booth (*shewing his fingers*) here – d—n me should be his nostrils, he should breathe through my hands, and breathe his last – d—n me.'

Booth answered, 'I think colonel I may appeal to your testimony that I dare do myself justice; since he who dare draw his sword against you, can hardly be supposed to fear any other person; but I repeat to you again that I love Colonel James so well, and am so greatly obliged to him, that it would be almost indifferent to me, whether I directed my sword against his breast, or my own.'

The colonel's muscles were considerably softened by Booth's last speech; but he again contracted them into a vast degree of fierceness, before he cryed out – 'Boy, thou hast reason enough to be vain; for thou are the first person that ever could proudly say he gained an advantage over me in combat. I believe indeed, thou art not afraid of any man breathing, and as I know thou hast some obligations to my brother, I do not discommend thee; for nothing more becomes the dignity of man than gratitude. Besides, as I am satisfied my brother can produce the author of the slander – I say, I am satisfied of that, d—n me, if any man alive dares assert the contrary; for that would be to make my brother himself a liar, I will make him produce his author; and then, my dear boy, your doing yourself proper justice there, will bring you finely out of the whole affair. As soon as my surgeon gives me leave to go abroad, which, I hope, will be in a few days, I will bring my brother James to a tavern, where you shall meet us; and I will engage my honour, my whole dignity to you, to make you friends.'

This assurance of the colonel gave Booth great pleasure; for few persons ever loved a friend better than he did James; and as for doing military justice on the author of that scandalous report which had incensed his friend against him, not Bath himself was ever more ready on such an occasion than Booth to execute it. He soon after took his leave, and returned home in high spirits to his Amelia, whom he found in Mrs Ellison's apartment, engaged in a party at ombre[25] with that lady, and her right honourable cousin.

His lordship had, it seems, had a second interview with the great man, and having obtained further hopes (for I think there was not yet an absolute promise) of success in Mr Booth's affairs, his usual good nature brought him immediately to acquaint Mr Booth with it. As he did not therefore find him at home, and as he met with the two ladies together, he resolved to stay till his friend's return, which he was assured would not be long, especially as he was so lucky, he said, to have no particular engagement that whole evening.

We remarked before, that his lordship, at the first interview with Amelia, had distinguished her by a more particular address from the other ladies; but that now appeared to be rather owing to his perfect good breeding, as she was then to be considered as the mistress of the house, than from any other preference. His present behaviour made this still more manifest; for as he was now in Mrs Ellison's apartment, tho' she was his relation and old acquaintance, he applied his conversation rather more to her than to Amelia. His eyes indeed were now and then guilty of the contrary distinction, but this was only by stealth; for they constantly withdrew the moment they were discovered. In short, he treated Amelia with the greatest distance, and at the same time with the most profound and awful[26] respect; his conversation was so general, so lively, and so obliging, that Amelia, when she added to his agreeableness the obligations she had to him for his friendship to Booth, was certainly as much pleased with his lordship, as any virtuous woman can possibly be with any man, besides her own husband.

CHAPTER 7

Containing various matters.

WE HAVE already mentioned the good humour in which Booth returned home; and the reader will easily believe it was not a little encreased by the good humour in which he found his company. My lord received him with the utmost marks of friendship and affection, and told him that his affairs went on as well almost as he himself could desire, and that he doubted not very soon to wish him joy of a company.

When Booth had made a proper return to all his lordship's unparallelled goodness, he whispered Amelia that the colonel was entirely out of danger, and almost as well as himself. This made her satisfaction complete, threw her into such spirits, and gave such a lustre to her eyes, that her face, as Horace says,[27] was too dazzling to be looked at; it was certainly too handsome to be looked at without the highest admiration.

His lordship departed about ten o'clock, and left the company in raptures with him, especially the two ladies, of whom it is difficult to say which exceeded the other in his commendations. Mrs Ellison swore she believed he was the best of all humankind; and Amelia, without making any exception, declared he was the finest gentleman, and most agreeable man she had ever seen in her life; adding, it was great pity he should remain single. 'That's true indeed,' cries Mrs Ellison, 'and I have often lamented it, nay I am astonished at it, considering the great liking he always shews for our sex, and he may certainly have the choice of all. The real reason, I believe, is his fondness for his sister's children. I declare, madam, if you was to see his behaviour to them, you would think they were his own. Indeed he is vastly fond of all manner of children.' 'Good creature,' cries Amelia, 'if ever he doth me the honour of another visit, I am resolved I will shew him my little things. I think, Mrs Ellison, as you say my lord loves children, I may say without vanity, he will not see many such.' 'No indeed, will he not,' answered Mrs Ellison, 'and now I think on't, madam, I wonder at my own stupidity in never making the offer before; but since you put it into my head, if you will give me leave, I'll take master and miss to wait on my lord's nephew and niece. They are very pretty behaved children; and little master and miss will be, I dare swear, very happy in their acquaintance; besides, if my lord himself should see them, I know what will happen; for he is the most generous of all human beings.'

Amelia very readily accepted the favour which Mrs Ellison offered her; but Booth exprest some reluctance. 'Upon my word, my dear,' said he, with a smile, 'this behaviour of ours puts me in mind of the common conduct of beggars; who, whenever they receive a favour, are sure to send other objects to the same fountain of charity. Don't we, my dear, repay our obligations to my lord in the same manner, by sending our children a begging to him?'

'O beastly!' cries Mrs Ellison, 'how could such a thought enter your brains! I protest, madam, I begin to grow ashamed of this husband of yours. How can you have so vulgar a way of thinking. Begging indeed! the poor little dear things a begging – If my lord was capable of such a thought, tho' he was my own brother instead of my cousin, I should scorn him too much ever to enter his doors.' – 'O dear madam,' answered Amelia, 'you take Mr Booth too seriously, when he was only in jest; and the children shall wait upon you whenever you please.'

Tho' Booth had been a little more in earnest than Amelia had represented him, and was not perhaps quite so much in the wrong as he was considered by Mrs Ellison; yet seeing there were two to one against him, he wisely thought proper to recede, and let his simile go off with that air of a jest, which his wife had given it.

Mrs Ellison however could not let it pass without paying some compliments to Amelia's understanding, nor without some obscure reflexions upon Booth, with whom she was more offended than the matter required. She was indeed a woman of most profuse generosity, and could not bear a thought which she deemed vulgar or sneaking. She afterwards launced forth the most profuse encomiums of his lordship's liberality, and concluded the evening with some instances which he had given of that virtue, which if not the noblest, is perhaps one of the most useful to society, with which great and rich men can be endowed.

The next morning early Serjeant Atkinson came to wait on Lieutenant Booth, and desired to speak with his honour in private. Upon which, the lieutenant and serjeant took a walk together in the Park. Booth expected every minute when the serjeant would open his mouth, under which expectation he continued till he came to the end of the Mall, and so he might have continued till he came to the end of the world: for tho' several words stood at the end of the serjeant's lips, there they were likely to remain for ever. He was indeed in the condition of a miser, whom a charitable impulse hath impelled to draw a few pence to the edge of his pocket, where they are altogether as secure, as if they were in the bottom: for, as the one hath not the heart to part with a farthing; so neither had the other the heart to speak a word.

Booth at length wondering that the serjeant did not speak, asked him what his business was, when the latter with a stammering voice began the following apology: 'I hope, sir, your honour will not be angry, nor take any thing amiss of me. I do assure you, it was not of my seeking, nay, I dare not proceed in the matter without first asking your leave. Indeed, if I had taken any liberties from the goodness you have been pleased to shew me, I should look upon myself as one of the most worthless and despicable of wretches; but nothing is farther from my thoughts. I know the distance which is between us; and because your honour hath been so kind and good as to treat me with more familiarity than any other officer ever did, if I had been base enough to take any freedoms, or to encroach upon your honour's goodness, I should deserve to be whipt through the regiment. I hope therefore, sir, you will not suspect me of any such attempt.'

'What can all this mean, Atkinson,' cries Booth, 'what mighty matter would you introduce with all this previous apology?'

'I am almost ashamed and afraid to mention it,' answered the serjeant, 'and yet I am sure, your honour will believe what I have said, and not think any thing owing to my own presumption; and at the same time I have no reason to think you would do any thing to spoil my fortune in an honest way, when it is dropt into my lap without my own seeking. For may I perish if it is not all the lady's own goodness, and I hope in Heaven with your honour's leave, I shall live to make her amends for it.' – In a word, that we may not detain the reader's curiosity quite so long as he did Booth's, he acquainted that gentleman that he had had an offer of marriage from a lady of his acquaintance, to whose company he had introduced him, and desired his permission to accept of it.

Booth must have been very dull indeed, if after what the serjeant had said, and after what he had heard Mrs Ellison say, he had wanted any information concerning the lady. He answered him briskly and chearfully, that he had his free consent to marry any woman whatever; 'and the greater and richer she is,' added he, 'the more I shall be pleased with the match. I don't enquire who the lady is,' said he, smiling, 'but I hope she will make as good a wife, as I am convinced her husband will deserve.'

'Your Honour hath been always too good to me,' cries Atkinson, 'but this I promise you, I will do all in my power to merit the kindness she is pleased to shew me. I will be bold to say she will marry an honest man, tho' he is but a poor one; and she shall never want any thing which I can give her or do for her, while my name is Joseph Atkinson.'

'And so her name is a secret, Joe; is it?' cries Booth.

'Why, sir,' answered the serjeant, 'I hope your honour will not insist upon knowing that, as I think it would be dishonourable in me to mention it.'

'Not at all,' replied Booth, 'I am the farthest in the world from any such desire. I know thee better than to imagine thou wouldst disclose the name of a fair lady.' Booth then shook Atkinson heartily by the hand, and assured him earnestly of the joy he had in his good fortune; for which the good serjeant failed not of making all proper acknowledgments. After which they parted, and Booth returned home.

As Mrs Ellison opened the door, Booth hastily rushed by; for he had the utmost difficulty to prevent laughing in her face. He ran directly up stairs, and throwing himself into a chair discharged such a fit of laughter as greatly surprized, and at first almost frightned his wife.

Amelia, it will be supposed, presently enquired into the cause of this phenomenon, with which Booth, as soon as he was able (for that was not within a few minutes) acquainted her. The news did not affect her in the same manner it had affected her husband. On the contrary, she cried, 'I protest I cannot guess what makes you see it in so ridiculous a light. I really think Mrs Ellison hath chosen very well. I am convinced Joe will make her one of the best of husbands; and in my opinion, that is the greatest blessing a woman can be possessed of.'

However, when Mrs Ellison came into her room a little while afterwards to fetch the children, Amelia became of a more risible disposition, especially when the former turning to Booth who was then present, said, 'So, captain, my *jantee*[28] serjeant was very early here this morning. I scolded my maid heartily for letting him wait so long in the entry like a *lacquais*, when she might have shewn him into my inner apartment.' At which words Booth burst out into a very loud laugh; and Amelia herself could no more prevent laughing than she could blushing.

'Heyday!' cries Mrs Ellison, 'what have I said to cause all this mirth?' and at the same time blushed, and looked very silly, as is always the case with persons who suspect themselves to be the objects of laughter, without absolutely taking what it is which makes them ridiculous.

Booth still continued laughing; but Amelia composing her muscles said, 'I ask your pardon, dear Mrs Ellison; but Mr Booth hath been in a strange gigling humour all this morning; and I really think it is infectious.'

'I ask your pardon too, madam,' cries Booth, 'but one is sometimes unaccountably foolish.'

'Nay, but seriously,' said she, 'what is the matter? – something I said about the serjeant, I believe; but you may laugh as much as you please, I am not ashamed of owning, I think him one of the prettiest fellows I ever saw in my life; and, I own, I scolded my maid at suffering him to wait in my entry; and where is the mighty ridiculous matter, pray?'

'None at all,' answered Booth, 'and, I hope, the next time he will be ushered into your inner apartment.'

'Why should he not, sir?' replied she. 'For wherever he is ushered, I am convinced he will behave himself as a gentleman should.'

Here Amelia put an end to the discourse, or it might have proceeded to very great lengths: for Booth was of a waggish inclination; and Mrs Ellison was not a lady of the nicest delicacy.

CHAPTER 8

The heroic behaviour of Colonel Bath.

BOOTH went this morning to pay a second visit to the colonel, where he found Colonel James. Both the colonel and the lieutenant appeared a little shocked at their first meeting; but matters were soon cleared up; for the former presently advanced to the latter, shook him heartily by the hand, and said – 'Mr Booth, I am ashamed to see you; for I have injured you, and I heartily ask your pardon. I am now perfectly convinced, that what I hinted to my brother, and which I find had like to have produced such fatal consequences, was entirely groundless. If you will be contented with my asking your pardon, and spare me the disagreeable remembrance of what led me into my error, I shall esteem it as the highest obligation.'

Booth answered, 'As to what regards yourself, my dear colonel, I am abundantly satisfied; but, as I am convinced, some rascal hath been my enemy with you in the cruellest manner, I hope, you will not deny me the opportunity of kicking him through the world.'

'By all the dignity of man,' cries Colonel Bath, 'the boy speaks with spirit, and his request is reasonable.'

Colonel James hesitated a moment, and then whispered Booth that he would give him all the satisfaction imaginable concerning the whole affair, when they were alone together; upon which Booth addressing himself to Colonel Bath, the discourse turned on other matters, during the remainder of the visit, which was but short, and then both went away together, leaving Colonel Bath as well as it was possible to expect, more to the satisfaction of Booth than of Colonel James, who would not have been displeased if his wound had been more dangerous: for he was grown somewhat weary of a disposition that he rather called captious than heroic, and which, as he every day more and more hated his wife, he apprehended might some time or other give him some trouble: for Bath was the most affectionate of brothers, and had often swore in the presence of James, that he would eat any man alive who should use his sister ill.

Colonel Bath was well satisfied that his brother and the lieutenant were gone out with a design of tilting, from which he offered not a syllable to dissuade them, as he was convinced it was right, and that Booth could not in honour take, nor the colonel give any less satisfaction. When they had been gone therefore about half an hour, he rang his bell, to enquire if there was any news of his brother; a question which he repeated every ten minutes, for the space of two hours, when having heard nothing of him, he began to conclude that both were killed on the spot.

While he was in this state of anxiety, his sister came to see him; for notwithstanding his desire of keeping it a secret, the duel had blazed all over the town. After receiving some kind congratulations on his safety, and some unkind hints concerning the warmth of his temper, the colonel asked her when she had seen her husband; she answered, not that morning. He then communicated to her his suspicion, told her he was convinced his brother had drawn his sword that day, and that as neither of them had heard any thing from him, he began to apprehend the worst that could happen.

Neither Miss Bellamy, nor Mrs Cibber,[29] were ever in a greater consternation on the stage, than now appeared in the countenance of Mrs James. 'Good Heavens! brother,' cries she, 'what do you tell me! you have frightened me to death. – Let your man get me a glass of water immediately, if you have not a mind to see me die before your face. When, where, how was this quarrel, why did you not prevent it, if you knew of it? Is it not enough to be every day tormenting me with hazarding your own life, but must you bring the life of one who you know must be and ought to be so much the dearest of all to me, into danger? Take your sword brother, take your sword, and plunge it into my bosom; it would be kinder of you than to fill it with such dreads and terrours.' – Here she swallowed the glass of water; and then threw herself back in her chair, as if she had intended to faint away.

Perhaps if she had so, the colonel would have lent her no assistance; for she had hurt him more than by ten thousand stabs. He sat erect in his chair, with his eye-brows knit, his forehead wrinkled, his eyes flashing fire, his teeth grating against each other, and breathing horrour all around him. In this posture he sat for some time silent, casting disdainful looks at his sister. At last, his voice found its way through a passion which had almost choaked him, and he cried out: 'Sister, what have I done to deserve the opinion you express of me? Which of my actions hath made you conclude that I am a rascal and a coward? Look at that poor sword, which never woman yet saw but in its sheath, what hath that done to merit your desire that it should be contaminated with the blood of a woman?'

'Alas! brother,' cried she, 'I know not what you say, you are desirous, I believe, to terrify me out of the little senses I have left. What can I have said in the agonies of grief, into which you threw me, to deserve this passion?'

'What have you said,' answered the colonel, 'you have said that which if a man had spoken, nay, d—n me, if he had but hinted that he durst even think, I would have made him eat my sword, by all the dignity of man, I would have crumbled his soul into powder. – But, I consider that the words were spoken by a woman, and I am calm again. Consider, my dear, that you are my sister, and behave yourself with more spirit. I have only mentioned to you my surmise. It may not have happened as I suspect; but let what will have happened, you will have the comfort that your husband hath behaved himself with becoming dignity, and lies in the bed of honour.'

'Talk not to me of such comfort,' replied the lady, 'it is a loss I cannot survive; but why do I sit here lamenting myself, I will go this instant and know the worst of my fate, if my trembling limbs will carry me to my coach. – Good morrow, dear brother, whatever becomes of me, I am glad to find you out of danger.' – The colonel paid her his proper compliments, and she then left the room, but returned instantly back; saying, 'Brother, I must beg the favour of you to let your footman step to my mantua-maker, I am sure it is a miracle in my present distracted condition, how it came into my head.' The footman was presently summoned, and Mrs James delivered him his message, which was to countermand the orders which she had given that very morning, to make her up a new suit of brocade. 'Heaven knows,' says she, 'now when I can wear brocade, or whether ever I shall wear it.' And now having repeated her message with great exactness, lest there should be any mistake, she again lamented her wretched situation, and then departed, leaving the colonel in full expectation of hearing speedy news of the fatal issue of the battle.

But tho' the reader should entertain the same curiosity, we must be excused from satisfying it, till we have first accounted for an incident which we have related in this very chapter, and which we think deserves some solution. The critic, I am convinced, already is apprized that I mean the friendly behaviour of James to Booth, which from what we had before recorded, seemed so little to be expected.

It must be remembered, that the anger which the former of these gentlemen had conceived against the latter, arose entirely from the false account given by Miss Mathews of Booth, whom that lady had accused to Colonel James of having as basely as wickedly traduced his character.

Now, of all the ministers of vengeance, there are none with whom the devil deals so treacherously, as with those whom he employs in executing the mischievous purposes of an angry mistress; for no sooner is revenge executed on an offending lover, than it is sure to be repented, and all the anger which before raged against the beloved object, returns with double fury on the head of his assassin.

Miss Mathews therefore no sooner heard that Booth was killed, (for so was the report at first, and by a colonel of the army) than she immediately concluded it to be James. She was extremely shock'd with the news, and her heart instantly began to relent. All the reasons on which she had founded her love, recurred in the strongest and liveliest colours to her mind, and all the causes of her hatred sunk down and disappeared; or if the least remembrance of any thing which had disobliged her remained, her heart became his zealous advocate, and soon satisfied her that her own fates were more to be blamed than he, and that without being a villain, he could have acted no otherwise than he had done.

In this temper of mind, she looked on herself as the murderer of an innocent man, and what to her was much worse, of the man she had loved, and still did love with all the violence imaginable. She looked on James as the tool with which she had done this murder; and as it is usual for people who have rashly or inadvertently made any animate or inanimate thing the instrument of mischief, to hate the innocent means by which the mischief was effected: (for this is a subtle method which the mind invents to excuse ourselves, the last objects on whom we would willingly wreak our vengeance;) so Miss Mathews now hated and cursed James as the efficient cause of that act which she herself had contrived, and laboured to carry into execution.

She sat down therefore in a furious agitation, little short of madness, and wrote the following letter:

> I hope this will find you in the hands of justice, for the murder of one of the best friends that ever man was blest with. In one sense indeed, he may seem to have deserved his fate, by chusing a fool for a friend; for who but a fool would have believed what the anger and rage of an injured woman suggested; a story so improbable, that I could scarce be thought in earnest when I mentioned it.
>
> Know then, cruel wretch, that poor Booth loved you of all men breathing, and was, I believe, in your commendation, guilty of as much falsehood, as I was in what I told you concerning him.
>
> If this knowledge makes you miserable, it is no more than you have made
>
> The unhappy
> F. MATHEWS.

CHAPTER 9

Being the last chapter of the fifth book.

WE SHALL now return to Colonel James and Mr Booth, who walked together from Colonel Bath's lodging with much more peaceable intention than that gentleman had conjectured, who dreamt of nothing but swords and guns, and implements of wars.

The Birdcage Walk[30] in the Park was the scene appointed by James for unburthening his mind. Thither they came, and there James acquainted Booth with all that which the reader knows already, and gave him the letter which we have inserted at the end of the last chapter.

Booth exprest great astonishment at this relation, not without venting some detestation of the wickedness of Miss Mathews; upon which James took him up, saying, he ought not to speak with such abhorrence of faults, which love for him had occasioned.

'Can you mention love, my dear colonel,' cried Booth, 'and such a woman in the same breath?'

'Yes, faith! can I,' says James; 'for the devil take me, if I know a more lovely woman in the world.' Here he began to describe her whole person; but as we cannot insert all the description, so we shall omit it all; and concluded with saying, 'curse me, if I don't think her the finest creature in the universe. I would give half my estate, Booth, she loved me as well as she doth you. Tho', on second consideration, I believe I should repent that bargain; for then, very possibly, I should not care a farthing for her.'

'You will pardon me, dear colonel,' answered Booth; 'but to me there appears somewhat very singular in your way of thinking. Beauty is indeed the object of liking, great qualities of admiration, good ones of esteem; but the devil take me, if I think any thing but love to be the object of love.'

'Is there not something too selfish,' replied James, 'in that opinion; but without considering it in that light, is it not of all things the most insipid? all oil! all sugar! zounds! it is enough to cloy the sharp-set appetite of a parson. Acids surely are the most likely to quicken.'

'I do not love reasoning in allegories,' cries Booth, 'but with regard to love, I declare I never found any thing cloying in it. I have lived almost alone with my wife near three years together, was never tired with her company, nor ever wished for any other; and I am sure, I never tasted any of the acid you mention to quicken my appetite.'

'This is all very extraordinary and romantic to me,' answered the colonel. 'If I was to be shut up three years with the same woman, which heaven forbid! nothing, I think, could keep me alive, but a temper as violent as that of Miss Mathews. As to love, it would make me sick to death, in the twentieth part of that time. If I was so condemned, let me see, what would I wish the woman to be! I think no one virtue would be sufficient. With the spirit of a tigress, I would have her be a prude, a scold, a scholar, a critic, a wit, a politician, and a Jacobite; and then perhaps eternal opposition would keep up our spirits; and wishing one another daily at the devil, we should make a shift to drag on a damnable state of life, without much spleen or vapours.'[31]

'And so you do not intend,' cries Booth, 'to break with this woman.'

'Not more than I have already, if I can help it,' answered the colonel.

'And you will be reconciled to her?' said Booth.

'Yes, faith! will I, if I can,' answered the colonel – 'I hope you have no objection.'

'None, my dear friend,' said Booth, 'unless on your account.'

'I do believe you,' said the colonel, 'and yet let me tell you, you are a very extraordinary man, not to desire me to quit her on your own account. Upon my soul, I begin to pity the woman, who hath placed her affection perhaps on the only man in England of your age, who would not return it. But for my part, I promise you I like her beyond all other women; and whilst that is the case, my boy, if her mind was as full of iniquity as Pandora's box[32] was of diseases, I'd hug her close in my arms, and only take as much care as possible to keep the lid down for fear of mischief. – But come, dear Booth,' said he, 'let us consider your affairs; for I am ashamed of having neglected them so long; and the only anger I have against this wench is, that she was the occasion of it.'

Booth then acquainted the colonel with the promises he had receiv'd from the noble lord, upon which James shook him by the hand, and heartily wish'd him joy, crying, 'I do assure you if you have his interest, you will need no other; I did not know you was acquainted with him.'

To which Mr Booth answered that he was but a new acquaintance, and that he was recommended to him by a lady.

'A lady,' cries the colonel, – 'well, I don't ask her name. You are a happy man, Booth, amongst the women; and I assure you, you could have no stronger recommendation. The peer loves the ladies, I believe, as well as ever Mark Antony did; and it is not his fault, if he hath not spent as much upon them. If he once fixes his eye upon a woman, he will stick at nothing to get her.'

'Ay, indeed!' cries Booth. 'Is that his character?'

'Ay, faith!' answered the colonel, 'and the character of most men beside him. Few of them, I mean, will stick at any thing beside their money. *Jusque a la bourse*,[33] is sometimes the boundary of love as well as friendship. And, indeed, I never knew any other man part with his money so very freely on these occasions. You see, dear Booth, the confidence I have in your honour.'

'I hope, indeed, you have,' cries Booth, 'but I don't see what instance you now give me of that confidence.'

'Have not I shewn you,' answered James, 'where you may carry your goods to market? I can assure you, my friend, that is a secret I would not impart to every man in your situation, and all circumstances considered.'

'I am very sorry, sir,' cries Booth very gravely, and turning as pale as death, 'you should entertain a thought of this kind. A thought which hath almost frozen up my blood. I am unwilling to believe there are such villains in the world; but there is none of them whom I should detest half so much as myself, if my own mind had ever suggested to me a hint of that kind. I have tasted of some distresses of life, and I know not to what greater I may be driven; but my honour, I thank Heaven, is in my own power, and I can boldly say to Fortune, she shall not rob me of it.'

'Have I not exprest that confidence, my dear Booth?' answered the colonel. 'And what you say now well justifies my opinion; for I do agree with you, that considering all things, it would be the highest instance of dishonour.'

'Dishonour indeed!' returned Booth. 'What to prostitute my wife! – Can I think there is such a wretch breathing?'

'I don't know that,' said the colonel; 'but I am sure, it was very far from my intention to insinuate the least hint of any such matter to you. Nor can I imagine how you yourself could conceive such a thought. The goods I meant, were no other than the charming person of Miss Mathews; for whom I am convinced my lord would bid a swinging price against me.'

Booth's countenance greatly cleared up at this declaration, and he answered with a smile, that he hoped he need not give the colonel any assurances on that head. However, tho' he was satisfied with regard to the colonel's suspicions; yet some chimeras now arose in his brain, which gave him no very agreeable sensations. What these were the sagacious reader may probably suspect; but if he should not, we may perhaps have occasion to open them in the sequel. Here we will put an end to this dialogue, and to the fifth book of this history.

BOOK VI

CHAPTER 1

Panegyrics on beauty, with other grave matters.

THE colonel and Booth walked together to the latter's lodging; for as it was not that day in the week in which all parts of the town are indifferent, Booth could not wait on the colonel.

When they arrived in Spring Garden, Booth to his great surprize found no one at home but the maid. In truth, Amelia had accompanied Mrs Ellison and her children to his lordship's; for as her little girl shewed a great unwillingness to go without her, the fond mother was easily persuaded to make one of the company.

Booth had scarce ushered the colonel up to his apartment, when a servant from Mrs James knocked hastily at the door. The lady not meeting with her husband at her return home began to despair of him, and performed every thing which was decent on the occasion. An apothecary was presently called with hartshorn and sal volatile, a doctor was sent for, and messengers were dispatched every way, amongst the rest one was sent to enquire at the lodgings of his supposed antagonist.

The servant hearing that his master was alive and well above stairs, ran up eagerly to acquaint him with the dreadful situation in which he left his miserable lady at home, and likewise with the occasion of all her distress, saying that his lady had been at her brother's, and had there heard that his honour was killed in a duel by Captain Booth.

The colonel smiled at this account, and bid the servant make haste back to contradict it. – And then turning to Booth he said, 'Was there ever such another fellow as this brother of mine? I thought indeed his behaviour was somewhat odd at the time. I suppose he overheard me whisper that I would give you satisfaction, and thence concluded we went together with a design of tilting. – D—n the fellow, I begin to grow heartily sick of him, and wish I could get well rid of him without cutting his throat, which I sometimes apprehend he will insist on my doing, as a return for my getting him made a lieutenant-colonel.'

Whilst these two gentlemen were commenting on the character of the third, Amelia and her company returned, and all presently came up stairs, not only the children, but the two ladies, laden with trinkets as if they had been come from a fair. Amelia, who had been highly delighted all the morning with the excessive pleasure which her children enjoyed, when she saw Colonel James with her husband, and perceived the most manifest marks of that reconciliation, which she knew had been so long and so earnestly wished by Booth, became so transported with joy that her happiness was scarce capable of addition. Exercise had painted her face with vermilion; and the highest good-humour had so sweetened every feature, and a vast flow of spirits had so lightened up her bright eyes, that she was all a blaze of beauty. She seemed indeed, as Milton sublimely describes Eve,[1]

– adorned
With what all Earth or Heaven could bestow
To make her amiable –

Again,

Grace was in all her steps, Heaven in her eye,
In ev'ry gesture, dignity and love.

Or, as Waller[2] sweetly, though less sublimely, sings:

Sweetness, truth, and every grace,
Which time and use are wont to teach,
The eye may in a moment reach,
And read distinctly in her face.

Or to mention one poet more, and him of all the sweetest, she seemed to be the very person of whom Suckling[3] wrote the following lines, where, speaking of Cupid, he says,

– All his lovely looks, his pleasing fires,
All his sweet motions, all his taking smiles,

All that awakes, all that inflames desires,
All that sweetly commands, all that beguiles,
He does into one pair of eyes convey,
And there begs leave that he himself may stay.

Such was Amelia at this time when she entered the room, and having paid her respects to the colonel, she went up to her husband, and cried, 'O my dear! never were any creatures so happy as your little things have been this whole morning; and all owing to my lord's goodness; sure never was any thing so good-natur'd and so generous!' – She then made the children produce their presents, the value of which amounted to a pretty large sum; for there was a gold watch amongst the trinkets that cost above twenty guineas.

Instead of discovering so much satisfaction on this occasion as Amelia expected, Booth very gravely answered, 'And pray, my dear, how are we to repay all these obligations to his lordship?' 'How can you ask so strange a question?' cries Mrs Ellison, 'how little do you know of the soul of generosity (for sure my cousin deserves that name) when you call a few little trinkets given to children, an obligation?' 'Indeed, my dear,' cries Amelia, 'I would have stopped his hand, if it had been possible; nay, I was forced at last absolutely to refuse, or I believe he would have laid a hundred pound out on the children: for I never saw any one so fond of children, which convinces me he is one of the best of men; but I ask your pardon, colonel,' said she, turning to him, 'I should not entertain you with these subjects; yet I know you have goodness enough to excuse the folly of a mother.'

The colonel made a very low assenting bow; and soon after they all sat down to a small repast; for the colonel had promised Booth to dine with him when they first came home together; and what he had since heard from his own house, gave him still less inclination than ever to repair thither.

But beside both these, there was a third and stronger inducement to him to pass the day with his friend; and this was the desire of passing it with his friend's wife. When the colonel had first seen Amelia in France, she was but just recovered from a consumptive habit, and looked pale and thin; besides, his engagements with Miss Bath at that time took total possession of him, and guarded his heart from the impressions of another woman; and when he had dined with her in town, the vexations through which she had lately passed had somewhat deadned her beauty; besides, he was then engaged, as we have seen, in a very warm pursuit of a new mistress; but now he had no such impediment: for though the reader hath just before seen his warm declarations of a passion for Miss Mathews; yet it may be remember'd that he had been in possession of her for above a fortnight; and one of the happy properties of this kind of passion is, that it can with equal violence love half a dozen, or half a score, different objects at one and the same time.

But indeed such were the charms now displayed by Amelia, of which we endeavoured above to draw some faint resemblance, that perhaps no other beauty could have secured him from their influence; and here to confess a truth in his favour, however the grave, or rather the hypocritical part of mankind may censure it, I am firmly persuaded that to withdraw admiration from exquisite beauty, or to feel no delight in gazing at it, is as impossible as to feel no warmth from the most scorching rays of the sun. To run away is all that is in our power; and yet in the former case if it must be allowed we have the power of running away, it must be allowed also that it requires the strongest resolution to execute it: for when, as Dryden[4] says,

All paradise is opened in a face,

how natural is the desire of going thither! and how difficult to quit the lovely prospect!

And yet however difficult this may be, my young readers, it is absolutely necessary, and that immediately too: flatter not yourselves that fire will not scorch as well as warm; and the longer we stay within its reach, the more we shall burn. The admiration of a beautiful woman, though the wife of our dearest friend, may at first perhaps be innocent; but let us not flatter ourselves it will always remain so; desire is sure to succeed; and wishes, hopes, designs, with a long train of mischiefs, tread close at our heels. In affairs of this kind we may most properly apply the well-known remark of *nemo repente fuit turpissimus.*[5] It fares indeed with us on this occasion, as with the unwary traveller in some parts of Arabia the desart, whom the treacherous sands imperceptibly betray till he is overwhelmed and lost. In both cases the only safety is by withdrawing our feet the very first moment we perceive them sliding.

This digression may appear impertinent to some readers; we could not however avoid the opportunity of offering the above hints; since of all passions there is none against which we should so strongly fortify ourselves as this, which is generally called love: for no other lays before us, especially in the tumultuous days of youth, such sweet, such strong, and almost irresistible temptations; none hath produced in private life such fatal and lamentable tragedies; and what is worst of all, there is none to whose poison and infatuation the best of minds are so liable. Ambition scarce ever produces any evil, but when it reigns in cruel and savage bosoms; and avarice seldom flourishes at all but in the basest and poorest soil. Love, on the contrary, sprouts usually up in the richest and noblest minds; but there unless nicely watched, pruned, and cultivated, and carefully kept clear of those vicious weeds which are too apt to surround it, it branches forth into wildness and disorder, produces nothing desirable, but choaks up and kills whatever is good and noble in the mind where it so abounds. In short, to drop the allegory, not only tenderness and good-nature, but bravery, generosity, and every virtue are often made the instruments of effecting the most atrocious purposes of this all-subduing tyrant.

CHAPTER 2

Which will not appear, we presume, unnatural to all married readers.

IF the table of poor Booth afforded but an indifferent repast to the colonel's hunger, here was most excellent entertainment of a much higher kind. The colonel began now to wonder within himself at his not having before discovered such incomparable beauty and excellence. This wonder was indeed so natural, that lest it should arise likewise in the reader, we thought proper to give the solution of it in the preceding chapter.

During the first two hours, the colonel scarce ever had his eyes off from Amelia; for he was taken by surprize, and his heart was gone before he suspected himself to be in any danger. His mind however no sooner suggested a certain secret to him, than it suggested some degree of prudence to him at the same time; and the knowledge that he had thoughts to conceal, and the care of concealing them, had birth at one and the same instant. During the residue of the day therefore, he grew more circumspect, and contented himself with now and then stealing a look by chance, especially as the more than ordinary gravity of Booth made him fear that his former behaviour had betrayed to Booth's observation the great and sudden liking he had conceived for his wife, even before he had observed it in himself.

Amelia continued the whole day in the highest spirits, and highest good humour imaginable; never once remarking that appearance of discontent in her husband, of which the colonel had taken notice; so much more quick-sighted, as we have somewhere else hinted, is guilt than innocence. Whether Booth had in reality made any such observations on the colonel's behaviour as he had suspected, we will not undertake to determine; yet so far may be material to say, as we can with sufficient certainty, that the change in Booth's behaviour that day, from what was usual with him, was remarkable enough. None of his former vivacity appeared in his conversation; and his countenance was altered from being the picture of sweetness and good humour, not indeed to sourness or moroseness, but to gravity and melancholy.

Tho' the colonel's suspicion had the effect which we have mentioned on his behaviour; yet it could not persuade him to depart. In short, he sat in his chair as if confined to it by enchantment, stealing looks now and then, and humouring his growing passion, without having command enough over his limbs to carry him out of the room, till decency at last forced him to put an end to his preposterous visit. When the husband and wife were left alone together; the latter resumed the subject of her children, and gave Booth a particular narrative of all that had past at his lordship's, which he, tho' something had certainly disconcerted him, affected to receive with all the pleasure he could; and this affectation, however aukwardly he acted his part, passed very well on Amelia: for she could not well conceive a displeasure, of which she had not the least hint of any cause; and indeed at a time when from his reconciliation with James, she imagined her husband to be entirely and perfectly happy.

The greatest part of that night Booth past awake; and if during the residue he might be said to sleep, he could scarce be said to enjoy repose; his eyes were no sooner closed, than he was pursued and haunted by the most frightful and terrifying dreams, which threw him into so restless a condition, that he soon disturbed his Amelia, and greatly alarmed her with apprehensions that he had been seized by some dreadful disease, tho' he had not the least symptoms of a fever by any extraordinary heat, or any other indication, but was rather colder than usual.

As Booth assured his wife that he was very well, but found no inclination to sleep, she likewise bid adieu to her slumbers, and attempted to entertain him with her conversation. Upon which his lordship occurred as the first topic; and she repeated to him all the stories which she had heard from Mrs Ellison of the peer's goodness to his sister and his nephew and niece. 'It is impossible, my dear,' says she, 'to describe their fondness for their uncle, which is to me an incontestable sign of a parent's goodness.' – In this manner she ran on for several minutes, concluding at last that it was pity so very few had such generous minds joined to immense fortunes.

Booth instead of making a direct answer to what Amelia had said, cried coldly, 'But do you think, my dear, it was right to accept all those expensive toys which the children brought home? And I ask you again, what return we are to make for these obligations?'

'Indeed, my dear,' cries Amelia, 'you see this matter in too serious a light. Though I am the last person in the world who would lessen his lordship's goodness, (indeed I shall always think we are both infinitely obliged to him) yet sure you must allow the expence to be a mere trifle to such a vast fortune. As for return, his own benevolence, in the satisfaction it receives more than repays itself, and I am convinced he expects no other.'

'Very well, my dear,' cries Booth, 'you shall have it your way; I must confess, I never yet saw any reason to blame your discernment; and perhaps I have been in the wrong to give myself so much uneasiness on this account.'

'Uneasiness! child,' said Amelia eagerly. 'Good Heavens! hath this made you uneasy?'

'I do own it hath,' answered Booth, 'and it hath been the only cause of breaking my repose.'

'Why then I wish,' cries Amelia, 'all the things had been at the devil, before ever the children had seen them; and whatever I may think myself, I promise you they shall never more accept the value of a farthing – If upon this occasion, I have been the cause of your uneasiness, you will do me the justice to believe that I was totally innocent.'

At those words Booth caught her in his arms, and with the tenderest embrace, emphatically repeating the word innocent, cried – 'Heaven forbid I should think otherwise, O thou art the best of creatures that ever blessed a man.'

'Well but,' said she smiling – 'Do confess, my dear, the truth; I promise you I won't blame you nor disesteem you for it; but is not pride really at the bottom of this fear of an obligation?'

'Perhaps it may,' answered he, 'or if you will, you may call it fear. I own I am afraid of obligations, as the worst kind of debts; for I have generally observed those who confer them, expect to be repaid ten thousand fold.'

Here ended all that is material of their discourse; and a little time afterwards, they both fell fast asleep in one another's arms; from which time Booth had no more restlessness, nor any further perturbation in his dreams.

Their repose however had been so much disturbed in the former part of the night, that, as it was very late before they enjoyed that sweet sleep I have just mentioned, they lay a-bed the next day till noon, when they both rose with the utmost chearfulness; and while Amelia bestirred herself in the affairs of her family, Booth went to visit the wounded colonel.

He found that gentleman still proceeding very fast in his recovery, with which he was more pleased than he had reason to be with his reception; for the colonel received him very coldly indeed, and when Booth told him he had received perfect satisfaction from his brother, Bath erected his head, and answered with a sneer, 'Very well, sir, if you think these matters can be so made up, d—n me, if it is any business of mine. My dignity hath not been injured.'

'No one, I believe,' cries Booth, 'dare injure it.'

'You believe so!' said the colonel, 'I think, sir, you might be assured of it; but this, at least, you may be assured of, that if any man did, I would tumble him down the precipice of hell, d—n me, that you may be assured of.'

As Booth found the colonel in this disposition, he had no great inclination to lengthen out his visit, nor did the colonel himself seem to desire it; so he soon returned back to his Amelia, whom he found performing the office of a cook, with as much pleasure as a fine lady generally enjoys in dressing herself out for a ball.

CHAPTER 3

In which the history looks a little backwards.

BEFORE we proceed farther in our history, we shall recount a short scene to our reader which passed between Amelia and Mrs Ellison, whilst Booth was on his visit to Colonel Bath. We have already observed, that Amelia had conceived an extraordinary affection for Mrs Bennet, which had still encreased every time she saw her; she thought she discovered something wonderfully good and gentle in her countenance and disposition, and was very desirous of knowing her whole history.

She had a very short interview with that lady this morning in Mrs Ellison's apartment. As soon therefore as Mrs Bennet was gone, Amelia acquainted Mrs Ellison with the good opinion she had conceived of her friend, and likewise with her curiosity to know her story: 'For there must be something uncommonly good,' said she, 'in one who can so truly mourn for a husband above three years after his death.'

'O,' cries Mrs Ellison, 'to be sure the world must allow her to have been one of the best of wives. And indeed, upon the whole she is a good sort of woman; and what I like her the best for is a strong resemblance that she bears to yourself in the form of her person, and still more in her voice. But for my own part, I know nothing remarkable in her fortune unless what I have told you, that she was the daughter of a clergyman, had little or no fortune, and married a poor parson for love, who left her in the utmost distress. If you please, I will shew you a letter which she writ to me at that time, tho' I insist upon your promise never to mention it to her; indeed, you will be the first person I ever shewed it to.' She then opened her scrutore,[6] and taking out the letter delivered it to Amelia, saying, 'There, madam, is, I believe, as fine a picture of distress as can well be drawn.'

Dear Madam,

As I have no other friend on earth but yourself, I hope you will pardon my writing to you at this season; tho' I do not know that you can relieve my distresses, or if you can, have I any pretence to expect that you should. My poor dear, O Heavens! – my — lies dead in the house, and after I had procured sufficient to bury him, a set of ruffians have entered my house, seized all I have, have seized his dear, dear corpse, and threaten to deny it burial. For Heaven's sake, send me, at least, some advice; little Tommy stands now by me crying for bread, which I have not to give him. – I can say no more than that I am,

Your most distressed humble servant,

M. BENNET.

Amelia read the letter over twice, and then returning it, with tears in her eyes, asked how the poor creature could possibly get through such distress.

'You may depend upon it, madam,' said Mrs Ellison, 'the moment I read this account, I posted away immediately to the lady. As to the seizing the body, that I found was a mere bugbear; but all the rest was literally true. I sent immediately for the same gentleman, that I recommended to Mr Booth, left the care of burying the corpse to him, and brought my friend and her little boy immediately away to my own house, where she remained some months in the most miserable condition. I then prevailed with her to retire into the country, and procured her a lodging with a friend at St Edmundsbury,[7] the air and gayety of which place by degrees recovered her; and she returned in about a twelvemonth to town, as well, I think, as she is at present.'

'I am almost afraid to ask,' cries Amelia; 'and yet I long methinks to know what is become of the poor little boy.'

'He hath been dead,' said Mrs Ellison, 'a little more than half a year; and the mother lamented him at first almost as much as she did her husband; but I found it indeed rather an easier matter to comfort her, tho' I sat up with her near a fortnight upon the latter occasion.'

'You are a good creature,' said Amelia, 'and I love you dearly.'

'Alas! madam,' cries she, 'what could I have done, if it had not been for the goodness of that best of men, my noble cousin! His lordship no sooner heard of the widow's distress from me, than he immediately settled £150 a year upon her during her life.'

'Well! how noble, how generous was that!' said Amelia, 'I declare I begin to love your cousin, Mrs Ellison.'

'And I declare if you do,' answered she, 'there is no love lost, I verily believe; if you had heard what I heard him say yesterday behind your back –'

'Why, what did he say, Mrs Ellison?' cries Amelia.

'He said,' answered the other, 'that you was the finest woman his eyes ever beheld. – Ah! it is in vain to wish, and yet, I cannot help wishing too. – O Mrs Booth! if you had been a single woman, I firmly believe I could have made you the happiest in the world. And I sincerely think, I never saw a woman who deserved it more.'

'I am obliged to you, madam,' cries Amelia, 'for your good opinion; but I really look on myself already as the happiest woman in the world. Our circumstances it is true might have been a little more fortunate; but, O my dear Mrs Ellison, what fortune can be put in the balance with such a husband as mine?'

'I am afraid, dear madam,' answered Mrs Ellison, 'you would not hold the scale fairly. – I acknowledge indeed, Mr Booth is a very pretty gentleman; heaven forbid I should endeavour to lessen him in your opinion; yet if I was to be brought to confession, I could not help saying, I see where the superiority lies, and that the men have more reason to envy Mr Booth, than the women have to envy his lady.'

'Nay, I will not bear this,' replied Amelia. 'You will forfeit all my love, if you have the least disrespectful opinion of my husband. – You do not know him Mrs Ellison, he is the best, the kindest, the worthiest of all his sex. I have observed indeed once or twice before that you have taken some dislike to him. I can't conceive for what reason. If he hath said or done any thing to disoblige you, I am sure I can justly acquit him of design. His extreme vivacity makes him sometimes a little too heedless; but, I am convinced, a more innocent heart, or one more void of offence, was never in a human bosom.'

'Nay, if you grow serious,' cries Mrs Ellison, 'I have done. How is it possible you should suspect I had taken any dislike to a man, to whom I have always shewn so perfect a regard! But to say I think him, or almost any other man in the world worthy of yourself, is not within my power with truth. And since you force the confession from me, I declare, I think such beauty, such sense, and such goodness united, might aspire without vanity to the arms of any monarch in Europe.'

'Alas! my dear Mrs Ellison,' answered Amelia, 'do you think happiness and a crown so closely united? How many miserable women have lain in the arms of kings? – Indeed, Mrs Ellison, if I had all the merit you compliment me with, I should think it all fully rewarded with such a man as I thank heaven hath fallen to my lot; nor would I, upon my soul, exchange that lot with any queen in the universe.'

'Well, there are enow of our sex,' said Mrs Ellison, 'to keep you in countenance; but I shall never forget the beginning of a song of Mr Congreve's,[8] that my husband was so fond of, that he was always singing it.

Love's but a frailty of the mind,
When 'tis not with ambition join'd.

Love without interest makes but an unsavory dish in my opinion.'

'And pray how long hath this been your opinion?' said Amelia, smiling.

'Ever since I was born,' answered Mrs Ellison, 'at least, ever since I can remember.'

'And have you never,' said Amelia, 'deviated from this generous way of thinking?'

'Never once,' answered the other, 'in the whole course of my life.'

'O Mrs Ellison! Mrs Ellison!' cries Amelia, 'why do we ever blame those who are disingenuous in confessing their faults, when we are so often ashamed to own ourselves in the right. Some women now, in my situation, would be angry that you had not made confidantes of them; but I never desire to know more of the secrets of others, than they are pleased to entrust me with. You must believe however, that I should not have given you these hints of my knowing all, if I had disapproved your choice. On the contrary, I assure you, I highly approve it. The gentility he wants, it will be easily in your power to procure for him; and as for his good qualities, I will myself be bound for them: and I make not the least doubt, as you have owned to me yourself that you have placed your affections on him, you will be one of the happiest women in the world.'

'Upon my honour,' cries Mrs Ellison, very gravely, 'I do not understand one word of what you mean.'

'Upon my honour, you astonish me,' said Amelia, 'but I have done.'

'Nay then,' said the other, 'I insist upon knowing what you mean.'

'Why, what can I mean,' answered Amelia, 'but your marriage with Serjeant Atkinson?'

'With Serjeant Atkinson!' cries Mrs Ellison eagerly, 'my marriage with a serjeant!'

'Well, with Mr Atkinson then, Captain Atkinson, if you please; for so I hope to see him.'

'And have you really no better opinion of me,' said Mrs Ellison, 'than to imagine me capable of such condescension?[9] What have I done, dear Mrs Booth, to deserve so low a place in your esteem? I find indeed, as Solomon says,[10] *Women ought to watch the door of their lips*. How little did I imagine that a little harmless freedom in discourse, could persuade any one that I could entertain a serious intention of disgracing my family! for of a very good family am I come, I assure you, madam, tho' I now let lodgings. Few of my lodgers, I believe, ever came of a better.'

'If I have offended you, madam,' said Amelia, 'I am very sorry, and ask your pardon; but besides what I heard from yourself, Mr Booth told me.'

'O yes,' answered Mrs Ellison, 'Mr Booth, I know, is a very good friend of mine. – Indeed, I know you better than to think it could be your own suspicion. – I am very much obliged to Mr Booth truly.'

'Nay,' cries Amelia, 'the serjeant himself is in fault; for Mr Booth, I am positive, only repeated what he had from him.'

'Impudent coxcomb!' cries Mrs Ellison. 'I shall know how to keep such fellows at a proper distance for the future. – I will tell you, dear madam, all that happened. When I rose in the morning, I found the fellow waiting in the entry; and as you had exprest some regard for him as your foster-brother, nay, he is a very genteel fellow that I must own, I scolded my maid for not shewing him into my little back-room; and I then asked him to walk into the parlour. Could I have imagined he would have construed such little civility into an encouragement?'

'Nay, I will have justice done to my poor brother too,' said Amelia. 'I myself have seen you give him much greater encouragement than that.'

'Well, perhaps I have,' said Mrs Ellison. 'I have been always too unguarded in my speech, and can't answer for all I have said.' She then began to change her note, and with an affected laugh turned all into ridicule; and soon afterwards the two ladies separated, both in apparent good humour; and Amelia went about those domestic offices, in which Mr Booth found her engaged at the end of the preceding chapter.

CHAPTER 4

Containing a very extraordinary incident.

IN THE afternoon, Mr Booth with Amelia and her children went to refresh themselves in the Park. The conversation now turned on what past in the morning with Mrs Ellison, the latter part of the dialogue, I mean, recorded in the last chapter. Amelia told her husband, that Mrs Ellison so strongly denied all intentions to marry the serjeant, that she had convinced her the poor fellow was under an error, and had mistaken a little too much levity for serious encouragement; and concluded, by desiring Booth not to jest with her any more on that subject.

Booth burst into a laugh, at what his wife said. 'My dear creature,' said he, 'how easy is thy honesty and simplicity to be imposed on! how little dost thou guess at the art and falsehood of women! I knew a young lady, who against her father's consent, was married to a brother officer of mine. And as I often used to walk with her, (for I knew her father intimately well) she would of her own accord take frequent occasions to ridicule and vilify her husband (for so he was at the time) and express great wonder and indignation at the report which she allowed to prevail, that she should condescend ever to look at such a fellow, with any other design than of laughing at, and despising him. The marriage afterwards became publicly owned, and the lady was reputably brought to bed. Since which, I have often seen her; nor hath she ever appeared to be in the least ashamed of what she had formerly said, tho' indeed I believe she hates me heartily for having heard it.'

'But for what reason,' cries Amelia, 'should she deny a fact, when she must be so certain of our discovering it, and that immediately?'

'I can't answer what end she may propose,' said Booth. 'Sometimes one would be almost persuaded that there was a pleasure in lying itself. But this I am certain, that I would believe the honest serjeant on his bare word, sooner than I would fifty Mrs Ellisons on oath. I am convinced he would not have said what he did to me, without the strongest encouragement; and, I think, after what we have been both witnesses to, it requires no great confidence in his veracity, to give him an unlimited credit with regard to the lady's behaviour.'

To this Amelia made no reply; and they discoursed of other matters during the remainder of a very pleasant walk.

When they returned home, Amelia was surprized to find an appearance of disorder in her apartment. Several of the trinkets, which his lordship had given the children, lay about the room; and a suit of her own cloaths which she had left in her drawers, was now displayed upon the bed.

She immediately summoned her little girl up stairs, who, as she plainly perceived the moment she came up with a candle, had half cried her eyes out: for though the girl had opened the door to them, as it was almost dark, she had not taken any notice of this phenomenon in her countenance.

The girl now fell down upon her knees, and cry'd, – 'For heaven's sake, madam, do not be angry with me. Indeed I was left alone in the house; and hearing somebody knock at the door, I opened it, I am sure thinking no harm. I did not know but it might have been you, or my master, or Madam Ellison; and immediately as I did, the rogue burst in and ran directly up stairs, and what he hath robbed you of I can't tell; but I am sure I could not help it: for he was a great swinging man with a pistol in each hand; and if I had dared to call out, to be sure he would have killed me. I am sure I was never in such a fright in my born days, whereof I am hardly come to myself yet. I believe he is somewhere about the house yet; for I never saw him go out.'

Amelia discovered some little alarm at this narrative, but much less than many other ladies would have shewn: for a fright is, I believe, some time laid hold of as an opportunity of disclosing several charms peculiar to that occasion. And which, as Mr Addison[11] says of certain virtues,

> *– shun the day, and lie concealed*
> *In the smooth seasons, and the calms of life.*

Booth having opened the window, and summoned in two chairmen to his assistance, proceeded to search the house; but all to no purpose; the thief was flown, though the poor girl in her state of terror had not seen him escape.

But now a circumstance appeared which greatly surprized both Booth and Amelia; indeed I believe it will have the same effect on the reader; and this was, that the thief had taken nothing with him. He had indeed tumbled over all Booth and Amelia's clothes, and the childrens toys, but had left all behind him.

Amelia was scarce more pleased than astonished at this discovery, and re-examined the girl, assuring her of an absolute pardon, if she confessed the truth, but grievously threatning her if she was found guilty of the least falsehood. 'As for a thief, child,' says she, 'that is certainly not true; you have had somebody with you, to whom you have been shewing the things; therefore tell me plainly who it was.'

The girl protested in the solemnest manner that she knew not the person; but as to some circumstances she began to vary a little from her first account, particularly as to the pistols; concerning which being strictly examined by Booth she at last cried, – 'To be sure, sir, he must have had pistols about him.' And instead of persisting in his having rushed in upon her, she now confessed, that he had asked at the door for her master and mistress; and that at his desire she had shewn him up stairs, where he at first said he would stay till their return home; 'but indeed,' cry'd she, 'I thought no harm; for he looked like a gentlemanlike sort of man. And indeed so I thought he was for a good while, whereof he sat down and behaved himself very civilly, till he saw some of master's and miss's things upon the chest of drawers; whereof he cry'd, "hey-day! what's here?" and then he fell to tumbling about the things like any mad. Then I thinks, thinks I to myself, to be sure he's a highwayman, whereof I did not dare speak to him: for I knew Madam Ellison and her maid was gone out, and what could such a poor girl as I do against a great strong man? And besides, thinks I, to be sure he hath got pistols about him, though I can't indeed, (that I will not do for the world,) take my Bible-oath that I saw any; yet to be sure he would have soon pulled them out, and shot me dead, if I had ventured to have said any thing to offend him.'

'I know not what to make of this,' cries Booth. 'The poor girl I verily believe speaks to the best of her knowledge. A thief it could not be; for he hath not taken the least thing; and it is plain he had the girl's watch in his hand. – If it had been a bailiff, surely he would have staid till our return. I can conceive no other from the girl's account, than that it must have been some madman.' –

'O good sir,' said the girl, 'now you mention it, if he was not a thief, to be sure he must have been a madman; for indeed he looked and behaved himself too, very much like a madman: for now I remember it, he talked to himself, and said many strange kind of words, that I did not understand. Indeed he looked altogether as I have seen people in Bedlam,[12] besides, if he was not a madman, what good could it do him to throw the things all about the room, in such a manner? and he said something too about my master, just before he went down stairs, I was in such a fright, I can't remember particularly; but I am sure they were very ill words, he said *he would do for him*, I am sure he said that, and other wicked bad words too, if I could but think of them.'

'Upon my word,' said Booth, 'this is the most probable conjecture; but still I am puzzled to conceive who it should be: for I have no madman to my knowledge of my acquaintance; and it seems, as the girl says, he asked for me.' He then turned to the child, and asked her if she was certain of that circumstance.

The poor maid after a little hesitation, answered. 'Indeed, sir, I cannot be very positive; for the fright he threw me into afterwards drove every thing almost out of my mind.'

'Well, whatever he was,' cries Amelia, 'I am glad the consequence is no worse; but let this be a warning to you, little Betty, and teach you to take more care for the future. If ever you should be left alone in the house again, be sure to let no persons in, without first looking out at the window, and seeing who they are. I promised not to chide you any more on this occasion, and I will keep my word; but it is very plain you desired this person to walk up into our apartment, which was very wrong in our absence.'

Betty was going to answer – but Amelia would not let her, saying, 'don't attempt to excuse yourself; for I mortally hate a liar, and can forgive any fault sooner than falsehood.'

The poor girl then submitted; and now Amelia with her assistance began to replace all things in their order; and little Emily hugging her watch with great fondness declared she would never part with it any more.

Thus ended this odd adventure, not entirely to the satisfaction of Booth: for, besides his curiosity, which when thoroughly roused is a very troublesome passion, he had as is, I believe, usual with all persons in his circumstances, several doubts and apprehensions of he knew not what. Indeed fear is never more uneasy, than when it doth not certainly know its object: for on such occasions the mind is ever employed in raising a thousand bugbears and fantoms, much more dreadful than any realities, and like children, when they tell tales of hobgoblins, seems industrious in terrifying itself.

CHAPTER 5

Containing some matters not very unnatural.

MATTERS were scarce sooner reduced into order and decency, than a violent knocking was heard at the door, such indeed as would have persuaded any one not accustomed to the sound, that the madman was returned in the highest spring-tide of his fury.

Instead, however, of so disagreeable an appearance, a very fine lady presently came into the room, no other indeed than Mrs James herself; for she was resolved to shew Amelia by the speedy return of her visit, how unjust all her accusation had been of any failure in the duties of friendship; she had moreover another reason to accelerate this visit, and that was, to congratulate her friend on the event of the duel between Colonel Bath and Mr Booth.

The lady had so well profited by Mrs Booth's remonstrance, that she had now no more of that stiffness and formality which she had worn on a former occasion. On the contrary, she now behaved with the utmost freedom and good-humour, and made herself so very agreeable, that Amelia was highly pleased and delighted with her company.

An incident happened during this visit, that may appear to some too inconsiderable in itself to be recorded; and yet, as it certainly produced a very strong consequence in the mind of Mr Booth, we cannot prevail on ourselves to pass it by.

Little Emily, who was present in the room while Mrs James was there, as she stood near that lady, happened to be playing with her watch, which she was so greatly overjoyed had escaped safe from the madman. Mrs James, who exprest great fondness for the child, desired to see the watch, which she commended as the prettiest of the kind she had ever seen.

Amelia caught eager hold of this opportunity to spread the praises of her benefactor. She presently acquainted Mrs James with the donor's name, and ran on with great encomiums on his lordship's goodness, and particularly on his generosity. To which Mrs James answered, 'O certainly, madam, his lordship hath universally the character of being extremely generous – where he likes.'

In uttering these words, she laid a very strong emphasis on the three last monosyllables, accompanying them at the same time with a very sagacious look, a very significant leer, and a great flirt with her fan.

The greatest genius[13] the world hath ever produced, observes in one of his most excellent plays, that

> *– Trifles light as air*
> *Are to the jealous confirmations strong*
> *As proofs of holy writ.*

That Mr Booth began to be possessed by this worst of fiends admits, I think, no longer doubt; for at this speech of Mrs James, he immediately turned pale, and from a high degree of chearfulness, was all on a sudden struck dumb, so that he spoke not another word till Mrs James left the room.

The moment that lady drove from the door, Mrs Ellison came up stairs. She entered the room with a laugh, and very plentifully rallied both Booth and Amelia concerning the madman, of which she had received a full account below stairs, and at last asked Amelia, if she could not guess who it was, but without receiving an answer went on, saying, 'for my own part, I fancy it must be some lover of yours; some person that hath seen you, and so is run mad with love. Indeed, I should not wonder if all mankind were to do the same. La! Mr Booth, what makes you grave? why, you are as melancholy as if you had been robbed in earnest. Upon my word, tho' to be serious, it is a strange story; and as the girl tells it, I know not what to make of it. Perhaps it might be some rogue that intended to rob the house, and his heart failed him; yet even that would be very extraordinary. What, did you lose nothing, madam?'

'Nothing at all,' answered Amelia. 'He did not even take the child's watch.'

'Well, captain,' cries Mrs Ellison, 'I hope you will take more care of the house to-morrow; for your lady and I shall leave you alone to the care of it. Here, madam,' said she, 'here is a present from my lord to us; here are two tickets for the masquerade at

Ranelagh.[14] You will be so charmed with it. It is the sweetest of all diversions.'

'May I be damned, madam,' cries Booth, 'if my wife shall go thither!'

Mrs Ellison stared at these words, and indeed so did Amelia: for they were spoke with great vehemence. At length the former cried out with an air of astonishment, 'Not let your lady go to Ranelagh, sir?'

'No, madam,' cries Booth, 'I will not let my wife go to Ranelagh.'

'You surprize me,' cries Mrs Ellison. 'Sure you are not in earnest.'

'Indeed, madam,' returned he, 'I am seriously in earnest. And what is more, I am convinced she would of her own accord refuse to go.'

'Now, madam,' said Mrs Ellison, 'you are to answer for yourself; and I will for your husband, that if you have a desire to go he will not refuse you.'

'I hope, madam,' answered Amelia with great gravity, 'I shall never desire to go to any place contrary to Mr Booth's inclinations.'

'Did ever mortal hear the like?' said Mrs Ellison, 'you are enough to spoil the best husband in the universe. Inclinations! What, is a woman to be governed then by her husband's inclinations, tho' they are never so unreasonable?'

'Pardon me, madam,' said Amelia, 'I will not suppose Mr Booth's inclinations ever can be unreasonable. I am very much obliged to you for the offer you have made me; but I beg you will not mention it any more: for after what Mr Booth hath declared, if Ranelagh was a heaven upon earth, I would refuse to go to it.'

'I thank you, my dear,' cries Booth, 'I do assure you, you oblige me beyond my power of expression by what you say; but I will endeavour to shew you both my sensibility of such goodness, and my lasting gratitude to it.'

'And pray, sir,' cries Mrs Ellison, 'what can be your objection to your lady's going to a place, which I will venture to say is as reputable as any about town, and which is frequented by the best company?'

'Pardon me, good Mrs Ellison,' said Booth. 'As my wife is so good to acquiesce without knowing my reasons, I am not, I think, obliged to assign them to any other person.'

'Well,' cries Mrs Ellison, 'if I had been told this, I would not have believed it. What, refuse your lady an innocent diversion, and that too when you have not the pretence to say it would cost you a farthing?'

'Why will you say any more on this subject, dear madam?' cries Amelia. 'All diversions are to me matters of such indifference, that the bare inclinations of any one for whom I have the least value, would at all times turn the balance of mine. I am sure then after what Mr Booth hath said –'

'My dear,' cries he, taking her up hastily, 'I sincerely ask your pardon, I spoke inadvertently and in a passion – I never once thought of controuling you – nor ever would. – Nay, I said in the same breath you would not go; and upon my honour I meant nothing more.'

'My dear,' said she, 'you have no need of making any apology. I am not in the least offended, and am convinced you will never deny me what I shall desire.'

'Try him, try him, madam,' cries Mrs Ellison, 'I will be judged by all the women in town, if it is possible for a wife to ask her husband any thing more reasonable. You can't conceive what a sweet, charming, elegant, delicious place it is. – Paradise itself can hardly be equal to it.'

'I beg you will excuse me, madam,' said Amelia, 'nay, I intreat you will ask me no more: for be assured I must and will refuse – Do let me desire you to give the ticket to poor Mrs Bennet. I believe it would greatly oblige her.' –

'Pardon me, madam,' said Mrs Ellison. 'If you will not accept of it, I am not so distressed for want of company as to go to such a public place with all sort of people neither. I am always very glad to see Mrs Bennet at my own house; because I look upon her as a very good sort of woman; but I don't chuse to be seen with such people in public places.'

Amelia exprest some little indignation at this last speech, which she declared to be entirely beyond her comprehension; and soon after Mrs Ellison, finding all her efforts to prevail on Amelia were ineffectual, took her leave, giving Mr Booth two or three sarcastical words, and a much more sarcastical look at her departure.

CHAPTER 6

A scene, in which some ladies will possibly think Amelia's conduct exceptionable.

BOOTH and his wife being left alone, a solemn silence prevailed during a few minutes. At last Amelia, who though a good, was yet a human creature, said to her husband, 'Pray, my dear, do inform me, what could put you into so great a passion when Mrs Ellison first offered me the tickets for this masquerade?'

'I had rather you would not ask me,' said Booth. 'You have obliged me greatly in your ready acquiescence with my desire, and you will add greatly to the obligation by not enquiring the reason of it. This you may depend upon, Amelia, that your good and happiness are the great objects of all my wishes, and the end I propose in all my actions. This view alone could tempt me to refuse you any thing, or to conceal any thing from you.'

'I will appeal to yourself,' answered she, 'whether this be not using me too much like a child, and whether I can possibly help being a little offended at it.'

'Not in the least,' replied he. 'I use you only with the tenderness of a friend. I would only endeavour to conceal that from you, which I think would give you uneasiness if you knew. These are called the pious frauds of friendship.'

'I detest all fraud,' says she; 'and pious is too good an epithet to be joined to so odious a word. You have often, you know, tried these frauds with no better effect than to teize and torment me. You cannot imagine, my dear, but that I must have a violent desire to know the reason of words, which, I own, I never expected to have heard. And the more you have shewn a reluctance to tell me, the more eagerly I have longed to know. Nor can this be called a vain curiosity; since I seem so much interested in this affair. If after all this, you still insist on keeping the secret, I will convince you, I am not ignorant of the duty of a wife, by my obedience; but I cannot help telling you at the same time, you will make me one of the most miserable of women.'

'That is,' cries he, 'in other words, my dear Emily, to say, I will be contented without the secret; but I am resolved to know it nevertheless.'

'Nay, if you say so,' cries she, 'I am convinced you will tell me – Positively, dear Billy, I must and will know.'

'Why then positively,' says Booth, 'I will tell you. And I think I shall then shew you, that however well you may know the duty of a wife, I am not always able to behave like a husband. In a word then, my dear, the secret is no more than this; I am unwilling you should receive any more presents from my lord.'

'Mercy upon me!' cries she, with all the marks of astonishment – 'what, a masquerade ticket!' –

'Yes, my dear,' cries he, 'that is perhaps the very worst and most dangerous of all. Few men make presents of those tickets to ladies, without intending to meet them at the place. And what do we know of your companion? To be sincere with you, I have not liked her behaviour for some time. What might be the consequence of going with such a woman to such a place, to meet such a person, I tremble to think – And now, my dear, I have told you my reason of refusing her offer with some little vehemence, and, I think, I need explain myself no farther.'

'You need not indeed, sir,' answered she. 'Good Heavens! did I ever expect to hear this! I can appeal to Heaven, nay, I will appeal to yourself, Mr Booth, if I have ever done any thing to deserve such a suspicion. If ever any action of mine, nay, if ever any thought had stained the innocence of my soul, I could be contented.'

'How cruelly do you mistake me,' said Booth – 'what suspicion have I ever shewn?'

'Can you ask it,' answered she, 'after what you have just now declared?'

'If I have declared any suspicion of you,' replied he, 'or if ever I entertained a thought leading that way, may the worst of evils that ever afflicted human nature attend me. I know the pure innocence of that tender bosom, I do know it, my lovely angel, and adore it. The snares which might be laid for that innocence, were alone the cause of my apprehension. I feared what a wicked and voluptuous man, resolved to sacrifice every thing to the gratification of a sensual appetite with the most delicious repast, might attempt. If ever I injured the unspotted whiteness of thy virtue in my imagination, may hell –'

'Do not terrify me,' cries she interrupting him, 'with such imprecations. O Mr Booth, Mr Booth, you must well know that a woman's virtue is always her sufficient guard. No husband without suspecting that can suspect any danger from those snares you mention – And why, if you are liable to take such things into your head, may not your suspicions fall on me, as well as on any other? for sure nothing was ever more unjust, I will not say ungrateful, than the suspicions which you have bestowed on his lordship. I do solemnly declare, in all the times I have seen the poor man, he hath never once offered the least forwardness. His behaviour hath been polite indeed, but rather remarkably distant than otherwise. Particularly when we played at cards together. I don't remember he spoke ten words to me all the evening; and when I was at his house, tho' he shewed the greatest fondness imaginable to the children, he took so little notice of me, that a vain woman would have been very little pleased with him. And if he gave them many presents, he never offered me one. The first indeed which he ever offered me was that, which you in that kind manner forced me to refuse.'

'All this may be only the effect of art,' said Booth. 'I am convinced he doth, nay I am convinced he must like you; and my good friend James, who perfectly well knows the world, told me, that his lordship's character was that of the most profuse in his pleasures with women; nay, what said Mrs James this very evening, "his lordship is extremely generous – where he likes." I shall never forget the sneer with which she spoke those last words.'

'I am convinced they injure him,' cries Amelia. 'As for Mrs James, she was always given to be censorious. I remarked it in her long ago, as her greatest fault. And for the colonel, I believe, he may find faults enow of this kind in his own bosom, without searching after them among his neighbours. I am sure he hath the most impudent look of all the men I know; and I solemnly declare, the very last time he was here, he put me out of countenance more than once.'

'Colonel James,' answered Booth, 'may have his faults very probably. I do not look upon him as a saint, nor do I believe he desires I should; but what interest could he have in abusing this lord's character to me: or why should I question his truth, when he assured me that my lord had never done an act of beneficence in his life, but for the sake of some woman whom he lusted after?'

'Then I myself can confute him,' replied Amelia: 'for besides his services to you, which for the future I shall wish to forget, and his kindness to my little babes, how inconsistent is the character which James gives of him, with his lordship's behaviour to his own nephew and niece, whose extreme fondness of their uncle sufficiently proclaims his goodness to them. – I need not mention all that I have heard from Mrs Ellison, every word of which I believe: for I have great reason to think, notwithstanding some little levity, which to give her her due she sees and condemns in herself, she is a very good sort of woman.'

'Well, my dear,' cries Booth, 'I may have been deceived, and I heartily hope I am so; but in cases of this nature it is always good to be on the surest side: for as Congreve[15] says,

The wise too jealous are. Fools too secure.'

Here Amelia burst into tears, upon which Booth immediately caught her in his arms, and endeavoured to comfort her. – Passion however for a while obstructed her speech, and at last she cried, – 'O Mr Booth, can I bear to hear the word jealousy from your mouth?'

'Why, my love,' said Booth, 'will you so fatally misunderstand my meaning? How often shall I protest that it is not of you, but of him that I was jealous. If you could look into my breast, and there read all the most secret thoughts of my heart, you would not see one faint idea to your dishonour.'

'I don't misunderstand you, my dear,' said she, 'so much as I am afraid you misunderstand yourself. What is it you fear? – you mention not force but snares. Is not this to confess, at least, that you have some doubt of my understanding? Do you then really imagine me so weak as to be cheated of my virtue? Am I to be deceived into an affection for a man, before I perceive the least inward hint of my danger? No, Mr Booth, believe me a woman must be a fool indeed, who can have in earnest such an excuse for her actions. I have not, I think, any very high opinion of my judgment; but so far I shall rely upon it, that no man breathing could have any such designs as you have apprehended, without my immediately seeing them; and how I should then act, I hope my whole conduct to you hath sufficiently declared.'

'Well, my dear,' cries Booth, 'I beg you will mention it no more, if possible forget it. I hope, nay I believe, I have been in the wrong, pray forgive me. –'

'I will, I do forgive you, my dear,' said she. 'If forgiveness be a proper word for one whom you have rather made miserable than angry; but let me entreat you to banish for ever all such suspicions from your mind. I hope Mrs Ellison hath not discovered the real cause of your passion; but poor woman, if she had, I am convinced it would go no farther. Oh Heavens! I would not for the world it should reach his lordship's ears. You would lose the best friend that ever man had. Nay, I would not for his own sake, poor man! for I really believe it would affect him greatly, and I must, I cannot help having an esteem for so much goodness. An esteem which by this dear hand,' said she, taking Booth's hand and kissing it, 'no man alive shall ever obtain by making love to me.'

Booth caught her in his arms and tenderly embraced her. After which the reconciliation soon became complete; and Booth in the contemplation of his happiness entirely buried all his jealous thoughts.

CHAPTER 7

A chapter in which there is much learning.

THE next morning whilst Booth was gone to take his morning-walk, Amelia went down into Mrs Ellison's apartment, where though she was received with great civility, yet she found that lady was not at all pleased with Mr Booth; and by some hints which dropt from her in conversation, Amelia very greatly apprehended that Mrs Ellison had too much suspicion of her husband's real uneasiness. For that lady declared very openly, she could not help perceiving what sort of man Mr Booth was; 'and though I have the greatest regard for you, madam, in the world,' said she, 'yet I think myself in honour obliged not to impose on his lordship, who, I know very well, hath conceived his greatest liking to the captain, on my telling him that he was the best husband in the world.'

Amelia's fears gave her much disturbance, and when her husband returned, she acquainted him with them; upon which occasion, as it was natural, she resumed a little the topic of their former discourse, nor could she help casting, tho' in very gentle terms, some slight blame on Booth, for having entertained a suspicion, which she said, might in its consequence very possibly prove their ruin, and occasion the loss of his lordship's friendship.

Booth became highly affected with what his wife said, and the more as he had just received a note from Colonel James, informing him that the colonel had heard of a vacant company in the regiment which Booth had mentioned to him, and that he had been with his lordship about it, who had promised to use his utmost interest to obtain him the command.

The poor man now exprest the utmost concern for his yesterday's behaviour, said, 'he believed the devil had taken possession of him,' and concluded with crying out, 'sure I was born, my dearest creature, to be your torment.'

Amelia no sooner saw her husband's distress, than she instantly forebore whatever might seem likely to aggravate it, and applied herself with all her power to comfort him. 'If you will give me leave to offer my advice, my dearest soul,' said she, 'I think all might yet be remedied. I think you know me too well, to suspect that the desire of diversion should induce me to mention, what I am now going to propose. And in that confidence, I will ask you to let me accept my lord's and Mrs Ellison's offer, and go to the masquerade. No matter how little while I stay there: if you desire it, I will not be an hour from you. I can make a hundred excuses to come home, or tell a real truth, and say I am tired with the place. The bare going will cure every thing.'

Amelia had no sooner done speaking, than Booth immediately approved her advice, and readily gave his consent. He could not however help saying, 'that the shorter her stay was there, the more agreeable it would be to him: for you know, my dear,' said he, 'I would never willingly be a moment out of your sight.'

In the afternoon Amelia sent to invite Mrs Ellison to a dish of tea; and Booth undertook to laugh off all that had past yesterday, in which attempt, the abundant good humour of that lady gave him great hopes of success.

Mrs Bennet came that afternoon to make a visit, and was almost an hour with Booth and Amelia, before the entry of Mrs Ellison.

Mr Booth had hitherto rather disliked this young lady, and had wondered at the pleasure which Amelia declared she took in her company. This afternoon, however, he changed his opinion, and liked her almost as much as his wife had done. She did indeed behave at this time with more than ordinary gaiety; and good-humour gave a glow to her countenance that set off her features, which were very pretty, to the best advantage, and lessened the deadness that had usually appeared in her complexion.

But if Booth was now pleased with Mrs Bennet, Amelia was still more pleased with her than ever. For when their discourse turned on love, Amelia discovered that her new friend had all the same sentiments on that subject with herself. In the course of their conversation, Booth gave Mrs Bennet a hint of wishing her a good husband, upon which both the ladies declaimed against second marriages, with equal vehemence.

Upon this occasion, Booth and his wife discovered a talent in their visitant, to which they had been before entirely strangers, and for which they both greatly admired her; and this was that the lady was a good scholar, in which indeed she had the advantage of poor Amelia, whose reading was confined to English plays, and poetry; besides which, I think, she had conversed only with the divinity of the great and learned Dr Barrow,[16] and with the histories of the excellent Bishop Burnet.[17]

Amelia delivered herself on the subject of second marriages with much eloquence and great good sense; but when Mrs Bennet came to give her opinion, she spoke in the following manner, 'I shall not enter into the question concerning the legality of bigamy.[18] Our laws certainly allow it, and so, I think, doth our religion. We are now debating only on the decency of it, and in this light, I own myself as strenuous an advocate against it, as any Roman matron would have been in those ages of the commonwealth, when it was held to be infamous.[19] For my own part, how great a paradox soever my opinion may seem, I solemnly declare, I see but little difference between having two husbands at one time, and at several times; and of this I am very confident, that the same degree of love for a first husband, which preserves a woman in the one case, will preserve her in the other. There is one argument, which I scarce know how to deliver before you, sir; but – if a woman hath lived with her first husband without having children, I think it unpardonable in her to carry barrenness into a second family. On the contrary, if she hath children by her first husband, to give them a second father is still more unpardonable.'

'But suppose, madam,' cries Booth, interrupting her, with a smile, 'she should have had children by her first husband, and have lost them.'

'That is a case,' answered she, with a sigh, 'which I did not desire to think of, and, I must own it, the most favourable light in which a second marriage can be seen. But the scriptures, as Petrarch observes,[20] rather suffer them than commend them; and St Jerome[21] speaks against them with the utmost bitterness.' 'I remember,' cries Booth, (who was willing either to shew his learning, or to draw out the lady's,) a very wise law of Charondas[22] the famous lawgiver of Thurium, by which men, who married a second time, were removed from all public councils: for it was scarce reasonable to suppose, that he who was so great a fool in his own family, should be wise in public affairs. And tho' second marriages were permitted among the Romans, yet they were at the same time discouraged; and those Roman widows who refused them, were held in high esteem, and honoured with what Valerius Maximus[23] calls the *corona pudicitiae*. In the noble family of Camilli,[24] there was not, in many ages, a single instance of this, which Martial[25] calls adultery:

Quae toties nubit, non nubit; adultera lege est.'

'True, sir,' says Mrs Bennet, 'and Virgil[26] calls this a violation of chastity, and makes Dido speak of it with the utmost detestation:

Sed mihi vel tellus optem prius ima dehiscat;
Vel Pater omnipotens adigat me fulmine ad umbras,
Pallentes umbras Erebi, noctemque profundam,
Ante, Pudor, quam te violo, aut tua jura resolvo.
Ille meos, primum qui me sibi junxit, amores,
Ille habeat semper secum, servetque sepulchro.'

She repeated these lines with so strong an emphasis, that she almost frightned Amelia out of her wits, and not a little staggered Booth, who was himself no contemptible scholar. – He expressed great admiration of the lady's learning; upon which she said it was all the fortune given her by her father, and all the dower left her by her husband; 'and sometimes,' said she, 'I am inclined to think I enjoy more pleasure from it, than if they had bestowed on me what the world would in general call more valuable.' She then took occasion from the surprize which Booth had affected to conceive at her repeating Latin with so good a grace, to comment on that great absurdity, (for so she termed it,) of excluding women from learning; for which they were equally qualified with the men, and in which so many had made so notable a proficiency: for a proof of which, she mentioned Madam Dacier,[27] and many others.

Tho' both Booth and Amelia outwardly concurred with her sentiments, it may be a question whether they did not assent rather out of complaisance, than from their real judgment.

CHAPTER 8

Containing some unaccountable behaviour in Mrs Ellison.

MRS ELLISON made her entrance at the end of the preceding discourse. At her first appearance she put on an unusual degree of formality and reserve; but when Amelia had acquainted her that she designed to accept the favour intended her, she soon began to alter the gravity of her muscles, and presently fell in with that ridicule which Booth thought proper to throw on his yesterday's behaviour.

The conversation now became very lively and pleasant, in

which Booth having mentioned the discourse that passed in the last chapter, and having greatly complimented Mrs Bennet's speech on that occasion, Mrs Ellison who was as strenuous an advocate on the other side, began to rally that lady extremely, declaring it was a certain sign she intended to marry again soon. 'Married ladies,' cries she, 'I believe, sometimes think themselves in earnest in such declarations, tho' they are oftner perhaps meant as compliments to their husbands; but when widows exclaim loudly against second marriages, I would always lay a wager, that the man, if not the wedding-day, is absolutely fixed on.'

Mrs Bennet made very little answer to this sarcasm. Indeed she had scarce opened her lips from the time of Mrs Ellison's coming into the room, and had grown particularly grave at the mention of the masquerade. Amelia imputed this to her being left out of the party, a matter which is often no small mortification to human pride, and in a whisper asked Mrs Ellison if she could not procure a third ticket; to which she received an absolute negative.

During the whole time of Mrs Bennet's stay, which was above an hour afterwards, she remained perfectly silent, and looked extremely melancholy. This made Amelia very uneasy, as she concluded she had guest the cause of her vexation. In which opinion she was the more confirmed from certain looks of no very pleasant kind, which Mrs Bennet now and then cast on Mrs Ellison, and the more than ordinary concern that appeared in the former lady's countenance, whenever the masquerade was mentioned, and which unfortunately was the principal topic of their discourse: for Mrs Ellison gave a very elaborate description of the extreme beauty of the place, and elegance of the diversion.

When Mrs Bennet was departed, Amelia could not help again solliciting Mrs Ellison for another ticket, declaring she was certain Mrs Bennet had a great inclination to go with them; but Mrs Ellison again excused herself from asking it of his lordship. 'Besides, madam,' says she, 'if I would go thither with Mrs Bennet, which, I own to you, I don't chuse, as she is a person whom *no body knows*, I very much doubt whether she herself would like it: for she is a woman of a very unaccountable turn. All her delight lies in books; and as for public diversions, I have heard her often declare her abhorrence of them.'

'What then,' said Amelia, 'could occasion all that gravity from the moment the masquerade was mentioned?'

'As to that,' answered the other, 'there is no guessing. You have seen her altogether as grave before now. She hath had these fits of gravity at times ever since the death of her husband.'

'Poor creature!' cries Amelia. 'I heartily pity her. For she must certainly suffer a great deal on these occasions. I declare I have taken a strange fancy to her.'

'Perhaps you would not like her so well, if you knew her thoroughly,' answered Mrs Ellison. 'She is upon the whole but of a whimsical temper; and, if you will take my opinion, you should not cultivate too much intimacy with her. I know you will never mention what I say; but she is like some pictures which please best at a distance.'

Amelia did not seem to agree with these sentiments, and she greatly importuned Mrs Ellison to be more explicit; but to no purpose; she continued to give only dark hints to Mrs Bennet's disadvantage; and, if ever she let drop something a little too harsh, she failed not immediately to contradict herself, by throwing some gentle commendations into the other scale; so that her conduct appeared utterly unaccountable to Amelia, and upon the whole, she knew not whether to conclude Mrs Ellison to be a friend or enemy to Mrs Bennet.

During this latter conversation Booth was not in the room: for he had been summoned down stairs by the serjeant, who came to him with news from Murphy whom he had met that evening, and who assured the serjeant, that if he was desirous of recovering the debt, which he had before pretended[28] to have on Booth, he might shortly have an opportunity; for that there was to be a very strong petition to the board, the next time they sat. Murphy said further, that he need not fear having his money: for that to his certain knowledge the captain had several things of great value, and even his children had gold-watches.

This greatly alarmed Booth, and still more, when the serjeant reported to him from Murphy, that all these things had been seen in his possession within a day last past. He now plainly perceived, as he thought, that Murphy himself, or one of his emissaries, had been the supposed madman; and he now very well accounted to himself in his own mind, for all that had happened, conceiving that the design was to examine into the state of his effects, and to try whether it was worth his creditors' while to plunder him by law.

At his return to his apartment, he communicated what he had heard to Amelia and Mrs Ellison, not disguising his apprehensions of the enemy's intentions; but Mrs Ellison endeavoured to laugh him out of his fears, calling him faint-hearted, and assuring him he might depend on her lawyer. – 'Till you hear from him,' said she, 'you may rest entirely contented: for take my word for it, no danger can happen to you, of which you will not be timely apprized by him. And as for the fellow that had the impudence to come into your room, if he was sent on such an errand as you mention, I heartily wish I had been at home; I would have secured him safe with a constable, and have carried him directly before Justice Thrasher. I know the Justice is an enemy to bailiffs on his own account.'[29]

This heartening speech a little roused the courage of Booth, and somewhat comforted Amelia, tho' the spirits of both had been too much hurried, to suffer them either to give or receive much entertainment that evening; which Mrs Ellison perceiving, soon took her leave, and left this unhappy couple to seek relief from sleep, that powerful friend to the distressed, tho' like other powerful friends, he is not always ready to give his assistance to those who want it most.

CHAPTER 9

Containing a very strange incident.

WHEN the husband and wife were alone, they again talked over the news which the serjeant had brought; on which occasion, Amelia did all she could to conceal her own fears, and to quiet those of her husband. At last she turned the conversation to another subject, and poor Mrs Bennet was brought on the carpet. 'I should be sorry,' cries Amelia, 'to find I had conceived an affection for a bad woman; and yet I begin to fear Mrs Ellison knows something of her more than she cares to discover; why else should she be unwilling to be seen with her in public? Besides, I have observed that Mrs Ellison hath been always backward to introduce her to me, nor would ever bring her to my apartment, though I have often desired her. Nay, she hath given me frequent hints not to cultivate the acquaintance. What do you think, my dear? – I should be very sorry to contract an intimacy with a wicked person.'

'Nay, my dear,' cries Booth, 'I know no more of her, nor indeed hardly so much as yourself. But this I think, that if Mrs Ellison knows any reason why she should not have introduced Mrs Bennet into your company, she was very much in the wrong in introducing her into it.'

In discourses of this kind they past the remainder of the evening. In the morning Booth rose early, and going down stairs received from little Betty a sealed note, which contained the following words:

> *Beware, beware, beware,*
> *For I apprehend a dreadful snare*
> *Is laid for virtuous innocence,*
> *Under a friend's false pretence.*

Booth immediately enquired of the girl who brought this note, and was told it came by a chairman, who having delivered it departed without saying a word.

He was extremely staggered at what he read, and presently referred the advice to the same affair on which he had received those hints from Atkinson the preceding evening; but when he came to consider the words more maturely, he could not so well reconcile the two last lines of this poetical epistle, if it may be so called, with any danger which the law gave him reason to apprehend. Mr Murphy and his gang could not well be said to attack either his innocence or virtue; nor did they attack him under any colour or pretence of friendship.

After much deliberation on this matter, a very strange suspicion came into his head; and this was, that he was betrayed by Mrs Ellison. He had for some time conceived no very high opinion of that good gentlewoman, and he now began to suspect that she was bribed to betray him. By this means he thought he could best account for the strange appearance of the supposed madman. And when this conceit once had birth in his mind, several circumstances nourished and improved it. Among these were her jocose behaviour and raillery on that occasion, and her attempt to ridicule his fears from the message which the serjeant had brought him.

This suspicion was indeed preposterous, and not at all warranted by, or even consistent with the character and whole behaviour of Mrs Ellison; but it was the only one which at that time suggested itself to his mind; and however blameable it might be, it was certainly not unnatural in him to entertain it: for so great a torment is anxiety to the human mind, that we always endeavour to relieve ourselves from it, by guesses however doubtful or uncertain; on all which occasions dislike and hatred are the surest guides to lead our suspicion to its object.

When Amelia rose to breakfast, Booth produced the note which he had received, saying, 'my dear, you have so often blamed me for keeping secrets from you, and I have so often indeed endeavoured to conceal secrets of this kind from you with such ill success, that, I think, I shall never more attempt it.' Amelia read the letter hastily, and seemed not a little discomposed; then turning to Booth with a very disconsolate countenance she said, 'sure Fortune takes a delight in terrifying us! what can be the meaning of this?' – Then fixing her eyes attentively on the paper, she perused it for some time, till Booth cried – 'How is it possible, my Emily, you can read such stuff patiently! The verses are certainly as bad as ever were written.' 'I was trying, my dear,' answered she, 'to recollect the hand; for I will take my oath, I have seen it before, and that very lately' – and suddenly she cried out with great emotion, 'I remember it perfectly now – It is Mrs Bennet's hand. Mrs Ellison shewed me a letter from her but a day or two ago. It is a very remarkable hand, and I am positive it is hers.'

'If it be hers,' cries Booth, 'what can she possibly mean by the latter part of her caution? Sure Mrs Ellison hath no intention to betray us.'

'I know not what she means,' answered Amelia, 'but I am resolved to know immediately; for I am certain of the hand. By the greatest luck in the world, she told me yesterday where her lodgings were, when she pressed me exceedingly to come and see her. She lives but a very few doors from us, and I will go to her this moment.'

Booth made not the least objection to his wife's design. His curiosity was indeed as great as hers, and so was his impatience to satisfy it, tho' he mentioned not this his impatience to Amelia; and perhaps it had been well for him if he had.

Amelia therefore presently equipped herself in her walking dress, and leaving her children to the care of her husband, made all possible haste to Mrs Bennet's lodgings.

Amelia waited near five minutes at Mrs Bennet's door, before any one came to open it; at length a maid-servant appeared, who being asked if Mrs Bennet was at home, answered with some confusion in her countenance, that she did not know; 'but, madam,' said she, 'if you will send up your name, I will go and see.' Amelia then told her name, and the wench, after staying a considerable time, returned and acquainted her that Mrs Bennet was at home. She was then ushered into a parlour, and told that the lady would wait on her presently.

In this parlour, Amelia cooled her heels, as the phrase is, near a quarter of an hour. She seemed indeed at this time, in the miserable situation of one of those poor wretches, who make their morning visits to the great, to solicit favours, or perhaps to solicit the payment of a debt: for both are alike treated as beggars, and the latter sometimes considered as the more troublesome beggars of the two.

During her stay here, Amelia observed the house to be in great confusion; a great bustle was heard above stairs, and the maid ran up and down several times in a great hurry.

At length Mrs Bennet herself came in. She was greatly disordered in her looks, and had, as the women call it, huddled on her cloaths in much haste; for in truth, she was in bed when Amelia first came. Of this fact she informed her, as the only apology she could make for having caused her to wait so long for her company.

Amelia very readily accepted her apology, but asked her with a smile, if these early hours were usual with her. Mrs Bennet turned as red as scarlet at the question, and answered, 'no indeed, dear madam. I am, for the most part, a very early riser; but I happened accidentally to sit up very late last night. I am sure I had little expectation of your intending me such a favour this morning.'

Amelia looking very stedfastly at her, said: 'Is it possible, madam, you should think such a note as this would raise no curiosity in me?' She then gave her the note, asking her if she did not know the hand.

Mrs Bennet appeared in the utmost surprize and confusion at this instant. Indeed if Amelia had conceived but the slightest suspicion before, the behaviour of the lady would have been a sufficient confirmation to her of the truth. She waited not therefore for an answer, which indeed the other seemed in no haste to give; but conjured her in the most earnest manner, to explain to her the meaning of so extraordinary an act of friendship: 'for so,' said she, 'I esteem it; being convinced you must have sufficient reason for the warning you have given me.'

Mrs Bennet after some hesitation, answered: 'I need not, I believe, tell you how much I am surprized at what you have shewn me, and the chief reason of my surprize is; how you came to discover my hand. Sure, madam, you have not shewn it to Mrs Ellison.'

Amelia declared she had not; but desired she would question her no farther. 'What signifies how I discovered it, since your hand it certainly is?'

'I own it is,' cries Mrs Bennet, recovering her spirits, 'and since you have not shewn it to that woman, I am satisfied. I begin to guess now whence you might have your information; but no matter, I wish I had never done any thing of which I ought to be more ashamed. – No one can, I think, justly accuse me of a crime on that account; and I thank Heaven, my shame will never be directed by the false opinion of the world. – Perhaps it was wrong to shew my letter; but when I consider all circumstances, I can forgive it.'

'Since you have guessed the truth,' said Amelia, 'I am not obliged to deny it. She indeed shewed me your letter; but I am sure you have not the least reason to be ashamed of it. On the contrary, your behaviour on so melancholy an occasion was highly praiseworthy; and your bearing up under such afflictions, as the loss of a husband in so dreadful a situation, was truly great and heroical.'

'So Mrs Ellison then hath shewn you my letter?' cries Mrs Bennet eagerly.[30]

'Why, did not you guess it yourself?' answered Amelia, 'otherwise I am sure I have betrayed my honour in mentioning it. I hope you have not drawn me inadvertent into any breach of my promise. Did you not assert, and that with an absolute certainty, that you knew she had shewn me your letter, and that you was not angry with her for so doing?'

'I am so confused,' replied Mrs Bennet, 'that I scarce know what I say; yes, yes, I remember I did say so – I wish I had no greater reason to be angry with her than that.'

'For Heaven's sake,' cries Amelia, 'do not delay my request any longer! what you say now greatly increases my curiosity; and my mind will be on the rack till you discover your whole meaning: for I am more and more convinced, that something of the utmost importance was the purport of your message.'

'Of the utmost importance indeed,' cries Mrs Bennet, 'at least you will own my apprehensions were sufficiently well founded – O gracious Heaven, how happy shall I think myself, if I should have proved your preservation! I will indeed explain my meaning; but in order to disclose all my fears in their just colours, I must unfold my whole history to you. Can you have patience, madam, to listen to the story of the most unfortunate of women?'

Amelia assured her of the highest attention; and Mrs Bennet soon after began to relate what is written in the seventh book of this history.

BOOK VII

CHAPTER 1

A very short chapter, and consequently requiring no preface.

MRS BENNET having fastened the door, and both the ladies having taken their places, she once or twice offered to speak, when passion stopt her utterance; and after a minute's silence she burst into a flood of tears. Upon which Amelia expressing the utmost tenderness of her, as well by her look as by her accent; cry'd – 'What can be the reason, dear madam, of all this emotion?' – 'O Mrs Booth,' answered she, – 'I find I have undertaken what I am not able to perform – You would not wonder at my emotion, if you knew you had an adulteress and a murderer now standing before you.'

Amelia turned pale as death at these words, which Mrs Bennet observing, collected all the force she was able, and a little composing her countenance, cry'd, 'I see, madam, I have terrified you with such dreadful words; but I hope you will not think me guilty of these crimes in the blackest degree.' – 'Guilty!' cries Amelia. 'Oh Heavens!' 'I believe indeed your candour,' continued Mrs Bennet, 'will be readier to acquit me than I am to acquit myself – Indiscretion, at least, the highest, most unpardonable indiscretion, I shall always lay to my own charge; and when I reflect on the fatal consequences, I can never, never forgive myself.' Here she again began to lament in so bitter a manner, that Amelia endeavoured, as much as she could (for she was herself greatly shocked) to sooth and comfort her; telling her, that if indiscretion was her highest crime, the unhappy consequences made her rather an unfortunate than a guilty person; and concluded by saying, – 'Indeed, madam, you have raised my curiosity to the highest pitch, and I beg you will proceed with your story.'

Mrs Bennet then seemed a second time going to begin her relation, when she cried out, 'I would, if possible, tire you with no more of my unfortunate life than just with that part which leads to catastrophe, in which I think you may yourself be interested; but I protest I am at a loss where to begin.'

'Begin wherever you please, dear madam,' cries Amelia; 'but I beg you will consider my impatience.' 'I do consider it,' answered Mrs Bennet; 'And therefore would begin with that part of my story which leads directly to what concerns yourself: for how, indeed, should my life produce any thing worthy your notice?' – 'Do not say so, madam,' cries Amelia, 'I assure you I have long suspected there were some very remarkable incidents in your life, and have only wanted an opportunity to impart to you my desire of hearing them: – I beg therefore you would make no more apologies.' – 'I will not, madam,' cries Mrs Bennet, 'and yet I would avoid any thing trivial; tho', indeed, in stories of distress, especially where love is concerned, many little incidents may appear trivial to those who have never felt the passion, which to delicate minds are the most interesting part of the whole.' – 'Nay but, dear madam,' cries Amelia, 'This is all preface.' –

'Well, madam,' answered Mrs Bennet, 'I will consider your impatience.' She then rallied all her spirits in the best manner she could, and began as is written in the next chapter.

And here possibly the reader will blame Mrs Bennet for taking her story so far back, and relating so much of her life in which Amelia had no concern; but in truth, she was desirous of inculcating a good opinion of herself, from recounting those transactions where her conduct was unexceptionable, before she came to the more dangerous and suspicious part of her character. This I really suppose to have been her intention: for to sacrifice the time and patience of Amelia at such a season, to the mere love of talking of herself, would have been as unpardonable in her, as the bearing it was in Amelia a proof of the most perfect good breeding.

CHAPTER 2

The beginning of Mrs Bennet's history.

'I WAS the younger of two daughters of a clergyman in Essex; of one in whose praise if I should indulge my fond heart in speaking, I think my invention could not outgo the reality. He was indeed well worthy of the cloth he wore; and that, I think, is the highest character a man can obtain.

'During the first part of my life, even till I reached my sixteenth year, I can recollect nothing to relate to you. All was one long serene day, in looking back upon which, as when we cast our eyes on a calm sea, no object arises to my view. All appears one scene of happiness and tranquillity.

'On the day, then, when I became sixteen years old, must I begin my history; for on that day, I first tasted the bitterness of sorrow.

'My father, besides those prescribed by our religion, kept five festivals every year. These were on his wedding-day, and on the birth-day of each of his little family. On these occasions he used to invite two or three neighbours to his house, and to indulge himself, as he said, in great excess: for so he called drinking a pint of very small punch; and indeed it might appear excess to one who on other days rarely tasted any liquor stronger than small beer.

'Upon my unfortunate birth-day then, when we were all in a high degree of mirth, my mother having left the room after dinner, and staying away pretty long, my father sent me to see for her. I went according to his orders; but tho' I searched the whole house, and called after her without doors, I could neither see nor hear her. I was a little alarmed at this (tho' far from suspecting any great mischief had befallen her) and ran back to acquaint my father, who answered coolly, (for he was a man of the calmest temper,) "Very well, my dear, I suppose she is not gone far, and will be here immediately." Half an hour or more past after this, when, she not returning, my father himself expressed some surprize at her stay; declaring, it must be some matter of importance which could detain her at that time from her company. His surprize now encreased every minute; and he began to grow uneasy, and to shew sufficient symptoms in his countenance of what he felt within. He then dispatched the servant maid to enquire after her mistress in the parish; but waited not her return; for she was scarce gone out of doors, before he begged leave of his guests to go himself on the same errand. The company now all broke up, and attended my father, all endeavouring to give him hopes that no mischief had happened. They searched the whole parish; but in vain: they could neither see my mother nor hear any news of her. My father returned home in a state little short of distraction. His friends in vain attempted to administer either advice or comfort; he threw himself on the floor in the most bitter agonies of despair.

'Whilst he lay in this condition, my sister and myself lying by him all equally, I believe, and completely miserable, our old servant maid came into the room, and cried out, her mind misgave her that she knew where her mistress was. Upon these words my father sprung from the floor, and asked her eagerly, where? – But oh! Mrs Booth, how can I describe the particulars of a scene to you, the remembrance of which chills my blood with horror, and which the agonies of my mind, when it past, made all a scene of confusion! The fact then in short was this; my mother, who was a most indulgent mistress to one servant, which was all we kept, was unwilling, I suppose, to disturb her at her dinner; and therefore went herself to fill her tea-kettle at a well, into which stretching herself too far, as we imagine, the water then being very low, she fell with the tea-kettle in her hand. The missing this gave the poor old wretch the first hint of her suspicion, which upon examination was found to be too well grounded.

'What we all suffered on this occasion may more easily be felt than described.' – 'It may indeed,' answered Amelia, 'and I am so sensible of it, that unless you have a mind to see me faint before your face, I beg you will order me something; a glass of water, if you please.' Mrs Bennet immediately complied with her friend's request; a glass of water was brought, and some hartshorn drops infused into it: which Amelia having drank off, declared she found herself much better; and then Mrs Bennet proceeded thus:

'I will not dwell on a scene which I see hath already so much affected your tender heart, and which is as disagreeable to me to relate, as it can be to you to hear. I will therefore only mention to you the behaviour of my father on this occasion, which was indeed becoming a philosopher and a Christian divine. On the day after my mother's funeral, he sent for my sister and myself into his room; where, after many caresses, and every demonstration of fatherly tenderness, as well in silence as in words, he began to exhort us to bear with patience the great calamity that had befallen us; saying, "That as every human accident, how terrible soever, must happen to us by divine permission at least, a due sense of our duty to our great Creator, must teach us an absolute submission to his will. Not only religion, but common sense must teach us this: for oh! my dear children," cries he, "How vain is all resistance, all repining! Could tears wash back again my angel from the grave, I should drain all the juices of my body through my eyes; but oh, could we fill up that cursed well with our tears, how fruitless would be all our sorrow!" – I think I repeat you his very words: for the impression they made on me is never to be obliterated. – He then proceeded to comfort us with the chearful thought that the loss was entirely our own, and that my mother was greatly a gainer by the accident which we lamented. "I have a wife," cries he, "my children, and you have a mother now amongst the heavenly choir: how selfish therefore is all our grief! How cruel to her are all our wishes!" – In this manner he talked to us near half an hour, tho' I must frankly own to you, his arguments had not the immediate good effect on us which they deserved: for we retired from him very little the better for his exhortations; however, they became every day more and more forcible upon our recollection; indeed they were greatly strengthened by his example: for in this, as in all other instances, he practised the doctrines which he taught. From this day he never mentioned my mother more, and soon after recovered his usual cheerfulness in public; tho' I have reason to think he paid many a bitter sigh in private to that remembrance which neither philosophy nor Christianity could expunge.

'My father's advice, enforced by his example, together with the kindness of some of our friends, assisted by that ablest of all the mental physicians, time, in a few months pretty well restored my tranquillity, when Fortune made a second attack on my quiet. My sister, whom I dearly loved, and who as warmly returned my affection, had fallen into an ill state of health some time before the fatal accident which I have related. She was indeed at that time so much better, that we had great hopes of her perfect recovery; but the disorders of her mind on that dreadful occasion so affected her body, that she presently relapsed to her former declining state, and thence grew continually worse and worse, till after a decay of near seven months, she followed my poor mother to the grave.

'I will not tire you, dear madam, with repetitions of grief; I will only mention two observations which have occurred to me from reflections on the two losses I have mentioned. The first is, that a mind once violently hurt grows, as it were, callous to any future impressions of grief; and is never capable of feeling the same pangs a second time. The other observation is, that the arrows of fortune, as well as all others, derive their force from the velocity with which they are discharged: for when they approach you by slow and perceptible degrees, they have but very little power to do you mischief.

'The truth of these observations I experienced, not only in my own heart, but in the behaviour of my father, whose philosophy seemed to gain a complete triumph over this latter calamity.

'Our family was now reduced to two; and my father grew extremely fond of me, as if he had now conferred an entire stock of affection on me, that had before been divided. His words indeed testified no less: for he daily called me his only darling, his whole comfort, his all. He committed the whole charge of his house to my care, and gave me the name of his little house-keeper, an appellation of which I was then as proud as any minister of state can be of his titles. But tho' I was very industrious in the discharge of my occupation, I did not, however, neglect my studies, in which I had made so great a proficiency, that I was become a pretty good mistress of the Latin language, and had made some progress in the Greek. I believe, madam, I have formerly acquainted you, that learning was the chief estate I inherited of my father, in which he had instructed me from my earliest youth.

'The kindness of this good man had at length wiped off the remembrance of all losses; and I, during two years, led a life of great tranquillity, I think I might almost say of perfect happiness.

'I was now in the nineteenth year of my age, when my father's good fortune removed us from the county of Essex into Hampshire, where a living was conferred on him by one of his old school-fellows, of twice the value of what he was before possessed of.

'His predecessor in this new living had died in very indifferent circumstances, and had left behind him a widow with two small children. My father, therefore, who with great economy had a most generous soul, bought the whole furniture of the parsonage-house at a very high price; some of it indeed he would have wanted: for tho' our little habitation in Essex was most completely furnished; yet it bore no proportion to the largeness of that house in which he was now to dwell.

'His motive, however, to the purchase was, I am convinced, solely generosity; which appeared sufficiently by the price he gave, and may be farther inforced by the kindness he shewed the widow in another instance: for he assigned her an apartment for the use of herself and her little family; which he told her, she was welcome to enjoy as long as it suited her conveniency.

'As this widow was very young, and generally thought to be tolerably pretty, tho' I own she had a cast with her eyes which I never liked, my father, you may suppose, acted from a less noble principle than I have hinted: but I must in justice acquit him; for these kind offers were made her before ever he had seen her face; and I have the greatest reason to think, that for a long time after he had seen her, he beheld her with much indifference.

'This act of my father's gave me, when I first heard it, great satisfaction: for I may, at least with the modesty of the ancient philosophers, call myself a lover of generosity; but when I became acquainted with the widow, I was still more delighted with what my father had done: for tho' I could not agree with those who thought her a consummate beauty, I must allow that she was very fully possessed of the power of making herself agreeable; and this power she exerted with so much success, with such indefatigable industry to oblige, that within three months I became in the highest manner pleased with my new acquaintance, and had contracted the most sincere friendship for her.

'But if I was so pleased with the widow, my father was by this time enamoured of her. She had, indeed, by the most artful conduct in the world, so insinuated herself into his favour, so entirely infatuated him, that he never shewed the least marks of cheerfulness in her absence, and could, in truth, scarce bear that she should be out of his sight.

'She had managed this matter so well, (O she is the most artful of women!) that my father's heart was gone before I ever suspected it was in danger. The discovery, you may easily believe, madam, was not pleasing. The name of a mother-in-law sounded dreadful in my ears, nor could I bear the thought of parting again with a share in those dear affections, of which I had purchased the whole by the loss of a beloved mother and sister.

'In the first hurry and disorder of my mind on this occasion, I committed a crime of the highest kind against all the laws of prudence and discretion. I took the young lady herself very roundly to task, treated her designs on my father as little better than a design to commit a theft; and in my passion, I believe, said she might be ashamed to think of marrying a man old enough to be her grandfather: for so in reality he almost was.

'The lady on this occasion acted finely the part of a hypocrite. She affected to be highly affronted at my unjust suspicions, as she called them, and proceeded to such asseverations of her innocence, that she almost brought me to discredit the evidence of my own eyes and ears.

'My father, however, acted much more honestly: for he fell the next day into a more violent passion with me than I had ever seen him in before, and asked me, whether I intended to return his paternal fondness by assuming the right of controlling his inclinations? with more of the like kind, which fully convinced me what had passed between him and the lady, and how little I had injured her in my suspicions.

'Hitherto I frankly own my aversion to this match had been principally on my own account: for I had no ill opinion of the woman, tho' I thought neither her circumstances nor my father's age promised any kind of felicity from such an union; but now I learnt some particulars, which, had not our quarrel become public in the parish, I should perhaps have never known. In short, I was informed, that this gentle obliging creature, as she had at first appeared to me, had the spirit of a tigress, and was by many believed to have broken the heart of her first husband.

'The truth of this matter being confirmed to me upon examination, I resolved not to suppress it. On this occasion fortune seemed to favour me, by giving me a speedy opportunity of seeing my father alone and in good humour. He now first began to open his intended marriage, telling me that he had formerly had some religious objections to bigamy, but he had very fully considered the matter, and had satisfied himself of its legality. He then faithfully promised me, that no second marriage should in the least impair his affection for me; and concluded with the highest elogiums on the goodness of the widow, protesting that it was her virtues and not her person with which he was enamoured.

'I now fell upon my knees before him, and bathing his hand in my tears, which flowed very plentifully from my eyes, acquainted him with all I had heard; and was so very imprudent, I might almost say so cruel, to disclose the author of my information.

'My father heard me without any indication of passion; and answered coldly, that if there was any proof of such facts, he should decline any further thoughts of his match; "But child," said he, "tho' I am far from suspecting the truth of what you tell me, as far as regards your knowledge; yet you know the inclination of the world to slander." However, before we parted he promised to make a proper enquiry into what I had told him. – But I ask your pardon, dear madam, I am running minutely into those particulars of my life, in which you have not the least concern.'

Amelia stopt her friend short in her apology, and tho', perhaps, she thought her impertinent enough, yet, (such was her good breeding) she gave her many assurances of a curiosity to know every incident of her life which she could remember; after which Mrs Bennet proceeded as in the next chatper.

CHAPTER 3

Continuation of Mrs Bennet's story.

'I THINK, madam,' said Mrs Bennet, 'I told you my father promised me to enquire farther into the affair; but he had hardly time to keep his word: for we separated pretty late in the evening, and early the next morning he was married to the widow.

'But tho' he gave no credit to my information, I had sufficient reason to think he did not forget it, by the resentment which he soon discovered to both the persons whom I had named as my informers.

'Nor was it long before I had good cause to believe, that my father's new wife was perfectly well acquainted with the good opinion I had of her, not only from her usage of me, but from certain hints which she threw forth with an air of triumph. One day particularly I remember she said to my father, upon his mentioning his age, "O, my dear, I hope you have many years yet to live; unless, indeed, I should be so cruel as to break your heart." She spoke these words looking me full in the face, and accompanied them with a sneer, in which the highest malice was visible under a thin covering of affected pleasantry.

'I will not entertain you, madam, with any thing so common as the cruel usage of a step-mother; nor of what affected me much more, the unkind behaviour of a father under such an influence. It shall suffice only to tell you, that I had the mortification to perceive the gradual and daily decrease of my father's affection. His smiles were converted into frowns; the tender appellations of child, and dear, were exchanged for plain Molly, that girl, that creature, and sometimes much harder names. I was at first turned all at once into a cypher, and at last seemed to be considered as a nuisance in the family.

'Thus altered was the man of whom I gave you such a character at the entrance on my story; but alas! he no longer acted from his own excellent disposition; but was in every thing governed and directed by my mother-in-law. In fact, whenever there is great disparity of years between husband and wife, the younger is, I believe, always possessed of absolute power over the elder: For superstition itself is a less firm support of absolute power than dotage.

'But tho' his wife was so entirely mistress of my father's will, that she could make him use me ill, she could not so perfectly subdue his understanding, as to prevent him from being conscious of such ill usage; and from this consciousness he began inveterately to hate me. Of this hatred he gave me numberless instances, and I protest to you, I know not any other reason for it than what I have assigned; and the cause, as experience hath convinced me, is adequate to the effect.

'While I was in this wretched situation, my father's unkindness having almost broken my heart, he came one day into my room with more anger in his countenance than I had ever seen; and after bitterly upbraiding me with my undutiful behaviour both to himself and his worthy consort, he bid me pack up my alls, and immediately prepare to quit his house; at the same time gave me a letter, and told me that would acquaint me where I might find a home; adding, that he doubted not but I expected and had indeed solicited the invitation; and left me with a declaration that he would have no spies in his family.

'The letter I found on opening it, was from my father's own sister; but before I mention the contents, I will give you a short sketch of her character, as it was somewhat particular. Her personal charms were not great; for she was very tall, very thin, and very homely. Of the defect of her beauty she was perhaps sensible; her vanity therefore retreated into her mind, where there is no looking-glass, and consequently where we can flatter ourselves with discovering almost whatever beauties we please. This is an encouraging circumstance; and yet I have observed, dear Mrs Booth, that few women ever seek these comforts from within, till they are driven to it by despair of finding any food for their vanity from without. Indeed, I believe, the first wish of our whole sex is to be handsome.'

Here both the ladies fixed their eyes on the glass, and both smiled.

'My aunt, however,' continued Mrs Bennet, 'from despair of

gaining any applause this way, had applied herself entirely to the contemplation of her understanding, and had improved this to such a pitch, that at the age of fifty, at which she was now arrived, she had contracted a hearty contempt for much the greater part of both sexes; for the women, as being idiots, and for the men, as the admirers of idiots. That word and fool were almost constantly in her mouth, and were bestowed with great liberality among all her acquaintance.

'This lady had spent one day only at my father's house in near two years. It was about a month before his second marriage. At her departure she took occasion to whisper me her opinion of the widow, whom she called a pretty idiot, and wondered how her brother could bear such company under his roof; for neither she nor I had at that time any suspicion of what afterwards happened.

'The letter which my father had just received, and which was the first she had sent him since his marriage, was of such a nature, that I should be unjust if I blamed him for being offended; fool and idiot were both plentifully bestowed in it as well on himself as on his wife. But what, perhaps, had principally offended him, was that part which related to me: for after much panegyric on my understanding, and saying he was unworthy of such a daughter, she considered his match not only as the highest indiscretion, as it related to himself; but as a downright act of injustice to me. One expression in it I shall never forget. "You have placed," said she, "a woman above your daughter, who, in understanding, the only valuable gift of nature, is the lowest in the whole class of pretty idiots." After much more of this kind, it concluded with inviting me to her house.

'I can truly say, that when I had read the letter, I entirely forgave my father's suspicion, that I had made some complaints to my aunt of his behaviour: for tho' I was indeed innocent, there was surely colour enough to suspect the contrary.

'Tho' I had never been greatly attached to my aunt, nor indeed had she formerly given me any reason for such an attachment; yet I was well enough pleased with her present invitation. To say the truth, I led so wretched a life where I then was, that it was impossible not to be a gainer by any exchange.

'I could not, however, bear the thoughts of leaving my father with an impression on his mind against me which I did not deserve. I endeavoured therefore to remove all his suspicion of my having complained to my aunt by the most earnest asseverations of my innocence; but they were all to no purpose. All my tears, all my vows, and all my entreaties were fruitless. My new mother indeed appeared to be my advocate; but she acted her part very poorly, and far from counterfeiting any desire of succeeding in my suit, she could not conceal the excessive joy which she felt on the occasion.

'Well, madam, the next day I departed for my aunt's, where after a long journey of forty miles, I arrived without having once broke my fast on the road: for grief is as capable as food of filling the stomach; and I had too much of the former to admit any of the latter. The fatigue of my journey and the agitation of my mind, joined to my fasting, so overpowered my spirits, that when I was taken from my horse, I immediately fainted away, in the arms of the man who helped me from my saddle. My aunt express'd great astonishment at seeing me in this condition, with my eyes almost swollen out of my head with tears; but my father's letter, which I delivered her soon after I came to myself, pretty well, I believed, cured her surprize. She often smiled with a mixture of contempt and anger, while she was reading it; and having pronounced her brother to be a fool, she turned to me, and with as much affability as possible, (for she is no great mistress of affability) said, "Don't be uneasy, dear Molly; for you are come to the house of a friend; of one who hath sense enough to discern the author of all the mischief; depend upon it, child, I will ere long make some people ashamed of their folly." This kind reception gave me some comfort, my aunt assuring me that she would convince him how unjustly he had accused me of having made any complaints to her. A paper war was now begun between these two, which not only fixed an irreconcileable hatred between them; but confirmed my father's displeasure against me, and in the end, I believe, did me no service with my aunt: for I was considered by both as the cause of their dissension; tho' in fact, my step-mother, who very well knew the affection my aunt had for her, had long since done her business with my father; and as for my aunt's affection towards him, it had been abating several years, from an apprehension that he did not pay sufficient deference to her understanding.

'I had lived about half a year with my aunt, when I heard of my step-mother's being delivered of a boy, and the great joy my father expressed on that occasion; but, poor man, he lived not long to enjoy his happiness; for within a month afterwards I had the melancholy news of his death.

'Notwithstanding all the disobligations I had lately received from him, I was sincerely afflicted at my loss of him. All his kindness to me in my infancy, all his kindness to me while I was growing up, recurred to my memory, raised a thousand tender, melancholy ideas, and totally obliterated all thoughts of his latter behaviour, for which I made also every allowance and every excuse in my power.

'But what may perhaps appear more extraordinary, my aunt began soon to speak of him with concern. She said, he had some understanding formerly, tho' his passion for that vile woman had in a great measure obscured it; and one day, when she was in an ill humour with me, she had the cruelty to throw out a hint, that she had never quarrelled with her brother, if it had not been on my account.

'My father during his life had allowed my aunt very handsomely for my board; for generosity was too deeply rivetted in his nature to be plucked out by all the power of his wife. So far, however, she prevailed, that tho' he died possessed of upwards of £2000 he left me no more than £100 which, as he expressed in his will, was to set me up in some business, if I had the grace to take to any.

'Hitherto my aunt had in general treated me with some degree of affection; but her behaviour began now to be changed. She soon took an opportunity cf giving me to understand, that her fortune was insufficient to keep me; and as I could not live on the interest of my own, it was high time for me to consider about going into the world. She added, that her brother having mentioned my setting up in some business, in his will, was very foolish; that I had been bred to nothing; and besides, that the sum was too trifling to set me up in any way of reputation; she desired me therefore to think of immediately going into service.

'This advice was perhaps right enough; and I told her I was very ready to do as she directed me; but I was at that time, in an ill state of health; I desired her therefore to let me stay with her, till my legacy, which was not to be paid till a year after my father's death, was due; and I then promised to satisfy her for my board; to which she readily consented.

'And now, madam,' said Mrs Bennet sighing, 'I am going to open to you those matters which lead directly to that great catastrophe of my life, which hath occasioned my giving you this trouble, and of trying your patience in this manner.'

Amelia, notwithstanding her impatience, made a very civil answer to this; and then Mrs Bennet proceeded to relate what is written in the next chapter.

CHAPTER 4

Further continuation.

'THE curate of the parish where my aunt dwelt was a young fellow of about four and twenty. He had been left an orphan in his infancy, and entirely unprovided for; when an uncle had the goodness to take care of his education, both at school and at the university. As the young gentleman was intended for the church, his uncle, tho' he had two daughters of his own, and no very large fortune, purchased for him the next presentation[1] of a living of near £200 a year. The incumbent, at the time of the purchase, was under the age of sixty, and in apparent good health; notwithstanding which he died soon after the bargain, and long before the nephew was capable of orders; so that the uncle was obliged to give the living to a clergyman, to hold it till the young man came of proper age.

'The young gentleman had not attained his proper age of taking orders,[2] when he had the misfortune to lose his uncle and only friend; who, thinking he had sufficiently provided for his nephew by the purchase of the living, considered him no farther in his will, but divided all the fortune of which he died possessed, between his two daughters; recommending it to them, however, on his death-bed, to assist their cousin with money sufficient to keep him at the university, till he should be capable of ordination.

'But as no appointment of this kind was in the will, the young ladies, who received about £2000 each, thought proper to disregard the last words of their father: for besides that both of them were extremely tenacious of their money, they were great enemies to their cousin, on account of their father's kindness to him, and thought proper to let him know that they thought he had robbed them of too much already.

'The poor young fellow was now greatly distrest: for he had yet above a year to stay at the university, without any visible means of sustaining himself there.

'In this distress, however, he met with a friend, who had the good-nature to lend him the sum of twenty pounds, for which he only accepted his bond for forty,[3] and which was to be paid within a year after his being possessed of his living; that is, within a year after his becoming qualified to hold it.

'With this small sum thus hardly[4] obtained, the poor gentleman made a shift to struggle with all difficulties, till he became of due age to take upon himself the character of a deacon. He then repaired to that clergyman, to whom his uncle had given the living upon the conditions above-mentioned, to procure a title to ordination;[5] but this, to his great surprize and mortification, was absolutely refused him.

'The immediate disappointment did not hurt him so much, as the conclusion he drew from it: for he could have but little hopes, that the man who could have the cruelty to refuse him a title, would vouchsafe afterwards to deliver up to him a living of so considerable a value; nor was it long before this worthy incumbent told him plainly, that he valued his uncle's favours at too high a rate to part with them to any one; nay, he pretended scruples of conscience, and said that if he had made any slight promises, which he did not now well remember, they were wicked and void; that he looked upon himself as married to his parish, and he could no more give it up, than he could give up his wife, without sin.

'The poor young fellow was now obliged to seek farther for a title, which at length he obtained from the rector of the parish where my aunt lived.

'He had not long been settled in the curacy, before an intimate acquaintance grew between him and my aunt: for she was a great admirer of the clergy, and used frequently to say they were the only conversable creatures in the country.

'The first time she was in this gentleman's company was at a neighbour's christning, where she stood god-mother. Here she displayed her whole little stock of knowledge, in order to captivate Mr Bennet (I suppose, madam, you already guess that to have been his name) and before they parted gave him a very strong invitation to her house.

'Not a word passed at this christning between Mr Bennet and myself; but our eyes were not unemployed. Here, madam, I first felt a pleasing kind of confusion, which I know not how to describe. I felt a kind of uneasiness; yet did not wish to be without it. I longed to be alone; yet dreaded the hour of parting. I could not keep my eyes off from the object which caused my confusion, and which I was at once afraid of and enamoured with. – But why do I attempt to describe my situation to one who must, I am sure, have felt the same?'

Amelia smiled, and Mrs Bennet went on thus, 'O, Mrs Booth, had you seen the person of whom I am now speaking, you would not condemn the suddenness of my love. Nay, indeed, I had seen him there before, tho' this was the first time I had ever heard the music of his voice. – O! it was the sweetest that was ever heard.

'Mr Bennet came to visit my aunt the very next day. She imputed this respectful haste to the powerful charms of her understanding, and resolved to lose no opportunity in improving the opinion which she imagined he had conceived of her. She became by his desire quite ridiculous, and ran into absurdities and a gallimatia[6] scarce credible.

'Mr Bennet, as I afterwards found, saw her in the same light with myself; but as he was a very sensible and well-bred man, he so well concealed his opinion from us both, that I was almost angry, and she was pleased even to raptures, declaring herself charmed with his understanding; tho' indeed he had said very little, but I believe he heard himself into her good opinion, while he gazed himself into love.

'The two first visits which Mr Bennet made to my aunt, tho' I was in the room all the time, I never spoke a word; but on the third, on some argument which arose between them, Mr Bennet referred himself to me. I took his side of the question, as indeed I must to have done justice, and repeated two or three words of Latin. My aunt reddened at this, and exprest great disdain of my opinion, declaring she was astonished that a man of Mr Bennet's understanding could appeal to the judgment of a silly girl: "Is she," said my aunt bridling herself, "fit to decide between us?" Mr Bennet spoke very favourably of what I had said; upon which my aunt burst almost into a rage, treated me with downright scurrility, called me conceited fool, abused my poor father for having taught me Latin, which, she said, had made me a downright coxcomb, and made me prefer myself to those who were a hundred times my superiors in knowledge. She then fell foul on the learned languages, declared they were totally useless, and concluded that she had read all that was worth reading, tho' she thanked heaven she understood no language but her own.

'Before the end of his visit, Mr Bennet reconciled himself very well to my aunt, which, indeed, was no difficult task for him to accomplish; but from that hour she conceived a hatred and rancour towards me, which I could never appease.

'My aunt had, from my first coming into her house, expressed great dislike to my learning. In plain truth, she envied me that advantage. This envy I had long ago discovered; and had taken great pains to smother it, carefully avoiding ever to mention a Latin word in her presence, and always submitting to her authority; for indeed I despised her ignorance too much to dispute with her. By these means I had pretty well succeeded, and we lived tolerably together. But the affront paid to her understanding by Mr Bennet in my favour was an injury never to be forgiven to me. She took me severely to task that very evening, and reminded me of going to service, in such earnest terms, as almost amounted to literally turning me out of doors; advising me, in the most insulting manner, to keep my Latin to myself; which, she said, was useless to any one; but ridiculous, when pretended to by a servant.

'The next visit Mr Bennet made at our house, I was not suffered to be present. This was much the shortest of all his visits; and when he went away, he left my aunt in a worse humour than ever I had seen her. The whole was discharged on me in the usual manner, by upbraiding me with my learning, conceit, and poverty; reminding me of obligations, and insisting on my going immediately to service. With all this I was greatly pleased, as it assured me, that Mr Bennet had said something to her in my favour; and I would have purchased a kind expression of his at almost any price.

'I should scarce, however, have been so sanguine as to draw this conclusion, had I not received some hints, that I had not unhappily placed my affections on a man who made me no return: for tho' he had scarce addressed a dozen sentences to me (for, indeed, he had no opportunity) yet his eyes had revealed certain secrets to mine, with which I was not displeased.

'I remained, however, in a state of anxiety near a month; sometimes pleasing myself, with thinking Mr Bennet's heart was in the same situation with my own; sometimes doubting that my wishes had flattered and deceived me; and not in the least questioning that my aunt was my rival: for I thought no woman could be proof against the charms that had subdued me. Indeed, Mrs Booth, he was a charming young fellow; I must, I must pay this tribute to his memory – O, gracious Heaven! why, why did I ever see him! why was I doom'd to such misery!' – Here she burst into a flood of tears, and remained incapable of speech for some time; during which, the gentle Amelia endeavoured all she could to soothe her; and gave sufficient marks of sympathizing in the tender affliction of her friend.

Mrs Bennet, at length, recovered her spirits, and proceeded, as in the next chapter.

CHAPTER 5

The story of Mrs Bennet continued.

'I SCARCE know where I left off – Oh! I was, I think, telling you, that I esteemed my aunt as my rival; and it is not easy to conceive a greater degree of detestation than I had for her; and what may, perhaps, appear strange, as she daily grew more and more civil to me, my hatred encreased with her civility: for I imputed it all to her triumph over me, and to her having secured, beyond all apprehension, the heart I longed for.

'How was I surprised, when one day, with as much good humour as she was mistress of, (for her countenance was not very pleasing) she asked me, how I liked Mr Bennet? The question, you will believe, madam, threw me into great confusion; which she plainly perceived, and without waiting for my answer, told me, she was very well satisfied; for that it did not require her discernment to read my thoughts in my countenance. "Well, child," said she, "I have suspected this a great while, and I believe it will please you to know, that I yesterday made the same discovery in your lover." This, I confess to you, was more than I could well bear, and I begged her to say no more to me at that time, on that subject. – "Nay, child," answered she, "I must tell you all, or I should not act a friendly part. Mr Bennet, I am convinced, hath a passion for you; but it is a passion which I think you should not encourage. For, to be plain with you, I fear he is in love with your person[7] only. Now this is a love, child, which cannot produce that rational happiness, which a woman of sense ought to expect." – In short, she ran on with a great deal of stuff about rational happiness, and women of sense, and concluded, with assuring me, that after the strictest scrutiny, she could not find that Mr Bennet had an adequate opinion of my understanding; upon which she vouchsafed to make me many compliments, but mixed with several sarcasms concerning my learning.

'I hope, madam, however,' said she to Amelia, 'you have not so bad an opinion of my capacity, as to imagine me dull enough to be offended with Mr Bennet's sentiments; for which I presently knew so well to account. I was, indeed, charmed with his ingenuity, who had discovered, perhaps, the only way of reconciling my aunt to those inclinations, which I now assured myself he had for me.

'I was not long left to support my hopes by my sagacity. He soon found an opportunity of declaring his passion. He did this in so forcible, tho' gentle, a manner, with such a profusion of fervency and tenderness at once, that his love, like a torrent, bore every thing before it; and I am almost ashamed to own to you, how very soon he prevailed upon me to – to – in short, to be an honest woman, and to confess to him the plain truth.

'When we were upon a good footing together, he gave me a long relation of what had past, at several interviews with my aunt, at which I had not been present. He said, he had discovered, that as she valued herself chiefly on her understanding, so she was extremely jealous of mine, and hated me on account of my learning. That as he had loved me passionately from his first seeing me, and had thought of nothing, from that time, but of throwing himself at my feet, he saw no way so open to propitiate my aunt as that which he had taken; by commending my beauty, a perfection to which she had long resigned all claim, at the expence of my understanding, in which he lamented my deficiency to a degree almost of ridicule. This he imputed chiefly to my learning; on this occasion he advanced a sentiment, which so pleased my aunt, that she thought proper to make it her own: for I heard it afterwards more than once from her own mouth. *Learning*, he said, *had the same effect on the mind, that strong liquors have on the constitution; both tending to eradicate all our natural fire and energy*. His flattery had made such a dupe of my aunt, that she assented, without the least suspicion of his sincerity, to all he said; so sure is vanity to weaken every fortress of the understanding, and to betray us to every attack of the enemy.

'You will believe, madam, that I readily forgave him all he had said, not only from that motive which I have mentioned, but as I was assured he had spoke the reverse of his real sentiments. I was not, however, quite so well pleased with my aunt, who began to treat me as if I was really an idiot. Her contempt, I own, a little piqued me; and I could not help often expressing my resentment, when we were alone together, to Mr Bennet; who never failed to gratify me, by making her conceit the subject of his wit; a talent which he possessed in the most extraordinary degree.

'This proved of very fatal consequence: for one day, while we were enjoying my aunt in a very thick arbour in the garden, she stole upon us unobserved, and overheard our whole conversation. I wish, my dear, you understood Latin, that I might repeat you a sentence, in which the rage of a tigress, that hath lost her young, is described.[8] No English poet, as I remember, hath come up to it; nor am I myself equal to the undertaking. She burst in upon us, open-mouthed, and after discharging every abusive word almost, in the only language she understood, on poor Mr Bennet, turned us both out of doors; declaring, she would send my rags after me, but would never more permit me to set my foot within her threshold.

'Consider, dear madam, to what a wretched condition we were now reduced. I had not yet received the small legacy left me by my father; nor was Mr Bennet master of five pounds in the whole world.

'In this situation, the man I doated on to distraction had but little difficulty to persuade me to a proposal, which, indeed, I thought generous in him to make; as it seemed to proceed from that tenderness for my reputation, to which he ascribed it; indeed, it could proceed from no motive with which I should have been displeased. – In a word, within two days we were man and wife.

'Mr Bennet now declared himself the happiest of men; and for my part, I sincerely declare, I envied no woman upon earth. – How little, alas! did I then know, or suspect the price I was to pay for all my joys. – A match of real love is, indeed, truly paradise; and such perfect happiness seems to be the forbidden fruit to mortals, which we are to lament having tasted, during the rest of our lives.

'The first uneasiness which attacked us after our marriage was on my aunt's account. It was very disagreeable to live under the nose of so near a relation, who did not acknowledge us; but, on the contrary, was ever doing us all the ill turns in her power; and making a party against us in the parish, which is always easy enough to do amongst the vulgar, against persons who are their superiors in rank, and, at the same time, their inferiors in fortune. This made Mr Bennet think of procuring an exchange, in which intention he was soon after confirmed by the arrival of the rector. It was the rector's custom to spend three months every year at his living; for which purpose he reserved an apartment in his parsonage-house, which was full large enough for two such little families as then occupied it: we, at first, promised ourselves some little convenience from his boarding with us; and Mr Bennet began to lay aside his thoughts of leaving his curacy, at least for some time. But these golden ideas presently vanished: for tho' we both used our utmost endeavours to please him, we soon found the impossibility of succeeding. He was, indeed, to give you his character in a word, the most peevish of mortals. This temper, notwithstanding that he was both a good and a pious man, made his company so insufferable, that nothing could compensate it. If his breakfast was not ready to a moment, if a dish of meat was too much or too little done; in short, if any thing failed of exactly hitting his taste, he was sure to be out of humour all that day; so that, indeed, he was scarce ever in a good temper a whole day together: for Fortune seems to take a delight in thwarting this kind of disposition, to which human life, with its many crosses and accidents, is in truth by no means fitted.

'Mr Bennet was now, by my desire, as well as his own, determined to quit the parish; but when he attempted to get an exchange, he found it a matter of more difficulty than he had apprehended: for the rector's temper was so well known among the neighbouring clergy, that none of them could be brought to think of spending three months in a year with him.

'After many fruitless enquiries, Mr Bennet thought best to remove to London, the great mart of all affairs ecclesiastical and civil. This project greatly pleased him; and he resolved, without more delay, to take his leave of the rector; which he did in the most friendly manner possible, and preached his farewel sermon; nor was there a dry eye in the church, except among the few whom my aunt, who remained still inexorable, had prevailed upon to hate us without any cause.

'To London we came, and took up our lodging the first night at the inn where the stage coach set us down; the next morning my husband went out early on his business, and returned with the good news of having heard of a curacy, and of having equipped himself with a lodging in the neighbourhood of a worthy peer, "who," said he, "was my fellow collegiate; and what is more, I have a direction to a person who will advance your legacy at a very reasonable rate."

'This last particular was extremely agreeable to me; for our last guinea was now broached; and the rector had lent my husband ten pounds to pay his debts in the country: for with all his peevishness he was a good and a generous man, and had indeed so many valuable qualities, that I lamented his temper, after I knew him thoroughly, as much on his account, as on my own.

'We now quitted the inn, and went to our lodgings, where my

husband having placed me in safety, as he said, he went about the business of the legacy, with good assurance of success.

'My husband returned elated with his success, the person to whom he applied having undertaken to advance the legacy, which he fulfilled as soon as the proper enquiries could be made, and proper instruments prepared for that purpose.

'This, however, took up so much time, that as our fund was so very low, we were reduced to some distress, and obliged to live extremely penurious; nor would all do, without my taking a most disagreeable way of procuring money, by pawning one of my gowns.

'Mr Bennet was now settled in a curacy in town, greatly to his satisfaction; and our affairs seemed to have a prosperous aspect, when he came home to me one morning in much apparent disorder, looking as pale as death, and begged me by some means or other to get him a dram; for that he was taken with a sudden faintness and lowness of spirits.

'Frighted as I was, I immediately ran down stairs, and procured some rum of the mistress of the house; the first time indeed I ever knew him drink any. When he came to himself, he begged me not to be alarmed; for it was no distemper, but something that had vexed him, which had caused his disorder, which he had now perfectly recovered.

'He then told me the whole affair. He had hitherto deferred paying a visit to the lord whom I mentioned to have been formerly his fellow collegiate, and was now his neighbour, till he could put himself in decent rigging. He had now purchased a new cassock, hat and wig, and went to pay his respects to his old acquaintance, who had received from him many civilities and assistances in his learning at the university, and had promised to return them fourfold hereafter.

'It was not without some difficulty that Mr Bennet got into the antichamber. Here he waited, or, as the phrase is, cooled his heels for above an hour, before he saw his lordship; nor had he seen him then, but by an accident: for my lord was going out, when he casually intercepted him in his passage to his chariot. He approached to salute him with some familiarity, tho' with respect, depending on his former intimacy, when my lord stepping short very gravely told him, he had not the pleasure of knowing him. "How! my lord," said he, "can you have so soon forgot your old acquaintance Tom Bennet?" "O Mr Bennet," cries his lordship, with much reserve, "is it you? You will pardon my memory. I am glad to see you, Mr Bennet; but you must excuse me at present: for I am in very great haste." He then broke from him, and without more ceremony, or any further invitation, went directly into his chariot.

'This cold reception from a person for whom my husband had a real friendship, and from whom he had great reason to expect a very warm return of affection, so affected the poor man, that it caused all those symptoms which I have mentioned before.

'Tho' this incident produced no material consequence, I could not pass it over in silence, as of all the misfortunes which ever befel him, it affected my husband the most. I need not, however, to a woman of your delicacy, make any comments on a behaviour, which, tho' I believe it is very common, is nevertheless cruel and base beyond description, and is diametrically opposite to true honour, as well as to goodness.

'To relieve the uneasiness which my husband felt on account of his false friend, I prevailed with him to go every night, almost for a fortnight together, to the play; a diversion of which he was greatly fond, and from which he did not think his being a clergyman excluded him; indeed, it is very well if those austere persons who would be inclined to censure him on this head, have themselves no greater sins to answer for.

'From this time during three months, we past our time very agreeably, a little too agreeably perhaps for our circumstances: for however innocent diversions may be in other respects, they must be owned to be expensive. When you consider then, madam, that our income from the curacy was less than forty pounds a year, and that after payment of the debt to the rector, and another to my aunt, with the costs in law which she had occasioned by suing for it, my legacy was reduced to less than seventy pounds, you will not wonder that in diversions, cloaths, and the common expences of life, we had almost consumed our whole stock.

'The inconsiderate manner in which we had lived for some time will, I doubt not, appear to you to want some excuse; but I have none to make for it. Two things, however, now happened which occasioned much serious reflexion to Mr Bennet; the one was, that I grew near my time; the other, that he now received a letter from Oxford demanding the debt of forty pounds, which I mentioned to you before. The former of these he made a pretence of obtaining a delay for the payment of the latter, promising in two months to pay off half the debt, by which means he obtained a forbearance during that time.

'I was now delivered of a son, a matter which should in reality have encreased our concern; but on the contrary it gave us great pleasure; greater indeed could not have been conceived at the birth of an heir to the most plentiful estate. So entirely thoughtless were we, and so little forecast had we of those many evils and distresses to which we had rendered a human creature, and one so dear to us, liable. The day of a christening is in all families, I believe, a day of jubilee and rejoicing; and yet, if we consider the interest of that little wretch, who is the occasion, how very little reason would the most sanguine persons have for their joy.

'But tho' our eyes were too weak to look forward, for the sake of our child, we could not be blinded to those dangers that immediately threatened ourselves. Mr Bennet, at the expiration of the two months, received a second letter from Oxford, in a very peremptory stile, and threatning a suit without any farther delay. This alarmed us in the strongest manner; and my husband, to secure his liberty, was advised for a while to shelter himself in the verge of the court.

'And now, madam, I am entring on that scene which directly leads to all my misery.' – Here she stopped, and wiped her eyes, – and then begging Amelia to excuse her for a few minutes ran hastily out of the room, leaving Amelia by herself, while she refreshed her spirits with a cordial to enable her to relate what follows in the next chapter.

CHAPTER 6

Farther continued.

MRS BENNET returning into the room, made a short apology for her absence, and then proceeded in these words:

'We now left our lodging, and took a second floor in that very house where you now are; to which we were recommended by the woman where we had before lodged: for the mistresses of both houses were acquainted; and, indeed, we had been all at the play together. To this new lodging then, (such was our wretched destiny) we immediately repaired, and were received by Mrs Ellison (how can I bear the sound of that detested name!) with much civility; she took care, however, during the first fortnight of our residence, to wait upon us every Monday morning for her rent: such being it seems the custom of this place, which as it was inhabited chiefly by persons in debt, is not the region of credit.

'My husband, by the singular goodness of the rector, who greatly compassionated his case, was enabled to continue in his curacy, tho' he could only do the duty on Sundays. He was, however, sometimes obliged to furnish a person to officiate at his expence; so that our income was very scanty, and the poor little remainder of the legacy being almost spent, we were reduced to some difficulties, and what was worse, saw still a prospect of greater before our eyes.

'Under these circumstances, how agreeable to poor Mr Bennet must have been the behaviour of Mrs Ellison, who, when he carried her her rent on the usual day, told him, with a benevolent smile, that he needed not to give himself the trouble of such exact punctuality. She added, that, if it was at any time inconvenient to him, he might pay her when he pleased. "To say the truth," says she, "I never was so much pleased with any lodgers in my life, – I am convinced, Mr Bennet, you are a very worthy man, and you are a very happy one too; for you have the prettiest wife and the prettiest child I ever saw." – These, dear madam, were the words she was pleased to make use of; and I am sure she behaved to me with such an appearance of friendship and affection, that, as I could not perceive any possible views of interest which she could have in her professions, I easily believed them real.

'There lodged in the same house, O Mrs Booth! the blood runs cold to my heart, and should run cold to yours when I name him: – There lodged in the same house a lord – the lord indeed whom I have since seen in your company. This lord, Mrs Ellison told me, had taken a great fancy to my little Charly:[9] Fool that I was, and blinded by my own passion, which made me conceive that an infant, not three months old, could be really the object of affection to any besides a parent; and more especially to a gay young fellow! But if I was silly in being deceived, how wicked was the wretch who deceived me; who used such art, and employed such pains, such incredible pains to deceive me! He acted the part of a nurse to my little infant; he danced it, he lulled it, he kissed it; declared it was the very picture of a nephew of his, his favourite sister's child; and said so many kind and fond things of its beauty, that I myself, tho', I believe, one of the tenderest and fondest of mothers, scarce carried my own ideas of my little darling's perfection, beyond the compliments which he paid it.

'My lord, however, perhaps from modesty before my face, fell far short of what Mrs Ellison reported from him. And now, when she found the impression which was made on me by these means, she took every opportunity of insinuating to me his lordship's many virtues, his great goodness to his sister's children in particular; nor did she fail to drop some hints, which gave me the most simple and groundless hopes of strange consequences from his fondness to my Charly.

'When by these means, which, simple as they may appear, were, perhaps, the most artful, my lord had gained something more, I think, than my esteem, he took the surest method to confirm himself in my affection. This was, by professing the highest friendship for my husband: for, as to myself, I do assure you, he never shewed me more than common respect; and I hope you will believe, I should have immediately startled and flown off if he had. Poor I accounted for all the friendship which he expressed for my husband, and all the fondness which he shewed to my boy, from the great prettiness of the one, and the great merit of the other;

foolishly conceiving, that others saw with my eyes, and felt with my heart. Little did I dream, that my own unfortunate person was the fountain of all this lord's goodness, and was the intended price of it.

'One evening, as I was drinking tea with Mrs Ellison by my lord's fire, (a liberty which she never scrupled taking when he was gone out) my little Charly, now about half a year old, sitting in her lap; my lord, accidentally no doubt; indeed, I then thought it so, came in. I was confounded and offered to go; but my lord declared, if he disturbed Mrs Ellison's company, as he phrased it, he would himself leave the room. When I was thus prevailed on to keep my seat, my lord immediately took my little baby into his lap, and gave it some tea there, not a little at the expence of his embroidery: for he was very richly drest; indeed, he was as fine a figure as, perhaps, ever was seen. His behaviour on this occasion gave me many ideas in his favour. I thought he discovered good sense, good-nature, condescension,[10] and other good qualities, by the fondness he shewed to my child, and the contempt he seemed to express for his finery, which so greatly became him: for I cannot deny, but that he was the handsomest and genteelest person in the world; tho' such considerations advanced him not a step in my favour.

'My husband now returned from church, (for this happened on a Sunday) and was, by my lord's particular desire, ushered into the room. My lord received him with the utmost politeness, and with many professions of esteem; which, he said, he had conceived from Mrs Ellison's representations of his merit. He then proceeded to mention the living, which was detained from my husband, of which Mrs Ellison had likewise informed him; and said, he thought it would be no difficult matter, to obtain a restoration of it by the authority of the bishop, who was his particular friend, and to whom he would take an immediate opportunity of mentioning it. This, at last, he determined to do the very next day; when he invited us both to dinner, where we were to be acquainted with his lordship's success.

'My lord now insisted on my husband's staying supper with him, without taking any notice of me; but Mrs Ellison declared, he should not part man and wife; and that she herself would stay with me. The motion was too agreeable to me to be rejected; and, except the little time I retired to put my child to bed, we spent together the most agreeable evening imaginable; nor was it, I believe, easy to decide, whether Mr Bennet or myself were most delighted with his lordship and Mrs Ellison; but this I assure you, the generosity of the one, and the extreme civility and kindness of the other were the subjects of our conversation all the ensuing night, during which we neither of us closed our eyes.

'The next day, at dinner, my lord acquainted us, that he had prevailed with the bishop to write to the clergyman in the country; indeed, he told us, that he had engaged the bishop to be very warm in our interest, and had not the least doubt of success. This threw us both into a flow of spirits,[11] and in the afternoon, Mr Bennet, at Mrs Ellison's request, which was seconded by his lordship, related the history of our lives, from our first acquaintance. My lord seemed much affected with some tender scenes, which, as no man could better feel, so none could better describe than my husband. When he had finished, my lord begged pardon for mentioning an occurrence which gave him such a particular concern, as it had disturbed that delicious state of happiness in which we had lived at our former lodging. "It would be ungenerous," said he, "to rejoice at an accident, which, tho' it brought me fortunately acquainted with two of the most agreeable people in the world, was yet at the expence of your mutual felicity. The circumstance I mean is your debt at Oxford; pray how doth that stand? I am resolved it shall never disturb your happiness hereafter." At these words, the tears burst from my poor husband's eyes; and in an ecstasy of gratitude, he cried out, "Your lordship overcomes me with generosity. If you go on in this manner, both my wife's gratitude and mine must be bankrupt." He then acquainted my lord with the exact state of the case, and received assurances from him, that the debt should never trouble him. My husband was again breaking out into the warmest expressions of gratitude; but my lord stopt him short; saying, "if you have any obligation, it is to my little Charly here, from whose little innocent smiles I have received more than the value of this trifling debt in pleasure." I forgot to tell you, that when I offered to leave the room after dinner, upon my child's account, my lord would not suffer me; but ordered the child to be brought to me. He now took it out of my arms, placed it upon his own knee, and fed it with some fruit from the dessert. In short, it would be more tedious to you than to myself, to relate the thousand little tendernesses he shewed to the child. He gave it many baubles; amongst the rest was a coral,[12] worth, at least, three pounds; and when my husband was confined near a fortnight to his chamber with a cold, he visited the child every day; (for to this infant's account were all the visits placed) and seldom failed of accompanying his visit with a present to the little thing.

'Here, Mrs Booth, I cannot help mentioning a doubt which hath often arisen in my mind, since I have been enough mistress of myself to reflect on this horrid train, which was laid to blow up my innocence. Wicked and barbarous it was to the highest degree, without any question; but my doubt is, whether the art or folly of it be the more conspicuous: for however delicate and refined the art must be allowed to have been, the folly, I think, must, upon a fair examination, appear no less astonishing: for to lay all considerations of cruelty and crime out of the case, what a foolish bargain doth the man make for himself, who purchases so poor a pleasure at so high a price!

'We had lived near three weeks, with as much freedom as if we had been all of the same family; when one afternoon, my lord proposed to my husband to ride down himself to solicit the surrender: for he said, the bishop had received an unsatisfactory answer from the parson, and had writ a second letter more pressing; which his lordship now promised us to strengthen by one of his own that my husband was to carry with him. Mr Bennet agreed to this proposal with great thankfulness; and the next day was appointed for his journey. The distance was near seventy miles.

'My husband set out on his journey; and he had scarce left me before Mrs Ellison came into my room, and endeavoured to comfort me in his absence; to say the truth, tho' he was to be from me but a few days, and the purpose of his going was to fix our happiness on a sound foundation for all our future days, I could scarce support my spirits under this first separation. But tho' I then thought Mrs Ellison's intentions to be most kind and friendly; yet the means she used were utterly ineffectual, and appeared to me injudicious. Instead of soothing my uneasiness, which is always the first physic to be given to grief, she rallied me upon it, and began to talk in a very unusual stile of gaiety, in which she treated conjugal love with much ridicule.

'I gave her to understand, that she displeased me by this discourse; but she soon found means to give such a turn to it, as made a merit of all she had said. And now, when she had worked me into a good humour, she made a proposal to me, which I at first rejected; but at last fatally, – too fatally suffered myself to be over-persuaded. This was to go to a masquerade at Ranelagh, for which my lord had furnished her with tickets.'

At these words Amelia turned pale as death, and hastily begged her friend to give her a glass of water, some air, or any thing. Mrs Bennet having thrown open the window, and procured the water, which prevented Amelia from fainting, looked at her with much tenderness, and cried, 'I do not wonder, my dear madam, that you are affected with my mentioning that fatal masquerade; since I firmly believe the same ruin was intended for you at the same place. The apprehension of which occasioned the letter I sent you this morning, and all the trial of your patience which I have made since.'

Amelia gave her a tender embrace, with many expressions of the warmest gratitude; assured her, she had pretty well recovered her spirits, and begged her to continue her story; which Mrs Bennet then did. However, as our readers may likewise be glad to recover their spirits also, we shall here put an end to this chapter.

CHAPTER 7

The story farther continued.

MRS BENNET proceeded thus:

'I was at length, prevailed on to accompany Mrs Ellison to the masquerade. Here, I must confess, the pleasantness of the place, the variety of the dresses, and the novelty of the thing gave me much delight, and raised my fancy to the highest pitch. As I was entirely void of all suspicion, my mind threw off all reserve, and pleasure only filled my thoughts. Innocence, it is true, possessed my heart; but it was innocence unguarded, intoxicated with foolish desires, and liable to every temptation. During the first two hours, we had many trifling adventures, not worth remembering. At length my lord joined us, and continued with me all the evening; and we danced several dances together.

'I need not, I believe, tell you, madam, how engaging his conversation is. I wish I could with truth say, I was not pleased with it; or, at least, that I had a right to be pleased with it. But I will disguise nothing from you: I now began to discover, that he had some affection for me; but he had already too firm a footing in my esteem, to make the discovery shocking. I will – I will own the truth; I was delighted with perceiving a passion in him, which I was not unwilling to think he had had from the beginning, and to derive his having concealed it so long, from his awe of my virtue, and his respect to my understanding. I assure you, madam, at the same time, my intentions were never to exceed the bounds of innocence. I was charmed with the delicacy of his passion; and in the foolish thoughtless turn of mind, in which I then was, I fancied I might give some very distant encouragement to such a passion in such a man, with the utmost safety; that I might indulge my vanity and interest at once, without being guilty of the least injury.

'I know Mrs Booth will condemn all these thoughts, and I condemn them no less myself; for it is now my stedfast opinion, that the woman who gives up the least out-work of her virtue, doth, in that very moment, betray the citadel.

'About two o'clock we returned home, and found a very handsome collation provided for us. I was asked to partake of it; and I did not, I could not refuse. I was not, however, entirely void of all suspicion, and I made many resolutions; one of which was, not to drink a drop more than my usual stint. This was, at the utmost, little more than half a pint of small punch.

'I adhered strictly to my quantity; but in the quality, I am convinced, I was deceived: for, before I left the room, I found my head giddy. What the villain gave me, I know not; but besides being intoxicated, I perceived effects from it, which are not to be described.

'Here, madam, I must draw a curtain over the residue of that fatal night. Let it suffice, that it involved me in the most dreadful ruin; a ruin, to which, I can truly say, I never consented; and of which I was scarce conscious, when the villanous man avowed it to my face in the morning.

'Thus I have deduced my story to the most horrid period; happy had I been, had this been the period of my life; but I was reserved for greater miseries: but before I enter on them, I will mention something very remarkable, with which I was now acquainted, and that will shew there was nothing of accident which had befallen me; but that all was the effect of a long, regular, premeditated design.

'You may remember, madam, I told you, that we were recommended to Mrs Ellison by the woman at whose house we had before lodged. This woman, it seems, was one of my lord's pimps, and had before introduced me to his lordship's notice.

'You are to know then, madam, that this villain, this lord, now confest to me, that he had first seen me in the galery at the oratorio; whither I had gone with tickets, with which the woman where I first lodged, had presented me, and which were, it seems, purchased by my lord. Here I first met the vile betrayer, who was disguised in a rug-coat, and a patch upon his face.'

At these words, Amelia cried, 'O gracious Heavens!' and fell back in her chair. Mrs Bennet, with proper applications, brought her back to life; and then Amelia acquainted her, that she herself had first seen the same person, in the same place, and in the same disguise. 'O! Mrs Bennet,' cried she, 'how am I indebted to you! What words, what thanks, what actions can demonstrate the gratitude of my sentiments! I look upon you, and always shall look upon you, as my preserver from the brink of a precipice; from which I was falling into the same ruin, which you have so generously, so kindly, and so nobly disclosed for my sake.'

Here the two ladies compared notes; and it appeared, that his lordship's behaviour at the oratorio had been alike to both: that he had made use of the very same words, the very same actions to Amelia, which he had practised over before on poor unfortunate Mrs Bennet. It may, perhaps, be thought strange, that neither of them could afterwards recollect him; but so it was. And, indeed, if we consider the force of disguise, the very short time that either of them was with him at this first interview, and the very little curiosity that must have been supposed in the minds of the ladies, together with the amusement in which they were then engaged, all wonder will, I apprehend, cease. Amelia, however, now declared, she remembered his voice and features perfectly well; and was thoroughly satisfied he was the same person. She then accounted for his not having visited in the afternoon, according to his promise, from her declared resolutions to Mrs Ellison not to see him. She now burst forth into some very satirical invectives against that lady, and declared she had the art, as well as the wickedness, of the devil himself.

Many congratulations now past from Mrs Bennet to Amelia, which were returned with the most hearty acknowledgments from that lady. But, instead of filling our paper with these, we shall pursue Mrs Bennet's story; which she resumed, as we shall find in the next chapter.

CHAPTER 8

Further continuation.

'NO SOONER,' said Mrs Bennet, continuing her story, 'was my lord departed, than Mrs Ellison came to me. She behaved in such a manner, when she became acquainted with what had past, that tho' I was at first satisfied[13] of her guilt, she began to stagger[14] my opinion; and, at length, prevailed upon me entirely to acquit her. She raved like a madwoman against my lord, swore he should not stay a moment in her house, and that she would never speak to him more. In short, had she been the most innocent woman in the world, she could not have spoke, nor acted any otherwise; nor could she have vented more wrath and indignation against the betrayer.

'That part of her denunciation of vengeance, which concerned my lord's leaving the house, she vowed should be executed immediately; but then, seeming to recollect herself, she said, "Consider, my dear child; it is for your sake alone I speak; will not such a proceeding give some suspicion to your husband?" I answered, that I valued not that; that I was resolved to inform my husband of all, the moment I saw him; with many expressions of detestation of myself, and an indifference for life, and for every thing else.

'Mrs Ellison, however, found means to soothe me, and to satisfy me with my own innocence; a point, in which, I believe, we are all easily convinced. In short, I was persuaded to acquit both myself and her, to lay the whole guilt upon my lord, and to resolve to conceal it from my husband.

'That whole day I confined myself to my chamber, and saw no person but Mrs Ellison. I was, indeed, ashamed to look any one in the face. Happily for me, my lord went into the country without attempting to come near me; for I believe his sight would have driven me to madness.

'The next day, I told Mrs Ellison, that I was resolved to leave her lodgings the moment my lord came to town; not on her account: (for I really inclined to think her innocent;) but on my lord's, whose face I was resolved, if possible, never more to behold. She told me, I had no reason to quit her house on that score: for that my lord himself had left her lodgings that morning, in resentment, she believed, of the abuses which she had cast on him the day before.

'This confirmed me in the opinion of her innocence; nor hath she from that day to this, till my acquaintance with you, madam, done any thing to forfeit my opinion. On the contrary, I owe her many good offices; amongst the rest I have an annuity of £150 a year from my lord, which I know was owing to her solicitations: for she is not void of generosity or good-nature; tho' by what I have lately seen, I am convinced she was the cause of my ruin, and hath endeavoured to lay the same snares for you.

'But to return to my melancholy story. My husband returned at the appointed time; and I met him with an agitation of mind not to be described. Perhaps the fatigue which he had undergone in his journey, and his dissatisfaction at his ill success, prevented his taking notice of what I feared was too visible. All his hopes were entirely frustrated; the clergyman had not received the bishop's letter; and as to my lord's he treated it with derision and contempt. Tired as he was, Mr Bennet would not sit down till he had enquired for my lord, intending to go and pay his compliments: poor man! he little suspected that he had deceived him, as I have since known, concerning the bishop; much less did he suspect any other injury. But the lord – the villain was gone out of town, so that he was forced to postpone all his gratitude.

'Mr Bennet returned to town late on the Saturday night, nevertheless he performed his duty at church the next day; but I refused to go with him. This, I think, was the first refusal I was guilty of since our marriage; but I was become so miserable, that his presence, which had been the source of all my happiness, was become my bane. I will not say I hated to see him; but I can say I was ashamed, indeed afraid to look him in the face. I was conscious of I knew not what – guilt I hope it cannot be called.'

'I hope not, nay I think not,' cries Amelia.

'My husband,' continued Mrs Bennet, 'perceived my dissatisfaction, and imputed it to his ill success in the country. I was pleased with this self-delusion; and yet when I fairly compute the agonies I suffered at his endeavours to comfort me on that head, I paid most severely for it. O my dear Mrs Booth, happy is the deceived party between true lovers, and wretched indeed is the author of the deceit.

'In this wretched condition I past a whole week, the most miserable, I think, of my whole life, endeavouring to humour my husband's delusion, and to conceal my own tortures; but I had reason to fear I could not succeed long; for on the Saturday night I perceived a visible alteration in his behaviour to me. He went to bed in an apparent ill humour, turned sullenly from me; and if I offered at any endearments, he gave me only peevish answers.

'After a restless turbulent night, he rose early on Sunday morning and walked down stairs. I expected his return to breakfast, but was soon informed by the maid that he was gone forth; and that it was no more than seven o'clock. All this, you may believe, madam, alarmed me. I saw plainly he had discovered the fatal secret, tho' by what means I could not divine. The state of my mind was very little short of madness. Sometimes I thought of running away from my injured husband, and sometimes of putting an end to my life.

'In the midst of such perturbations, I spent the day. My husband returned in the evening. – O Heavens, can I describe what followed. – It is impossible, I shall sink under the relation. – He entered the room, with a face as white as a sheet, his lips trembling, and his eyes red as coals of fire, and starting as it were from his head. – "Molly," cries he, throwing himself into his chair, "are you well?" – "Good Heavens," says I, "what's the matter? – Indeed, I can't say I am well." "No!" says he, – starting from his chair, "false monster, you have betrayed me, destroyed me, you have ruined your husband." Then looking like a fury he snatched off a large book from the table, and with the malice of a madman, threw it at my head, and knocked me down backwards. He then caught me up in his arms, and kissed me with most extravagant tenderness; then looking me stedfast in the face for several moments, the tears gushed in a torrent from his eyes, and with his utmost violence he threw me again on the floor – kicked me, stamped upon me. I believe, indeed, his intent was to kill me, and I believe he thought he had accomplished it.

'I lay on the ground for some minutes I believe, deprived of my senses. When I recovered myself, I found my husband lying by my side on his face, and the blood running from him. It seems when he thought he had dispatched me, he ran his head with all his force against a chest of drawers which stood in the room, and gave himself a dreadful wound in his head.

'I can truly say, I felt not the least resentment for the usage I had received; I thought I deserved it all; tho' indeed I little guessed what he had suffered from me. I now used the most earnest entreaties to him to compose himself; and endeavoured with my feeble arms to raise him from the ground. At length, he broke from me, and springing from the ground flung himself into a chair, when looking wildly at me, he cried, – "Go from me, Molly. I beseech you leave me, I would not kill you." – He then discovered to me – O Mrs Booth, can you not guess it? – I was indeed polluted by the villain – I had infected my husband – O Heaven! why do I live to relate any thing so horrid – I will not, I cannot yet survive it. I cannot forgive myself. Heaven cannot forgive me. –'

Here she became inarticulate with the violence of her grief, and fell presently into such agonies, that the frighted Amelia began to call aloud for some assistance. Upon this a maid servant came up, who seeing her mistress in a violent convulsion fit, presently screamed out she was dead. Upon which one of the other sex made his appearance; and who should this be but the honest serjeant? whose countenance soon made it evident, that tho' a soldier and a brave one too, he was not the least concerned of all the company on this occasion.

The reader, if he hath been acquainted with scenes of this kind, very well knows that Mrs Bennet in the usual time returned again to the possession of her voice; the first use of which she made, was to express her astonishment at the presence of the serjeant, and with a frantic air, to enquire who he was.

The maid concluding that her mistress was not yet returned to her senses, answered, 'Why 'tis my master, madam. Heaven preserve your senses, madam – Lord, sir, my mistress must be very bad not to know you.'

What Atkinson thought at this instant, I will not say; but certain it is he looked not over wise. He attempted twice to take hold of Mrs Bennet's hand; but she withdrew it hastily, and presently after rising up from her chair, she declared herself pretty well again, and desired Atkinson and the maid to withdraw. Both of whom presently obeyed; the serjeant appearing by his countenance to want comfort almost as much as the lady did to whose assistance he had been summoned.

It is a good maxim to trust a person entirely or not at all: for a secret is often innocently blabbed out by those who know but half of it. Certain it is that the maid's speech communicated a suspicion to the mind of Amelia, which the behaviour of the serjeant did not tend to remove; what that is the sagacious readers may likewise probably suggest to themselves; if not, they must wait our time for disclosing it. We shall now resume the history of Mrs Bennet, who after many apologies, proceeded to the matters in the next chapter.

CHAPTER 9

The conclusion of Mrs Bennet's history.

'WHEN I became sensible,' cries Mrs Bennet, 'of the injury I had done my husband, I threw myself at his feet, and embracing his knees, while I bathed them with my tears, I begged a patient hearing, declaring if he was not satisfied with what I should say, I would become a willing victim of his resentment. I said, and I said truly, that if I owed my death that instant to his hands, I should have no other terrour, but of the fatal consequence which it might produce to himself.

'He seemed a little pacified, and bid me say whatever I pleased.

'I then gave him a faithful relation of all that had happened. He heard me with great attention, and at the conclusion, cried, with a deep sigh – "O Molly, I believe it all. – You must have been betrayed as you tell me; you could not be guilty of such baseness, such cruelty, such ingratitude." – He then – O 'tis impossible to describe his behaviour – he exprest such kindness, such tenderness, such concern, for the manner in which he had used me – I cannot dwell on this scene – I shall relapse – You must excuse me.'

Amelia begged her to omit any thing which so affected her; and she proceeded thus:

'My husband, who was more convinced than I was of Mrs Ellison's guilt, declared he would not sleep that night in her house. He then went out to see for a lodging; he gave me all the money he had, and left me to pay her bill, and put up the cloaths, telling me if I had not money enough, I might leave the cloaths as a pledge; but he vowed he could not answer for himself, if he saw the face of Mrs Ellison.

'Words cannot scarce express the behaviour of that artful woman, it was so kind and so generous. She said she did not blame my husband's resentment, nor could she expect any other, but that he and all the world should censure her – that she hated her house almost as much as we did, and detested her cousin, if possible, more. In fine, she said I might leave my cloaths there that evening;

but that she would send them to us the next morning. That she scorned the thought of detaining them; and as for the paultry debt, we might pay her whenever we pleased: for to do her justice with all her vices, she hath some good in her.'

'Some good in her, indeed!' cried Amelia, with great indignation.

'We were scarce settled in our new lodgings,' continued Mrs Bennet, 'when my husband began to complain of a pain in his inside. He told me he feared he had done himself some injury in his rage, and had burst something within him. As to the odious – I cannot bear the thought, the great skill of his surgeon soon entirely cured him; but his other complaint instead of yielding to any application, grew still worse and worse, nor ever ended till it brought him to his grave.

'O Mrs Booth, could I have been certain that I had occasioned this, however innocently I had occasioned it, I could never have survived it; but the surgeon who opened him after his death assured me, that he died, of what they called a polypus[15] in his heart, and that nothing which had happened on account of me was in the least the occasion of it.

'I have, however, related the affair truly to you. The first complaint I ever heard of the kind, was within a day or two after we left Mrs Ellison's; and this complaint remained till his death, which might induce him perhaps to attribute his death to another cause; but the surgeon, who is a man of the highest eminence, hath always declared the contrary to me, with the most positive certainty; and this opinion hath been my only comfort.

'When my husband died, which was about ten weeks after we quitted Mrs Ellison's, of whom I had then a different opinion from what I have now, I was left in the most wretched condition imaginable. I believe, madam, she shewed you my letter. Indeed she did every thing for me at that time, which I could have expected from the best of friends. She supplied me with money from her own pocket, by which means I was preserved from a distress in which I must have otherwise inevitably perished.

'Her kindness to me in this season of distress prevailed on me to return again to her house. Why, indeed, should I have refused an offer so very convenient for me to accept, and which seemed so generous in her to make? Here I lived a very retired life, with my little babe, seeing no company but Mrs Ellison herself, for a full quarter of a year. At last Mrs Ellison brought me a parchment from my lord, in which he had settled upon me, at her instance, as she told me, and as I believe it was, an annuity of £150 a year. This was, I think, the very first time she had mentioned his hateful name to me since my return to her house. And she now prevailed upon me, tho' I assure you, not without much difficulty, to suffer him to execute the deed in my presence.

'I will not describe our interview, – I am not able to describe it, and I have often wondered how I found spirits to support it. This I will say for him, that if he was not a real penitent, no man alive could act the part better.

'Beside resentment, I had another motive of my backwardness to agree to such a meeting. And this was fear. I apprehended, and surely not without reason, that the annuity was rather meant as a bribe than a recompence, and that further designs were laid against my innocence: But in this I found myself happily deceived; for neither then, nor at any time since, have I ever had the least solicitation of that kind. Nor indeed have I seen the least occasion to think my lord had any such desires.

'Good Heavens! what are these men! what is this appetite, which must have novelty and resistance for its provocatives; and which is delighted with us no longer than while we may be considered in the light of enemies.'

'I thank you, madam,' cries Amelia, 'for relieving me from my fears on your account; I trembled at the consequence of this second acquaintance with such a man, and in such a situation.'

'I assure you, madam, I was in no danger,' returned Mrs Bennet: 'for besides that I think I could have pretty well relied on my own resolution, I have heard since, at St Edmundsbury, from an intimate acquaintance of my lord's, who was an entire stranger to my affairs, that the highest degree of inconstancy is his character; and that few of his numberless mistresses have ever received a second visit from him.

'Well, madam,' continued she, 'I think I have little more to trouble you with; unless I should relate to you, my long ill state of health; from which, I am lately, I thank Heaven, recovered: or, unless I should mention to you the most grievous accident that ever befel me, the loss of my poor dear Charly.' – Here she made a full stop, and the tears ran down into her bosom.

Amelia was silent a few minutes, while she gave the lady time to vent her passion; after which, she began to pour forth a vast profusion of acknowledgements for the trouble she had taken in relating her history; but chiefly, for the motive which had induced her to it; and for the kind warning which she had given her by the little note which Mrs Bennet had sent her that morning.

'Yes, madam,' cries Mrs Bennet, 'I am convinced, by what I have lately seen, that you are the destined sacrifice to this wicked lord; and that Mrs Ellison, whom I no longer doubt to have been the instrument of my ruin, intended to betray you in the same manner. The day I met my lord in your apartment, I began to entertain some suspicions, and I took Mrs Ellison very roundly to task upon them: her behaviour, notwithstanding many asseverations to the contrary, convinced me I was right; and I intended, more than once, to speak to you, but could not; till last night the mention of the masquerade determined me to delay it no longer. I therefore sent you that note this morning; and am glad you so luckily discovered the writer, as it hath given me this opportunity of easing my mind, and of honestly shewing you, how unworthy I am of your friendship, at the same time that I so earnestly desire it.'

CHAPTER 10

Being the last chapter of the seventh book.

AMELIA did not fail to make proper compliments to Mrs Bennet, on the conclusion of her speech in the last chapter. She told her, that from the first moment of her acquaintance, she had the strongest inclination to her friendship; and that her desires of that kind were much increased by hearing her story. 'Indeed, madam,' says she, 'you are much too severe a judge on yourself: for they must have very little candour, in my opinion, who look upon your case with any severe eye. To me, I assure you, you appear highly the object of compassion; and I shall always esteem you, as an innocent and an unfortunate woman.'

Amelia would then have taken her leave; but Mrs Bennet so strongly pressed her to stay to breakfast, that at length she complied: indeed she had fasted so long, and her gentle spirits had been so agitated with variety of passions, that nature very strongly seconded Mrs Bennet's motion.

Whilst the maid was preparing the tea-equipage, Amelia, with a little slyness in her countenance, asked Mrs Bennet, if Serjeant Atkinson did not lodge in the same house with her. The other reddened so extremely at the question, repeated the serjeant's name with such hesitation, and behaved so aukwardly, that Amelia wanted no further confirmation of her suspicions. She would not, however, declare them abruptly to the other; but began a dissertation on the serjeant's virtues; and after observing the great concern which he had manifested, when Mrs Bennet was in her fit, concluded with saying, she believed the serjeant would make the best husband in the world: for that he had great tenderness of heart, and a gentleness of manners, not often to be found in any man; and much seldomer in persons of his rank.

'And why not in his rank?' said Mrs Bennet, 'Indeed, Mrs Booth, we rob the lower order of mankind of their due. I do not deny the force and power of education; but when we consider how very injudicious is the education of the better sort in general, how little they are instructed in the practice of virtue, we shall not expect to find the heart much improved by it. And even as to the head, how very slightly do we commonly find it improved, by what is called a genteel education! I have myself, I think, seen instances of as great goodness, and as great understanding too, among the lower sort of people, as among the higher. Let us compare your serjeant now, with the lord who hath been the subject of conversation; on which side would an impartial judge decide the balance to incline?'

'How monstrous then,' cries Amelia, 'is the opinion of those, who consider our matching ourselves the least below us in degree, as a kind of contamination!'

'A most absurd and preposterous sentiment,' answered Mrs Bennet warmly, 'how abhorrent from justice, from common sense, and from humanity – but how extremely incongruous with a religion, which professes to know no difference of degree; but ranks all mankind on the footing of brethren! Of all kinds of pride, there is none so unchristian as that of station; in reality, there is none so contemptible. Contempt, indeed, may be said to be its own object: for my own part, I know none so despicable as those who despise others.'

'I do assure you,' said Amelia, 'you speak my own sentiments. I give you my word, I should not be ashamed of being the wife of an honest man in any station. – Nor, if I had been much higher than I was, should I have thought myself degraded, by calling our honest serjeant my husband.'

'Since you have made this declaration,' cries Mrs Bennet, 'I am sure you will not be offended at a secret I am going to mention to you.' –

'Indeed, my dear,' answered Amelia smiling, 'I wonder rather you have concealed it so long; especially after the many hints I have given you.'

'Nay, pardon me, madam,' replied the other, 'I do not remember any such hints; and, perhaps, you do not even guess what I am going to say. My secret is this; that no woman ever had so sincere, so passionate a lover, as you have had in the serjeant.'

'I a lover in the serjeant! I!' cries Amelia a little surprized.

'Have patience,' answered the other, – 'I say you, my dear. As much surprized as you appear, I tell you no more than the truth; and yet it is a truth you could hardly expect to hear from me, especially with so much good humour; since I will honestly confess to you – But what need have I to confess, what I know you guess already? – Tell me now sincerely, don't you guess?' –

'I guess, indeed, and hope,' said she, 'that he is your husband.'

'He is, indeed, my husband,' cries the other, 'and I am most happy in your approbation. In honest truth, you ought to approve my choice; since you was every way the occasion of my making it. What you said of him, very greatly recommended him to my opinion; but he endeared himself to me most, by what he said of you. In short, I have discovered, that he hath always loved you, with such a faithful, honest, noble, generous passion, that I was consequently convinced his mind must possess all the ingredients of such a passion; and what are these, but true honour, goodness, modesty, bravery, tenderness, and, in a word, every human virtue. – Forgive me, my dear; but I was uneasy till I became myself the object of such a passion.'

'And do you really think,' said Amelia smiling, 'that I shall forgive you robbing me of such a lover? Or, supposing what you banter me with, was true, do you really imagine you could change such a passion?'

'No, my dear,' answered the other, 'I only hope I have changed the object: for be assured, there is no greater vulgar error, than that it is impossible for a man who loves one woman, ever to love another. On the contrary, it is certain, that a man who can love one woman so well at a distance, will love another better that is nearer to him. Indeed, I have heard one of the best husbands in the world, declare, in the presence of his wife, that he had always loved a princess with adoration. These passions which reside only in very amorous and very delicate minds, feed only on the delicacies there growing; and leave all the substantial food, and enough of the delicacy too for the wife.'

The tea being now ready, Mrs Bennet, or if you please, for the future, Mrs Atkinson, proposed to call in her husband; but Amelia objected. She said, she should be glad to see him any other time; but was then in the utmost hurry, as she had been three hours absent from all she most loved. However, she had scarce drank a dish of tea before she changed her mind; and saying, she would not part man and wife, desired Mr Atkinson might apear.

The maid answered, that her master was not at home; which words she had scarce spoken, when he knocked hastily at the door; and immediately came runing into the room, all pale and breathless; and addressing himself to Amelia, cried out, 'I am sorry, my dear lady, to bring you ill news; but Captain Booth –' 'What! what!' cries Amelia, dropping the tea-cup from her hand, 'is any thing the matter with him!' – 'Don't be frightened, my dear lady,' said the serjeant – 'He is in very good health; but a misfortune hath happened.' – 'Are my children well?' said Amelia. – 'O, very well,' answered the serjeant. – 'Pray, madam, don't be frightened; I hope it will signify nothing – he is arrested – but I hope to get him out of their damned hands immediately.' 'Where is he,' cries Amelia, 'I will go to him this instant!' 'He begs you will not,' answered the serjeant. 'I have sent his lawyer to him, and am going back with Mrs Ellison this moment; but I beg your ladyship, for his sake, and for your own sake, not to go.' 'Mrs Ellison! what is Mrs Ellison to do?' cries Amelia, – 'I must and will go.' Mrs Atkinson then interposed, and begged that she would not hurry her spirits; but compose herself, and go home to her children; whither she would attend her. She comforted her with the thoughts, that the captain was in no immediate danger, that she could go to him when she would; and desired her, to let the serjeant return with Mrs Ellison; saying, she might be of service; and that there was much wisdom, and no kind of shame, in making use of bad people on certain occasions.

'And who,' cries Amelia a little come to herself, 'hath done this barbarous action?'

'One I am ashamed to name,' cries the serjeant; 'indeed, I had always a very different opinion of him; I could not have believed any thing but my own ears and eyes; but Dr Harrison is the man who hath done the deed.'

'Dr Harrison!' cries Amelia. – 'Well then, there is an end of all goodness in the world. I will never have a good opinion of any human being more.'

The serjeant begged, that he might not be detained from the captain; and that if Amelia pleased to go home, he would wait upon her. But she did not chuse to see Mrs Ellison at this time; and after a little consideration, she resolved to stay where she was; and Mrs Atkinson agreed to go and fetch her children to her, it being not many doors distant.

The serjeant then departed; Amelia, in her confusion, never having once thought of wishing him joy on his marriage.

BOOK VIII

CHAPTER 1

Being the first chapter of the eighth book.

THE history must now look a little backwards to those circumstances, which led to the catastrophe mentioned at the end of the last book.

When Amelia went out in the morning, she left her children to the care of her husband. In this amiable office he had been engaged near an hour; and was at that very time lying along on the floor, and his little things crawling and playing about him, when a most violent knock was heard at the door; and immediately a footman running up stairs, acquainted him, that his lady was taken violently ill, and carried into Mrs Chenevix's toy-shop.[1]

Booth no sooner heard this account, which was delivered with great appearance of haste and earnestness, than he leapt suddenly from the floor; and leaving his children roaring at the news of their mother's illness, in strict charge with his maid, he ran as fast as his legs could carry him to the place; or towards the place rather: for, before he arrived at the shop, a gentleman stopt him full butt, crying, 'captain, whither so fast?' – Booth answered eagerly, 'whoever you are, friend, don't ask me any questions now.' – 'You must pardon me, captain,' answered the gentleman; 'but I have a little business with your honour – In short, captain, I have a small warrant here in my pocket against your honour, at the suit of one Dr Harrison.' 'You are a bailiff[2] then,' says Booth. 'I am an officer, sir,' answered the other. – 'Well, sir, it is in vain to contend,' cries Booth; 'but let me beg you will permit me only to step to Mrs Chenevix's – I will attend you, upon my honour, wherever you please; but my wife lies violently ill there.' – 'O, for that matter,' answered the bailiff, 'you may set your heart at ease. Your lady, I hope, is very well. I assure you, she is not there; you will excuse me, captain, these are only stratagems of war. *Bolus and virtus, quis in a hostess equirit?*'[3] – 'Sir, I honour your learning,' cries Booth, 'and could almost kiss you for what you tell me. I assure you, I would forgive you five hundred arrests for such a piece of news. Well, sir, and whither am I to go with you?' – 'O, any where; where your honour pleases,' cries the bailiff. 'Then suppose we go to Brown's coffee-house,' said the prisoner. 'No,' answered the bailiff, 'that will not do; that's in the verge of the court.' 'Why then, to the nearest tavern,' said Booth. 'No, not to a tavern,' cries the other, 'that is not a place of security; and you know, captain, your honour is a shy cock; I have been after your honour these three months – come, sir, you must go to my house, if you please.' 'With all my heart,' answered Booth, 'if it be any where hereabouts.' 'O, it is but a little ways off,' replied the bailiff; 'it is only in Gray's Inn Lane,[4] just by almost.' He then called a coach, and desired his prisoner to walk in.

Booth entered the coach without any resistance, which had he been inclined to make, he must have plainly perceived would have been ineffectual, as the bailiff appeared to have several followers at hand, two of whom, beside the commander in chief, mounted with him into the coach. As Booth was a sweet-tempered man, as well as somewhat of a philosopher, he behaved with all the good humour imaginable, and, indeed, with more than his companions; who, however, shewed him what they call civility, that is, they neither struck him nor spit in his face.

Notwithstanding the pleasantry which Booth endeavoured to preserve, he in reality envied every labourer whom he saw pass by him in his way. The charms of liberty against his will rushed on his mind; and he could not avoid suggesting to himself, how much more happy was the poorest wretch who without controul could repair to his homely habitation, and to his family; compared to him, who was thus violently, and yet lawfully torn away from the company of his wife and children. And their condition, especially that of his Amelia, gave his heart many a severe and bitter pang.

At length he arrived at the bailiff's mansion, and was ushered into a room; in which were several persons. Booth desired to be alone, upon which the bailiff waited on him up stairs, into an apartment, the windows of which were well fortified with iron bars; but the walls had not the least outwork raised before them; they were, indeed, what is generally called naked, the bricks having been only covered with a thin plaister, which in many places was mouldered away.

The first demand made upon Booth was for coach-hire, which amounted to two shillings, according to the bailiff's account; that being just double the legal fare. He was then asked if he did not chuse a bowl of punch; to which he having answered in the negative, the bailiff replied, 'Nay, sir, just as you please. I don't ask you to drink, if you don't chuse it; but certainly you know the custom, the house is full of prisoners, and I can't afford gentlemen a room to themselves for nothing.'

Booth presently took this hint, indeed it was a pretty broad one, and told the bailiff, he should not scruple to pay him his price; but in fact, he never drank unless at his meals. 'As to that, sir,' cries the bailiff, 'it is just as your honour pleases. I scorn to impose upon any gentleman in misfortunes: I wish you well out of them for my part. Your honour can take nothing amiss of me, I only does my duty, what I am bound to do; and as you says you don't care to drink any thing, what will you be pleased to have for dinner?'

Booth then complied in bespeaking a dish of meat, and told the bailiff, he would drink a bottle with him after dinner. He then desired the favour of pen, ink and paper, and a messenger; all which were immediately procured him, the bailiff telling him he might send wherever he pleased, and repeating his concern for Booth's misfortunes, and a hearty desire to see the end of them.

The messenger was just dispatched with the letter, when who should arrive but honest Atkinson? A soldier of the Guards, belonging to the same company with the serjeant, and who had known Booth at Gibraltar, had seen the arrest, and heard the orders given to the coachman. This fellow accidentally meeting Atkinson had acquainted him with the whole affair.

At the appearance of Atkinson, joy immediately overspread the countenance of Booth. The ceremonials which past between them are unnecessary to be repeated. Atkinson was soon dispatched to the attorney, and to Mrs Ellison, as the reader hath before heard from his own mouth.

Booth now greatly lamented that he had writ to his wife. He

thought she might have been acquainted with the affair better by the serjeant. Booth begged him, however, to do every thing in his power to comfort her, to assure her that he was in perfect health and good spirits, and to lessen as much as possible the concern, which he knew she would have at the reading his letter.

The serjeant, however, as the reader hath seen, brought himself the first account of the arrest. Indeed, the other messenger did not arrive till a full hour afterwards. This was not owing to any slowness of his, but to many previous errands which he was to execute before the delivery of the letter: for, notwithstanding the earnest desire which the bailiff had declared to see Booth out of his troubles, he had ordered the porter, who was his follower, to call upon two or three other bailiff's and as many attornies, to try to load his prisoner with as many actions as possible.

Here the reader may be apt to conclude, that the bailiff, instead of being a friend, was really an enemy to poor Booth; but in fact, he was not so. His desire was no more than to accumulate bail bonds; for the bailiff was reckoned an honest and good sort of man in his way, and had no more malice against the bodies in his custody, than a butcher hath to those in his; and as the latter when he takes his knife in hand, hath no idea but of the joints into which he is to cut the carcase; so the former when he handles his writ, hath no other design but to cut out the body into as many bail bonds as possible. As to the life of the animal, or the liberty of the man, they are thoughts which never obtrude themselves on either.

CHAPTER 2

Containing an account of Mr Booth's fellow sufferers.

BEFORE we return to Amelia, we must detain our reader a little longer with Mr Booth, in the custody of Mr Bondum the bailiff, who now informed his prisoner, that he was welcome to the liberty of the house with the other gentlemen.

Booth asked who those gentlemen were. 'One of them, sir,' says Mr Bondum, 'is a very great writer or author, as they call him – He hath been here these five weeks, at the suit of a bookseller, for eleven pound odd money; but he expects to be discharged in a day or two: for he hath writ out the debt. He is now writing for five or six booksellers, and he will get you sometimes, when he sits to it, a matter of fifteen shillings a day. For he is a very good pen, they say; but is apt to be idle. Some days he won't write above five hours; but at other times I have known him at it above sixteen.' – 'Ay!' cries Booth, 'Pray what are his productions? – What doth he write?' 'Why sometimes,' answered Bondum, 'he writes your history books for your numbers,[5] and sometimes your verses, your poems, what do you call them? And then again he writes news for your news papers.' – 'Ay indeed! he is a most extraordinary man truly – How doth he get his news here?' – 'Why he makes it, as he doth your parliament speeches for your magazines.[6] He reads them to us sometimes over a bowl of punch. – To be sure it is all one as if one was in the parliament house – It is about liberty and freedom, and about the constitution of England. I say nothing for my part: for I will keep my neck out of a halter; but faith he makes it out plainly to me, that all matters are not as they should be. I am for liberty, for my part.' 'Is that so consistent with your calling?' cries Booth, 'I thought, my friend, you had lived by depriving men of their liberty.' 'That's another matter,' cries the bailiff, 'that's all according to law, and in the way of business. To be sure men must be obliged to pay their debts, or else there would be an end of every thing.' Booth desired the bailiff to give him his opinion of liberty. Upon which he hesitated a moment, and then cried out, 'O 'tis a fine thing, 'tis a very fine thing, and the constitution of England.' Booth told him that by the old constitution of England, he had heard that men could not be arrested for debt;[7] to which the bailiff answered, that must have been in very bad times. 'Because as why,' says he, 'would it not be the hardest thing in the world if a man could not arrest another for a just and lawful debt? Besides, sir, you must be mistaken: for, how could that ever be! is not liberty the constitution of England? Well, and is not the constitution, as a man may say, – whereby the constitution, that is the law and liberty, and all that –.'

Booth had a little mercy upon the poor bailiff, when he found him rounding in this manner, and told him he had made the matter very clear. Booth then proceeded to enquire after the other gentlemen, his fellows in affliction; upon which Bondum acquainted him that one of the prisoners was a poor fellow. 'He calls himself a gentleman,' said Bondum; 'but I am sure I never saw any thing genteel by him. In a week that he hath been in my house, he hath drank only part of one bottle of wine. I intend to carry him to Newgate within a day or two, if he can't find bail, which I suppose he will not be able to do: for every body says he is an undone man. He hath run out all he hath by losses in business, and one way or other; and he hath a wife and seven children. – Here was the whole family here the other day, all howling together. I never saw such a beggarly crew; I was almost ashamed to see them in my house. I thought they seemed fitter for Bridewell than any other place. To be sure, I do not reckon him as proper company for such as you, sir; but there is another prisoner in the house that I dare say you will like very much. He is, indeed, very much of a gentleman, and spends his money like one. I have had him only three days, and I am afraid he won't stay much longer. They say, indeed, he is a gamester; but what is that to me or any one, as long as a man appears as a gentleman? I always love to speak by people as I find. And, in my opinion, he is fit company for the greatest lord in the land; for he hath very good cloaths, and money enough. He is not here for debt, but upon a judge's warrant for an assault and battery; for the tipstaff[8] locks up here.'

The bailiff was thus haranguing, when he was interrupted by the arrival of the attorney, whom the trusty serjeant had, with the utmost expedition, found out, and dispatched to the relief of his distressed friend; but before we proceed any further with the captain, we will return to poor Amelia, for whom, considering the situation in which we left her, the good-natured reader may be, perhaps, in no small degree sollicitous.

CHAPTER 3

Containing some extraordinary behaviour in Mrs Ellison.

THE serjeant being departed to convey Mrs Ellison to the captain, his wife went to fetch Amelia's children to their mother.

Amelia's concern for the distresses of her husband was aggravated at the sight of her children. 'Good Heavens!' she cry'd, 'what will, what can become of these poor little wretches! Why have I produced these little creatures only to give them a share of poverty and misery!' At which words she embraced them eagerly in her arms, and bedew'd them both with her tears.

The children's eyes soon overflowed as fast as their mother's, tho' neither of them knew the cause of her affliction. The little boy, who was the elder, and much the sharper of the two, imputed the agonies of his mother to her illness, according to the account brought to his father in his presence.

When Amelia became acquainted with the child's apprehensions, she soon satisfied him that she was in a perfect state of health; at which the little thing express'd great satisfaction, and said, he was glad she was well again. – Amelia told him she had not been in the least disordered. – Upon which the innocent cry'd out, 'La! how can people tell such fibs! A great tall man told my papa you was taken very ill at Mrs Somebody's shop; and my poor papa presently ran down stairs, I was afraid he would have broke his neck to come to you.'

'O the villains,' cries Mrs Atkinson, 'what a stratagem was here to take away your husband!'

'Take away!' answered the child – 'What hath any body taken away papa? – Sure that naughty fibbing man hath not taken away papa?'

Amelia begged Mrs Atkinson to say something to her children; for that her spirits were over-powered. She then threw herself into a chair, and gave a full vent to a passion almost too strong for her delicate constitution.

The scene that followed, during some minutes, is beyond my

power of description: I must beg the readers' hearts to suggest it to themselves. The children hung on their mother, whom they endeavour'd in vain to comfort; as Mrs Atkinson did in vain attempt to pacify them, telling them, all would be well, and they would soon see their papa again.

At length, partly by the persuasions of Mrs Atkinson, partly from consideration of her little ones, and more, perhaps, from the relief which she had acquired by her tears, Amelia became a little composed.

Nothing worth notice past in this miserable company from this time till the return of Mrs Ellison from the bailiff's house; and to draw out scenes of wretchedness to too great a length is a task very uneasy to the writer, and for which none but readers of a most gloomy complexion will think themselves ever obliged to his labours.

At length, Mrs Ellison arrived, and entered the room with an air of gaiety, rather misbecoming the occasion. When she had seated herself in a chair, she told Amelia that the captain was very well, and in good spirits; and that he earnestly desired her to keep up hers. 'Come, madam,' said she, 'don't be disconsolate; I hope we shall soon be able to get him out of his troubles. The debts, indeed, amount to more than I expected; however, ways may be found to redeem him. He must own himself guilty of some rashness in going out of the verge, when he knew to what he was liable; but that is now not to be remedied. If he had followed my advice, this had not happened; but men will be headstrong.'

'I cannot bear this,' cries Amelia; 'shall I hear that best of creatures blamed for his tenderness to me?'

'Well, I will not blame him,' answered Mrs Ellison, 'I am sure I propose nothing but to serve him: and if you will do as much to serve him yourself, he will not long be a prisoner.'

'I do!' cries Amelia, 'Oh Heavens! is there a thing upon earth –'

'Yes, there is a thing upon earth,' said Mrs Ellison, 'and a very easy thing too. – And yet I will venture my life, you start when I propose it. And yet when I consider that you are a woman of understanding, I know not why I should think so; for sure you must have too much good sense to imagine that you can cry your husband out of prison. If this would have done, I see you have almost cried your eyes out already. And yet you may do the business by a much pleasanter way than by crying and bawling.'

'What do you mean, madam!' cries Amelia. – 'For my part I cannot guess your meaning.'

'Before I tell you then, madam,' answered Mrs Ellison, 'I must inform you, if you do not already know it, that the captain is charged with actions to the amount of near £500. I am sure I would willingly be his bail; but I know my bail would not be taken for that sum. You must consider, therefore, madam, what chance you have of redeeming him; unless you chuse, as perhaps some wives would, that he should lie all his life in prison.'

At these words, Amelia discharged a shower of tears, and gave every mark of the most frantic grief.

'Why there now,' cries Mrs Ellison, 'while you will indulge these extravagant passions, how can you be capable of listening to the voice of reason. I know I am a fool in concerning myself thus with the affairs of others. I know the thankless office I undertake; and yet I love you so, my dear Mrs Booth, that I cannot bear to see you afflicted, and I would comfort you, if you would suffer me. Let me beg you to make your mind easy; and within these two days, I will engage to set your husband at liberty.

'Harkee, child, only behave like a woman of spirit this evening, and keep your appointment, notwithstanding what hath happened; and I am convinced there is one, who hath the power and the will to serve you.'

Mrs Ellison spoke the latter part of her speech in a whisper; so that Mrs Atkinson, who was then engaged with the children, might not hear her; but Amelia answered aloud, and said, 'What appointment would you have me keep this evening?'

'Nay, nay, if you have forgot,' cries Mrs Ellison, 'I will tell you more another time; but come, will you go home? my dinner is ready by this time, and you shall dine with me.'

'Talk not to me of dinners,' cries Amelia. 'My stomach is too full already.'

'Nay, but, dear madam,' answered Mrs Ellison, – 'let me beseech you to go home with me. I do not care,' says she, whispering, 'to speak before some folks.'

'I have no secret, madam, in the world,' reply'd Amelia aloud, 'which I would not communicate to this lady: for I shall always acknowledge the highest obligations to her for the secrets she hath imparted to me.'

'Madam,' said Mrs Ellison, 'I do not interfere with obligations. I am glad the lady hath obliged you so much; and I wish all people were equally mindful of obligations. I hope I have omitted no opportunity of endeavouring to oblige Mrs Booth, as well as I have some other folks.'

'If by other folks, madam, you mean me,' cries Mrs Atkinson, 'I confess, I sincerely believe you intended the same obligation to us both: and I have the pleasure to think it is owing to me that this lady is not as much obliged to you as I am.'

'I protest, madam, I can hardly guess your meaning,' said Mrs Ellison. – 'Do you really intend to affront me, madam?'

'I intend to preserve innocence and virtue, if it be in my power, madam,' answered the other. 'And sure nothing but the most eager resolution to destroy it, could induce you to mention such an appointment at such a time.'

'I did not expect this treatment from you, madam,' cries Mrs Ellison: 'such ingratitude I could not have believed, had it been reported to me by any other.'

'Such impudence,' answered Mrs Atkinson, 'must exceed, I think, all belief; but when women once abandon that modesty which is the characteristic of their sex, they seldom set any bounds to their assurance.'

'I could not have believed this to have been in human nature;' cries Mrs Ellison. 'Is this the woman whom I have fed, have cloathed, have supported? who owes to my charity, and my intercessions, that she is not at this day destitute of all the necessaries of life!'

'I own it all,' answered Mrs Atkinson. – 'And I add the favour of a masquerade ticket to the number. Could I have thought, madam, that you would, before my face, have asked another lady to go to the same place with the same man! – But I ask your pardon, I impute rather more assurance to you than you are mistress of – You have endeavoured to keep the assignation a secret from me; and it was by mere accident only that I discovered it; unless there are some guardian angels, that in general protect innocence and virtue, tho' I may say I have not always found them so watchful.'

'Indeed, madam,' said Mrs Ellison, 'you are not worth my answer, nor will I stay a moment longer with such a person. – So, Mrs Booth, you have your choice, madam, whether you will go with me, or remain in the company of this lady.'

'If so, madam,' answered Mrs Booth, 'I shall not be long in determining to stay where I am.'

Mrs Ellison then casting a look of great indignation at both the ladies, made a short speech full of invectives against Mrs Atkinson, and not without oblique hints of ingratitude against poor Amelia; after which she burst out of the room, and out of the house; and made haste to her own home, in a condition of mind, to which fortune without guilt cannot, I believe, reduce any one.

Indeed, how much the superiority of misery is on the side of wickedness, may appear to every reader who will compare the present situation of Amelia, with that of Mrs Ellison. Fortune had attack'd the former with almost the highest degree of her malice. She was involved in a scene of most exquisite distress; and her husband, her principal comfort, torn violently from her arms; yet her sorrow, however exquisite, was all soft and tender; nor was she without many consolations. Her case, however hard, was not absolutely desperate; for scarce any condition of fortune can be so. Art and industry, chance and friends have often relieved the most distrest circumstances, and converted them into opulence. In all these she had hopes on this side the grave, and perfect virtue and innocence gave her the strongest assurances on the other. Whereas in the bosom of Mrs Ellison all was storm and tempest; anger, revenge, fear, and pride, like so many raging furies, possessed her mind, and tortured her with disappointment and shame. Loss of reputation, which is generally irreparable, was to be her lot; loss of friends is of this the certain consequence; all on this side the grave appeared dreary and comfortless; and endless misery on the other, closed the gloomy prospect.

Hence, my worthy reader, console thyself, that however few of the other good things of life are thy lot; the best of all things, which is innocence, is always within thy own power; and tho'

Fortune may make thee often unhappy, she can never make thee completely and irreparably miserable without thy own consent.

CHAPTER 4

Containing, among many matters, the exemplary behaviour of Colonel James.

WHEN Mrs Ellison was departed, Mrs Atkinson began to apply all her art to soothe and comfort Amelia; but was presently prevented by her: 'I am ashamed, dear madam,' said Amelia, 'of having indulged my affliction so much at your expence. The suddenness of the occasion is my only excuse; for had I had time to summon my resolution to my assistance, I hope I am mistress of more patience than you have hitherto seen me exert. I know, madam, in my unwarrantable excesses, I have been guilty of many transgressions. First, against that divine will and pleasure, without whose permission at least, no human accident can happen; in the next place, madam, if any thing can aggravate such a fault, I have transgressed the laws of friendship, as well as decency, in throwing upon you some part of the load of my grief; and again I have sinned against common sense, which should teach me instead of weakly and heavily lamenting my misfortunes, to rouse all my spirits to remove them. In this light I am shocked at my own folly, and am resolved to leave my children under your care, and go directly to my husband. I may comfort him. I may assist him. I may relieve him. There is nothing now too difficult for me to undertake.'

Mrs Atkinson greatly approved and complimented her friend on all the former part of her speech, except what related to herself, on which she spoke very civilly, and I believe with great truth; but as to her determination of going to her husband, she endeavoured to dissuade her, at least she begged her to defer it for the present, and till the serjeant returned home. She then reminded Amelia that it was now past five in the afternoon, and that she had not taken any refreshment but a dish of tea the whole day, and desired she would give her leave to procure her a chick, or any thing she liked better for her dinner.

Amelia thanked her friend, and said, she would sit down with her to whatever she pleased; 'but if I do not eat,' said she, 'I would not have you impute it to any thing but want of appetite: for I assure you all things are equally indifferent to me. I am more solicitous about these poor little things, who have not been used to fast so long. Heaven knows what may hereafter be their fate.'

Mrs Atkinson bid her hope the best, and then recommended the children to the care of her maid.

And now arrived a servant from Mrs James, with an invitation to Captain Booth and his lady, to dine with the colonel the day after the next. This a little perplexed Amelia; but after a short consideration she dispatched an answer to Mrs James, in which she concisely informed her of what had happened.

The honest serjeant, who had been on his legs almost the whole day, now returned, and brought Amelia a short letter from her husband; in which he gave her the most solemn assurances of his health and spirits, and begged her with great earnestness to take care to preserve her own; which if she did, he said he had no doubt but that they should shortly be happy. He added something of hopes from my lord, with which Mrs Ellison had amused him; and which served only to destroy the comfort that Amelia received from the rest of his letter.

Whilst Amelia, the serjeant and his lady were engaged in a cold collation, for which purpose a cold chicken was procured from the tavern for the ladies, and two pound of cold beef for the serjeant; a violent knocking was heard at the door, and presently afterwards Colonel James entered the room. After proper compliments had past, the colonel told Amelia, that her letter was brought to Mrs James while they were at table, and that on her shewing it him, he had immediately rose up, made an apology to his company, and took a chair[9] to her. He spoke to her with great tenderness on the occasion, and desired her to make herself easy; assuring her, that he would leave nothing in his power undone to serve her husband. He then gave her an invitation, in his wife's name, to his own house, in the most pressing manner.

Amelia returned him very hearty thanks for all his kind offers; but begged to decline that of an apartment in his house. She said, as she could not leave her children, so neither could she think of bringing such a trouble with her into his family; and tho' the colonel gave her many assurances that her children as well as herself would be very welcome to Mrs James, and even betook himself to entreaties, she still persisted obstinately in her refusal.

In real truth, Amelia had taken a vast affection for Mrs Atkinson, of the comfort of whose company she could not bear to be deprived in her distress; nor to exchange it for that of Mrs James, to whom she had lately conceived no little dislike.

The colonel, when he found he could not prevail with Amelia to accept his invitation, desisted from any further solicitations. He then took a bank-bill of fifty pounds from his pocket-book, and said, – 'You will pardon me, dear madam, if I chuse to impute your refusal of my house, rather to a dislike of my wife, who I will not pretend to be the most agreeable of women, (all men,' said he sighing, 'have not Captain Booth's fortune) than to any aversion or anger to me. I must insist upon it therefore, to make your present habitation as easy to you as possible. – I hope, madam, you will not deny me this happiness; I beg you will honour me with the acceptance of this trifle.' He then put the note into her hand, and declared that the honour of touching it was worth a hundred times that sum.

'I protest, Colonel James,' cried Amelia blushing, 'I know not what to do or say, your goodness so greatly confounds me. Can I, who am so well acquainted with the many great obligations Mr Booth already hath to your generosity, consent that you should add more to a debt we never can pay? –'

The colonel stopt her short, protesting that she misplaced the obligation: for that if to confer the highest happiness was to oblige, he was obliged to her acceptance. 'And I do assure you, madam,' said he, 'if this trifling sum, or a much larger, can contribute to your ease, I shall consider myself as the happiest man upon earth, in being able to supply it; and you, madam, my greatest benefactor in receiving it.'

Amelia then put the note in her pocket; and they entered into a conversation, in which many civil things were said on both sides; but what was chiefly worth remark, was that Amelia had almost her husband constantly in her mouth, and the colonel never mentioned him: the former seemed desirous to lay all obligations, as much as possible, to the account of her husband; and the latter endeavoured with the utmost delicacy to insinuate that her happiness was the main, and indeed only point which he had in view.

Amelia had made no doubt, at the colonel's first appearance, but that he intended to go directly to her husband. When he dropt therefore a hint of his intention to visit him next morning, she appeared visibly shocked at the delay. The colonel perceiving this, said, 'However inconvenient it may be; yet, madam, if it will oblige you, or if you desire it, I will even go to-night.' Amelia answered, 'My husband would be far from desiring to derive any good from your inconvenience; but if you put it to me, I must be excused for saying, I desire nothing more in the world than to send him so great a comfort as I know he will receive from the presence of such a friend.' 'Then to shew you, madam,' cries the colonel, 'that I desire nothing more in the world than to give you pleasure, I will go to him immediately.'

Amelia then bethought herself of the serjeant, and told the colonel, his old acquaintance Atkinson whom he had known at Gibraltar, was then in the house, and would conduct him to the place. The serjeant was immediately called in, paid his respects to the colonel, and was acknowledged by him. They both immediately set forward, Amelia to the utmost of her power pressing their departure.

Mrs Atkinson now returned to Amelia, and was by her acquainted with the colonel's late generosity: for her heart so boiled over with gratitude, that she could not conceal the ebullition. Amelia likewise gave her friend a full narrative of the colonel's former behaviour and friendship to her husband, as well abroad as in England; and ended with declaring, that she believed him to be the most generous man upon earth.

Mrs Atkinson agreed with Amelia's conclusion, and said she was glad to hear there was any such man. They then proceeded with the children to the tea table, where panegyric, and not scandal, was the topic of their conversation; and of this panegyric the colonel was the subject; both the ladies seeming to vie with each other in celebrating the praises of his goodness.

CHAPTER 5
Comments upon authors.

HAVING left Amelia in as comfortable a situation as could possibly be expected, her immediate distresses relieved, and her heart filled with great hopes from the friendship of the colonel; we will now return to Booth, who when the attorney and serjeant had left him, received a visit from that great author of whom honourable mention is made in our second chapter.

Booth, as the reader may be pleased to remember, was a pretty good master of the classics: for his father, tho' he designed his son for the army, did not think it necessary to breed him up a blockhead. He did not perhaps imagine that a competent share of Latin and Greek would make his son either a pedant or a coward. He considered likewise, probably, that the life of a soldier is in general a life of idleness, and might think that the spare hours of an officer in country quarters would be as well employed with a book, as in sauntring about the streets, loitering in a coffee house, sotting in a tavern, or in laying schemes to debauch and ruin a set of harmless ignorant country girls.

As Booth was therefore what might well be called, in this age at least, a man of learning, he began to discourse our author on subjects of literature. 'I think, sir,' says he, 'that Doctor Swift[10] hath been generally allowed by the critics in this kingdom, to be the greatest master of humour that ever wrote. Indeed, I allow him to have possessed most admirable talents of this kind; and if Rabelais was his master, I think he proves the truth of the common Greek proverb – that the scholar is often superior to the master. As to Cervantes, I do not think we can make any just comparison; for tho' Mr Pope compliments him with sometimes taking Cervantes' serious air –' 'I remember the passage,' cries the author:

'Oh thou, whatever title please thy ear,
Dean, Drapier, Bickerstaff or Gulliver;
Whether you take Cervantes' serious air,
Or laugh and shake in Rabelais' easy chair.'[11]

'You are right, sir,' said Booth, 'but tho' I should agree that the doctor hath sometimes condescended to imitate Rabelais, I do not remember to have seen in his works the least attempt in the manner of Cervantes. But there is one in his own way, and whom I am convinced he studied above all others – You guess, I believe, I am going to name Lucian.[12] This author, I say, I am convinced he followed; but I think he followed him at a distance; as, to say the truth, every other writer of this kind hath done in my opinion: for none, I think, hath yet equalled him. I agree, indeed, entirely with Mr Moyle[13] in his discourse on the age of the Philopatris, when he gives him the epithet of the incomparable Lucian; and incomparable I believe he will remain as long as the language in which he wrote shall endure. What an inimitable piece of humour is his *Cock*.'[14] – 'I remember it very well,' cries the author, 'his story of a cock and a bull is excellent.' Booth stared at this, and asked the author what he meant by the bull? 'Nay,' answered he, 'I don't know very well upon my soul. It is a long time since I read him. I learnt him all over at school, I have not read him much since. And pray, sir,' said he, 'how do you like his *Pharsalia*? Don't you think Mr Rowe's translation[15] a very fine one?' Booth replied, 'I believe we are talking of different authors. The *Pharsalia* which Mr Rowe translated was written by Lucan; but I have been speaking of Lucian, a Greek writer, and in my opinion the greatest in the humorous way, that ever the world produced.' 'Ay!' cries the author, 'he was indeed so, a very excellent writer indeed. I fancy a translation of him would sell very well.' 'I do not know, indeed,' cries Booth. 'A good translation[16] of him would be a valuable book. I have seen a wretched one published by Mr Dryden, but translated by others,[17] who in many places have misunderstood Lucian's meaning, and have no where preserved the spirit of the original.' 'That is great pity,' says the author. 'Pray, sir, is he well translated into French?' Booth answered, he could not tell; but that he doubted it very much, having never seen a good version into that language, out of the Greek. 'To confess the truth, I believe,' said he, 'the French translators have generally consulted the Latin only,[18] which, in some of the few Greek writers I have read, is intolerably bad. And as the English translators, for the most part, pursue the French, we may easily guess, what spirit those copies of bad copies of bad copies must preserve of the original.'

'Egad, you are a shrewd guesser,' cries the author, 'I am glad the booksellers have not your sagacity. But how should it be otherwise, considering the price they pay by the sheet? The Greek, you will allow, is a hard language; and there are few gentlemen that write, who can read it without a good lexicon. Now, sir, if we were to afford time to find out the true meaning of words, a gentleman would not get bread and cheese by his work. If one was to be paid, indeed, as Mr Pope was for his Homer.[19] – Pray, sir, don't you think that the best translation in the world?'

'Indeed, sir,' cries Booth, 'I think, tho' it is certainly a noble paraphrase, and of itself a fine poem, yet, in some places, it is no translation at all. In the very beginning, for instance, he hath not rendered the true force of the author. Homer invokes his muse in the five first lines of the Iliad; and, at the end of the fifth, he gives his reason:

Διὸς δ' ἐτελείετο βουλή

For all these things,' says he, 'were brought about by the decree of Jupiter; and, therefore, he supposes their true sources are known only to the deities. Now, the translation takes no more notice of the ΔE,[20] than if no such word had been there.'

'Very possibly,' answered the author; 'it is a long time since I read the original. Perhaps, then, he followed the French translations. I observe, indeed, he talks much in the notes of Madam Dacier and Monsieur Eustathius.'[21]

Booth had now received conviction enough of his friend's knowledge of the Greek language; without attempting, therefore, to set him right, he made a sudden transition to the Latin. 'Pray, sir,' said he, 'as you have mentioned Rowe's translation of the *Pharsalia*; do you remember, how he hath rendered that passage in the character of Cato?

– Venerisque huic maximus usus
Progenies; urbi pater est, urbique maritus.[22]

For I apprehend that passage is generally misunderstood.'

'I really do not remember,' answered the author. – 'Pray, sir, what do you take to be the meaning?'

'I apprehend, sir,' replied Booth, 'that, by these words, *Urbi pater est, urbique maritus*, Cato is represented as the father and husband to the city of Rome.'

'Very true, sir,' cries the author, 'very fine, indeed. – Not only the father of his country, but the husband too; very noble, truly.'

'Pardon me, sir,' cries Booth, 'I do not conceive that to have been Lucan's meaning. If you please to observe the context: Lucan having commended the temperance of Cato, in the instances of diet and clothes, proceeds to venereal pleasures; of which, says the poet, his principal use was procreation: then he adds, *Urbi pater est, urbique maritus*, that he became a father and a husband, for the sake only of the city.'

'Upon my word, that's true,' cries the author, 'I did not think of it. It is much finer than the other. – *Urbis pater est* – what is the other? – ay – *urbis maritus*. – It is certainly as you say, sir.'

Booth was, by this, pretty well satisfied of the author's profound learning; however, he was willing to try him a little further. He asked him, therefore, what was his opinion of Lucan in general, and in what class of writers he ranked him.

The author stared a little at this question; and after some hesitation, answered, 'Certainly, sir, I think he is a fine writer, and a very great poet.'

'I am very much of the same opinion,' cries Booth; 'but where do you class him, next to what poet do you place him?'

'Let me see,' cries the author, 'where do I class him! next to whom do I place him! – Ay! – why! – why, pray, where do you yourself place him?'

'Why, surely,' cries Booth, 'if he is not to be placed in the first rank, with Homer, and Virgil, and Milton – I think clearly, he is at the head of the second; before either Statius,[23] or Silius Italicius.[24] – Tho' I allow to each of these their merits; but, perhaps, an epic poem was beyond the genius of either. I own I have often thought, if Statius had ventured no farther than Ovid or Claudian,[25] he would have succeeded better: for his *Sylvae* are, in my opinion, much better than his *Thebaïs*.'

'I believe I was of the same opinion formerly,' said the author.

'And for what reason have you altered it?' cries Booth.

'I have not altered it,' answered the author; 'but, to tell you the truth, I have not any opinion at all about these matters at present. I do not trouble my head much with poetry: for there is no encouragement to such studies in this age. It is true, indeed, I have now and then wrote a poem or two for the magazines; but I never intend to write any more: for a gentleman is not paid for his time. A sheet is a sheet with the booksellers; and, whether it be in prose or verse, they make no difference; tho' certainly there is as much difference to a gentleman in the work, as there is to a taylor, between making a plain and a laced suit. Rhimes are difficult things; they are stubborn things, sir. I have been sometimes longer in tagging a couplet, than I have been in writing a speech on the side of the opposition, which hath been read with great applause all over the kingdom.'

'I am glad you are pleased to confirm that,' cries Booth: 'for I protest, it was an entire secret to me till this day. I was so perfectly ignorant, that I thought the speeches, published in the magazines, were really made by the members themselves.'

'Some of them, and I believe I may, without vanity, say, the best,' cries the author, 'are all the production of my own pen; but, I believe, I shall leave it off soon, unless a sheet of speech will fetch more than it does at present. In truth, the romance writing[26] is the only branch of our business now, that is worth following. Goods of that sort have had so much success lately in the market, that a bookseller scarce cares what he bids for them. And it is certainly the easiest work in the world; you may write it almost as fast as you can set pen to paper; and if you interlard it with a little scandal, a little abuse on some living characters of note, you cannot fail of success.'

'Upon my word, sir,' cries Booth, 'you have greatly instructed me. I could not have imagined, there had been so much regularity in the trade of writing, as you are pleased to mention; by what I can perceive, the pen and ink is likely to become the staple commodity of the kingdom.'

'Alas! sir,' answered the author, 'it is over-stocked – The market is over-stocked. There is no encouragement to merit, no patrons. I have been these five years soliciting a subscription for my new translation of Ovid's *Metamorphoses*, with notes explanatory, historical, and critical; and I have scarce collected five hundred names yet.'

The mention of this translation a little surprised Booth; not only as the author had just declared his intentions to forsake the tuneful muses; but for some other reasons, which he had collected from his conversation with our author, he little expected to hear of a proposal to translate any of the Latin poets. He proceeded, therefore, to catechise him a little farther; and by his answers was fully satisfied, that he had the very same acquaintance with Ovid, that he had appeared to have with Lucan.

The author then pulled out a bundle of papers, containing proposals for his subscription, and receipts; and addressing himself to Booth, said, 'Tho' the place in which we meet, sir, is an improper place to solicit favours of this kind; yet, perhaps, it may be in your power to serve me, if you will charge your pockets with some of these.' Booth was just offering at an excuse, when the bailiff introduced Colonel James, and the serjeant.

The unexpected visit of a beloved friend to a man in affliction, especially in Mr Booth's situation, is a comfort which can scarce be equalled; not barely from the hopes of relief, or redress, by his assistance; but, as it is an evidence of sincere friendship, which scarce admits of any doubt or suspicion. Such an instance doth, indeed, make a man amends for all ordinary troubles and distresses; and we ought to think ourselves gainers, by having had such an opportunity of discovering, that we are possessed of one of the most valuable of all human possessions.

Booth was so transported at the sight of the colonel, that he dropt the proposals which the author had put into his hand, and burst forth into the highest professions of gratitude to his friend, who behaved very properly on his side, and said every thing which became the mouth of a friend on the occasion.

It is true, indeed, he seemed not moved equally, either with Booth or the serjeant; both whose eyes watered at the scene. In truth, the colonel, tho' a very generous man, had not the least grain of tenderness in his disposition. His mind was formed of those firm materials, of which nature formerly hammered out the Stoic, and upon which the sorrows of no man living could make an impression. A man of this temper, who doth not much value danger, will fight for the person he calls his friend; and the man that hath but little value for his money will give it him; but such friendship is never to be absolutely depended on: for whenever the favourite passion interposes with it, it is sure to subside and vanish into air. Whereas, the man, whose tender disposition really feels the miseries of another, will endeavour to relieve them for his own sake; and, in such a mind, friendship will often get the superiority over every other passion.

But from whatever motive it sprung, the colonel's behaviour to Booth seemed truly amiable; and so it appeared to the author, who took the first occasion to applaud it in a very florid oration; which the reader, when he recollects that he was a speech-maker by profession, will not be surprised at; nor, perhaps, will be much more surprised, that he soon after took an occasion of clapping a proposal into the colonel's hands; holding at the same time a receipt very visible in his own.

The colonel received both, and gave the author a guinea in exchange, which was double the sum mentioned in the receipt; for which the author made a low bow, and very politely took his leave, saying, 'I suppose, gentlemen, you may have some private business together; I heartily wish a speedy end to your confinement; and I congratulate you on the possessing so great, so noble, and so generous a friend.'

CHAPTER 6

Which inclines rather to satire than panegyric.

THE colonel had the curiosity to ask Booth the name of the gentleman, who, in the vulgar language, had struck, or taken him in for a guinea, with so much ease and dexterity. Booth answered, he did not know his name; all that he knew of him was, that he was the most impudent and illiterate fellow he had ever seen; and that, by his own account, he was the author of most of the wonderful productions of the age. 'Perhaps,' said he, 'it may look uncharitable in me, to blame you for your generosity; but I am convinced the fellow hath not the least merit or capacity; and you have subscribed to the most horrid trash that ever was published.'

'I care not a farthing what he publishes,' cries the colonel. 'Heaven forbid, I should be obliged to read half the nonsense I have subscribed to.'

'But, don't you think,' said Booth, 'that by such indiscriminate encouragement of authors, you do a real mischief to the society? By propagating the subscriptions of such fellows, people are tired out, and with-hold their contributions to men of real merit; and, at the same time, you are contributing to fill the world, not only with nonsense, but with all the scurrility, indecency, and profaneness with which the age abounds; and with which all bad writers supply the defect of genius.'

'Pugh!' cries the colonel, 'I never consider these matters. Good or bad, it is all one to me; but there's an acquaintance of mine, and a man of great wit too, that thinks the worst the best, as they are the surest to make him laugh.'

'I ask pardon, sir,' says the serjeant; 'but I wish your honour would consider your own affairs a little; for it grows late in the evening.'

'The serjeant says true,' answered the colonel. 'What is it you intend to do?'

'Faith, colonel, I know not what I shall do. My affairs seem so irreparable, that I have been driving them, as much as possibly I could from my mind. If I was to suffer alone, I think, I could bear them with some philosophy; but when I consider who are to be the sharers in my fortune – the dearest of children; and the best, the worthiest, and the noblest of women. Pardon me, my dear friend, these sensations are above me, they convert me into a woman; they drive me to despair, to madness.'

The colonel advised him to command himself; and told him, this was not the way to retrieve his fortune. 'As to me, my dear Booth,' said he, 'you know, you may command me as far as is really within my power.'

Booth answered eagerly, that he was so far from expecting any more favours from the colonel, that he had resolved not to let him know any thing of his misfortune. 'No, my dear friend,' cries he, 'I am too much obliged to you already;' and then burst into many fervent expressions of gratitude; till the colonel himself stopt him, and begged him to give an account of the debt or debts, for which he was detained in that horrid place.

Booth answered, he could not be very exact; but he feared it was upwards of four hundred pounds.

'It is but three hundred pounds, indeed, sir,' cries the serjeant; 'if you can raise three hundred pounds, you are a free man this moment.'

Booth, who did not apprehend the generous meaning of the serjeant, as well as, I believe, the reader will, answered, he was mistaken; that he had computed his debts, and they amounted to upwards of four hundred pounds: nay, that the bailiff had shewn him writs for above that sum.

'Whether your debts are three or four hundred,' cries the colonel, 'the present business is to give bail only; and then you will have some time to try your friends. I think you might get a company abroad; and then I would advance the money on the security of half your pay: and, in the mean time, I will be one of your bail with all my heart.'

Whilst Booth poured forth his gratitude for all this kindness, the serjeant ran down stairs for the bailiff; and shortly after returned with him into the room.

The bailiff, being informed that the colonel offered to be bail for his prisoner, answered a little surlily, 'Well, sir, and who will be the other? You know, I suppose, there must be two; and I must have time to enquire after them.'

The colonel replied, 'I believe, sir, I am well known to be responsible for a much larger sum than your demand on this gentleman; but if your forms require two, I suppose the serjeant here will do for the other.'

'I don't know the serjeant, nor you either, sir,' cries Bondum, 'and if you propose yourselves bail for the gentleman, I must have time to enquire after you.'

'You need very little time to enquire after me,' says the colonel; 'for I can send for several of the law, whom I suppose you know, to satisfy you; but consider it is very late.'

'Yes, sir,' answered Bondum, 'I do consider it is too late for the captain to be bailed to-night.'

'What do you mean by too late?' cries the colonel.

'I mean, sir, that I must search the office,[27] and that is now shut up: for if my Lord Mayor and the court of aldermen would be bound for him, I would not discharge him, till I had searched the office.'

'How, sir,' cries the colonel, 'hath the law of England no more regard for the liberty of the subject, than to suffer such fellows as you to detain a man in custody for debt, when he can give undeniable security?'

'Don't fellow me,' said the bailiff, 'I am as good a fellow as yourself, I believe, tho' you have that ribbond in your hat there.'

'Do you know who you are speaking to?' said the serjeant. 'Do you know you are talking to a colonel of the army?'

'What's a colonel of the army to me!' – cries the bailiff. 'I have had as good as he in my custody before now.'

'And a Member of Parliament' – cries the serjeant.

'Is the gentleman a Member of Parliament? – Well, and what harm have I said – I am sure I meant no harm, and if his honour is offended, I ask his pardon; to be sure his honour must know that the sheriff is answerable for all the writs in the office, tho' they were never so many, and I am answerable to the sheriff. I am sure the captain can't say that I have shewn him any manner of incivility since he hath been here. – And I hope, honourable sir,' cries he turning to the colonel, 'you don't take any thing amiss that I said, or meant by way of disrespect, or any such matter. I did not, indeed, as the gentleman here says, know who I was speaking to; but I did not say any thing uncivil as I know of, and I hope no offence.'

The colonel was more easily pacified than might have been expected, and told the bailiff that if it was against the rules of law to discharge Mr Booth that evening, he must be contented. He then addressed himself to his friend, and began to prescribe comfort and patience to him; saying he must rest satisfied with his confinement that night, and the next morning he promised to visit him again.

Booth answered, that as for himself, the lying one night in any place was very little worth his regard. 'You and I, my dear friend, have both spent our evening in a worse situation than I shall in this house. All my concern is for my poor Amelia, whose sufferings on account of my absence I know, and I feel with unspeakable tenderness. Could I be assured she was tolerably easy, I could be contented in chains or in a dungeon.'

'Give yourself no concern on her account,' said the colonel, 'I will wait on her myself, tho' I break an engagement for that purpose, and will give her such assurances as I am convinced will make her perfectly easy.'

Booth embraced his friend, and weeping over him paid his acknowledgment with tears, for all his goodness. In words, indeed, he was not able to thank him; for gratitude joining with his other passions almost choaked him, and stopt his utterance.

After a short scene, in which nothing past worth recounting, the colonel bid his friend good-night; and leaving the serjeant with him made the best of his way back to Amelia.

CHAPTER 7

Worthy a very serious perusal.

THE colonel found Amelia sitting very disconsolate with Mrs Atkinson. He entered the room with an air of great gaiety, assured Amelia that her husband was perfectly well, and that he hoped the next day he would again be with her.

Amelia was a little comforted at this account; and vented many grateful expressions to the colonel, for his unparallelled friendship, as she was pleased to call it. She could not, however, help giving way soon after to a sigh, at the thoughts of her husband's bondage, and declared that night would be the longest she had ever known.

'This lady, madam,' cries the colonel, 'must endeavour to make it shorter. And if you will give me leave, I will join in the same endeavour.' Then after some more consolatory speeches, the colonel attempted to give a gay turn to the discourse; and said, 'I was engaged to have spent this evening disagreeably at Ranelagh, with a set of company I did not like. How vastly am I obliged to you, dear Mrs Booth, that I pass it so infinitely more to my satisfaction!'

'Indeed, colonel,' said Amelia, 'I am convinced that to a mind so rightly turned as yours, there must be a much sweeter relish in the highest offices of friendship, than in any pleasures which the gayest public places can afford.'

'Upon my word, madam,' said the colonel, 'you now do me more than justice. I have, and always had the utmost indifference for such pleasures. Indeed, I hardly allow them worthy of that name, or if they are so at all, it is in a very low degree. In my opinion, the highest friendship must always lead us to the highest pleasure.'

Here Amelia entered into a long dissertation on friendship, in which she pointed several times directly at the colonel as the hero of her tale.

The colonel highly applauded all her sentiments; and when he could not avoid taking the compliment to himself, he received it with a most respectful bow. He then tried his hand likewise at description, in which he found means to repay all Amelia's panegyric in kind. This tho' he did with all possible delicacy; yet a curious observer might have been apt to suspect that it was chiefly on her account that the colonel had avoided the masquerade.

In discourses of this kind they past the evening, till it was very late, the colonel never offering to stir from his chair before the clock had struck one; when he thought, perhaps, that decency obliged him to take his leave.

As soon as he was gone, Mrs Atkinson said to Mrs Booth, 'I think, madam, you told me this afternoon, that the colonel was married.'

Amelia answered, she did so.

'I think likewise, madam,' said Mrs Atkinson, 'you was acquainted with the colonel's lady.'

Amelia answered, that she had been extremely intimate with her abroad.

'Is she young, and handsome,' said Mrs Atkinson, 'In short, pray, was it a match of love or convenience?'

Amelia answered, entirely of love, she believed, on his side: for that the lady had little or no fortune.

'I am very glad to hear it,' said Mrs Atkinson: 'For I am sure the colonel is in love with somebody. I think, I never saw a more luscious picture of love drawn than that which he was pleased to give us, as the portraiture of friendship. I have read, indeed, of Pylades and Orestes, Damon and Pythias,[28] and other great friends of old; nay, I sometimes flatter myself that I am capable of being a friend myself; but as for that fine, soft, tender, delicate passion, which he was pleased to describe, I am convinced there must go a he and a she to the composition.'

'Upon my word, my dear, you are mistaken,' cries Amelia. 'If you had known the friendship which hath always subsisted between the colonel and my husband, you would not imagine it possible for any description to exceed it. Nay, I think his behaviour this very day is sufficient to convince you.'

'I own what he hath done to-day hath great merit,' said Mrs Atkinson; 'and yet from what he hath said to-night – You will pardon me, dear madam; perhaps I am too quick-sighted in my observations, nay, I am afraid I am even impertinent.'

'Fie! upon it,' cries Amelia, 'how can you talk in that strain? Do you imagine I expect ceremony? – Pray speak what you think with the utmost freedom.'

'Did he not then,' said Mrs Atkinson, 'repeat the words, the finest woman in the world, more than once? Did he not make use of an expression which might have become the mouth of Oroondates[29] himself? – If I remember, the words were these, "That had he been Alexander the Great, he should have thought it more glory to have wiped off a tear from the bright eyes of Statira, than to have conquered fifty worlds."'

'Did he say so?' cries Amelia – 'I think he did say something like it; but my thoughts were so full of my husband that I took little notice. But what would you infer from what he said? I hope you don't think he is in love with me!'

'I hope he doth not think so himself,' answered Mrs Atkinson, 'tho' when he mentioned the bright eyes of Statira, he fixed his own eyes on yours with the most languishing air I ever beheld.'

Amelia was going to answer, when the serjeant arrived, and then she immediately fell to enquiring after her husband; and received such satisfactory answers to all her many questions concerning him, that she expressed great pleasure. These ideas so possessed her mind, that without once casting her thoughts on any other matters, she took her leave of the serjeant and his lady, and repaired to bed to her children, in a room which Mrs Atkinson had provided her in the same house; where we will at present wish her a good night.

CHAPTER 8

Consisting of grave matters.

WHILE innocence and chearful hope, in spite of the malice of Fortune, closed the eyes of the gentle Amelia, on her homely bed, and she enjoyed a sweet and profound sleep; the colonel lay restless all night on his down: his mind was affected with a kind of ague fit; sometimes scorched up with flaming desires, and again chilled with the coldest despair.

There is a time, I think, according to one of our poets, *when lust and envy sleep*.[30] This, I suppose, is when they are well gorged with the food they most delight in; but while either of these are hungry,

Nor poppy, nor mandragora,
Nor all the drousy syrups of the East
Will ever medicine them to slumber.[31]

The colonel was, at present, unhappily tormented by both these fiends. His last evening's conversation with Amelia had done his business effectually. The many kind words she had spoken to him, the many kind looks she had given him, as being, she conceived, the friend and preserver of her husband, had made an entire conquest of his heart. Thus, the very love which she bore him, as the person to whom her little family were to owe their preservation and happiness, inspired him with thoughts of sinking them all in the lowest abyss of ruin and misery; and while she smiled with all her sweetness on the supposed friend of her husband, she was converting that friend into his most bitter enemy.

> *Friendship, take heed; if woman interfere,*
> *Be sure the hour of thy destruction's near.*[32]

These are the lines of Vanbrugh; and the sentiment is better than the poetry. To say the truth, as a handsome wife is the cause and cement of many false friendships, she is often too liable to destroy the real ones.

Thus the object of the colonel's lust very plainly appears; but the object of his envy may be more difficult to discover. Nature and Fortune had seemed to strive with a kind of rivalship, which should bestow most on the colonel. The former had given him person, parts, and constitution, in all which he was superior to almost every other man. The latter had given him rank in life, and riches, both in a very eminent degree. Whom then should this happy man envy? Here, lest ambition should mislead the reader to search the palaces of the great, we will direct him at once to Gray's Inn Lane, where in a miserable bed, in a miserable room, he will see a miserable broken lieutenant, in a miserable condition, with several heavy debts on his back, and without a penny in his pocket. This, and no other, was the object of the colonel's envy. And why? because this wretch was possessed of the affections of a poor little lamb; which all the vast flocks that were within the power and reach of the colonel, could not prevent that glutton's longing for. And sure this image of the lamb[33] is not improperly adduced on this occasion: for what was the colonel's desire but to lead this poor lamb, as it were, to the slaughter, in order to purchase a feast of a few days by her final destruction, and to tear her away from the arms of one where she was sure of being fondled and caressed all the days of her life.

While the colonel was agitated with these thoughts, his greatest comfort was, that Amelia and Booth were now separated, and his greatest terror was of their coming again together. From wishes therefore he began to meditate designs; and so far was he from any intention of procuring the liberty of his friend, that he began to form schemes of prolonging his confinement, till he could procure some means of sending him away far from her; in which case he doubted not but of succeeding in all he desired.

He was forming this plan in his mind, when a servant informed him, that one Serjeant Atkinson desired to speak with his honour. The serjeant was immediately admitted, and acquainted the colonel, that if he pleased to go and become bail for Mr Booth, another unexceptionable housekeeper[34] would be there to join with him. This person the serjeant had procured that morning, and had, by leave of his wife, given him a bond of indemnification for the purpose.

The colonel did not seem so elated with this news as Atkinson expected. On the contrary, instead of making a direct answer to what Atkinson said, the colonel began thus: 'I think, serjeant, Mr Booth hath told me that you was foster-brother to his lady. She is really a charming woman, and it is a thousand pities she should ever have been placed in the dreadful situation she is now in. There is nothing so silly as for subaltern officers of the army to marry, unless where they meet with women of very great fortunes indeed. What can be the event of their marrying otherwise, but entailing misery and beggary on their wives and their posterity?'

'Ah! sir!' cries the serjeant, 'it is too late to think of those matters now. To be sure my lady might have married one of the top gentlemen in the country: for she is certainly one of the best, as well as one of the handsomest, women in the kingdom; and if she had been fairly dealt by, would have had a very great fortune into the bargain. Indeed she is worthy of the greatest prince in the world; and if I had been the greatest prince in the world, I should have thought myself happy with such a wife; but she was pleased to like the lieutenant, and certainly there can be no happiness in marriage without liking.'

'Lookee, serjeant,' said the colonel, 'you know very well that I am the lieutenant's friend. I think I have shewn myself so.'

'Indeed, your honour hath,' quoth the serjeant, 'more than once, to my knowledge.'

'But I am angry with him for his imprudence, greatly angry with him for his imprudence; and the more so, as it affects a lady of so much worth.'

'She is, indeed, a lady of the highest worth,' cries the serjeant. 'Poor dear lady, I knew her, an't please your honour, from her infancy; and the sweetest-temper'd, best-natured lady she is, that ever trod on English ground. I have always loved her as if she was my own sister. – Nay, she hath very often called me brother; and I have taken it to be a greater honour than if I was to be called a general officer.'

'What pity it is,' said the colonel, 'that this worthy creature should be exposed to so much misery by the thoughtless behaviour of a man, who, though I am his friend, I cannot help saying, hath been guilty of imprudence, at least. Why could he not live upon his half-pay? What had he to do to run himself into debt in this outrageous manner?'

'I wish indeed,' cries the serjeant, 'he had been a little more considerative; but, I hope, this will be a warning to him.'

'How am I sure of that,' answered the colonel; 'or what reason is there to expect it? Extravagance is a vice of which men are not so easily cured. I have thought a great deal of this matter, Mr Serjeant; and upon the most mature deliberation, I am of opinion, that it will be better both for him and his poor lady, that he should smart a little more.'

'Your honour, sir, to be sure is in the right,' reply'd the serjeant; 'but yet, sir, if you will pardon me for speaking, I hope you will be pleased to consider my poor lady's case. She suffers, all this while, as much or more than the lieutenant; for I know her so well, that I am certain she will never have a moment's ease till her husband is out of confinement.'

'I know women better than you, serjeant,' cries the colonel: 'they sometimes place their affections on a husband, as children do on their nurse; but they are both to be weaned. I know you, serjeant, to be a fellow of sense as well as spirit, or I should not speak so freely to you; but I took a fancy to you a long time ago, and I intend to serve you; but first I ask you this question, is your attachment to Mr Booth, or to his lady?'

'Certainly, sir,' said the serjeant, 'I must love my lady best. Not but I have a great affection for the lieutenant too, because I know my lady hath the same; and, indeed, he hath been always very good to me, as far as was in his power. A lieutenant, your honour knows, can't do a great deal; but I have always found him my friend upon all occasions.'

'You say true,' cries the colonel, 'a lieutenant can do but little; but I can do much to serve you, and will too – But let me ask you one question – Who was the lady whom I saw last night with Mrs Booth at her lodgings?'

Here the serjeant blushed, and repeated, 'The lady, sir!'

'Ay, a lady, a woman,' cries the colonel, 'who supped with us last night. She looked rather too much like a gentlewoman for the mistress of a lodging house.'

The serjeant's cheeks glowed at this compliment to his wife, and he was just going to own her, when the colonel proceeded. 'I think I never saw in my life so ill-looking, sly, demure a b—. I would give something, methinks, to know who she was.'

'I don't know, indeed,' cries the serjeant in great confusion. – 'I know nothing about her.'

'I wish you would enquire,' said the colonel, 'and let me know her name, and likewise what she is. I have a strange curiosity to know, and let me see you again this evening exactly at seven.'

'And will not your honour then go to the lieutenant this morning?' said Atkinson.

'It is not in my power,' answered the colonel: 'I am engaged another way. Besides there is no haste in this affair. If men will be imprudent, they must suffer the consequences. Come to me at seven, and bring me all the particulars you can concerning that ill-look'd jade, I mentioned to you; for I am resolved to know who she is. And so, good-morrow to you, serjeant; be assured I will take an opportunity to do something for you.'

Tho' some readers may, perhaps, think the serjeant not unworthy of the freedom with which the colonel treated him, yet that haughty officer would have been very backward to have condescended to such familiarity with one of his rank, had he not proposed some design from it. In truth, he began to conceive hopes of making the serjeant instrumental to his design on Amelia; in other words, to convert him into a pimp; an office in which the colonel had been served by Atkinson's betters; and which, as he knew it was in his power very well to reward him, he had no apprehension that the serjeant would decline: an opinion which the serjeant might have pardon'd, though he had never given the least grounds for it, since the colonel borrowed it from the knowledge of his own heart. This dictated to him, that he, from a bad motive, was capable of desiring to debauch his friend's wife; and the same heart inspired him to hope that another from another bad motive, might be guilty of the same breach of friendship, in assisting him. Few men, I believe, think better of others than of themselves; nor do they easily allow the existence of any virtue of which they perceive no traces in their own minds: for which reason I have observed, that it is extremely difficult to persuade a rogue that you are an honest man; nor would you ever succeed in the attempt by the strongest evidence, was it not for the comfortable conclusion which the rogue draws, that he who proves himself to be honest, proves himself to be a fool at the same time.

CHAPTER 9

A curious chapter, from which a curious reader may draw sundry observations.

THE serjeant retired from the colonel in a very dejected state of mind; in which, however, we must leave him awhile, and return to Amelia; who as soon as she was up, had dispatched Mrs Atkinson to pay off her former lodgings, and to bring off all cloaths and other moveables.

The trusty messenger returned without performing her errand: for Mrs Ellison had locked up all her rooms, and was gone out very early that morning, and the servant knew not whither she was gone.

The two ladies now sat down to breakfast, together with Amelia's two children; after which Amelia declared she would take a coach and visit her husband. To this motion Mrs Atkinson soon agreed, and offered to be her companion. To say truth, I think it was reasonable enough; and the great abhorrence which Booth had of seeing his wife in a bailiff's house, was, perhaps, rather too nice and delicate.

When the ladies were both drest, and just going to send for their vehicle, a great knocking was heard at the door, and presently Mrs James was usher'd into the room.

This visit was disagreeable enough to Amelia, as it detained her from the sight of her husband, for which she so eagerly longed. However, as she had no doubt but that the visit would be reasonably short, she resolved to receive the lady with all the complaisance in her power.

Mrs James now behaved herself so very unlike the person that she lately appeared, that it might have surprised any one who doth not know, that besides that of a fine lady, which is all mere art and mummery, every such woman hath some real character at the bottom, in which, whenever nature gets the better of her, she acts. Thus the finest ladies in the world will sometimes love, and sometimes scratch, according to their different natural dispositions, with great fury and violence, tho' both of these are equally inconsistent with a fine lady's artificial character.

Mrs James then was at the bottom a very good-natured woman; and the moment she heard of Amelia's misfortune, was sincerely grieved at it. She had acquiesced on the very first motion with the colonel's design of inviting her to her house; and this morning at breakfast, when he had acquainted her that Amelia made some difficulty in accepting the offer, very readily undertook to go herself and persuade her friend to accept the invitation.

She now pressed this matter with such earnestness, that Amelia, who was not extremely versed in the art of denying, was hardly able to refuse her importunity; nothing, indeed, but her affection to Mrs Atkinson could have prevailed on her to refuse; that point, however, she would not give up, and Mrs James, at last, was contented with a promise, that as soon as their affairs were settled, Amelia, with her husband and family, would make her a visit, and stay some time with her in the country, whither she was soon to retire.

Having obtained this promise, Mrs James, after many very friendly professions, took her leave; and stepping into her coach, re-assumed the fine lady, and drove away to join her company at an auction.

The moment she was gone, Mrs Atkinson, who had left the room upon the approach of Mrs James, returned into it, and was informed by Amelia of all that had past.

'Pray, madam,' said Mrs Atkinson, 'do this colonel and his lady live, as it is called, well together?'

'If you mean to ask,' cries Amelia, 'whether they are a very fond couple, I must answer that I believe they are not.'

'I have been told,' says Mrs Atkinson, 'that there have been instances of women who have become bawds to their own husbands, and the husbands pimps for them.'

'Fie upon it,' cries Amelia. 'I hope there are no such people. Indeed, my dear, this is being a little too censorious.'

'Call it what you please,' answered Mrs Atkinson. 'It arises from my love to you, and my fears for your danger. You know the proverb of a burnt child,[35] and if such a one hath any good-nature it will dread the fire, on the account of others as well as on its own. And if I may speak my sentiments freely, I cannot think you will be in safety at this colonel's house.'

'I cannot but believe your apprehensions to be sincere,' replied Amelia, 'and I must think myself obliged to you for them; but I am convinced you are entirely in an error. I look on Colonel James as the most generous and best of men. He was a friend, and an excellent friend too, to my husband, long before I was acquainted with him, and he hath done him a thousand good offices. What do you say of his behaviour yesterday?'

'I wish,' cries Mrs Atkinson, 'that his behaviour to-day had been equal. What I am now going to undertake is the most disagreeable office of friendship, but it is a necessary one. I must tell you therefore what past this morning between the colonel and Mr Atkinson; for tho' it will hurt you, you ought, on many accounts to know it.' Here she related the whole which we have recorded in the preceding chapter, and with which the serjeant had acquainted her, while Mrs James was paying her visit to Amelia. And as the serjeant had painted the matter rather in stronger colours than the colonel; so Mrs Atkinson again a little improved on the serjeant. Neither of these good people, perhaps, intended to aggravate any circumstance; but such is, I believe, the unavoidable consequence of all reports. Mrs Atkinson, indeed, may be supposed not to see what related to James in the most favourable light, as the serjeant, with more honesty than prudence, had suggested to his wife, that the colonel had not the kindest opinion of her, and had called her a sly and demure —; it is true he omitted ill-looking b—; two words, which are, perhaps, superior to the patience of any Job in petticoats that ever lived. He made amends, however, by substituting some other phrases in their stead, not extremely agreeable to a female ear.

It appeared to Amelia, from Mrs Atkinson's relation, that the colonel had grossly abused Booth to the serjeant, and had absolutely refused to become his bail. Poor Amelia became a pale and motionless statue at this account. At length, she cry'd, 'If this be true, I and mine are all, indeed, undone. We have no comfort, no hope, no friend left. – I cannot disbelieve you. – I know you would not deceive me. – Why should you, indeed, deceive me? – But what can have caused this alteration since last night? – Did I say or do any thing to offend him?'

'You said and did rather, I believe, a great deal too much to please him,' answered Mrs Atkinson. 'Besides, he is not in the least offended with you. On the contrary, he said many kind things.' –

'What can my poor love have done?' said Amelia. 'He hath not seen the colonel since last night. Some villain hath set him against my husband; he was once before suspicious of such a person. Some cruel monster hath belied his innocence.'

'Pardon me, dear madam,' said Mrs Atkinson, 'I believe the person, who hath injured the captain with this friend of his, is one of the worthiest and best of creatures – nay, do not be surprised; the person I mean, is even your fair self: sure you would not be so dull in any other case; but in this, gratitude, humility, modesty, every virtue shuts your eyes.

Mortales hebetant visus,

as Virgil says.[36] What in the world can be more consistent, than his desire to have you at his own house; and to keep your husband confined in another? All that he said, and all that he did yesterday; and, what is more convincing to me than both, all that he looked last night, are very consistent with both these designs.'

'O Heavens!' cries Amelia, 'you chill my blood with horror! The idea freezes me to death: I can not, must not, will not think it. Nothing but conviction – Heaven forbid, I should ever have more conviction! And did he abuse my husband! What! did he abuse a poor, unhappy, distrest creature; opprest, ruined, torn from his children, torn away from his wretched wife; the honestest, worthiest, noblest, tenderest, fondest, best!' – Here she burst into an agony of grief, which exceeds the power of description.

In this situation, Mrs Atkinson was doing her utmost to support her, when a most violent knocking was heard at the door, and immediately the serjeant ran hastily into the room; bringing with him a cordial, which presently relieved Amelia. What this cordial was, we shall inform the reader in due time. In the mean while, he must suspend his curiosity; and the gentlemen at White's[37] may lay wagers, whether it was Ward's pill, or Dr James's powder.[38]

But before we close this chapter, and return back to the bailiff's house, we must do our best to rescue the character of our heroine from the dulness of apprehension, which several of our quick-sighted readers may lay more heavily to her charge than was done by her friend Mrs Atkinson.

I must inform, therefore, all such readers, that it is not, because innocence is more blind than guilt, that the former often overlooks and tumbles into the pit, which the latter foresees and avoids. The truth is, that it is almost impossible guilt should miss the discovering of all the snares in its way; as it is constantly prying closely into every corner, in order to lay snares for others. Whereas innocence, having no such purpose, walks fearlessly and carelessly through life; and is consequently liable to tread on the gins, which cunning hath laid to entrap it. To speak plainly, and without allegory or figure, it is not want of sense, but want of suspicion by which innocence is often betrayed. Again, we often admire at the folly of the dupe, when we should transfer our whole surprize to the astonishing guilt of the betrayer. In a word, many an innocent person hath owed his ruin to this circumstance alone, that the degree of villany was such as must have exceeded the faith of every man who was not himself a villain.

CHAPTER 10

In which are many profound secrets of philosophy.

BOOTH, having had enough of the author's company the preceding day, chose now another companion. Indeed the author was not very solicitous of a second interview: for, as he could have no hope from Booth's pocket, so he was not likely to receive much increase to his vanity from Booth's conversation: for, low as this wretch was in virtue, sense, learning, birth and fortune, he was by no means low in his vanity. This passion, indeed, was so high in him, and at the same time so blinded him to his own demerits, that he hated every man, who did not either flatter him or give him money. In short, he claimed a strange kind of right; either to cheat all his acquaintance of their praise, or to pick their pockets of their pence; in which latter case, he himself repaid very liberally with panegyric.

A very little specimen of such a fellow must have satisfied a man of Mr Booth's temper. He chose, therefore, now to associate himself with that gentleman, of whom Bondum had given so shabby a character. In short, Mr Booth's opinion of the bailiff was such, that he recommended a man most, where he least intended it. Nay, the bailiff, in the present instance, tho' he had drawn a malicious conclusion, honestly avowed, that this was drawn only from the poverty of the person; which is never, I believe, any forcible disrecommendation to a good mind: but he must have had a very bad mind, indeed, who, in Mr Booth's circumstances, could have disliked or dispised another man, because that other man was poor.

Some previous conversation having past between this gentleman and Booth, in which they had both opened their several situations to each other; the former casting an affectionate look on the latter, exprest great compassion for his circumstances; for which Booth thanking him said, 'You must have a great deal of compassion, and be a very good man, in such a terrible situation as you describe yourself, to have any pity to spare for other people.'

'My affairs, sir,' answered the gentleman, 'are very bad, it is true; and yet there is one circumstance, which makes you appear to me more the object of pity than I am to myself; and it is this, that you must from your years be a novice in affliction; whereas I have served a long apprenticeship to misery, and ought by this time, to be a pretty good master of my trade. To say the truth, I believe, habit teaches men to bear the burthens of the mind, as it enures them to bear heavy burthens on their shoulders. Without use and experience, the strongest minds and bodies both will stagger under a weight, which habit might render easy, and even contemptible.'

'There is great justice,' cries Booth, 'in the comparison; and, I think, I have myself experienced the truth of it: for I am not that tyro in affliction which you seem to apprehend me. And, perhaps, it is from the very habit you mention, that I am able to support my present misfortunes a little like a man.'

The gentleman smiled at this, and cried, 'Indeed, captain, you are a young philosopher.'

'I think,' cries Booth, 'I have some pretensions to that philosophy which is taught by misfortunes; and you seem to be of opinion, sir, that is one of the best schools of philosophy.'

'I mean no more, sir,' said the gentleman, 'than that in the days of our affliction, we are inclined to think more seriously, than in those seasons of life, when we are engaged in the hurrying pursuits of business or pleasure, when we have neither leisure nor inclination to sift and examine things to the bottom. Now there are two considerations, which, from my having long fixed my thoughts upon them, have greatly supported me under all my afflictions. The one is the brevity of life, even at its longest duration, which the wisest of men hath compared to the short dimension of a span.[39] One of the Roman poets compares it to the duration of a race;[40] and another, to the much shorter transition of a wave.[41]

'The second consideration is the uncertainty of it. Short as its utmost limits are, it is far from being assured of reaching those limits. The next day, the next hour, the next moment may be the end of our course. Now of what value is so uncertain, so precarious a station? This consideration, indeed, however lightly it is passed over in our conception, doth, in a great measure, level all fortunes and conditions; and gives no man a right to triumph in the happiest state, or any reason to repine in the most miserable. Would the most worldly men see this, in the light in which they examine all other matters, they would soon feel and acknowledge the force of this way of reasoning: for which of them would give any price for an estate, from which they were liable to be immediately ejected; or, would they not laugh at him as a madman, who accounted himself rich from such an uncertain possession! This is the fountain, sir, from which I have drawn my philosophy. Hence it is, that I have learnt to look on all those things, which are esteemed the blessings of life, and those which are dreaded as its evils, with such a degree of indifference, that as I should not be elated with possessing the former, so neither am I greatly dejected and depressed by suffering the latter. Is the actor esteemed happier, to whose lot it falls to play the principal part, than he who plays the lowest? And yet the drama may run twenty nights together, and by consequence may out-last our lives; but, at the best, life is only a little longer drama; and the business of the great stage is consequently a little more serious than that which is performed at the Theatre Royal. But even here, the catastrophes and calamities which are represented, are capable of affecting us. The wisest men can deceive themselves into feeling the distresses of a tragedy, tho' they know them to be merely imaginary; and children will often lament them as realities: what wonder then, if these tragical scenes, which I allow to be a little more serious, should a little more affect us? Where then is the remedy, but in the philosophy I have mentioned; which, when once by a long course of meditation it is reduced to a habit, teaches us to set a just value on every thing; and cures at once all eager wishes and abject fears, all violent joy and grief concerning objects which cannot endure long, and may not exist a moment.'

'You have exprest yourself extremely well,' cries Booth,' and I entirely agree with the justice of your sentiments; but, however true all this may be in theory, I still doubt its efficacy in practice. And the cause of the difference between these two is this; that we reason from our heads, but act from our hearts:

– Video meliora, proboque;
Deteriora sequor.[42]

Nothing can differ more widely than wisemen and fools, in their estimation of things; but as both act from their uppermost passion, they both often act alike. What comfort then can your philosophy give to an avaricious man, who is deprived of his riches; or, to an ambitious man, who is stript of his power? To the fond lover, who is torn from his mistress; or, to the tender husband, who is dragged from his wife? Do you really think, that any meditations on the shortness of life will soothe them in their afflictions? Is not this very shortness itself one of their afflictions?[43] And if the evil they suffer be a temporary deprivation of what they love, will they not think their fate the harder, and lament the more, that they are to lose any part of an enjoyment, to which there is so short and so uncertain a period?'

'I beg leave, sir,' said the gentleman, 'to distinguish here. By philosophy, I do not mean the bare knowledge of right and wrong; but an energy, a habit, as Aristotle calls it;[44] and this I do firmly believe, with him and with the stoics, is superior to all the attacks of fortune.'

He was proceeding, when the bailiff came in, and in a surly tone bad them both good-morrow; after which he asked the philosopher, if he was prepared to go to Newgate; for that he must carry him thither that afternoon.

The poor man seemed very much shocked with this news. 'I hope,' cries he, 'you will give me a little longer time, if not till the return of the writ. But I beg you particularly, not to carry me thither to-day: for I expect my wife and children here in the evening.'

'I have nothing to do with wives and children,' cried the bailiff; 'I never desire to see any wives and children here. I like no such company.'

'I entreat you,' said the prisoner, 'give me another day. I shall take it as a great obligation; and you will disappoint me in the cruellest manner in the world, if you refuse me.'

'I can't help people's disappointments,' cries the bailiff, 'I must consider myself and my own family. I know not where I shall be paid the money that's due already. I can't afford to keep prisoners at my own expence.'

'I don't intend it shall be at your expence,' cries the philosopher; 'my wife is gone to raise money this morning, and I hope to pay you all I owe you at her arrival. But we intend to sup together to-night at your house; and if you should remove me now, it would be the most barbarous disappointment to us both, and will make me the most miserable man alive.'

'Nay, for my part,' said the bailiff, 'I don't desire to do any thing barbarous. I know how to treat gentlemen with civility as well as another. And when people pay as they go, and spend their money like gentlemen, I am sure no body can accuse me of any incivility since I have been in the office. And if you intend to be merry to-night, I am not the man that will prevent it – Tho' I say it, you may have as good a supper drest here as at any tavern in town.'

'Since Mr Bondum is so kind, captain,' said the philosopher, 'I hope for the favour of your company. I assure you, if it ever be my fortune to go abroad into the world, I shall be proud of the honour of your acquaintance.'

'Indeed, sir,' cries Booth, 'it is an honour I shall be very ready to accept; but as for this evening, I cannot help saying, I hope to be engaged in another place.'

'I promise you, sir,' answered the other, 'I shall rejoice at your liberty, tho' I am a loser by it.'

'Why, as to that matter,' cries Bondum with a sneer, 'I fancy, captain, you may engage yourself to the gentleman without any fear of breaking your word: for I am very much mistaken if we part to-day.'

'Pardon me, my good friend,' said Booth, 'but I expect my bail every minute.'

'Lookee, sir,' cries Bondum, 'I don't love to see gentlemen in an error. I shall not take the serjeant's bail; and as for the colonel, I have been with him myself this morning; (for to be sure I love to do all I can for gentlemen) and he told me, he could not possibly be here to-day: besides, why should I mince the matter? there is more stuff in the office.'

'What do you mean by stuff?' cries Booth.

'I mean that there is another writ,' answered the bailiff, 'at the suit of Mrs Ellison, the gentlewoman that was here yesterday; and the attorney that was with her, is concerned against you. Some officers would not tell you all this; but I loves to shew civility to gentlemen, while they behave themselves as such. And I loves the gentlemen of the army in particular. I had like to have been in the army myself once; but I liked the commission I have better. Come, captain, let not your noble courage be cast down; what say you to a glass of white wine, or a tiff of punch, by way of whet?'

'I have told you, sir, I never drink in a morning,' cries Booth a little peevishly.

'No offence, I hope, sir,' said the bailiff. 'I hope I have not treated you with any incivility. I don't ask any gentleman to call for liquor in my house, if he doth not chuse it; nor I don't desire any body to stay here longer than they have a mind to. – Newgate, to be sure is the place for all debtors that can't find bail. I knows what civility is, and I scorn to behave myself unbecoming a gentleman; but I'd have you consider that the twenty-four hours appointed by Act of Parliament are almost out; and so it is time to think of removing. As to bail, I would not have you flatter yourself: for I knows very well there are other things coming against you. Besides, the sum you are already charged with is very large, and I must see you in a place of safety. My house is no prison, tho' I lock up for a little time in it. Indeed, when gentlemen are gentlemen, and likely to find bail, I don't stand for a day or two; but I have a good nose at a bit of carrion, captain; I have not carried so much carrion to Newgate, without knowing the smell of it.'

'I understand not your cant,' cries Booth; 'but I did not think to have offended you so much by refusing to drink in a morning.'

'Offended me, sir,' cries the bailiff. 'Who told you so? Do you think, sir, if I want a glass of wine I am under any necessity of asking my prisoners for it? Damn it, sir, I'll shew you, I scorn your words. I can afford to treat you with a glass of the best wine in England, if you comes to that.' – He then pulled out a handful of guineas, saying, 'There, sir, they are all my own; I owe no body a shilling. I am no beggar, nor no debtor. I am the king's officer, as well as you, and I will spend guinea for guinea as long as you please.'

'Harkee, rascal,' cries Booth, laying hold of the bailiff's collar,

'How dare you treat me with this insolence? Doth the law give you any authority to insult me in my misfortunes?' At which words he gave the bailiff a good shove, and threw him from him.

'Very well, sir,' cries the bailiff, 'I will swear both an assault and an attempt to a rescue. If officers are to be used in this manner, there is an end of all law and justice. But tho' I am not a match for you myself, I have those below that are.' He then ran to the door, and called up two ill-looking fellows, his followers, whom, as soon as they entered the room, he ordered to seize on Booth, declaring he would immediately carry him to Newgate; at the same time pouring out a vast quantity of abuse, below the dignity of history to record.

Booth desired the two dirty fellows to stand off, and declared he would make no resistance, at the same time bidding the bailiff carry him wherever he durst.

'I'll shew you what I dare,' cries the bailiff, and again ordered the followers to lay hold of their prisoner, saying, 'He hath assaulted me already, and endeavoured a rescue. I shan't trust such a fellow to walk at liberty. A gentleman, indeed! Ay, ay, Newgate is the properest place for such gentry; as arrant carrion as ever was carried thither.'

The fellows then both laid violent hands on Booth, and the bailiff stept to the door to order a coach; when on a sudden, the whole scene was changed in an instant: for now the serjeant came running, out of breath, into the room; and seeing his friend, the captain, roughly handled by two ill-looking fellows, without asking any questions, stept briskly up to his assistance, and instantly gave one of the assailants so violent a salute with his fist, that he directly measured his length on the floor.

Booth having by this means his right arm at liberty was unwilling to be idle, or entirely to owe his rescue from both the ruffians to the serjeant; he therefore imitated the example which his friend had set him, and with a lusty blow levelled the other follower with his companion on the ground.

The bailiff roared out, 'A rescue, a rescue'; to which the serjeant answered, there was no rescue intended. 'The captain,' said he, 'wants no rescue. Here are some friends coming who will deliver him in a better manner.'

The bailiff swore heartily he would carry him to Newgate, in spite of all the friends in the world.

'You carry him to Newgate!' cried the serjeant, with the highest indignation. 'Offer but to lay your hands on him, and I will knock your teeth down your ugly jaws.' – Then turning to Booth, he cried, – 'They will be all here within a minute, sir, we had much ado to keep my lady from coming herself; but she is at home in good health, longing to see your honour; and I hope you will be with her within this half hour.'

And now three gentlemen entered the room; these were an attorney, the person whom the serjeant had procured in the morning to be his bail with Colonel James, and lastly, Doctor Harrison himself.

The bailiff no sooner saw the attorney, with whom he was well acquainted (for the others he knew not) than he began, as the phrase is, to pull in his horns, and ordered the two followers, who were now got again on their legs, to walk down stairs.

'So, captain,' says the doctor, 'when last we parted, I believe we neither of us expected to meet in such a place as this.'

'Indeed, doctor,' cries Booth, 'I did not expect to have been sent hither by the gentleman who did me that favour.'

'How so, sir?' said the doctor, 'you was sent hither by some person, I suppose, to whom you was indebted. This is the usual place, I apprehend, for creditors to send their debtors to. But you ought to be more surprised that the gentleman who sent you hither is come to release you. – Mr Murphy, you will perform all the necessary ceremonials.'

The attorney then asked the bailiff with how many actions Booth was charged, and was informed there were five besides the doctor's, which was much the heaviest of all. Proper bonds were presently provided, and the doctor and the serjeant's friend signed them; the bailiff, at the instance of the attorney, making no objection to the bail.

Booth, we may be assured, made a handsome speech to the doctor for such extraordinary friendship, with which, however, we do not think proper to trouble the reader; and now every thing being ended, and the company ready to depart, the bailiff stepped up to Booth, and told him he hoped he would remember civility money.

'I believe,' cries Booth, 'you mean incivility money; if there are any fees due for rudeness, I must own you have a very just claim.'

'I am sure, sir,' cries the bailiff, 'I have treated your honour with all the respect in the world: no man, I am sure, can charge me with using a gentleman rudely. I knows what belongs to a gentleman better; but you can't deny that two of my men have been knocked down; and I doubt not but as you are a gentleman, you will give them something to drink.'

Booth was about to answer with some passion, when the attorney interfered, and whispered in his ear, that it was usual to make a compliment to the officer, and that he had better comply with the custom.

'If the fellow had treated me civilly,' answered Booth, 'I should have had no objection to comply with a bad custom in his favour; but I am resolved, I will never reward a man for using me ill, and I will not agree to give him a single farthing.'

''Tis very well, sir,' said the bailiff, 'I am rightly served for my good-nature; but if it had been to do again, I would have taken care you should not have been bailed this day.'

Doctor Harrison, to whom Booth referred the cause, after giving him a succinct account of what had past, declared the captain to be in the right. He said it was a most horrid imposition, that such fellows were ever suffered to prey on the necessitous; but that the example would be much worse to reward them where they had behaved themselves ill. 'And I think,' says he, 'the bailiff is worthy of great rebuke for what he hath just now said; in which I hope he hath boasted of more power than is in him. We do, indeed, with great justice and propriety, value ourselves on our freedom, if the liberty of the subject depends on the pleasure of such fellows as these.'

'It is not so neither altogether,' cries the lawyer: 'but custom hath established a present or fee to them at the delivery of a prisoner, which they call civility money, and expect as in a manner their due, tho' in reality they have no right.'

'But will any man,' cries Doctor Harrison, 'after what the captain hath told us, say that the bailiff hath behaved himself as he ought; and if he had, is he to be rewarded for not acting in an unchristian and inhuman manner? It is pity, that instead of a custom of feeing them out of the pockets of the poor and wretched, when they do not behave themselves ill, there was not both a law and a practice to punish them severely when they do. In the present case, I am so far from agreeing to give the bailiff a shilling, that if there be any method of punishing him for his rudeness, I shall be heartily glad to see it put in execution: for there are none whose conduct should be so strictly watched as that of these necessary evils in the society, as their office concerns for the most part those poor creatures who cannot do themselves justice, and as they are generally the worst of men who undertake it.'

The bailiff then quitted the room, muttering that he should know better what to do another time; and shortly after Booth and his friends left the house; but as they were going out, the author took Doctor Harrison aside, and slipt a receipt into his hand, which the doctor returned, saying he never subscribed when he neither knew the work nor the author; but that if he would call at his lodgings, he would be very willing to give all the encouragement to merit which was in his power.

The author took down the doctor's name and direction, and made him as many bows as he would have done had he carried off the half guinea, for which he had been fishing.

Mr Booth then took his leave of the philosopher, and departed with the rest of his friends.

BOOK IX

CHAPTER 1

In which the history looks backwards.

BEFORE we proceed farther with our history, it may be proper to look back a little, in order to account for the late conduct of Doctor Harrison; which, however inconsistent it may have hitherto appeared, when examined to the bottom, will be found, I apprehend, to be truly congruous with all the rules of the most perfect prudence, as well as with the most consummate goodness.

We have already partly seen in what light Booth had been represented to the doctor abroad. Indeed, the accounts which were sent of the captain, as well by the curate as by a gentleman of the neighbourhood, were much grosser and more to his disadvantage, than the doctor was pleased to set them forth in his letter to the person accused. What sense he had of Booth's conduct was, however, manifest by that letter. Nevertheless he resolved to suspend his final judgment till his return; and tho' he censured him, would not absolutely condemn him without ocular demonstration.

The doctor on his return to his parish found all the accusations which had been transmitted to him, confirmed by many witnesses, of which the curate's wife, who had been formerly a friend to Amelia, and still preserved the outward appearance of friendship, was the strongest. She introduced all with *I am sorry to say it*; and *it is friendship which bids me speak*; and *it is for their good it should be told you*; after which beginnings, she never concluded a single speech without some horrid slander and bitter invective.

Besides the malicious turn which was given to these affairs in the country, which were owing a good deal to misfortune, and some little perhaps to imprudence, the whole neighbourhood rung with several gross and scandalous lies, which were merely the inventions of his enemies, and of which the scene was laid in London since his absence.

Poisoned with all this malice, the doctor came to town, and learning where Booth lodged, went to make him a visit. Indeed, it was the doctor, and no other who had been at his lodgings that evening when Booth and Amelia were walking in the Park; and concerning which the reader may be pleased to remember so many strange and odd conjectures.

Here the doctor saw the little gold watch, and all those fine trinkets with which the noble lord had presented the children; and which from the answers given him by the poor ignorant innocent girl, he could have no doubt had been purchased within a few days by Amelia.

This account tallied so well with the ideas he had imbibed of Booth's extravagance in the country, that he firmly believed both the husband and wife to be the vainest, silliest, and most unjust people alive. It was, indeed, almost incredible, that two rational beings should be guilty of such absurdity; but monstrous and absurd as it was, ocular demonstration appeared to be the evidence against them.

The doctor departed from their lodgings enraged at this supposed discovery, and unhappily for Booth was engaged to supper that very evening with the country gentleman of whom Booth had rented a farm. As the poor captain happened to be the subject of conversation, and occasioned their comparing notes, the account which the doctor gave of what he had seen that evening, so incensed the gentleman to whom Booth was likewise a debtor, that he vowed he would take a writ out against him the next morning, and have his body alive or dead. And the doctor was at last persuaded to do the same. Mr Murphy was thereupon immediately sent for, and the doctor in his presence repeated again what he had seen at his lodgings, as the foundation of his suing him, which the attorney, as we have before seen, had blabbed to Atkinson.

But no sooner did the doctor hear that Booth was arrested, than the wretched condition of his wife and family began to affect his mind. The children, who were to be utterly undone with their father, were entirely innocent; and as for Amelia herself, though he thought he had most convincing proofs of very blameable levity; yet his former friendship and affection to her were busy to invent every excuse, till, by very heavily loading the husband, they lightened the suspicion against the wife.

In this temper of mind he resolved to pay Amelia a second visit, and was on his way to Mrs Ellison, when the serjeant met him, and made himself known to him. The doctor took his old servant into a coffee-house, where he received from him such an account of Booth and his family, that he desired the serjeant to shew him presently to Amelia; and this was the cordial which we mentioned at the end of the ninth chapter of the preceding book.

The doctor became soon satisfied concerning the trinkets which had given him so much uneasiness, and which had brought so much mischief on the head of poor Booth. Amelia likewise gave the doctor some satisfaction as to what he had heard of her husband's behaviour in the country; and assured him, upon her honour, that Booth could so well answer every complaint against his conduct, that she had no doubt but that a man of the doctor's justice and candour would entirely acquit him, and would consider him as an innocent unfortunate man, who was the object of a good man's compassion, not of his anger or resentment.

This worthy clergyman, who was not desirous of finding proofs to condemn the captain, or to justify his own vindictive proceedings, but, on the contrary, rejoiced heartily in every piece of evidence which tended to clear up the character of his friend, gave a ready ear to all which Amelia said. To this, indeed, he was induced by the love he always had for that lady, by the good opinion he entertained of her, as well as by pity for her present condition, than which nothing appeared more miserable; for he found her in the highest agonies of grief and despair, with her two little children crying over their wretched mother. These are, indeed, to a well disposed mind, the most tragical sights that human nature can furnish, and afford a juster motive to grief and tears in the beholder, than it would be to see all the heroes who have ever infested the earth, hanged all together in a string.

The doctor felt this sight as he ought. He immediately endeavoured to comfort the afflicted; in which he so well succeeded, that he restored to Amelia sufficient spirits to give him the satisfaction we have mentioned: after which, he declared he would go and release her husband; which he accordingly did, in the manner we have above related.

CHAPTER 2

In which the history goes forward.

WE NOW return to that period of our history, to which we had brought it at the end of our last book.

Booth and his friends arrived, from the bailiff's, at the serjeant's lodgings; where Booth immediately ran up stairs to his Amelia; between whom I shall not attempt to describe the meeting. Nothing certainly was ever more tender or more joyful. This however I will observe, that a very few of these exquisite moments, of which the best minds only are capable, do, in reality, over-balance the longest enjoyments which can ever fall to the lot of the worst.

Whilst Booth and his wife were feasting their souls with the most delicious mutual endearments, the doctor was fallen to play with the two little children below stairs. While he was thus engaged, the little boy did somewhat amiss; upon which the doctor said, 'If you do so any more, I will take your papa away from you again.' – 'Again, sir,' said the child, 'why, was it you then that took away my papa before?' 'Suppose it was,' said the doctor, 'would not you forgive me?' 'Yes,' cries the child, 'I would forgive you; because a Christian must forgive every body; but I should hate you as long as I live.'

The doctor was so pleased with the boy's answer, that he caught him in his arms, and kiss'd him, at which time, Booth and his wife returned. The doctor asked which of them was their son's instructor in his religion: Booth answered, that he must confess Amelia had all the merit of that kind. 'I should have rather thought he had learnt of his father,' cries the doctor, 'for he seems a good soldier-like Christian, and professes to hate his enemies with a very good grace.'

'How, Billy,' cries Amelia. 'I am sure I did not teach you so.'

'I did not say I would hate my enemies, madam,' cries the boy. 'I only said I would hate papa's enemies; sure, mamma, there is no harm in that: nay, I am sure there is no harm in it; for I have heard you say the same thing a thousand times.'

The doctor smiled on the child, and chucking him under the chin told him, he must hate no body: and now Mrs Atkinson, who had provided a dinner for them all, desired them to walk up, and partake of it.

And now it was that Booth was first made acquainted with the serjeant's marriage; as was Dr Harrison, both of whom greatly felicitated him upon it.

Mrs Atkinson, who was, perhaps, a little more confounded than she would have been had she married a colonel, said, 'If I have done wrong, Mrs Booth is to answer for it; for she made the match: indeed, Mr Atkinson, you are greatly obliged to the character which this lady gives of you.' 'I hope he will deserve it,' said the doctor; 'and if the army hath not corrupted a good boy, I believe I may answer for him.'

While our little company were enjoying that happiness which never fails to attend conversation, where all present are pleased with each other, a visitant arrived, who was, perhaps, not very welcome to any of them. This was no other than Colonel James, who entering the room with much gaiety went directly up to Booth, embraced him, and expressed great satisfaction at finding him there; he then made an apology for not attending him in the morning, which he said had been impossible; and that he had with the utmost difficulty put off some business of great consequence, in order to serve him this afternoon; 'but I am glad on your account,' cried he to Booth, 'that my presence was not necessary.'

Booth himself was extremely satisfied with this declaration, and failed not to return him as many thanks as he would have deserved, had he performed his promise; but the two ladies were not quite so well satisfied. As for the serjeant, he had slipt out of the room when the colonel entered, not entirely out of that bashfulness which we have remarked him to be tainted with; but, indeed, from what had past in the morning he hated the sight of the colonel, as well on the account of his wife as on that of his friend.

The doctor, on the contrary, on what he had formerly heard

from both Amelia and her husband of the colonel's generosity and friendship, had built so good an opinion of him, that he was very much pleased with seeing him, and took the first opportunity of telling him so. 'Colonel,' said the doctor, 'I have not the happiness of being known to you; but I have long been desirous of an acquaintance with a gentleman, in whose commendation I have heard so much from some present.' The colonel made a proper answer to this compliment, and they soon entered into a familiar conversation together: for the doctor was not difficult of access; indeed, he held the strange reserve, which is usually practised in this nation between people who are in any degree strangers to each other, to be very unbecoming the Christian character.

The two ladies soon left the room; and the remainder of the visit, which was not very long, past in discourse on various common subjects, not worth recording. In the conclusion, the colonel invited Booth and his lady, and the doctor, to dine with him the next day.

To give Colonel James his due commendation, he had shewn a great command of himself, and great presence of mind on this occasion: for to speak the plain truth, the visit was intended to Amelia alone; nor did he expect, or, perhaps, desire, any thing less than to find the captain at home. The great joy which he suddenly conveyed into his countenance at the unexpected sight of his friend, is to be attributed to that noble art which is taught in those excellent schools called the several courts of Europe. By this men are enabled to dress out their countenances as much at their own pleasure, as they do their bodies; and to put on friendship with as much ease as they can a laced coat.

When the colonel and doctor were gone, Booth acquainted Amelia with the invitation he had received. She was so struck with the news, and betrayed such visible marks of confusion and uneasiness, that they could not have escaped Booth's observation, had suspicion given him the least hint to remark: but this, indeed, is the great optic glass helping us to discern plainly almost all that passes in the minds of others, without some use of which nothing is more purblind than human nature.

Amelia having recovered from her first perturbation, answered, 'My dear, I will dine with you wherever you please to lay your commands on me.' – 'I am obliged to you, my dear soul,' cries Booth, 'your obedience shall be very easy; for my command will be, that you shall always follow your own inclinations.' 'My inclinations,' answered she, 'would, I am afraid, be too unreasonable a confinement to you; for they would always lead me to be with you and your children, with at most a single friend or two, now and then.' 'O my dear,' replied he, 'large companies give us a greater relish for our own society when we return to it; and we shall be extremely merry, for Dr Harrison dines with us.' 'I hope you will, my dear,' cries she; 'but I own I should have been better pleased to have enjoyed a few days with yourself and the children, with no other person but Mrs Atkinson, for whom I have conceived a violent affection, and who would have given us but little interruption. However, if you have promised, I must undergo the penance.' 'Nay, child,' cry'd he, 'I am sure I would have refused, could I have guessed it had been in the least disagreeable to you; tho' I know your objection.' – 'Objection!' cries Amelia eagerly, 'I have no objection.' 'Nay, nay,' said he, 'come be honest, I know your objection, tho' you are unwilling to own it.' 'Good Heavens!' cry'd Amelia, frighten'd, 'what do you mean? what objection?' 'Why,' answered he, 'to the company of Mrs James, and I must confess she hath not behaved to you lately as you might have expected; but you ought to pass all that by for the sake of her husband, to whom we have both so many obligations; who is the worthiest, honestest, and most generous fellow in the universe, and the best friend to me that ever man had.'

Amelia, who had far other suspicions, and began to fear that her husband had discovered them, was highly pleased when she saw him taking a wrong scent. She gave, therefore, a little into the deceit, and acknowledged the truth of what he had mentioned; but said, that the pleasure she should have in complying with his desires, would highly recompense any dissatisfaction, which might arise on any other account; and shortly after ended the conversation on this subject, with her chearfully promising to fulfil his promise.

In reality, poor Amelia had now a most unpleasant task to undertake; for she thought it absolutely necessary to conceal from her husband the opinion she had conceived of the colonel. For as she knew the characters, as well of her husband as of his friend, or rather enemy, (both being often synonymous in the language of the world) she had the utmost reason to apprehend something very fatal might attend her husband's entertaining the same thought of James, which filled and tormented her own breast.

And as she knew that nothing but these thoughts could justify the least unkind, or indeed, the least reserved behaviour to James; who had, in all appearance, conferred the greatest obligations upon Booth and herself, she was reduced to a dilemma, the most dreadful that can attend a virtuous woman, as it often gives the highest triumph, and sometimes no little advantage to the men of professed gallantry.

In short, to avoid giving any umbrage to her husband, Amelia was forced to act in a manner, which she was conscious must give encouragement to the colonel: a situation which, perhaps, requires as great prudence and delicacy, as any in which the heroic part of the female character can be exerted.

CHAPTER 3

A conversation between Dr Harrison and others.

THE next day, Booth and his lady, with the doctor, met at Colonel James's, where Colonel Bath likewise made one of the company.

Nothing very remarkable past at dinner, or till the ladies withdrew. During this time, however, the behaviour of Colonel James was such as gave some uneasiness to Amelia, who well understood his meaning, tho' the particulars were too refined and subtle to be observed by any other present.

When the ladies were gone, which was as soon as Amelia could prevail on Mrs James to depart, Colonel Bath, who had been pretty brisk with champagne at dinner, soon began to display his magnanimity. 'My brother tells me, young gentleman,' said he to Booth, 'that you have been used very ill lately by some rascals; and I have no doubt but you will do yourself justice.'

Booth answered, that he did not know what he meant. 'Since I must mention it then,' cries the colonel, 'I hear you have been arrested; and I think you know what satisfaction is to be required by a man of honour.'

'I beg, sir,' says the doctor, 'no more may be mentioned of that matter. I am convinced, no satisfaction will be required of the captain, till he is able to give it.'

'I do not understand what you mean by able,' cries the colonel – To which the doctor answered, that it was of too tender a nature to speak more of.

'Give me your hand, doctor,' cries the colonel, 'I see you are a man of honour, tho' you wear a gown. It is, as you say, a matter of a tender nature. Nothing, indeed, is so tender as a man's honour. Curse my liver, if any man; I mean, that is, if any gentleman, was to arrest me – I would as surely cut his throat as –'

'How, sir!' said the doctor, 'would you compensate one breach of the law by a much greater, and pay your debts by committing murder?'

'Why do you mention law between gentlemen?' says the colonel. 'A man of honour wears his law by his side. And can the resentment of an affront make a gentleman guilty of murder? and what greater affront can one man cast upon another, than by arresting him? I am convinced, that he who would put up an arrest, would put up a slap in the face.'

Here the colonel looked extremely fierce, and the divine stared with astonishment at this doctrine; when Booth, who well knew the impossibility of opposing the colonel's humour with success, began to play with it; and having first conveyed a private wink to the doctor, he said, there might be cases undoubtedly where such an affront ought to be resented; but that there were others, where any resentment was impracticable: 'As for instance,' said he, 'where the man is arrested by a woman.'

'I could not be supposed to mean that case,' cries the colonel, 'and you are convinced I did not mean it.'

'To put an end to this discourse at once, sir,' said the doctor, 'I was the plaintiff, at whose suit this gentleman was arrested.'

'Was you so, sir!' cries the colonel, 'then I have no more to say. Women and the clergy are upon the same footing. The long-robed gentry are exempted from the laws of honour.'

'I do not thank you for that exemption, sir,' cries the doctor;

'and if honour and fighting are, as they seem to be, synonymous words[1] with you, I believe there are some clergymen, who, in defence of their religion, or their country, or their friend, the only justifiable causes of fighting, except bare self-defence, would fight as bravely as yourself, colonel; and that without being paid for it.'

'Sir, you are privileged,' says the colonel with great dignity, 'and you have my leave to say what you please. I respect your order, and you cannot offend me.'

'I will not offend you, colonel,' cries the doctor, 'and our order is very much obliged to you; since you profess so much respect to us, and pay none to our Master.'

'What master, sir?' said the colonel.

'That Master,' answered the doctor, 'who hath expressly forbidden all that cutting of throats, to which you discover so much inclination.'

'O, your servant, sir,' said the colonel, 'I see what you are driving at; but you shall not persuade me to think, that religion forces me to be a coward.'

'I detest and despise the name as much as you can,' cries the doctor; 'but you have a wrong idea of the word, colonel. What were all the Greeks and Romans? Were these cowards; and yet did you ever hear of this butchery, which we call duelling, among them?'

'Yes, indeed, have I,' cries the colonel. 'What else is all Mr Pope's Homer full of, but duels? Did not, what's his name, one of the Agamemnons fight with that paultry rascal Paris? and Diomede with, what d'ye call him there; and Hector with, I forget his name, he that was Achilles's bosom-friend; and afterwards with Achilles himself? Nay, and in Dryden's Virgil,[2] is there any thing almost besides fighting?'

'You are a man of learning, colonel,' cries the doctor, 'but –'

'I thank you for that compliment,' said the colonel – 'No, sir, I do not pretend to learning; but I have some little reading, and I am not ashamed to own it.'

'But are you sure, colonel,' cries the doctor, 'that you have not made a small mistake? For I am apt to believe, both Mr Pope and Mr Dryden (tho' I cannot say I ever read a word of either of them) speak of wars between nations, and not of private duels: for of the latter, I do not remember one single instance in all the Greek or Roman story. In short, it is a modern custom, introduced by barbarous nations since the times of Christianity; tho' it is a direct and audacious defiance of the Christian law, and is consequently much more sinful in us, than it would have been in the heathens.'

'Drink about, doctor,' cries the colonel, 'and let us call a new cause: for I perceive we shall never agree on this. You are a churchman, and I don't expect you to speak your mind.'

'We are both of the same Church, I hope,' cries the doctor.

'I am of the Church of England, sir,' answered the colonel, 'and will fight for it to the last drop of my blood.'

'It is very generous in you, colonel,' cries the doctor, 'to fight so zealously for a religion by which you are to be damned.'

'It is well for you, doctor,' cries the colonel, 'that you wear a gown: for by all the dignity of a man, if any other person had said the words you have just uttered, I would have made him eat them – ay, d—n me, and my sword into the bargain.'

Booth began to be apprehensive that this dispute might grow too warm; in which case he feared that the colonel's honour, together with the champagne, might hurry him so far as to forget the respect due, and which he professed to pay, to the sacerdotal robe. Booth, therefore, interposed between the disputants, and said, the colonel had very rightly proposed to call a new subject: for that it was impossible to reconcile accepting a challenge with the Christian religion, or refusing it with the modern notion of honour. 'And you must allow it, doctor,' said he, 'to be a very hard injunction for a man to become infamous; and more especially for a soldier, who is to lose his bread into the bargain.'

'Ay, sir,' says the colonel with an air of triumph, 'what say you to that?'

'Why, I say,' cries the doctor, 'that it is much harder to be damned on the other side.'

'That may be,' said the colonel, 'but damn me, if I would take an affront of any man breathing for all that. And yet I believe myself to be as good a Christian as wears a head. My maxim is, never to give an affront, nor ever to take one; and I say that is the maxim of a good Christian; and no man shall ever persuade me to the contrary.'

'Well, sir,' said the doctor, 'since that is your resolution, I hope no man will ever give you an affront.'

'I am obliged to you for your hope, doctor,' cries the colonel with a sneer; 'and he that doth, will be obliged to you for lending him your gown: for by the dignity of a man, nothing out of petticoats I believe dares affront me.'

Colonel James had not hitherto joined in the discourse. In truth, his thoughts had been otherwise employed; nor is it very difficult for the reader to guess what had been the subject of them. Being waked, however, from his reverie, and having heard the two or three last speeches, he turned to his brother, and asked him, why he would introduce such a topic of conversation before a gentleman of Dr Harrison's character?

'Brother,' cried Bath, 'I own it was wrong, and I ask the doctor's pardon; I know not how it happened to arise: for you know, brother, I am not used to talk of these matters. They are generally poltroons that do. I think I need not be beholden to my tongue to declare I am none. I have shewn myself in a line of battle. I believe there is no man will deny that; I believe I may say, no man dares deny, that I have done my duty.' –

The colonel was thus proceeding to prove that his prowess was neither the subject of his discourse, nor the object of his vanity, when a servant entered, and summoned the company to tea with the ladies; a summons which Colonel James instantly obeyed, and was followed by all the rest.

But as the tea-table conversation, tho' extremely delightful to those who are engaged in it, may probably appear somewhat dull to the reader, we will here put an end to the chapter.

CHAPTER 4

A dialogue between Booth and Amelia.

THE next morning early, Booth went by appointment and waited on Colonel James; whence he returned to Amelia, in that kind of disposition which the great master of human passions[3] would describe in Andromache, when he tells us she cried and smiled at the same instant.

Amelia plainly perceived the discomposure of his mind, in which the opposite affections of joy and grief were struggling for the superiority, and begged to know the occasion; upon which Booth spoke as follows:

'My dear,' said he, 'I had no intention to conceal from you what hath past this morning between me and the colonel, who hath oppressed me, if I may use that expression, with obligations. Sure never man had such a friend; for never was there so noble, so generous a heart – I cannot help this ebullition of gratitude, I really cannot.' – Here he paused a moment and wiped his eyes, and then proceeded; 'You know, my dear, how gloomy the prospect was yesterday before our eyes, how inevitable ruin stared me in the face; and the dreadful idea of having entailed beggary on my Amelia and her posterity racked my mind: for, tho' by the goodness of the doctor I had regained my liberty, the debt yet remained; and if that worthy man had a design of forgiving me his share, this must have been my utmost hope; and the condition in which I must still have found myself need not to be expatiated on. In what light then shall I see, in what words shall I relate the colonel's kindness! O, my dear Amelia, he hath removed the whole gloom at once, hath driven all despair out of my mind, and hath filled it with the most sanguine, and at the same time, the most reasonable hopes of making a comfortable provision for yourself and my dear children. In the first place then, he will advance me a sum of money to pay off all my debts; and this on a bond to be repaid only when I shall become colonel of a regiment, and not before. In the next place, he is gone this very morning to ask a company for me, which is now vacant in the West Indies; and as he intends to push this with all his interest, neither he nor I have any doubt of his success. Now, my dear, comes the third, which, tho' perhaps it ought to give me the greatest joy, such is, I own, the weakness of my nature, it rends my very heart-strings asunder. – I cannot mention it: for I know it will give you equal pain – tho' I know on all proper occasions you can exert a manly resolution. – You will not, I am convinced, oppose it, whatever you must suffer in complying – O, my dear Amelia, I must suffer likewise; yet I have resolved to bear it – You know not what my poor heart hath suffered since he made the proposal – It is love for you alone which could persuade me to submit to it – Consider our situation, consider that of our children; reflect but on those poor babes, whose future happiness is at stake, and it must arm your resolution. It is your interest and theirs that reconciled me to a proposal, which, when the colonel first made it, struck me with the utmost horror: he hath, indeed, from these motives persuaded me into a resolution, which I thought impossible for any one to have persuaded me into – O, my dear Amelia, let me entreat you to give me up to the good of your children; as I have promised the colonel to give you up to their interest and your own. If you refuse these terms, we are still undone; for he insists absolutely upon them – Think then, my love, however hard they may be, necessity compels us to submit to them. I know in what light a woman who loves like you, must consider such a proposal; and yet how many instances have you of women, who, from the same motives, have submitted to the same!'

'What can you mean, Mr Booth?' cries Amelia trembling.

'Need I explain my meaning to you more?' answered Booth. – 'Did I not say, I must give up my Amelia?'

'Give me up!' said she.

'For a time only, I mean,' answered he; 'for a short time perhaps. The colonel himself will take care it shall not be long – for I know his heart; I shall scarce have more joy in receiving you back, than he will have in restoring you to my arms. In the mean time, he will not only be a father to my children, but a husband to you.'

'A husband to me!' said Amelia.

'Yes, my dear; a kind, a fond, a tender, an affectionate husband.

If I had not the most certain assurances of this, doth my Amelia think I could be prevailed on to leave her? – No, my Amelia, he is the only man on earth, who could have prevailed on me –; but I know his house, his purse, his protection will be all at your command – And as for any dislike you have conceived to his wife, let not that be any objection: for I am convinced he will not suffer her to insult you; besides she is extremely well-bred, and how much soever she may hate you in her heart, she will at least treat you with civility.

'Nay, the invitation is not his but hers; and I am convinced they will both behave to you with the greatest friendship; his I am sure will be sincere, as to the wife of a friend entrusted to his care; and hers will, from good breeding, have not only the appearances, but the effects of the truest friendship.'

'I understand you, my dear, at last,' said she, (indeed she had rambled into very strange conceits from some parts of his discourse) 'and I will give you my resolution in a word – I will do the duty of a wife; and that is, to attend her husband wherever he goes.'

Booth attempted to reason with her, but all to no purpose. She gave, indeed, a quiet hearing to all he said, and even to those parts which most displeased her ears; I mean those in which he exaggerated the great goodness and disinterested generosity of his friend; but her resolution remained inflexible, and resisted the force of all his arguments with a steadiness of opposition, which it would have been almost excusable in him to have construed into stubbornness.

The doctor arrived in the midst of the dispute, and having heard the merits of the cause on both sides, delivered his opinion in the following words:

'I have always thought it, my dear children, a matter of the utmost nicety, to interfere in any differences between husband and wife; but since you both desire me with such earnestness, to give you my sentiments on the present contest between you, I will give you my thoughts as well as I am able. In the first place then, can any thing be more reasonable than for a wife to desire to attend her husband? It is, as my favourite child observes, no more than a desire to do her duty; and I make no doubt but that is one great reason of her insisting on it. And how can you yourself oppose it?

Can love be its own enemy; or can a husband who is fond of his wife, content himself almost on any account with a long absence from her?'

'You speak like an angel, my dear Doctor Harrison,' answered Amelia; 'I am sure if he loved as tenderly as I do, he could on no account submit to it.'

'Pardon me, child,' cries the doctor, 'there are some reasons which would not only justify his leaving you, but which must force him, if he hath any real love for you, joined with common sense, to make that election. If it was necessary, for instance, either to your good, or to the good of your children, he would not deserve the name of a man, I am sure not that of a husband, if he hesitated a moment. Nay, in that case I am convinced, you yourself would be an advocate for what you now oppose. I fancy therefore I mistook him, when I apprehended he said that the colonel made his leaving you behind as the condition of getting him the commission: for I know my dear child hath too much goodness, and too much sense, and too much resolution to prefer any temporary indulgence of her own passions to the solid advantages of her whole family.'

'There, my dear,' cries Booth, 'I knew what opinion the doctor would be of. Nay I am certain, there is not a wise man in the kingdom who would say otherwise.'

'Don't abuse me, young gentleman,' said the doctor, 'with appellations I don't deserve.'

'I abuse you, my dear doctor!' cries Booth.

'Yes, my dear sir,' answered the doctor; 'you insinuated slily that I was wise, which, as the world understands the phrase, I should be ashamed of; and my comfort is, that no one can accuse me justly of it; I have just given an instance of the contrary, by throwing away my advice.'

'I hope, sir,' cries Booth, 'that will not be the case.'

'Yes, sir,' answered the doctor. 'I know it will be the case in the present instance; for either you will not go at all, or my little turtle here will go with you.'

'You are in the right, doctor,' cries Amelia.

'I am sorry for it,' said the doctor; 'for then I assure you, you are in the wrong.'

'Indeed,' cries Amelia, 'if you knew all my reasons, you would say they were very strong ones.'

'Very probably,' cries the doctor – 'The knowledge that they are in the wrong, is a very strong reason to some women to continue so.'

'Nay, doctor,' cries Amelia, 'you shall never persuade me of that. I will not believe that any human being ever did an action merely because they knew it to be wrong.'

'I am obliged to you, my dear child,' said the doctor, 'for declaring your resolution of not being persuaded. Your husband would never call me a wise man again, if after that declaration I should attempt to persuade you.'

'Well, I must be content,' cries Amelia, 'to let you think as you please.'

'That is very gracious, indeed,' said the doctor. 'Surely in a country where the Church suffers others to think as they please, it would be very hard if they had not themselves the same liberty. And yet, as unreasonable as the power of controuling men's thoughts is represented, I will shew you how you shall controul mine whenever you desire it.'

'How, pray!' cries Amelia. 'I should greatly esteem that power.'

'Why, whenever you act like a wise woman,' cries the doctor, 'you will force me to think you so; and whenever you are pleased to act as you do now, I shall be obliged, whether I will or no, to think as I do now.'

'Nay, dear doctor,' cries Booth, 'I am convinced my Amelia will never do any thing to forfeit your good opinion. Consider but the cruel hardship of what she is to undergo; and you will make allowances for the difficulty she makes in complying. To say the truth, when I examine my own heart, I have more obligations to her than appear at first sight: for by obliging me to find arguments to persuade her, she hath assisted me in conquering myself. Indeed, if she had shewn more resolution, I should have shewn less.'

'So you think it necessary then,' said the doctor, 'that there should be one fool at least in every married couple. A mighty resolution truly, and well worth your valuing yourself upon, to part with your wife for a few months in order to make the fortune of her and your children. When you are to leave her too in the care and protection of a friend that gives credit to the old stories of friendship, and doth an honour to human nature. What, in the name of goodness, do either of you think that you have made a union to endure for ever? How will either of you bear that separation which must some time or other, and perhaps very soon, be the lot of one of you? Have you forgot that you are both mortal? – As for Christianity, I see you have resigned all pretensions to it: for I make no doubt, but that you have so set your hearts on the happiness you enjoy here together, that neither of you ever think a word of hereafter.'

Amelia now burst into tears, upon which Booth begged the doctor to proceed no further. Indeed, he would not have wanted the caution: for, however blunt he appeared in his discourse, he had a tenderness of heart which is rarely found among men; for which I know no other reason, than that true goodness is rarely found among them: for I am firmly persuaded that the latter never possessed any human mind in any degree, without being attended by as large a portion of the former.

Thus ended the conversation on this subject; what followed is not worth relating till the doctor carried off Booth with him to take a walk in the Park.

CHAPTER 5

A conversation between Amelia and Doctor Harrison, with the result.

AMELIA being left alone, began to consider seriously of her condition; she saw it would be very difficult to resist the importunities of her husband, backed by the authority of the doctor; especially as she well knew how unreasonable her declarations must appear to every one who was ignorant of her real motives to persevere in it. On the other hand, she was fully determined, whatever might be the consequence, to adhere firmly to her resolution of not accepting the colonel's invitation.

When she had turned the matter every way in her mind, and

vexed and tormented herself with much uneasy reflexion upon it, a thought at last occurred to her, which immediately brought her some comfort. This was, to make a confidant of the doctor, and to impart to him the whole truth. This method, indeed, appeared to her now to be so adviseable, that she wondered she had not hit upon it sooner; but it is the nature of despair to blind us to all the means of safety, however easy and apparent they may be.

Having fixed her purpose in her mind, she wrote a short note to the doctor, in which she acquainted him that she had something of great moment to impart to him, which must be an entire secret from her husband, and begged that she might have an opportunity of communicating it as soon as possible.

Doctor Harrison received the letter that afternoon, and immediately complied with Amelia's request in visiting her. He found her drinking tea with her husband and Mrs Atkinson, and sat down and joined the company.

Soon after the removal of the tea-table, Mrs Atkinson left the room. The doctor then turning to Booth, said, 'I hope, captain, you have a true sense of the obedience due to the Church, tho' our clergy do not often exact it. However, it is proper to exercise our power sometimes in order to remind the laity of their duty. I must tell you therefore, that I have some private business with your wife; and I expect your immediate absence.'

'Upon my word, doctor,' answered Booth, 'no popish confessor, I firmly believe, ever pronounced his will and pleasure with more gravity and dignity; none therefore was ever more immediately obeyed than you shall be.' Booth then quitted the room, and desired the doctor to recall him when his business with the lady was over.

Doctor Harrison promised he would, and then turning to Amelia, he said, 'Thus far, madam, I have obeyed your commands, and am now ready to receive the important secret which you mention in your note.'

Amelia now informed her friend of all she knew, all she had seen and heard, and all that she suspected of the colonel. The good man seemed greatly shocked at the relation, and remained in a silent astonishment. – Upon which, Amelia said, 'Is villany so rare a thing, sir, that it should so much surprize you?' 'No, child,' cries he; 'but I am shocked at seeing it so artfully disguised under the appearance of so much virtue. And to confess the truth, I believe my own vanity is a little hurt in having been so grossly imposed upon. Indeed, I had a very high regard for this man; for, besides the great character given him by your husband, and the many facts I have heard so much redounding to his honour, he hath the fairest and most promising appearance I have ever yet beheld – A good face they say, is a letter of recommendation.[4] O Nature, Nature, why art thou so dishonest, as ever to send men with these false recommendations into the world!'

'Indeed, my dear sir, I begin to grow entirely sick of it,' cries Amelia: 'for sure all mankind almost are villains in their hearts.'

'Fie, child,' cries the doctor. 'Do not make a conclusion so much to the dishonour of the great Creator. The nature of man is far from being in itself evil: it abounds with benevolence, charity and pity, coveting praise and honour, and shunning shame and disgrace. Bad education, bad habits, and bad customs, debauch our nature, and drive it headlong as it were into vice. The governors of the world, and I am afraid the priesthood, are answerable for the badness of it. Instead of discouraging wickedness to the utmost of their power, both are too apt to connive at it. In the great sin of adultery[5] for instance; hath the government provided any law to punish it; or doth the priest take any care to correct it? On the contrary, is the most notorious practice of it any detriment to a man's fortune or to his reputation in the world? Doth it exclude him from any preferment in the State, I had almost said in the Church? Is it any blot in his escutcheon? Any bar to his honour? Is he not to be found every day in the assemblies of women of the highest quality? In the closets of the greatest men, and even at the tables of bishops? What wonder then, if the community in general treat this monstrous crime as matter of jest, and that men give way to the temptations of a violent appetite, when the indulgence of it is protected by law and countenanced by custom. I am convinced there are good stamina[6] in the nature of this very man: for he hath done acts of friendship and generosity to your husband, before he could have any evil design on your chastity; and in a Christian society, which I no more esteem this nation to be, than I do any part of Turkey, I doubt not but this very colonel would have made a worthy and valuable member.'

'Indeed, my dear sir,' cries Amelia, 'you are the wisest as well as best man in the world –'

'Not a word of my wisdom,' cries the doctor. 'I have not a grain – I am not the least versed in the chrematistic* art, as an old friend of mine calls it. I know not how to get a shilling, nor how to keep it in my pocket, if I had it.'

'But you understand human nature to the bottom,' answered Amelia; 'and your mind is the treasury of all ancient and modern learning.'

'You are a little flatterer,' cries the doctor; 'but I dislike you not for it. And to shew you I don't, I will return your flattery; and tell you, you have acted with great prudence in concealing this affair from your husband; but you have drawn me into a scrape: for I have promised to dine with this fellow again to-morrow; and you have made it impossible for me to keep my word.'

'Nay but, dear sir,' cries Amelia, 'for Heaven's sake take care. If you shew any kind of disrespect to the colonel, my husband may be led into some suspicion – especially after our conference.'

'Fear nothing, child. I will give him no hint; and that I may be certain of not doing it, I will stay away. You do not think, I hope, that I will join in a chearful conversation with such a man; that I will so far betray my character as to give any countenance to such flagitious proceedings. Besides, my promise was only conditional; and I do not know whether I could otherwise have kept it: for I expect an old friend every day, who comes to town twenty miles on foot to see me; whom I shall not part with on any account: for as he is very poor, he may imagine I treat him with disrespect.'

'Well, sir,' cries Amelia, 'I must admire you, and love you for your goodness.'

'Must you love me?' cries the doctor. 'I could cure you now in a minute if I pleased.'

'Indeed, I defy you, sir,' said Amelia.

'If I could but persuade you,' answered he, 'that I thought you

* The art of getting wealth is so called by Aristotle in his *Politics*.[7]

not handsome, away would vanish all ideas of goodness in an instant. Confess honestly, would they not?'

'Perhaps I might blame the goodness of your eyes,' replied Amelia; 'and that is perhaps an honester confession than you expected. But do, pray, sir, be serious; and give me your advice what to do. Consider the difficult game I have to play: for I am sure, after what I have told you, you would not even suffer me to remain under the roof of this colonel.'

'No, indeed, would I not,' said the doctor, 'whilst I have a house of my own to entertain you.'

'But how to dissuade my husband,' continued she, 'without giving him any suspicion of the real cause, the consequences of his guessing at which, I tremble to think upon.'

'I will consult my pillow upon it,' said the doctor, 'and in the morning you shall see me again. In the mean time be comforted, and compose the perturbations of your mind.'

'Well, sir,' said she, 'I put my whole trust in you.'

'I am sorry to hear it,' cries the doctor. 'Your innocence may give you a very confident trust in a much more powerful assistance. However, I will do all I can to serve you; and now if you please we will call back your husband: for upon my word he hath shewn a good catholic patience. And where is the honest serjeant and his wife? I am pleased with the behaviour of you both to that worthy fellow, in opposition to the custom of the world; which instead of being formed on the precepts of our religion to consider each other as brethren, teaches us to regard those who are a degree below us, either in rank or fortune, as a species of beings of an inferior order in the creation.'

The captain now returned into the room, as did the serjeant and Mrs Atkinson; and the two couple, with the doctor, spent the evening together in great mirth and festivity; for the doctor was one of the best companions in the world; and a vein of cheerfulness, good-humour and pleasantry, ran through his conversation, with which it was impossible to resist being pleased.

CHAPTER 6

Containing as surprizing an accident as is perhaps recorded in history.

BOOTH had acquainted the serjeant with the great goodness of Colonel James, and with the cheerful prospects which he entertained from it. This Atkinson behind the curtain communicated to his wife. The conclusions which she drew from it, need scarce be hinted to the reader. She made, indeed, no scruple of plainly and bluntly telling her husband that the colonel had a most manifest intention to attack the chastity of Amelia.

This thought gave the poor serjeant great uneasiness, and after having kept him long awake, tormented him in his sleep with a most horrid dream, in which he imagined that he saw the colonel standing by the bed-side of Amelia, with a naked sword in his hand, and threatening to stab her instantly, unless she complied with his desires. Upon this, the serjeant started up in his bed, and catching his wife by the throat, cried out, 'D—n you, put up your sword this instant, and leave the room, or by heaven I'll drive mine to your heart's blood.'

This rough treatment immediately roused Mrs Atkinson from her sleep, who no sooner perceived the position of her husband, and felt his hand grasping her throat, than she gave a violent shriek, and presently fell into a fit.

Atkinson now waked likewise, and soon became sensible of the violent agitations of his wife. He immediately leapt out of bed, and running for a bottle of water began to sprinkle her very plentifully; but all to no purpose, she neither spoke nor gave any symptoms of recovery. Atkinson then began to roar aloud; upon which Booth, who lay under him, jumpt from his bed, and ran up with the lighted candle in his hand. The serjeant had no sooner taken the candle, than he ran with it to the bed-side. Here he beheld a sight which almost deprived him of his senses. The bed appeared to be all over blood, and his wife weltring in the midst of it. Upon this, the serjeant almost in a frenzy, cried out, 'O Heavens! I have killed my wife. I have stabbed her. I have stabbed her.' – 'What can be the meaning of all this?' said Booth. – 'O sir,' cries the serjeant, 'I dreamt I was rescuing your lady from the hands of Colonel James, and I have killed my wife.' – Here he threw himself upon the bed by her, caught her in his arms, and behaved like one frantic with despair.

By this time, Amelia had thrown on a wrapping gown, and was come up into the room, where the serjeant and his wife were lying on the bed, and Booth standing like a motionless statue by the bed-side. Amelia had some difficulty to conquer the effects of her own surprize on this occasion; for a more ghastly and horrible sight than the bed presented, could not be conceived.

Amelia sent Booth to call up the maid of the house, in order to lend her assistance; but before his return, Mrs Atkinson began to come to herself: and soon after, to the inexpressible joy of the serjeant, it was discovered she had no wound. Indeed, the delicate nose of Amelia soon made that discovery, which the grosser smell of the serjeant, and perhaps his fright had prevented him from making: for now it appeared that the red liquor with which the bed was stained, tho' it may perhaps sometimes run through the veins of a fine lady, was not what is properly called blood; but was, indeed, no other than cherry brandy, a bottle of which Mrs Atkinson always kept in her room to be ready for immediate use; and to which she used to apply for comfort in all her afflictions. This the poor serjeant, in his extreme hurry, had mistaken for a bottle of water. Matters were now soon accommodated, and no other mischief appeared to be done, unless to the bed-cloaths. Amelia and Booth returned back to their room; and Mrs Atkinson rose from her bed, in order to equip it with a pair of clean sheets.

And thus this adventure would have ended without producing any kind of consequence, had not the words which the serjeant uttered in his frenzy, made some slight impression on Booth: so much, at least, as to awaken his curiosity; so that in the morning when he arose, he sent for the serjeant, and desired to hear the particulars of this dream, since Amelia was concerned in it.

The serjeant, at first, seem'd unwilling to comply, and endeavoured to make excuses. This, perhaps, encreased Booth's curiosity, and he said, 'Nay I am resolved to hear it. Why, you simpleton, do you imagine me weak enough to be affected by a dream, however terrible it may be?'

'Nay, sir,' cries the serjeant, 'as for that matter dreams have sometimes fallen out to be true. – One of my own, I know, did so, concerning your honour: for when you courted my young lady, I dreamt you was married to her; and yet it was at a time when neither I myself, nor any of the country, thought you would ever obtain her. But Heaven forbid this dream should ever come to pass.'

'Why, what was this dream?' cries Booth. 'I insist on knowing.'

'To be sure, sir,' cries the serjeant, 'I must not refuse you; but, I hope, you will never think any more of it. Why then, sir, I dreamt that your honour was gone to the West Indies, and had left my lady in the care of Colonel James; and last night, I dreamt, the colonel came to my lady's bed-side, offering to ravish her; and with a drawn sword in his hand, threatening to stab her that moment, unless she would comply with his desires. How I came to be by, I know not; but, I dreamt, I rushed upon him, caught him by the throat, and swore I would put him to death, unless he instantly left the room. – Here I waked, and this was my dream. I never paid any regard to a dream in my life – but, indeed, I never dreamt any thing so very plain as this. It appeared downright reality. I am sure I have left the marks of my fingers in my wife's throat. I would not have taken a hundred pound to have used her so.'

'Faith,' cries Booth, 'it was an odd dream – and not so easily to be accounted for, as that you had formerly of my marriage; for as Shakespear says,[8] *Dreams denote a foregone conclusion.* Now it is impossible you should ever have thought of any such matter as this.'

'However, sir,' cries the serjeant, 'it is in your honour's power to prevent any possibility of this dream's coming to pass, by not leaving my lady to the care of the colonel: if you must go from her, certainly there are other places where she may be with great safety; and since my wife tells me that my lady is so very unwilling, whatever reasons she may have, I hope your honour will oblige her.'

'Now I recollect it,' cries Booth, 'Mrs Atkinson hath once or twice dropt some disrespectful words of the colonel. He hath done something to disoblige her.'

'He hath, indeed, sir,' replied the serjeant: 'He hath said that of her which she doth not deserve, and for which, if he had not been my superior officer, I would have cut both his ears off. – Nay, for that matter, he can speak ill of other people besides her.'

'Do you know, Atkinson,' cries Booth, very gravely, 'that you are talking of the dearest friend I have?'

'To be honest then,' answered the serjeant, 'I do not think so. If I did, I should love him much better than I do.'

'I must and will have this explained,' cries Booth. 'I have too good an opinion of you, Atkinson, to think you would drop such things as you have, without some reason – and I will know it.'

'I am sorry I have dropt a word,' cries Atkinson. 'I am sure I did not intend it; and your honour hath drawn it from me unawares.'

'Indeed, Atkinson,' cries Booth, 'you have made me very uneasy, and I must be satisfied.'

'Then, sir,' said the serjeant, 'you shall give me your word of honour; or I will be cut into ten thousand pieces before I will mention another syllable.'

'What shall I promise?' said Booth.

'That you will not resent any thing I shall lay to the colonel,' answered Atkinson.

'Resent! – Well, I give you my honour,' said Booth.

The serjeant made him bind himself over and over again; and then related to him the scene which formerly past between the colonel and himself, as far as concerned Booth himself; but concealed all that more immediately related to Amelia.

'Atkinson,' cries Booth, 'I cannot be angry with you; for I know you love me, and I have many obligations to you; but you have done wrong in censuring the colonel for what he said of me. I deserve all that he said; and his censures proceeded from his friendship.'

'But it was not so kind, sir,' said Atkinson, 'to say such things to me who am but a serjeant, and at such a time too.'

'I will hear no more,' cries Booth. 'Be assured you are the only man I would forgive on this occasion; and I forgive you only on condition you never speak a word more of this nature. – This silly dream hath intoxicated you.'

'I have done, sir,' cries the serjeant. 'I know my distance, and whom I am to obey; but I have one favour to beg of your honour, never to mention a word of what I have said to my lady; for I know she never would forgive me; I know she never would, by what my wife hath told me. Besides, you need not mention it, sir, to my lady; for she knows it all already, and a great deal more.'

Booth presently parted from the serjeant, having desired him to close his lips on this occasion, and repaired to his wife, to whom he related the serjeant's dream.

Amelia turned as white as snow, and fell into so violent a trembling, that Booth plainly perceived her emotion, and immediately partook of it himself. – 'Sure, my dear,' said he, staring wildly, 'there is more in this than I know. A silly dream could not so discompose you. I beg you, I intreat you to tell me – hath ever Colonel James –'

At the very mention of the colonel's name, Amelia fell on her knees, and begged her husband not to frighten her.

'What do I say, my dear love,' cried Booth, 'that can frighten you?'

'Nothing, my dear,' said she. – 'But my spirits are so discomposed with the dreadful scene I saw last night, that a dream, which, at another time, I should have laughed at, hath shocked me. Do but promise me that you will not leave me behind you, and I am easy.'

'You may be so,' cries Booth; 'for I will never deny you any thing. – But make me easy too. I must know, if you have seen any thing in Colonel James to displease you.'

'Why should you suspect it?' cries Amelia.

'You torment me to death,' cries Booth. 'By Heavens! I will know the truth. Hath he ever said or done anything which you dislike?'

'How, my dear,' said Amelia, 'can you imagine I should dislike a man, who is so much your friend? Think of all the obligations you have to him, and then you may easily resolve yourself. Do you think, because I refuse to stay behind you in his house, that I have any objection to him? – No, my dear, had he done a thousand times more than he hath, was he an angel instead of a man, I would not quit my Billy. – There's the sore, my dear; there's the misery, to be left by you.'

Booth embraced her with the most passionate raptures, and looking on her with inexpressible tenderness, cry'd – 'Upon my soul, I am not worthy of you. – I am a fool, and yet you cannot blame me. – If the stupid miser hoards, with such care, his worthless treasure; if he watches it with such anxiety; if every apprehension of another's sharing the least part, fills his soul with such agonies; O Amelia! what must be my condition, what terrors must I feel while I am watching over a jewel of such real, such inestimable worth?'

'I can, with great truth, return the compliment,' cries Amelia. 'I have my treasure too; and am so much a miser, that no force shall ever tear me from it.'

'I am ashamed of my folly,' cries Booth; 'and yet it is all from extreme tenderness. Nay, you yourself are the occasion. – Why will you ever attempt to keep a secret from me? Do you think I should have resented to my friend his just censure of my conduct?' –

'What censure, my dear love?' cries Amelia.

'Nay, the serjeant hath told me all,' cries Booth – 'Nay, and that he hath told it to you – Poor soul! thou couldst not endure to hear me accused, tho' never so justly, and by so good a friend. Indeed, my dear, I have discovered the cause of that resentment to the colonel, which you could not hide from me. – I love you, I adore you for it. Indeed I could not forgive a slighting word on you. – But why do I compare things so unlike? What the colonel said of me was just and true; every reflexion on my Amelia must be false and villanous.'

The discernment of Amelia was extremely quick; and she now perceived what had happened, and how much her husband knew of the truth. She resolved therefore to humour him, and fell severely on Colonel James for what he had said to the serjeant, which Booth endeavoured all he could to soften; and thus ended this affair, which had brought Booth to the very brink of a discovery, which must have given him the highest torment, if it had not produced any of those tragical effects which Amelia apprehended.

CHAPTER 7

In which the author appears to be master of that profound learning called the knowledge of the town.

MRS JAMES now came to pay a morning's visit to Amelia. She entered the room with her usual gaiety, and after a slight preface, addressing herself to Booth, said, she had been quarrelling with her husband on his account. 'I know not,' said she, 'what he means by thinking of sending you the Lord knows whither. I have insisted on his asking something for you nearer home. And it would be the hardest thing in the world, if he should not obtain it. Are we resolved never to encourage merit; but to throw away all our preferments on those who do not deserve them? What a set of contemptible wretches do we see strutting about the town in scarlet!'

Booth made a very low bow, and modestly spoke in disparagement of himself. To which she answered, 'Indeed, Mr Booth, you have merit. I have heard it from my brother, who is a judge of those matters; and I am sure cannot be suspected of flattery. He is your friend as well as myself; and we will never let Mr James rest till he hath got you a commission in England.'

Booth bowed again, and was offering to speak, but she interrupted him, saying, 'I will have no thanks, nor no fine speeches. If I can do you any service, I shall think I am only paying the debt of friendship to my dear Mrs Booth.'

Amelia, who had long since forgot the dislike she had taken to Mrs James at her first seeing her in town, had attributed it to the right cause, and had begun to resume her former friendship for her, expressed very warm sentiments of gratitude on this occasion. She told Mrs James, she should be eternally obliged to her if she could succeed in her kind endeavours; for that the thoughts of parting again with her husband had given her the utmost concern. 'Indeed,' added she 'I cannot help saying, he hath some merit in the service: for he hath received two dreadful wounds in it, one of which very greatly endangered his life; and, I am convinced, if his pretensions were backed with any interest, he would not fail of success.'

'They shall be backed with interest,' cries Mrs James, 'if my husband hath any. He hath no favour to ask for himself, nor for any other friend that I know of; and, indeed, to grant a man his just due, ought hardly to be thought a favour. Resume your old gaiety, therefore, my dear Emily. Lord! I remember the time when you was much the gayer creature of the two. But you make an arrant mope of yourself, by confining yourself at home. One never meets you any where. Come, you shall go with me to the Lady Betty Castleton's.'

'Indeed, you must excuse me, my dear,' answered Amelia, 'I do not know Lady Betty.'

'Not know Lady Betty! How is that possible? – But no matter, I will introduce you – She keeps a morning rout; hardly a rout, indeed; a little bit of a drum[9] – only four or five tables. – Come, take your capuchine;[10] you positively shall go – Booth, you shall go with us too. Tho' you are with your wife, another woman will keep you in countenance.'

'La! child,' cries Amelia, 'how you rattle!'

'I am in spirits,' answered Mrs James, 'this morning: for I won four rubbers together last night; and betted the things, and won almost every bet. I am in luck, and we will contrive to be partners – come.'

'Nay, child, you shall not refuse Mrs James,' said Booth.

'I have scarce seen my children to-day,' answered Amelia. 'Besides, I mortally detest cards.'

'Detest cards!' cries Mrs James. 'How can you be so stupid? I would not live a day without them – nay, indeed, I do not believe I should be able to exist. Is there so delightful a sight in the world, as the four honours in one's own hand, unless it be three natural aces at bragg[11] – And you really hate cards!'

'Upon reflexion,' cries Amelia, 'I have sometimes had great pleasure in them – in seeing my children build houses with them. My little boy is so dexterous, that he will sometimes build up the whole pack.'

'Indeed, Booth,' cries Mrs James, 'this good woman of yours is strangely altered since I knew her first; but she will always be a good creature.'

'Upon my word, my dear,' cries Amelia, 'you are altered too very greatly; but I doubt not to live to see you alter again, when you come to have as many children as I have.'

'Children!' cries Mrs James, 'you make me shudder. How can you envy me the only circumstance which makes matrimony comfortable?'

'Indeed, my dear,' said Amelia, 'you injure me: for I envy no woman's happiness in marriage.' At these words, such looks past between Booth and his wife as, to a sensible by-stander, would have made all the airs of Mrs James appear in the highest degree contemptible, and would have rendered herself the object of compassion. Nor could that lady avoid looking a little silly on the occasion.

Amelia now, at the earnest desire of her husband, accoutered herself to attend her friend; but first she insisted on visiting her children, to whom she gave several hearty kisses, and then recommending them to the care of Mrs Atkinson, she and her husband accompanied Mrs James to the rout; where few of my fine readers will be displeased to make part of the company.

The two ladies and Booth then entered an apartment beset with card-tables, like the rooms at Bath and Tunbridge.[12] Mrs James immediately introduced her friends to Lady Betty; who received them very civilly, and presently engaged Booth and Mrs James in a party at whist: for, as to Amelia, she so much declined playing, that as the party could be filled without her, she was permitted to sit by.

And now, who should make his appearance but the noble peer, of whom so much honourable mention hath already been made in this history. He walked directly up to Amelia, and addressed her with as perfect a confidence, as if he had not been in the least conscious of having in any manner displeased her; tho' the reader will hardly suppose, that Mrs Ellison had kept any thing a secret from him.

Amelia was not, however, so forgetful. She made him a very distant curtesy, would scarce vouchsafe an answer to any thing he said; and took the first opportunity of shifting her chair, and retiring from him.

Her behaviour, indeed, was such, that the peer plainly perceived, that he should get no advantage by pursuing her any farther at present. Instead, therefore, of attempting to follow her, he turned on his heel, and addressed his discourse to another lady; tho' he could not avoid often casting his eyes towards Amelia as long as she remained in the room.

Fortune, which seems to have been generally no great friend to Mr Booth, gave him no extraordinary marks of her favour at play. He lost two full rubbers, which cost him five guineas; after which, Amelia, who was uneasy at his lordship's presence, begged him in a whisper to return home; with which request he directly complied.

Nothing, I think, remarkable happened to Booth, unless the renewal of his acquaintance with an officer whom he had known abroad, and who made one of his party at the whist-table.

The name of this gentleman, with whom the reader will hereafter be better acquainted, was Trent. He had formerly been in the same regiment with Booth, and there was some intimacy between them. Captain Trent exprest great delight in meeting his brother officer, and both mutually promised to visit each other.

The scenes which had past the preceding night and that morning, had so confused Amelia's thoughts, that in the hurry in which she was carried off by Mrs James, she had entirely forgot her appointment with Dr Harrison. When she was informed at her return home, that the doctor had been to wait upon her, and had expressed some anger at her being gone out, she became greatly uneasy, and begged of her husband to go to the doctor's lodgings, and make her apology.

But lest the reader should be as angry with the doctor, as he had declared himself with Amelia, we think proper to explain the matter. Nothing then was farther from the doctor's mind than the conception of any anger towards Amelia. On the contrary, when the girl answered him, that her mistress was not at home, the doctor said with great good humour, 'How! not at home! then tell your mistress she is a giddy vagabond, and I will come to see her no more till she sends for me.' – This the poor girl, from misunderstanding one word, and half forgetting the rest, had construed into great passion, several very bad words, and a declaration that he would never see Amelia any more.

CHAPTER 8

In which two strangers make their appearance.

BOOTH went to the doctor's lodgings, and found him engaged with his country-friend and his son, a young gentleman who was lately in orders; both whom the doctor had left, to keep his appointment with Amelia.

After what we mentioned at the end of the last chapter, we need take little notice of the apology made by Booth, or the doctor's reception of it, which was in his peculiar manner. 'Your wife,' said he, 'is a vain hussy to think herself worth my anger; but tell her, I have the vanity myself to think I cannot be angy without a better cause. And yet tell her, I intend to punish her for her levity: for if you go abroad, I have determined to take her down with me into the country, and make her do penance there till your return.'

'Dear sir,' said Booth, 'I know not how to thank you, if you are in earnest.'

'I assure you then I am in earnest,' cries the doctor; 'but you need not thank me, however, since you know not how.' –

'But would not that, sir,' said Booth, 'be shewing a slight to the colonel's invitation? and you know I have so many obligations to him.'

'Don't tell me of the colonel,' cries the doctor, 'the Church is to be first served. Besides, sir, I have priority of right, even to you yourself. You stole my little lamb from me: for I was her first love.'

'Well, sir,' cries Booth, 'if I should be so unhappy to leave her to any one, she must herself determine; and, I believe, it will not be difficult to guess where her choice will fall: for of all men, next to her husband, I believe, none can contend with Dr Harrison in her favour.'

'Since you say so,' cries the doctor, – 'fetch her hither to dinner with us: for I am at least so good a Christian to love those that love me – I will shew you my daughter, my old friend; for I am really proud of her – and you may bring my grand-children with you, if you please.'

Booth made some compliments, and then went on his errand. As soon as he was gone, the old gentleman said to the doctor, 'Pray, my good friend, what daughter is this of yours? I never so much as heard that you was married.'

'And what then,' cries the doctor, 'did you ever hear that a pope was married? and yet some of them have had sons and daughters, I believe; but, however, this young gentleman will absolve me without obliging me to penance.'

'I have not yet that power,' answered the young clergyman: 'for I am only in deacon's orders.'

'Are you not?' cries the doctor; 'why then I will absolve myself. You are to know then, my good friend, that this young lady was the daughter of a neighbour of mine, who is since dead, and whose sins I hope are forgiven: for she had too much to answer for on her child's account. Her father was my intimate acquaintance and friend; a worthier man, indeed, I believe never lived. He died suddenly when his children were infants; and, perhaps, to the suddenness of his death it was owing, that he did not recommend any care of them to me. However, I, in some measure, took that charge upon me; and particularly of her whom I call my daughter. Indeed, as she grew up, she discovered[13] so many good qualities, that she wanted not the remembrance of her father's merit to recommend her. I do her no more than justice, when I say, she is one of the best creatures I ever knew. She hath a sweetness of temper, a generosity of spirit, an openness of heart – in a word, she hath a true Christian disposition. I may call her *an Israelite indeed, in whom there is no guile.*'[14]

'I wish you joy of your daughter,' cries the old gentleman: 'for to a man of your disposition, to find out an adequate object of your benevolence, is, I acknowledge, to find a treasure.'

'It is, indeed, a happiness,' cries the doctor.

'The greatest difficulty,' added the gentleman, 'which persons of your turn of mind meet with, is in finding proper objects of their goodness: for nothing sure can be more irksome to a generous mind, than to discover, that it hath thrown away all its good offices on a soil that bears no other fruit than ingratitude.'

'I remember,' cries the doctor, 'Phocylides[15] saith,

Μὴ κακὸν εὖ ἔρξῃς· σπείρειν ἴσον ἐστ' ἐνὶ πόντῳ.*

'But he speaks more like a philosopher than a Christian. I am more pleased with a French writer, one of the best, indeed, that I ever read; who blames men for lamenting the ill return which is so often made to the best offices.† A true Christian can never be disappointed if he doth not receive his reward in this world: the labourer might as well complain, that he is not paid his hire[17] in the middle of the day.'

'I own, indeed,' said the gentleman, 'if we see it in that light –'

'And in what light should we see it?' answered the doctor. 'Are we like Agrippa,[18] only almost Christians? or, is Christianity a matter of bare theory, and not a rule for our practice?'

'Practical undoubtedly, undoubtedly practical,' cries the gentleman. 'Your example might indeed have convinced me long ago, that we ought to do good to every one.'

'Pardon me, father,' cries the young divine, 'that is rather a heathenish than a Christian doctrine. Homer, I remember, introduces in his Iliad one Axylus,[19] of whom he says,

– Φίλος δ' ἦν ἀνθρώποισι,
Πάντας γὰρ φιλέεσκεν.§

But Plato, who of all the heathens came nearest to the Christian philosophy, condemned this as impious doctrine; so Eustathius[20] tells us, folio 474.'

'I know he doth,' cries the doctor, 'and so Barnes[21] tells us, in his note upon the place; but if you remember the rest of the quotation, as well as you do that from Eustathius, you might have added the observation which Mr Dryden[22] makes in favour of this passage, that he found not in all the Latin authors so admirable an instance of extensive humanity. You might have likewise remembred the

* To do a kindness to a bad man, is like sowing your seed in the sea.
† D'Esprit.[16]
§ He was a friend to mankind, for he loved them all.

noble sentiment, with which Mr Barnes ends his note, the sense of which is taken from the fifth chapter of Matthew,[23]

– ὃς καὶ φάος ἠελίοιο
Μίγδ' ἀγαθοῖσι κακοῖσί τ' ἐπ' ἀνδράσιν ἐξανατέλλει.

It seems, therefore, as if this character rather became a Christian than a heathen: for Homer could not have transcribed it from any of his deities. Whom is it, therefore, we imitate by such extensive benevolence?'

'What a prodigious memory you have!' cries the old gentleman. 'Indeed, son, you must not contend with the doctor in these matters.'

'I shall not give my opinion hastily,' cries the son. 'I know again what Mr Poole,[24] in his Annotations, says on that verse of St Matthew – That it is only to *heap coals of fire upon their heads* – How are we to understand, pray, the text immediately preceding? *Love your enemies, bless them that curse you, do good to them that hate you.*'

'You know, I suppose, young gentleman,' said the doctor, 'how these words are generally understood – the commentator you mention, I think, tells us, that love is not here to be taken in the strict sense, so as to signify the complacency of the heart; you may hate your enemies as God's enemies, and seek due revenge of them for his honour; and for your own sakes too you may seek moderate satisfaction of them; but then, you are to love them with a love consistent with these things – that is to say, in plainer words, you are to love them and hate them, and bless and curse, and do them good and mischief.'

'Excellent! admirable!' said the old gentleman, 'you have a most inimitable turn to ridicule.'

'I do not approve ridicule,' said the son, 'on such subjects.'

'Nor I neither,' cries the doctor, 'I will give you my opinion, therefore, very seriously. The two verses taken together contain a very positive precept, delivered in the plainest words, and yet illustrated by the clearest instance, in the conduct of the Supreme Being; and lastly, the practice of this precept is most nobly inforced by the reward annexed – *that ye may be the children*, and so forth. No man, who understands what it is to love, and to bless, and to do good, can mistake the meaning. But if they required any comment, the Scripture itself affords enow. *If thine enemy hunger, feed him; if he thirst, give him drink;*[25] *not rendering evil for evil, or railing for railing, but contrariwise, blessing*[26] – They do not, indeed, want the comments of men, who, when they cannot bend their minds to the obedience of Scripture, are desirous to wrest Scripture to a compliance with their own inclinations.'

'Most nobly and justly observed,' cries the old gentleman. 'Indeed, my good friend, you have explained the text with the utmost perspicuity.'

'But if this be the meaning,' cries the son, 'there must be an end of all law and justice – for I do not see how any man can prosecute his enemy in a court of justice.'

'Pardon me, sir,' cries the doctor. 'Indeed, as an enemy merely, and from a spirit of revenge, he cannot, and he ought not to prosecute him; but as an offender against the laws of his country, he may and it is his duty so to do: is there any spirit of revenge in the magistrates or officers of justice, when they punish criminals? Why do such, ordinarily I mean, concern themselves in inflicting punishments, but because it is their duty? And why may not a private man deliver an offender into the hands of justice, from the same laudable motive? Revenge, indeed, of all kinds is strictly prohibited; wherefore, as we are not to execute it with our own hands, so neither are we to make use of the law as the instrument of private malice, and to worry each other with inveteracy and rancour. And where is the great difficulty in obeying this wise, this generous, this noble precept? If revenge be, as a certain divine,[27] not greatly to his honour, calls it, the most luscious morsel the devil ever dropt into the mouth of a sinner, it must be allowed at least to cost us often extremely dear. It is a dainty, if indeed it be one, which we come at with great inquietude, with great difficulty, and with great danger. However pleasant it may be to the palate, while we are feeding on it, it is sure to leave a bitter relish behind it; and so far, indeed, it may be called a luscious morsel, that the most greedy appetites are soon glutted, and the most eager longing for it is soon turned into loathing and repentance. I allow there is something tempting in its outward appearance; but it is like the beautiful colour of some poisons, from which, however they may attract our eyes, a regard to our own welfare commands us to abstain. And this is an abstinence to which wisdom alone, without any divine command, hath been often found adequate; with instances of which, the Greek and Latin authors every where abound. May not a Christian, therefore, be well ashamed of making a stumbling-block of a precept, which is not only consistent with his wordly interest, but to which so noble an incentive is proposed?'

The old gentleman fell into raptures at this speech, and after making many compliments to the doctor upon it, he turned to his son, and told him, he had an opportunity now of learning more in one day, than he had learnt at the university in a twelve-month.

The son replied, that he allowed the doctrine to be extremely good in general, and that he agreed with the greater part; 'but I must make a distinction,' said he. However, he was interrupted from his distinction at present; for now Booth returned with Amelia and the children.

CHAPTER 9

A scene of modern wit and humour.

IN THE afternoon, the old gentleman proposed a walk to Vauxhall;[28] a place of which, he said, he had heard much, but had never seen it.

The doctor readily agreed to his friend's proposal, and soon after ordered two coaches to be sent for to carry the whole company. But when the servant was gone for them, Booth acquainted the doctor that it was yet too early. 'Is it so?' said the doctor; 'why then I will carry you first to one of the greatest and highest entertainments in the world.'

The children pricked up their ears at this; nor did any of the company guess what he meant; and Amelia asked what entertainment he could carry them to at that time of the day.

'Suppose,' says the doctor, 'I should carry you to court.'

'At five o'clock in the afternoon!' cries Booth.

'Ay, suppose I should have interest enough to introduce you into the Presence.'

'You are jesting, dear sir,' cries Amelia.

'Indeed, I am serious,' answered the doctor. 'I will introduce you into that Presence, compared to whom the greatest emperor on the earth is many millions of degrees meaner than the most contemptible reptile is to him. What entertainment can there be to a rational being equal to this? Was not the taste of mankind most wretchedly depraved, where would the vain man find an honour, or where would the love of pleasure propose so adequate an object as divine worship? With what ecstasy must the contemplation of being admitted to such a Presence fill the mind! The pitiful courts of princes are open to few, and to those only at particular seasons; but from this glorious and gracious Presence, we are none of us, and at no time excluded.'

The doctor was proceeding thus, when the servant returned, saying the coaches were ready; and the whole company with the greatest alacrity attended the doctor to St James's church.[29]

When the service was ended, and they were again got into their coaches, Amelia returned the doctor many thanks for the light in which he had placed divine worship; assuring him, that she had never before had so much transport in her devotion as at this time, and saying, she believed she should be the better for this notion he had given her, as long as she lived.

The coaches being come to the water side, they all alighted, and getting into one boat proceeded to Vauxhall.

The extreme beauty and elegance of this place is well known to almost every one of my readers; and happy is it for me that it is so; since to give an adequate idea of it, would exceed my power of description. To delineate the particular beauties of these gardens, would, indeed, require as much pains and as much paper too, as to rehearse all the good actions of their master; whose life proves the truth of an observation which I have read in some ethic writer, that a truly elegant taste is generally accompanied with an excellency of heart; or in other words, that true virtue is, indeed, nothing else but true taste.

Here our company diverted themselves, with walking an hour or two before the music began. Of all the seven, Booth alone had ever been here before; so that to all the rest, the place with its other charms, had that of novelty. When the music played, Amelia, who stood next to the doctor, said to him in a whisper, 'I hope I am not guilty of profaneness; but in pursuance of that cheerful chain of thoughts with which you have inspired me this afternoon, I was just now lost in a reverie, and fancied myself in those blissful mansions which we hope to enjoy hereafter. The delicious sweetness of the place, the enchanting charms of the music, and the satisfaction which appears in every one's countenance, carried my soul almost to Heaven in its ideas. I could not have, indeed, imagined there had been anything like this in this world.'

The doctor smiled, and said, 'You see, dear madam, there may be pleasures of which you could conceive no idea, till you actually enjoyed them.'

And now the little boy, who had long withstood the attractions of several cheese-cakes that passed to and fro, could contain no longer, but asked his mother to give him one; saying, 'I am sure my sister would be glad of another, tho' she is ashamed to ask.' The doctor overhearing the child proposed that they should all retire to some place where they might sit down and refresh themselves, which they accordingly did. Amelia now missed her husband; but as she had three men in her company, and one of them was the doctor, she concluded herself and her children to be safe, and doubted not but that Booth would soon find her out.

They now sat down, and the doctor very gallantly desired Amelia to call for what she liked. Upon which the children were supplied with cakes; and some ham and chicken were provided for the rest of the company. With which while they were regaling themselves with the highest satisfaction, two young fellows walking arm in arm came up, and when they came opposite to Amelia, they stood still, staring Amelia full in the face, and one of them cried aloud to the other, 'D—n me, my lord, if she is not an angel!' – My lord stood still staring likewise at her, without speaking a word – when two others of the same gang came up – and one of them cried – 'Come along, Jack, I have seen her before; but she is too well manned already. Three — are enough for one woman, or the devil is in it.'

'D—n me,' says he that spoke first, and whom they called Jack, 'I will have a brush at her, if she belonged to the whole convocation.' And so saying he went up to the young clergyman, and cried – 'Doctor, sit up a little, if you please, and don't take up more room in a bed than belongs to you.' At which words, he gave the young man a push, and seated himself down directly over-against Amelia, and leaning both his elbows on the table, he fixed his eyes on her in a manner with which modesty can neither look, nor bear to be looked at.

Amelia seemed greatly shocked at this treatment; upon which the doctor removed her within him, and then facing the gentleman, asked him what he meant by this rude behaviour. – Upon which my lord stept up and said, 'Don't be impertinent, old gentleman. Do you think such fellows as you, are to keep, d—n me, such fine wenches, d—n me, to yourselves, d—n me?'

'No, no,' cries Jack, 'the old gentleman is more reasonable. Here's the fellow that eats up the tithe pig.[30] Don't you see how his mouth waters at her – Where's your slabbering bib?'[31] For tho' the gentleman had rightly guessed he was a clergyman; yet, he had not any of those insignia on, with which it would have been improper to have appeared there.

'Such boys as you,' cries the young clergyman, 'ought to be well whipped at school, instead of being suffered to become nuisances in the society.'

'Boys, sir!' says Jack, 'I believe I am as good a man as yourself, Mr — and as good a scholar too. *Bos fur sus quotque sacerdos*.[32] – Tell me what's next. D—n me, I'll hold you fifty pounds – you don't tell me what's next.'

'You have him, Jack,' cries my lord, 'It's over with him, d—n me. He can't strike another blow.'

'If I had you in a proper place,' cries the clergyman, 'you should find I would strike a blow, and a pretty hard one too.'

'There,' cries my lord, 'there is the meekness of the clergyman – there spoke the wolf in the sheep's cloathing.[33] D—n me, how big he looks – You must be civil to him, faith! or else he will burst with pride.'

'Ay, ay,' cries Jack, 'let the clergy alone for pride, there's not a lord in the kingdom now hath half the pride of that fellow.'

'Pray, sir,' cries the doctor, turning to the other, 'are you a lord?'

'Yes, Mr—,' cries he, 'I have that honour, indeed.'

'And I suppose you have pride too,' said the doctor.

'I hope I have, sir,' answered he, 'at your service.'

'If such a one as you, sir,' cries the doctor, 'who are not only a scandal to the title you bear as a lord, but even as a man, can pretend to pride, why will you not allow it to a clergyman? I suppose, sir, by your dress you are in the army, and by the ribbon in your hat, you seem to be proud of that too. How much greater and more honourable is the service in which that gentleman is enlisted than yours. Why then should you object to the pride of the clergy, since the lowest of the function is in reality every way so much your superior?'

'Tida tidu tidum,'[34] – cries my lord.

'However, gentlemen,' cries the doctor, 'if you have the least pretension to that name, I beg you will put an end to your frolick; since you see it gives so much uneasiness to the lady. Nay, I entreat you, for your own sakes; for here is one coming who will talk to you in a very different stile from ours.'

'One coming!' cries my lord – 'what care I who is coming?'

'I suppose it is the devil,' cries Jack: 'for here are two of his livery servants already.'

'Let the devil come as soon as he will,' cries my lord, 'd—n me if I have not a kiss.'

Amelia now fell a trembling, and her children perceiving her fright, both hung on her, and began to cry – when Booth and Captain Trent both came up.

Booth seeing his wife disordered asked eagerly what was the matter. At the same time, the lord and his companion seeing Captain Trent, whom they well knew – said both together – 'What, doth this company belong to you?' When the doctor with presence of mind, as he was apprehensive of some fatal consequence if Booth should know what had past, said, 'So, Mr Booth, I am glad you are returned; your poor lady here began to be frighted out of her wits. But now you have him again,' said he to Amelia, 'I hope you will be easy.'

Amelia, frighted as she was, presently took the hint, and greatly chid her husband for leaving her; but the little boy was not so quick-sighted, and cried – 'Indeed, papa, those naughty men there have frighted my mamma out of her wits.'

'How!' cries Booth, a little moved. 'Frighten'd! hath any one frighten'd you, my dear?'

'No, my love,' answered she, 'nothing. I know not what the child means. Every thing is well, now I see you safe.'

Trent had been all the while talking aside with the young sparks; and now addressing himself to Booth, said, 'Here hath been some little mistake; I believe my lord mistook Mrs Booth for some other lady.'

'It is impossible,' cries my lord, 'to know every one. – I am sure, if I had known the lady to be a woman of fashion, and an acquaintance of Captain Trent, I should have said nothing disagreeable to her; but if I have, I ask her pardon, and the company's.'

'I am in the dark,' cries Booth. 'Pray, what is all this matter?'

'Nothing of any consequence,' cries the doctor, 'nor worth your enquiring into – You hear it was a mistake of the person; and I really believe his lordship, that all proceeded from his not knowing to whom the lady belonged.'

'Come, come,' says Trent, 'there is nothing in the matter, I assure you. I will tell you the whole another time.'

'Very well, since you say so,' cries Booth, 'I am contented.' So ended the affair, and the two sparks made their congee[35] and sneaked off.

'Now they are gone,' said the young gentleman, 'I must say, I never saw two worse-bred jackanapes, nor fellows that deserved to be kick'd more. If I had had them in another place, I would have taught them a little more respect to the Church.'

'You took rather a better way,' answered the doctor, 'to teach them that respect.'

Booth now desired his friend Trent to sit down with them, and proposed to call for a fresh bottle of wine; but Amelia's spirits were too much disconcerted to give her any prospect of pleasure that evening. She therefore laid hold of the pretence of her children, for whom she said the hour was already too late; with which the doctor agreed. So they paid their reckoning, and departed; leaving to the two rakes, the triumph of having totally dissipated the mirth of this little innocent company, who were before enjoying complete satisfaction.

CHAPTER 10

A curious conversation between the doctor, the young clergyman, and the young clergyman's father.

THE next morning when the doctor and his two friends were at breakfast, the young clergyman, in whose mind the injurious treatment he had received the evening before, was very deeply impressed, renewed the conversation on that subject. 'It is a scandal,' said he, 'to the government, that they do not preserve more respect to the clergy, by punishing all rudeness to them with the utmost severity. It was very justly observed of you, sir,' says he to the doctor, 'that the lowest clergyman in England is in real dignity superior to the highest nobleman. What then can be so shocking as to see that gown, which ought to entitle us to the veneration of all we meet, treated with contempt and ridicule? Are we not, in fact, ambassadors from Heaven,[36] to the world; and do they not, therefore, in denying us our due respect, deny it in reality to him that sent us?'

'If that be the case,' says the doctor; 'it behoves them to look to themselves; for he who sent us is able to exact most severe vengeance for the ill treatment of his ministers.'

'Very true, sir,' cries the young one; 'and I heartily hope he will; but those punishments are at too great a distance to infuse terror into wicked minds. The government ought to interfere with its immediate censures. Fines and imprisonments and corporal punishments operate more forcibly on the human mind than all the fears of damnation.'

'Do you think so?' cries the doctor; 'then I am afraid men are very little in earnest in those fears.'

'Most justly observed,' says the old gentleman. 'Indeed, I am afraid that is too much the case.'

'In that,' said the son, 'the government is to blame. Are not books of infidelity, treating our holy religion as a mere imposture; nay, sometimes, as a mere jest, published daily, and spread abroad amongst the people with perfect impunity?'

'You are certainly in the right,' says the doctor, 'there is a most blameable remissness with regard to these matters; but the whole blame doth not lie there; some little share of the fault is, I am afraid, to be imputed to the clergy themselves.'

'Indeed, sir,' cries the young one, 'I did not expect that charge from a gentleman of your cloth: Do the clergy give any encouragement to such books? Do they not, on the contrary, cry loudly out against the suffering them? This is the invidious aspersion of the laity; and I did not expect to hear it confirmed by one of our own cloth.'

'Be not too impatient, young gentleman,' said the doctor. 'I do not absolutely confirm the charge of the laity. It is much too general, and too severe; but even the laity themselves do not attack them in that part to which you have applied your defence. They are not supposed such fools as to attack that religion to which they owe their temporal welfare. They are not taxed with giving any other support to infidelity, than what it draws from the ill examples of their lives; I mean of the lives of some of them. Here too the laity carry their censures too far: for there are very few or none of the clergy, whose lives, if compared with those of the laity, can be called profligate; but such, indeed, is the perfect purity of our religion; such is the innocence and virtue, which it exacts to entitle us to its glorious rewards, and to screen us from its dreadful punishments, that he must be a very good man indeed who lives up to it. Thus then these persons argue. This man is educated in a perfect knowledge of religion, is learned in its laws, and is by his profession obliged in a manner to have them always before his eyes. The rewards which it promises to the obedience of these laws are so great, and the punishments threatned on disobedience so dreadful, that it is impossible but all men must fearfully fly from the one, and as eagerly pursue the other. If therefore such a person lives in direct opposition to, and in a constant breach of these laws, the inference is obvious. There is a pleasant story in Matthew Paris,[37] which I will tell you as well as I can remember it. Two young gentlemen, I think they were priests, agreed together, that whosoever died first, should return and acquaint his friend with the secrets of the other world. One of them died soon after, and fulfilled his promise. The whole relation he gave is not very material, but among other things he produced one of his hands which Satan had made use of, to write upon as the moderns do on a card, and had sent his compliments to the priests, for the number of souls, which the wicked examples of their lives daily sent to hell. This story is the more remarkable, as it was written by a priest, and a great favourer of his order.'

'Excellent,' cried the old gentleman, 'what a memory you have!'

'But, sir,' cries the young one, 'a clergyman is a man as well as another; and if such perfect purity be expected –'

'I do not expect it,' cries the doctor, 'and I hope it will not be expected of us. The Scripture itself gives us this hope, where the best of us are said to fall twenty times a day.[38] But sure, we may not allow the practice of any of those grosser crimes which contaminate the whole mind. We may expect an obedience to the Ten Commandments, and an abstinence from such notorious vices; as in the first place, avarice, which indeed can hardly subsist without the breach of more Commandments than one; indeed it would be excessive candour to imagine, that a man, who so visibly sets his whole heart not only on this world, but on one of the most worthless things in it, (for so is money without regard to its uses,) should be at the same time laying up his treasure in Heaven.[39] Ambition is a second vice of this sort; we are told we cannot serve God and Mammon.[40] I might have applied this to avarice, but I chose rather to mention it here. When we see a man sneaking about in courts and levees, and doing the dirty work of great men from the hopes of preferment, can we believe that a fellow, whom we see to have so many hard taskmasters upon earth, ever thinks of his Master which is in Heaven? Must he not himself think, if he ever reflects at all, that so glorious a Master will disdain and disown a servant, who is the dutiful tool of a court favourite; and employed either as the pimp of his pleasure, or sometimes perhaps made a dirty channel, to assist in the conveyance of that corruption, which is clogging up and destroying the very vitals of his country?

'The last vice which I shall mention, is pride. There is not in the universe a more ridiculous, nor a more contemptible animal than a proud clergyman; a turkey-cock or a jackdaw, are objects of veneration when compared with him. I don't mean by pride, that noble dignity of mind, to which goodness can only administer an adequate object, which delights in the testimony of its own conscience, and could not without the highest agonies bear its condemnation. By pride, I mean, that saucy passion, which exults in every little eventual pre-eminence over other men; such are the ordinary gifts of nature, and the paultry presents of fortune, wit, knowledge, birth, strength, beauty, riches, titles and rank. That passion which is ever-aspiring, like a silly child, to look over the heads of all about them; which while it servilely adheres to the great, flies from the poor, as if afraid of contamination; devouring greedily every murmur of applause, and every look of admiration, pleased and elated with all kind of respect, and hurt and enflamed with the contempt of the lowest and most despicable of fools, even with such as treated you last night disrespectfully at Vauxhall. Can such a mind as this be fixed on things above? Can such a man reflect that he hath the ineffable honour to be employed in the immediate service of his great Creator, or can he please himself with the heart-warming hope, that his ways are acceptable in the sight of that glorious, that incomprehensible Being?'

'Hear, child, hear,' cries the old gentleman, 'hear and improve your understanding. Indeed, my good friend, no one retires from you without carrying away some good instructions with him. Learn of the doctor, Tom, and you will be the better man as long as you live.'

'Undoubtedly, sir,' answered Tom, 'the doctor hath spoken a great deal of excellent truth, and, without a compliment to him, I was always a great admirer of his sermons, particularly of their oratory. But,

Nec tamen hoc tribuens dederim quoque caetera.[41]

I cannot agree that a clergyman is obliged to put up with an affront, any more than another man, and more especially when it is paid to the order.'

'I am very sorry, young gentleman,' cries the doctor, 'that you should be ever liable to be affronted, as a clergyman; and, I do assure you, if I had known your disposition formerly, the order should never have been affronted through you.'

The old gentleman now began to check his son, for his opposition to the doctor, when a servant delivered the latter a note from

Amelia, which he read immediately to himself, and it contained the following words:

> My dear Sir,
>
> Something hath happened since I saw you, which gives me great uneasiness, and I beg the favour of seeing you as soon as possible, to advise with you upon it.
>
> I am,
> your most obliged,
> and dutiful daughter,
> Amelia Booth.

The doctor's answer was, that he would wait on the lady directly; and then turning to his friend, he asked him if he would not take a walk in the Park before dinner. 'I must go,' says he, 'to the lady who was with us last night, for I am afraid by her letter, some bad accident hath happened to her. Come, young gentleman, I spoke a little too hastily to you just now, but I ask your pardon. Some allowance must be made to the warmth of your blood. I hope we shall in time both think alike.'

The old gentleman made his friend another compliment, and the young one declared, he hoped he should always think, and act too, with the dignity becoming his cloth. After which, the doctor took his leave for a while, and went to Amelia's lodgings.

As soon as he was gone, the old gentleman fell very severely on his son. 'Tom,' says he, 'how can you be such a fool, to undo by your perverseness all that I have been doing? Why will you not learn to study mankind with the attention which I have employed to that purpose? Do you think, if I had affronted this obstinate old fellow as you do, I should ever have engaged his friendship?'

'I cannot help it, sir,' said Tom, 'I have not studied six years at the university, to give up my sentiments to every one. It is true, indeed, he put together a set of sounding words; but, in the main, I never heard any one talk more foolishly.'

'What of that,' cries the father, 'I never told you he was a wise man, nor did I ever think him so. If he had any understanding, he would have been a bishop long ago, to my certain knowledge. But, indeed, he hath been always a fool in private life; for I question whether he is worth £100 in the world, more than his annual income. He hath given away above half his fortune to the Lord knows who. I believe I have had above £200 of him, first and last; and would you lose such a milch-cow as this for want of a few compliments? Indeed, Tom, thou art as great a simpleton as himself. How do you expect to rise in the Church, if you can't temporize, and give into the opinion of your superiors?'

'I don't know, sir,' cries Tom, 'what you mean by my superiors. In one sense, I own, a Doctor of Divinity is superior to a Batchelor of Arts, and so far I am ready to allow his superiority; but I understand Greek and Hebrew as well as he, and will maintain my opinion against him, or any other in the Schools.'

'Tom,' cries the old gentleman, 'till thou gettest the better of thy conceit, I shall never have any hopes of thee. If thou art wise, thou wilt think every man thy superior, of whom thou canst get any thing; at least thou wilt persuade him that thou thinkest so, and that is sufficient. Tom, Tom, thou hast no policy in thee.'

'What have I been learning these seven years,' answered he, 'in the university? However, father, I can account for your opinion. It is the common failing of old men to attribute all wisdom to themselves. Nestor[42] did it long ago; but, if you will enquire my character at college, I fancy you will not think I want to go to school again.'

The father and son then went to take their walk, during which the former repeated many good lessons of policy to his son, not greatly, perhaps, to his edification. In truth, if the old gentleman's fondness had not, in a great measure, blinded him to the imperfections of his son, he would have soon perceived that he was sowing all his instructions in a soil so choaked with self-conceit, that it was utterly impossible they should ever bear any fruit.

BOOK X

CHAPTER 1

To which we will prefix no preface.

THE doctor found Amelia alone, for Booth was gone to walk with his new revived acquaintance, Captain Trent, who seemed so pleased with the renewal of his intercourse with his old brother officer, that he had been almost continually with him from the time of their meeting at the drum.

Amelia acquainted the doctor with the purport of her message, as follows: 'I ask your pardon, my dear sir, for troubling you so often with my affairs; but I know your extreme readiness as well as ability to assist any one with your advice. The fact is, that my husband hath been presented by Colonel James with two tickets for a masquerade,[1] which is to be in a day or two; and he insists so strongly on my going with him, that I really do not know how to refuse, without giving him some reason; and I am not able to invent any other than the true one, which you would not, I am sure, advise me to communicate to him. Indeed I had a most narrow escape the other day; for I was almost drawn in inadvertently, by a very strange accident, to acquaint him with the whole matter.' She then related the serjeant's dream, with all the consequences that attended it.

The doctor considered a little with himself, and then said, 'I am really, child, puzzled as well as you about this matter. I would by no means have you go to the masquerade: I do not indeed like the diversion itself, as I have heard it described to me: not that I am such a prude to suspect every woman who goes there of any evil intentions; but it is a pleasure of too loose and disorderly a kind for the recreation of a sober mind. Indeed you have still a stronger and more particular objection. I will try myself to reason him out of it.'

'Indeed it is impossible,' answered she; 'and therefore I would not set you about it. I never saw him more set on any thing. There is a party, as they call it, made on the occasion; and he tells me my refusal will disappoint all.'

'I really do not know what to advise you,' cries the doctor: 'I have told you I do not approve these diversions; but yet, as your husband is so very desirous, I cannot think there will be any harm in going with him. However, I will consider of it, and do all in my power for you.'

Here Mrs Atkinson came in, and the discourse on this subject ceased; but soon after Amelia renewed it, saying, there was no occasion to keep any thing a secret from her friend. They then fell to debating on the subject; but could not come to any resolution: but Mrs Atkinson, who was in an unusual flow of spirits, cried out, 'Fear nothing, my dear Amelia; two women surely will be too hard for one man. I think, doctor, it exceeds Virgil:

Una dolo divum si femina victa duorum est.'[2]

'Very well repeated indeed,' cries the doctor. 'Do you understand all Virgil as well as you seem to do that line?'

'I hope I do, sir,' said she, 'and Horace too; or else my father threw away his time to very little purpose in teaching me.'

'I ask your pardon, madam,' cries the doctor, 'I own it was an impertinent question.'

'Not at all, sir,' says she; 'and if you are one of those who imagine women incapable of learning, I shall not be offended at it. I know the common opinion; but

Interdum vulgus rectum videt, est ubi peccat.'[3]

'If I was to profess such an opinion, madam,' said the doctor, 'Madam Dacier[4] and yourself would bear testimony against me. The utmost indeed that I should venture would be to question the utility of learning in a young lady's education.'

'I own,' said Mrs Atkinson, 'as the world is constituted, it cannot be as serviceable to her fortune, as it will be to that of a man; but you will allow, doctor, that learning may afford a woman at least a reasonable and an innocent entertainment.'

'But I will suppose,' cried the doctor, 'it may have its inconveniencies. As for instance, if a learned lady should meet with an unlearned husband, might she not be apt to despise him?'

'I think not,' cries Mrs Atkinson – 'and if I may be allowed the instance – I think I have shewn myself that women who have learning themselves, can be contented without that qualification in a man.'

'To be sure,' cries the doctor, 'there may be other qualifications which may have their weight in the balance. But let us take the other side of the question, and suppose the learned of both sexes to meet in the matrimonial union, may it not afford one excellent subject of disputation, which is the most learned?'

'Not at all,' cries Mrs Atkinson; 'for, if they had both learning and good sense, they would soon see on which side the superiority lay.'

'But if the learned man,' said the doctor, 'should be a little unreasonable in his opinion, are you sure that the learned woman would preserve her duty to her husband, and submit?'

'But why,' cries Mrs Atkinson, 'must we necessarily suppose that a learned man would be unreasonable?'

'Nay, madam,' said the doctor, 'I am not your husband; and you shall not hinder me from supposing what I please. Surely it is not such a paradox to conceive that a man of learning should be unreasonable. Are there no unreasonable opinions in very learned authors, even among the critics themselves? For instance, what can be a more strange, and indeed unreasonable opinion, than to prefer the *Metamorphoses* of Ovid to the *Aeneid* of Virgil?'[5]

'It would be indeed so strange,' cries the lady, 'that you shall not persuade me it was ever the opinion of any man.'

'Perhaps not,' cries the doctor; 'and I believe you and I should not differ in our judgments of any person who maintained such an opinion – what a taste must he have?'

'A most contemptible one indeed,' cries Mrs Atkinson.

'I am satisfied,' cries the doctor. 'And in the words of your own Horace, *Verbum non amplius addam.*'[6]

'But how provoking is this!' cries Mrs Atkinson, 'to draw one in in such a manner. I protest I was so warm in the defence of my favourite Virgil, that I was not aware of your design; but all your triumph depends on a supposition that one should be so unfortunate as to meet with the silliest fellow in the world.'

'Not in the least,' cries the doctor. 'Dr Bentley was not such a person; and yet he would have quarrelled, I am convinced, with any wife in the world, in behalf of one of his corrections. I don't suppose he would have given up his *ingentia fata*[7] to an angel.'

'But do you think,' said she, 'if I had loved him, I would have contended with him?'

'Perhaps you might sometimes,' said the doctor, 'be of these sentiments; but you remember your own Virgil – *varium et mutabile semper femina*.'[8]

'Nay, Amelia,' said Mrs Atkinson, 'you are now concern'd as well as I am; for he hath now abused the whole sex, and quoted the severest thing that ever was said against us, though I allow it is one of the finest.'

'With all my heart, my dear,' cries Amelia. 'I have the advantage of you however, for I don't understand him.'

'Nor doth she understand much better than yourself,' cries the doctor; 'or she would not admire nonsense even though in Virgil.'

'Pardon me, sir,' said she.

'And pardon me, madam,' cries the doctor with a feigned seriousness, 'I say a boy in the fourth form at Eton would be whipt, or would deserve to be whipt at least, who made the neuter gender agree with the feminine.[9] You have heard however, that Virgil left his Aeneid incorrect; and perhaps had he lived to correct it, we should not have seen the faults we now see in it.'

'Why, it is very true as you say, doctor,' cries Mrs Atkinson – 'There seems to be a false concord. I protest I never thought of it before.'

'And yet this is the Virgil,' answered the doctor, 'that you are so fond of, who hath made you all of the neuter gender; or as we say in English, he hath made mere animals of you: for if we translate it thus;

Woman is a various and changeable animal,

there will be no fault, I believe, unless in point of civility to the ladies.'

Mrs Atkinson had just time to tell the doctor he was a provoking creature, before the arrival of Booth and his friend put an end to that learned discourse, in which neither of the parties had greatly recommended themselves to each other, the doctor's opinion of the lady being not at all heightened by her progress in the classics; and she on the other hand, having conceived a great dislike in her heart towards the doctor, which would have raged, perhaps, with no less fury from the consideration that he had been her husband.

CHAPTER 2

What happened at the masquerade.

FROM this time to the day of the masquerade, nothing happened of consequence enough to have a place in this history.

On that day Colonel James came to Booth's about nine in the evening, where he stay'd for Mrs James, who did not come till near eleven. The four masques then set out together in several chairs; and all proceeded to the Haymarket.

When they arrived at the Opera House, the Colonel and Mrs James presently left them; nor did Booth and his lady remain long together, but were soon divided from each other by different masques.

A domino soon accosted the lady and had her away to the upper end of the furthest room on the right hand, where both the masques sat down: nor was it long before the he domino began to make very fervent love to the she. It would perhaps be tedious to the reader to run thro' the whole process, which was not indeed in the most romantick stile. The lover seemed to consider his mistress as a mere woman of this world, and seemed rather to apply to her avarice and ambition than to her softer passions.

As he was not so careful to conceal his true voice as the lady was, she soon discovered that this lover of hers was no other than her old friend the peer, and presently a thought suggested itself to her of making an advantage of this accident. She gave him therefore an intimation that she knew him, and expressed some astonishment at his having found her out. 'I suspect,' says she, 'my lord, that you have a friend in the woman where I now lodge, as well as you had in Mrs Ellison.' My lord protested the contrary – To which she answered, 'Nay, my lord, do not defend her so earnestly till you are sure I should have been angry with her.'

At these words, which were accompanied with a very bewitching softness, my lord flew into raptures rather too strong for the place he was in. These the lady gently checked, and begged him to take care they were not observed; for that her husband, for aught she knew, was then in the room.

Colonel James came now up, and said, 'So, madam, I have the good fortune to find you again; I have been extremely miserable since I lost you.' The lady answered in her masquerade voice that she did not know him. 'I am Colonel James,' said he, in a whisper. 'Indeed, sir,' answer'd she, 'you are mistaken, I have no acquaintance with any Colonel James.' 'Madam,' answer'd he, in a whisper likewise, 'I am positive I am not mistaken, you are certainly Mrs Booth.' – 'Indeed, sir,' said she, 'you are very impertinent, and I beg you will leave me.' My lord then interposed, and speaking in his own voice, assur'd the colonel that the lady was a woman of quality, and that they were engaged in a conversation together; upon which the colonel asked the lady's pardon; for as there was nothing remarkable in her dress, he really believ'd he had been mistaken.

He then went again a hunting through the rooms, and soon after found Booth, walking without his mask between two ladies, one of whom was in a blue domino, and the other in the dress of a shepherdess. 'Will,' cries the colonel, 'do you know what is become of our wives; for I have seen neither of them since we have been in the room?' Booth answered, 'that he supposed they were both together, and they should find them by and by.' 'What,' cries the lady in the blue domino, 'are you both come upon duty then with your wives? As for yours, Mr Alderman,' said she to the colonel, 'I make no question but she is got into much better company than her husband's.' 'How can you be so cruel, madam,' said the shepherdess, 'you will make him beat his wife by and by, for he is a military man I assure you.' 'In the trained bands[10] I presume,' cries the domino, 'for he is plainly dated from the city.' – 'I own, indeed,' cries the other, 'the gentleman smells strongly of Thames Street,[11] and, if I may venture to guess, of the honourable calling of a taylor.'

'Why, what the devil hast thou pick'd up here?' cries James.

'Upon my soul, I don't know,' answered Booth; 'I wish you would take one of them at least.'

'What say you, madam,' cries the domino, 'will you go with the colonel? I assure you, you have mistaken your man, for he is no less a person than the great Colonel James himself.'

'No wonder, then, that Mr Booth gives him his choice of us; it is the proper office of a caterer, in which capacity Mr Booth hath, I am told, the honour to serve the noble colonel.'

'Much good may it do you with your ladies,' said James, 'I will go in pursuit of better game.' At which words he walked off.

'You are a true sportsman,' cries the shepherdess; 'for your only pleasure, I believe, lies in the pursuit.'

'Do you know the gentleman, madam?' cries the domino.

'Who doth not know him?' answered the shepherdess.

'What is his character?' cries the domino; 'for though I have jested with him I only know him by sight.'

'I know nothing very particular in his character,' cries the shepherdess. 'He gets every handsome woman he can, and so they do all.'

'I suppose then he is not married,' said the domino.

'O yes, and married for love too,' answered the other; 'but he hath loved away all his love for her long ago, and now, he says, she makes as fine an object of hatred. – I think if the fellow ever appears to have any wit, it is when he abuses his wife, and luckily for him, that is his favourite topick. – I don't know the poor wretch, but as he describes her, it is a miserable animal.'

'I know her very well,' cries the other, 'and I am much mistaken if she is not even with him: but hang him, what is become of Booth?'

At this instant a great noise arose near that part where the two ladies were. This was occasioned by a large assembly of young fellows, whom they call bucks, who were got together and were enjoying, as the phrase is, a letter, which one of them had found in the room.

Curiosity hath its votaries among all ranks of people, whenever therefore an object of this appears, it is as sure of attracting a croud in the assemblies of the polite, as in those of their inferiors.

When this croud was gathered together, one of the bucks, at the desire of his companions, as well as of all present, perform'd the part of a public orator, and read out the following letter, which we shall give the reader, together with the comments of the orator himself, and of all his audience.

The orator then being mounted on a bench began as follows:

'Here beginneth the first chapter of[12] – Saint – Pox on't, Jack, what is the saint's name? I have forgot.'

'Timothy, you blockhead,' answer'd another – 'Timothy.'

'Well, then,' cries the orator, 'of Saint Timothy.

'"Sir, I am very sorry to have any occasion of writing on the following subject, in a country that is honoured with the name of Christian; much more am I concern'd to address myself to a man whose many advantages derived both from nature and fortune should demand the highest return of gratitude to the great Giver of all those good things. Is not such a man guilty of the highest ingratitude to that most beneficent Being, by a direct and avowed disobedience of his most positive laws and commands?

'"I need not tell you that adultery is forbid in the laws of the Decalogue,[13] nor need I, I hope, mention, that it is as expressly forbid in the New Testament."[14]

'*You see therefore*,' said the orator, '*what the law is, and therefore none of you will be able to plead ignorance when you come to the Old Bailey*[15] *in the other world. – But here goes again.* –

'"If it had not been so expressly forbidden in Scripture, still the law of nature would have yielded light enough for us to have discovered the great horror and atrociousness of this crime.

'"And accordingly we find, that nations where the sun of righteousness hath yet never shined, have punished the adulterer with the most exemplary pains and penalties, not only the polite heathens, but the most barbarous nations have concurred in these; in many places the most severe and shameful corporal punishments, and in some, and those not a few, death itself hath been inflicted on this crime.

'"And sure in a human sense there is scarce any guilt which deserves to be more severely punished. It includes in it almost every injury and every mischief which one man can do to, or can bring on another. It is robbing him of his property."

'*Mind that, ladies*,' said the orator, '*you are all the property of your husbands*; "and of that property, which, if he is a good man, he values above all others. It is poisoning that fountain whence he hath a right to derive the sweetest and most innocent pleasure, the most cordial comfort, the most solid friendship, and most faithful assistance in all his affairs, wants and distresses. It is the destruction of his peace of mind, and even of his reputation. The ruin of both wife and husband, and sometimes of the whole family, are the probable consequence of this fatal injury. Domestic happiness is the end of almost all our pursuits, and the common reward of all our pains. When men find themselves for ever barred from this delightful fruition, they are lost to all industry, and grow careless of all their worldly affairs. Thus they become bad subjects, bad relations, bad friends and bad men. Hatred and revenge are the wretched passions which boil in their minds. Despair and madness very commonly ensue, and murder and suicide often close the dreadful scene."

'*Thus, gentlemen and ladies, you see the scene is closed. So here ends the first act – and thus begins the second.*

'"I have here attempted to lay before you a picture of this vice, the horror of which no colours of mine can exaggerate. But what pencil can delineate the horrors of that punishment which the Scripture denounces against it?

'"And for what will you subject yourself to this punishment? Or for what reward will you inflict all this misery on another? I will add on your friend? For the possession of a woman; for the pleasure of a moment? But if neither virtue nor religion can restrain your inordinate appetites, are there not many women as handsome as your friend's wife, whom, though not with innocence, you may possess with a much less degree of guilt? What motive then can thus hurry you on to the destruction of yourself and your friend? Doth the peculiar rankness of the guilt add any zest to the sin? Doth it enhance the pleasure as much as we may be assured it will the punishment?

'"But if you can be so lost to all sense of fear, and of shame, and of goodness, as not to be debarred by the evil which you are to bring on yourself, by the extreme baseness of the action, nor by the ruin in which you are to involve others, let me still urge the difficulty, I may say the impossibility of the success. You are attacking a fortress on a rock; a chastity so strongly defended, as well by a happy natural disposition of mind, as by the strongest principles of religion and virtue, implanted by education, and nourished and improved by habit, that the woman must be invincible even without that firm and constant affection of her husband, which would guard a much looser and worse disposed heart. What therefore are you attempting but to introduce distrust, and perhaps disunion between an innocent and a happy couple, in which too you cannot succeed without bringing, I am convinced, certain destruction on your own head?

'"Desist, therefore, let me advise you, from this enormous crime; retreat from the vain attempt of climbing a precipice which it is impossible you should ever ascend, where you must probably soon fall into utter perdition, and can have no other hope but of dragging down your best friend into perdition with you.

'"I can think of but one argument more, and that indeed a very bad one: you throw away that time in an impossible attempt, which might, in other places, crown your sinful endeavours with success."

'*And so ends the dismal ditty.*'

'D—n me,' cries one, 'did ever mortal hear such d—nd stuff?'

'Upon my soul,' said another, 'I like the last argument well enough. There is some sense in that: for d—n me if I had not rather go to D—g—ss[16] at any time, than follow a virtuous b— for a fortnight.'

'Tom,' says one of them, 'let us set the ditty to musick; let us subscribe to have it set by Handel, it will make an excellent oratorio.'

'D—n me, Jack,' says another, 'we'll have it set to a psalm tune, and we'll sing it next Sunday at St James's church, and I'll bear a bob,[17] d—n me.'

'Fie upon it, gentlemen, fie upon it,' said a friar who came up, 'do you think there is any wit and humour in this ribaldry; or if there were, would it make any atonement for abusing religion and virtue?'

'Hey day!' cries one, 'this is a friar in good earnest.'

'Whatever I am,' said the friar, 'I hope at least, you are what you appear to be. Heaven forbid, for the sake of our posterity, that you should be gentlemen.'

'Jack,' cries one, 'let us toss the friar in a blanket.'

'Me in a blanket!' said the friar, 'by the dignity of man, I will twist the neck of every one of you as sure as ever the neck of a dunghill-cock was twisted.' At which words he pulled off his masque, and the tremendous majesty of Colonel Bath appear'd, from which the bucks fled away as fast as the Trojans heretofore from the face of Achilles. The colonel did not think it worth while to pursue any other of them except him who had the letter in his hand, which the colonel desired to see, and the other delivered, saying it was very much at his service.

The colonel being possess'd of the letter retired as privately as he could, in order to give it a careful perusal; for badly as it had been read by the orator, there were some passages in it which had pleased the colonel. He had just gone through it when Booth passed by him; upon which the colonel called to him, and delivering him the letter, bid him put it in his pocket, and read it at his leisure. He made many encomiums upon it, and told Booth it would be of service to him, and was proper for all young men to read.

Booth had not yet seen his wife; but as he concluded she was safe with Mrs James, he was not uneasy. He had been prevented from searching farther after her, by the lady in the blue domino, who had joined him again. Booth had now made these discoveries; that the lady was pretty well acquainted with him; that she was a woman of fashion; and that she had a particular regard for him. But though he was a gay man, he was in reality so fond of his Amelia, that he thought of no other woman; wherefore, though not absolutely a Joseph,[18] as we have already seen; yet could he not be guilty of premeditated inconstancy. He was indeed so very cold and insensible to the hints which were given him, that the lady began to complain of his dulness. When the shepherdess again came up, and heard this accusation against him, she confirmed it, saying: 'I do assure you, madam, he is the dullest fellow in the world. Indeed I should almost take you for his wife, by finding you a second time with him; for I do assure you the gentleman very seldom keeps any other company.' 'Are you so well acquainted with him, madam?' said the domino. 'I have had that honour longer than your ladyship, I believe,' answered the shepherdess. 'Possibly you may, madam,' cries the domino, 'but I wish you would not interrupt us at present; for we have some business together.' 'I believe, madam,' answered the shepherdess, 'my business with the gentleman is altogether as important as yours; and therefore your ladyship may withdraw if you please.' – 'My dear ladies,' cries Booth, 'I beg you will not quarrel about me.' – 'Not at all,' answered the domino, 'since you are so indifferent, I resign my pretensions with all my heart. If you had not been the dullest fellow upon earth, I am convinced you must have discovered me.' – She then went off muttering to herself, that she was satisfied the shepherdess was some wretched creature whom no body knew.

The shepherdess overheard the sarcasm, and answered it, by asking Booth what contemptible wretch he had picked up. 'Indeed, madam,' said he, 'you know as much of her as I do; she is a masquerade acquaintance like yourself.' 'Like me!' repeated she, 'Do you think if this had been our first acquaintance, I should have wasted so much time with you as I have? For your part indeed, I believe a woman will get very little advantage by her having been formerly intimate with you.' 'I do not know, madam,' said Booth, 'that I deserve that character, any more than I know the person that now gives it me.' 'And you have the assurance then,' said she in her own voice, 'to affect not to remember me.' 'I think,' cries Booth, 'I have heard that voice before; but upon my soul I do not recollect it.' 'Do you recollect,' said she, 'no woman that you have used with the highest barbarity? I will not say ingratitude.' 'No, upon my honour,' answered Booth. 'Mention not honour,' said she, 'thou wretch: for hardened as thou art, I could shew thee a face, that in spite of thy consummate impudence, would confound thee with shame and horrour. Do'st thou not yet know me?' 'I do, madam, indeed,' answered Booth, 'and I confess, that of all women in the world you have the most reason for what you said.'

Here a long dialogue ensued between the gentleman and the lady, whom, I suppose, I need not mention to have been Miss Mathews; but as it consisted chiefly of violent upbraidings on her side, and excuses on his, I despair of making it entertaining to the reader, and shall therefore return to the colonel, who having searched all the rooms with the utmost diligence, without finding the woman he looked for, began to suspect that he had before fixed on the right person, and that Amelia had denied herself to him, being pleased with her paramour, whom he had discovered to be the noble peer.

He resolved therefore, as he could have no sport himself, to spoil that of others; accordingly he found out Booth, and asked him again what was become of both their wives; for that he had searched all over the rooms, and could find neither of them?

Booth was now a little alarmed at this account, and parting with Miss Mathews, went along with the colonel in search of his wife. As for Miss Mathews, he had at length pacified her with a promise to make her a visit; which promise she extorted from him, swearing bitterly in the most solemn manner, unless he made it to her, she would expose both him and herself at the masquerade.

As he knew the violence of the lady's passions, and to what heights they were capable of rising, he was obliged to come into these terms; for he had, I am convinced, no fear upon earth equal to that of Amelia's knowing what it was in the power of Miss Mathews to communicate to her, and which to conceal from her, he had already undergone so much uneasiness.

The colonel led Booth directly to the place where he had seen the peer and Amelia (such he was now well convinced she was) sitting together. Booth no sooner saw her, than he said to the colonel, 'sure that is my wife in conversation with that masque.' – 'I took her for your lady myself,' said the colonel; 'but I found I was mistaken. – (Hark ye, that is my lord —, and I have seen that very lady with him all this night.)'

This conversation past at a little distance, and out of the hearing of the supposed Amelia; when Booth looking stedfastly at the lady, declared with an oath that he was positive the colonel was in the right. She then beckon'd to him with her fan; upon which he went directly to her; and she asked him to go home, which he very readily consented to. The peer then walked off, the colonel went in pursuit of his wife, or of some other woman; and Booth and his lady returned in two chairs to their lodgings.

CHAPTER 3

Consequences of the masquerade, not uncommon nor surprising.

THE lady getting first out of her chair ran hastily up into the nursery to the children; for such was Amelia's constant method at her return home, at whatever hour. Booth then walked into the dining-room, where he had not been long before Amelia came down to him, and with a most chearful countenance said, 'My dear, I fancy we have neither of us supped, shall I go down and see whether there is any cold meat in the house?'

'For yourself, if you please,' answered Booth; 'but I shall eat nothing.'

'How, my dear,' said Amelia, 'I hope you have not lost your appetite at the masquerade?' For supper was a meal at which he generally eat very heartily.

'I know not well what I have lost,' said Booth; 'I find myself disordered. My head aches. I know not what is the matter with me.'

'Indeed, my dear, you frighten me,' said Amelia; 'you look indeed disordered. I wish the masquerade had been far enough, before you had gone thither.'

'Would to Heaven it had,' cries Booth; 'but that is over now. But pray, Amelia, answer me one question, who was that gentleman with you, when I came up to you?'

'The gentleman, my dear,' said Amelia, 'what gentleman?'

'The gentleman, the nobleman, when I came up; sure I speak plain.'

'Upon my word, my dear, I don't understand you,' answered she; 'I did not know one person at the masquerade.'

'How!' said he, 'what, spend the whole evening with a masque without knowing him?'

'Why, my dear,' said she, 'you know we were not together.'

'I know we were not?' said he; 'but what is that to the purpose?

sure you answer me strangely. I know we were not together; and therefore I ask you whom you were with?'

'Nay but, my dear,' said she, 'can I tell people in masques?'

'I say again, madam,' said he, 'would you converse two hours or more with a masque whom you did not know?'

'Indeed, child,' says she, 'I know nothing of the methods of a masquerade; for I never was at one in my life.'

'I wish to Heaven you had not been at this,' cries Booth. 'Nay you will wish so yourself, if you tell me truth – What have I said? do I, can I suspect you of not speaking truth? – Since you are ignorant then I will inform you, the man you have conversed with was no other than Lord —.'

'And is that the reason,' said she, 'you wish I had not been there?'

'And is not that reason,' answered he, 'sufficient? Is he not the last man upon earth with whom I would have you converse?'

'So you really wish then that I had not been at the masquerade?'

'I do,' cried he, 'from my soul.'

'So may I ever be able,' cried she, 'to indulge you in every wish as in this. – I was not there.'

'Do not trifle, Amelia,' cried he, 'you would not jest with me if you knew the situation of my mind.'

'Indeed I do not jest with you,' said she. 'Upon my honour I was not there. Forgive me this first deceit I ever practised, and indeed it shall be the last; for I have paid severely for this by the uneasiness it hath given me.' She then revealed to him the whole secret, which was thus:

I think it hath been already mentioned in some part of this history, that Amelia and Mrs Atkinson were exactly of the same make and stature, and that there was likewise a very near resemblance between their voices. When Mrs Atkinson therefore found that Amelia was so extremely averse to the masquerade, she proposed to go thither in her stead, and to pass upon Booth for his own wife.

This was afterwards very easily executed; for when they left Booth's lodgings, Amelia, who went last to her chair, ran back to fetch her masque, as she pretended, which she had purposely left behind. She then whipt off her domino, and threw it over Mrs Atkinson, who stood ready to receive it, and ran immediately down stairs, and stepping into Amelia's chair proceeded with the rest to the masquerade.

As her stature exactly suited that of Amelia, she had very little difficulty to carry on the imposition; for besides the natural resemblance of their voices, and the opportunity of speaking in a feigned one, she had scarce an intercourse of six words with Booth during the whole time; for the moment they got into the crowd, she took the first opportunity of slipping from him. And he, as the reader may remember, being seized by other women, and concluding his wife to be safe with Mrs James, was very well satisfied, till the Colonel set him upon the search, as we have seen before.

Mrs Atkinson, the moment she came home, ran up stairs to the nursery, where she found Amelia, and told her in haste that she might very easily carry on the deceit with her husband; for that she might tell him what she pleased to invent, as they had not been a minute together during the whole evening.

Booth was no sooner satisfied that his wife had not been from home that evening, than he fell into raptures with her, gave her a thousand tender caresses, blamed his own judgment, acknowledged the goodness of hers, and vowed never to oppose her will more in any one instance during his life.

Mrs Atkinson, who was still in the nursery with her masquerade dress, was then summoned down stairs; and when Booth saw her, and heard her speak in her mimic tone, he declared he was not surprised at his having been imposed upon; for that if they were both in the same disguise, he should scarce be able to discover the difference between them.

They then sat down to half an hour's chearful conversation; after which they retired all in the most perfect good humour.

CHAPTER 4

Consequences of the masquerade.

WHEN Booth rose in the morning, he found in his pocket that letter which had been delivered to him by Colonel Bath, which, had not chance brought to his remembrance, he might possibly have never recollected.

He had now however the curiosity to open the letter, and beginning to read it the matter of it drew him on, till he perused the whole; for notwithstanding the contempt cast upon it by those learned critics the bucks, neither the subject, nor the manner in which it was treated, was altogether contemptible.

But there was still another motive which induced Booth to read the whole letter; and this was, that he presently thought he knew the hand. He did indeed immediately conclude it was Dr Harrison; for the doctor wrote a very remarkable one; and this letter contained all the particularities of the doctor's character.

He had just finished a second reading of this letter, when the doctor himself entered the room. The good man was impatient to know the success of Amelia's stratagem; for he bore towards her all that love which esteem can create in a good mind, without the assistance of those selfish considerations, from which the love of wives and children may be ordinarily deduced. The latter of which Nature, by very subtle and refined reasoning, suggests to us to be part of our dear selves; and the former, as long as they remain the objects of our liking, that same Nature is furnished with very plain and fertile arguments, to recommend to our affections. But to raise that affection in the human breast, which the doctor had for Amelia, Nature is forced to use a kind of logic, which is no more understood by a bad man, than Sir Isaac Newton's doctrine of colours[19] is by one born blind. And yet in reality it contains nothing more abstruse than this, that an injury is the object of anger, danger of fear, and praise of vanity: for in the same simple manner it may be asserted, that goodness is the object of love.

The doctor enquired immediately for his child (for so he often called Amelia;) Booth answered that he had left her asleep; for that she had had but a restless night. 'I hope she is not disordered by the masquerade,' cries the doctor. Booth answered, he believed she would be very well when she waked. 'I fancy,' said he, 'her gentle spirits were a little too much fluttered last night; that is all.'

'I hope then,' said the doctor, 'you will never more insist on her going to such places, but know your own happiness in having a wife that hath the discretion to avoid those places; which, though perhaps they may not be as some represent them, such brothels of vice and debauchery, as would impeach the character of every virtuous woman who was seen at them, are certainly however scenes of riot, disorder, and intemperance, very improper to be frequented by a chaste and sober Christian matron.'

Booth declared, that he was very sensible of his error; and that so far from soliciting his wife to go to another masquerade, he did not intend ever to go thither any more himself.

The doctor highly approved the resolution; and then Booth said: 'And I thank you, my dear friend, as well as my wife's discretion, that she was not at the masquerade last night.' He then related to the doctor the discovery of the plot; and the good man was greatly pleased with the success of the stratagem, and that Booth took it in such good part.

'But, sir,' says Booth, 'I had a letter given me by a noble colonel there, which is written in a hand so very like yours, that I could almost swear to it. Nor is the stile, as far as I can guess, unlike your own. Here it is, sir. Do you own the letter, doctor, or do you not?'

The doctor took the letter, and having looked at it a moment, said – 'And did the colonel himself give you this letter?'

'The colonel himself,' answered Booth.

'Why then,' cries the doctor, 'he is surely the most impudent fellow that the world ever produced. What, did he deliver it with an air of triumph?'

'He delivered it me with air enough,' cries Booth, 'after his own manner, and bid me read it for my edification. To say the truth, I am a little surprised that he should single me out of all mankind to deliver the letter to; I do not think I deserve the character of such a husband. It is well I am not so very forward to take an affront as some folks.'

'I am glad to see you are not,' said the doctor; 'and your behaviour in this affair becomes both the man of sense and the Christian: for it would be surely the greatest folly, as well as the most daring impiety, to risque your own life for the impertinence of a fool. As long as you are assured of the virtue of your own wife, it is wisdom in you to despise the efforts of such a wretch. Not indeed that your wife accuses him of any downright attack, though she hath observed enough in his behaviour to give offence to her delicacy.'

'You astonish me, doctor,' said Booth. 'What can you mean? My wife dislike his behaviour! Hath the colonel ever offended her?'

'I do not say he hath ever offended her by any open declarations. – Nor hath he done any thing which, according to the most romantic notion of honour, you can or ought to resent; but there is something extremely nice in the chastity of a truly virtuous woman.'

'And hath my wife really complained of any thing of that kind in the colonel?'

'Look ye, young gentleman,' cries the doctor, 'I will have no quarrelling, or challenging; I find I have made some mistake, and therefore I insist upon it, by all the rights of friendship, that you give me your word of honour you will not quarrel with the colonel on this account.'

'I do with all my heart,' said Booth; 'for if I did not know your character, I should absolutely think you was jesting with me. I do not think you have mistaken my wife; but I am sure she hath mistaken the colonel; and hath misconstrued some overstrained point of gallantry, something of the Quixote kind, into a design against her chastity; but I have that opinion of the colonel, that I hope you will not be offended, when I declare I know not which of you two I should be the sooner jealous of.'

'I would by no means have you jealous of any one,' cries the doctor; 'for I think my child's virtue may be firmly relied on; but I am convinced she would not have said what she did to me, without a cause; nor should I, without such a conviction, have written that letter to the colonel, as I own to you I did. However, nothing I say hath yet past which, even in the opinion of false honour, you are at liberty to resent; but as to declining any great intimacy, if you will take my advice, I think that would be prudent.'

'You will pardon me, my dearest friend,' said Booth, 'but I have really such an opinion of the colonel, that I would pawn my life upon his honour; and as for women, I do not believe he ever had an attachment to any.'

'Be it so,' said the doctor. 'I have only two things to insist on. The first is, that if ever you change your opinion, this letter may not be the subject of any quarrelling or fighting: the other is, that you never mention a word of this to your wife. By the latter I shall see whether you can keep a secret; and if it is no otherwise material, it will be a wholesome exercise to your mind; for the practice of any virtue is a kind of mental exercise, and serves to maintain the health and vigour of the soul.'

'I faithfully promise both,' cries Booth. And now the breakfast entered the room, as did soon after Amelia, and Mrs Atkinson.

The conversation ran chiefly on the masquerade; and Mrs Atkinson gave an account of several adventures there; but whether she told the whole truth with regard to herself, I will not determine. For certain it is, she never once mentioned the name of the noble peer. Amongst the rest, she said there was a young fellow that had preached a sermon there upon a stool, in praise of adultery she believed; for she could not get near enough to hear the particulars.

During that transaction, Booth had been engaged with the blue domino in another room, so that he knew nothing of it; so that what Mrs Atkinson now said, only brought to his mind the doctor's letter to Colonel Bath; for to him he supposed it was written; and the idea of the colonel being a lover to Amelia struck him in so ridiculous a light, that it threw him into a violent fit of laughter.

The doctor, who, from the natural jealousy of an author, imputed the agitation of Booth's muscles to his own sermon, or letter on that subject, was a little offended, and said gravely: 'I should be glad to know the reason of this immoderate mirth. Is adultery a matter of jest in your opinion?'

'Far otherwise,' answer'd Booth. 'But how is it possible to

refrain from laughter at the idea of a fellow preaching a sermon in favour of it at such a place.'

'I am very sorry,' cries the doctor, 'to find the age is grown to so scandalous a degree of licentiousness; that we have thrown off not only virtue, but decency. How abandoned must be the manners of any nation where such insults upon religion and morality can be committed with impunity? No man is fonder of true wit and humour than myself; but to profane sacred things with jest and scoffing is a sure sign of a weak and a wicked mind. It is the very vice which Homer attacks in the odious character of Thersites.[20] The ladies must excuse my repeating the passage to you, as I know you have Greek enough to understand it.

> Ὃς ῥ' ἔπεα φρεσὶν ησιν ἄκοσμά τε, πολλά τε ηδη.
> Μὰψ, ἀτὰρ οὐ κατὰ κόσμον ἐριζέμεναι βασιλεῦσιν,
> 'Αλλ' ὅ, τι οἷ εἴσαιτο γελοΐον 'Αργείοισιν
> Ἔμμεναι.*

And immediately adds,

> —αἴσχιστος δὲ ανὴρ ὑπὸ Ἴλιον ἦλθε.†

Horace[21] again describes such a rascal.

> – *Solutos*
> *Qui captat risus hominum famamque dicacis.*§

And says of him,

> —*Hic niger est, hunc tu, Romane, caveto.*'‖

'O charming Homer,' said Mrs Atkinson, 'how much above all other writers!'

'I ask your pardon, madam,' said the doctor, 'I forgot you was a

* Thus paraphrased by Mr Pope.
Aw'd by no shame, by no respect controll'd,
In scandal busy, in reproaches bold:
With witty malice studious to defame,
Scorn all his joy, and laughter all his aim.

† *He was the greatest scoundrel in the whole army.*

§ *Who trivial bursts of laughter strives to raise,*
And courts of prating petulance the praise.
FRANCIS.[22]

‖ *This man is black, do thou, O Roman, shun this man.*

scholar; but indeed I did not know you understood Greek as well as Latin.'

'I do not pretend,' said she, 'to be a critic in the Greek; but I think I am able to read a little of Homer, at least with the help of looking now and then into the Latin.'[23]

'Pray, madam,' said the doctor, 'how do you like this passage in the speech of Hector to Andromache?

—Εἰς οἶκον ἰουσα τὰ σαυτῆς ἔργα κόμιζε,
Ἱστόν τ' ἠλακάτην τε, καὶ ἀμφιπόλοισι κέλευε
Ἔργον ἐποίχεσθαι.*

'Or how do you like the character of Hippodamia, who, by being the prettiest girl, and best workwoman of her age, got one of the best husbands in all Troy? – I think, indeed, Homer[25] enumerates her discretion with her other qualifications; but I do not remember he gives us one character of a woman of learning. – Don't you conceive this to be a great omission in that charming poet? However, Juvenal[26] makes you amends, for he talks very abundantly of the learning of the Roman ladies in his time.'

'You are a provoking man, doctor,' said Mrs Atkinson, 'Where is the harm in a woman's having learning as well as a man?'

'Let me ask you another question,' said the doctor. 'Where is the harm in a man's being a fine performer with a needle as well as a woman? And yet, answer me honestly, would you greatly chuse to marry a man with a thimble upon his finger? Would you in earnest think a needle became the hand of your husband as well as a halberd?'

'As to war, I am with you,' said she. 'Homer himself, I well remember, makes Hector tell his wife, that warlike works – what is the Greek word – pollemy[27] – something – belonged to men only; and I readily agree to it. I hate a masculine woman, an amazon, as much as you can do; but what is there masculine in learning?'

'Nothing so masculine, take my word for it. As for your Pollemy, I look upon it to be the true characteristic of a devil. So Homer every where characterizes Mars.'

* *Go home and mind your own business. Follow your spinning, and keep your maids to their work.*[24]

'Indeed, my dear,' cries the serjeant, 'you had better not dispute with the doctor; for upon my word, he will be too hard for you.'

'Nay, I beg *you* will not interfere,' cries Mrs Atkinson, 'I am sure *you* can be no judge in these matters.'

At which the doctor and Booth burst into a loud laugh; and Amelia, though fearful of giving her friend offence, could not forbear a gentle smile.

'You may laugh, gentlemen, if you please,' said Mrs Atkinson; 'but I thank Heaven, I have married a man who is not jealous of my understanding. I should have been the most miserable woman upon earth with a starched pedant, who was possessed of that nonsensical opinion, that the difference of sexes causes any difference in the mind. Why don't you honestly avow the Turkish notion, that women have no souls;[28] for you say the same thing in effect?'

'Indeed, my dear,' cries the serjeant, greatly concerned to see his wife so angry, 'you have mistaken the doctor.'

'I beg, my dear,' cried she, '*you* will say nothing upon these subjects. – I hope *you* at least do not despise my understanding.'

'I assure you, I do not,' said the serjeant, 'and I hope you will never despise mine; for a man may have some understanding, I hope, without learning.'

Mrs Atkinson reddened extremely at these words; and the doctor fearing he had gone too far began to soften matters, in which Amelia assisted him. By these means the storm rising in Mrs Atkinson before was in some measure laid, at least suspended from bursting at present; but it fell afterwards upon the poor serjeant's head in a torrent; who had learn'd perhaps one maxim from his trade, that a cannon-ball always doth mischief in proportion to the resistance it meets with; and that nothing so effectually deadens its force as a wool-pack. The serjeant therefore bore all with patience; and the idea of a wool-pack perhaps bringing that of a featherbed into his head, he at last not only quieted his wife; but she cried out with great sincerity, 'Well, my dear, I will say one thing for you, that I believe from my soul, though you have no learning, you have the best understanding of any man upon earth; and I must own I think the latter far the more profitable of the two.'

Far different was the idea she entertained of the doctor, whom, from this day, she considered as a conceited pedant, nor could all Amelia's endeavours ever alter her sentiments.

The doctor now took his leave of Booth and his wife for a week, he intending to set out within an hour or two with his old friend, with whom our readers were a little acquainted at the latter end of the ninth book, and of whom perhaps they did not then conceive the most favourable opinion.

Nay I am aware that the esteem which some readers before had for the doctor, may be here lessened; since he may appear to have been too easy a dupe to the gross flattery of the old gentleman. If there be any such critics, we are heartily sorry as well for them as for the doctor; but it is our business to discharge the part of a faithful historian, and to describe human nature as it is, not as we would wish it to be.

CHAPTER 5

In which Colonel Bath appears in great glory.

THAT afternoon, as Booth was walking in the Park, he met with Colonel Bath, who presently asked him for the letter which he had given him the night before, upon which Booth immediately returned it.

'Don't you think,' cries Bath, 'it is writ with great dignity of expression and emphasis of – of – of judgment?'

'I am surprised though,' cries Booth, 'that any one should write such a letter to you, colonel.'

'To me?' said Bath. – 'What do you mean, sir, I hope you don't imagine any man durst write such a letter to me? D—n me, if I knew a man who thought me capable of debauching my friend's wife, I would — d—n me.'

'I believe indeed, sir,' cries Booth, 'that no man living dares put his name to such a letter: But you see it is anonymous.'

'I don't know what you mean by *ominous*,' cries the colonel; 'but, blast my reputation, if I had received such a letter, if I would not have searched the world to have found the writer. D—n me, I would have gone to the East Indies to have pulled off his nose.'

'He would indeed have deserved it,' cries Booth. – 'But pray, sir, how came you by it?'

'I took it,' said the colonel, 'from a set of idle young rascals, one of whom was reading it out aloud upon a stool, while the rest were attempting to make a jest, not only of the letter, but of all decency, virtue and religion. A set of fellows that you must have seen or heard of about town, that are, d—n me, a disgrace to the dignity of manhood; puppies that mistake noise and impudence, rudeness and profaneness for wit. If the drummers of my company had not more understanding than twenty such fellows, I'd have them both whipt out of the regiment.'

'So then you do not know the person to whom it was writ,' said Booth.

'Lieutenant,' cries the colonel, 'your question deserves no answer. I ought to take time to consider whether I ought not to resent the supposition. Do you think, sir, I am acquainted with a rascal?'

'I do not suppose, Colonel,' cries Booth, 'that you would willingly cultivate an intimacy with such a person; but a man must have good luck who hath any acquaintance, if there are not some rascals among them.'

'I am not offended with you, child,' says the colonel. 'I know you did not intend to offend me.'

'No man, I believe, dares intend it,' said Booth.

'I believe so too,' said the colonel, 'd—n me, I know it. But you know, child, how tender I am on this subject. If I had been ever married myself, I should have cleft the man's scull who had dar'd look wantonly at my wife.'

'It is certainly the most cruel of all injuries,' said Booth. 'How finely doth Shakespeare express it in his Othello![29]

But there, where I had treasur'd up my soul.'

'That Shakespeare,' cries the colonel, 'was a fine fellow. He was a very pretty poet indeed. Was it not Shakespeare that wrote the play about Hotspur? You must remember these lines. I got them almost by heart at the play-house; for I never missed that play whenever it was acted, if I was in town.

By heav'n it was an easy leap,
To pluck bright honour into the full moon.
Or drive into the bottomless deep.[30]

'And – and – faith, I have almost forgot them; but I know it is something about saving your honour from drowning – O it is very fine. I say, d—n me, the man that writ those lines was the greatest poet the world ever produced. There is dignity of expression and emphasis of thinking, d—n me.'

Booth assented to the colonel's criticism, and then cried, 'I wish, colonel, you would be so kind to give me that letter.' The colonel answered, if he had any particular use for it, he would give it him with all his heart, and presently delivered it; and soon afterwards they parted.

Several passages now struck all at once upon Booth's mind, which gave him great uneasiness. He became confident now that he had mistaken one colonel for another; and though he could not account for the letter's getting into those hands from whom Bath had taken it (indeed James had dropt it out of his pocket) yet a thousand circumstances left him no room to doubt the identity of the person, who was a man much more liable to raise the suspicion of a husband than honest Bath, who would at any time have rather fought with a man than lain with a woman.

The whole behaviour of Amelia now rushed upon his memory. Her resolution not to take up her residence at the colonel's house; her backwardness even to dine there, her unwillingness to go to the masquerade, many of her unguarded expressions, and some where she had been more guarded, all joined together to raise such an idea in Mr Booth, that he had almost taken a resolution to go and cut the colonel to pieces in his own house. Cooler thoughts, however, suggested themselves to him in time. He recollected the promise he had so solemnly made to the doctor. He considered moreover, that he was yet in the dark, as to the extent of the colonel's guilt. Having nothing therefore to fear from it, he contented himself to postpone a resentment which he nevertheless resolved to take of the colonel hereafter, if he found he was in any degree a delinquent.

The first step he determined to take was, on the first opportunity, to relate to Colonel James the means by which he became possessed of the letter, and to read it to him. On which occasion he thought he should easily discern by the behaviour of the colonel, whether he had been suspected either by Amelia or the doctor without a cause: but as for his wife, he fully resolved not to reveal the secret to her till the doctor's return.

While Booth was deeply engaged by himself in these meditations, Captain Trent came up to him, and familiarly slapp'd him on the shoulder.

They were soon joined by a third gentleman, and presently afterwards by a fourth, both acquaintances of Mr Trent, and all having walked twice the length of the Mall[31] together, it being now past nine in the evening, Trent proposed going to the tavern, to which the strangers immediately consented; and Booth himself, after some resistance, was at length persuaded to comply.

To the King's Arms then they went, where the bottle went very briskly round till after eleven; at which time Trent proposed a game at cards, to which proposal likewise Booth's consent was obtain'd, though not without much difficulty; for though he had naturally some inclination to gaming, and had formerly a little indulged it; yet he had entirely left it off for many years.

Booth and his friend were partners, and had at first some success; but Fortune, according to her usual conduct, soon shifted about, and persecuted Booth with such malice, that in about two hours he was strip'd of all the gold in his pocket, which amounted to twelve guineas, being more than half the cash which he was at that time worth.

How easy it is for a man who is at all tainted with the itch of gaming, to leave off play in such a situation, especially when he is likewise heated with liquor, I leave to the gamesters to determine. Certain it is, that Booth had no inclination to desist; but, on the contrary, was so eagerly bent on playing on, that he called his friend out of the room, and asked him for ten pieces, which he promised punctually to pay the next morning.

Trent chid him for using so much formality on the occasion. 'You know,' said he, 'dear Booth, you may have what money you please of me. Here is a £20 note, at your service, and if you want five times the sum, it is at your service. We will never let these fellows go away with our money in this manner; for we have so much the advantage, that if the knowing ones were here, they would lay odds of our side.'

But if this was really Mr Trent's opinion, he was very much mistaken; for the other two honourable gentlemen were not only greater masters of the game, and somewhat soberer than poor Booth, having with all the art in their power evaded the bottle; but they had moreover another small advantage over their adversaries, both of them, by means of some certain private signs, previously agreed upon between them, being always acquainted with the principal cards in each other's hands. It cannot be wonder'd therefore, that Fortune was on their side; for however she may be reported to favour fools, she never I believe shews them any countenance when they engage in play with knaves.

The more Booth lost, the deeper he made his bets; the consequence of which was, that about two in the morning, besides the loss of his own money, he was £50 indebted to Trent. A sum indeed, which he would not have borrowed, had not the other, like a very generous friend, push'd it upon him.

Trent's pockets became at last dry, by means of these loans. His own loss indeed was trifling; for the stakes of the games were no higher than crowns; and betting, (as it is called) was that to which Booth owed his ruin. The gentlemen therefore, pretty well knowing Booth's circumstances, and being kindly unwilling to win more of a man than he was worth, declined playing any longer, nor did Booth once ask them to persist; for he was ashamed of the debt which he had already contracted to Trent, and very far from desiring to encrease it.

The company then separated. The two victors and Trent went off in their chairs to their several houses near Grosvenor Square;[32] and poor Booth, in a melancholy mood, walk'd home to his lodgings. He was indeed in such a fit of despair, that it more than once came into his head to put an end to his miserable being.

But before we introduce him to Amelia, we must do her the justice to relate the manner in which she spent this unhappy evening. It was about seven when Booth left her to walk in the Park: from this time till past eight she was employ'd with her children, in playing with them, in giving them their supper, and in putting them to bed.

When these offices were performed, she employ'd herself another hour in cooking up a little supper for her husband, this being, as we have already observed, his favourite meal, as indeed it was hers; and in a most pleasant and delightful manner they generally passed their time at this season, though their fare was very seldom of the sumptuous kind.

It now grew dark, and her hashed mutton was ready for the table, but no Booth appear'd. Having waited therefore for him a full hour, she gave him over for that evening; nor was she much alarmed at his absence, as she knew he was in a night or two to be at the tavern with some brother officers. She concluded therefore that they had met in the Park, and had agreed to spend this evening together.

At ten then she sat down to supper by herself; for Mrs Atkinson was then abroad. And here we cannot help relating a little incident, however trivial it may appear to some. Having sat some time alone reflecting on their distress'd situation, her spirits grew very low; and she was once or twice going to ring the bell to send her maid for half a pint of white-wine, but check'd her inclination in order to save the little sum of sixpence; which she did the more resolutely as she had before refused to gratify her children with tarts for their supper from the same motive. And this self-denial she was very probably practising, to save sixpence, while her husband was paying a debt of several guineas incurred by the ace of trumps being in the hands of his adversary.

Instead therefore of this cordial she took up one of the excellent Farquhar's comedies,[33] and read it half through, when the clock striking twelve, she retired to bed, leaving the maid to sit up for her master. She would indeed have much more willingly sat up herself; but the delicacy of her own mind assured her that Booth would not thank her for the compliment. This is indeed a method which some wives take of upbraiding their husbands for staying abroad till too late an hour, and of engaging them, thro' tenderness and good-nature, never to enjoy the company of their friends too long, when they must do this at the expence of their wives' rest.

To bed then she went, but not to sleep. Thrice indeed she told the dismal clock, and as often heard the more dismal watchman, till her miserable husband found his way home, and stole silently, like a thief, to bed to her; at which time pretending then first to awake she threw her snowy arms around him; though, perhaps, the more witty property of snow, according to Addison,[34] that is to say, its coldness, rather belonged to the poor captain.

CHAPTER 6

Read, gamester, and observe.

BOOTH could not so well disguise the agitations of his mind from Amelia, but that she perceived sufficient symptoms to assure her that some misfortune had befallen him. This made her in her turn so uneasy, that Booth took notice of it, and after breakfast said, 'Sure, my dear Emily, something hath fallen out to vex you.'

Amelia looking tenderly at him answered, 'Indeed, my dear, you are in the right. I am indeed extremely vexed.' 'For Heaven's sake,' said he, 'what is it?' 'Nay, my love,' cries she, 'that you must answer yourself. Whatever it is which hath given you all that disturbance that you in vain endeavour to conceal from me, this it is which causes all my affliction.'

'You guess truly, my sweet,' replied Booth; 'I am indeed afflicted, and I will not, nay I cannot conceal the truth from you. I have undone myself, Amelia.'

'What have you done, child?' said she, in some consternation, 'pray tell me.'

'I have lost my money at play,' answered he.

'Pugh!' said she, recovering herself, – 'what signifies the trifle you had in your pocket? Resolve never to play again, and let it give you no further vexation. I warrant you we will contrive some method to repair such a loss.'

'Thou heavenly angel, thou comfort of my soul,' cried Booth tenderly embracing her. – Then starting a little from her arms, and looking with eager fondness in her eyes, he said, 'Let me survey thee, art thou really human, or art thou not rather an angel in a human form? – O, no,' cried he, flying again into her arms, 'thou art my dearest woman, my best, my beloved wife.'

Amelia having returned all his caresses with equal kindness told him she had near eleven guineas in her purse, and asked how much she should fetch him. – 'I would not advise you, Billy, to carry too much in your pocket, for fear it should be a temptation to you to return to gaming, in order to retrieve your past losses. Let me beg you, on all accounts, never to think more, if possible, on the trifle you have lost, any more than if you had never possessed it.'

Booth promised her faithfully he never would, and refused to take any of the money. He then hesitated a moment – and cried – 'You say, my dear, you have eleven guineas; you have a diamond ring likewise, which was your grandmother's, I believe that is worth twenty pound; and your own and the child's watch are worth as much more.'

'I believe they would sell for as much,' cried Amelia; 'for a pawnbroker of Mrs Atkinson's acquaintance offered to lend me thirty-five pounds upon them, when you was in your last distress – But why are you computing their value now?'

'I was only considering,' answered he, 'how much we could raise in any case of exigency.'

'I have computed it myself,' said she; 'and I believe all we have in the world, besides our bare necessary apparel, would produce about sixty pounds: and suppose, my dear,' said she, 'while we have that little sum, we should think of employing it some way or other to procure some small subsistence for ourselves and our family. As for your dependance on the colonel's friendship, it is all vain, I am afraid, and fallacious. Nor do I see any hopes you have from any other quarter, of providing for yourself again in the army. And though the sum which is now in our power is very small; yet we may possibly contrive with it to put ourselves into some mean way of livelihood. I have a heart, my Billy, which is capable of undergoing any thing for your sake; and I hope my hands are as able to work, as those which have been more inured to it. But think, my dear, think what must be our wretched condition, when the very little we now have, is all moulder'd away, as it will soon be in this town.'

When poor Booth heard this, and reflected that the time which Amelia foresaw was already arrived (for that he had already lost every farthing they were worth) it touched him to the quick; he turned pale, gnashed his teeth, and cried out, 'Damnation! this is too much to bear.'

Amelia was thrown into the utmost consternation by this behaviour, and with great terror in her countenance cried out, 'Good Heavens, my dear love, what is the reason of this agony?'

'Ask me no questions,' cried he, 'unless you would drive me to madness.'

'My Billy, my love,' said she, 'what can be the meaning of this? – I beg you will deal openly with me, and tell me all your griefs.'

'Have you dealt fairly with me, Amelia?' said he.

'Yes surely,' said she, 'Heaven is my witness how fairly.'

'Nay, do not call Heaven,' cried he, 'to witness a falsehood. You have not dealt openly with me, Amelia. You have concealed secrets from me; secrets which I ought to have known, and which if I had known, it had been better for us both.'

'You astonish me, as much as you shock me,' cried she. 'What falsehood, what treachery have I been guilty of?'

'You tell me,' said he, 'that I can have no reliance on James, why did you not tell me so before?'

'I call Heaven again,' said she, 'to witness; nay I appeal to yourself for the truth of it; I have often told you so. I have told you I disliked the man, notwithstanding the many favours he had done you. I desired you not to have too absolute a reliance upon him. I own I had once an extreme good opinion of him, but I changed it, and I acquainted you that I had so –'

'But not,' cries he, 'with the reasons why you had changed it.'

'I was really afraid, my dear,' said she, 'of going too far. I knew the obligations you had to him; and if I suspected that he acted rather from vanity than true friendship –'

'Vanity!' cries he, 'take care, Amelia, you know his motive to be much worse than vanity – a motive, which if he had piled obligations on me till they had reached the skies, would tumble all down to hell. It is in vain to conceal it longer – I know all – your confidant hath told me all.'

'Nay then,' cries she, 'on my knees I entreat you to be pacified, and hear me out. It was, my dear, for you, my dread of your jealous honour, and the fatal consequences.'

'Is not Amelia then,' cried he, 'equally jealous of my honour!

Would she, from a weak tenderness for my person, go privately about to betray, to undermine the most invaluable treasure of my soul? Would she have me pointed at as the credulous dupe, the easy fool, the tame, the kind cuckold of a rascal, with whom I conversed as a friend?'

'Indeed you injure me,' said Amelia. 'Heaven forbid I should have the trial; but I think I could sacrifice all I hold most dear to preserve your honour. I think I have shewn I can. But I will – when you are cool, I will – satisfy you I have done nothing you ought to blame.'

'I am cool then,' cries he – 'I will with the greatest coolness hear you. – But do not think, Amelia, I have the least jealousy, the least suspicion, the least doubt of your honour. It is your want of confidence in me alone which I blame.'

'When you are calm,' cried she, 'I will speak, and not before.'

He assured her he was calm; and then she said – 'You have justified my conduct by your present passion, in concealing from you my suspicions; for they were no more, nay it is possible they were unjust: for since the doctor, in betraying the secret to you, hath so far falsified my opinion of him, why may I not be as well deceived in my opinion of the colonel; since it was only formed on some particulars in his behaviour, which I disliked? for upon my honour he never spoke a word to me, nor hath been ever guilty of any direct action which I could blame.' She then went on, and related most of the circumstances which she had mentioned to the doctor, omitting one or two of the strongest, and giving such a turn to the rest, that if Booth had not had some of Othello's blood in him, his wife would have almost appeared a prude in his eyes. Even he, however, was pretty well pacified by this narrative, and said he was glad to find a possibility of the colonel's innocence, but that he greatly commended the prudence of his wife, and only wished she would for the future make him her only confidant.

Amelia upon that expressed some bitterness against the doctor for breaking his trust, when Booth in his excuse related all the circumstances of the letter, and plainly convinced her, that the secret had dropt by mere accident from the mouth of the doctor.

Thus the husband and wife became again reconciled, and poor

Amelia generously forgave a passion, of which the sagacious reader is better acquainted with the real cause, than was that unhappy lady.

CHAPTER 7

In which Booth receives a visit from Captain Trent.

WHEN Booth grew perfectly cool, and began to reflect that he had broken his word to the doctor, in having made the discovery to his wife, which we have seen in the last chapter, that thought gave him great uneasiness; and now to comfort him, Captain Trent came to make him a visit. This was indeed almost the last man in the world, whose company he wished for; for he was the only man he was ashamed to see, for a reason well known to gamesters; among whom the most dishonourable of all things, is not to pay a debt, contracted at the gaming-table, the next day, or the next time at least that you see the party.

Booth made no doubt, but that Trent was come on purpose to receive this debt; the latter had been therefore scarce a minute in the room, before Booth began, in an aukward manner, to apologize; but Trent immediately stopt his mouth, and said, 'I do not want the money, Mr Booth, and you may pay it me whenever you are able; and if you are never able, I assure you I will never ask you for it.'

This generosity raised such a tempest of gratitude in Booth (if I may be allowed the expression) that the tears burst from his eyes, and it was some time before he could find any utterance for those sentiments with which his mind overflowed; but when he began to express his thankfulness, Trent immediately stopt him, and gave a sudden turn to their discourse.

Mrs Trent had been to visit Mrs Booth on the masquerade evening, which visit Mrs Booth had not yet returned. Indeed this was only the second day since she had received it. Trent therefore now told his friend, that he should take it extremely kind if he and his lady would wave all ceremony, and sup at their house the next evening. Booth hesitated a moment – but presently said, 'I am pretty certain my wife is not engaged, and I will undertake for her. I am sure she will not refuse any thing Mr Trent can ask.' And soon after Trent took Booth with him to walk in the Park.

There were few greater lovers of a bottle than Trent; he soon proposed therefore to adjourn to the King's Arms tavern, where Booth, though much against his inclination, accompanied him. But Trent was very importunate, and Booth did not think himself at liberty to refuse such a request to a man, from whom he had so lately received such obligations.

When they came to the tavern, however, Booth recollected the omission he had been guilty of the night before. He wrote a short note therefore to his wife, acquainting her that he should not come home to supper; but comforted her with a faithful promise that he would on no account engage himself in gaming.

The first bottle past in ordinary conversation; but when they had tapped the second, Booth, on some hints which Trent gave him, very fairly laid open to him his whole circumstances, and declared he almost despaired of mending them. 'My chief relief,' said he, 'was in the interest of Colonel James; but I have given up those hopes.'

'And very wisely too,' said Trent. 'I say nothing of the colonel's good will. Very likely he may be your sincere friend; but I do not believe he hath the interest he pretends to. He hath had too many favours in his own family, to ask any more yet a while. But I am mistaken, if you have not a much more powerful friend than the colonel; one who is both able and willing to serve you. I dined at his table within these two days, and I never heard kinder nor warmer expressions from the mouth of man, than he made use of towards you. I make no doubt you know whom I mean.'

'Upon my honour I do not,' answered Booth; 'nor did I guess that I had such a friend in the world as you mention.'

'I am glad then,' cries Trent, 'that I have the pleasure of informing you of it.' He then named the noble peer, who hath been already so often mentioned in this history.

Booth turned pale and started at his name. 'I forgive you, my dear Trent,' cries Booth, 'for mentioning his name to me, as you are a stranger to what hath past between us.'

'Nay, I know nothing that hath past between you,' answered

Trent. 'I am sure if there is any quarrel between you of two days standing, all is forgiven on his part.'

'D—n his forgiveness,' said Booth. 'Perhaps I ought to blush at what I have forgiven.'

'You surprise me,' cries Trent. 'Pray, what can be the matter?'

'Indeed, my dear Trent,' cries Booth very gravely, 'he would have injured me in the tenderest part. I know not how to tell it you; but he would have dishonoured me with my wife.'

'Sure you are not in earnest,' answered Trent; 'but if you are, you will pardon me for thinking that impossible.'

'Indeed,' cries Booth, 'I have so good an opinion of my wife, as to believe it impossible for him to succeed; but that he should intend me the favour you will not, I believe, think an impossibility.'

'Faith! not in the least,' said Trent. 'Mrs Booth is a very fine woman; and if I had the honour to be her husband, I should not be angry with any man for liking her.'

'But you would be angry,' said Booth, 'with a man, who should make use of stratagems and contrivances to seduce her virtue; especially if he did this under the colour of entertaining the highest friendship for yourself.'

'Not at all,' cries Trent. 'It is human nature.'

'Perhaps it is,' cries Booth; 'but it is human nature depraved, stript of all its worth, and loveliness and dignity, and degraded down to a level with the vilest brutes.'

'Look ye, Booth,' cries Trent, 'I would not be misunderstood. I think, when I am talking to you, I talk to a man of sense, and to an inhabitant of this country; not to one who dwells in a land of saints. If you have really such an opinion as you express of this noble lord, you have the finest opportunity of making a complete fool and bubble of him that any man can desire, and of making your own fortune at the same time. I do not say that your suspicions are groundless; for of all men upon earth I know, my lord is the greatest bubble to women, though I believe he hath had very few. And this I am confident of, that he hath not the least jealousy of these suspicions. Now, therefore, if you will act the part of a wise man, I will undertake that you shall make your fortune without the least injury to the chastity of Mrs Booth.'

'I do not understand you, sir,' said Booth.

'Nay,' cries Trent, 'if you will not understand me I have done. I meant only your service; and I thought I had known you better.'

Booth begged him to explain himself. 'If you can,' said he, 'shew me any way to improve such circumstances as I have opened to you, you may depend on it I shall readily embrace it, and own my obligations to you.'

'That is spoken like a man,' cries Trent. 'Why, what is it more than this? Carry your suspicions in your own bosom. Let Mrs Booth, in whose virtue I am sure you may be justly confident, go to the public places; there let her treat my lord with common civility only; I am sure he will bite. And thus without suffering him to gain his purpose, you will gain yours. I know several who have succeeded with him in this manner.'

'I am very sorry, sir,' cries Booth, 'that you are acquainted with any such rascals. I do assure you, rather than I would act such a part I would submit to the hardest sentence that Fortune could pronounce against me.'

'Do as you please, sir,' said Trent; 'I have only ventured to advise you as a friend. But do you not think your nicety is a little over-scrupulous?'

'You will excuse me, sir,' said Booth; 'but I think no man can be too scrupulous in points which concern his honour.'

'I know many men of very nice honour,' answered Trent, 'who have gone much farther; and no man, I am sure, had ever a better excuse for it than yourself. – You will forgive me, Booth, since what I speak proceeds from my love to you; nay, indeed, by mentioning your affairs to me, which I am heartily sorry for, you have given me a right to speak. You know best what friends you have to depend upon; but if you have no other pretensions than your merit, I can assure you, you would fail if it was possible you could have ten times more merit than you have. And if you love your wife, as I am convinced you do, what must be your condition, in seeing her want the necessaries of life?'

'I know my condition is very hard,' cries Booth; 'but I have one comfort in it, which I will never part with, and that is innocence. As to the mere necessaries of life, however, it is pretty difficult to deprive us of them; this I am sure of, no one can want them long.'

'Upon my word, sir,' cries Trent, 'I did not know you had been so great a philosopher; but believe me, these matters look much less terrible at a distance, than when they are actually present. You will then find, I am afraid, that honour hath no more skill in cookery, than Shakespeare tells us it hath in surgery.[35] – D—n me if I don't wish his lordship loved my wife as well as he doth yours, I promise you I would trust her virtue; and if he should get the better of it, I should have people of fashion enough to keep me in countenance.'

Their second bottle being now almost out, Booth, without making any answer, called for a bill. Trent prest very much the drinking another bottle; but Booth absolutely refused, and presently afterwards they parted, not extremely well satisfied with each other. They appeared indeed one to the other in disadvantageous lights of a very different kind. Trent concluded Booth to be a very silly fellow; and Booth began to suspect that Trent was very little better than a scoundrel.

CHAPTER 8

Contains a letter and other matters.

WE WILL now return to Amelia, to whom immediately upon her husband's departure to walk with Mr Trent, a porter brought the following letter, which she immediately opened and read.

MADAM,

The quick dispatch which I have given to your first commands will, I hope, assure you of the diligence with which I shall always obey every command that you are pleased to honour me with. I have indeed in this trifling affair, acted as if my life itself had been at stake, nay, I know not but it may be so: for this insignificant matter you was pleased to tell me would oblige the charming person in whose power is not only my happiness; but as I am well persuaded my life too. Let me reap therefore some little advantage in your eyes as you have in mine from this trifling occasion: for if any thing could add to the charms of which you are mistress; it would be perhaps that amiable zeal with which you maintain the cause of your friend. I hope indeed she will be my friend and advocate with the most lovely of her sex, as I think she hath reason, and as you was pleased to insinuate she had been: Let me beseech you, madam, let not that dear heart whose tenderness is so inclin'd to compassionate the miseries of others, be harden'd only against the sufferings which itself occasions. Let not that man alone have reason to think you cruel, who of all others would do the most to procure your kindness. How often have I lived over in my reflections, in my dreams, those two short minutes we were together? but alas! how faint are these mimickries of the imagination! What would I not give to purchase the reality of such another blessing! This, madam, is in your power to bestow on the man who hath no wish, no will, no fortune, no heart, no life, but what are at your disposal. Grant me only the favour to be at Lady —'s assembly. – You can have nothing to fear from indulging me with a moment's sight, a moment's conversation. I will ask no more. I know your delicacy, and had rather die than offend it. Could I have seen you sometimes, I believe the fear of offending you would have kept my love for ever buried in my own bosom; but to be totally excluded even from the sight of what my soul doats on is what I cannot bear. It is that alone which hath extorted the fatal secret from me. Let that obtain your forgiveness for me. I need not sign this letter, otherwise than with that impression of my heart which I hope it bears; and to conclude it in any form, no language hath words of devotion strong enough to tell you with what truth, what anguish, what zeal, what adoration I love you.

Amelia had just strength to hold out to the end, when her trembling grew so violent, that she dropt the letter, and had probably dropt herself, had not Mrs Atkinson come timely in to support her.

'Good Heavens!' cries Mrs Atkinson, 'What is the matter with you, madam?'

'I know not what is the matter,' cries Amelia, 'but I have receiv'd a letter at last from that infamous colonel.'

'You will take my opinion again then, I hope, madam,' cries Mrs Atkinson. 'But don't be so affected; the letter cannot eat you, or run away with you. – Here it lies, I see, will you give me leave to read it?'

'Read it with all my heart,' cries Amelia, 'and give me your advice how to act; for I am almost distracted.'

'Hey day!' says Mrs Atkinson, 'here is a piece of parchment too – what is that?' In truth this parchment had dropt from the letter when Amelia first open'd it, but her attention was so fixed by the contents of the letter itself that she had never read the other. Mrs Atkinson had now opened the parchment first, and after a moment's perusal, the fire flash'd from her eyes, and the blood flush'd into her cheeks, and she cried out in a rapture, 'It is a commission for my husband; upon my soul it is a commission for my husband;' and at the same time began to jump about the room in a kind of frantic fit of joy.

'What can be the meaning of all this?' cries Amelia, under the highest degree of astonishment.

'Do not I tell you, my dear madam,' cried she, 'that it is a commission for my husband, and can you wonder at my being overjoyed at what I know will make him so happy? – And now it is all out. The letter is not from the colonel, but from that noble lord of whom I have told you so much. But indeed, madam, I have some pardons to ask of you. – However I know your goodness, and I will tell you all.

'You are to know then, madam, that I had not been in the opera house six minutes before a masque came up, and taking me by the hand led me aside. I gave the masque my hand, and seeing a lady at that time lay hold on Captain Booth, I took that opportunity of slipping away from him; for tho' by the help of the squeaking voice, and by attempting to mimic yours, I had pretty well disguised my own, I was still afraid, if I had much conversation with your husband, he would discover me. I walk'd therefore away with this masque, to the upper end of the farthest room, where we sat down in a corner together. He presently discover'd to me that he took me for you; and I soon after found out who he was; indeed, so far from attempting to disguise himself, he spoke in his own voice, and in his own person. He now began to make very violent love to me, but it was rather in the stile of a great man of the present age, than of an arcadian swain. In short, he laid his whole fortune at my feet, and bade me make whatever terms I pleased, either for myself or for others. By others I suppose he meant your husband. This however put a thought into my head, of turning the present occasion to advantage. I told him, there were two kinds of persons, the fallaciousness of whose promises had become proverbial in the world. These were lovers and great men. What reliance then could I have on the promise of one who united in himself both those characters? That I had seen a melancholy instance in a very worthy woman of my acquaintance, (meaning myself, madam) of his want of generosity. I said I knew the obligations that he had to this woman, and the injuries he had done her, all which I was convinced she forgave: for that she had said the handsomest things in the world of him to me. He answer'd that he thought he had not been deficient in generosity to this lady, (for I explain'd to him whom I meant) but that indeed if she had spoke well of him to me, (meaning yourself, madam) he would not fail to reward her for such an obligation. I then told him, she had married a very deserving man, who had served long in the army abroad as a private man, and who was a serjeant in the Guards, that I knew it was so very easy for him to get him a commission, that I should not think he had any honour or goodness in the world, if he neglected it. I declar'd this step must be a preliminary to any good opinion he must ever hope for of mine. I then professed the greatest friendship to that lady (in which I am convinced you will think me serious) and assured him he would give me one of the highest pleasures, in letting me be the instrument of doing her such a service. He promised me in a moment to do what you see, madam, he hath since done. And to you I shall always think myself indebted for it.'

'I know not how you are indebted to me,' cries Amelia. 'Indeed, I am very glad of any good fortune that can attend poor Atkinson; but I wish it had been obtain'd some other way. Good Heavens! what must be the consequence of this? What must this lord think of me, for listning to his mention of love, nay, for making any terms with him? For what must he suppose those terms mean? Indeed, Mrs Atkinson, you carried it a great deal too far. No wonder he had the assurance to write to me in the manner he hath done. It is too plain what he conceives of me, and who knows what he may say to others. You may have blown up[36] my reputation by your behaviour.'

'How is that possible?' answer'd Mrs Atkinson. 'Is it not in my power to clear up all matters? If you will but give me leave to make an appointment in your name, I will meet him myself, and declare the whole secret to him.'

'I will consent to no such appointment,' cries Amelia, 'I am heartily sorry I ever consented to practise any deceit. I plainly see the truth of what Dr Harrison hath often told me, that if one steps ever so little out of the ways of virtue and innocence, we know not how we may slide; for all the ways of vice are a slippery descent.'

'That sentiment,' cries Mrs Atkinson, 'is much older than Dr Harrison. *Omne vitium in proclivi est*.'[37]

'However new or old it is, I find it is true,' cries Amelia. – 'But pray, tell me all, though I tremble to hear it.'

'Indeed, my dear friend,' said Mrs Atkinson, 'you are terrified at nothing – indeed, indeed, you are too great a prude.'

'I do not know what you mean by prudery,' answered Amelia. 'I shall never be ashamed of the strictest regard to decency, to reputation, and to that honour in which the dearest of all human creatures hath his share. But pray give me the letter, there is an expression in it which alarmed me when I read it. – Pray, what doth he mean by his two short minutes, and by purchasing the reality of such another blessing?'

'Indeed I know not what he means by two minutes,' cries Mrs Atkinson, 'unless he calls two hours so; for we were not together much less. – And as for any blessing he had – I am a stranger to it. Sure I hope you have a better opinion of me than to think I granted him the last favour.'

'I don't know what favours you granted him, madam,' answer'd Amelia peevishly; 'but I am sorry you granted him any in my name.'

'Upon my word,' cries Mrs Atkinson, 'you use me unkindly – and it is a usage I did not expect at your hands; nor do I know that I have deserved it. I am sure I went to the masquerade with no other view than to oblige you; nor did I say or do any thing there which any woman, who is not the most confounded prude upon earth, would have started at on a much less occasion than what induced me. Well, I declare upon my soul then that if I was a man, rather than be married to a woman who makes such a fuss with her virtue, I would wish my wife was without such a troublesome companion.'

'Very possibly, madam, these may be your sentiments,' cries Amelia, 'and I hope they are the sentiments of your husband.'

'I desire, madam,' cries Mrs Atkinson, 'you would not reflect on my husband. He is as worthy a man, and as brave a man as yours; yes, madam, and he is now as much a captain.'

She spoke those words with so loud a voice, that Atkinson, who was accidentally going up stairs, heard them, and being surprised at the angry tone of his wife's voice, he entered the room, and with a look of much astonishment, begged to know what was the matter.

'The matter, my dear,' cries Mrs Atkinson, 'is, that I have got a commission for you, and your good old friend here is angry with me for getting it.'

'I have not spirits enow,' cries Amelia, 'to answer you as you deserve, and if I had you are below my anger.'

'I do not know, Mrs Booth,' answered the other, 'whence this great superiority over me is derived; but if your virtue gives it you I would have you to know, madam, that I despise a prude, as much as you can do a —'

'Though you have several times,' cries Amelia, 'insulted me with that word, I scorn to give you any ill language in return. If you deserve any bad appellation, you know it without my telling it you.'

Poor Atkinson, who was more frightned than he had ever been in his life, did all he could to procure peace. He fell upon his knees to his wife, and begged her to compose herself; for indeed she seemed to be in a most furious rage.

While he was in this posture, Booth, who had knocked so gently at the door, for fear of disturbing his wife, that he had not been heard in the tempest, came into the room. The moment Amelia saw him, the tears which had been gathering for some time, burst in a torrent from her eyes, which however she endeavoured to conceal with her handkerchief. The entry of Booth turn'd all in an instant into a silent picture; in which the first figure which struck the eyes of the captain was the serjeant on his knees to his wife.

Booth immediately cried – 'What's the meaning of this?' – but received no answer. He then cast his eyes towards Amelia, and plainly discerning her condition, he ran to her, and in a very tender phrase begged to know what was the matter. To which she answered – 'Nothing, my dear, nothing of any consequence.' He replied – that he would know, and then turned to Atkinson, and asked the same question.

Atkinson answered, 'Upon my honour, sir, I know nothing of it. – Something hath passed between madam and my wife, but what it is I know no more than your honour.'

'Your wife,' said Mrs Atkinson, 'hath used me cruelly ill, Mr Booth. If you must be satisfied, that is the whole matter.'

Booth rapt out a great oath, and cried, 'It is impossible, my wife is not capable of using any one ill.'

Amelia then cast herself upon her knees to her husband, and cried, 'For Heaven's sake, do not throw yourself into a passion – some few words have past – perhaps I may be in the wrong.'

'Damnation seize me if I think so,' cries Booth. 'And I wish whoever hath drawn these tears from your eyes, may pay it with as many drops of their heart's blood.'

'You see, madam,' cries Mrs Atkinson, 'you have your bully to take your part; so I suppose you will use your triumph.'

Amelia made no answer, but still kept hold of Booth, who, in a violent rage, cried out, – 'My Amelia triumph over such a wretch as thee! – What can lead thy insolence to such presumption? Serjeant, I desire you'll take that monster out of the room, or I cannot answer for myself.'

The serjeant was beginning to beg his wife to retire, (for he perceived very plainly, that she had, as the phrase is, taken a sip too much that evening,) when, with a rage little short of madness, she cried out, – 'And do you tamely see me insulted in such a manner, now that you are a gentleman and upon a footing with him?'

'It is lucky for us all, perhaps,' answer'd Booth, 'that he is not my equal.'

'You lie, sirrah,' said Mrs Atkinson, 'he is every way your equal; he is as good a gentleman as yourself, and as much an officer. – No, I retract what I say – he hath not the spirit of a gentleman, nor of a man neither – or he would not bear to see his wife insulted.'

'Let me beg of you, my dear,' cries the serjeant, 'to go with me and compose yourself.'

'Go with thee, thou wretch,' – cries she, looking with the utmost disdain upon him, – 'no, nor ever speak to thee more.' – At which words she burst out of the room; and the serjeant, without saying a word, followed her.

A very tender and pathetic scene now passed between Booth and his wife, in which, when she was a little composed, she related to him the whole story. For besides that it was not possible for her otherwise to account for the quarrel which he had seen, Booth was now possessed of the letter that lay on the floor.

Amelia having emptied her mind to her husband, and obtained his faithful promise that he would not resent the affair to my lord, was pretty well composed, and began to relent a little towards Mrs Atkinson; but Booth was so highly incensed with her, that he declared he would leave her house the next morning; which they both accordingly did, and immediately accommodated themselves with convenient apartments within a few doors of their friend the doctor.

CHAPTER 9

Containing some things worthy observation.

NOTWITHSTANDING the exchange of his lodgings, Booth did not forget to send an excuse to Mr Trent, of whose conversation he had taken a full surfeit the preceding evening.

That day in his walks Booth met with an old brother-officer, who had served with him at Gibraltar, and was on half-pay as well as himself. He had not indeed had the fortune of being broke with his regiment,[38] as was Booth; but had gone out, as they call it, on half-pay as a lieutenant, a rank to which he had risen in five and thirty years.

This honest gentleman, after some discourse with Booth, desir'd him to lend him half a crown; which he assured him he would faithfully pay the next day, when he was to receive some money for his sister. This sister was the widow of an officer that had been killed in the sea service; and she and her brother lived together, on their joint stock, out of which they maintained likewise an old mother, and two of the sister's children, the eldest of which was about nine years old. 'You must know,' said the old lieutenant, 'I have been disappointed this morning by an old scoundrel, who wanted fifteen per cent for advancing my sister's pension; but I have now got an honest fellow, who hath promised it me to-morrow, at ten per cent.'

'And enough too of all conscience,' cries Booth.

'Why indeed, I think so too,' answer'd the other, 'considering it is sure to be paid one time or other. To say the truth, it is a little hard the government doth not pay those pensions better; for my sister's hath been due almost these two years; that is my way of thinking.'

Booth answered he was ashamed to refuse him such a sum; but 'Upon my soul,' said he, 'I have not a single half-penny in my pocket; for I am in a worse condition if possible than yourself; for I have lost all my money, and what is worse, I owe Mr Trent, whom you remember at Gibraltar, £50.'

'Remember him! yes, d—n him, I remember him very well,' cries the old gentleman, 'though he will not remember me. He is grown so great now, that he will not speak to his old acquaintance; and yet I should be ashamed of myself to be great in such a manner.'

'What manner do you mean?' cries Booth a little eagerly.

'Why, by pimping,' answered the other, 'He is pimp in ordinary to my lord—who keeps his family; or how the devil he lives else I don't know; for his place is not worth £300 a year, and he and his wife spend a thousand at least. But she keeps an assembly, which, I believe, if you was to call a bawdy-house, you would not miss-name it. But d—n me if I had not rather be an honest man, and walk on foot, with holes in my shoes, as I do now, or go without a dinner, as I and all my family will to day, than ride in a chariot, and feast by such means. I am honest Bob Bound, and always will be;

that's my way of thinking; and there's no man shall call me otherwise; for if he doth, I will knock him down for a lying rascal; that is my way of thinking.'

'And a very good way of thinking too,' cries Booth. 'However you shall not want a dinner to day; for if you will go home with me, I will lend you a crown with all my heart.'

'Lookee,' said the old man, 'if it be any wise inconvenient to you, I will not have it; for I will never rob another man of his dinner, to eat myself – that is my way of thinking.'

'Pooh,' said Booth, 'never mention such a trifle twice between you and me. Besides you say you can pay it me to-morrow; and I promise you that will be the same thing.'

They then walked together to Booth's lodgings, where Booth, from Amelia's pocket, gave his friend double the little sum he had asked. Upon which the old gentleman shook him heartily by the hand, and repeating his intention of paying him the next day, made the best of his way to a butcher's, whence he carried off a leg of mutton to a family that had lately kept Lent without any religious merit.

When he was gone, Amelia asked her husband who that old gentleman was. Booth answered, he was one of the scandals of his country. That the Duke of Marlborough[39] had about thirty years before made him an ensign from a private man, for very particular merit, and that he had not long since gone out of the army with a broken heart, upon having several boys put over his head. He then gave her an account of his family, which he had heard from the old gentleman in their way to his house, and with which we have already in a concise manner acquainted the reader.

'Good Heavens!' cries Amelia, 'what are our great men made of! Are they in reality a distinct species from the rest of mankind? Are they born without hearts?'

'One would indeed sometimes,' cries Booth, 'be inclined to think so. In truth they have no perfect idea of those common distresses of mankind which are far removed from their own sphere. Compassion, if thoroughly examined, will, I believe, appear to be the fellow-feeling only of men of the same rank and degree of life for one another, on account of the evils to which they themselves are liable. Our sensations are, I am afraid, very cold towards those who are at a great distance from us, and whose calamities can consequently never reach us.'

'I remember,' cries Amelia, 'a sentiment of Dr Harrison's, which he told me was in some Latin book; *I am a man myself, and my heart is interested in whatever can befal the rest of mankind.*[40] That is the sentiment of a good man, and whoever thinks otherwise is a bad one.'

'I have often told you, my dear Emily,' cries Booth, 'that all men, as well the best as the worst, act alike from the principle of self-love. Where benevolence therefore is the uppermost passion, self-love directs you to gratify it by doing good, and by relieving the distresses of others; for they are then in reality your own. But where ambition, avarice, pride, or any other passion governs the man, and keeps his benevolence down, the miseries of all other men affect him no more than they would a stock or a stone. And thus the man and his statue have often the same degree of feeling or compassion.'

'I have often wished, my dear,' cries Amelia, 'to hear you converse with Dr Harrison on this subject; for I am sure he would convince you, though I can't, that there are really such things as religion and virtue.'

This was not the first hint of this kind which Amelia had given; for she sometimes apprehended from his discourse that he was little better than an atheist. A consideration which did not diminish her affection for him; but gave her great uneasiness. On all such occasions Booth immediately turned the discourse to some other subject; for tho' he had in other points a great opinion of his wife's capacity; yet as a divine or a philosopher he did not hold her in a very respectable light, nor did he lay any great stress on her sentiments in such matters. He now therefore gave a speedy turn to the conversation, and began to talk of affairs below the dignity of this history.

BOOK XI

CHAPTER 1

Containing a very polite scene.

WE WILL now look back to some personages, who, though not the principal characters in this history, have yet made too considerable a figure in it to be abruptly dropt. And these are Colonel James and his lady.

This fond couple never met till dinner the day after the masquerade, when they happened to be alone together in an antichamber before the arrival of the rest of the company.

The conversation began with the colonel's saying, 'I hope, madam, you got no cold last night at the masquerade.' To which the lady answered by much the same kind of question.

They then sat together near five minutes without opening their mouths to each other. At last Mrs James said, 'Pray, sir, who was that masque with you in the dress of a shepherdess? How could you expose yourself by walking with such a trollop in public; for certainly no woman of any figure would appear there in such a dress. You know, Mr James, I never interfere with your affairs; but I would methinks for my own sake, if I was you, preserve a little decency in the face of the world.'

'Upon my word,' said James, 'I do not know whom you mean. A woman in such a dress might speak to me for aught I know – A thousand people speak to me at a masquerade. But I promise you, I spoke to no woman acquaintance there that I know of – Indeed I now recollect there was a woman in a dress of a shepherdess; and there was another aukward thing in a blue domino that plagued me a little, but I soon got rid of them.'

'And I suppose you do not know the lady in the blue domino neither? –'

'Not I, I assure you,' said James. 'But pray, why do you ask me these questions? It looks so like jealousy.'

'Jealousy,' cries she, 'I jealous! No, Mr James, I shall never be jealous I promise you, especially of the lady in the blue domino; for to my knowledge she despises you of all the human race.'

'I am heartily glad of it,' said James; 'for I never saw such a tall aukward monster in my life.'

'That is a very cruel way of telling me you knew me. –'

'You, madam,' said James – 'you was in a black domino.'

'It is not so unusual a thing, I believe, you yourself know, to change dresses, – I own I did it to discover some of your tricks. I did not think you could have distinguish'd the tall aukward monster so well.'

'Upon my soul,' said James, 'if it was you, I did not even suspect it; so you ought not to be offended at what I have said ignorantly.'

'Indeed, sir,' cries she, 'you cannot offend me by any thing you can say to my face – no, by my soul, I despise you too much. But I wish, Mr James, you would not make me the subject of your conversation amongst your wenches. I desire I may not be afraid of meeting them for fear of their insults: that I may not be told by a dirty trollop, you make me the subject of your wit amongst them, of which it seems I am the favourite topic. Tho' you have married a tall aukward monster, Mr James, I think she hath a right to be treated, as your wife, with respect at least – Indeed I shall never require any more: indeed, Mr James, I never shall. – I think a wife hath a title to that.'

'Who told you this, madam?' said James.

'Your slut,' said she, 'your wench, your shepherdess.'

'By all that's sacred,' cries James, 'I do not know who the shepherdess was.'

'By all that's sacred then,' says she – 'she told me so – and I am convinced she told me truth. – But I do not wonder at your denying it; for that is equally consistent with honour as to behave in such a manner to a wife who is a gentlewoman. – I hope you will allow me that, sir. – Because I had not quite so great a fortune, I hope you do not think me beneath you, or that you did me any honour in marrying me. I am come of as good a family as yourself,

Mr James; and if my brother knew how you treated me, he would not bear it.'

'Do you threaten me with your brother, madam?' said James.

'I will not be ill treated, sir,' answered she.

'Nor I neither, madam,' cries he; 'and therefore I desire you will prepare to go into the country to-morrow morning.'

'Indeed, sir,' said she, 'I shall not.'

'By Heavens, madam, but you shall,' answered he, 'I will have my coach at the door to-morrow morning by seven; and you shall either go into it or be carried.'

'I hope, sir, you are not in earnest,' said she.

'Indeed, madam,' answered he, 'but I am in earnest, and resolved; and into the country you go to-morrow.'

'But why into the country,' said she, 'Mr James? Why will you be so barbarous to deny me the pleasures of the town?'

'Because you interfere with my pleasures,' cried James; 'which I have told you long ago I would not submit to. It is enough for fond couples to have these scenes together. I thought we had been upon a better footing, and had cared too little for each other to become mutual plagues. I thought you had been satisfied with the full liberty of doing what you please.'

'So I am. I defy you to say I have ever given you any uneasiness.'

'How,' cries he, 'have you not just now upbraided me with what you heard at the masquerade?'

'I own,' said she, 'to be insulted by such a creature to my face stung me to the soul. I must have had no spirit to bear the insults of such an animal. Nay she spoke of you with equal contempt. Whoever she is, I promise you, Mr Booth is her favourite. But indeed she is unworthy any one's regard: for she behaved like an arrant dragoon.'

'Hang her,' cries the colonel, 'I know nothing of her.'

'Well but, Mr James – I am sure you will not send me into the country. Indeed I will not go into the country.'

'If you was a reasonable woman,' cries James, 'perhaps I should not desire it. – And on one consideration –'

'Come name your consideration,' said she.

'Let me first experience your discernment,' said he – 'Come,

Molly, let me try your judgment. Can you guess at any woman of your acquaintance that I like?'

'Sure,' said she, 'it cannot be Mrs Booth!'

'And why not Mrs Booth?' answer'd he. 'Is she not the finest woman in the world?'

'Very far from it,' replied she, 'in my opinion.'

'Pray, what faults,' said he, 'can you find in her?'

'In the first place,' cries Mrs James, 'her eyes are too large; and she hath a look with them that I don't know how to describe; but I know I don't like it. Then her eyebrows are too large; therefore indeed she doth all in her power to remedy this with her pincers: for if it was not for those, her eyebrows would be preposterous. – Then her nose, as well proportioned as it is, hath a visible scar on one side. – Her neck likewise is too protuberant for the genteel size, especially as she laces herself: for no woman in my opinion can be genteel who is not entirely flat before. And lastly, she is both too short and too tall. – Well, you may laugh, Mr James, I know what I mean, tho' I cannot well express it. – I mean that she is too tall for a pretty woman, and too short for a fine woman. – There is such a thing as a kind of insipid medium – a kind of something that is neither one thing or another. I know not how to express it more clearly; but when I say such a one is a pretty woman, a pretty thing, a pretty creature, you know very well I mean a little woman; and when I say such a one is a very fine woman, a very fine person of a woman, to be sure I must mean a tall woman. Now a woman that is between both, is certainly neither the one nor the other.'

'Well, I own,' said he, 'you have explain'd yourself with great dexterity; but with all these imperfections, I cannot help liking her.'

'That you need not tell me, Mr James,' answer'd the lady; 'for that I knew before you desir'd me to invite her to your house. And nevertheless, did not I, like an obedient wife, comply with your desires? Did I make any objection to the party you proposed for the masquerade, tho' I knew very well your motive? What can the best of wives do more? To procure you success is not in my power; and if I may give you my opinion, I believe you never will succeed with her.'

'Is her virtue so very impregnable?' said he, with a sneer.

'Her virtue,' answer'd Mrs James, 'hath the best guard in the world, which is a most violent love for her husband.'

'All pretence, and affectation,' cries the colonel. 'It is impossible she should have so little taste, or indeed so little delicacy as to like such a fellow.'

'Nay I do not much like him myself,' said she – 'He is not indeed at all such a sort of man as I should like; but I thought he had been generally allow'd to be handsome.'

'He handsome?' cries James. 'What, with a nose like the proboscis of an elephant, with the shoulders of a porter, and the legs of a chairman? The fellow hath not in the least the look of a gentleman; and one would rather think he had followed the plough than the camp all his life.'

'Nay now I protest,' said she, 'I think you do him injustice. He is genteel enough, in my opinion. It is true indeed he is not quite of the most delicate make; but whatever he is, I am convinced she thinks him the finest man in the world.'

'I cannot believe it,' answer'd he peevishly. – 'But will you invite her to dinner here to-morrow?'

'With all my heart, and as often as you please,' answer'd she. – 'But I have some favours to ask of you. – First, I must hear no more of going out of town till I please.'

'Very well,' cried he.

'In the next place,' said she, 'I must have two hundred guineas within these two or three days.'

'Well – I agree to that too,' answered he.

'And when I do go out of town, I go to Tunbridge – I insist upon that; and from Tunbridge I go to Bath – positively to Bath. And I promise you faithfully I will do all in my power to carry Mrs Booth with me.'

'On that condition,' answer'd he, 'I promise you you shall go wherever you please. – And to shew you, I will even prevent your wishes by my generosity, as soon as I receive the five thousand pounds, which I am going to take up on one of my estates, you shall have two hundred more.'

She thanked him with a low curtesie; and he was in such good humour that he offered to kiss her. To this kiss she coldly turn'd her cheek – and then flirting her fan, said – 'Mr James, there is one thing I forgot to mention to you – I think you intended to get a commission in some regiment abroad for this young man. – Now if you would take my advice, I know this will not oblige his wife; and besides I am positive she resolves to go with him. – But if you can provide for him in some regiment at home, I know she will dearly love you for it; and when he is order'd to quarters, she will be left behind – and Yorkshire or Scotland I think is as good a distance as either of the Indies.'

'Well, I will do what I can,' answer'd James; 'but I cannot ask any thing yet: for I got two places of £100 a year each for two of my footmen, within this fortnight.'

At this instant a violent knock at the door signified the arrival of their company; upon which both husband and wife put on their best looks to receive their guests; and from their behaviour to each other during the rest of the day, a stranger might have concluded he had been in company with the fondest couple in the universe.

CHAPTER 2

Matters political.

BEFORE we return to Booth, we will relate a scene in which Dr Harrison was concern'd.

This good man whilst in the country happen'd to be in the neighbourhood of a nobleman of his acquaintance, and whom he knew to have very considerable interest with the ministers at that time.

The doctor who was very well known to this nobleman, took this opportunity of paying him a visit in order to recommend poor Booth to his favour. Nor did he much doubt of his success, the favour he was to ask being a very small one, and to which he thought the service of Booth gave him so just a title.

The doctor's name soon gain'd him an admission to the presence of this great man, who indeed receiv'd him with much courtesy and politeness; not so much perhaps from any particular regard to the sacred function, nor from any respect to the doctor's personal merit, as from some considerations which the reader will perhaps guess anon. After many ceremonials, and some previous discourse on different subjects, the doctor open'd his business, and told the great man, that he was come to him to solicit a favour for a young gentleman who had been an officer in the army, and was now on half-pay. 'All the favour I ask, my lord,' said he, 'is, that this gentleman may be again admitted *ad eundem*.[1] I am convinced your lordship will do me the justice to think I would not ask for a worthless person; but indeed the young man I mean, hath very extraordinary merit. He was at the siege of Gibraltar, in which he behav'd with distinguish'd bravery; and was dangerously wounded at two several times in the service of his country. I will add, that he is at present in great necessity, and hath a wife and several children, for whom he hath no other means of providing; and if it will recommend him further to your lordship's favour, his wife, I believe, is one of the best and worthiest of all her sex.'

'As to that, my dear doctor,' cries the nobleman, 'I shall make no doubt. Indeed any service I shall do the gentleman will be upon your account. As to necessity, it is the plea of so many, that it is impossible to serve them all. – And with regard to the personal merit of these inferior officers, I believe, I need not tell you that it is very little regarded. But if you recommend him, let the person be what he will, I am convinced it will be done: for I know it is in your power at present to ask for a greater matter than this.'

'I depend entirely upon your lordship,' answer'd the doctor.

'Indeed, my worthy friend,' replied the lord, 'I will not take a merit to myself, which will so little belong to me. You are to depend on yourself. It falls out very luckily too at this time when you have it in your power so greatly to oblige us.'

'What, my lord, is in my power?' cries the doctor.

'You certainly know,' answer'd his lordship, 'how hard Colonel Trompington is run at your town, in the election of a mayor; they tell me it will be a very near thing, unless you join us. But we know it is in your power to do the business, and turn the scale. I heard your name mention'd the other day on that account; and I know you may have any thing in reason, if you will give us your interest.'

'Sure, my lord,' cries the doctor, 'you are not in earnest in asking my interest for the colonel.'

'Indeed I am,' answer'd the peer. 'Why should you doubt it?'

'For many reasons,' answer'd the doctor. 'First, I am an old friend and acquaintance of Mr Fairfield, as your lordship, I believe, very well knows. The little interest, therefore, that I have, you may be assured, will go in his favour. Indeed I do not concern myself deeply in these affairs: for I do not think it becomes my cloth so to do. But as far as I think it decent to interest myself, it will certainly be on the side of Mr Fairfield. Indeed I should do so, if I was acquainted with both the gentlemen, only by reputation: the one being a neighbouring gentleman, of a very large estate, a very sober and sensible man, of known probity and attachment to the true interest of his country. The other is a mere stranger, a boy, a soldier of fortune, and as far as I can discern from the little conversation I have had with him, of a very shallow capacity, and no education.'

'No education! my dear friend,' cries the nobleman. 'Why he hath been educated in half the courts of Europe.'

'Perhaps so, my lord,' answer'd the doctor; 'but I shall always be so great a pedant as to call a man of no learning, a man of no education. – And from my own knowledge, I can aver, that I am persuaded there is scarce a foot soldier in the army who is more illiterate than the colonel.'

'Why as to Latin and Greek, you know,' replied the lord, 'they are not much requir'd in the army.'

'It may be so,' said the doctor. 'Then let such persons keep to their own profession. It is a very low civil capacity indeed for which an illiterate man can be qualified. And to speak a plain truth, if your lordship is a friend to the colonel, you would do well to advise him to decline an attempt, in which I am certain he hath no probability of success.'

'Well, sir,' said the lord, 'if you are resolv'd against us, I must deal as freely with you, and tell you plainly I cannot serve you in your affair. Nay it will be the best thing I can do, to hold my tongue: for if I should mention his name with your recommendation after what you have said, he would perhaps never get provided for as long as he lives.'

'Is his own merit then, my lord, no recommendation?' cries the doctor.

'My dear, dear sir,' cries the other – 'what is the merit of a subaltern officer?'

'Surely, my lord,' cries the doctor, 'it is the merit which should recommend him to the post of a subaltern officer. And it is a merit which will hereafter qualify him to serve his country in a higher capacity. And I do assure you of this young man, that he hath not only a good heart, but a good head too. And I have been told by those who are judges, that he is for his age an excellent officer.'

'Very probably!' cries my lord – 'And there are abundance with the same merit, and the same qualifications, who want a morsel of bread for themselves and their families.'

'It is an infamous scandal on the nation,' cries the doctor; 'and I am heartily sorry it can be said even with a colour of truth.'

'How can it be otherwise?' says the peer. 'Do you think it is possible to provide for all men of merit?'

'Yes, surely do I,' said the doctor. 'And very easily too.'

'How pray? –' cries the lord – 'Upon my word I shall be glad to know.'

'Only by not providing for those who have none – The men of merit in any capacity are not I am afraid so extremely numerous, that we need starve any of them, unless we wickedly suffer a set of worthless fellows to eat their bread.'

'This is all mere Utopia,' cries his lordship. 'The chimerical system of Plato's commonwealth with which we amused ourselves at the university; politics which are inconsistent with the state of human affairs.'

'Sure, my lord,' cries the doctor, 'we have read of states where such doctrines have been put in practice. What is your lordship's opinion of Rome in the earlier ages of the commonwealth, of Sparta, and even of Athens itself, in some periods of its history?'

'Indeed, doctor,' cries the lord, 'all these notions are obsolete and long since exploded. To apply maxims of government drawn from the Greek and Roman histories, to this nation, is absurd and impossible. But if you will have Roman examples, fetch them from those times of the republic that were most like our own. Do you not know, doctor, that this is as corrupt a nation as ever existed under the sun? And would you think of governing such a people by the strict principles of honesty and morality?'

'If it be so corrupt,' said the doctor, 'I think it is high time to amend it. Or else it is easy to foresee that Roman and British liberty will have the same fate; for corruption in the body politic as naturally tends to dissolution as in the natural body.'

'I thank you for your simile,' cries my lord: 'for in the natural body, I believe, you will allow there is the season of youth, the season of manhood, and the season of old age; and that, when the last of these arrives, it will be an impossible attempt by all the means of art to restore the body again to its youth, or to the vigour of its middle age. The same periods happen to every great kingdom. In its youth it rises by arts and arms to power and prosperity. This it enjoys and flourishes with a while; and then it may be said to be in the vigour of its age, enrich'd at home with all the emoluments and blessings of peace, and formidable abroad with all the terrors of war. At length this very prosperity introduces corruption; and then comes on its old age. Virtue and learning, art and industry, decay by degrees. The people sink into sloth and luxury, and prostitution. It is enervated at home, becomes contemptible abroad; and such indeed is its misery and wretchedness, that it resembles a man in the last decrepid stage of life, who looks with unconcern at his approaching dissolution.'

'This is a melancholy picture indeed,' cries the doctor; 'and if the latter part of it can be applied to our case, I see nothing but religion, which would have prevented this decrepid state of the constitution, should prevent a man of spirit from hanging himself out of the way of so wretched a contemplation.'

'Why so?' said the peer; 'Why, hang myself, doctor? Would it not be wiser, think you, to make the best of your time, and the most you can in such a nation?'

'And is religion then to be really laid out of the question?' cries the doctor.

'If I am to speak my own opinion, sir,' answered the peer, 'you know I shall answer in the negative. – But you are too well acquainted with the world to be told, that the conduct of politicians is not formed upon the principles of religion.'

'I am very sorry for it,' cries the doctor; 'but I will talk to them then of honour and honesty: this is a language which I hope they will at least pretend to understand. Now to deny a man the preferment which he merits, and to give it to another man who doth not merit it, is a manifest act of injustice; and is consequently inconsistent with both honour and honesty. Nor is it only an act of injustice to the man himself, but to the public, for whose good principally all public offices are, or ought to be instituted. Now this good can never be completed, nor obtained, but by employing all persons according to their capacities. Wherever true merit is liable to be superseded by favour and partiality, and men are intrusted with offices, without any regard to capacity or integrity, the affairs of that state will always be in a deplorable situation. Such, as Livy tells us,[2] was the state of Capua, a little before its final destruction; and the consequence your lordship well knows. But, my lord, there is another mischief which attends this kind of injustice, and that is, it hath a manifest tendency to destroy all virtue and all ability among the people, by taking away all that encouragement and incentive, which should promote emulation, and raise men to aim at excelling in any art, science, or profession. Nor can any thing, my lord, contribute more to render a nation contemptible among its neighbours; for what opinion can other countries have of the councils, or what terror can they conceive of the arms of such a people? And it was chiefly owing to the avoiding this error, that Oliver Cromwell carried the reputation of England higher than it ever was at any other time. I will add only one argument more, and that is founded on the most narrow and selfish system of politics; and this is, that such a conduct is sure to create universal discontent and grumbling at home: for nothing can bring men to rest satisfied, when they see others preferred to them, but an opinion that they deserve that elevation; for as one of the greatest men this country ever produced, observes,

One worthless man that gains what he pretends,
Disgusts a thousand unpretending friends.[3]

With what heartburnings then must any nation see themselves obliged to contribute to the support of a set of men, of whose incapacity to serve them they are well apprized, and who do their country a double diskindness; by being themselves employed in posts to which they are unequal, and by keeping others out of those employments, for which they are qualified!'

'And do you really think, doctor,' cries the nobleman, 'that any minister could support himself in this country upon such principles as you recommend? Do you think he would be able to baffle an opposition, unless he should oblige his friends by conferring places, often contrary to his own inclinations, and his own opinion?'

'Yes, really do I,' cries the doctor. 'Indeed if a minister is resolved to make good his confession in the liturgy,[4] *by leaving undone all those things which he ought to have done, and by doing all those things which he ought not to have done*: Such a minister, I grant, will be obliged to baffle opposition, as you are pleased to term it, by these arts; for as Shakespeare somewhere says,

Things ill begun strengthen themselves by ill.[5]

'But if, on the contrary, he will please to consider the true interest of his country, and that only in great and national points; if he will engage his country in neither alliances or quarrels, but where it is really interested; if he will raise no money but what is wanted; nor employ any civil or military officers but what are useful; and place in these employments men of the highest integrity, and of the greatest abilities; if he will employ some few of his hours to advance our trade, and some few more to regulate our domestic government: if he would do this, my lord, I will answer for it he shall either have no opposition to baffle, or he shall baffle it by a fair appeal to his conduct. Such a minister may, in the language of the law, put himself on his country[6] when he pleases and he shall come off with honour and applause.'

'And do you really believe, doctor,' cries the peer, 'there ever was such a minister, or ever will be?'

'Why not, my lord?' answered the doctor. 'It requires no very extraordinary parts, nor any extraordinary degree of virtue. He need practise no great instances of self-denial. He shall have power, and honour, and riches, and perhaps all in a much greater degree than he can ever acquire, by pursuing a contrary system. He shall have more of each, and much more of safety.'

'Pray, doctor,' said my lord, 'let me ask you one simple question. Do you really believe any man upon earth was ever a rogue out of choice?'

'Really, my lord,' says the doctor, 'I am ashamed to answer in the affirmative; and yet I am afraid experience would almost justify me if I should. Perhaps the opinion of the world may sometimes mislead men to think those measures necessary, which in reality are not so. Or the truth may be, that a man of good inclinations finds his office filled with such corruption by the iniquity of his predecessors, that he may despair of being capable of purging it; and so sits down contented, as Augeas did with the filth of his stables, not because he thought them the better, or that such filth was really necessary to a stable; but that he despaired of sufficient force to cleanse them.'

'I will ask you one question more, and I have done,' said the nobleman. 'Do you imagine that if any minister was really as good as you would have him, that the people in general would believe that he was so?'

'Truly, my lord,' said the doctor, 'I think they may be justified in not believing too hastily. But I beg leave to answer your lordship's question by another. Doth your lordship believe that the people of Greenland, when they see the light of the sun, and feel his warmth, after so long a season of cold and darkness, will really be persuaded that he shines upon them?'

My lord smiled at the conceit; and then the doctor took an opportunity to renew his suit, to which his lordship answered he would promise nothing, and could give him no hopes of success: 'But you may be assured,' said he with a leering countenance, 'I shall do him all the service in my power.' A language which the doctor well understood, and soon after took a civil, but not a very ceremonious leave.

CHAPTER 3

The history of Mr Trent.

WE WILL now return to Mr Booth and his wife. The former had spent his time very uneasily, ever since he had discovered what sort of man he was indebted to; but lest he should forget it, Mr Trent thought now proper to remind him, in the following letter, which he read the next morning after he had put off the appointment.

SIR,

I am sorry the necessity of my affairs obliges me to mention that small sum which I had the honour to lend you the other night at play; and which I shall be much obliged to you, if you will let me have some time either to day, or to-morrow. I am,

SIR,

Your most obedient,

most humble servant,

Geo. Trent.

This letter a little surprized Booth, after the genteel, and indeed, as it appeared, generous behaviour of Trent. But lest it should have the same effect upon the reader, we will now proceed to account for this, as well as for some other phenomena that have appeared in this history, and which perhaps we shall be forgiven, for not having opened more largely before.

Mr Trent then was a gentleman, possibly of a good family; for it was not certain whence he sprung on the father's side. His mother, who was the only parent he ever knew or heard of, was a single gentlewoman, and for some time carried on the trade of milliner in Covent Garden.[7] She sent her son, at the age of eight years old, to a charity-school,[8] where he remained till he was of the age of fourteen, without making any great proficiency in learning. Indeed it is not very probable he should; for the master who, in preference to a very learned and proper man, was chosen by a party into this school, the salary of which was upwards of £100 a year, had himself never travelled through the Latin grammar, and was in truth a most consummate blockhead.

At the age of fifteen Mr Trent was put clerk to an attorney, where he remained a very short time before he took leave of his master; rather, indeed, departed without taking leave; and having broke open his mother's escritoire, and carried off with him all the valuable effects he there found, to the amount of about fifty pound, he marched off to sea, and went on board a merchantman, whence he was afterwards pressed into a man of war.

In this service he continued above three years; during which time he behaved so ill in his moral character, that he twice underwent a very severe discipline for thefts in which he was detected; but at the same time, he behaved so well as a sailor in an engagement with some pirates, that he wiped off all former scores, and greatly recommended himself to his captain.

At his return home, he being then about twenty years of age, he found that the attorney had in his absence married his mother, had buried her, and secured all her effects, to the amount, as he was inform'd, of about fifteen hundred pound. Trent applied to his step-father, but to no purpose; the attorney utterly disowned him, nor would he suffer him to come a second time within his doors.

It happened that the attorney had, by a former wife, an only daughter, a great favourite, who was about the same age with Trent himself; and had, during his residence at her father's house, taken a very great liking to this young fellow, who was extremely handsome, and perfectly well made. This her liking was not, during his absence, so far extinguished, but that it immediately revived on his return. Of this she took care to give Mr Trent proper intimation; for she was not one of those backward and delicate ladies, who can die rather than make the first overture. Trent was overjoyed at this, and with reason; for she was a very lovely girl in her person, the only child of a rich father; and the prospect of so complete a revenge on the attorney charmed him above all the rest. To be as short in the matter as the parties, a marriage was soon consummated between them.

The attorney at first raged and was implacable; but at last fondness for his daughter so far overcame resentment, that he advanced a sum of money to buy his son-in-law (for now he acknowledged him as such) an ensign's commission in a marching regiment then ordered to Gibraltar; at which place the attorney heartily hoped that Trent might be knocked on the head: for in that case he thought he might marry his daughter more agreeably to his own ambition, and to her advantage.

The regiment into which Trent purchased, was the same with that in which Booth likewise served; the one being an ensign, and the other a lieutenant in the two additional companies.

Trent had no blemish in his military capacity. Though he had had but an indifferent education, he was naturally sensible and genteel, and nature, as we have said, had given him a very agreeable person. He was likewise a very bold fellow, and as he really behaved himself every way well enough, while he was at Gibraltar, there was some degree of intimacy between him and Booth.

When the siege was over, and the additional companies were again reduced, Trent returned to his wife, who received him with great joy and affection. Soon after this an accident happened, which proved the utter ruin of his father-in-law, and ended in breaking his heart. This was nothing but making a mistake pretty common at this day, of writing another man's name to a deed instead of his own. In truth, this matter was no less than what the law calls forgery, and was just then made capital by an Act of Parliament.[9] From this offence indeed the attorney was acquitted by not admitting the proof of the party who was to avoid his own deed, by his evidence; and therefore no witness, according to those excellent rules, called the law of evidence;[10] a law very excellently calculated for the preservation of the lives of his majesty's roguish subjects, and most notably used for that purpose.

But tho' by common law the attorney was honourably acquitted; yet as common sense manifested to every one that he was guilty, he unhappily lost his reputation, and of consequence his business; the chagrin of which latter soon put an end to his life.

This prosecution had been attended with a very great expence; for besides the ordinary costs of avoiding the gallows by the help of the law, there was a very high article of no less than a thousand pounds paid down to remove out of the way a witness, against whom there was no legal exception. The poor gentleman had besides suffered some losses in business; so that to the surprise of all his acquaintance, when his debts were paid there remained no more than a small estate of fourscore pounds a year, which he settled upon his daughter, far out of the reach of her husband, and about two hundred pounds in money.

The old gentleman had not long been in his grave, before Trent set himself to consider seriously of the state of his affairs. He had lately begun to look on his wife with a much less degree of liking and desire than formerly; for he was one of those who think too much of one thing is good for nothing. Indeed he had indulged these speculations so far, that I believe his wife, though one of the prettiest women in town, was the last subject that he would have chose for any amorous dalliance.

Many other persons however, greatly differed from him in this opinion. Amongst the rest was the illustrious peer of amorous memory. This noble peer having therefore got a view of Mrs Trent one day in the street, did, by means of an emissary then with him, make himself acquainted with her lodging, to which he immediately laid siege in form, setting himself down in a lodging directly opposite to her, from whence the battery of ogles began to play the very next morning.

This siege had not continued long before the governor of the garrison became sufficiently apprised of all the works which were carrying on, and having well reconnoitred the enemy, and discovered who he was, notwithstanding a false name, and some disguise of his person, he called a council of war within his own breast. In fact, to drop all allegory, he began to consider whether his wife was not really a more valuable possession than he had lately thought her. In short, as he had been disappointed in her fortune, he now conceived some hopes of turning her beauty itself into a fortune.

Without communicating these views to her, he soon scraped an acquaintance with his opposite neighbour by the name which he there usurped, and counterfeited an entire ignorance of his real name and title. On this occasion Trent had his disguise likewise, for he affected the utmost simplicity; of which affectation, as he was a very artful fellow, he was extremely capable.

The peer fell plumb into this snare; and when, by the simplicity, as he imagined, of the husband he became acquainted with the wife, he was so extravagantly charmed with her person, that he resolved, whatever was the cost or the consequence, he would possess her.

His lordship, however, preserved some caution in his management of this affair; more, perhaps, than was necessary. As for the husband, none was requisite; for he knew all he could; and with regard to the wife herself, as she had, for some time, perceived the decrease of her husband's affection, (for few women are, I believe, to be imposed upon in that matter) she was not displeased to find the return of all that complaisance and endearment, of those looks and languishments from another agreeable person which she had formerly received from Trent, and which she now found she should receive from him no longer.

My lord, therefore, having been indulged with as much opportunity as he could wish from Trent, and having received rather more encouragement than he could well have hoped from the lady, began to prepare all matters for a storm, when luckily Mr Trent declaring he must go out of town for two days, he fix'd on the first day of his departure as the time of carrying his design into execution.

And now, after some debate with himself in what manner he should approach his love, he at last determined to do it in his own person; for he conceived, and perhaps very rightly, that the lady, like Semele,[11] was not void of ambition, and would have preferred Jupiter in all his glory to the same deity in the disguise of an humble shepherd. He dressed himself therefore in the richest embroidery of which he was master, and appeared before his mistress array'd in all the brightness of peerage. A sight whose charms she had not the power to resist, and the consequences are only to be imagined. In short, the same scene which Jupiter acted with his abovementioned mistress of old, was more than beginning, when Trent burst from the closet into which he had convey'd himself, and unkindly interrupted the action.

His lordship presently run to his sword; but Trent, with great calmness, answered, that as it was very well known he durst fight, he should not draw his sword on this occasion: 'For sure,' says he, 'my lord, it would be the highest imprudence in me to kill a man who is now become so considerably my debtor.' At which words he fetched a person from the closet, who had been confined with him, telling him he had done his business, and might now, if he pleased, retire.

It would be tedious here to amuse the reader with all that passed on the present occasion; the rage and confusion of the wife, or the perplexity in which my lord was involved. We will omit therefore all such matters, and proceed directly to business, as Trent and his lordship did soon after. And in the conclusion, my lord stipulated to pay a good round sum, and to provide Mr Trent with a good place on the first opportunity.

On the side of Mr Trent were stipulated absolute remission of all past, and full indulgence for the time to come.

Trent now immediately took a house at the polite end of the town, furnished it elegantly, and set up his equipage, rigged out both himself and his wife with very handsome cloaths, frequented all publick places where he could get admission, pushed himself into acquaintance, and his wife soon afterwards began to keep an assembly, or in the fashionable phrase, to be at home once a week; when, by my lord's assistance, she was presently visited by most men of the first rank, and by all such women of fashion as are not very nice in their company.

My lord's amour with this lady lasted not long; for as we have before observed, he was the most inconstant of all human race. Mrs Trent's passion was not however of that kind which leads to any very deep resentment of such fickleness. Her passion indeed was principally founded upon interest; so that foundation served to support another superstructure; and she was easily prevailed upon, as well as her husband, to be useful to my lord in a capacity, which, though very often exerted in the polite world, hath not, as yet, to my great surprise, acquired any polite name, or indeed any which is not too coarse to be admitted in this history.

After this preface, which we thought necessary to account for a character of which some of my country and collegiate readers might possibly doubt the existence, I shall proceed to what more immediately regards Mrs Booth. The reader may be pleased to remember that Mr Trent was present at the assembly to which Booth and his wife were carried by Mrs James, and where Amelia was met by the noble peer.

His lordship seeing there that Booth and Trent were old acquaintance, failed not, to use the language of sportsmen, to put Trent on upon the scent of Amelia. For this purpose that gentleman visited Booth the very next day, and had pursued him close ever since. By his means therefore my lord learn'd that Amelia was to be at the masquerade, to which place she was dogg'd by Trent in a sailor's jacket, who meeting my lord according to agreement, at the entrance of the opera-house, like the fourlegged gentlemen of the same vocation,[12] made a dead point, as it is called, at the game.

My lord was so satisfied and delighted with his conversation at the masquerade with the supposed Amelia, and the encouragement which in reality she had given him, that when he saw Trent the next morning, he embraced him with great fondness, gave him a bank note of £100 and promised him both the Indies on his success, of which he began now to have no manner of doubt.

The affair that happened at the gaming table, was likewise a scheme of Trent's, on a hint given by my lord to him to endeavour to lead Booth into some scrape or distress, his lordship promising to pay whatever expence Trent might be led into by such means. Upon his lordship's credit therefore the money lent to Booth was really advanced. And hence arose all that seeming generosity, and indifference as to the payment, Trent being satisfied with the obligation conferred on Booth, by means of which he hoped to effect his purpose.

But now the scene was totally changed; for Mrs Atkinson, the morning after the quarrel, beginning seriously to recollect that she had carried the matter rather too far, and might really injure Amelia's reputation, a thought to which the warm pursuit of her own interest had a good deal blinded her at the time, resolved to visit my lord himself, and to let him into the whole story; for, as she had succeeded already in her favourite point, she thought she had no reason to fear any consequence of the discovery. This resolution she immediately executed.

Trent came to attend his lordship just after Mrs Atkinson had left him. He found the peer in a very ill humour, and brought no news to comfort or recruit his spirits; for he had himself just received a billet from Booth, with an excuse for himself and his wife, from accepting the invitation at Trent's house that evening, where matters had been previously concerted for their entertainment; and when his lordship was by accident to drop into the room where Amelia was, while Booth was to be engaged at play in another.

And now after much debate, and after Trent had acquainted my lord with the wretched situation of Booth's circumstances, it was resolved, that Trent should immediately demand his money of Booth, and upon his not paying it, for they both concluded it impossible he should pay it, to put the note which Trent had for the money, in suit against him by the genteel means of paying it away to a nominal third person;[13] and this they both conceived must end immediately in the ruin of Booth, and consequently in the conquest of Amelia.

In this project, and with this hope, both my lord and his setter, or (if the sportsmen please) setting-dog, both greatly exulted, and it was next morning executed, as we have already seen.

CHAPTER 4

Containing some distress.

TRENT'S letter drove Booth almost to madness. To be indebted to such a fellow, at any rate, had stuck much in his stomach, and had given him very great uneasiness; but to answer this demand in any other manner, than by paying the money, was absolutely what he could not bear. Again, to pay this money he very plainly saw there was but one way; and this was by stripping his wife not only of every farthing, but almost of every rag she had in the world; a thought so dreadful, that it chilled his very soul with horrour; and yet pride at last seemed to represent this as the lesser evil of the two.

But how to do this was still a question. It was not sure, at least he feared it was not, that Amelia herself would readily consent to this; and so far from persuading her to such a measure, he could not bear even to propose it. At length his determination was to acquaint his wife with the whole affair, and to ask her consent by way of asking her advice; for he was well assured she could find no other means of extricating him out of his dilemma. This he accordingly did, representing the affair as bad as he could; though indeed it was impossible for him to aggravate the real truth.

Amelia heard him patiently without once interrupting him. When he had finished, she remained silent some time: indeed the shock she received from this story, almost deprived her of the power of speaking. At last she answered: 'Well, my dear, you ask my advice; I certainly can give you no other than that the money must be paid.'

'But how must it be paid?' cries he. 'Oh Heavens! thou sweetest creature, what, not once upbraid me for bringing this ruin on thee!'

'Upbraid you, my dear!' said she – 'Would to Heaven I could prevent your upbraiding yourself. But do not despair. I will endeavour by some means or other to get you the money.'

'Alas! my dear love,' cries Booth, 'I know the only way by which you can raise it. How can I consent to that? Do you forget the fears you so lately expressed of what would be our wretched condition, when our little all was mouldered away? – O, my Amelia, they cut my very heart-strings, when you spoke then; for I had then lost this little all. Indeed I assure you I have not played since, nor ever will more.'

'Keep that resolution,' said she, 'my dear, and I hope we shall yet recover the past' – At which words casting her eyes on the children, the tears burst from her eyes, and she cry'd – 'Heaven will, I hope, provide for us.'

A pathetic scene now ensued between the husband and wife, which would not perhaps please many readers to see drawn at too full a length. It is sufficient to say, that this excellent woman not only used her utmost endeavours to stifle and conceal her own concern, but said, and did every thing in her power to allay that of her husband.

Booth was at this time to meet a person whom we have formerly mentioned in the course of our history. This gentleman had a place in the War Office, and pretended to be a man of great interest and consequence; by which means he did not only receive great respect and court from the inferiour officers, but actually bubbled several of their money, by undertaking to do them services which, in reality, were not within his power. In truth, I have known few great men who have not been beset with one or more such fellows as these, through whom the inferiour part of mankind are obliged to make their court to the great men themselves; by which means, I believe principally, persons of real merit have been often deterred from the attempt; for these subaltern coxcombs ever assume an equal state with their masters, and look for an equal degree of respect to be paid to them; to which men of spirit, who are in every light their betters, are not easily brought to submit. These fellows indeed themselves have a jealous eye towards all great abilities, and are sure, to the utmost of their power, to keep all who are so endowed, from the presence of their masters. They use their masters, as bad ministers have sometimes used a prince; they keep all men of merit from his ears, and daily sacrifice his true honour and interest to their own profit, and their own vanity.

As soon as Booth was gone to his appointment with this man, Amelia immediately betook herself to her business with the highest resolution. She packed up not only her own little trinkets, and those of the children, but the greatest part of her own poor cloaths, (for she was but barely provided) and then drove in a hackney-coach to the same pawnbroker's, who had before been recommended to her by Mrs Atkinson: who advanced her the money she desired.

Being now provided with her sum she returned well pleased home; and her husband coming in soon after, she with much chearfulness delivered him all the money.

Booth was so overjoyed with the prospect of discharging his debt to Trent, that he did not perfectly reflect on the distress to which his family was now reduced. The good humour which appeared in the countenance of Amelia, was perhaps another help to stifle those reflexions; but above all were the assurances he had received from the great man, whom he had met at a coffee-house, and who had promised to do him all the service in his power; which several halfpay subaltern officers assured him was very considerable.

With this comfortable news he acquainted his wife, who either was, or seemed to be extremely well pleased with it. And now he set out with the money in his pocket to pay his friend Trent, who unluckily for him happened not to be at home.

On his return home he met his old friend the lieutenant, who thankfully paid him his crown, and insisted on his going with him and taking part of a bottle. This invitation was so eager and pressing, that poor Booth, who could not resist much importunity, complied.

While they were over this bottle, Booth acquainted his friend with the promises he had received that afternoon at the coffee-house, with which the old gentleman was very well pleased: 'For I have heard,' says he, 'that gentleman hath very powerful interest;' but he informed him likewise, that he had heard that the great man must be touched;[14] for that he never did any thing without touching. Of this, indeed, the great man himself had given some oblique hints, by saying, with great sagacity and slyness, that he knew where fifty pound might be deposited to much advantage.

Booth answered that he would very readily advance a small sum, if he had it in his power, but that at present it was not so; for that he had no more in the world than the sum of fifty pounds, which he owed Trent, and which he intended to pay him the next morning.

'It is very right undoubtedly to pay your debts,' says the old gentleman; 'but sure, on such an occasion, any man but the rankest usurer would be contented to stay a little while for his money; and it will be only a little while I am convinced: for if you deposite this sum in the great man's hands, I make no doubt but you will succeed immediately in getting your commission; and then I will help you to a method of taking up such a sum as this.' The old gentleman persisted in this advice, and backed it with every argument he could invent; declaring, as was indeed true, that he gave the same advice which he would pursue, was the case his own.

Booth long rejected the opinion of his friend; till, as they had not argued with dry lips, he became heated with wine, and then at last the old gentleman succeeded. Indeed, such was his love either for Booth, or for his own opinion, and perhaps for both, that he omitted nothing in his power. He even endeavoured to palliate the character of Trent, and unsaid half what he had before said of that gentleman. In the end he undertook to make Trent easy, and to go to him the very next morning for that purpose.

Poor Booth at last yielded, though with the utmost difficulty. Indeed had he known quite as much of Trent as the reader doth, no motive whatsoever would have prevailed on him to have taken the old gentleman's advice.

CHAPTER 5

Containing more wormwood, and other ingredients.

IN THE morning Booth communicated the matter to Amelia, who told him she would not presume to advise him in an affair, of which he was so much the better judge.

While Booth remained in a doubtful state what conduct to pursue, Bound came to make him a visit, and informed him that he had been at Trent's house, but found him not at home; adding, that he would pay him a second visit that very day, and would not rest till he found him.

Booth was ashamed to confess his wavering resolution, in an affair in which he had been so troublesome to his friend; he therefore dressed himself immediately, and together they both went to wait on the little great man, to whom Booth now hoped to pay his court in the most effectual manner.

Bound had been longer acquainted with the modern methods of business than Booth; he advised his friend therefore to begin with tipping (as it is called) the great man's servant. He did so, and by that means got speedy access to the master.

The great man received the money, not as a gudgeon doth a bait, but as a pike receives a poor gudgeon into his maw. To say the truth, such fellows as these may well be likened to that voracious fish, who fattens himself by devouring all the little inhabitants of the river. As soon as the great man had pocketed the cash, he shook Booth by the hand, and told him he would be sure to slip no opportunity of serving him, and would send him word as soon as any offered.

Here I shall stop one moment, and so perhaps will my good-natured reader; for surely it must be a hard heart which is not affected, with reflecting on the manner in which this poor little sum was raised, and on the manner in which it was bestowed. A worthy family, the wife and children of a man who had lost his blood abroad in the service of his country, parting with their little all, and exposed to cold and hunger, to pamper such a fellow as this.

And if any such reader, as I mention, should happen to be in reality a great man, and in power, perhaps the horrour of this picture may induce him to put a final end to this abominable practice of touching, as it is called; by which indeed a set of leaches are permitted to suck the blood of the brave and the indigent; of the widow and the orphan.

Booth now returned home, where he found his wife with Mrs James. Amelia had, before the arrival of her husband, absolutely refused Mrs James's invitation to dinner the next day; but when Booth came in, the lady renewed her application, and that in so pressing a manner, that Booth seconded her; for tho' he had enough of jealousy in his temper; yet such was his friendship to the colonel, and such his gratitude to the obligations which he had received from him, that his own unwillingness to believe any thing of him, co-operating with Amelia's endeavours to put every thing in the fairest light, had brought him to acquit his friend of any ill design. To this perhaps the late affair concerning my lord had moreover contributed: for it seems to me, that the same passion cannot much energize on two different objects at one and the same time: an observation which I believe will hold as true, with regard to the cruel passions of jealousy and anger, as to the gentle passions of love, in which one great and mighty object is sure to engage the whole passion.

When Booth grew importunate, Amelia answered, 'My dear, I should not refuse you whatever was in my power; but this is absolutely out of my power; for since I must declare the truth, I cannot dress myself.'

'Why so?' said Mrs James, 'I am sure you are in good health.'

'Is there no other impediment to dressing but want of health, madam?' answered Amelia.

'Upon my word none that I know of,' replied Mrs James.

'What do you think of want of cloaths, madam?' said Amelia.

'Ridiculous!' cried Mrs James. 'What need have you to dress yourself out? – You will see no body but our own family, and I promise you I don't expect it. – A plain night-gown will do very well.'

'But if I must be plain with you, madam,' said Amelia, 'I have no other cloaths but what I have now on my back. – I have not even a clean shift in the world: for you must know, my dear,' said she to Booth, 'that little Betty is walk'd off this morning, and hath carried all my linen with her.'

'How, my dear,' cries Booth, 'little Betty robb'd you!'

'It is even so,' answer'd Amelia. Indeed she spoke truth; for little Betty having perceiv'd the evening before that her mistress was moving her goods, was willing to lend all the assistance in her power, and had accordingly mov'd off early that morning, taking with her whatever she could lay her hands on.

Booth expressed himself with some passion on the occasion, and swore he would make an example of the girl. 'If the little slut be above ground,' cried he, 'I will find her out and bring her to justice.'

'I am really sorry for this accident,' said Mrs James, 'and (tho' I know not how to mention it) I beg you'll give me leave to offer you any linen of mine, till you can make new of your own.'

Amelia thank'd Mrs James, but declin'd the favour, saying she should do well enough at home; and that as she had no servant now to take care of her children, she could not, nor would not leave them on any account.

'Then bring master and miss with you,' said Mrs James. 'You shall positively dine with us to-morrow.'

'I beg, madam, you will mention it no more,' said Amelia; 'for besides the substantial reasons I have already given, I have some things on my mind at present which made me unfit for company; and I am resolved nothing shall prevail on me to stir from home.'

Mrs James had carried her invitation already to the very utmost limits of good-breeding if not beyond them. She desisted therefore from going any further, and after some short stay longer took her leave, with many expressions of concern, which however, great as it was, left her heart and her mouth together, before she was out of the house.

Booth now declar'd that he would go in pursuit of little Betty, against whom he vowed so much vengeance, that Amelia endeavour'd to moderate his anger by representing to him the girl's youth, and that this was the first fault she had ever been guilty of.

'Indeed,' says she, 'I should be very glad to have my things again, and I would have the girl too punish'd in some degree, which might possibly be for her own good; but I tremble to think of taking away her life:' for Booth in his rage had sworn he would hang her.

'I know the tenderness of your heart, my dear,' said Booth, 'and I love you for it; but I must beg leave to dissent from your opinion. I do not think the girl in any light an object of mercy. She is not only guilty of dishonesty, but of cruelty: for she must know our situation, and the very little we had left. She is besides guilty of ingratitude to you, who have treated her with so much kindness, that you have rather acted the part of a mother than of a mistress. And so far from thinking her youth an excuse, I think it rather an aggravation. It is true indeed there are faults which the youth of the party very strongly recommends to our pardon. Such are all those which proceed from carelessness, and want of thought; but crimes of this black die, which are committed with deliberation and imply a bad mind, deserve a more severe punishment in a young person than in one of riper years: for what must the mind be in old age which hath acquir'd such a degree of perfection in villainy so very early! Such persons as these it is really a charity to the public to put out of the society; and indeed a religious man would put them out of the world for the sake of themselves; for whoever understands any thing of human nature must know, that such people the longer they live, the more they will accumulate vice and wickedness.'

'Well, my dear,' cries Amelia, 'I cannot argue with you on these subjects. I shall always submit to your superior judgment, and I know you too well to think that you will ever do any thing cruel.'

Booth then left Amelia to the care of her children, and went in pursuit of the thief.

CHAPTER 6

A scene of the tragic kind.

HE HAD not been long gone, before a thundring knock was heard at the door of the house where Amelia lodged, and presently after a figure all pale, ghastly, and almost breathless, rush'd into the room where she then was with her children.

This figure Amelia soon recognized to be Mrs Atkinson, tho' indeed she was so disguised that at her first entrance Amelia scarce knew her. Her eyes were sunk in her head, her hair dishevelled, and not only her dress but every feature in her face was in the utmost disorder.

Amelia was greatly shock'd at this sight, and the little girl was much frightned; as for the boy he immediately knew her, and running to Amelia, he cried, 'La! mamma, what is the matter with poor Mrs Atkinson?'

As soon as Mrs Atkinson recover'd her breath, she cried out – 'O Mrs Booth, I am the most miserable of women; I have lost the best of husbands.'

Amelia looking at her with all the tenderness imaginable; forgetting, I believe, that there had ever been any quarrel between them – said – 'Good Heavens, madam, what's the matter?'

'O Mrs Booth,' answer'd she, 'I fear I have lost my husband. The doctor says, there is but little hope of his life. O madam, however I have been in the wrong I am sure you will forgive me and pity me. I am sure I am severely punish'd: for to that cursed affair I owe all my misery.'

'Indeed, madam,' cries Amelia, 'I am extremely concern'd for your misfortune. But pray tell me hath any thing happen'd to the serjeant?'

'O madam,' cries she, 'I have the greatest reason to fear I shall lose him. The doctor hath almost given him over. – He says he hath scarce any hopes. – O madam, that evening that the fatal quarrel happen'd between us, my dear captain took it so to heart, that he sat up all night and drank a whole bottle of brandy. – Indeed, he said, he wish'd to kill himself: for nothing could have hurt him so much in the world, he said, as to have any quarrel between you and me. His concern and what he drank together threw him into a high fever. – So that when I came home from my lord's – (for indeed, madam, I have been and set all to rights – your reputation is now in no danger.) When I came home, I say, I found the poor man in a raving delirious fit, and in that he hath continued ever since till about an hour ago, when he came perfectly to his senses; but now he says he is sure he shall die, and begs for Heaven's sake to see you first. Would you, madam, would you have the goodness to grant my poor captain's desire; consider he is a dying man, and neither he nor I shall ever ask you a second favour. He says he hath something to say to you that he can mention to no other person, and that he cannot die in peace unless he sees you.'

'Upon my word, madam,' cries Amelia, 'I am extremely concern'd at what you tell me. I knew the poor serjeant from his infancy, and always had an affection for him, as I think him to be one of the best-natur'd and honestest creatures upon earth. I am sure if I could do him any service, – but of what use can my going be? –'

'Of the highest in the world,' answer'd Mrs Atkinson. 'If you knew how earnestly he entreated it, how his poor breaking heart begged to see you, you would not refuse. –'

'Nay, I do not absolutely refuse,' cries Amelia. – 'Something to say to me of consequence, and that he could not die in peace, unless he said it – did he say that, Mrs Atkinson?'

'Upon my honour he did,' answer'd she, 'and much more than I have related.'

'Well, I will go with you,' cries Amelia. 'I cannot guess what this should be; but I will go.'

Mrs Atkinson then poured out a thousand blessings and thanksgivings; and taking hold of Amelia's hand, and eagerly kissing it, cried out – 'How could that fury passion drive me to quarrel with such a creature?'

Amelia told her she had forgiven and forgot it; and then calling up the mistress of the house, and committing to her the care of the children, she cloaked herself up as well as she could, and set out with Mrs Atkinson.

When they arrived at the house, Mrs Atkinson said she would go first and give the captain some notice; for that if Amelia entered the room unexpectedly, the surprize might have an ill effect. She left therefore Amelia in the parlour, and proceeded directly up stairs.

Poor Atkinson, weak and bad as was his condition, no sooner heard that Amelia was come, than he discovered great joy in his countenance, and presently afterwards she was introduced to him.

Atkinson exerted his utmost strength to thank her for this goodness to a dying man, (for so he called himself.) He said he should not have presumed to give her this trouble, had he not had something, which he thought of consequence, to say to her, and which he could not mention to any other person. He then desired his wife to give him a little box, of which he always kept the key himself, and afterwards begged her to leave the room for a few minutes; at which neither she, nor Amelia, expressed any dissatisfaction.

When he was alone with Amelia, he spoke as follows: 'This, madam, is the last time my eyes will ever behold what – do pardon me, madam, I will never offend you more.' – Here he sunk down in his bed, and the tears gushed from his eyes.

'Why should you fear to offend me, Joe?' said Amelia; 'I am sure you never did any thing willingly to offend me.'

'No, madam,' answered he, 'I would die a thousand times, before I would have ventured it in the smallest matter. But – I cannot speak – and yet I must. You cannot pardon me, and yet perhaps as I am a dying man, and never shall see you more. – Indeed, if I was to live after this discovery, I should never dare to look you in the face again – and yet, madam, to think I shall never see you more is worse than ten thousand deaths.'

'Indeed, Mr Atkinson,' cries Amelia, blushing, and looking down on the floor, 'I must not hear you talk in this manner. If you have any thing to say, tell it me, and do not be afraid of my anger; for I think I may promise to forgive whatever it was possible you should do.'

'Here then, madam,' said he, 'is your picture, I stole it when I was eighteen years of age, and have kept it ever since. It is set in gold, with three little diamonds; and yet I can truly say, it was not the gold nor the diamonds which I stole – it was that face which, if I had been the emperor of the world –'

'I must not hear any more of this;' said she, – 'comfort yourself, Joe, and think no more of this matter. Be assured I freely and heartily forgive you – But pray compose yourself; come, let me call in your wife. –'

'First, madam, let me beg one favour' – cried he, 'consider it is the last, and then I shall die in peace – let me kiss that hand before I die.'

'Well, nay,' says she, 'I don't know what I am doing – well – there –' she then carelessly gave him her hand, which he put gently to his lips, and then presently let it drop and fell back in the bed.

Amelia now summoned Mrs Atkinson, who was indeed no further off than just without the door. She then hastened down stairs and called for a great glass of water, which having drank off, she threw herself into a chair, and the tears ran plentifully from her eyes with compassion for the poor wretch she had just left in his bed.

To say the truth, without any injury to her chastity, that heart which had stood firm as a rock to all the attacks of title and equipage, of finery and flattery, and which all the treasures of the universe could not have purchased, was yet a little softened by the plain, honest, modest, involuntary, delicate, heroic passion of this poor and humble swain; for whom, in spite of herself, she felt a momentary tenderness and complacence, at which Booth, if he had known it, would perhaps have been displeased.

Having staid some time in the parlour, and not finding Mrs Atkinson come down, (for indeed her husband was then so bad she could not quit him) Amelia left a message with the maid of the house for her mistress, purporting that she should be ready to do any thing in her power to serve her, and then left the house with a confusion on her mind that she had never felt before, and which any chastity that is not hewn out of marble must feel on so tender and delicate an occasion.

CHAPTER 7

In which Mr Booth meets with more than one adventure.

BOOTH having hunted about for two hours at last saw a young lady in a tattered silk gown, stepping out of a shop in Monmouth Street[15] into a hackney coach. This lady, notwithstanding the disguise of her dress, he presently discovered to be no other than little Betty.

He instantly gave the alarm of 'stop thief, stop coach;' upon which, Mrs Betty was immediately stopt in her vehicle, and Booth and his myrmidons laid hold of her.

The girl no sooner found that she was seised by her master, than the consciousness of her guilt overpowered her; for she was not yet an experienced offender, and she immediately confessed her crime.

She was then carried before a Justice of Peace, where she was searched, and there was found in her possession four shillings and sixpence in money, besides the silk gown, which was indeed proper furniture for rag fair,[16] and scarce worth a single farthing, though the honest shopkeeper in Monmouth Street had sold it for a crown to this simple girl.

The girl being examined by the magistrate, spoke as follows: 'Indeed, sir, an't please your worship, I am very sorry for what I have done; and to be sure, an't please your honour, my lord, it must have been the devil that put me upon it; for to be sure, please your majesty, I never thought upon such a thing in my whole life before, any more than I did of my dying day; but indeed, sir, an't please your worship –'

She was running on in this manner when the Justice interrupted her, and desir'd her to give an account what she had taken from her master, and what she had done with it.

'Indeed, an't please your majesty,' said she, 'I took no more than two shifts of madam's, and I pawned them for five shillings, which I gave for the gown that's upon my back; and as for the money in my pocket, it is every farthing of it my own. I am sure I intended to carry back the shifts too as soon as ever I could get money to take them out.'

The girl having told them where the pawnbroker lived, the Justice sent to him, to produce the shifts, which he presently did; for he expected that a warrant to search his house would be the consequence of his refusal.

The shifts being produced, on which the honest pawnbroker had lent five shillings, appeared plainly to be worth above thirty: indeed when new they had cost much more. So that by their goodness, as well as by their size, it was certain they could not have belonged to the girl.

Booth grew very warm against the pawnbroker. 'I hope, sir,' said he to the Justice, 'there is some punishment for this fellow likewise, who so plainly appears to have known that these goods were stolen. The shops of these fellows may indeed be called the fountains of theft: for it is in reality the encouragement which they meet with from these receivers of their goods that induces men very often to become thieves; so that these deserve equal, if not severer punishment than the thieves themselves.'

The pawnbroker protested his innocence. And denied the taking in the shifts. Indeed in this he spoke truth; for he had slipt into an inner room, as was always his custom on these occasions, and left a little boy to do the business; by which means he had carried on the trade of receiving stolen goods for many years with impunity, and had been twice acquitted at the Old Bailey, though the juggle appeared upon the most manifest evidence.

As the Justice was going to speak he was interrupted by the girl, who falling upon her knees to Booth with many tears begged his forgiveness.

'Indeed, Betty,' cries Booth, 'you do not deserve forgiveness; for you know very good reasons why you should not have thought of robbing your mistress, particularly at this time. And what further aggravates your crime is, that you have robbed the best and kindest mistress in the world. Nay, you are not only guilty of felony, but of a felonious breach of trust; for you know very well every thing your mistress had, was intrusted to your care.'

Now it happened by very great accident that the Justice before whom the girl was brought, understood the law. Turning therefore to Booth he said, 'Do you say, sir, that this girl was intrusted with the shifts?'

'Yes, sir,' said Booth, 'she was intrusted with every thing.'

'And will you swear that the goods stolen,' said the Justice, 'are worth forty shillings?'

'No indeed, sir,' answered Booth, 'nor that they are worth thirty either.'

'Then, sir,' cries the justice, 'the girl cannot be guilty of felony.'

'How, sir,' said Booth, 'is it not a breach of trust? And is not a breach of trust felony, and the worst felony too?'

'No, sir,' answered the Justice, 'a breach of trust is no crime in our law, unless it be in a servant; and then the Act of Parliament requires the goods taken to be of the value of forty shillings.'

'So then a servant,' cries Booth, 'may rob his master of thirty-nine shillings whenever he pleases, and he can't be punished.'

'If the goods are under his care, he can't,' cries the Justice.

'I ask your pardon, sir,' says Booth. 'I do not doubt what you say; but sure this is a very extraordinary law.'

'Perhaps I think so too,' said the Justice; 'but it belongs not to my office to make or to mend laws. My business is only to execute them. If therefore the case be as you say, I must discharge the girl.'

'I hope however, you will punish the pawnbroker,' cries Booth.

'If the girl is discharged,' cries the Justice, 'so must be the pawnbroker: for if the goods are not stolen, he cannot be guilty of receiving them, knowing them to be stolen. And besides as to his offence, to say the truth, I am almost weary of prosecuting it; for such are the difficulties laid in the way of this prosecution, that it is almost impossible to convict any one on it. And to speak my opinion plainly, such are the laws, and such the method of proceeding, that one would almost think our laws were rather made for the protection of rogues, than for the punishment of them.'

Thus ended this examination; the thief and the receiver went about their business; and Booth departed, in order to go home to his wife.

In his way home, Booth was met by a lady in a chair; who, immediately upon seeing him, stopt her chair, bolted out of it, and going directly up to him, said: 'So, Mr Booth, you have kept your word with me.'

This lady was no other than Miss Mathews; and the speech she meant was of a promise made to her at the masquerade, of visiting her within a day or two; which whether he ever intended to keep I cannot say; but in truth the several accidents that had since happened to him, had so discomposed his mind, that he had absolutely forgot it.

Booth however was too sensible, and too well bred, to make the excuse of forgetfulness to a lady; nor could he readily find any other. While he stood therefore hesitating, and looking not over wise, Miss Mathews said: 'Well, sir, since by your confusion I see you have some grace left; I will pardon you on one condition, and that is, that you will sup with me this night. But if you fail me now, expect all the revenge of an injured woman.' She then bound herself by a most outrageous oath, that she would complain to his wife – 'And I am sure,' says she, 'she is so much a woman of honour, as to do me justice. – And tho' I miscarried in my first attempt, be assured I will take care of my second.'

Booth asked what she meant by her first attempt; to which she answered, that she had already writ his wife an account of his ill usage of her, but that she was pleased it had miscarried. She then repeated her asseverations, that she would now do it effectually, if he disappointed her.

This threat she reckoned would most certainly terrify poor Booth; and indeed she was not mistaken; for I believe it would have been impossible, by any other menace, or by any other means, to have brought him once even to balance in his mind on this question. But by this threat she prevailed; and Booth promised, upon his word and honour, to come to her at the hour she appointed. After which she took leave of him with a squeeze by the hand, and a smiling countenance, and walked back to her chair.

But however she might be pleased with having obtained this promise, Booth was far from being delighted with the thoughts of having given it. He looked indeed upon the consequences of this meeting with horrour; but as to the consequence which was so apparently intended by the lady, he resolved against it. At length he came to this determination; to go according to his appointment, to argue the matter with the lady, and to convince her, if possible, that from a regard to his honour only, he must discontinue her acquaintance. If this failed to satisfy her, and she still persisted in her threats to acquaint his wife with the affair, he then resolved, whatever pains it cost him, to communicate the whole truth himself to Amelia, from whose goodness he doubted not but to obtain an absolute remission.

CHAPTER 8

In which Amelia appears in a light more amiable than gay.

WE WILL now return to Amelia, whom we left in some perturbation of mind departing from Mrs Atkinson.

Though she had before walked through the streets in a very improper dress with Mrs Atkinson, she was unwilling, especially as she was alone, to return in the same manner. Indeed she was scarce able to walk in her present condition; for the case of poor Atkinson had much affected her tender heart, and her eyes had overflown with many tears.

It occurred likewise to her at present, that she had not a single shilling in her pocket, or at home, to provide food for herself and her family. In this situation she resolved to go immediately to the pawnbroker whither she had gone before, and to deposite her picture for what she could raise upon it. She then immediately took a chair, and put her design in execution.

The intrinsic value of the gold, in which this picture was set, and of the little diamonds which surrounded it, amounted to nine guineas. This therefore was advanced to her; and the prettiest face in the world (such is often the fate of beauty) was deposited, as of no value into the bargain.

When she came home, she found the following letter from Mrs Atkinson:

My dearest Madam,

As I know your goodness, I could not delay a moment acquainting you with the happy turn of my affairs since you went. The doctor, on his return to visit my husband, has assured me, that the captain was on the recovery, and in very little danger; and I really think he is since mended. I hope to wait on you soon with better news. Heaven bless you, dear madam, and believe me to be, with the utmost sincerity,

Your most obliged,

obedient humble servant,

Atkinson.

Amelia was really pleased with this letter; and now it being past four o'clock, she despaired of seeing her husband till the evening. She therefore provided some tarts for her children; and then eating nothing but a slice of bread and butter herself, she began to prepare for the captain's supper.

There were two things of which her husband was particularly fond, which, though it may bring the simplicity of his taste into great contempt with some of my readers, I will venture to name. These were a fowl and egg sauce, and mutton broth; both which Amelia immediately purchased.

As soon as the clock struck seven, the good creature went down into the kitchin, and began to exercise her talents of cookery, of which she was a great mistress, as she was of every economical[17] office, from the highest to the lowest; and as no woman could outshine her in a drawing-room, so none could make the drawing-room itself shine brighter than Amelia. And if I may speak a bold truth, I question whether it be possible to view this fine creature in a more amiable light, than while she was dressing her husband's supper with her little children playing round her.

It was now half an hour past eight, and the meat almost ready, the table likewise neatly spread with materials, borrowed from her landlady, and she began to grow a little uneasy at Booth's not returning; when a sudden knock at the door roused her spirits, and she cried, 'There, my dear, there is your good papa;' at which words she darted swiftly up stairs, and opened the door to her husband.

She desired her husband to walk up into the dining-room, and she would come to him in an instant; for she was desirous to encrease his pleasure, by surprising him with his two favourite dishes. She then went down again to the kitchin, where the maid of the house undertook to send up the supper, and she with her children returned to Booth.

He then told her concisely what had happened, with relation to the girl – to which she scarce made any answer; but asked him if he had not dined. He assured her he had not eat a morsel the whole day. 'Well,' says she, 'my dear, I am a fellow-sufferer; but we shall both enjoy our supper the more: for I have made a little provision for you, as I guessed what might be the case. I have got you a bottle of wine too. And here is a clean cloth and a smiling countenance, my dear Will. Indeed I am in unusual good spirits to-night, and I have made a promise to the children, which you must confirm; I have promised to let them sit up this one night to supper with us. – Nay, don't look so serious; cast off all uneasy thoughts – I have a present for you here – no matter how I came by it.' – At which words she put eight guineas into his hand, crying: 'Come, my dear Bill, be gay – Fortune will yet be kind to us – at least let us be happy this night. Indeed the pleasures of many women, during their whole lives, will not amount to my happiness this night, if you will be in good humour.'

Booth fetched a deep sigh, and cried – 'How unhappy am I, my dear, that I can't sup with you to-night!'

As in the delightful month of June, when the sky is all serene, and the whole face of nature looks with a pleased and smiling aspect, suddenly a dark cloud spreads itself over the hemisphere, the sun vanishes from our sight, and every object is obscured by a dark and horrid gloom. So happened it to Amelia; the joy that had enlightened every feature disappeared in a moment; the lustre forsook her shining eyes; and all the little loves, that played and wantoned in her cheeks, hung their drooping heads, and with a faint trembling voice she repeated her husband's words: 'Not sup with me to night, my dear!'

'Indeed, my dear,' answered he, 'I cannot. I need not tell you how uneasy it makes me, or that I am as much disappointed as yourself; but I am engaged to sup abroad. I have absolutely given my honour; and besides, it is on business of importance.'

'My dear,' said she, 'I say no more. I am convinced you would not willingly sup from me. I own it is a very particular disappointment to me to night, when I had proposed unusual pleasure; but the same reason which is sufficient to you, ought to be so to me.'

Booth made his wife a compliment on her ready compliance, and then asked her, what she intended by giving him that money, or how she came by it.

'I intend, my dear,' said she, 'to give it you; that is all. As to the manner in which I came by it, you know, Billy, that is not very material. You are well assured I got it by no means which would displease you; and perhaps another time I may tell you.'

Booth asked no farther questions; but he returned her, and insisted on her taking all but one guinea, saying she was the safest treasurer. He then promised her to make all the haste home in his power, and he hoped, he said, to be with her in an hour and half at farthest, and then took his leave.

When he was gone, the poor disappointed Amelia sat down to supper with her children; with whose company she was forced to console herself for the absence of her husband.

CHAPTER 9

A very tragic scene.

THE clock had struck eleven, and Amelia was just proceeding to put her children to bed, when she heard a knock at the street door. Upon which the boy cried out, 'There's papa, mamma, pray let me stay and see him before I go to bed.' This was a favour very easily obtained; for Amelia instantly ran down stairs, exulting in the goodness of her husband for returning so soon, though half an hour was already elapsed beyond the time in which he promised to return.

Poor Amelia was now again disappointed; for it was not her husband at the door, but a servant with a letter for him, which he delivered into her hands. She immediately returned up stairs, and said – 'It was not your papa, my dear; but I hope it is one who hath brought us some good news.' For Booth had told her, that he hourly expected to receive such from the great man, and had desired her to open any letter which came to him in his absence.

Amelia therefore broke open the letter, and read as follows:

SIR,

After what hath past between us, I need only tell you that I know you supped this very night alone with Miss Mathews: a fact which will upbraid you sufficiently, without putting me to that trouble; and will very well account for my desiring the favour of seeing you to-morrow in Hyde Park at six in the morning. You will forgive me reminding you once more how inexcusable this behaviour is in you who are possessed in your own wife of the most inestimable jewel.

Yours, &c.

T. James.

I shall bring pistols with me.

It is not easy to describe the agitation of Amelia's mind when she read this letter. She threw herself into her chair, turned as pale as death, began to tremble all over, and had just power enough left to tap the bottle of wine, which she had hitherto preserved entire for her husband, and to drink off a large bumper.

The little boy perceived the strange symptoms which appeared in his mother; and running to her, he cried, 'What's the matter, my dear mamma, you don't look well? – No harm hath happened to poor papa, I hope – Sure that bad man hath not carried him away again.'

Amelia answered, 'No, child, nothing – nothing at all.' – And then a large shower of tears came to her assistance; which presently after produced the same in the eyes of both the children.

Amelia, after a short silence, looking tenderly at her children, cry'd out, 'It is too much, too much to bear. Why did I bring these little wretches into the world! Why were these innocents born to such a fate!' – She then threw her arms round them both, (for they were before embracing her knees) and cried, 'O my children! my children! forgive me, my babes – Forgive me that I have brought you into such a world as this. You are undone – my children are undone.'

The little boy answered with great spirit, 'How undone, mamma? my sister and I don't care a farthing for being undone – don't cry so upon our accounts – we are both very well; indeed we are – but do pray tell us. I am sure some accident hath happened to poor papa.'

'Mention him no more,' cries Amelia – 'your papa is – indeed he is a wicked man – he cares not for any of us – O Heavens, is this the happiness I promised myself this evening!' – At which words she fell into an agony, holding both her children in her arms.

The maid of the house now entered the room, with a letter in her hand, which she had received from a porter, whose arrival the reader will not wonder to have been unheard by Amelia in her present condition.

The maid, upon her entrance into the room, perceiving the situation of Amelia, cried out, 'Good Heavens! madam, what's the matter?' Upon which Amelia, who had a little recovered herself after the last violent vent of her passion, started up and cried – 'Nothing, Mrs Susan – nothing extraordinary. I am subject to these fits sometimes; but I am very well now. Come, my dear children, I am very well again; indeed I am. You must now go to bed; Mrs Susan will be so good as to put you to bed.'

'But why doth not papa love us?' cries the little boy, 'I am sure we have none of us done any thing to disoblige him.'

This innocent question of the child so stung Amelia, that she had the utmost difficulty to prevent a relapse. However she took another dram of wine; for so it might be called to her, who was the most temperate of women, and never exceeded three glasses on any occasion. In this glass she drank her children's health, and soon after so well soothed, and composed them, that they went quietly away with Mrs Susan.

The maid, in the shock she had conceived at the melancholy, indeed frightful scene, which had presented itself to her at her first coming into the room, had quite forgot the letter, which she held in her hand. However, just at her departure, she recollected it, and delivered it to Amelia; who was no sooner alone, than she opened it, and read as follows:

My dearest sweetest Love,

I write this from the bailiff's house, where I was formerly, and to which I am again brought at the suit of that villain, Trent. I have the misfortune to think I owe this accident (I mean that it happened to night) to my own folly, in endeavouring to keep a secret from you – O my dear, had I had resolution to confess my crime to you, your forgiveness would, I am convinced, have cost me only a few blushes, and I had now been happy in your arms. Fool that I was to leave you on such an account, and to add to a former transgression a new one. – Yet by heavens I mean not a transgression of the like kind; for of that I am not, nor ever will be guilty; and when you know the true reason of my leaving you to-night, I think you will pity, rather than upbraid me. I am sure you would, if you knew the compunction with which I left you to go to the most worthless, the most infamous – Do guess the rest – guess that crime with which I cannot stain my paper – but still believe me no more guilty than I am – or, if it will lessen your vexation at what hath befallen me, believe me as guilty as you please, and think me, for a while at least, as undeserving of you, as I think myself. This paper and pen are so bad, I question whether you can read what I write. I almost doubt whether I wish you should. Yet this I will endeavour to make as legible as I can – Be comforted, my dear love, and still keep up your spirits with the hopes of better days. The doctor will be in town to-morrow, and I trust on his goodness for my delivery once more from this place, and that I shall soon be able to repay him. That Heaven may bless and preserve you, is the prayer of,

My dearest love,
Your ever fond affectionate,
and hereafter, faithful husband,

W. Booth.

Amelia pretty well guessed the obscure meaning of this letter, which though at another time it might have given her unspeakable torment, was at present rather of the medicinal kind, and served to allay her anguish. Her anger to Booth too began a little to abate, and was softened by her concern for his misfortune. Upon the whole, however, she past a miserable and sleepless night, her gentle mind torn and distracted with various and contending passions, distressed with doubts, and wandring in a kind of twilight, which presented her only objects of different degrees of horrour, and where black despair closed at a small distance the gloomy prospect.

BOOK XII

CHAPTER 1

The book begins with polite history.

BEFORE we return to the miserable couple, whom we left at the end of the last book, we will give our reader the more chearful view of the gay and happy family of Colonel James.

Mrs James when she could not, as we have seen, prevail with Amelia to accept that invitation, which at the desire of the colonel she had so kindly and obediently carried her, returned to her husband, and acquainted him with the ill success of her embassy; at which, to say the truth, she was almost as much disappointed as the colonel himself: for he had not taken a much stronger liking to Amelia, than she herself had conceived for Booth. This will account for some passages, which may have a little surprised the reader in the former chapters of this history, as we were not then at leisure to communicate to them a hint of this kind: it was indeed on Mr Booth's account that she had been at the trouble of changing her dress at the masquerade.

But her passions of this sort, happily for her, were not extremely strong; she was therefore easily baulked, and as she met with no encouragement from Booth, she soon gave way to the impetuosity of Miss Mathews; and from that time scarce thought more of the affair, till her husband's design against the wife revived hers likewise; insomuch, that her passion was, at this time, certainly strong enough for Booth, to produce a good hearty hatred for Amelia, whom she now abused to the colonel in very gross terms; both on the account of her poverty, and her insolence: for so she termed the refusal of all her offers.

The colonel seeing no hopes of soon possessing his new mistress, began, like a prudent and wise man, to turn his thoughts towards the securing his old one. From what his wife had mentioned, concerning the behaviour of the shepherdess, and particularly her preference of Booth, he had little doubt but that this was the identical Miss Mathews. He resolved therefore to watch her closely, in hopes of discovering Booth's intrigue with her. In this, besides the remainder of affection which he yet preserved for that lady, he had another view, as it would give him a fair pretence to quarrel with Booth; who, by carrying on this intrigue, would have broke his word and honour given to him. And he began now to hate poor Booth heartily, from the same reason from which Mrs James had contracted her aversion to Amelia.

The colonel therefore employed an inferior kind of pimp to watch the lodgings of Miss Mathews, and to acquaint him if Booth, whose person was known to the pimp, made any visit there.

The pimp faithfully performed his office, and having last night made the wish'd for discovery, immediately acquainted his master with it.

Upon this news the colonel presently dispatched to Booth the short note which we have before seen. He sent it to his own house instead of Miss Mathews's, with hopes of that very accident which actually did happen. Not that he had any ingredient of the bully in him, and desired to be prevented from fighting, but with a prospect of injuring Booth in the affection and esteem of Amelia, and of recommending himself somewhat to her by appearing in the light of her champion; for which purpose he added that compliment to Amelia in his letter. He concluded upon the whole, that, if Booth himself opened the letter, he would certainly meet him the next morning; but if his wife should open it before he came home, it might have the effects before mentioned; and for his future expostulation with Booth, it would not be in Amelia's power to prevent it.

Now it happened, that this pimp had more masters than one. Amongst these was the worthy Mr Trent, for whom he had often done business of the pimping vocation. He had been employed indeed in the service of the great peer himself, under the direction of the said Trent, and was the very person who had assisted the said Trent in dogging Booth and his wife to the opera-house on masquerade night.

This subaltern pimp was with his superior Trent yesterday morning, when he found a bailiff with him in order to receive his instructions for the arresting Booth; when the bailiff said it would be a very difficult matter to take him; for that to his knowledge he was as shy a cock as any in England. The subaltern immediately acquainted Trent with the business in which he was employ'd by the colonel, upon which Trent enjoined him the moment he had set him to give immediate notice to the bailiff; which he agreed to, and performed accordingly.

The bailiff, on receiving the notice, immediately set out for his stand at an alehouse within three doors of Miss Mathews's lodgings. At which, unfortunately for poor Booth, he arrived a very few minutes before Booth left that lady in order to return to Amelia.

These were several matters, of which we thought necessary our reader should be informed; for, besides that it conduces greatly to a perfect understanding of all history, there is no exercise of the mind of a sensible reader more pleasant than the tracing the several small and almost imperceptible links in every chain of events by which all the great actions of the world are produced. We will now in the next chapter proceed with our history.

CHAPTER 2

In which Amelia visits her husband.

AMELIA, after much anxious thinking, in which she sometimes flattered herself that her husband was less guilty than she had at first imagined him, and that he had some good excuse to make for himself; (for indeed she was not so able as willing to make one for him,) at length resolved to set out for the bailiff's castle. Having therefore strictly recommended the care of her children to her good landlady, she sent for a hackney coach, and ordered the coachman to drive to Gray's Inn Lane.

When she came to the house, and ask'd for the captain, the bailiff's wife, who came to the door, guessing by the greatness of her beauty, and the disorder of her dress, that she was a young lady of pleasure, answered surlily, 'Captain! I do not know of any captain that is here, not I.' For this good woman was, as well as Dame Purgante in Prior,[1] a bitter enemy to all whores; especially to those of the handsome kind; for some such she suspected to go shares with her in a certain property to which the law gave her the sole right.

Amelia replied, she was certain that Captain Booth was there. 'Well, if he is so,' cries the bailiff's wife, 'you may come into the kitchin if you will – and he shall be called down to you if you have any business with him.' At the same time she mutter'd something to herself, and concluded a little more intelligibly, tho' still in a muttering voice, that she kept no such house.

Amelia, whose innocence gave her no suspicion of the true cause of this good woman's sullenness, was frightened, and began to fear she knew not what. At last she made a shift to totter into the kitchin, when the mistress of the house asked her, 'Well, madam, who shall I tell the captain wants to speak with him?'

'I ask your pardon, madam,' cries Amelia, 'in my confusion I really forgot you did not know me – tell him, if you please, that I am his wife.'

'And are you indeed his wife, madam?' cries Mrs Bailiff, a little softened.

'Yes, indeed, and upon my honour,' answers Amelia.

'If this be the case,' cries the other, 'you may walk up stairs if you please. Heaven forbid I should part man and wife. Indeed I think they can never be too much together. But I never will suffer any bad doings in my house, nor any of the town ladies to come to gentlemen here.'

Amelia answered, that she liked her the better; for indeed, in her present disposition, Amelia was as much exasperated against wicked women as the virtuous mistress of the house, or any other virtuous woman could be.

The bailiff's wife then ushered Amelia up stairs, and having unlocked the prisoner's door, cried, 'Captain, here is your lady, sir, come to see you.' At which words Booth started up from his chair, and caught Amelia in his arms, embracing her for a considerable time with so much rapture, that the bailiff's wife, who was an eye-witness of this violent fondness, began to suspect whether

Amelia had really told her truth. However she had some little awe of the captain, and for fear of being in the wrong did not interfere, but shut the door and turned the key.

When Booth found himself alone with his wife, and had vented the first violence of his rapture in kisses and embraces, he looked tenderly at her, and cried, 'Is it possible, Amelia, is it possible you can have this goodness to follow such a wretch as me to such a place as this – or do you come to upbraid me with my guilt, and to sink me down to that perdition I so justly deserve?'

'Am I so given to upbraiding then,' says she, in a gentle voice, 'have I ever given you occasion to think I would sink you to perdition?'

'Far be it from me, my love, to think so,' answered he. 'And yet you may forgive the utmost fears of an offending, penitent sinner. I know indeed the extent of your goodness, and yet I know my guilt so great –'

'Alas! Mr Booth,' said she, 'what guilt is this which you mention, and which you writ to me of last night – sure by your mentioning to me so much, you intend to tell me more, nay indeed to tell me all. – And not leave my mind open to suspicions perhaps ten times worse than the truth.'

'Will you give me a patient hearing?' said he.

'I will indeed,' answered she, 'nay I am prepared to hear the worst you can unfold; nay perhaps the worst is short of my apprehensions.'

Booth then, after a little further apology, began and related to her the whole that had pass'd between him and Miss Mathews, from their first meeting in the prison to their separation the preceding evening. All which, as the reader knows it already, it would be tedious and unpardonable to transcribe from his mouth. He told her likewise all that he had done and suffered, to conceal his transgression from her knowledge. This he assured her was the business of his visit last night, the consequence of which was, he declared in the most solemn manner, no other than an absolute quarrel with Miss Mathews, of whom he had taken a final leave.

When he had ended his narration, Amelia, after a short silence, answered, – 'Indeed, I firmly believe every word you have said – but I cannot now forgive you the fault you have confessed – and my reason is – because I have forgiven it long ago. Here, my dear,' said she, 'is an instance that I am likewise capable of keeping a secret.' – She then delivered her husband a letter which she had some time ago received from Miss Mathews, and which was the same which that lady had mentioned, and supposed, as Booth had never heard of it, that it had miscarried; for she sent it by the penny-post.[2] In this letter, which was sign'd by a feigned name, she had acquainted Amelia with the infidelity of her husband, and had besides very greatly abused him; taxing him with many falsehoods; and, among the rest, with having spoken very slightingly and disrespectfully of his wife.

Amelia never shin'd forth to Booth in so amiable and great a light; nor did his own unworthiness ever appear to him so mean and contemptible, as at this instant. However when he had read the letter, he uttered many violent protestations to her, that all which related to herself was absolutely false.

'I am convinced it is,' said she. 'I would not have a suspicion of the contrary for the world. I assure you I had, till last night revived it in my memory, almost forgot the letter; for as I well knew from whom it came, by her mentioning obligations which she had conferred on you, and which you had more than once spoken to me of: I made large allowances for the situation you was then in; and I was the more satisfied, as the letter itself, as well as many other circumstances, convinced me the affair was at an end.'

Booth now utter'd the most extravagant expressions of admiration and fondness that his heart could dictate, and accompanied them with the warmest embraces. All which warmth and tenderness she return'd; and tears of love and joy gush'd from both their eyes. So ravish'd indeed were their hearts, that for some time they both forgot the dreadful situation of their affairs.

This however was but a short reverie. It soon recurr'd to Amelia that tho' she had the liberty of leaving that house when she pleased, she could not take her beloved husband with her. This thought stung her tender bosom to the quick, and she could not so far command herself, as to refrain from many sorrowful exclamations against the hardship of their destiny; but when she saw the effect they had upon Booth, she stifled her rising grief, forced a little cheerfulness into her countenance, and exerting all the spirits she could raise within herself, expressed her hopes of seeing a speedy end to their sufferings. She then ask'd her husband what she should do for him, and to whom she should apply for his deliverance.

'You know, my dear,' cries Booth, 'that the doctor is to be in town some time to day. My hopes of immediate redemption are only in him; and if that can be obtain'd, I make no doubt but of the success of that affair which is in the hands of a gentleman who hath faithfully promised, and in whose power I am so well assured it is to serve me.'

Thus did this poor man support his hopes by a dependance on that ticket which he had so dearly purchased of one who pretended to manage the wheels in the great state lottery[3] of preferment. A lottery indeed which hath this to recommend it, that many poor wretches feed their imaginations with the prospect of a prize during their whole lives, and never discover they have drawn a blank.

Amelia, who was of a pretty sanguine temper, and was entirely ignorant of these matters, was full as easy to be deceived into hopes as her husband; but in reality at present she turn'd her eyes to no distant prospect; the desire of regaining her husband's liberty having engrossed her whole mind.

While they were discoursing on these matters, they heard a violent noise in the house, and immediately after several persons passed by their door up stairs to the apartment over their head. This greatly terrified the gentle spirit of Amelia, and she cried – 'Good Heavens, my dear, must I leave you in this horrid place? I am terrified with a thousand fears concerning you.'

Booth endeavoured to comfort her, saying, that he was in no manner of danger, and that he doubted not but that the doctor would soon be with him. – 'And stay, my dear,' cries he, 'now I recollect, suppose you should apply to my old friend James; for I believe you are pretty well satisfied, that your apprehensions of him were groundless. I have no reason to think but that he would be as ready to serve me as formerly.'

Amelia turned pale as ashes at the name of James, and instead of making a direct answer to her husband, she laid hold of him, and cried, 'My dear, I have one favour to beg of you, and I insist on your granting it me.'

Booth readily swore he would deny her nothing.

'It is only this, my dear,' said she, 'that if that detested colonel comes, you will not see him. Let the people of the house tell him you are not here.'

'He knows nothing of my being here,' answer'd Booth; 'but why should I refuse to see him, if he should be kind enough to come hither to me? Indeed, my Amelia, you have taken a dislike to that man without sufficient reason.'

'I speak not upon that account,' cries Amelia; 'but I have had dreams last night about you two. Perhaps you will laugh at my folly; but pray indulge it. Nay I insist on your promise of not denying me.'

'Dreams! my dear creature,' answer'd he. 'What dream can you have had of us?'

'One too horrible to be mention'd,' reply'd she. – 'I cannot think of it without horror, and unless you will promise me not to see the colonel till I return, I positively will never leave you.'

'Indeed, my Amelia,' said Booth, 'I never knew you unreasonable before. How can a woman of your sense talk of dreams?'

'Suffer me to be once at least unreasonable,' said Amelia; 'as you are so good-natur'd to say I am not often so. Consider, what I have lately suffer'd, and how weak my spirits must be at this time.'

As Booth was going to speak, the bailiff without any ceremony enter'd the room; and cried, 'No offence, I hope, madam, my wife, it seems, did not know you. She thought the captain had a mind for a bit of flesh by the bye. But I have quieted all matters: for I know you very well; I have seen that handsome face many a time, when I have been waiting upon the captain formerly. No offence, I hope, madam; but if my wife was as handsome as you are – I should not look for worse goods abroad.'

Booth conceived some displeasure at this speech; but he did not think proper to express more than a pish. – And then ask'd the bailiff what was the meaning of the noise they heard just now.

'I know of no noise,' answer'd the bailiff. 'Some of my men have been carrying a piece of bad luggage up stairs; a poor rascal that resisted the law and justice; so I gave him a cut or two with a hanger.[4] If they should prove mortal, he must thank himself for it.

If a man will not behave like a gentleman to an officer, he must take the consequence; but I must say that for you, captain, you behave yourself like a gentleman; and therefore I shall always use you as such; and I hope you will find bail soon with all my heart. This is but a paultry sum to what the last was; and I do assure you, there is nothing else against you in the office.'

The latter part of the bailiff's speech somewhat comforted Amelia, who had been a little frightned by the former; and she soon after took leave of her husband, to go in quest of the doctor, who, as Amelia had heard that morning, was expected in town that very day, which was somewhat sooner than he had intended at his departure.

Before she went, however, she left a strict charge with the bailiff, who usher'd her very civilly down stairs, that if one Colonel James came there to enquire for her husband, he should deny that he was there.

She then departed; and the bailiff immediately gave a very strict charge to his wife, his maid, and his followers, that if one Colonel James, or any one from him, should enquire after the captain, they should let him know he had the captain above stairs: for he doubted not but that the colonel was one of Booth's creditors; and he hoped for a second bail bond by his means.

CHAPTER 3

Containing matter pertinent to the history.

AMELIA in her way to the doctor's determin'd just to stop at her own lodgings which lay a little out of the road, and to pay a momentary visit to her children.

This was fortunate enough; for had she call'd at the doctor's house, she would have heard nothing of him, which would have caused in her some alarm and disappointment; for the doctor was set down at Mrs Atkinson's, where he was directed to Amelia's lodgings, to which he went before he called at his own; and here Amelia now found him playing with her two children.

The doctor had been a little surprized at not finding Amelia at home, or any one that could give an account of her. He was now more surprized to see her come in in such a dress, and at the disorder which he very plainly perceived in her pale and melancholy countenance. He addressed her first (for indeed she was in no great haste to speak) and cry'd, 'My dear child, what is the matter? where is your husband? Some mischief I am afraid hath happen'd to him in my absence.'

'O, my dear doctor,' answer'd Amelia, 'sure some good angel hath sent you hither. My poor Will is arrested again. I left him in the most miserable condition in the very house whence your goodness formerly redeem'd him.'

'Arrested!' cries the doctor. 'Then it must be for some very inconsiderable trifle.'

'I wish it was,' said Amelia; 'but it is for no less than £50.'

'Then,' cries the doctor, 'he hath been disingenuous with me. He told me he did not owe ten pounds in the world for which he was liable to be sued.'

'I know not what to say,' cries Amelia. 'Indeed I am afraid to tell you the truth.'

'How, child,' said the doctor – 'I hope you will never disguise it to any one, especially to me. Any prevarication, I promise you, will forfeit my friendship for ever.'

'I will tell you the whole,' cries Amelia, 'and rely entirely on your goodness.' She then related the gaming story, not forgetting to set in the fullest light, and to lay the strongest emphasis on his promise never to play again.

The doctor fetched a deep sigh when he had heard Amelia's relation, and cried, 'I am sorry, child, for the share you are to partake in your husband's sufferings; but as for him, I really think he deserves no compassion. You say he hath promised never to play again; but I must tell you he hath broke his promise to me already: for I had heard he was formerly addicted to this vice, and had given him sufficient caution against it. You will consider, child, I am already pretty largely engaged for him, every farthing of which I am sensible I must pay. You know I would go to the utmost verge of prudence to serve you; but I must not exceed my ability, which is not very great; and I have several families on my hands, who are by misfortune alone brought to want. I do assure you I cannot at present answer for such a sum as this, without distressing my own circumstances.'

'Then Heaven have mercy upon us all,' cries Amelia; 'for we have no other friend on earth – my husband is undone; and these poor little wretches must be starved.'

The doctor cast his eyes on the children, and then cried – 'I hope not so. I told you I must distress my circumstances, and I will distress them this once on your account, and on the account of these poor little babes – But things must not go on any longer in this way – You must take an heroic resolution. I will hire a coach for you to-morrow morning, which shall carry you all down to my parsonage-house. There you shall have my protection, till something can be done for your husband; of which, to be plain with you, I at present see no likelihood.'

Amelia fell upon her knees in an ecstasy of thanksgiving to the doctor, who immediately raised her up and placed her in her chair. She then recollected herself and said – 'O my worthy friend, I have still another matter to mention to you, in which I must have both your advice and assistance. My soul blushes to give you all this trouble; but what other friend have I – indeed what other friend could I apply to so properly on such an occasion?'

The doctor, with a very kind voice and countenance, desired her to speak. She then said – 'O sir, that wicked colonel, whom I have mentioned to you formerly, hath picked some quarrel with my husband,' (for she did not think proper to mention the cause) 'and hath sent him a challenge. It came to my hand last night after he was arrested; I opened and read it.'

'Give it me, child,' said the doctor.

She answered she had burnt it; as was indeed true. 'But I remember it was an appointment to meet at sword and pistol this morning at Hyde Park.'

'Make yourself easy, my dear child,' cries the doctor, 'I will take care to prevent any mischief.'

'But consider, my dear sir,' said she, 'this is a tender matter. My husband's honour is to be preserved as well as his life.'

'And so is his soul, which ought to be the dearest of all things,' cries the doctor. 'Honour! Nonsense. Can honour dictate to him to disobey the express commands of his maker, in compliance with a custom established by a set of blockheads, founded on false principles of virtue, in direct opposition to the plain and positive precepts of religion, and tending manifestly to give a sanction to ruffians, and to protect them in all the ways of impudence and villany?'

'All this, I believe, is very true,' cries Amelia; 'but yet you know, doctor, the opinion of the world.'

'You talk simply, child,' cries the doctor. 'What is the opinion of the world opposed to religion and virtue? But you are in the wrong. It is not the opinion of the world; it is the opinion of the idle, ignorant, and profligate. It is impossible it should be the opinion of one man of sense, who is in earnest in his belief of our religion. Chiefly indeed it hath been upheld by the nonsense of women; who either from their extreme cowardice, and desire of protection, or, as Mr Bayle thinks,[5] from their excessive vanity, have been always forward to countenance a set of hectors and bravoes, and to despise all men of modesty and sobriety; tho' these are often, at the bottom, not only the better but the braver men.'

'You know, doctor,' cries Amelia, 'I have never presumed to argue with you; your opinion is to me always instruction, and your word a law.'

'Indeed, child,' cries the doctor, 'I know you are a good woman; and yet I must observe to you, that this very desire of feeding the passion of female vanity with the heroism of her man, old Homer seems to make the characteristic of a bad and loose woman. He introduces Helen upbraiding her gallant with having quitted the fight, and left the victory to Menelaus, and seeming to be sorry that she had left her husband, only because he was the better duellist of the two;[6] but in how different a light doth he represent the tender and chaste love of Andromache to her worthy Hector! She dissuades him from exposing himself to danger, even in a just cause.[7] This is indeed a weakness; but it is an amiable one, and becoming the true feminine character; but a woman, who out of heroic vanity (for so it is) would hazard not only the life, but the soul too of her husband in a duel, is a monster, and ought to be painted in no other character but that of a fury.'

'I assure you, doctor,' cries Amelia, 'I never saw this matter in the odious light, in which you have truly represented it, before. I am ashamed to recollect what I have formerly said on this subject. – And yet whilst the opinion of the world is as it is, one would wish to comply as far as possible – especially as my husband is an officer of the army. If it can be done therefore with safety to his honour –'

'Again honour!' cries the doctor, 'indeed I will not suffer that noble word to be so basely and barbarously prostituted. I have known some of these men of honour, as they call themselves, to be the most arrant rascals in the universe.'

'Well. I ask your pardon,' said she, – 'reputation then, if you please – or any other word you like better – you know my meaning very well.'

'I do know your meaning,' cries the doctor, 'and Virgil knew it a great while ago. The next time you see your friend Mrs Atkinson, ask her what it was made Dido fall in love with Aeneas.'[8]

'Nay, dear sir,' said Amelia, 'do not rally me so unmercifully; think where my poor husband is now.'

'He is,' answered the doctor, 'where I will presently be with him. In the mean time, do you pack up every thing in order for your journey to-morrow; for, if you are wise, you will not trust your husband a day longer in this town – therefore to packing –'

Amelia promised she would – though indeed she wanted not any warning for her journey on this account; for when she packed up herself in the coach, she packed up her all. However she did not think proper to mention this to the doctor; for as he was now in pretty good humour, she did not care to venture again discomposing his temper.

The doctor then set out for Gray's Inn Lane; and, as soon as he was gone, Amelia began to consider of her incapacity to take a journey in her present situation, without even a clean shift. At last she resolved, as she was possessed of seven guineas and a half, to go to her friend and redeem some of her own and her husband's linen out of captivity; indeed just so much, as would render it barely possible for them to go out of town with any kind of decency. And this resolution she immediately executed.

As soon as she had finished her business with the pawnbroker, (if a man who lends under thirty per cent deserves that name) he said to her, 'Pray, madam, did you know that man who was here yesterday, when you brought the picture?' Amelia answered in the negative. 'Indeed, madam,' said the broker, 'he knows you, though he did not recollect you while you was here, as your hood was drawn over your face; but the moment you was gone, he begged to look at the picture, which I thinking no harm permitted. He had scarce looked upon it, when he cried out – "By heaven and earth it is her picture." He then asked me if I knew you – "Indeed," says I, "I never saw the lady before."'

In this last particular, however, the pawnbroker a little savoured of his profession, and made a small deviation from the truth: for when the man had asked him if he knew the lady, he answered she was some poor undone woman, who had pawned all her cloaths to him the day before; 'and I suppose,' says he, 'this picture is the last of her goods and chattels.' This hint we thought proper to give the reader, as it may chance to be material.

Amelia answered coldly, that she had taken so very little notice of the man, that she scarce remembered he was there.

'I assure you, madam,' says the pawnbroker, 'he hath taken very great notice of you; for the man changed countenance upon what I said, and presently after begged me to give him a dram. Oho! thinks I to myself, are you thereabouts? I would not be so much in love with some folks, as some people are, for more interest than I shall ever make of a thousand pound.'

Amelia blushed, and said with some peevishness that she knew nothing of the man; but supposed he was some impertinent fellow or other.

'Nay, madam,' answered the pawnbroker, 'I assure you he is not worthy your regard. He is a poor wretch, and I believe I am possessed of most of his moveables. However I hope you are not offended; for indeed he said no harm; but he was very strangely disordered, that is the truth of it.'

Amelia was very desirous of putting an end to this conversation, and altogether as eager to return to her children; she therefore bundled up her things as fast as she could, and calling for a hackney-coach directed the coachman to her lodgings, and bid him drive her home with all the haste he could.

CHAPTER 4

In which Dr Harrison visits Colonel James.

THE doctor, when he left Amelia, intended to go directly to Booth; but he presently changed his mind and determined first to call on the colonel, as he thought it was proper to put an end to that matter, before he gave Booth his liberty.

The doctor found the two colonels, James and Bath, together. They both received him very civilly; for James was a very well bred man; and Bath always shewed a particular respect to the clergy, he being indeed a perfect good Christian, except in the articles of fighting and swearing.

Our divine sat some time without mentioning the subject of his errand, in hopes that Bath would go away; but when he found no likelihood of that, (for indeed Bath was of the two much the most pleased with his company) he told James that he had something to say to him relating to Mr Booth, which he believed he might speak before his brother.

'Undoubtedly, sir,' said James; 'for there can be no secrets between us which my brother may not hear.'

'I come then to you, sir,' said the doctor, 'from the most unhappy woman in the world, to whose afflictions you have very greatly and very cruelly added, by sending a challenge to her husband, which hath very luckily fallen into her hands; for had the man, for whom you designed it, received it, I am afraid you would not have seen me upon this occasion.'

'If I writ such a letter to Mr Booth, sir,' said James, 'you may be assured I did not expect this visit in answer to it.'

'I do not think you did,' cries the doctor; 'but you have great reason to thank Heaven for ordering this matter contrary to your expectations. I know not what trifle may have drawn this challenge from you; but after what I have some reason to know of you, sir, I must plainly tell you, that if you had added to your guilt already committed against this man that of having his blood upon your hands, your soul would have become as black as hell itself.'

'Give me leave to say,' cries the colonel, 'this is a language which I am not used to hear; and if your cloth was not your protection, you should not give it me with impunity. After what you know of me, sir! What do you presume to know of me to my disadvantage?'

'You say my cloth is my protection, colonel,' answered the doctor, 'therefore pray lay aside your anger; I do not come with any design of affronting or offending you. –'

'Very well,' cries Bath, 'that declaration is sufficient from a clergyman, let him say what he pleases.'

'Indeed, sir,' says the doctor, very mildly, 'I consult equally the good of you both, and, in a spiritual sense, more especially yours; for you know you have injured this poor man.'

'So far on the contrary,' cries James, 'that I have been his greatest benefactor; I scorn to upbraid him; but you force me to it. Nor have I ever done him the least injury.'

'Perhaps not,' said the doctor; 'I will alter what I have said. – But for this I apply to your honour – Have you not intended him an injury, the very intention of which cancels every obligation?'

'How, sir,' answered the colonel – 'what do you mean?'

'My meaning,' replied the doctor, 'is almost too tender to mention – Come, colonel, examine your own heart; and then answer me on your honour, if you have not intended to do him the highest wrong which one man can do another.'

'I do not know what you mean by the question,' answered the colonel.

'D—n me, the question is very transparent,' cries Bath. 'From any other man it would be an affront with the strongest emphasis, but from one of the doctor's cloth it demands a categorical answer.'

'I am not a papist, sir,' answered Colonel James, 'nor am I obliged to confess to my priest. But if you have any thing to say, speak openly – for I do not understand your meaning.'

'I have explained my meaning to you already,' said the doctor, 'in a letter I wrote to you on the subject – a subject which I am sorry I should have any occasion to write upon to a Christian.'

'I do remember now,' cries the colonel, 'that I received a very impertinent letter something like a sermon, against adultery; but I did not expect to hear the author own it to my face.'

'That brave man then, sir,' answered the doctor, 'stands before you who dares own he wrote that letter, and dares affirm too, that it was writ on a just and strong foundation. But if the hardness of your heart could prevail on you to treat my good intention with contempt and scorn, what pray could induce you to shew it, nay to give it Mr Booth? What motive could you have for that, unless you meant to insult him, and to provoke your rival to give you that opportunity of putting him out of the world, which you have since wickedly sought by your challenge?'

'I give him the letter!' said the colonel.

'Yes, sir,' answered the doctor, 'he shewed me the letter, and affirmed that you gave it him at the masquerade.'

'He is a lying rascal then,' said the colonel very passionately. 'I scarce took the trouble of reading the letter, and lost it out of my pocket.'

Here Bath interfered, and explain'd this affair in the manner in which it happen'd, and with which the reader is already acquainted. He concluded by great eulogiums on the performance, and declared it was one of the most enthusiastic[9] (meaning perhaps ecclesiastic) letters that ever was written. 'And d—n me,' says he, 'if I do not respect the author with the utmost emphasis of thinking.'

The doctor now recollected what had passed with Booth, and perceived he had made a mistake of one colonel for another. This he presently acknowledged to Colonel James, and said that the mistake had been his and not Booth's.

Bath now collected all his gravity, and dignity, as he called it, into his countenance, and addressing himself to James, said – 'And was that letter writ to you, brother? – I hope you never deserved any suspicion of this kind.'

'Brother,' cries James, 'I am accountable to myself for my actions, and shall not render an account either to you, or to that gentleman.'

'As to me, brother,' answered Bath, 'you say right; but I think this gentleman may call you to an account; nay I think it is his duty so to do. And let me tell you, brother, there is ONE much greater than he to whom you must give an account. Mrs Booth is really a fine woman, a lady of most imperious and majestick presence. I have heard you often say, that you liked her; and if you have quarrelled with her husband upon this account, by all the dignity of man, I think you ought to ask his pardon.'

'Indeed, brother,' cries James, 'I can bear this no longer – you will make me angry presently.'

'Angry! Brother James,' cries Bath – 'angry! – I love you, brother, and have obligations to you. I will say no more – but I hope you know I do not fear making any man angry.'

James answered, he knew it well; and then the doctor apprehending that while he was stopping up one breach, he should make another, presently interfered and turned the discourse back to Booth. 'You tell me, sir,' said he to James, 'that my gown is my protection; let it then at least protect me where I have had no design in offending; where I have consulted your highest welfare, as in truth I did in writing this letter. And if you did not in the least deserve any such suspicion, still you have no cause for resentment. Caution against sin, even to the innocent, can never be unwholesome. But this I assure you, whatever anger you have to me, you can have none to poor Booth, who was entirely ignorant of my writing to you, and who, I am certain, never entertain'd the least suspicion of you; on the contrary, reveres you with the highest esteem, and love and gratitude. Let me therefore reconcile all matters between you, and bring you together before he hath even heard of this challenge.'

'Brother,' cries Bath, 'I hope I shall not make you angry – I lie when I say so; for I am indifferent to any man's anger – Let me be an accessary to what the doctor hath said. I think I may be trusted with matters of this nature, and it is a little unkind that if you intended to send a challenge you did not make me the bearer. But indeed, as to what appears to me, this matter may be very well made up; and as Mr Booth doth not know of the challenge, I don't see why he ever should, any more than your giving him the lie just now; but that he shall never have from me, nor I believe from this gentleman; for indeed if he should, it would be incumbent upon him to cut your throat.'

'Lookee, doctor,' said James, 'I do not deserve the unkind suspicion you just now threw out against me. I never thirsted after any man's blood, and as for what hath passed, since this discovery hath happened, I may perhaps not think it worth my while to trouble myself any more about it.'

The doctor was not contented with perhaps, he insisted on a firm promise, to be bound with the colonel's honour. This at length he obtained, and then departed well satisfied.

In fact, the colonel was ashamed to avow the real cause of the quarrel to this good man, or indeed to his brother Bath, who would not only have condemned him equally with the doctor, but would possibly have quarrelled with him on his sister's account, whom, as the reader must have observed, he loved above all things; and in plain truth, though the colonel was a brave man, and dared to fight, yet he was altogether as willing to let it alone; and this made him now and then give a little way to the wrongheadedness of Colonel Bath, who, with all the other principles of honour and humanity made no more of cutting the throat of a man upon any of his punctilio's than a butcher doth of killing sheep.

CHAPTER 5

What passed at the bailiff's house.

THE doctor now set forwards to his friend Booth, and as he past by the door of his attorney in the way, he called upon him, and took him with him.

The meeting between him and Booth need not be expatiated on. The doctor was really angry, and tho' he deferred his lecture to a more proper opportunity, yet as he was no dissembler (indeed he was incapable of any disguise) he could not put on a show of that heartiness with which he had formerly used to receive his friend.

Booth at last began himself in the following manner: 'Doctor, I am really ashamed to see you; and if you knew the confusion of my soul on this occasion, I am sure you would pity rather than upbraid me – And yet I can say with great sincerity, I rejoice in this last instance of my shame, since I am like to reap the most solid advantage from it.' The doctor stared at this, and Booth thus proceeded: 'Since I have been in this wretched place, I have employ'd my time almost entirely in reading over a series of sermons, which are contained in that book,' (meaning Dr Barrow's works,[10] which then lay on the table before him,) 'in proof of the Christian religion, and so good an effect have they had upon me, that I shall, I believe, be the better man for them as long as I live. I have not a doubt, (for I own I have had such) which remains now unsatisfied. – If ever an angel might be thought to guide the pen of a writer, surely the pen of that great and good man had such an assistant.' The doctor readily concurred in the praises of Dr Barrow, and added – 'You say you have had your doubts, young gentleman, indeed I did not know that – And pray, what were your doubts?' 'Whatever they were, sir,' said Booth, 'they are now satisfied, as I believe those of every impartial and sensible reader will be, if he will, with due attention, read over these excellent sermons.' 'Very well,' answer'd the doctor, 'tho' I have conversed, I find, with a false brother hitherto, I am glad you are reconciled to truth at last, and I hope your future faith will have some influence on your future life.' 'I need not tell you, sir,' replied Booth, 'that will always be the case, where faith is sincere, as I assure you mine is. Indeed I never was a rash disbeliever; my chief doubt was founded on this, that as men appeared to me to act entirely from their passions, their actions could have neither merit nor demerit.' 'A very worthy conclusion truly,' cries the doctor; 'but if men act, as I believe they do, from their passions, it would be fair to conclude that religion to be true which applies immediately to the strongest of these passions, hope and fear, chusing rather to rely on its rewards and punishments, than on that native beauty of virtue which some of the antient philosophers thought proper to recommend to their disciples. – But we will defer this discourse till another opportunity; at present, as the devil hath thought proper to set you free, I will try if I can prevail on the bailiff to do the same.'

The doctor had really not so much money in town as Booth's debt amounted to, and therefore though he would otherwise very willingly have paid it, he was forced to give bail to the action. For which purpose, as the bailiff was a man of great form, he was obliged to get another person to be bound with him.[11] This person, however, the attorney undertook to procure, and immediately set out in quest of him.

During his absence the bailiff came into the room, and addressing himself to the doctor, said, 'I think, sir, your name is Dr Harrison.' The doctor immediately acknowledged his name. Indeed the bailiff had seen it to a bail-bond before. 'Why then, sir,' said the bailiff, 'there is a man above in a dying condition, that desires the favour of speaking to you; I believe he wants you to pray by him.'

The bailiff himself was not more ready to execute his office on all occasions for his fee, than the doctor was to execute his for nothing. Without making any further enquiry therefore into the condition of the man, he immediately went up stairs.

As soon as the bailiff returned down stairs, which was immediately after he had lodged the doctor in the room, Booth had the curiosity to ask him who this man was. 'Why, I don't know much of him,' said the bailiff, 'I had him once in custody before now, I remember it was when your honour was here last; and now I remember too, he said then he knew your honour very well. Indeed I had some opinion of him at that time; for he spent his money very much like a gentleman; but I have discovered since, that he is a poor fellow, and worth nothing. He is a mere shy cock. I have had the stuff about me this week, and could never get at him till this morning; nay, I don't believe we should ever have found out his lodgings, had it not been for the attorney that was here just now, who gave us information. And so we took him this morning by a comical way enough. For we dressed up one of my men in women's cloaths, who told the people of the house, that he was his sister just come to town: for we were told by the attorney, that he had such a sister, upon which he was let up stairs; and so kept the door a-jar till I and another rush'd in. Let me tell you, captain, there are as good stratagems made use of in our business as any in the army.'

'But pray, sir,' said Booth, 'did not you tell me this morning that the poor fellow was desperately wounded; nay, I think you told the doctor that he was a dying man?'

'I had like to have forgot that,' cries the bailiff. – 'Nothing would serve the gentleman but that he must make resistance, and he gave my man a blow with a stick; but I soon quieted him, by giving him a wipe or two with a hanger. Not that I believe I have done his business neither; but the fellow is faint-hearted, and the surgeon, I fancy, frightens him more than he need. – But however, let the worst come to the worst, the law is all on my side, and it is only *se fendendo*.[12] The attorney that was here just now told me so, and bid me fear nothing: for that he would stand my friend, and undertake the cause; and he is a devilish good one at a defence at the Old Bailey I promise you. I have known him bring off several that every body thought would have been hang'd.'

'But suppose you should be acquitted,' said Booth; 'would not the blood of this poor wretch lie a little heavy at your heart?'

'Why should it, captain?' said the bailiff. 'Is it not all done in a lawful way? Why will people resist the law when they know the consequence? To be sure, if a man was to kill another in an unlawful manner as it were, and what the law calls murder, that is quite and clear another thing. I should not care to be convicted of murder any more than another man. Why now, captain, you have been abroad in the wars they tell me, and to be sure must have killed men in your time. Pray, was you ever afraid afterwards of seeing their ghosts?'

'That is a different affair,' cries Booth; 'but I would not kill a man in cold blood for all the world.'

'There is no difference at all, as I can see,' cries the bailiff. 'One is as much in the way of business as the other. When gentlemen behave themselves like unto gentlemen, I know how to treat them as such as well as any officer the king hath. – And when they do not, why they must take what follows, and the law doth not call it murder.'

Booth very plainly saw that the bailiff had squared his conscience exactly according to law, and that he could not easily subvert his way of thinking. He therefore gave up the cause, and desir'd the bailiff to expedite the bonds, which he promised to do, saying, he hoped he had used him with proper civility this time if he had not the last, and that he should be remember'd for it.

But before we close this chapter, we shall endeavour to satisfy an enquiry which may arise in our most favourite readers, (for so are the most curious) how it came to pass that such a person as was Dr Harrison should employ such a fellow as this Murphy.

The case then was thus. This Murphy had been clerk to an attorney in the very same town in which the doctor liv'd, and when he was out of his time[13] had set up with a character fair enough, and had married a maid servant of Mrs Harris, by which means he had all the business to which that lady and her friends, in which number was the doctor, could recommend him.

Murphy went on with his business, and thrived very well, till he happen'd to make an unfortunate slip, in which he was detected by a brother of the same calling. But tho' we call this by the gentle name of a slip, in respect to its being so extremely common, it was a matter in which the law if it had ever come to its ears would have passed a very severe censure, being indeed no less than perjury and subornation of perjury.

This brother attorney being a very good-natur'd man, and unwilling to bespatter his own profession, and considering perhaps that the consequence did in no wise affect the public, who had no manner of interest in the alternative, whether A. in whom the right was, or B. to whom Mr Murphy by the means aforesaid, had transferr'd it, succeeded in an action. We mention this particular, because as this brother attorney was a very violent party man, and a professed stickler for the public, to suffer any injury to have been done to that, would have been highly inconsistent with his principles.

This gentleman therefore came to Mr Murphy, and after shewing him that he had it in his power to convict him of the aforesaid crime, very generously told him that he had not the least delight in bringing any man to destruction, nor the least animosity against him. All that he insisted upon was, that he would not live in the same town or county with one who had been guilty of such an action. He then told Mr Murphy that he would keep the secret on two conditions; the one was that he immediately quitted that country, the other was, that he should convince him he deserved this kindness by his gratitude, and that Murphy should transfer to the other all the business which he then had in those parts, and to which he could possibly recommend him.

It is the observation of a very wise man, that it is a very common exercise of wisdom in this world, of two evils to chuse the least.[14] The reader therefore cannot doubt but that Mr Murphy complied with the alternative proposed by his kind brother, and accepted the terms on which secrecy was to be obtain'd.

This happen'd while the doctor was abroad, and with all this, except the departure of Murphy, not only the doctor, but the whole town (save his aforesaid brother alone) were to this day unacquainted.

The doctor at his return hearing that Mr Murphy was gone, applied to the other attorney in his affairs, who still employ'd this Murphy as his agent in town, partly perhaps out of good-will to him, and partly from the recommendation of Miss Harris; for as he had married a servant of the family, and a particular favourite of hers, there can be no wonder that she who was entirely ignorant of the affair above related, as well as of his conduct in town, should continue her favour to him. It will appear therefore, I apprehend, no longer strange, that the doctor who had seen this man but three times since his removal to town, and then conversed with him only on business, should remain as ignorant of his life and character, as a man generally is of the character of the hackney coachman who drives him. Nor doth it reflect more on the honour or understanding of the doctor under these circumstances to employ Murphy, than it would if he had been driven about the town by a thief or a murderer.

CHAPTER 6

What passed between the doctor and the sick man.

WE LEFT the doctor in the last chapter with the wounded man, to whom the doctor in a very gentle voice spoke as follows:

'I am sorry, friend, to see you in this situation, and am very ready to give you any comfort or assistance within my power.'

'I thank you kindly, doctor,' said the man. 'Indeed I should not have presumed to have sent to you had I not known your character: for tho' I believe I am not at all known to you, I have lived many years in that town where you yourself had a house: my name is Robinson. I used to write for the attorneys in those parts, and I have been employ'd on your business in my time.'

'I do not recollect you, nor your name;' said the doctor, 'but consider, friend, your moments are precious, and your business, as I am inform'd, is to offer up your prayers to that Great Being, before whom you are shortly to appear. – But first let me exhort you earnestly to a most serious repentance of all your sins.'

'O doctor,' said the man – 'pray, what is your opinion of a death-bed repentance?'

'If repentance is sincere,' cries the doctor, 'I hope through the mercies and merits of our most powerful and benign intercessor it will never come too late.'

'But do not you think, sir,' cries the man, 'that in order to obtain forgiveness of any great sin we have committed by an injury done to our neighbours, it is necessary, as far as in us lies, to make all the amends we can to the party injur'd, and to undo if possible the injury we have done.'

'Most undoubtedly,' cries the doctor, 'our pretence to repentance would otherwise be gross hypocrisy, and an impudent attempt to deceive and impose upon our Creator himself.'

'Indeed I am of the same opinion,' cries the penitent; 'and I think further, that this is thrown in my way, and hinted to me by that great Being: for an accident happened to me yesterday, by which, as things have fallen out since, I think I plainly discern the hand of Providence. I went yesterday, sir, you must know, to a pawnbroker's, to pawn the last moveable, which, except the poor cloaths you see on my back, I am worth in the world. While I was there, a young lady came in to pawn her picture. She had disguised herself so much, and pulled her hood so over her face, that I did not know her while she staid, which was scarce three minutes. As soon as she was gone, the pawnbroker taking the picture in his hand, cried out – *Upon my word this is the handsomest face I ever saw in my life*. I desired him to let me look on the picture, which he readily did – and I no sooner cast my eyes upon it, than the strong resemblance struck me, and I knew it to be Mrs Booth.'

'Mrs Booth! what Mrs Booth?' cries the doctor.

'Captain Booth's lady, the captain who is now below,' said the other.

'How!' cries the doctor with great impetuosity.

'Have patience,' said the man, 'and you shall hear all. I expressed some surprize to the pawnbroker, and asked the lady's name. He answered that he knew not her name, but that she was some undone wretch, who had the day before left all her cloaths with him in pawn. My guilt immediately flew in my face, and told me I had been accessary to this lady's undoing. The sudden shock so affected me, that had it not been for a dram which the pawnbroker gave me, I believe I should have sunk on the spot.'

'Accessary to her undoing! How accessary?' said the doctor. 'Pray tell me, for I am impatient to hear.'

'I will tell you all, as fast as I can,' cries the sick man. 'You know, good doctor, that Mrs Harris of our town had two daughters, this Mrs Booth and another. Now, sir, it seems the other daughter had, some way or other, disobliged her mother, a little before the old lady died; therefore she made a will, and left all her fortune, except one thousand pound, to Mrs Booth; to which will Mr Murphy, myself, and another, who is now dead, were the witnesses. Mrs Harris afterwards died suddenly; upon which it was contrived, by her other daughter and Mr Murphy to make a new will, in which Mrs Booth had a legacy of £10 and all the rest was given to the other. To this will Murphy, myself, and the same third person, again set our hands.'

'Good Heaven! how wonderful is thy providence,' cries the doctor – 'Murphy say you?'

'He himself, sir,' answered Robinson; 'Murphy, who is the greatest rogue I believe now in the world.'

'Pray, sir, proceed,' cries the doctor.

'For this service, sir,' said Robinson, 'myself and the third person, one Carter, received £200 each. What reward Murphy himself had, I know not. Carter died soon afterwards; and from that time, at several payments, I have by threats extorted above £100 more – And this, sir, is the whole truth, which I am ready to testify, if it would please Heaven to prolong my life. –'

'I hope it will,' cries the doctor; 'but something must be done for fear of accidents – I will send to counsel immediately, to know how to secure your testimony. – Whom can I get to send? – Stay, ay – he will do – but I know not where his house or his chambers are – I will go myself – but I may be wanted here.'

While the doctor was in this violent agitation, the surgeon made his appearance. The doctor stood still in a meditating posture, while the surgeon examined his patient. After which the doctor begged him to declare his opinion, and whether he thought the wounded man in any immediate danger of death. 'I do not know,' answered the surgeon, 'what you call immediate. He may live several days – nay he may recover. It is impossible to give any certain opinion in these cases.' He then launched forth into a set of terms, which the doctor, with all his scholarship, could not understand. To say the truth, many of them were not to be found in any dictionary or lexicon.

One discovery however the doctor made, and that was, that the surgeon was a very ignorant, conceited fellow, and knew nothing of his profession. He resolved therefore to get better advice for the sick; but this he postponed at present, and applying himself to the surgeon, said he should be very much obliged to him, if he knew where to find such a counsellor, and would fetch him thither. 'I should not ask such a favour of you, sir,' says the doctor, 'if it was not on business of the last importance, or if I could find any other messenger.'

'I fetch – sir!' said the surgeon very angrily. 'Do you take me for a footman, or a porter? I don't know who you are; but I believe you are full as proper to go on such an errand as I am;' (for as the doctor, who was just come off his journey, was very roughly dressed, the surgeon held him in no great respect.) The surgeon then called aloud from the top of the stairs, 'Let my coachman draw up,' and strutted off without any ceremony, telling his patient he would call again the next day.

At this very instant arrived Murphy with the other bail, and finding Booth alone, he asked the bailiff at the door, what was become of the doctor. 'Why, the doctor,' answer'd he, 'is above stairs, praying with —' 'How!' cries Murphy. 'How came you not to carry him directly to Newgate, as you promised me?' 'Why, because he was wounded,' cries the bailiff. 'I thought it was charity to take care of him; and besides, why should one make more noise about the matter than is necessary.' 'And Dr Harrison with him?' said Murphy. 'Yes, he is,' said the bailiff; 'he desired to speak with the doctor very much, and they have been praying together almost this hour.' – 'All is up, and undone,' cries Murphy. 'Let me come by, I have thought of something which I must do immediately.'

Now as by means of the surgeon's leaving the door open, the doctor heard Murphy's voice naming Robinson peevishly, he drew softly to the top of the stairs, where he heard the foregoing dialogue; and as soon as Murphy had uttered his last words, and was moving downwards, the doctor immediately sallied from his post, running as fast as he could, and crying 'stop the villain, stop the thief.'

The attorney wanted no better hint to accelerate his pace; and having the start of the doctor, got down stairs, and out into the street; but the doctor was so close at his heels, and being in foot the nimbler of the two, he soon overtook him, and laid hold of him, as he would have done on either Broughton or Slack[15] in the same cause.

This action in the street, accompanied with the frequent cry of 'stop thief' by the doctor, during the chace, presently drew together a large mob,[16] who began, as is usual, to enter immediately upon business, and to make strict enquiry into the matter, in order to proceed to do justice in their summary way.

Murphy, who knew well the temper of the mob, cried out, 'If you are a bailiff, shew me your writ. Gentlemen, he pretends to arrest me here without a writ.'

Upon this one of the sturdiest and forwardest of the mob, and who by a superior strength of body, and of lungs, presided in this assembly, declared he would suffer no such thing. 'D—n me,' says he, 'away to the pump with the catch-pole directly – shew me your writ, or let the gentleman go – you shall not arrest a man contrary to law.'

He then laid his hands on the doctor, who still fast griping the attorney, cried out: 'He is a villain – I am no bailiff, but a clergyman, and this lawyer is guilty of forgery, and hath ruined a poor family.'

'How!' cries the spokesman – 'a lawyer! – that alters the case –'

'Yes, faith,' cries another of the mob, 'it is lawyer Murphy. I know him very well.'

'And hath he ruined a poor family? Like enough, faith, if he's a lawyer. – Away with him to the justice immediately.'

The bailiff now came up desiring to know what was the matter; to whom Doctor Harrison answered, that he had arrested that villain for forgery. 'How can you arrest him,' cries the bailiff, 'you are no officer, nor have any warrant? Mr Murphy is a gentleman, and he shall be used as such.'

'Nay to be sure,' cries the spokesman, 'there ought to be a warrant; that's the truth on't.'

'There needs no warrant,' cries the doctor. 'I accuse him of felony; and I know so much of the law of England, that any man may arrest a felon without any warrant whatever. This villain hath undone a poor family; and I will die on the spot before I part with him.'

'If the law be so,' cries the orator, 'that is another matter. And to be sure, to ruin a poor man is the greatest of sins. And being a lawyer too, makes it so much the worse – He shall go before the Justice, d—n me if he shan't go before the Justice. I says the word he shall.'

'I say he is a gentleman, and shall be used according to law,' cries the bailiff. 'And though you are a clergyman,' said he to Harrison, 'you don't shew yourself as one by your actions.'

'That's a bailiff,' cries one of the mob – 'one lawyer will always stand by another: but I think the clergyman is a very good man, and acts becoming a clergyman to stand by the poor.'

At which words the mob all gave a great shout, and several cried out: 'Bring him along, away with him to the Justice.'

And now a constable appeared, and with an authoritative voice declared what he was, produced his staff, and demanded the peace.

The doctor then delivered his prisoner over to the officer, and charged him with felony; the constable received him; the attorney submitted; the bailiff was hushed; and the waves of the mob immediately subsided.

The doctor now balanced with himself how he should proceed; at last he determined to leave Booth a little longer in captivity, and not to quit sight of Murphy, before he had lodged him safe with a magistrate. They then all moved forwards to the Justice; the constable and his prisoner marching first, the doctor and the bailiff following next, and about five thousand mob, (for no less number were assembled in a very few minutes) following in the procession.

They found the magistrate just sitting down to his dinner; however, when he was acquainted with the doctor's profession, he immediately admitted him, and heard his business. Which he no sooner perfectly understood, with all its circumstances, than he resolved, tho' it was then very late, and he had been fatigued all the morning with public business, to postpone all refreshment till he had discharged his duty. He accordingly adjourned the prisoner and his cause to the bailiff's house, whither he himself with the doctor immediately repaired, and whither the attorney was followed by a much larger number of attendants than he had been honoured with before.

CHAPTER 7

In which the history draws towards a conclusion.

NOTHING could exceed the astonishment of Booth at the behaviour of the doctor, at the time when he sallied forth in pursuit of the attorney; for which it was so impossible for him to account in any manner whatever. He remained a long time in the utmost torture of mind, till at last the bailiff's wife came to him, and asked him if the doctor was not a mad-man; and in truth he could hardly defend him from that imputation.

While he was in this perplexity, the maid of the house brought him a message from Robinson, desiring the favour of seeing him above stairs. With this he immediately complied.

When these two were alone together, and the key turned on them (for the bailiff's wife was a most careful person, and never omitted that ceremony in the absence of her husband, having always at her tongue's end that excellent proverb of 'Safe bind, safe find',) Robinson looking stedfastly upon Booth, said, 'I believe, sir, you scarce remember me.'

Booth answered, that he thought he had seen his face somewhere before; but could not then recollect when or where.

'Indeed, sir,' answered the man, 'it was a place which no man can remember with pleasure. But do you not remember, a few weeks ago, that you had the misfortune to be in a certain prison in this town, where you lost a trifling sum at cards to a fellow prisoner?'

This hint sufficiently awakened Booth's memory, and he now recollected the features of his old friend Robinson. He answered him a little surlily, 'I know you now very well; but I did not imagine you would ever have reminded me of that transaction.'

'Alas, sir!' answered Robinson, 'whatever happened then was very trifling, compared to the injuries I have done you; but if my life be spared long enough, I will now undo it all; and as I have been one of your worst enemies, I will now be one of your best friends.'

He was just entering upon his story, when a noise was heard below, which might be almost compared to what hath been heard in Holland, when the dykes have given way, and the ocean in an inundation breaks in upon the land. It seemed indeed as if the whole world was bursting into the house at once.

Booth was a man of great firmness of mind, and he had need of it all at this instant. As for poor Robinson, the usual concomitants of guilt attended him, and he began to tremble in a violent manner.

The first person who ascended the stairs was the doctor, who no sooner saw Booth than he ran to him and embraced him, crying, 'My child, I wish you joy with all my heart. Your sufferings are all at an end; and providence hath done you the justice at last, which it will one day or other render to all men. – You will hear all presently; but I can now only tell you, that your sister is discovered,[17] and the estate is your own.'

Booth was in such confusion, that he scarce made any answer; and now appeared the Justice and his clerk, and immediately afterwards the constable with his prisoner, the bailiff, and as many more as could possibly crowd up stairs.

The doctor now addressed himself to the sick man, and desired him to repeat the same information before the Justice which he had made already; to which Robinson readily consented.

While the clerk was taking down the information, the attorney expressed a very impatient desire to send instantly for his clerk; and expressed so much uneasiness at the confusion in which he had left his papers at home, that a thought suggested itself to the doctor, that if his house was searched, some lights, and evidence, relating to this affair, would certainly be found; he therefore desired the Justice to grant a search-warrant immediately, to search his house.

The Justice answered that he had no such power. That if there was any suspicion of stolen goods, he could grant a warrant to search for them.

'How, sir!' said the doctor, 'can you grant a warrant to search a man's house for a silver tea-spoon, and not in a case like this, where a man is robbed of his whole estate?'

'Hold, sir,' says the sick man, 'I believe I can answer that point; for I can swear he hath several title deeds of the estate now in his possession, which I am sure were stolen from the right owner.'

The Justice still hesitated. He said title deeds savoured of the realty,[18] and it was not felony to steal them. If indeed they were taken away in a box, then it would be felony to steal the box.

'Savour of the realty! savour of the fartalty,' said the doctor, 'I never heard such incomprehensible nonsense. This is impudent, as well as childish trifling with the lives and properties of men.'

'Well, sir,' said Robinson, 'I now am sure I can do his business; for I know he hath a silver cup in his possession, which is the property of this gentleman,' (meaning Booth) 'and how he got it but by stealth, let him account if he can.'

'That will do,' cries the Justice with great pleasure. 'That will do; and if you will charge him on oath with that, I will instantly grant my warrant to search his house for it.' 'And I will go and see it executed,' cries the doctor: for it was a maxim of his, that no man could descend below himself in doing any act which may contribute to protect an innocent person, or to bring a rogue to the gallows.

The oath was instantly taken, the warrant signed, and the doctor attended the constable in the execution of it.

The clerk then proceeded in taking the information of Robinson, and had just finished it, when the doctor returned with the utmost joy in his countenance, and declared that he had sufficient evidence of the fact in his possession. He had indeed two or three letters from Miss Harris, in answer to the attorney's frequent demands of money for secrecy, that fully explained the whole villainy.

The Justice now asked the prisoner what he had to say for himself, or whether he chose to say any thing in his own defence.

'Sir,' said the attorney with great confidence, 'I am not to defend myself here. It will be of no service to me; for I know you neither can, nor will discharge me. But I am extremely innocent of all this matter, as I doubt not but to make appear to the satisfaction of a court of justice.'

The legal previous ceremonies were then gone through of binding over the prosecutor, etc. and then the attorney was committed to Newgate; whither he was escorted amidst the acclamations of the populace.

When Murphy was departed, and a little calm restored in the house, the Justice made his compliments of congratulation to Booth; who, as well as he could in his present tumult of joy, returned his thanks to both the magistrate and the doctor. They were now all preparing to depart, when Mr Bondum stept up to Booth, and said: 'Hold, sir, you have forgot one thing – you have not given bail yet.'

This occasioned some distress at this time; for the attorney's friend was departed; but when the Justice heard this, he immediately offered himself as the other bondsman; and thus ended the affair.

It was now past six o'clock, and none of the gentlemen had yet dined. They very readily therefore accepted the magistrate's invitation, and went all together to his house.

And now the very first thing that was done, even before they set down to dinner, was to dispatch a messenger to one of the best surgeons in town, to take care of Robinson; and another messenger to Booth's lodgings, to prevent Amelia's concern at their staying so long.

The latter however was to little purpose; for Amelia's patience had been worn out before, and she had taken a hackney-coach, and driven to the bailiff's, where she arrived a little after the departure of her husband, and was thence directed to the Justice's.

Though there was no kind of reason for Amelia's fright at hearing that her husband and Doctor Harrison were gone before the Justice; and though she indeed imagined that they were there in the light of complainants, not of offenders; yet so tender were her fears for her husband, and so much had her gentle spirits been lately agitated, that she had a thousand apprehensions of she knew not what. When she arrived therefore at the house, she ran directly into the room, where all the company were at dinner, scarce knowing what she did, or whither she was going.

She found her husband in such a situation, and discovered such chearfulness in his countenance, that so violent a turn was given to her spirits, that she was just able, with the assistance of a glass of water, to support herself. She soon however recovered her calmness, and in a little time began to eat what might indeed be almost called her breakfast.

The Justice now wished her joy of what had happened that day; for which she kindly thanked him, apprehending he meant the liberty of her husband. His worship might perhaps have explained himself more largely, had not the doctor given him a timely wink; for this wise and good man was fearful of making such a discovery all at once to Amelia, lest it should overpower her; and luckily the Justice's wife was not well enough acquainted with the matter to say any thing more on it than barely to assure the lady that she joined in her husband's congratulation.

Amelia was then in a clean white gown, which she had that day redeemed, and was indeed dressed all over with great neatness and exactness; with the glow therefore which arose in her features from finding her husband released from his captivity, she made so charming a figure, that she attracted the eyes of the magistrate and of his wife, and they both agreed when they were alone, that they had never seen so charming a creature; nay Booth himself afterwards told her that he scarce ever remembered her to look so extremely beautiful as she did that evening.

Whether Amelia's beauty, or the reflexion on the remarkable act of justice he had performed, or whatever motive filled the magistrate with extraordinary good humour, and opened his heart and cellars, I will not determine; but he gave them so hearty a welcome, and they were all so pleased with each other, that Amelia, for that one night, trusted the care of her children to the woman where they lodged, nor did the company rise from table till the clock struck eleven.

They then separated. Amelia and Booth having been set down at their lodgings retired into each other's arms; nor did Booth that evening, by the doctor's advice, mention one word of the grand affair to his wife.

CHAPTER 8

Thus this history draws nearer to a conclusion.

IN THE morning early Amelia received the following letter from Mrs Atkinson.

> The surgeon of the regiment, to which the captain my husband lately belonged, and who came this evening to see the captain, hath almost frightened me out of my wits by a strange story of your husband being committed to prison by a Justice of Peace for forgery. For Heaven's sake send me the truth. If my husband can be of any service, weak as he is, he will be carried in a chair to serve a brother officer for whom he hath a regard, which I need not mention. Or if the sum of £20 will be of any service to you, I will wait upon you with it the moment I can get my cloaths on, the morning you receive this; for it is too late to send to night. The captain begs his hearty service and respects, and believe me,
>
> Dear madam,
>
> Your ever affectionate friend,
>
> and humble servant,
>
> F. Atkinson.

When Amelia read this letter to Booth they were both equally surprised, she at the commitment for forgery, and he at seeing such a letter from Mrs Atkinson; for he was a stranger yet to the reconciliation that had happened.

Booth's doubts were first satisfied by Amelia, from which he received great pleasure; for he really had a very great affection and fondness for Mr Atkinson, who indeed so well deserved it. 'Well, my dear,' said he to Amelia smiling, 'shall we accept this generous offer?'

'O fy! no certainly,' answered she.

'Why not,' cries Booth, 'it is but a trifle; and yet it will be of great service to us?'

'But consider, my dear,' said she, 'how ill these poor people can spare it.'

'They can spare it for a little while,' said Booth, 'and we shall soon pay it them again.'

'When, my dear?' said Amelia. 'Do, my dear Will, consider our wretched circumstances. I beg you let us go into the country immediately, and live upon bread and water, till Fortune pleases to smile upon us.'

'I am convinced that day is not far off,' said Booth. 'However, give me leave to send an answer to Mrs Atkinson, that we shall be glad of her company immediately to breakfast.'

'You know I never contradict you,' said she, 'but I assure you it is contrary to my inclinations to take this money.'

'Well, suffer me,' cries he, 'to act this once contrary to your inclinations.' He then writ a short note to Mrs Atkinson, and dispatched it away immediately; which when he had done, Amelia said, 'I shall be glad of Mrs Atkinson's company to breakfast; but yet I wish you would oblige me in refusing this money. Take five guineas only. That is indeed such a sum, as, if we never should pay it, would sit light on my mind. The last persons in the world from whom I would receive favours of that sort, are the poor and generous.'

'You can receive favours only from the generous,' cries Booth; 'and, to be plain with you, there are very few who are generous that are not poor.'

'What think you,' said she, 'of Dr Harrison?'

'I do assure you,' said Booth, 'he is far from being rich. The doctor hath an income of little more than £600 a year; and I am convinced he gives away four of it. Indeed he is one of the best economists in the world; but yet I am positive he never was at any time possessed of £500 since he hath been a man. Consider, dear Emely, the late obligations we have to this gentleman, it would be unreasonable to expect more, at least at present; my half-pay is mortgaged for a year to come. – How then shall we live?'

'By our labour,' answered she, 'I am able to labour, and I am sure I am not ashamed of it.'

'And do you really think you can support such a life?'

'I am sure I could be happy in it,' answered Amelia. 'And why not I as well as a thousand others, who have not the happiness of such a husband to make life delicious? Why should I complain of my hard fate, while so many, who are much poorer than I, enjoy theirs. Am I of a superior rank of being to the wife of the honest labourer? Am I not partaker of one common nature with her?'

'My angel,' cries Booth, 'it delights me to hear you talk thus, and for a reason you little guess; for I am assured that one who can so heroically endure adversity, will bear prosperity with equal greatness of soul; for the mind that cannot be dejected by the former, is not likely to be transported with the latter.'

'If it had pleased Heaven,' cried she, 'to have tried me, I think, at least I hope I should have preserved my humility.'

'Then, my dear,' said he, 'I will relate you a dream I had last night. You know you lately mentioned a dream of yours.'

'Do so,' said she, 'I am attentive.'

'I dreamt,' said he, 'this night that we were in the most miserable situation imaginable. Indeed in the situation we were yesterday morning, or rather worse, that I was laid in a prison for debt, and that you wanted a morsel of bread to feed the mouths of your hungry children. At length (for nothing you know is quicker than the transition in dreams) Dr Harrison methought came to me, with chearfulness and joy in his countenance. The prison doors immediately flew open; and Dr Harrison introduced you, gayly tho' not richly dressed. That you gently chid me for staying so long; all on a sudden appear'd a coach with four horses to it, in which was a maid servant with our two children. We both immediately went into the coach, and taking our leave of the doctor, set out towards your country house: for yours I dreamt it was. – I only ask you now if this was real, and the transition almost as sudden, could you support it? –'

Amelia was going to answer when Mrs Atkinson came into the room, and after very little previous ceremony presented Booth with a bank note, which he received of her, saying, he would very soon repay it; a promise that a little offended Amelia, as she thought he had no chance of keeping it.

The doctor presently arrived, and the company sat down to

breakfast, during which Mrs Atkinson entertained them with the history of the doctors that had attended her husband, by whose advice Atkinson was recovered from every thing but the weakness which his distemper had occasioned.

When the tea-table was removed, Booth told the doctor that he had acquainted his wife with a dream he had last night. 'I dreamt, doctor,' said he, 'that she was restored to her estate.'

'Very well,' said the doctor; 'and if I am to be the *Oneiropolos*,[19] I believe the dream will come to pass. To say the truth, I have rather a better opinion of dreams than Horace had.[20] Old Homer says they came from Jupiter;[21] and as to your dream, I have often had it in my waking thoughts, that some time or other that roguery (for so I was always convinced it was) would be brought to light: for the same Homer says, as you, madam,' (meaning Mrs Atkinson) 'very well know,

> Εἴπερ γάρ τε καὶ αὐτίκ' Ὀλύμπιος οὐκ ἐτέλεσσεν,
> Ἔκ τε καὶ ὀψὲ τελεῖ· σύν τε μεγάλῳ ἀπέτισαν
> Σὺν σφῇσιν κεφαλῇσι, γυναιξί τε καὶ τεκέεσσιν.*

'I have no Greek ears, sir,' said Mrs Atkinson. 'I believe I could understand it in the Delphin Homer.'[23]

'I wish,' cries he, 'my dear child,' (to Amelia) 'you would read a little in the Delphin Aristotle, or else in some Christian divine, to learn a doctrine which you will one day have a use for, I mean to bear the hardest of all human conflicts, and support with an even temper and without any violent transports of mind, a sudden gust of prosperity.'

'Indeed,' cries Amelia, 'I should almost think my husband and you, doctor, had some very good news to tell me, by your using, both of you, the same introduction. As far as I know myself, I think I can answer, I can support any degree of prosperity, and I think I yesterday shew'd I could: for I do assure you, it is not in the power of Fortune to try me with such another transition from grief to joy, as I conceived from seeing my husband in prison and at liberty.'

* If Jupiter doth not immediately execute his vengeance; he will however execute it at last; and their transgressions shall fall heavily on their own heads, and on their wives and children.[22]

'Well, you are a good girl,' cries the doctor, 'and after I have put on my spectacles I will try you.'

The doctor then took out a news paper, and read as follows:

'"Yesterday one Murphy, an eminent attorney at law, was committed to Newgate, for the forgery of a will under which an estate hath been for many years detain'd from the right owner."

'Now in this paragraph there is something very remarkable, and that is – that it is true: but *opus est explanatum.*[24] In the Delphin edition of this news paper, there is the following note upon the words right owner: "The right owner of this estate is a young lady of the highest merit, whose maiden name was Harris, and who some time since was married to an idle fellow, one Lieutenant Booth. And the best historians assure us, that letters from the elder sister of this lady, which manifestly prove the forgery, and clear up the whole affair, are in the hands of an old parson, call'd Dr Harrison."'

'And is this really true?' cries Amelia.

'Yes, really, and sincerely,' cries the doctor. 'The whole estate: for your mother left it you all, and is as surely yours, as if you was already in possession.'

'Gracious Heaven,' cries she, falling on her knees, 'I thank you.' – And then starting up, she ran to her husband, and embracing him, cried, 'My dear love, I wish you joy: and I ought in gratitude to wish it you: for you are the cause of mine. It is upon yours, and my children's account, that I principally rejoice.'

Mrs Atkinson rose from her chair, and jumped about the room for joy, repeating,

> *'Turne, quod optanti divûm promittere nemo*
> *Auderet, volvenda dies, en, attulit ultro.'**

Amelia now threw herself into a chair, complain'd she was a little faint, and begg'd a glass of water. The doctor advis'd her to be blooded;[26] but she refused, saying she requir'd a vent of another kind. – She then desir'd her children to be brought to her, whom she immediately caught in her arms, and having profusely cried

* What none of all the gods could grant thy vows,
That, Turnus, this auspicious day bestows.[25]

over them for several minutes, declar'd she was easy. After which she soon regain'd her usual temper and complexion.

That day they din'd together, and in the afternoon they all, except the doctor, visited Captain Atkinson; he repair'd to the bailiff's house to visit the sick man, whom he found very chearful, the surgeon having assur'd him that he was in no danger.

The doctor had a long spiritual discourse with Robinson, who assur'd him that he sincerely repented of his past life, that he was resolv'd to lead his future days in a different manner, and to make what amends he could for his sins to the society by bringing one of the greatest rogues in it to justice. There was a circumstance which much pleased the doctor, and made him conclude that, however Robinson had been corrupted by his old master, he had naturally a good disposition. This was, that Robinson declared he was chiefly induced to the discovery by what had happened at the pawnbroker's, and by the miseries which he there perceived he had been instrumental in bringing on Booth and his family.

The next day Booth and his wife, at the doctor's instance, din'd with Colonel James and his lady, where they were receiv'd with great civility, and all matters were accommodated, without Booth ever knowing a syllable of the challenge even to this day.

The doctor insisted very strongly on having Miss Harris taken into custody, and said, if she was his sister, he would deliver her to justice. He added besides, that it was impossible to screen her, and carry on the prosecution, or indeed recover the estate. Amelia at last begg'd the delay of one day only, in which time she wrote a letter to her sister informing her of the discovery and the danger in which she stood, and begg'd her earnestly to make her escape, with many assurances that she would never suffer her to know any distress. This letter she sent away express, and it had the desir'd effect: for Miss Harris having receiv'd sufficient information from the attorney to the same purpose, immediately set out for Pool, and from thence to France, carrying with her all her money, most of her cloaths, and some few jewels. She had indeed pack'd up plate and jewels to the value of £2000 and upwards. But Booth to whom Amelia communicated the letter, prevented her, by ordering the man that went with the express, (who had been a serjeant of the Foot Guards recommended to him by Atkinson) to suffer the lady to go whither she pleased, but not to take any thing with her except her cloaths, which he was carefully to search. These orders were obey'd punctually, and with these she was oblig'd to comply.

Two days after the bird was flown, a warrant from the Lord Chief Justice arriv'd to take her up, the messenger of which return'd with the news of her flight, highly to the satisfaction of Amelia, and consequently of Booth, and indeed not greatly to the grief of the doctor.

About a week afterwards Booth and Amelia, with their children, and Captain Atkinson and his lady, all set forwards together for Amelia's house, where they arriv'd amidst the acclamations of all the neighbours, and every public demonstration of joy.

They found the house ready prepar'd to receive them by Atkinson's friend, the old serjeant, and a good dinner prepar'd for them by Amelia's old nurse, who was addressed with the utmost duty by her son and daughter, most affectionately caress'd by Booth and his wife, and by Amelia's absolute command seated next to herself at the table. At which perhaps were assembled some of the best and happiest people then in the world.

CHAPTER 9

In which the history is concluded.

HAVING brought our history to a conclusion, as to those points in which we presume our reader was chiefly interested, in the foregoing chapter; we shall in this, by way of epilogue, endeavour to satisfy his curiosity, as to what hath since happened to the principal personages of whom we have treated in the foregoing pages.

Colonel James and his lady, after living in a polite manner for many years together, at last agreed to live in as polite a manner asunder. The colonel hath kept Miss Mathews ever since, and is at length grown to doat on her (though now very disagreeable in her person, and immensely fat) to such a degree, that he submits to be treated by her in the most tyrannical manner.

He allows his lady £800 a year, with which she divides her time between Tunbridge, Bath and London, and passes about nine hours in the twenty-four at cards. Her income is lately increased by £3000 left her by her brother Colonel Bath, who was killed in a duel about six years ago, by a gentleman who told the colonel he differed from him in opinion.

The noble peer and Mrs Ellison have been both dead several years, and both of the consequences of their favourite vices; Mrs Ellison having fallen a martyr to her liquor, and the other to his amours, by which he was at last become so rotten, that he stunk above ground.

The attorney, Murphy, was brought to his trial at the Old Bailey, where, after much quibbling about the meaning of a very plain Act of Parliament, he was at length convicted of forgery, and was soon afterwards hanged at Tyburn.

The witness for some time seemed to reform his life, and received a small pension from Booth; after which he returned to vicious courses, took a purse on the highway, was detected and taken, and followed the last steps of his old master. So apt are men, whose manners have been once thoroughly corrupted, to return, from any dawn of an amendment, into the dark paths of vice.

As to Miss Harris, she lived three years with a broken heart at Boulogne, where she received annually fifty pounds from her sister, who was hardly prevailed on by Dr Harrison not to send her a hundred, and then died in a most miserable manner.

Mr Atkinson upon the whole hath led a very happy life with his wife, though he hath been sometimes obliged to pay proper homage to her superior understanding and knowledge. This, however, he chearfully submits to, and she makes him proper returns of fondness. They have two fine boys, of whom they are equally fond. He is lately advanced to the rank of captain, and last summer both he and his wife paid a visit of three months to Booth and his wife.

Dr Harrison is grown old in years, and in honour; beloved and respected by all his parishioners, and by all his neighbours. He divides his time between his parish, his old town, and Booth's – at which last place he had, two years ago, a gentle fit of the gout, being the first attack of that distemper. During this fit Amelia was his nurse, and her two oldest daughters sat up alternately with him for a whole week. The eldest of those girls, whose name is Amelia, is his favourite; she is the picture of her mother, and it is thought the doctor hath distinguished her in his will; for he hath declared that he will leave his whole fortune, except some few charities, among Amelia's children.

As to Booth and Amelia, Fortune seems to have made them large amends for the tricks she played them in their youth. They have, ever since the above period of this history, enjoyed an uninterrupted course of health and happiness. In about six weeks after Booth's first coming into the country, he went to London, and paid all his debts of honour; after which, and a stay of two days only, he returned into the country, and hath never since been thirty miles from home. He hath two boys and four girls; the eldest of the boys, he, who hath made his appearance in this history, is just come from the university, and is one of the finest gentlemen, and best scholars of his age. The second is just going from school, and is intended for the Church, that being his own choice. His eldest daughter is a woman grown, but we must not mention her age. A marriage was proposed to her the other day with a young fellow of a good estate, but she never would see him more than once; 'for Dr Harrison,' says she, 'told me he was illiterate, and I am sure he is ill natured.' The second girl is three years younger than her sister, and the others are yet children.

Amelia is still the finest woman in England of her age. Booth himself often avers she is as handsome as ever. Nothing can equal the serenity of their lives. Amelia declared to me the other day, that she did not remember to have seen her husband out of humour these ten years; and upon my insinuating to her, that he had the best of wives, she answered with a smile, that she ought to be so, for that he had made her the happiest of women.

FINIS.

APPENDIX

Chapter 2, Book v, of the first edition, deleted in Murphy's edition of Fielding's *Works* (1762), and in all subsequent editions

CHAPTER 2

Containing a brace of doctors, and much physical matter.

SUCH was the end of this present interview, so little to the content of Booth, that he was heartily concerned he had ever mentioned a syllable of the matter. He now returned with all his uneasiness to his Amelia, whom he found in a condition very little adapted to relieve or comfort him. That poor woman was now indeed under very great apprehensions for her child, whose fever now began to rage very violently: and what was worse, an apothecary had been with her, and frightened her almost out of her wits. He had indeed represented the case of the child to be very desperate, and had prevailed on the mother to call in the assistance of a doctor.

Booth had been a very little time in the room before this doctor arrived, with the apothecary close at his heels, and both approached the bed, where the former felt the pulse of the sick, and performed several other physical ceremonies. He then began to enquire of the apothecary what he had already done for the patient; all which, as soon as informed, he greatly approved. The doctor then sat down, called for a pen and ink, filled a whole side of a sheet of paper with physic, then took a guinea, and took his leave; the apothecary waiting upon him down stairs, as he had attended him up.

All that night both Amelia and Booth sat up with their child, who rather grew worse than better. In the morning Mrs Ellison found the infant in a raging fever, burning hot, and very light-headed, and the mother under the highest dejection: for the distemper had not given the least ground to all the efforts of the apothecary and doctor, but seemed to defy their utmost power, with all that tremendous apparatus of phials and gallypots, which were ranged in battle-array all over the room.

Mrs Ellison seeing the distressed, and indeed distracted condition of Amelia's mind, attempted to comfort her by giving her hopes of the child's recovery. 'Upon my word, madam,' says she, 'I saw a child of much the same age with miss, who, in my opinion was much worse, restored to health in a few days by a physician of my acquaintance; nay, I have known him cure several others of very bad fevers; and, if miss was under his care, I dare swear she would do very well.' 'Good Heavens! madam,' answered Amelia, 'why would you not mention him to me? for my part, I have no acquaintance with any London physicians, nor do I know whom the apothecary hath brought me.' 'Nay, madam,' cries Mrs Ellison, 'it is a tender thing you know, to recommend a physician; and as for my doctor, there are abundance of people who give him an ill name; indeed it is true, he hath cured me twice of fevers, and so he hath several others to my knowledge; nay, I never heard of any more than one of his patients that died; and yet as the doctors and apothecaries all give him an ill character, one is fearful, you know, dear madam.' – Booth enquired the doctor's name, which he no sooner heard, than he begged his wife to send for him immediately, declaring he had heard the highest character imaginable of him at the tavern, from an officer of very good understanding. Amelia presently complied, and a messenger was dispatched accordingly.

But before the second doctor could be brought, the first returned with the apothecary attending him, as before. He again surveyed and handled the sick; and when Amelia begged him to tell her, if there was any hopes, he shook his head, and said, 'To be sure, madam, miss is in a very dangerous condition, and there is no time to lose. If the blisters, which I shall now order her, should not relieve her, I fear – we can do no more.' – 'Would not you please, sir,' says the apothecary, 'to have the powders and the draught repeated?' – 'How often were they ordered?' cries the doctor. – 'Only *tertia quaq. hora*,'[1] says the apothecary. – 'Let them be taken every hour, by all means,' cries the doctor; 'and – let me see, pray get me a pen and ink.' – 'If you think the child in such imminent danger,' said Booth, 'would you give us leave to call in another physician to your assistance? – Indeed my wife –' 'O by all means,' said the doctc ', 'it is what I very much wish. Let me see, Mr Arsenic, whom shall we call?' – 'What do you think of Dr Dosewell?' said the apothecary. – 'No body better,' cries the physician. – 'I should have no objection to the gentleman,' answered Booth, 'but another hath been recommended to my wife.' He then mentioned the physician, for whom they had just before sent. 'Who, sir?' cries the doctor, dropping his pen; and when Booth repeated the name of Thompson,[2] 'Excuse me, sir,' cries the doctor hastily, 'I shall not meet him.' – 'Why so, sir?' answered Booth. 'I will not meet him,' replied the doctor, 'shall I meet a man who pretends to know more than the whole College, and would overturn the whole method of practice, which is so well established, and from which no one person hath pretended to deviate?' 'Indeed, sir,' cries the apothecary, 'you do not know what you are about, asking your pardon; why, he kills every body he comes near.' 'That is not true,' said Mrs Ellison, 'I have been his patient twice, and I am alive yet.' – 'You have had good luck then, madam,' answered the apothecary; 'for he kills every body he comes near.' – 'Nay, I know above a dozen others of my own acquaintance,' replied Mrs Ellison,' 'who have been all cured by him.' – 'That may be, madam,' cries Arsenic, 'but he kills every body for all that – why, madam, did you never hear of Mr – I can't think of the gentleman's name, tho' he was a man of great fashion, but every body knows whom I mean.' 'Every body indeed must know whom you mean,' answered Mrs Ellison, 'for I never heard but of one, and that many years ago.'

Before the dispute was ended, the doctor himself entered the room. As he was a very well-bred and a very good-natured man, he addressed himself with much civility to his brother physician, who was not quite so courteous on his side. However, he suffered the new comer to be conducted to the sick bed, and at Booth's earnest request to deliver his opinion.

The dispute which ensued between the two physicians would perhaps be unintelligible to any but to those of the faculty, and not very entertaining to them. The character which the officer and Mrs Ellison had given of the second doctor, had greatly prepossessed Booth in his favour; and indeed his reasoning seemed to be the juster. Booth therefore declared he would abide by his advice; upon which the former operator, with his zany[3] the apothecary, quitted the field, and left the other in full possession of the sick.

The first thing the new doctor did was (to use his own phrase) to blow up the physical magazine. All the powders and potions instantly disappeared at his command: for he said there was a much readier and nearer way to convey such stuff to the vault, than by first sending it through a human body. He then ordered the child to be blooded, gave it a clyster,[4] and some cooling physic; and, in short, (that I may not dwell too long on so unpleasing a part of history) within three days cured the little patient of her distemper, to the great satisfaction of Mrs Ellison, and to the vast joy of Amelia.

Some readers will perhaps think this whole chapter might have been omitted; but though it contains no great matter of amusement, it may at least serve to inform posterity concerning the present state of physic.

NOTES

TITLE-PAGE

Felices . . . copula: 'Thrice happy and more are they whom an unbroken bond unites' (Horace, *Odes*, I, xiii, 17–18). Γυναικὸς . . . κακῆς: 'A man can possess nothing better than a virtuous woman, nor any thing worse than a bad one' (Simonides, *Iambics*, iii).

DEDICATION

1. *Ralph Allen, Esq*: Ralph Allen (1693–1764) of Prior Park, Bath. Of humble origins, he became extremely wealthy as postmaster of Bath by improving the system of cross-posts (which avoided London) in England and Wales, and later by the purchase of valuable stone quarries. A philanthropist and generous patron of writers, Allen befriended Fielding, who often compliments him in his writing, notably by making him one of the models for Squire Allworthy in *Tom Jones*. After Fielding's death, Allen continued to contribute to the family, providing for the children's education and leaving legacies for members of the family.
2. *Detur Optimo*: 'Let it be given to the best man.' In suggesting a letter so addressed would be given to Allen, Fielding alludes to Allen's position as postmaster of Bath.
3. *their usual design*: i.e. to attract financial support.

BOOK I

1. (p. 14) *the liberty of Westminster*: properly speaking, the City of Westminster consisted of only two parishes, St Margaret's and St John the Evangelist's; another seven parishes (and the precinct of the Savoy) made up the liberty (or liberties) of Westminster, an area beyond the bounds of the city but subject to its control.
2. (p. 14) *writer of three letters*: Henry St John, Viscount Bolingbroke (1678–1751), author of *Letters, On the Spirit of Patriotism, On the Idea of*

a Patriot King, and On the State of Politics at the Accession of King George the First (1747).

3. (p. 14) *Lord Coke*: Sir Edward Coke (1552–1634), commonly called Lord Coke, the celebrated jurist and parliamentarian, admired and frequently cited by Fielding. In his later years he was a staunch upholder of the common law against the royal prerogative and the Church. Fielding paraphrases Coke's remarks in his *Commentary upon Littleton* (II, vi, 138).
4. (p. 15) *Graham*: George Graham (1673–1751), the distinguished instrument-maker and inventor, and Fellow of the Royal Society.
5. (p. 15) *economical*: household.
6. (p. 15) *watchmen*: until the Police Act of 1839, all towns were patrolled from sunset to sunrise by the watch, a body of men often much as Fielding describes them. From the time that he was first appointed a magistrate (1748) Fielding strove to improve the effectiveness of the watch by organizing the more capable Bow Street Runners, an initiative eventually supported by the government in 1753. The story is told by Fielding's brother John in his *Account of the Origin and Effects of a Police* (1758).
7. (p. 16) *Quae . . . conveniunt*: 'a boon which does not befit thy strength' (Ovid, *Metamorphoses*, II, 54–5). Fielding facetiously compares the young and inexperienced Phaeton (who has asked his father Apollo for permission to drive his chariot and winged horses across the sky for a day) with the decrepit but equally incapable watch.
8. (p. 16) *Rochefoucault*: François, 6th Duc de La Rochefoucauld (1613–80), whose cynical and witty *Maximes* appeared in 1665.
9. (p. 17) *Bridewell*: a penitentiary in London, used particularly as a house of correction for vagabonds and loose women. The word was often employed as a synonym for prison.
10. (p. 18) *Opus est Interprete*: 'an interpreter is necessary'.
11. (p. 18) *in the year 1749*: i.e., when Fielding was on the bench. Fielding's account of the laws against rioting and of the Riot Act is to be found in his *A True State of the Case of Boscavern Penlez* (1749).
12. (p. 19) *round-house*: overnight lock-up for prisoners awaiting trial.
13. (p. 20) *free of the place*: allowed to move freely about the prison.
14. (p. 21) *Nose she had none*: the result of the ravages of tertiary syphilis.
15. (p. 21) *St Giles's*: the parish of St Giles-in-the-Fields (depicted at this time in Hogarth's 'Gin Lane') was one of the seediest areas of London.
16. (p. 23) *Dr Clarke*: the Revd Samuel Clarke (1675–1729), philosopher and divine, chaplain to Queen Anne and rector of St James's, Piccadilly (1708–29). Fielding refers to Clarke's Boyle Lectures of 1704 and 1705, in which he refutes the arguments of Hobbes, Spinoza, and other freethinkers whose fatalism Robinson espouses.
17. (p. 23) *labefacta . . . nostri*: from the opening lines of Claudian's invective *Against Rufinus*. Claudian (*c*.370–*c*.410), wavering between belief in divine direction in the world and purposeless chance, tells how he fell into Epicureanism ('that other philosophy'):

. . . my belief in God was weakened and failed, and even against mine own will I embraced the tenets of that other philosophy which teaches that atoms drift in purposeless motion and that new forms throughout the vast void are shaped by chance and not design – that philosophy which believes in God in an ambiguous sense, or holds that there be no gods, or that they are careless of our doings.

18. (p. 23) *Brutus*: Marcus Junius Brutus (84–42 BC), before committing suicide after his defeat by Antony at Philippi, called valour the slave of fortune. The story is told in Dio's *Roman History* (XLVII, 49).
19. (p. 25) *to be stolen*: for Fielding's expression of outrage at the cruelty and inequity of the law, and of the need for law reform, see his *Covent-Garden Journal* (8 and 25 February 1752).
20. (p. 26) *traversable*: a traversable offence is one that may be formally denied at law.
21. (p. 26) *certiorari*: a writ issued from a higher court by which the records of a case are transferred from a lower court. The defendant in a case of perjury was often able to avail himself of this process on the grounds that he could not have an impartial trial in the lower court. By the time the novel was published the use of the writ *certiorari* in a case of perjury was no longer available, having been prohibited by an Act of Parliament (March 1750).
22. (p. 26) *the siege of Gibraltar*: Spanish resentment over the British possession of Gibraltar, confirmed by the Treaty of Utrecht (1713), was one of the causes of a war (1727–9) between Spain and England and her allies, during which Gibraltar was besieged.
23. (p. 26) *Chelsea*: the Royal Hospital, Chelsea, established by Charles II in 1682 for old and wounded soldiers.
24. (p. 26) *his fees*: discharge fees extracted by the gaoler, often illegally. It was this abuse that first stimulated John Howard to begin his campaign for prison reform.
25. (p. 27) *cull*: novice (in the criminal underworld).
26. (p. 27) *a Methodist*: Fielding's antipathy to Methodism, frequently expressed in his writing (notably, in *Shamela* (1741), *Joseph Andrews* (1742), and *Tom Jones* (1749)), rested on his detestation of their emphasis upon justification by faith alone, and consequent denial of the efficacy of good works for salvation. In his novels Methodists are generally represented as hypocrites, like Blifil in *Tom Jones*, who is eventually converted to the movement.
27. (p. 30) *Belides*: in fulfilment of a promise to their father, the Danaïds (after Danaus, their father – Belus was their grandfather) killed their husbands on their wedding night and, according to later legend, were eternally punished in Hades by having to collect water in leaking jugs. The story is told by Pindar in one of his *Triumphal Odes* (the Ninth Pythian), as well as in Ovid's *Metamorphoses* and Horace's *Odes*.
28. (p. 32) *four by honours*: the ace, king, queen, and knave of trumps in whist.

29. (p. 33) *disorder and hurry of spirits*: the regular flow throughout the body of the animal spirits (thought of as subtle, highly refined particles distilled from the blood in the rational faculty of the brain) was considered essential for human life. If disrupted or agitated the spirits would cause severe nervous disorder and eventually death.
30. (p. 34) *materia medica*: medical knowledge or subject matter.
31. (p. 34) *philosophy*: natural philosophy or science.
32. (p. 35) *Clive*: Catherine ('Kitty') Clive (1711–85), the greatly admired comic actress. Both Kitty Clive and William Hogarth (1697–1764) were friends of Fielding. Kitty Clive, to whom he dedicated *The Intriguing Chambermaid* (1733), played the leading female role in many of his plays. Hogarth is frequently complimented in Fielding's works, and his satiric designs are compared with Fielding's own caricatures (e.g., *Tom Jones*, I, xi; II, iii; and III, vi).
33. (p. 35) *heroine of the tender sex*: for *Dalila* and *Jezebel* see Judges xvi and 1 Kings xvi–2 Kings ix. Other domineering or vindictive women in this list include: (1) *Medea*, whose story is told in tragedies by Euripides and by Seneca, and by Ovid in his *Metamorphoses*; (2) *Semiramis* (9th century BC), legendary founder of Nineveh with her husband Ninus, whom she ordered to be executed when he granted her his power for a few days; (3) *Parysatis* (5th century BC), daughter of Artaxerxes I and Queen of Persia, notorious for her cruelty; (4) *Tanaquil*, wife of L. Tarquinus Priscus, legendary founder of the Roman Tarquinian dynasty; (5) *Livilla* (13 BC–31 AD), who poisoned her husband Drusus at the urging of her lover, Sejanus; (5) *Messalina*, wife of the Emperor Claudius, infamous for her avarice, lust, and cruelty, was finally executed by her husband in 48 AD; (6) *Agrippina* (16–59 AD), married the Emperor Claudius as her third husband, whom she poisoned along with various rivals and enemies so that her son Nero, by a previous marriage, would succeed; (7) *Brunichilde*, either Brunhilda (567–613), ruler of the Merovingian kingdom (after the death of her husband, King Sigbert, and her rival Fredegond), or Brunhild, the Valkyrie and heroine of the *Volsungasaga* and the *Niebelungenlied*; (8) *Elfrida*, or Aelfthryth (*c.*945–1000), second wife of King Edgar, who secured the succession for her own son, Aethelred the Unready, by arranging for the death of Edward the Martyr, her stepson and the heir; (9) *Joan of Naples*, or Queen Joanna II (1371–1435), notorious for her licentiousness and misrule; (10) *Christina of Sweden* (1626–89), daughter of Gustavus Adolphus, she was crowned 'King' of Sweden and was known for her arrogance; (11) *Katharine Hays*, or Hayes (1690–1726), burned at the stake for the gruesome murder of her husband with a hatchet; (12) *Sarah Malcolm* (*c.*1710–33), hanged for murdering her wealthy employer and two servants; and (13) *Con. Philips*, or Teresa Constantia Phillips (1709–65), an infamous courtesan and literary blackmailer, she concluded the *Apology* for her life (3 vols., 1748–9)

with a vicious attack on Fielding. On Con Phillips see note 5 to p. 148.

34. (p. 36) *the lovely 10th of June*: the birthday of James Francis Edward Stuart (1688–1766, the only son of James II, known as the 'Old Pretender') and hence a favourite day for Jacobite celebrations. The white rose was a Jacobite emblem.
35. (p. 36) *Boreas*: the north wind.
36. (p. 36) *the Revolution*: the 'Glorious' Revolution of 1688, and the constitutional adjustments that followed it, ensured the Protestant succession. For Jacobites the failure of the rebellions of 1715 and 1745 (the two attempts to restore the House of Stuart) were the 'dreadful' consequences.
37. (p. 36) *the young adventurer*: i.e. Charles Edward Stuart (1720–88), known as the 'Young Pretender' and 'Bonny Prince Charlie'.
38. (p. 36) *the inimitable B—y C—s*: Betty Careless (d. 1752), a notorious Covent Garden beauty and keeper of a bagnio (brothel) in Covent Garden, who ended her days in a poorhouse. In the last plate of Hogarth's *The Rake's Progress* (the Bedlam scene) her name can be seen carved on a banister.
39. (p. 37) *standing uppermost*: i.e. taking the leading position in a dance.
40. (p. 38) *a cornet*: a commissioned officer who carried the colours in a troop of cavalry.
41. (p. 39) *delight in music*: Miss Mathews's unmusical nature is probably meant as a sign of her emotional instability.
42. (p. 41) *jointure*: dower, that is, the annual income which a man at marriage settled on his wife in case she survived him. Hebbers, by marrying the widow, would get his hands on her dower from her previous husband.
43. (p. 47) *person*: outward appearance, bodily form.
44. (p. 52) *manslaughter and cold iron*: first offenders could claim 'benefit of clergy' in case of manslaughter (unpremeditated murder committed in passion) which, when granted, reduced the punishment from hanging to branding on the left thumb (often done only nominally, i.e. with cold iron). Benefit of clergy, originally available only to those who could read, had been made universal by the reign of Anne.
45. (p. 52) *chance-medley, or se defendendo*: chance-medley is manslaughter by misadventure; *se defendendo* is a plea of self-defence.
46. (p. 52) *and such stuff*: an indictment is the legal process by which a formal accusation is brought before a jury; an abatement is a defendant's plea showing technical reasons for not being prosecuted; a plea in bar is an objection sufficiently strong to stop an action at law; an ejectment is an action to recover possession of land from a lessee, or to try the title; trover is an action to recover personal property from someone who is in possession of it.
47. (p. 52) *summa totidis*: 'sum total' (properly, *summa totalis*).
48. (p. 52) *de non . . . est ratio*: 'that which is not seen must be treated as if it

did not exist' (properly, *de non apparentibus et non existentibus eadem est ratio*).

49. (p. 53) *Tace . . . is Latin for a candle*: a conventional hint to keep quiet. The point is that *tace* (Latin for 'be quiet') is *not* Latin for candle, as anyone with even a smattering of Latin would know, and so understand the hint.
50. (p. 53) *darken her day-lights*: give her black eyes.
51. (p. 53) *mill doll*: Bridewell – from the thieves' slang for beating hemp (mill dolly) in a house of correction.
52. (p. 54) *malice prepensive*: malice aforethought. If malice aforethought could be proved, Miss Mathews would be guilty of murder, rather than of the less serious crime of manslaughter. In the discussion that follows Booth points out, correctly, that homicide by stabbing is an exception to the rule that permitted benefit of clergy to be claimed in cases of manslaughter. In the reign of James I, homicide by stabbing, even without malice aforethought, was made a felony without benefit of clergy.
53. (p. 54) *contra formam statutis*: 'against the form of the statute', the concluding words of an indictment for an offence created by statute.
54. (p. 54) *implicit*: Murphy means explicit. His English, like his Latin, is sometimes comically incorrect.
55. (p. 55) *the book*: the Bible, on which oaths are sworn in a court of law.
56. (p. 55) *the crier*: an officer of the court.

BOOK II

1. (p. 69) *Order of the Rag*: i.e. poor, with not much more than rags to their name.
2. (p. 70) *put red liveries upon all the saints in my closet*: paint (military) uniforms on all the pictures of the saints in my private room.
3. (p. 70) *settled every penny which the mother should lay down*: agreed to a deed of settlement to secure Amelia's marriage portion (provided by her mother). In II, 8, we learn that this agreement was not carried out.
4. (p. 70) *an express*: a specially sent message.
5. (p. 72) *equipage*: coach and footmen.
6. (p. 76) *Who calls the wretched thing that was Alphonso?*: William Congreve, *The Mourning Bride* (1697), II, ii, 35. The play retained its popularity throughout the eighteenth century, as the ability of both Booth and Amelia to quote from it attests.
7. (p. 80) *parts*: abilities.
8. (p. 83) *my mother*: my mother-in-law.
9. (p. 88) *to touch*: to be bribed.
10. (p. 89) *wind*: slang for strong drink (generally gin or rum).
11. (p. 89) *the Lord of Oxford's Horse*: the Royal Regiment of Horse Guards, formed in 1661 under Aubrey de Vere, Earl of Oxford.
12. (p. 89) *peery*: fearful.

13. (p. 89) *the mob*: the semi-criminal London mob, which was particularly hard on anyone who informed on law-breakers. For Fielding's account of the mob see *The Covent-Garden Journal* (20 June 1752), and for his account of the difficulty in taking felons because of the popular hostility to informers see his *An Enquiry into the Causes of the Late Increase of Robbers* (1751), VII.
14. (p. 89) *a good part of the reward*: thieves who turned king's evidence could escape punishment and claim a share of the reward for the capture of their comrades.
15. (p. 90) *upon the snaffling lay*: a cant term for robbery on the highway.
16. (p. 90) *impeach*: give evidence against.
17. (p. 90) *the road*: gentlemen of the road, highwaymen, often popularly romanticized, like Captain Macheath in Gay's *Beggar's Opera* (1728).
18. (p. 90) *an evidence*: a witness, one who gives evidence.
19. (p. 91) *Noscitur a sosir*: 'you may know him by the company he keeps' (properly, *noscitur a socio*).
20. (p. 92) *The blackest . . . a blot*: George Villiers, 2nd Duke of Buckingham, *The Rehearsal* (1672), III, ii (slightly misquoted).

BOOK III

1. (p. 101) *Lady Bountiful*: the wealthy and beneficent gentlewoman in George Farquhar's *The Beaux' Stratagem* (1707).
2. (p. 103) *Scilly*: the Scilly Isles, off Land's End, Cornwall.
3. (p. 108) *Mandevil*: Bernard Mandeville (1670–1733), whose cynical *The Fable of the Bees* (1714) was designed to illustrate the self-interest and rapacity of human nature.
4. (p. 114) *the hysterics*: various names for severe melancholy (or psychotic depression), to which women were thought to be particularly susceptible. Based on the concept of humoral medicine laid down by Galen in the second century, the notion still persisted that both physical and mental disorders were caused by an imbalance or corruption of the body's four fluids, or 'humours' (blood, phlegm, choler, and black bile). Corruption of the black bile was thought to produce the 'vapours', which rose from the lower organs (specifically, the spleen) to the head, causing depression, headaches, and insomnia. For the spirits see note 29 to p. 33.
5. (p. 114) *the curses of Egypt*: Exodus vii, 16–xii, 30.
6. (p. 114) *the Governor*: at this time Sir David Colyear, 1st Earl of Portmore.
7. (p. 114) *Montpelier*: Montpellier in southern France, known for its salubrious climate, was a popular medical resort.
8. (p. 116) *jacta est alia*: 'the die is cast' (properly, *jacta est alea*), Julius Caesar's famous statement as he crossed the Rubicon on his way to conquer Rome.

9. (p. 116) *a knapsack*: the poor cannot afford to suffer from such fashionable conditions as the vapours.
10. (p. 117) *discounted the captain's draught*: cashed his money draft (with a discount for interest).
11. (p. 118) *the sun of righteousness*: Malachi iv, 2.
12. (p. 121) *the ridiculous*: for Fielding's idea that vanity is the true source of the ridiculous see his Preface to *Joseph Andrews* and his essay in *The Champion* (15 April 1740).
13. (p. 122) *a surfeit*: sickness caused by over-indulgence in food or drink.
14. (p. 122) *caudle*: a warm drink, usually thin gruel sweetened and mixed with wine or ale, given as a restorative to the sick.
15. (p. 123) *posset*: hot milk mixed with ale, wine, or other liquid, often sweetened and spiced, taken for colds.
16. (p. 125) *Porcia*: the affection of Marcus Junius Brutus for his wife, Portia, is recorded by Plutarch. See also Shakespeare, *Julius Caesar*, II, i, and IV, iii.
17. (p. 125) *the great King of Sweden*: Charles XII (1682–1716), often taken in the eighteenth century as a type of the fierce and over-ambitious conqueror. His story was familiar from Voltaire's *Histoire de Charles XII* (1732, immediately translated into English), and from Johnson's *The Vanity of Human Wishes* (1749), ll. 191–222. The story of his grief over the death of his sister is told in an appendix to Gustave Adlerfeld's *The Military History of Charles XII, King of Sweden* (1740), which Fielding helped translate from the French.
18. (p. 125) *Xerxes*: king of Persia (485–465 BC). Among other instances of his impulsive nature, Herodotus tells of Xerxes' tears at the thought of the brevity of human life as he reviewed his army. In Johnson's *Vanity of Human Wishes*, published shortly before *Amelia*, the story of Xerxes also immediately follows that of Charles XII.
19. (p. 126) *party quarrée*: a party of four (properly, *partie carrée*).
20. (p. 129) *luxuriously delicate*: extremely delightful.
21. (p. 129) *'Had I . . . out again'*: Matthew Prior, 'To a Young Gentleman in Love. A Tale' (1720), ll. 43–6.
22. (p. 129) *Calista*: Nicholas Rowe, *The Fair Penitent*, IV, i (slightly misquoted).
23. (p. 130) *consistent with your honour*: duelling (practised by officers in defence of their 'honour') was frequently attacked as unchristian by, among others, Defoe, Addison, Steele, Richardson, and Fielding. For Fielding's comments see *The Temple Beau* (II, xii), *Jonathan Wild* (I, ii), *Tom Jones* (VII, xii-xiv) and below, IX, iii.
24. (p. 132) *The burden becomes light by being well borne*: Ovid, *Amores*, I, ii, 10. Cf. *Tom Jones*, II, iii, where the notion is also Partridge's 'usual recipe of patience'.
25. (p. 132) *Aristotle*: by the eighteenth century the new empirical philosophy of writers such as Bacon and Locke had brought the rationalist philosophy of Aristotle into disrepute.

26. (p. 132) *can be called happy*: in his *Nicomachean Ethics* (I, ix, 10–11) Aristotle cites the case of Priam, King of Troy, who fell from the height of prosperity into utter misery when his city was taken and sacked by the Greeks.
27. (p. 132) *To look down on all human affairs as matters below his consideration*: *Tusculan Disputations*, III, vii, 15.
28. (p. 132) *short transitory evils*: Dr Harrison's argument that the divine assurance of immortality assists the Christian to rise above wordly calamity more readily than the pagan philosopher is traditional in Christian consolation.
29. (p. 133) *court of requests*: first established in the reign of Henry VIII, the courts of requests (or of conscience) dealt with cases of debt or damage under forty shillings.
30. (p. 133) *at Garaway's or at White's*: the former was a famous auction-room and coffee-house located in Exchange Alley, Cornhill, and frequented by wealthy merchants; the latter a chocolate-house which became a private club with a largely aristocratic membership well-known for gambling at very high stakes.
31. (p. 133) *Bedlam*: the common name for the Hospital of St Mary of Bethlehem, the principal London lunatic asylum.
32. (p. 133) *A set of beggarly philosophers*: the *Aretalogi* are mentioned in Juvenal, *Satires*, XV, 16, and in Suetonius, *Lives of the Caesars*, II, lxxiv.
33. (p. 134) *Thucydides observes*: in his *History of the Peloponnesian War*, II, 61. Dr Harrison refers to the speech of Pericles to the Athenians exhorting them to cast their minds beyond present disasters to eventual triumph.
34. (p. 136) *Miss Harris*: the eighteenth-century convention was to refer to (and address) the eldest daughter by her surname before her marriage. Amelia as a younger sister would have been called Miss Amelia and referred to as Miss Amelia Harris.
35. (p. 136) *saluted*: kissed.
36. (p. 137) *Miss Emily*: Emily was often used as a variant of Amelia, as here, where her spiteful sister rudely refuses to accord Amelia her proper name.
37. (p. 142) *his patron the earl*: the patron of an ecclesiastical benefice held the advowson, or right of presentation of his candidate to the bishop for institution into a vacant benefice (or living). By the eighteenth century a patron was usually able to appoint a clergyman to a vacant living, even against the will of the bishop of the diocese.
38. (p. 144) *the verge of the court*: originally an area extending twelve miles around the king's court, by the eighteenth century the verge of the court consisted of the neighbourhood around Whitehall and St James's Palace under the jurisdiction of the Lord Steward of the Royal Household. As the civil officers of the law had no authority there,

offenders were free from arrest and the area became a natural haven for debtors.

BOOK IV

1. (p. 146) *Anthony*: Fielding refers to Dryden's *All for Love* (1678), III, 168–71, which had virtually replaced Shakespeare's version of the story of Antony and Cleopatra on the eighteenth-century stage.
2. (p. 147) *locking-up time*: 9 p.m. in Newgate prison.
3. (p. 147) *rack-punch*: punch made with arrack (strong spirits imported from the Levant).
4. (p. 148) *bagnio*: bath-house or brothel.
5. (p. 148) *gay*: immoral, dissolute. The notorious courtesan Con Phillips had published her *Apology* in 1748–9 (see note 33 to p. 35), and the *Memoirs* of Laetitia Pilkington (1712–50), which also attracted much notoriety, appeared in 1748. More recently, in 1751 the sensational revelations of Frances Anne, Viscountess Vane, were published as Chapter 88 ('The Memoirs of a Lady of Quality') of Smollett's *Peregrine Pickle*.
6. (p. 149) *conversation*: intimacy
7. (p. 151) *Calista*: see note 22 to p. 129.
8. (p. 152) *to touch*: to be bribed.
9. (p. 154) *agitation of her spirits*: see note 29 to p. 33.
10. (p. 154) *Till all the whores were burnt alive*: from Matthew Prior, 'Paulo Purganti and his Wife' (1708), ll. 45–6. Also quoted by Fielding in *The Covent-Garden Journal* (1 August 1752).
11. (p. 156) *melancholy*: often used in a much stronger sense in Fielding's day to suggest severe depression.
12. (p. 158) *a hack*: hackney coach (i.e. one let out for hire).
13. (p. 159) *the church*: St Anne's, Soho.
14. (p. 159) *N.S.*: New Style, that is, according to the Gregorian Calendar, in use in the greater part of Europe from 1582. Until 2 September 1752 (Old Style) England adhered to the old or Julian Calendar, which by the eighteenth century had fallen eleven days behind the Gregorian Calendar and which also recognized Lady Day (25 March) as the beginning of the new year. To avoid confusion writers often indicated which calendar they were using.
15. (p. 160) *favourite Greek historian*: Thucydides. Dr Harrison paraphrases Pericles' funeral oration from the *Peloponnesian War*, II, 40.
16. (p. 164) *a memorial of his pretensions*: a statement of his claims.
17. (p. 164) *pieces*: gold pieces or guineas.
18. (p. 165) *the only day he could venture*: by a law of the reign of Charles II arrests could not be made, or processes of law served, on Sunday, except in cases of treason, felony, or breach of the peace.
19. (p. 165) *the chairman*: porters of sedan chairs (or chairmen) could be hired to carry letters.

20. (p. 166) *furens quid femina possit*: 'what a woman can do in frenzy' (Virgil, *Aeneid*, V, 6).
21. (p. 167) *Spring Garden*: a garden between St James's Park and Charing Cross and Whitehall, which served as a popular resort. The coffee-house was probably Brown's.
22. (p. 168) *the King's Arms*: a tavern on the north side of Pall Mall.
23. (p. 170) *Tully*: Marcus Tullius Cicero.
24. (p. 176) *a rout*: a large and fashionable evening assembly or party.
25. (p. 177) *the Parade*: an open space in St James's Park beside the Horse Guards, or guard-house of the royal palace.
26. (p. 178) *a Latin author*: Cicero, in *De oratore*, II, iii, 10, comments on the diffidence of the well-bred. 'Ingenuous' originally signified the qualities of the noble or free-born man.
27. (p. 178) *in the Guards*: that is, in one of the three regiments of the foot guards (the Grenadier Guards, the Coldstream Guards, and the Scots Guards) responsible for the protection of the monarch.
28. (p. 179) *about fifteen years of age*: Fielding (as here) often protested against the practice of commissioning mere boys from wealthy families, while experienced soldiers were passed over for promotion. Cf *Tom Jones*, VIII, xii.
29. (p. 181) *the great man*: a phrase often used facetiously by Fielding, as in *Jonathan Wild* (1741). During the period of Walpole's ascendancy as prime minister (1721–42) the word 'great' was frequently used by the opposition to suggest the connection between power and corruption.
30. (p. 181) *necessity*: lack of means, poverty.
31. (p. 182) *the oratorio*: because of its sacred or semi-sacred subject matter, its English text, and its lack of dramatic staging or acting, the oratorio in England was considered a more rational and more respectable form of entertainment than the Italian opera, then in decline. Associated particularly with the name of Handel (1685–1759, resident in England from 1712) and with his most famous work, *The Messiah* (1742), the oratorio flourished in London from the 1730s.
32. (p. 183) *the pun*: Fielding, playing on the word 'broken', suggests that the half-pay officers are physically enfeebled as well as financially bankrupt.
33. (p. 184) *the industrious bee*: the analogy of human society and the beehive is the fundamental metaphor of Bernard de Mandeville's *The Grumbling Hive* (1703) and of his *The Fable of the Bees* (1714, and later revised editions), but the comparison is at least as old as Virgil's fourth *Georgic*.
34. (p. 186) *Board of Green-Cloth*: a division of the Household Department under the Lord Steward, the Board of Green Cloth (so called from the colour of the cloth on the table at which its officers sat) could function as a court of justice responsible for keeping the peace within the verge of the court. To avoid a writ of summons from this court (or from the Marshal's Court, with which it shared jurisdiction within the royal

precinct), Booth would have to remain in his own lodgings. In the event, as the Palace Court (the popular name for the two courts) was virtually dormant in the eighteenth century, Murphy's threat is essentially idle.

35. (p. 188) *in very indifferent circumstances*: as the widows of clergymen were not eligible for a pension, they were often desperately poor and dependent upon charities. Fielding, like a number of his contemporaries, was zealous in campaigning for improved charitable provision for such women and their children. See his *The Jacobite's Journal* (23 April; 18 and 25 June; and 2 and 9 July 1748), *The Covent-Garden Journal* (6 January 1752), and *Tom Jones* (IV, xiv).

BOOK V

1. (p. 191) *we term modesty*: the Greek word αἰδώς signifies a sense of shame or modesty, as well as a feeling of honour, self-respect, and respect for others.
2. (p. 194) *a scrag*: the lean end of the neck.
3. (p. 195) *Beau Fribble*: byword for an effeminate fop, from the character in David Garrick's theatrical afterpiece, *Miss in Her Teens* (1747).
4. (p. 195) *mauvaise honte*: self-consciousness, bashfulness.
5. (p. 195) *Mr Essex*: John Essex, the well-known dancing master and author of several treatises on the art of dancing.
6. (p. 197) *leading-strings*: reins used to guide and support children who are learning to walk.
7. (p. 198) *And whatsoever the sages . . . and our own too from falling*: the lines which Mrs Ellison imperfectly remembers are from Farquhar's *The Beaux' Stratagem* (1707), II, ii. Mrs Ellison suggests that, like Archer in Farquhar's play, pride (in her superior social class) prevents a greater emotional entanglement.
8. (p. 199) *economy*: prudent management.
9. (p. 200) *All for Love, or the World well Lost*: the title of Dryden's famous version of the tragedy of Antony and Cleopatra.
10. (p. 200) *Nec quenquam . . . parem*: 'Caesar could no longer endure a superior, nor Pompey an equal' (Lucan, *Pharsalia*, I, 125–6).
11. (p. 202) *the Marshal's Court*: also called the Court of Marshalsea. One of the two courts which comprised the Palace Court, the sole jurisdiction within the verge of the court. See note 34 to p. 186.
12. (p. 204) *the Monument*: the column (202 ft high) designed by Christopher Wren to commemorate the Great Fire of London (1666) can be ascended by an internal staircase.
13. (p. 205) *the City*: the ancient City of London was the home of prosperous tradesmen and merchants, but not of people of fashion, who preferred to live near the royal court in Westminster.
14. (p. 206) *the Ring*: a circle in Hyde Park, laid out in the reign of Charles I, which served as a fashionable place to ride or promenade. The Ring

(and the area around it) was well-known in the eighteenth century as a duelling-ground.

15. (p. 206) *a Spaniard*: a slow or deliberate walking pace with an air of gravity was thought to be a Spanish affectation, and was frequently ridiculed.
16. (p. 207) *the house by the water*: possibly a building known as Price's Lodge, which was taken down about 1733 to permit the completion of the Serpentine in Hyde Park.
17. (p. 208) *Grosvenor Gate*: one of the few entrances into Hyde Park, which was surrounded by a brick wall in the eighteenth century. Sir Richard Grosvenor constructed the gate in 1724 for the residents of Grosvenor Square, near by.
18. (p. 208) *a very eminent surgeon*: Fielding's friend and surgeon, John Ranby (1703–73), lived in Bond Street at the time of the novel. He was made sergeant-surgeon to George II in 1740. Cf. *Tom Jones*, VIII, xiii and XVII, ix.
19. (p. 208) *complexion*: temperament, nature.
20. (p. 210) *the Philistines*: facetiously used, by analogy with the Philistines in the Old Testament, of those considered 'the enemy'.
21. (p. 210) *qui vive*: originally a sentry's challenge (requiring the answer *vive le roi*), the expression has come to signify anyone on the alert or lookout.
22. (p. 212) *resentment*: the injury done to another, and hence, a sense of loss or regret.
23. (p. 212) *resentment*: acknowledgement.
24. (p. 212) *grinned horribly a ghastly smile*: Milton, *Paradise Lost*, II, 846.
25. (p. 213) *ombre*: a game of cards, fashionable in the seventeenth and eighteenth centuries.
26. (p. 214) *awful*: scrupulous, reverential.
27. (p. 214) *as Horace says*: Odes, I, xix, 5–8.
28. (p. 218) *jantee*: obsolete variant of jaunty.
29. (p. 220) *Miss Bellamy, nor Mrs Cibber*: the celebrated rival actresses. The theatrical 'war' began when George Anne Bellamy (1731?–88) played Juliet to Garrick's Romeo at Drury Lane (28 September – 11 October 1750) while Susannah Cibber (née Arne, 1714–66) played Juliet to Barry's Romeo at Covent Garden. Fielding may have been thinking of the scene in which Juliet learns of the death of her cousin Tybalt, killed by Romeo in a duel.
30. (p. 224) *The Birdcage Walk*: along the south side of St James's Park, so called from the royal aviary there.
31. (p. 225) *spleen or vapours*: see note 4 to p. 114.
32. (p. 225) *Pandora's box*: the gift of Jupiter to Pandora, the box contained all human ills, which escaped when Pandora, against her husband's orders, opened it.
33. (p. 226) *Jusque a la bourse*: (properly, *jusqu'à la bourse*) 'as far as the purse', suggesting the limits of friendship.

BOOK VI

1. (p. 229) *as Milton sublimely describes Eve*: *Paradise Lost*, VIII, 482–4, 488–9.
2. (p. 229) *Waller*: Edmund Waller (1606–87), 'Of Loving at First Sight', ll. 11–14.
3. (p. 229) *Suckling*: Sir John Suckling (1609–42), 'The crafty Boy, that had full oft essay'd', ll. 7–12.
4. (p. 231) *Dryden*: *Absalom and Achitophel*, l. 30.
5. (p. 231) *nemo repente fuit turpissimus*: 'no one reaches the depths of turpitude all at once' (Juvenal, *Satires*, II, 83).
6. (p. 237) *scrutore*: a corruption of the French *escritoire*, writing desk.
7. (p. 237) *St Edmundsbury*: in Suffolk (now generally called Bury St Edmunds), a fashionable resort in the eighteenth century.
8. (p. 239) *Mr Congreve's*: William Congreve (1670–1729), *The Way of the World*, III, xii.
9. (p. 240) *condescension*: stooping low (in social rank).
10. (p. 240) *as Solomon says*: actually David in Psalm 141, v. 3: 'Set a watch, O Lord, before my mouth, keep the door of my lips.'
11. (p. 243) *Mr Addison*: *Cato*, II, iv.
12. (p. 244) *Bedlam*: cf. note 31 to p. 133. The lunatic asylum could be visited for a small sum on Sunday afternoons and was one of the principal sights of London.
13. (p. 247) *The greatest genius*: Shakespeare. See *Othello*, III, iii, 319–21.
14. (p. 248) *Ranelagh*: a fashionable place of public entertainment, built by the river Thames on ground belonging to the first Earl of Ranelagh. Opened in 1742, Ranelagh is an anachronism in the novel, which is set in 1733. Ranelagh acquired a reputation, particularly with the introduction of masquerade parties, for licentiousness. Fielding was among those who objected to public masquerades as encouragements to debauchery. See his *A Charge Delivered to the Grand Jury* (1749).
15. (p. 253) *Congreve*: *The Way of the World*, III, xviii.
16. (p. 256) *Dr Barrow*: The Revd Isaac Barrow, DD (1630–77), the eminent Cambridge mathematician and theologian, Master of Trinity College (1672–7), was one of the greatest Anglican divines of the seventeenth century and a leader of the latitudinarian (or liberal) school in the English Church. As his 'favourite divine' (*The Covent-Garden Journal*, 11 April 1752), Barrow had a strong influence on Fielding's moral philosophy, especially his belief in the supreme value of good nature. His sermons are the cause of Booth's conversion in the final book of the novel (see Book XII, chapter 5).
17. (p. 256) *Bishop Burnet*: Gilbert Burnet (1643–1715), Bishop of Salisbury and a powerful figure in court and church circles, who played a significant role in the Revolution of 1688, accompanying William of Orange on his march to London. He was the author of *The History of the Reformation of the Church of England* (1679–1714) and a *History of My*

Own Times (published posthumously, 1723–4). Fielding's partiality to Burnet, whose Whig views of the Protestant succession and of religious toleration he shared, is evident in the words of the first edition of *Amelia* where Burnet is called 'almost the only *English* Historian that is likely to be known to Posterity, by whom he will be most certainly ranked amongst the greatest Writers of Antiquity'.

18. (p. 256) *bigamy*: remarriage after the death of a first husband or wife.
19. (p. 257) *held to be infamous*: 'Among the old Romans it was thought infamous in a Widow to marry' (Fielding in *The Covent-Garden Journal*, No. 66, 14 October 1752). There are other parallels between that number of the *Journal* and this chapter of the novel.
20. (p. 257) *as Petrarch observes*: *De remediis utriusque fortuna*, translated by T. Twyne as *Physicke against Fortune* (1579), Book I, Dialogue LXXVI ('Of seconde Marriage').
21. (p. 257) *St Jerome*: The reference is to St Jerome's letter 'To Furia on the Duty of Remaining a Widow' (Letter 54), cited by Petrarch.
22. (p. 257) *Charondas*: The celebrated lawgiver of Catania in Sicily, who flourished about 550 BC. The account of this law is given by Diodorus Siculus (who mistakenly associates Charondas with Thurium) in his *Library of History*, XII, xii.
23. (p. 257) *Valerius Maximus*: in his *Factorum et dictorum memorabilium libri*, II, i, 3, Valerius Maximus declares that those who were content with one husband were honoured with the crown of chastity (*corona pudicitiae*).
24. (p. 257) *the noble family of Camilli*: Furia, to whom St Jerome's letter against remarriage (see note above) is addressed, belonged to this family, of which Jerome asserts that few or none of the women had known a second husband's bed.
25. (p. 257) *Martial*: 'She who marries so often does not marry; she is an adulteress by form of law' (*Epigrams*, VI, vii, 5).
26. (p. 257) *Virgil*: 'But rather, I would pray, may earth yawn for me to its depths, or may the Almighty Father hurl me with his bolt to the shades – the pale shades and abysmal night of Erebus – before, O Shame, I violate thee or break thy laws! He, who first linked me to himself, has taken away my heart; may he keep it with him, and guard it in the grave!' (slightly misquoted from the *Aeneid*, IV, 24–9).
27. (p. 258) *Madam Dacier*: like her husband André, Anne Dacier (1654–1720, née Lefèvre) was a classical scholar, translator, and editor. She acquired fame throughout Europe, particularly for her translations of the *Iliad* (1699) and the *Odyssey* (1708).
28. (p. 260) *pretended*: claimed (not necessarily with a sense of feigning).
29. (p. 261) *on his own account*: the hint is that, in the dishonest cooperation between the bailiffs and the Justice, the Justice did not always receive what he considered his fair share.
30. (p. 266) *eagerly*: anxiously.

BOOK VII

1. (p. 281) *the next presentation*: before the Benefices Act of 1898 it was possible to purchase from the holder of an advowson (cf. note 37 to p. 142) the right of 'next presentation' to an ecclesiastical benefice. Such a sale, however, would be considered simony (the corrupt buying or selling of benefices) and severely punished by ecclesiastical law, if the benefice were vacant, if the incumbent were not in good health, or if the sale were to a clergyman who intended to present himself. The right of next presentation had to be exercised within six months of the vacancy, after which it passed to the bishop.
2. (p. 281) *his proper age of taking orders*: twenty-three years of age for the deaconate; twenty-four for the priesthood.
3. (p. 282) *only accepted his bond for forty*: Fielding is sarcastic. The young clergyman will be obliged to repay double the amount of money he borrowed.
4. (p. 282) *hardly*: painfully, on hard terms.
5. (p. 282) *a title to ordination*: before he could be ordained, a candidate for holy orders was usually required by the bishop to provide a guarantee of support in the form of a title or valid claim to a benefice or other ecclesiastical preferment.
6. (p. 283) *a gallimatia*: gibberish ('galimatias' is the usual form).
7. (p. 286) *person*: outward appearance, bodily form.
8. (p. 287) *a tigress, that hath lost her young, is described*: a common topos in Latin literature.
9. (p. 294) *my little Charly*: earlier (p. 237) Mrs Bennet refers to her son 'Tommy'.
10. (p. 295) *condescension*: affability, graciousness (to one's social inferiors).
11. (p. 296) *threw us both into a flow of spirits*: made us both very cheerful. The flow of animal spirits, essential to life, determined the emotional condition. See note 29 to p. 33.
12. (p. 297) *a coral*: a teething ring (made of polished coral).
13. (p. 301) *satisfied*: convinced.
14. (p. 301) *stagger*: shake, unsettle.
15. (p. 307) *polypus*: blood clot.

BOOK VIII

1. (p. 314) *Mrs Chenevix's toy-shop*: Elizabeth Chenevix (née Deard, d. 1755), wife of Paul Daniel Chenevix, ran a fashionable toy shop (located in Powell's Building at the corner of Cockspur Street and Warwick Street) frequently mentioned in the period.
2. (p. 314) *a bailiff*: an officer of justice under a sheriff, who executes writs and processes, distraints and arrests. His house, known as a sponging house, was used as a place of preliminary confinement for debtors.

3. (p. 315) *Bolus . . . equirit*: properly, '*dolus an virtus, quis in hoste requirat*' (*Aeneid*, II, 390): 'whether deceit or valour, who would ask in the enemy?'
4. (p. 315) *Gray's Inn Lane*: now part of Gray's Inn Road (beside the Inn of Court of that name), some distance from the place of Booth's arrest.
5. (p. 318) *your history books for your numbers*: the practice of issuing books in portions, often weekly, is ridiculed by Fielding in *Joseph Andrews* (II, i) and *Tom Jones* (XIII, i).
6. (p. 318) *Parliament speeches for your magazines*: in 1738 the House of Commons forbade the publication of parliamentary debates, forcing political journals like *The London Magazine* and *The Gentleman's Magazine* to disguise their reports. *The Gentleman's Magazine*, for example, published the 'Debates of the Senate of Lilliput' and from 1741 to 1743 it employed Samuel Johnson to write the speeches.
7. (p. 318) *men could not be arrested for debt*: in *The Champion* (19 February 1739/40) Fielding argues that imprisonment for debt is an innovation not consonant with the ancient constitution of England.
8. (p. 319) *tipstaff*: an officer of the court (so called from his silver-tipped staff of office), who waits upon the judge and takes charge of committed prisoners.
9. (p. 326) *took a chair*: hired a sedan chair.
10. (p. 329) *Doctor Swift*: Fielding often expressed his high regard for Swift, notably in the obituary of Swift he wrote for *The True Patriot* (5 November 1745).
11. (p. 330) *Rabelais' easy chair*: the passage is slightly misquoted from *The Dunciad* (1728), I, 17–20.
12. (p. 330) *Lucian*: the Greek writer (*c.*115–*c.*180) remembered for his witty satires on the follies and superstitions of his day.
13. (p. 330) *Mr Moyle*: Walter Moyle (1672–1721), a politician and scholar whose *Works* in two volumes were published in 1726. Moyle's epithet for Lucian was actually 'matchless'.
14. (p. 330) *his Cock*: Lucian's *The Dream: or, The Cock*.
15. (p. 330) *Mr Rowe's translation*: Nicholas Rowe's translation of Lucan's epic poem, *Pharsalia*, appeared in 1718.
16. (p. 330) *A good translation*: such as the one that Fielding planned to publish with the Revd William Young and which he promoted in *The Covent-Garden Journal* (27 and 30 June 1752). The project was abandoned.
17. (p. 330) *translated by others*: Dryden provided the preface to an edition of Lucian's *Works* (1710–11) translated by Walter Moyle, Tom Brown, Charles Gildon, John Phillips, Lawrence Echard, and Nahum Tate.
18. (p. 331) *consulted the Latin only*: it was the normal publishing practice of the day to print the works of Greek authors in bilingual editions, Greek on one page and Latin on the other. Fielding was familiar with

at least two French translations, those by Jean Baudouin and by Perrot d'Ablancourt, which were in his library.

19. (p. 331) *as Mr Pope was for his Homer*: Pope achieved financial independence through the success of his publication by subscription of the *Iliad* (1715–20) and the *Odyssey* (1725–6), which together brought him £9,000.

20. (p. 331) *the translation takes no more notice of the* ΔE: the conjunctive particle, δέ, is frequently redundant and omitted in translation. Booth's quibble is that Pope's translation ('Such was the Sov'reign Doom, and such the Will of Jove') ignores the implied causal relationship between the will of Jove and its fulfilment through the wrath of Achilles.

21. (p. 331) *Madam Dacier and Monsieur Eustathius*: Pope's translation of Homer was accomplished with the help of earlier translations, including Mme Dacier's (see above, note 27 to p. 258), and of the famous commentary of Eustathius, Archbishop of Thessalonica (1160–*c.*1198).

22. (p. 332) *Venerisque . . . maritus*: *Pharsalia*, II, 387–8, translated by Rowe as:

> He sought no end of marriage, but increase,
> Nor wish'd a pleasure, but his country's peace:
> That took up all the tend'rest part of life,
> His country was his children and his wife.

23. (p. 332) *Statius*: Publius Papinius Statius (*c.*40–*c.*96) a Roman poet, author of the *Thebaid* and a collection of poems called *Silvae*, admired from the Middle Ages until well into the eighteenth century, when he was translated by both Pope and Gray.

24. (p. 332) *Silius Italicus*: Tiberius Catius Silius Italicus (25–101), a Roman poet, author of a long epic, the *Punica*, generally considered uninspired.

25. (p. 333) *Claudian*: Claudius Claudianus (*c.*370–*c.*404), the last great poet of ancient Rome.

26. (p. 333) *romance writing*: fictitious stories with incidents remote from ordinary life, often containing sexual intrigues and personal allusions.

27. (p. 338) *search the office*: the bailiff declares himself obliged to check with the sheriff's office to be certain that all Booth's debts will be covered by the bail.

28. (p. 341) *Pylades and Orestes, Damon and Pythias*: classical types of male friendship. Orestes, the son of Agamemnon and Clytemnestra, raised by his uncle Strophius, King of Phocis (after the murder of Agamemnon by Clytemnestra and Aegisthus), formed a close friendship with his cousin Pylades. The friends Damon and Pythias were proverbial for their devotion.

29. (p. 341) *Oroondates*: the hero of La Calprenède's French romance,

Cassandre (1644–50), who was sometimes cited in the period as a model of the devoted lover.

30. (p. 342) *when lust and envy sleep*: Dryden's *The Indian Emperor or, The Conquest of Mexico* (1665), III, ii.
31. (p. 342) *Nor poppy . . . slumber*: misquoted from *Othello*, III, iii, 327–9.
32. (p. 343) *Friendship . . . destruction's near*: Sir John Vanbrugh (1664–1726), *The False Friend* (1702), I, i.
33. (p. 343) *this image of the lamb*: probably an allusion to 2 Samuel xi and xii, especially xii, 1–4.
34. (p. 344) *unexceptionable housekeeper*: a householder to whom no objection on grounds of impecuniosity could be made. Atkinson is not sufficiently well off to stand bail, but has persuaded another householder to join Colonel James, giving him a 'bond of indemnification' against possible loss.
35. (p. 349) *the proverb of a burnt child*: the burnt child dreads the fire.
36. (p. 351) *as Virgil says*: properly, *mortales hebetat visus*, 'dulls thy mortal vision' (*Aeneid*, II, 603).
37. (p. 351) *White's*: the aristocratic club (see note 30 to p. 133).
38. (p. 351) *Ward's pill, or Dr James's powder*: popular patent medicines. Joshua 'Spot' Ward (1685–1761) was often satirized as a quack, a view Fielding shared until his final illness when he was treated by Ward. Dr Robert James (1705–76) is praised in the first edition of the novel as the creator of 'that powder, for the invention of which, my worthy and ingenious friend Dr James would, in almost any country but this, have received public honours and rewards'.
39. (p. 353) *the short dimension of a span*: cf. Psalm xxxix, 6, 'Behold, thou hast made my days as it were a span long' (as translated by Miles Coverdale, 1488–1568, whose version of the Psalms was retained in *The Book of Common Prayer*). In his 'Of the Remedy of Affliction for the Loss of Our Friends' Fielding attributes the comparison to Solomon.
40. (p. 353) *the duration of a race*: possibly Martial, *Epigrams*, X, 1,5–8, or Claudian, *Panegyric on the Consuls Probinus and Olybrius*, I, 68–70.
41. (p. 353) *transition of a wave*: probably Ovid, *Metamorphoses*, XV, 179–84.
42. (p. 355) *Video . . . sequor*: 'I see the better course and I approve it, but still I follow the worse' (Ovid, *Metamorphoses*, VII, 20–21).
43. (p. 355) *this very shortness itself one of their afflictions*: the famous reply of Solon to those who were consoling him with the customary topos of life's brevity. Cf. Diogenes Laertius, *Lives of Eminent Philosophers*, I, 63.
44. (p. 355) *as Aristotle calls it*: cf. *Nicomachean Ethics*, I, x, 9.

BOOK IX

1. (p. 371) *honour and fighting are . . . synonymous words*: in his 'A Modern Glossary' of abused words in *The Covent-Garden Journal* (14 January 1752) Fielding ironically defines 'Honour' as 'Duelling'. The campaign against duelling, waged by clergymen in sermons and by writers in newspapers, journals, and tracts, is a persistent theme in the literature of the eighteenth century (see note 23 to p. 130). One of the most important of the many publications was the Revd John Cockburn's *History and Examination of Duels. Shewing their Heinous Nature and the Necessity of Suppressing them* (1720), to which Fielding is indebted throughout Dr Harrison's argument.
2. (p. 371) *Dryden's Virgil*: published in 1697.
3. (p. 374) *the great master of human passions*: Homer in the *Iliad*, VI, 483–4.
4. (p. 381) *a letter of recommendation*: Addison, *The Spectator*, 221 (13 November 1711): 'It was a Saying of an Ancient Philosopher . . . That a good Face is a Letter of Recommendation.' The philosopher is identified as Aristotle by Diogenes Laertius, *Lives of Eminent Philosophers*, V, 18–19.
5. (p. 381) *the great sin of adultery*: Fielding evidently felt strongly about the need for laws against adultery, devoting two numbers of *The Covent-Garden Journal* (Nos. 67 and 68, 21 and 28 October 1752) to the subject.
6. (p. 381) *stamina*: rudiments, germs.
7. (p. 382) *Aristotle in his Politics*: *Politics*, I, ii, 2.
8. (p. 386) *as Shakespear says*: *Othello*, III, iii, 424–5.
9. (p. 391) *a drum*: an assembly of fashionable people at a private house. A larger and more public party was called a rout (see note 24 to p. 176).
10. (p. 391) *capuchine*: a hooded cloak in the style of the dress of a Capuchin friar.
11. (p. 391) *bragg*: a card game much like the modern game of poker.
12. (p. 392) *the rooms at Bath and Tunbridge*: the fashionable spas of Bath and Tunbridge Wells had public assembly rooms which provided entertainment for visitors.
13. (p. 395) *discovered*: revealed.
14. (p. 395) *in whom there is no guile*: John i, 47.
15. (p. 396) *Phocylides*: Phocylides of Miletus (*fl.* 6th century BC), author of gnomic verses, the *Sententiae*.
16. (p. 396) *D'Esprit*: Jacques Esprit (1611–78), author of *La Fausseté des vertus humaines* (1677–8), to which Dr Harrison refers.
17. (p. 396) *the labourer . . . not paid his hire*: Matthew xx, 1–16.
18. (p. 396) *Agrippa*: Acts xxvi, 28–9.
19. (p. 396) *Axylus*: *Iliad*, VI, 14–15.
20. (p. 396) *Eustathius*: see note 21 to p. 331.
21. (p. 396) *Barnes*: Joshua Barnes (1654–1712), the Cambridge professor

of Greek, published an edition of the *Iliad* and the *Odyssey* in two volumes (1711). See Vol. I, 232, for the note in question.

22. (p. 396) *Dryden*: Actually Knightly Chetwood (1650–1720), the author of 'The Life of Virgil' prefixed to Dryden's translation of Virgil (1697).
23. (p. 397) *the fifth chapter of Matthew*: Matthew v, 45: 'for he [God] makes his sun rise on the evil and on the good, and sends rain on the just and on the unjust.'
24. (p. 397) *Poole*: Matthew Poole (1624–79), *Annotations upon the Holy Bible* (1683–5). The commentary on Matthew v, 44–5, in Vol. II, is not by Poole himself but by those who continued his work.
25. (p. 398) *If thine enemy hunger . . . drink*: Romans xii, 20.
26. (p. 398) *not rendering evil . . . blessing*: 1 Peter iii, 9.
27. (p. 398) *a certain divine*: Robert South (1634–1716), the well-known high-church clergyman. Dr Harrison quotes from South's sermon on 1 Samuel xxv, 32–3.
28. (p. 399) *Vauxhall*: the fashionable pleasure gardens on the south side of the Thames, probably opened shortly before the Restoration (1660). Under the management (1728–67) of Fielding's friend, Jonathan Tyers, and especially after the visit of the Prince of Wales in 1732, Vauxhall became the most fashionable resort of the time.
29. (p. 400) *St James's church*: one of the principal parish churches in Westminster, designed by Christopher Wren and consecrated in 1684.
30. (p. 402) *the tithe pig*: a pig taken as tithe. Derogatory references to the clergy as eaters of tithe pigs were fairly common until the end of the eighteenth century.
31. (p. 402) *slabbering bib*: a derogatory allusion to his clerical vest.
32. (p. 402) *Bos fur sus quotque sacerdos*: a corruption of *bos et fus, atque sacerdos*, exceptions to the rules governing Latin nouns of the third declension.
33. (p. 402) *the wolf in the sheep's cloathing*: Matthew vii, 15.
34. (p. 403) *Tida tidu tidum*: meaningless pseudo-Latin, meant to provoke the clergyman.
35. (p. 404) *congee*: *congé*, parting bow.
36. (p. 405) *ambassadors from Heaven*: 2 Corinthians v, 20.
37. (p. 406) *Matthew Paris*: (*c.*1200–1259), Benedictine monk and the foremost chronicler of the thirteenth century. His principal work, the *Historia Major* (or *Chronica Majora*), is based in part on Roger of Wendover's *Flowers of History. Comprising the History of England from the Descent of the Saxons to A.D. 1235*, where the story of the two priests is to be found.
38. (p. 407) *fall twenty times a day*: probably a mistake for Proverbs xxiv, 16: 'a righteous man falls seven times a day'.
39. (p. 407) *treasure in Heaven*: Matthew vi, 19–20.
40. (p. 407) *God and Mammon*: Matthew vi, 24 and Luke xvi, 13.

41. (p. 408) *Nec . . . caetera*: 'Yet, while granting this virtue, I would not also allow him every other' (Horace, *Satires*, I, x, 5).
42. (p. 410) *Nestor*: King of Pylos, venerated in Homer for his wisdom.

BOOK X

1. (p. 411) *a masquerade*: large public masquerades were held at the Opera House in the Haymarket, under the management of John James Heidegger (*c.*1659–1749), appointed Master of the Revels by George II. A highly popular form of entertainment throughout the century, masquerades were denounced by moral reformers because of the indiscriminate mixing of social classes (since everyone was disguised) and for the sexual licence that was consequently thought to ensue. Fielding also satirized the masquerades in *The Masquerade* (1728), *The Champion* (19 February 1740), *Miss Lucy in Town* (1742) and *Tom Jones* (XIII, vii).
2. (p. 412) *Una dolo . . . duorum est*: 'if one woman is subdued by the guile of two gods' (*Aeneid*, IV, 95).
3. (p. 412) *Interdum . . . peccat*: 'At times the public see straight; sometimes they make mistakes' (Horace, *Epistles*, II, i, 63).
4. (p. 412) *Madam Dacier*: cf. note 27 to p. 258.
5. (p. 413) *the Aeneid of Virgil*: behind the dispute over female learning, a perennial subject of satire in Fielding's day, lies the quarrel between Mme Dacier and Antoine Houdar de la Motte (1672–1731) over Homer, to which Dr Harrison here alludes. Replying to Mme Dacier's attack upon his treatment of Homer, de la Motte had in some respects preferred Ovid to Homer. (See Étienne Fourmont, *Examen pacifique de la querelle de Madame Dacier et de Monsieur de la Motte sur Homer*, 1716).
6. (p. 413) *Verbum non amplius addam*: 'Not a word more will I add' (*Satires*, I, i, 22).
7. (p. 414) *his ingentia fata*: one of the many, and controversial, emendations made by Richard Bentley (1662–1742), the great classical scholar, in his edition of Horace (1711). Bentley maintained in a long note that *facta* ('deeds') should be *fata* ('the Fates').
8. (p. 414) *Varium et mutabile semper femina*: 'A fickle and changeful thing is woman ever' (Aeneid, IV, 569–70).
9. (p. 414) *neuter gender agree with the feminine*: the word *animal* must be understood in order to account for the grammar of Virgil's famous line – as Dr Harrison points out.
10. (p. 416) *the trained bands*: armed troops of citizens formed, from the sixteenth to the eighteenth century, to supplement the army, especially in times of danger.
11. (p. 416) *Thames Street*: one of the principal streets of the City of London, the prosperous but unfashionable part of London (as opposed to the more fashionable and aristocratic West End in the City of Westminster).

12. (p. 418) *Here beginneth the first chapter of*: the formula in *The Book of Common Prayer* used to introduce the biblical lessons read at Matins and Evensong.
13. (p. 418) *the Decalogue*: the Ten Commandments, Exodus xx, 2–17 and Deuteronomy v, 6–21.
14. (p. 418) *the New Testament*: Matthew v, 27–8.
15. (p. 418) *the Old Bailey*: the central criminal court.
16. (p. 420) D–g–ss: 'Mother' Jenny Douglas (d. 1761), a notorious Covent Garden procuress. Late in life she repented and was (probably) immortalized in Hogarth's satire on Methodism, *Enthusiasm Delineated* (1761).
17. (p. 420) *bear a bob*: join in the refrain.
18. (p. 421) *a Joseph*: the story of Joseph's rejection of the sexual advances of Potiphar's wife is told in Genesis xxxix. 'Joseph' is of course the name Fielding gave to the chaste hero of *Joseph Andrews*.
19. (p. 427) *Sir Isaac Newton's doctrine of colours*: the reference is to Newton's *Optics* (1704).
20. (p. 431) *Thersites*: *Iliad*, II, 213–16.
21. (p. 431) *Horace*: *Satires*, I, iv, 82–3, 85.
22. (p. 431) *Francis*: Philip Francis (*c.*1708–72), whose translation of Horace was published by Andrew Millar in 1746–7.
23. (p. 432) *looking now and then into the Latin*: most editions of Greek texts were published with a Latin translation on the facing page. See note 18 to p. 331.
24. (p. 432) *Go home . . . and keep your maids to their work*: *Iliad*, VI, 490–92.
25. (p. 432) *Homer*: *Iliad*, XIII, 431–3.
26. (p. 432) *Juvenal*: the reference to Juvenal's Roman ladies is facetious as the sixth *Satire* of Juvenal is well-known for its sarcastic attack on women, particularly those who pretend to learning.
27. (p. 432) *pollemy*: Mrs Atkinson struggles for the word *πόλεμος* (war) which Hector declares 'shall be for men' (*Iliad*, VI, 492).
28. (p. 433) *the Turkish notion, that women have no souls*: a common mistake of the time about Turkish beliefs. See, for example, Farquhar's *The Beaux' Stratagem* (1707), IV, i.
29. (p. 435) *Othello*: misquoted from IV, ii, 56, 'But there where I have garnered up my heart'.
30. (p. 436) *By heav'n . . . the bottomless deep*: Colonel Bath's garbled version of Hotspur's speech in *1 Henry IV*, I, iii, 201–5:

    By heaven, me thinks it were an easy leap
    To pluck bright honour from the pale-faced moon,
    Or dive into the bottom of the deep,
    Where fathom-line could never touch the ground,
    And pluck up drownèd honour by the locks.

    The last two lines are those which Colonel Bath is unable to remember.

31. (p. 437) *the Mall*: in St James's Park.
32. (p. 438) *Grosvenor Square*: the most fashionable square in the West End of London, developed between 1725 and 1731 as the show-piece of the Grosvenor estate in Mayfair.
33. (p. 439) *Farquhar's comedies*: George Farquhar (1678–1707), author of *The Recruiting Officer* (1706) and *The Beaux' Stratagem* (1707).
34. (p. 440) *Addison*: in *The Spectator*, No. 62 (11 May 1711), Addison, distinguishing between true and false wit, comments: 'When a Poet tells us, the Bosom of his Mistress is as white as Snow, there is no Wit in the Comparison; but when he adds, with a Sigh, that it is as cold too, it then grows into Wit.'
35. (p. 448) *than Shakespeare tells us it hath in surgery*: *1 Henry IV*, V, i, 135.
36. (p. 452) *blown up*: destroyed, ruined.
37. (p. 452) *Omne vitium in proclivi est*: probably a misquotation of Juvenal, '*Omne in praecipiti vitium stetit*' (*Satire* I, 149): 'all vice is at its acme'.
38. (p. 455) *being broke with his regiment*: lost his position when his regiment was dispersed.
39. (p. 457) *the Duke of Marlborough*: John Churchill (1650–1722), the 1st Duke of Marlborough, victor in the War of the Spanish Succession (1702–11) against Louis XIV. Fielding greatly admired Marlborough and wrote his *Full Vindication of the Dutchess Dowager of Marlborough* (1742) in defence of Sarah, his widow.
40. (p. 458) *I am a man myself . . . the rest of mankind*: '*Homo sum: humani nihil a me alienum puto*' (Terence, *Heauton Timorumenos*, l. 77).

BOOK XI

1. (p. 465) *ad eundem*: to the same rank.
2. (p. 469) *as Livy tells us*: *History of Rome*, XXVI, xii, 8. Capua fell in 211 BC, after the desertion of the state by the nobility, who refused to meet in the senate, and allowed power to fall into the hands of the unworthy magistrate, Seppius Loesius.
3. (p. 469) *One worthless man . . . unpretending friends*: George Bubb Dodington (1691–1762), *An Epistle to the Right Honourable Sir Robert Walpole* (1726), p. 8.
4. (p. 470) *his confession in the liturgy*: the 'General Confession' in *The Book of Common Prayer*.
5. (p. 470) *Things ill begun . . . by ill*: *Macbeth*, III, ii, 55 (slightly misquoted).
6. (p. 470) *put himself on his country*: stand trial by jury.
7. (p. 472) *the trade of milliner in Covent Garden*: i.e. she kept a brothel.
8. (p. 472) *a charity-school*: one dependent on voluntary contributions for the education of poor children.
9. (p. 474) *made capital by an Act of Parliament*: forgery was a capital crime from 1729 to 1832.

10. (p. 474) *those excellent rules, called the law of evidence*: for Fielding's view of the inadequacy of the laws of evidence see his *An Enquiry into the Causes of the Late Increase of Robbers* (Section IX).
11. (p. 476) *Semele*: beloved of Zeus, who came to her disguised as a mortal, Semele tricked Zeus into promising to appear to her as he did to his wife on Olympus.
12. (p. 477) *the fourlegged gentlemen of the same vocation*: pointers or setters (dogs used by sportsmen to indicate the presence of game).
13. (p. 479) *paying it away to a nominal third person*: the law making promissory notes for gambling debts void (Gaming Act of 1710) could be evaded by selling the notes to a third party.
14. (p. 481) *touched*: bribed.
15. (p. 491) *Monmouth Street*: throughout the eighteenth century Monmouth Street was well known for its old clothes shops.
16. (p. 491) *rag fair*: the old clothes market in Rosemary Lane near the Tower of London was a poorer and cheaper market than Monmouth Street.
17. (p. 496) *economical*: household.

BOOK XII

1. (p. 506) *Dame Purgante in Prior*: Matthew Prior, 'Paulo Purganti and his Wife.' Cf. note 10 to p. 154.
2. (p. 508) *the penny-post*: that is, a cheaper and less reliable service than that offered by the General Post Office.
3. (p. 509) *the great state lottery*: Fielding compares Booth's chance of getting preferment to the chance of holding a winning ticket in the annual state lotteries, authorized by Act of Parliament from 1709 to 1824 to raise money for public works.
4. (p. 510) *hanger*: sword (hung from the belt).
5. (p. 514) *as Mr Bayle thinks*: Pierre Bayle (1647–1706), author of the *Dictionnaire historique et critique*. See the article on the Duke of Guise.
6. (p. 514) *the better duellist of the two*: *Iliad*, III, 426–36.
7. (p. 514) *even in a just cause*: *Iliad*, VI, 405–39.
8. (p. 515) *what it was made Dido fall in love with Aeneas*: *Aeneid*, IV; Dido loved Aeneas for his valour.
9. (p. 519) *enthusiastic*: in the eighteenth century the word was often used pejoratively to suggest the effects of an overheated imagination or the display of violent passions.
10. (p. 522) *Dr Barrow's works*: see note 16 to p. 256. Barrow's sermons on the Apostles' Creed are evidently intended here, particularly the first sermon, 'Of the Evil and Unreasonableness of Infidelity'.
11. (p. 522) *to get another person to be bound with him*: the law required that bail be supplied by two persons, each able to pay the amount of the bond.
12. (p. 524) *se fendendo*: properly *se defendendo*, a plea of self-defence.

13. (p. 525) *was out of his time*: had finished his apprenticeship.
14. (p. 525) *of two evils to chuse the least*: proverbial wisdom.
15. (p. 530) *Broughton or Slack*: John Broughton (1705–89), considered the father of British pugilism, was eventually defeated by John Slack, 'the Butcher of Norwich', in 1750.
16. (p. 530) *mob*: the unruly element of the London populace, notorious in the eighteenth century for taking justice into its own hands.
17. (p. 533) *your sister is discovered*: your sister-in-law has been found out.
18. (p. 534) *title deeds savoured of the realty*: cf. Thomas Wood, *An Institute of the Laws of England*, III, i, where the phrasing is very close.
19. (p. 540) *the Oneiropolos*: the interpreter (of dreams). See *Iliad*, I, 63.
20. (p. 540) *better opinion of dreams than Horace had*: *Ars Poetica*, ll. 7–8, where idle fancies are compared to a sick man's dreams.
21. (p. 540) *they came from Jupiter*: *Iliad*, I, 63.
22. (p. 540) *If Jupiter . . . their wives and children*: *Iliad*, IV, 160–62.
23. (p. 540) *the Delphin Homer*: an edition of the Latin classics prepared at the command of Louis XIV *ad usum Delphini* (for the use of the Dauphin). As the Greek authors were not included, there was neither a Delphin Homer nor an Aristotle.
24. (p. 541) *opus est explanatum*: the work is explained.
25. (p. 541) *What none . . . auspicious day bestows*: *Aeneid*, IX, 6–7.
26. (p. 541) *to be blooded*: to be bled. Eighteenth-century physiological lore held that powerful emotions affected the body, causing the blood to boil or rage. This condition could be calmed by drinking water or, in more serious cases, by letting blood.

APPENDIX

1. (p. 548) *tertia quaq. hora*: *tertia quaque hora*, every third hour.
2. (p. 548) *Thompson*: Dr Thomas Thompson (*c.*1700–1763), an unorthodox and controversial physician whom, at least for a while, Fielding greatly admired.
3. (p. 549) *his zany*: attendant, underling (generally used in a derogatory sense).
4. (p. 549) *clyster*: enema.